*NOONDAY*

ROBERT PERRIN

# *NOONDAY*

Pan Books London and Sydney

First published 1985 by Pan Books Ltd,
Cavaye Place, London SW10 9PG
9 8 7 6 5 4 3 2 1
© Robert Perrin 1985
ISBN 0 330 28554 8
Printed and bound by
Richard Clay (The Chaucer Press) Ltd, Bungay, Suffolk

*For my dear friend and second father,*
*Bob Wyatt, who might read this elsewhere.*

'I have made their widows more in numbers
than the sands of the sea;
'I have brought against the mothers of
young men a destroyer at noonday;
'I have made anguish and terror fall upon
them suddenly.'

*Book of Jeremiah*, Chapter 15, Verse 8.

*BOOK ONE*

# Chapter 1 August, 1822

Jack Keane stripped off his clothes and stood naked under the warm midday sun. The paleness of his trunk and thighs contrasted with the ruddy, weather-beaten colour of the rest of his tall, husky body. He ran down the fine sands of the lonely Irish coast and laughed and whooped with joy as he kicked at the water. He walked out until the sea was up to his chest. Spluttering and gasping, he began to strike out with his own ungainly mixture of the breast-stroke and the crawl, arms and legs flailing. Soon, the sounds from the twin beaches of Ballybunnion faded behind him. To his right, once he'd left the headland at his back, he could see a huge, dark rock rising over 150 feet from the sea with a large, round tunnel running right through its middle. Here, the sea boiled and roared its way through. No man had ever swum the tunnel without drowning in its fierce undercurrents. Jack smiled to himself as he thought on the rock's name. A passage forced by no man, and thus the Virgin's Rock. He turned over to float on his back, raising his head slightly and looking down along his body, broad and long and without an ounce of fat, and then let his head fall back again, surrendering himself to the sway of the sea. He remembered his certainty that this day, 15 August 1822, was to be special.

Jack Keane had had the feeling ever since he'd been awoken that morning in the small cabin lit by the glow from the tamped-down peat fire. His mother and father were lying together on their straw bed in one corner; his older brothers, Michael and John, still asleep in the other. Jack quietly urged six chickens through the cabin doorway, pulling aside the brown hessian sack hanging across it. Next, he went to the large, wooden cage where the pig and sow lay with their four pigeens, opened it, and forced them out into the damp of the morning.

Outside, he dashed some cold water over his face and arms, scooping it from the wooden rainwater tub by the cabin doorway, alongside the bricks of peat, stacked neatly against the cabin's white-washed mud and clay walls. Now he felt ready for the day. He took a deep breath of fresh air, imagining that he could already smell the salt from the distant sea. Then he set off from the small huddle of cabins that made up the West Kerry townland of Drombeg, vaulting easily across dry-stone walls until he reached the broad track leading to Ballybunnion.

Jack could already hear the Atlantic rollers, now less than a mile away, and smell the salt in the air. He strode past the cabins that pointed the way to the sea. A woman in late middle age, a red shawl over her head and shoulders, looked up from the cow she was milking.

'Where are you from, boy?' she called. 'Come a long way for the pattern, have you?'

'From Drombeg,' Jack replied, stopping by the wicker gate set in the stone wall around her cabin.

'You must have a thirst on you.'

'I am a wee bit dry,' Jack conceded, a broad grin on his face, knowing that he would be offered a mug of warm, foaming milk. Custom dictated that he would drink only half of what he was offered.

When he'd finished his drink, he wiped his mouth with the back of his hand.

'Thank you, mother.'

'Thanks be to God and His Blessing on this day. And not too much noise at the crossroads tonight, you mind,' called the woman after him.

'I haven't even got a dancing partner yet,' Jack shouted back as he started up the broad track.

'You'll have no trouble there, my young friend,' muttered the woman to herself, continuing her milking. 'Not with your looks, you won't,' she sighed to herself. He'll break some pretty hearts, she thought, as she wearily rose from her milking stool and pushed her cow aside to grasp the handle of the brimming wooden pail.

The cabins ended thirty yards from the cliff-top and Jack saw the blueness of the sea stretching away from him; the ruined keep of Ballybunnion Castle on the headland and the curving bays of fine sand. He undid the knot in his red handkerchief, took out a large potato, and chewed on its cold, cooked flesh. The early morning sun was rising behind him, glinting off the small rock pools at the base of the deep grey cliffs shot through with streaks of red and yellow sulphur. Away to his left a lone figure worked amongst these rocks, picking mussels, lichens, and crabs from the small rock pools, and tossing them into a basket. The man's donkey stood patiently by, one filled basket already strapped to its back.

Now, his thoughts far away, he was almost lulled to sleep by the motion of the sea. If he floated long enough, would he be washed up in America, he wondered idly? Then, suddenly, something struck him hard in the side, pushing him off balance and under the water.

He coughed, struggling to the surface, arms and legs thrashing the water round him as he fought to keep afloat.

He heard a shriek of laughter and, blinking the salt from his eyes, saw a smiling face close to his, a girl's face with vivid green eyes, a snub nose, a generous mouth with red lips, all framed by long ringlets of gleaming black hair.

Angrily Jack grabbed at the girl's round bare shoulders, pulled her to him, and pushed her under the sea. He felt her firm breasts pressed against his body as she slid down under him. She bobbed to the surface, gasping for air and Jack, alarmed that he might have gone too far, held her closely to prevent her going under again.

'You divil,' she spluttered, her eyes blazing. Then she saw the genuine concern on his face and softened, feeling the strength of his arms around her.

'You dunderhead,' she began to laugh.

'You started it, ducking me.'

'No I didn't,' the girl protested, her voice low and melodious. 'I didn't see you lying there at all.'

'Anyway, what are you doing way out here?' Jack asked, still clutching her close to him. 'You'll drown out here, so you will.'

'And why, pray? I could swim when I was only five. I'm as safe as you are.'

Jack began to feel the warmth of her body against his, a disturbing, exciting warmth that he'd never known before. The girl, too, realized that he was still pressing close to her from her knees to her breasts. She felt his manhood lengthening and hardening against the soft curve of her belly.

'Now, get away from me,' she cried, pushing at him. 'A girl's supposed to have her privacy swimming from the women's beach.'

Jack peered back at the shore and realized she was speaking the truth. He must have drifted with the current and was well north of the men's beach.

The girl laughed again when she saw his perplexed expression. 'You're coming ashore on our beach then are you, you brazen lummock?'

'No, of course not.' Jack felt himself blush at the thought, aware of how the girl's soft body had physically excited him.

'Come on, I'm getting cold,' said the girl with the green eyes. 'I'll race you back to the headland.'

She thrust out of the water. Jack glimpsed her slim body and full breasts for a moment and then she was pushing through the water away from him and back towards the shore.

Jack didn't follow her immediately, admiring with excitement the twin globes of her buttocks and the divide between them as her legs kicked her through the water. He realized that she was a strong swimmer with a smoother style than his. He began thrashing after her, pulling at the water with all his strength, and started to close the gap between them. As they neared the headland separating the beaches he was swimming level with her. Her eyes smiled into his, glad to have him alongside her.

'Where do you come from?' she asked.

'Drombeg,' gasped Jack, panting with exertion. 'The name's Jack Keane.'

'Hello, Jack Keane. I'm Brigid Aherne from Gortacrossane.'

By now, the two youngsters were about twenty yards from the headland, near enough to hear the shouts and cries of the late comers enjoying themselves on the beach. They realized that, for decency's sake, they would have to go their different ways, to the beaches reserved for men and women. Jack stood up, the water reaching half-way up his chest. Brigid swam a few more yards and turned to face him, the sea lapping the upper swell of her breasts.

'Thanks for the swim, Jack Keane,' she smiled.

'Thank you, Brigid Aherne.' Jack liked the sound of her name.

They began moving apart towards their respective beaches. 'Brigid,' he blurted, 'are you dancing tonight?'

'I might be, and then again I mightn't be. Why?'

'Would you be my dancing partner?'

'And who says I haven't got one already?'

Jack's face fell with dismay. 'I just thought.'

She smiled softly at him. 'And then again I might not have a partner.'

'Meet me by the castle when you're dressed?'

'Perhaps, Jack Keane, perhaps.'

Brigid glanced quickly over her shoulder at the eighteen-year-old. In one look she took in the details of his strong, lean body, from his broad shoulders to his firm waist, and lower. She walked ashore, her head high, two red spots bright on her cheeks, a smile playing around her lips.

Jack sat on the warm stone by the ruined castle staring out over the twin bays of Ballybunnion, now fairly crowded with people enjoying their holiday after having made their devotions. Many were youngsters, playing naked in the pools and shallows, but here and there were dotted family groups sitting against the rocks, the grandmother always at their centre, invariably dressed in black with a shawl covering her grey head. He waited for more than half-an-hour, beginning to despair with each minute that passed that Brigid wouldn't keep their rendezvous. Perhaps she thought him just a farm boy with uncouth manners and, at this very moment was giggling about him with some of her friends? He was torn with the uncertainty of youth.

Two hands crossed his eyes, blotting out the sunlight. 'Hello, Jack Keane,' said a soft voice in his ear.

He swung round on the stone. Brigid Aherne smiled down at him, her black hair fluffed in curls, a brown woollen shawl across her shoulders falling over her green blouse, the full, bright red skirt covering her legs to mid-calf. Her feet, like Jack's, were bare.

'Brigid! I thought you weren't . . .'

'You thought I'd break my word, did you then? And hardly knowing me, too,' she exclaimed in mock indignation, putting her hands on her hips.

'Well, you didn't *promise* . . .'

'I'm here, aren't I?' She noticed his red handkerchief lying on the grass. 'What have you there?'

'Some lumpers.'

'That's good. I've got some seaweed to go with them.' She plunged her hand into a deep pocket near the hem of her skirt and pulled out a handful of dried seaweed. Together they shared the food in silence. The bitter sweetness of the edible seaweed flavoured the blandness of the large potatoes.

Brigid was the first to speak. 'And how many more are there at home like you?'

'Just me and me brothers, Michael and John. And me mam and dad, of course. They've gone to the fair in Listowel today.'

'So have mine.' She looked at him keenly. 'Have you much land?'

'Three acres or so with some wheat, some chickens and some potatoes. And we've got some pigs and pigeens and Siobhan.'

'Siobhan?'

'That what me mam calls her. Says the cow reminds her of me dad's Auntie Soibhan.'

Brigid laughed, a soft laugh that lit up her whole face. 'Well, it strikes me that with Siobhan and all, you're well off.'

'How many of you are there then?'

'There's Theresa and Bernadette, who are older than me,' Brigid ticked off her sisters on her fingers. 'And Mary and May who are younger. Me dad's got a conacre, and what with a cow and him working for Sir James Watson, we survive.'

Jack thought for a moment about Brigid's family. A man with a conacre was a cottier and was lower down the agrarian social scale than a tenant farmer like his father. A cottier, in return for his labours, was allowed by his landlord to farm a small plot by his rented cabin, invariably growing potatoes. The Ahernes would be a family, Jack thought, with little to fall back on in hard times.

'I suppose Jonathan Sandes is your agent as well, Brigid?'

'That he is and a hard man too. Me dad says he's got a smile like a brass plate on a coffin. If we didn't borrow ahead from the Cork butter men, or sell turf at the market, he'd have us out of our cabin as quick as a Kilkenny cat.'

Jack nodded glumly in agreement. 'The last time the potatoes failed, me dad had to go to the gombeen man for the rent, or the bailiffs would have had our roof off. What with his rates of interest, me dad's only just paid him off.'

'Why's it allowed to happen, Jack?' asked Brigid, tucking her knees under her chin. 'God knows we have little enough. Why do they always want more?'

'Because they're landlords, that's why,' he said angrily. 'Landlords are always like that. People like your man Sir James Watson sit in their fine houses in Dublin or London and let their agents like Sandes do their filthy work. They never see their land but they always want their rent on time. The most of them would rather see us living in the ditch first and the land turned over to cattle with no cabins in the way.'

'Me dad says that some people are ready to do something about it,' said Brigid.

'They are that. Me brothers, Michael and John, think so anyway.' He lowered his voice. 'They belong to the Whiteboys.'

'The Whiteboys!' Brigid sniffed disdainfully. 'And what do they do? All that burning and killing. Where does that get them?'

'It makes sure the landlords know that we're not beaten, that we'll fight them if needs be.'

'I thought the Whiteboys were supposed to be secret. How do you know your brothers belong?'

'That's just it. I don't know for sure. But they keep slipping away at dusk and then the next day or so we hear the Whiteboys have done this or that. I'm guessing that Michael and John had something to do with the burning of the farm over at Duagh last week.'

'I'm thinking you'd like to join them, Jack Keane,' Brigid said, her face set with concern.

'They won't let me,' he said, disconsolately. 'They say I'm too young for such things. But I'm as strong and quick as they are.'

Jack, like most young Kerrymen, held the Whiteboys in awe; a secret society with strange oaths and initiation ceremonies whose object was to harass and challenge the overwhelming power of the landlords and their agents. No one knew who they were, only that they identified themselves by wearing long white shirts when on their raids. They burned, stole, and killed, always directing their attacks at the landlords or those who supported them.

'Well, don't let me catch you running around in a white shirt, that's all,' said Brigid, breaking into his thoughts. 'You know what Father O'Sullivan says about all this violence.'

'You mean you'd care what I did?' he asked, looking up into her face for reassurance.

She laughed and ran her hands through his thick hair. 'And would I be sitting here jawing with you, if I didn't? You're a soft one, Jack Keane, that you are.'

He put up his hand and touched hers, and then grasped it tightly. She responded to the pressure, running her thumb along his hand. But, after a moment, she pulled away and jumped up from the stone where she'd been sitting.

'That's enough of that, Jack Keane. You're taking a liberty, that you are. First you grab me when I'm having a quiet swim on me own, and now you're trying to hold me hand with everyone looking at us.'

'But there's no one around,' said Jack, looking guiltily about him.

'Sure, and what difference does that make?'

Jack sat bewildered on the grass as Brigid moved over to the stones of the ruined keep. He couldn't fathom her changing moods. In the distance, a fiddler struck up a tune.

'That'll be Michael Coffey from Doon,' called Brigid. 'Are you coming to listen to him?'

'I'd prefer to be here with you.'

'Well, you can't. If you're not coming, I'll go on my own.'

'Oh, all right then,' he said reluctantly. He wished he could understand the ways of young women. One moment they were all affection and concern; the next, they were prancing away as if they didn't care. It was baffling.

By the time Brigid and Jack had reached the crossroads, a dozen other couples were already there, sitting on walls or on the ground, chatting quietly together. The men with partners stayed on one side of the road, while those without stood morosely across from them, only brightening when an unattached girl approached along the track. When she'd taken a partner and joined the other couples, the rejected men returned to stand in groups, making unflattering remarks about girls in general, though not in voices loud enough to carry across the road. No one wanted a fight at this stage of the evening. Later, perhaps, but not at dusk with the sky in the west glowing orange from the sinking sun.

When he'd judged enough people to be at the crossroads, a small, wizened man wearing a large, grey felt hat stepped into the middle of the track. From under his ragged tail coat, as if by sleight of hand, he produced a fiddle and bow. Michael Coffey, tinker and music man, was indispensable for any night's dancing at the crossroads. In fact, his fiddle went to every important event in the district, whether it was a birth, a wedding, or a death. He waited for the chattering to subside and then stroked a single chord of A out of his fiddle. Some at the crossroads dropped to their knees, others simply stood straight. All crossed themselves and waited in silence. Michael Coffey's fiddle had signalled the sunset 'Angelus'.

Brigid fell to her knees, pulling Jack down with her. There was silence and stillness everywhere without, it seemed, even a bird singing or flying. Jack looked towards the hills of Kerry in the east where yellow clouds drifted gently. In the falling light, the hollows of the hills were turning from blue to dark purple, and their fretted ridges to jet black. The high clouds changed colour perceptibly against a sky glowing with an incandescent light that was almost pale green.

Brigid's eyes were screwed tightly shut, her lips moving as she silently recited a prayer. The sunset picked her face out in perfect profile, and in Jack's later years when the world had had its way he was to remember that this was the moment when he realized he was enduringly in love with her.

After two minutes or so, Michael Coffey stroked another chord on his fiddle, and the spell was broken. Brigid's eyes opened and she looked directly into Jack's face. There was a misty sadness in her face and Jack knew that her prayer had been about the two of them.

16

He rose from his knees and held out his hand. Brigid grasped it tightly as he pulled her to her feet. For seconds, they stood closely together, pressing against each other. Then Brigid, still allowing Jack to hold her hand, pulled away to arm's length and dropped a deep curtsey. Her skirt formed a red circle on the grass by the side of the track as she sank before him and bowed her head, the ringlets of black hair dipping and bobbing. One or two of the girls standing nearby giggled shyly as they watched this open declaration of Brigid's love. It was a private moment of thoughts and vows, of overpowering warmth.

Michael Coffey saw Brigid's gesture and hesitated to begin playing his fiddle, not wanting to spoil precious moments for the young couple. But, as Brigid began to rise from her curtsey, he lifted his fiddle to his chin and, stamping his foot, launched into his first jig.

As the music rose into the evening, Jack pulled Brigid to him. 'Why?' he whispered into her ear.

'Because . . . Well, just because for now,' she answered shyly, standing on tip toe, pressing her mouth close to his ear.

Torches, made from damp bogland rushes dipped in candle grease, were lit and stuck in the walls on the four sides of the crossroads. Their smoky light flickered across the scene, casting wild, grotesque shadows as the dancers dipped and twirled into the eight-handed reel, 'The Siege of Ennis'.

Brigid's skirt flared up her strong and gleaming thighs, as she and Jack joined another couple in a four-handed reel, their feet pointing and darting in the complicated steps of the dance, their arms listed above their heads. Wild cries came from deep in their throats as the tempo increased, never slackening, and Michael Coffey's fingers moved in a blur up and down the strings of his fiddle.

As the stars began to glisten in the dark blue sky, the dancing grew wilder with more and more couples joining in the reels. Eventually Jack and Brigid sank to the grass by the crossroads, thoroughly exhausted.

'Tis about time we started home, Brigid,' said Jack softly. 'We've a long walk yet.'

'That's true, but I don't want this night to end. I'll always remember it.'

'So will I. Until I die, and that's the truth.'

The couple drifted off into the darkness and walked along the track towards Listowel in the east, hand in hand, letting the fiddle music and the whooping of the dancers fade behind them. Soon there were only the noises of the night for company. Brigid clung closely to Jack's arm, her head pressing against his chest.

'What happened to us today?' Jack whispered.

'I don't know, but I'm thinking it was blessed.'

Jack smiled in the darkness and pressed Brigid closer to him, nuzzling her hair and smelling the sea still in it. It took more than two hours to reach the cabins of the townland of Gortacrossane, on the edge of Listowel parish, about a mile or so from where Jack lived.

'Shall I see you to your cabin?'

'No, it would be better not,' Brigid replied.

'It's funny us living so close and never meeting before.'

'We have now and that's the most important thing. The very most important thing.'

Brigid stopped and lifted herself on to her toes. She kissed Jack lightly on the lips before he realized what was happening. Then she turned and ran off into the darkness.

'Brigid . . . Brigid,' Jack called into the night.

'Hush, not so loud,' came Brigid's voice, not many yards away. 'Hush . . . '

'But you just can't go like that.'

'I'll be at market next week.'

'I'll be there,' promised Jack. He could still taste her kiss on his lips.

'Goodnight, dear Jack Keane. Remember me till next week.'

'That I will. Surely.'

Jack wandered back along the track and across the fields to Drombeg, his mind whirling. He doubted if he would ever understand girls. He rubbed his fingers gently against his lips and smiled to himself. At that moment, he didn't care whether he understood or not. He'd known all along the day was going to be something special. And that's what really mattered.

## Chapter 2 September, 1822

An insistent murmer below his bedroom window awoke Jonathan Sandes, land agent to Sir James Watson. He rolled away from the warm, musky nakedness of the girl beside him, pulled aside the curtains of his four-poster bed, and shivered a little as his bare legs and feet struck the cold air. He padded over to the window, parted the heavy dark green curtains, and looked down on to Listowel market square, still lit by pale moonlight.

The country folk were already afoot, arriving for the day's market. He watched a drover, bent over his stick, following his cows, calling from time to time in a low early-morning voice to his subdued dog. A donkey, knock-kneed under the weight of its load, plodded along, wicker baskets full of turf tied either side of its spiny back. A woman carrying a basket of dried seaweed, a sleeping baby of a few months tied papoose-like to her back by her shawl, pushed two other young children in front of her. Still half-asleep, they stumbled along, their thin bodies covered only by·makeshift vests of sacking that fell to their thighs. The moon grew paler every moment, and the little chill wind that comes before the sun rattled the windows of Jonathan Sandes' house. The air outside grew grey.

Sandes turned back towards the bed, stretching his body, still vigorous and athletic in early middle age through constant riding and hunting. He smiled as he saw the bare back of the girl and her long, dark hair spread across the pillows. A pretty and plump serving girl called Finoola from his kitchen; a girl with some surprising tricks he recalled. Yes, it had certainly been worthwhile letting his wife go to Dublin. He felt himself growing excited at the memory of the night's love-making and the thought of the coming faction fight. He slipped back into bed, put his hand on the girl's shoulder and rolled her over on to her back. Instinctively, even in her waking moments, the girl opened and raised her thighs as he plunged between their satiny smoothness. She began uttering small cries of delight as he moved rhythmically in her, her ankles and

19

calves clasped tightly around his lean buttocks, thrusting upwards in unison with him, drawing him further and further into her. He groaned with pleasure.

Jack Keane thought nervously about the faction fight while he sat milking Siobhan the cow. He'd heard about it the night before, sitting with his family around the glowing red peat fire in the middle of their cabin, chomping on hot potatoes and drinking mugs of milk. His father had broken the news.

'I heard from tinker O'Brien that the Cooleens will be at market looking for a fight. It seems someone insulted your Cooleen man and it's being blamed on us Mulvihills.'

'But why a fight, Joe?' exclaimed Mary Keane.

'Well, I'm guessing it's almost a year since we pulped the Cooleens at Tralee Fair and they're just finding any old reason to catch us out.'

'How many will be there?' asked his wife anxiously.

'Your man O'Brien says no more than a hundred a side. That's why he was so late telling me. The Mulvihills had almost made up their numbers in Listowel alone. But they did their sums and decided on a few more, thanks be to God!'

Mary Keane grimaced with disapproval. 'It's no thanks to Him that you couldn't work for two weeks after the Tralee fight, what with your sore head and cracked ribs.'

'This one won't be like that, woman!' her husband said in exasperation. 'This'll just be a short spat, no more.'

But, despite his father's cheery optimism, Jack had spent a fitful night. He had never taken part in a faction fight before, although he'd heard many gory tales about them. The Cooleens, he knew, were the descendants of old Kerry families, settled in the county for centuries. The Mulvihills were from the neighbouring county of Clare and had moved to Kerry generations ago in search of better land. In the parishes south of the River Shannon, you were either a Cooleen or a Mulvihill, depending on your family's history. The Keanes were Mulvihills, and thus the sworn enemies of the opposing faction. It was as simple as that.

Joe Keane, a large man nearly six feet tall, wide leather belt holding up his breeches and containing his growing belly, was a veteran of many faction fights. Now he peered in the half-light at a broken piece of mirror pinned to the cabin wall, his chin raised, hacking at the last errant patch of stubble with a cut throat razor.

'Are you ready yet, Joe?' Mary Keane called from inside the

cabin, where she'd been carefully packing three dozen eggs and a round pat of butter in her wicker basket.

'Just coming, Mary. Is it all done?'

'It is that.'

Joe Keane rubbed his hand over his craggy face and thought his rough shave would suffice. 'Got everything, boyos?' he called to his sons. 'Jack, get the pigeen and don't forget your stick, either.'

'Must he, Joe?' protested his wife, wrapping her green shawl firmly round her head as she came out of the cabin. 'He's only a boy, after all.'

'He'll have to learn some time, Mary. Today's as good a day as any. It won't come to much; a few split heads at the most.'

'Father O'Sullivan won't be pleased. He'll be mortal angry, that he will. You know what he thinks of the factions.'

'Sure, and the priest should look after things he knows about and keep his pointy nose out of men's business.'

Joe picked up a thick, gnarled stick about three feet long that was resting against the cabin wall, and slapped it into his palm. He winced as the hard blackthorn wood, capped with lead, stung his hand.

His wife laughed at his discomfort. 'That'll show you, Joe Keane. You and your shillelagh. It'll be you ending up with a split head.'

'Not if I see a Cooleen first,' said her husband gruffly as he jammed a shapeless felt hat on his head. He turned to his three sons standing by him and saw each was carrying his shillelagh. 'That's good, boys. Now remember what I tell you. When the fight starts, stay together and then you won't get hurt. The Cooleens won't be pulping three big lads like you.'

As they approached the market town, the sun rising in their eyes, the Keanes passed travellers more heavily laden than themselves. The greeting was unvarying and inevitable.

'A fine morning, it is.'

'It is that, thanks be to God.'

'And is it to the market you're going?'

'Indeed it is. And you?'

'We've a little to sell.'

'And, sure, who has more in these hard days?'

Just outside Listowel, in sight of the town's ruined castle standing high on a hillock, the Keanes stopped for a few minutes. In front of them was the River Feale, shallow and clear in the gathering autumn. The grown-ups bathed their travel-stained feet in it, dried them roughly, and laced on their footwear. The sons looked at their father's shoes with envy, knowing that there wasn't the money in the family for them all to be shod. One day – not too soon, pray God, Michael thought – they'll be mine as the eldest son. He would treat his shoes just as sparingly.

In the market square hundreds of people were already milling about, setting out their wares for sale. Those with money enough were already gathering outside the coaching inn tucked away in a corner of the square, washing down a potato or two with draughts of black porter.

Jack began looking eagerly around for Brigid Aherne. At first he failed to see her in the crowd but then he spotted her standing by a large pile of turf at the far end of the square.

'Hang on to this, Michael,' he said, handing his brother the squealing pigeen. 'I've a call to pay.'

His brother followed his glance and saw Brigid. She stood out vividly from the crowds around her, a bright red shawl framing her clear beauty.

'So that's your dancing girl, is it, young Jack? I'm thinking she needs an older man. Perhaps John or meself would fit her better.'

Jack looked at him in alarm. Michael tried to keep a straight face but quickly broke into a broad grin.

'Go on. Off you trot and see your lady love. But mind yourself. Dad'll want you with us when the Cooleens arrive so just you watch out for their green ribbons. And listen for our shout.'

Jack approached Brigid shyly, uncertain of his reception. Their day together seemed so magical in his memory that he wasn't even certain what to say. Brigid had seen him arrive in the square long before he'd caught sight of her, but continued to stack her pile of turf as if she hadn't noticed him. Then he was standing behind her, shifting his feet awkwardly. He coughed once and she spun round, as if surprised.

'Oh, I didn't see you there. Creeping up on a girl like that!'

'Hello Brigid.'

'Just don't stand there, Jack Keane. Can't you see I'm having trouble piling this turf.'

Jack started nervously. 'To be sure. I'm sorry. Let me help.'

She handed him turfs from a cart and he piled them neatly on to the ever-growing stack.

'Haven't you anything to say then, you lummock?'

'It's good to see you again, Brigid. I've been thinking of you all week.'

She slipped her hand into his and gave it a squeeze. 'To be sure, I was awful worried that you wouldn't come today.'

'A regiment of soldiers wouldn't have kept me away.'

'Oh, it's just that boys are funny.'

'So you know all about boys, do you?'

'Well, I've heard enough to know some boys think girls are just out to trap them.'

'Trap them?'

'You know . . . ' Brigid said shyly, lowering her eyes. 'Trap them into marrying.'

'And what if the boy wanted to be trapped?'

'Well, that'd be different, wouldn't it? That'd be fair.'

'We can't wait a week again, can we, Brigid?'

'No, if you're asking . . . '

'What about meeting on Saturday at the old school?'

Before Brigid could reply, a woman, round and plump, came up to the pile of turf.

'Have you not finished yet, Brigid?' she snapped, angrily. 'We'll never get these turves sold if you keep chatting to every Tom, Dick and Harry.

'Mam, this is the boy I told you about. This is Jack.'

'Oh, your dancing boy, is it? Well, don't just stand there. Show me him.'

'Jack, this is me mam. Mam, this is Jack Keane.'

Jack held out his hand, then realizing it was grimy from the turf wiped it against his breeches before shaking hands with Brigid's mother.

'He has manners anyway, Brigid. I'll say that for him.'

'Oh, Mam,' Brigid protested. 'He's been helping with the turf.'

'Well, thank you for that, Jack. And I'm sorry I am that you had to do the work your man should be doing.'

'Where is Dad?' asked Brigid.

'With the rest of his cronies, supping some courage for this fight. I've been trying to find Father O'Sullivan to see if he can stop it before it starts but he's nowhere to be found.'

'Me dad says it won't be much of a fight,' Jack volunteered. 'He'll be in it too.'

'Well, more fool him,' said Brigid's mother. 'Men have less sense than the cattle.'

'Jack, Jack,' the call came from across the square. He turned and saw Michael waving at him.

'That's me brother. I've got to go.' He whispered, 'Saturday, Brigid?'

'Saturday afternoon, Jack,' she said shyly, looking at her mother for confirmation. But Mrs Aherne had turned away to serve a customer.

The calls from the market drifted through the half-open window of Jonathan Sandes' living room in his house on the market square. The cries of the countryfolk selling their wares meant money to him, money to pay Sir James Watson's rents. Sandes, elegantly dressed in a chocolate brown jacket with rounded tails, matching knee breeches, and fine white silk hose covering his muscular calves, was entertaining his fellow land agent, Dr Peter Church, who watched over the interests of Lord Listowel, the other great landowner in the area.

'Another glass, Peter?' he inquired, moving towards his guest with a decanter of his finest madeira. 'It won't be long now before the fight starts and that's a sight I want to see.'

'Gets rid of their energy, eh, Jonathan?' said Church, a stocky, red-faced man, dressed in black. 'Few broken heads keeps 'em quiet, eh?' He held out his glass to be refilled.

'Well, it's a damned sight better than letting them use their energy for those accursed Whiteboys.'

'Yes, I can imagine you're not too well pleased with them at present. Lost that farm over at Duagh a fortnight back, didn't you?'

'Yes, curse 'em. I gave the constabulary a stiff wigging over that. They didn't catch one of the devils. But I'm glad his Lordship has joined Sir James in asking for more militia from Dublin. The soldiers will soon stamp them out.'

'I'm not so sure, Jonathan,' said Church, rubbing his chin dubiously. 'Remember we've thought before that they've been finished, everything's gone quiet for a while, and then there they are again, white shirts and all.'

Sandes sank wearily back into the high-backed, silk-covered chair by the window. The dark rings under his eyes testified to the night's pleasurable exertions. 'There's only one thing these peasants understand, Peter and you know that as well as I. Strength! If once we let them suspect weakness, heaven knows what'll happen.'

'I'm wondering if that's altogether right. The poor devils have little enough,' replied Church. 'They've to use all their energies just to find enough food to fill their bellies, let alone anything else.'

'Well, they find enough energy to have these faction fights, don't they? And then join the Whiteboys.'

Sandes moved to the window. 'Ah, I thought so, Peter,' he said over his shoulder. 'There are the Cooleens at the far end of the square. They're putting the green ribbons on their shillelaghs. It won't be long now.'

Church levered himself out of his chair. 'Will the constabulary move between them?'

'Not if Inspector Kiddey values his rank. Faction fights are to be left alone. Those are his orders. Let them break their own heads open. If they weren't fighting each other, they'd be fighting us.'

'True enough,' Church agreed, 'Can you see the Mulvihills yet?'

'Down there by the coaching house, tying on the white ribbons. Don't seem to be as many of them as there are Cooleens.'

His eyes had not deceived him. About ninety of the Cooleens, ribbons fluttering from their shillelaghs, stood at the east end of the square, blocking the track leading to the bridge over the River Feale. Outside the Listowel Arms, about fifty Mulvihills were draining their mugs of porter and whiskey and handing them to the potmen, who were anxious to gather in all the inn's breakable property before the fight started. The last of the cattle were being herded out of the square and Jack Keane, standing nervously with his brothers, was glad to see Brigid Aherne and her mother move into a side alley, pushing their almost empty cart.

'Here, take these, Jack,' said his brother, Michael, handing him three jagged stones. 'Put them in your pocket. You'll soon be needing them.'

'But what can we do?' asked Jack anxiously. 'Can't you see we're outnumbered?'

'That's true enough, Jack, to be sure. But our boys know about these fights. They've got a few surprises yet. You just stand behind John and me and watch us.'

Jack saw the Cooleens beginning to approach in two groups, one on each side of the church in the middle of the square.

'They'll rush us when they've passed the church,' whispered John. 'Then we'll show them a trick or two, I'm thinking.'

'But we'll be cornered by the inn here,' protested Jack, looking nervously around him.

'Better to fight with a wall at your back. They can't sneak behind us then,' said Michael. 'Now stop your blathering and get ready.'

A strange sound began to fill the market square, empty now except for the fighters, as the Cooleens grouped into one body, no more than thirty yards from the waiting Mulvihills. It began low and grew in intensity.

'Coolee . . . coolee . . . coolee . . . coolee.' Rhythmic and menacing, it grew to a shout.

Jack heard his brothers and the men around him begin to answer. Deep in their chests at first, and then louder in their throats, to the stamp of their feet, they began chanting, 'Mmmulvi . . . mmmulvi . . . mmmulvi . . . mmulvi.'

'Coolee . . . mmmulvi . . . coolee . . . mmulvi.' The opposing chants mingled and grew to a crescendo. And then they suddenly stopped. For a few seconds the market square was silent, as if everyone was holding his breath.

Then the Cooleens charged, shouting wildly at the top of their voices.

'Now, Jack, now,' said Michael urgently. 'Get your stones.'

The shrieking Cooleens were no more than ten yards away and Jack could see the distorted grimaces of hate and drunken anger on their faces.

'Now, me boyos,' roared a voice from the side. Jack recognized it as his father's.

'Throw at their legs,' shouted Michael, hurling his first stone with all his strength.

A hail of jagged stones flew low across the narrowing gap between the factions, some skipping up from the hard-trodden earth of the market square. They crashed into the unprotected knees and shins of the running Cooleens, gashing flesh and splintering bone. The front rank of Cooleens leaped and tumbled under the onslaught, screaming with sudden agony, their contortions tripping the men behind them. Twice more, the hail of stones hurtled into the mob of men at waist and knee height. Some Cooleens doubled up, shouting in pain, dropping their shillelaghs to hold on to their genitals where the stones had ripped into them. In seconds, the Cooleens were a mass of tumbling, shrieking men. But the impetus of the unharmed men behind pushed the injured further forward as they tried to retreat.

'Pulp 'em now, boyos,' Jack heard his father cry. And the Mulvihills advanced, shillelaghs swinging at head height, into the disorganized mass of Cooleens, some lying groaning on the ground, others trying to hop backwards clutching their injuries, but all the time being pushed forward into their rivals' flailing shillelaghs.

For the first moments, as the two factions closed together, the unhurt Cooleens were unable to reach the Mulvihills because of the tangle of their own wounded. Cries of agony and panic mingled with oaths and the cracking sounds of the Mulvihill shillelaghs as they found their targets.

Jack felt his fear disappearing as the fight got under way. There was no time to think as the crowd of men pressed round him, cursing and grunting, wielding their heavy sticks. An irrational feeling of anger against the Cooleens grew inside him and he heard himself, almost involuntarily, mouthing the chants and shouts of the others.

'Mmmulvi . . . mmmulvi . . . mmulvi.'

He saw a man lurch in front of him clutching a shillelagh with a green ribbon tied round it, blood streaming from his gashed legs. Jack struck out automatically feeling the shiver of impact run up his stick into his shoulders. His shillelagh caught the Cooleen in the angle of his neck and shoulder and Jack heard the sickening crack as the man's collarbone smashed. The Cooleen dropped his shillelagh and screamed with pain, grabbing his injured shoulder, his knees bending as he began to fall. Without thinking, Jack raised his stick again, holding it with both hands, and brought it down with all his strength squarely on top of the man's head. He dropped without a cry. Jack leapt over him to seek a new opponent. He saw a man trying to drag himself away on one good leg and thwacked him flat across his shoulders. The man looked round into Jack's face, holding up his arms in a mute appeal for mercy but there was none in Jack's heart. He struck again at the man's upraised arm hearing it break just above the elbow. The Cooleen screamed and began writhing in agony on the earth. Jack paid no heed to his suffering, kicking him in the ribs with his hardened feet as he stepped over him. A mist had descended over his mind. All he could hear echoing in his brain was his father's shout, 'Pulp 'em, pulp 'em, pulp 'em.'

By now, though, the main throng of uninjured Cooleens had closed with the advancing Mulvihills. Jack glimpsed a thick-set man swinging his shillelagh at his head. He ducked, raising his own stick, and deflected the fearsome blow downwards. The Cooleen shillelagh thudded into him, skidding off the ribs on his right side. Jack could do nothing but bend double as the wind went out of him. He thrust out his own shillelagh and by luck, rather than judgement, caught the Cooleen a jabbing blow in the pit of his stomach. The man shouted with pain but raised his shillelagh again to strike at Jack, his features blazing with anger. But, before he could bring his stick down, his face went slack, his eyes glazing, and he toppled away towards the ground. Jack saw his brother, Michael, swing at the man again, striking him for the second time on the head.

'He almost got you, Jack,' shouted Michael, above the din of the battle. 'Start moving back now. And watch yourself.'

The two factions were pressed so close together now that it was almost impossible to find room enough to swing their shillelaghs. The man jabbed at each other with their sticks or resorted to using their fists. Jack caught one blow high up on his forehead and staggered back, but the press of Mulvihills behind him saved him from falling. He jabbed out with the shillelagh in his right hand and swung his left fist. The stick caught a Cooleen under his ribs and, as he bent forward, Jack's fist cracked him under his right eye. He looked quickly behind him and saw the Mulvihills being pressed further into the corner of the square. There seemed no chance of escape as the greater number of Cooleens bore down on them, their anger inflamed by their heavy casualties.

'Coolee . . . coolee . . . coolee.' Their cries had a triumphant note in them. They pressed forward until the Mulvihills could move back no further. The men at the back were crushed against the railings outside the coaching house and began to cry out in panic as they felt the breath being squeezed from their bodies.

Jack was pressed hard against a Cooleen, but neither of them was able to do more than hack at the other's shins with his bare feet and scrabble with his hands at the other's already tattered clothes.

'You bastard divil Mulvi.' The Cooleen spat into Jack's face, his fetid breath nauseous and hot.

'Back Coolee . . . back Coolee.' The shout came from the rear of the Cooleens. Jack realized that the enemy was going to retreat slightly to get space to use their shillelaghs against the helpless Mulvihills pinned in the corner. He looked wildly around him for any way of escape but could see none. Then he caught John's eye a few yards away. His brother saw the panic growing in Jack's expression and winked at him.

'Don't worry,' he mouthed. 'Don't worry, Jack.'

And then the pressure of the Cooleens eased. Jack raised his shillelagh again prepared, as he thought, to face the final, devastating attack. The hope flashed through his mind that he wouldn't be too badly beaten or scarred or else he wouldn't be able to meet Brigid Aherne on Saturday.

Suddenly he heard his father's voice booming out across the square. 'Now, boyos, at 'em. Get at 'em.'

Jack couldn't understand. There was no way that the trapped Mulvihills could advance. Then he saw a flurry away to his left. He jumped up to get a better view, catching a glimpse of about thirty men waving shillelaghs bearing white ribbons. They were running out of the entrance to the stables behind the coaching house, shouting the Mulvihill battlecry.

The reinforcements caught the Cooleens totally unaware as they attacked their rear lashing their shillelaghs into men still turning to meet the new threat. Dozens fell under the onslaught, limbs broken, scalps laid bare, their shouts and groans reaching the Cooleens facing Jack and his brothers. Bewilderment and then panic and fear flashed across their faces, as they realized they were caught in a trap, surrounded by Mulvihills on three sides with buildings on the fourth.

'Attack now,' cried Michael. 'Thump 'em into the next county.'

Jack's shillelagh caught a Cooleen high up on his face splitting his cheek. The man reeled away directly into his brothers' two flailing sticks which caught him high across his back and shoulders as he tried to duck away from them.

'Holy Mother . . . ' he gibbered as the blow caught him. 'No more, boys. No more. I'm beaten.'

But now the Mulvihills sensed victory and were in even less of a mood to give quarter. Jack watched Michael steady himself and then smash his shillelagh flat across the man's forehead. He collapsed in a crumpled heap on the ground, blood from his head wounds dripping on to the hard earth. The fight was turning into a rout with the Cooleens fighting desperately to get away from the market square.

The ground beneath their feet was growing slippery with blood and it was becoming difficult to reach those Cooleens who were now in full flight. Within minutes, the last twenty Cooleens were surrounded by more than fifty Mulvihills. Some sank to their knees, holding their shillelaghs over their heads with both hands, trying to ward off the blows. Others, stoically, offered no defence to their attackers, ready to accept the inevitable battering that would send them into unconsciousness. Like a pack of wolves, the Mulvihills bayed their cry of victory as they savaged their opponents.

'Mmmulvi . . . mmmulvi . . . mmmulvi.' There were no answering cries except those of pain and panic and fear.

The three Keane brothers surrounded one Cooleen who crouched low on the ground, his arms wrapped round his head and neck for protection.

Suddenly the brothers were thrust apart as a man burst between them, pushing them away with surprising strength. Jack swung round, ready to attack the intruder.

'Jack, Jack,' cried Michael. ''Tis the Father.'

Father O'Sullivan, thin and wiry with a shock of grey hair, burst his way through the Mulvihills to stand amongst the small group of

Cooleens still upright. He held his arms outstretched, as if putting a protective mantle above the fallen men around him.

'That's enough, boys,' he shouted. 'Stop it, I say. That's enough.'

His strong voice, surprisingly deep and resonant for such a thin man, rose above the hubbub. 'Stop this slaughter,' he exclaimed, spinning round and seeming to pierce every Mulvihill brain with his blazing eyes. 'Can't you see they're finished. Mercy on them!'

Shillelaghs hung in mid-air as the Mulvihills looked to their leaders for instructions. Jack Keane saw his father and two men with him nod their assent.

'Right, boyos,' cried Joe Keane. 'That's enough. The Father's right. They're finished. Come away now.'

The Mulvihills turned away, exhaustion making their shoulders slump as their nerves relaxed and the blood lust drained away. Jack Keane felt curiously tired and dispirited for a moment, but then a sense of victory swept over him. He lifted his head and, with the others, shouted a last Mulvihill battlecry.

'Mmmulvi . . . mmmulvi . . . mmmulvi . . . '

The victors began walking back towards the coaching house, stepping carefully over their fallen opponents, until they came to their own injured. Already the fallen men's womenfolk had hurried from their places of safety to begin tending their wounds.

Listowel market square seemed strangely silent after the violent noise of the fight. It had seemed to go on for hours to those, like Jack, who'd been in the thick of it. In fact, the fight had lasted barely twenty minutes.

'Didn't I tell you?' exulted Joe Keane, slapping his youngest son on his back. 'Didn't I say it'd be no more than a short spat. To be sure, it was.'

Jack smiled and began to untie the white ribbon around his shillelagh. It was red with blood, some of it his own.

Jonathan Sandes and Dr Peter Church stood at the window, their glasses still in their hands.

'The viciousness of them,' whispered Church in awe. 'They're just like wild animals.'

'And so they are, Peter. Wild animals. But cunning, too. Did you see how those Cooleens got themselves trapped. Good tactics by the Mulvihills. Cunning and vicious, that's what they are.'

The two men watched people from the coaching house throw buckets of water over the scores of men still lying on the ground. Some began sitting up, groaning, hands pressed against their bleeding wounds. A few lay still. The priest in his sweeping, black cassock, hurried among these, kneeling to feel their pulses and pressing his ear against their chests to listen to their heart beats. He rose from his knees after a few seconds to move on to the next injured man, satisfied that in time they would recover their senses.

'I wonder if I should go and help,' said Church, who treated patients in his apothecary shop.

'Wouldn't bother, Peter. The priest is very experienced in these things. He's done all there is to be done. They'll all soon be on their feet.'

They began turning away from the window when Sandes stopped. 'Look here a moment. Perhaps I was too hasty.'

Father O'Sullivan was making the sign of the cross above a man lying on the ground. Then he bent down and began whispering into the fallen man's ear. Two women hurried across to where the priest was, the elder wearing a black shawl.

'There's one even you can't help, I'm thinking, Peter,' said Sandes, sipping his glass of wine. 'If I'm not mistaken, the priest's giving him the last rites.'

'Do you think he's dead?' asked Church.

Sandes said in a bored voice, 'They can't all have thick skulls. Short as the fight was, there were some murderous blows struck.'

'To be sure,' agreed Church. 'That's true, I suppose.'

'Not even that unusual as you know,' said Sandes, watching the scene in the square with callous disinterest. 'There were three killed in that fight last year, you remember. Part of the hazards and that's the truth.'

The woman with the black shawl had thrown herself across the man's body, her back heaving with sobs. A younger woman knelt by the priest, her head bent low, praying and crying at the same time. Her red shawl contrasted vividly with the black of the priest's soutane.

Sandes rubbed his hands together. 'Now what about lunch, Peter? Watching that fight's given me quite an appetite. I've a brace of pheasant for us.'

Church moved reluctantly from the window. 'It really ought to be stopped, you know, Jonathan. Men getting killed for nothing.'

'It'll never be stopped. The peasants enjoy it too much. Personally, I think it's a thing to be encouraged.'

In the coaching house, the Mulvihills were drinking their fill, retailing their parts in the battle to each other. Jack Keane was flushed with excitement after having had three large mugs of whiskey forced down him.

'That'll ease your pain, me boyo,' boomed his father, slipping his arm around his son's shoulders and turning him to face the assembled Mulvihills.

'Now look at him, me bonny fighters. What a fighting man he's going to be with some more weight on him.'

The assembled faction roared with approval and Jack felt himself blushing. He felt no pain from his bruised face and ribs, nor from his split knuckles. He was on top of the world, accepted as a man who'd acquitted himself well in his first faction fight.

'Well, what do you say now, young Jack?' asked Michael. 'Twasn't as bad as all that.'

'I thought we were for it.'

'Ah, and didn't I say not to worry? We pulped those Cooleens and no mistake.'

Jack moved to the doorway, his brother still with him. They watched the injured being helped away, limping on sticks, or with arms draped around their family's shoulders. Potmen from the inn were busy sloshing water over the square, clearing the patches of blood away.

'Isn't that your dancing girl over there, Jack?' said Michael, pointing up the square. 'There, where Father O'Sullivan is with that cart. You want to go and show her your wounds. It'll be mighty impressed she'll be and that's the truth.'

'Do you think so?'

'I'm sure so. Off you go, but not too long else we'll be carrying your dad home with all the whiskey he's supping.'

Jack tucked his shillelagh under his arm and strolled across the square, trying to appear as nonchalant as possible. Brigid, with her red shawl and skirt, had her back to him and was helping Father O'Sullivan push something into the cart.

'Brigid, Brigid,' he called as he neared them.

She turned slowly round. Her face was puffy and lined with tears.

'Brigid, what's wrong?' He hurried the last few steps to her side. She said nothing, just nodded her head towards the cart. Jack moved round to stand between her and Father O'Sullivan. He looked into the cart. Two bare legs, grimy and covered with dried blood, protruded from under a pile of sacking.

Jack turned in bewilderment. First to the priest, who merely shook his head sadly, and then to Brigid. 'What? . . . Who? . . . ' he mumbled.

'Me dad,' said Brigid softly. 'He's dead. The fight. It happened in the fight.' She looked at Jack, tears welling in her eyes. 'The fight,' she repeated, beginning to sob. 'His head . . . oh, his poor head.'

Brigid moved a step towards him. Jack dropped his shillelagh and put his arms around her, feeling her tears on his bare chest. She cried quietly for a few moments, then looked up into Jack's face, noticing the bruised lump on his forehead. She stepped back and saw his hand bandaged with a kerchief. Then her eyes moved down his body to rest on the stained shillelagh lying at his feet.

She didn't move her eyes from the shillelagh. She seemed transfixed by it.

'You were in the fight, Jack Keane?' she asked quietly.

'Yes . . . but . . . but I didn't . . . '

'You can't be a Cooleen else I would have seen you,' Brigid reasoned aloud to herself, slowly. 'You're a Mulvihill.'

'Yes . . . but . . . '

'You're a Mulvihill, Jack Keane,' she repeated softly, her green eyes fixed wildly on the shillelagh lying on the ground between them. Then, suddenly, she raised her head and stared into his face. 'You killed him!' she shrieked. 'You killed me father.' Brigid leapt at him and began scratching at his face and chest, sobbing uncontrollably. 'You killed him . . . you . . . you. . .'

Jack tried to push her away but her demented strength was too much for him. He staggered back under her onslaught. 'Brigid, it was the fight,' he exclaimed, gripping her shoulders, trying to hold her away.

'Murderer!' she screeched. 'Murderer!'

She spat into his face as Father O'Sullivan thrust himself between the two youngsters, forcing them apart.

Suddenly, her strength dissolved. She crumpled to the ground, crying uncontrollably, hiding her face in her hands.

Jack moved again to comfort her, wiping the spittle from his cheeks.

The priest restrained him gently. 'Not now, son,' he said quietly. 'Not now. It'll do no good.'

Jack nodded, understanding, and turned away. He walked slowly back towards his family at the inn, his mind filled with the sounds of grief.

# Chapter 3 September, 1822

The sullen sky wept gently with rain. The keening notes of Michael Coffey's fiddle gave Gortacrossane the sound of mourning. The fiddler stood close by the rough walls of the Aherne cabin, his sodden felt hat jammed firmly over his head. Michael Coffey's eyes were fixed rheumily on the distance as he stroked the fiddle tucked under his chin, voicing the almost physical sense of bereavement that hung over the cabin. Sometimes he bowed his head in recognition as a woman, black shawl pulled tightly over her head, moved past him, ducking to enter the low doorway of the cabin. Coffey heard the low murmuring of voices within the cabin punctuated by frequent bouts of sobbing.

He had already been inside to pay his respects to the dead Cooleen. The women of the township had done their best to clean and hide his wounds by wrapping his head in bandages, but they had been unable to cover the dark bruises under his closed eyes. The Aherne women sat in a semi-circle before Tom Aherne's rough coffin, the daughters dry-eyed in their grief, trying to comfort their mother as she swayed and sobbed on the only high-backed chair in the cabin, clutching a cross intertwined with smooth rosary beads. Cooleen men would come with bottles tucked under their arms. Then the cabin would become raucous with noise and the fiddler would stop his laments and help dance Tom Aherne to his grave.

From his position outside the cabin , Michael Coffey noticed a movement by the wall of another cabin fifty yards away. A young man with a shock of black hair peered round the wall, and then emerged to walk slowly towards the Aherne cabin.

Jack Keane presented a sorry sight; his hair plastered to his skull; his clothes clinging like a second skin; mud spattering his calves and covering his bare feet. The memory of Brigid Aherne's contemptuous spittle running down his face while she screamed at him in the square after the faction fight still seared his brain.

His father had been sympathetic but firm in his advice. 'Sure,

Jack, and it's a terrible thing to have happened,' he'd said as the Keane family ate their supper the previous evening. ''Tis a real shame what with you being stuck on his wee girlie. But think if it was me in the box and not him. Would you like a Cooleen calling here to pay a respect? I doubt so. I really do. Better let time pass, I'm thinking.'

Jack had put down his mug of milk and gazed into the peat fire. 'But, Dad, if I don't go now, I'll never be able to ask her to walk with me. She needs comfort, doesn't she?'

He looked towards his mother for support. She nodded. 'He's right, Joe. The wound between them will fester with time, not heal.'

'I'll not be telling you what to do, Jack,' said Joe Keane, rising from his chair and hitching his trousers round his belly with an air of finality. ''Tis your life and your girl. Remember you're Mulvihill and she's Cooleen, no matter what. But you're a fighting man now, not a boy. Do what is in your mind and I pray you're right.'

Jack spent a restless night trying to decide whether he should visit the Ahernes. The next morning the rest of the family restrained themselves from giving him further advice. They let him wander around doing his chores and then watched him move off across the fields towards Gortacrossane.

As Jack neared the Aherne cabin, Michael Coffey recognized him from the night at the Ballybunnion crossroads, and remembered his link with the sorrowing womenfolk inside. He stopped playing and moved towards Jack. ''Tis only women in there, lad,' he said quietly, almost conspiratorially. 'Are you sure tis the right time?' Too well he knew the ritual of a wake; first women to comfort, then men to cheer. It was always that way.

'No,' muttered Jack. 'No, but when is it the right time for me? I have to go now or not at all.'

'Then let me help,' said the fiddler as they approached the damp sacking hanging across the cabin doorway. 'I'll come with you. That's only proper.'

Jack nodded dully. Michael Coffey pulled the sacking aside and entered the cabin first.

The two men stood inside the doorway unnoticed. Jack wiped the rain off his face, not knowing where to look first. Inevitably, his eyes were drawn towards the coffin in the corner of the tiny cabin. He crossed himself quickly as he peered through the half-light, desperately hoping that he wouldn't recognize the dead man as one of those he'd fought in Listowel. He searched his memory, remembering again the upturned faces distorted with panic and agony.

'Thanks be to God,' he murmured almost inaudibly to himself as he realized that he hadn't seen the dead Cooleen before. His shillelagh had not killed Brigid's father. Of that he was certain.

Jack's eyes moved away from the coffin and met those of the womenfolk. Two young girls sat on the earth floor looking at him curiously. They'd be May and Mary, he thought. His gaze flicked across Brigid's face, noting her surprised expression, to her elder sisters, Theresa and Bernadette. They looked at him suspiciously as they crouched on the floor by their mother. Mrs Aherne was bent over her rosary beads.

Brigid was the first to move. She rose from a wooden stool and crossed the cabin in half-a-dozen strides. She stood before Jack looking up into his face. 'Why did you let him in, fiddler?' she asked Michael Coffey quietly, never once moving her eyes from Jack.

The fiddler shuffled nervously. 'He just came. I said it wasn't time. I did say, to be sure. But he came.'

'Well?' asked Brigid, still staring at Jack, pain and bewilderment in her dark-ringed eyes.

'I had to,' he explained softly. 'I just had to, Brigid.'

He looked over her shoulder at the coffin. 'I'm terribly sorry. So are we all.'

'Yes?'

'I had to tell you that now. We're all sorry.' Jack saw a mistiness coming into Brigid's eyes. He leaned slightly towards her. 'What can I do?'

'There's nothing.' A tear formed at the corner of her right eye and began trickling down her cheek. 'Nothing at all anyone can do. It's done, isn't it?'

'Brigid,' Mrs Aherne spoke without looking up. Her voice was low and flat. 'Who is it here?'

Brigid half-turned away from Jack, her red skirt brushing his legs. ''Tis the fiddler and Jack.'

'Your young Jack? The one at the market? Bring him here for his respect then. And give the fiddler a mug.'

Jack walked slowly across the cabin to stand before the coffin. 'Rest in God, Tom Aherne.'

'Amen,' murmured Mrs Aherne vacantly. Her eyes were red from weeping. 'Thank you for coming, young Jack,' she said, glancing quickly up at him. 'It wouldn't be easy, I know. And don't be blaming yourself for it. We're not blaming anyone. Not even your man there.' She nodded towards her dead husband.

Her daughters huddled closer to her as Jack returned to the

doorway. He felt as if a great weight had been lifted from him.

The fiddler drained his mug of poteen and placed it back gently on the rough table. 'All done, lad?'

'Done,' said Jack, beginning to pull aside the sacking of the doorway.

Ten days later, Jack Keane, stripped to the waist, was rebuilding part of a dry-stone wall round the potato field near his family's cabin. In the warm midday sun he picked up the large stones which had fallen to the ground and fitted them back into place, stuffing in lumps of turf to make the wall secure before the fierce winter winds came off the Atlantic. It was a job he enjoyed. He worked steadily away, whistling to himself. It was some minutes before he realized he was being watched. He looked up and there was Brigid Aherne leaning on her elbows on the other side of the wall.

'Sure and aren't we busy now?' she smiled, her head cupped in her hands. 'Perhaps too busy for someone who's walked all this way to see him.'

Jack grabbed at his shirt, reddening with confusion. 'How long have you been there?'

'Long enough to feel I'm being ignored.'

'Wait. I'll come over.'

Jack vaulted over the wall brushing his hands together to rid them of the dirt from the stones and turf. ''Tis glad I am you came.'

Brigid plumped herself on to the ground, resting her back against the wall. She smoothed out the folds of her red skirt and looked up at Jack with an inviting smile. 'Well, don't just stand there. Sit down.' She patted the turf beside her.

'I've been thinking of you, Brigid,' said Jack as he sat beside her. He looked closely at her. He saw that her eyes were once again clear and bright. 'You look fine. Just fine.'

'Well, life has to go on. Me dad's buried and that's that.'

'I thought you were never going to see me again. After the fight you said . . . '

'I know. I am sorry for what I said, Jack.' She reached out a hand. Jack took it and gently squeezed. 'Forget it now.'

'Father O'Sullivan told me what I said. I don't remember at all. I must have gone half mad. I'm sorry.'

''Tis over. How's your mam now?'

'She misses me dad badly. She was always going at him when he was here and now that he's away she misses him. I suppose that's the way of love, isn't it?'

'Sure and it is.'

'But she's over the worst of it; and so are we all.'

Brigid giggled suddenly, spreading her free hand over her mouth. 'Truth, you should have been at the wake, Jack. That was fierce. I think the men were drunk for two days and me mam wasn't much better. Two of them fell in the dung heap and nobody knew they were there until the next day. And then the fiddler's dog went and cocked his leg over the coffin.'

She laughed out loud at Jack's shocked expression.

'You silly. Me dad would have enjoyed the joke looking down on it all. I just hope he had a bottle with him to join in.'

Jack smiled, 'Tis good to see you laughing.'

'And why not, pray? We've cried enough.'

'But how are you going to live now?' Jack asked anxiously, 'with your dad gone?'

'Well, the Cooleens gathered up some money for me mam. Nearly three pounds, they did. It'll keep us for some months at least.'

'And then?'

'We'll see. Us girls can keep the potato patch going. That'll give us food and the Cooleen money will pay the rent.'

'That's a relief for a bit then,' Jack said happily. 'I feel better for you.'

'Just better?' Brigid whispered, glancing down at her hand still clasped in his. 'You feel just better? And don't you remember the crossroads, you big lummock'

'I do that, Brigid.'

They smiled at each other. Brigid leaned towards him. Jack released her hand and put his arm round her shoulders, pulling her to his chest. He felt her breath on his skin where his shirt was unbuttoned.

'You smell nice,' she breathed against him. 'All warm and nice.'

'And you feel nice,' he muttered into the ringlets of her hair. 'All soft and round and nice.'

'Do I, Jack?' Brigid raised her head and looked up at him.

They gazed deeply into each other's eyes. Jack felt himself tremble as their faces were drawn towards each other. Their lips met, softly at first, then harder. Brigid's mouth opened under the pressure and Jack felt the tip of her warm tongue push between his teeth, gently exploring. They kissed until they were breathless, Brigid's eyes looking hugely into his. They were like green pools of Erin fire.

For long moments they gazed at each other. Then Brigid moved her head back on to his chest. 'There,' was all she said. And then again, 'There.'

The two youngsters rested against the wall, warmed by the sun and their love, both too happy to speak.

'I always knew this would be.' Brigid's quiet, wondering voice broke the silence. 'Ever since I first saw you, I just knew.'

'When I ducked you in the sea?'

'No. No, long before that.'

Jack started with surprise, pushing Brigid slightly away from him and turning her to face him. 'Before that?' he asked.

Brigid smiled mischievously. 'Oh, a year or so. Ever since I saw you with your mam and dad at market. It took a time to find your name, that it did.'

He grabbed her shoulders, feeling their firmness under her green blouse. A broad grin spread over his even features. 'You little divil! You . . .'

'Now aren't you glad, Jack Keane?' she interrupted. 'You said you didn't mind being trapped.'

Jack threw back his head and laughed. 'Trapped? That I am, but I'm wondering who trapped who?'

'We both did, didn't we?' said Brigid gently, putting her arms around his neck. 'And it's not bad. Tell me it's not bad.'

'No, not at all.'

They kissed again. But this time it was a different embrace. There was a sureness about it, a certainty. It was a kiss that sealed a bond as yet unspoken. They both knew that now their lives and loves were committed.

Jack pulled away first and stood up.

Brigid pouted, 'You're tired of me already then?'

'No, but I'm thinking you must be as hungry as me. Come to our cabin and eat. I'm sure me mam will have enough for you.'

He offered her his hands and, as she took them, pulled her to her feet.

'Are you sure it'll be all right with your mam and dad?' asked Brigid.

'I'm sure, mavourneen.' Jack savoured the endearment. 'Mavourneen Brigid,' he repeated.

'Avourneen Jack,' she whispered, smiling at him.

Together, hands clasped, they strolled towards the Keane cabin. Jack's mother was putting some washing over the cabin wall to dry and realized that her son was with the girl Cooleen. They made a handsome couple, she thought proudly. At the same moment she knew a strange sadness. Her youngest child was now grown up, she realized, and the long parting had begun.

Mistress Keane went forward and stood before Brigid. 'Welcome, little one.'

Tentatively, she bent forward and kissed the girl's cheek, noting the happiness shining in her eyes. She felt a twinge of envy, remembering suddenly when she'd first been in love with Joe Keane. She took Brigid's free hand and led her into the cabin.

Jack's father and brothers soon warmed to Brigid's infectious gaiety. By the time they'd finished their meal there was an unspoken but complete acceptance that here was a new member of the family.

Eventually, Michael, a broad grin on his face, spoke the words that were in everyone's thoughts. 'I'm thinking, Mam, we'll need feeding up like this through the winter if we're to build a new cabin in the spring.'

He looked directly at Jack and Brigid. 'If that's not too long a time, that is.'

The family laughed as they saw the two youngsters blush beet red. The small cabin was filled with happiness.

The winter winds howling off the pounding Atlantic transformed West Kerry into a bleak wilderness. People huddled around their peat fires, only half warm, as the relentless wind found every chink in the walls and windows. They rarely ventured out, hibernating like squirrels and living on the meagre supplies of potatoes and corn they'd managed to harvest during the summer and autumn. Their animals spent the winter inside the cabins too, bringing some precious warmth along with the pungent smell of fresh dung. To survive was enough. Sickly babies and frail old folk died from pneumonia and were buried with little ceremony in shallow graves hacked from the frozen earth. Those families which ran out of food begged handfuls of corn from their neighbours and searched potato patches for any left-over lumpers. Even wrapped in sacking, they froze to their bones as they scrabbled with stafans – large bent hoes – in deserted fields under the fast-moving, grey clouds from the west that brought biting rain or flurries of snow. By St Stephen's Day, the workhouse in Listowel was crowded to overflowing with families who had given up the struggle. Here, at least, was warmth and a daily chunk of bread and a bowl of thin gruel. Their deserted cabins were soon torn apart by the ever-searching wind.

For Jonathan Sandes, the winter was an equally difficult time. Rents went unpaid and he had either to reprieve families at a properly burdensome rate of interest on their arrears, or condemn them, with the workhouse full, to a makeshift home in a ditch with an inadequate roof made from branches covered with sods of turf. Thus it was, in early January, 1823, that the plight of the Aherne womenfolk came to his notice. Jonathan Sandes at sat a desk by a crackling log fire in the study of his home at Listowel hearing the weekly report from his rent collector, Finn Bowler.

'Tis my opinion, sir, that we shall get no more rent from them,' said Bowler, a stout figure in heavy, rough tweeds. 'I'm believing we should have had them out after their man died in last year's fight.'

'Is that so, Bowler?' said Sandes, his voice drawling with sarcasm and mulled wine. 'And, pray, would we not have aroused some wrath if we'd done that? I'd have had the Whiteboys through my front door and no mistake. What grounds would we have had for putting them in the ditch? The Cooleen's woman was able to pay her quarter's rent.'

'Well, that's not the case now, sir. They've no money, precious little food, and no prospect of getting either when spring comes. I'm thinking we should cut our losses.'

Sandes drained his pewter mug and poured himself some more wine. He rose from his desk a trifle unsteadily and walked over to the fireplace picking up a glowing poker which had been thrust into the burning wood. This he pushed into his mug of wine with a sizzle. As he did so, he reflected yet again on the harshness of Irishman to Irishman. The peasants call me heartless and cruel, he thought, and yet here's one of their own, a man only marginally higher in station than them, who'd be as ruthless as any land agent. The peasants were their own worst enemies, he reckoned. Squabbling among themselves, killing each other, betraying one another. What chance did they have? But what if they united against a common enemy? The thought made Jonathan Sandes shiver inwardly even in the sweating warmth of his study.

'So that's what you think should be done, Bowler?' he said aloud as he resumed his seat behind his desk.

'It is, sir. It is.'

Sandes looked at him curiously as he stood before him, perspiring in the heat of the fire. Bowler's judgement was usually correct. The rent collector drew on the cunning that had carried him unscathed through the wars against Bonaparte.

'I just wonder, Bowler. Remind me, how many there are?'

'The mother, sir and five strapping girls. One of them is set to jump over the broom in the spring with a lad from Drombeg, so it's really only four.'

'A marriage, eh? And the lad's family can't help?'

'Tis Joe Keane's boy, sir. The Keanes have little enough to spare, as you know. They've only just paid off the gombeen man.'

Jonathan Sandes smiled blearily at Bowler. 'Well then, we shall have to do something, won't we? The first fine day and we'll ride out there together and have a look at this gaggle of women'.

Four days later, Sandes, astride his favourite bay hunter, trotted among the battered and sorry-looking cabins of Gortacrossane. His high-crowned, silver-grey riding hat perfectly matched his thick coat. His brown leather boots gleamed with polish.

Finn Bowler, beside him on a shaggy, ungroomed horse that had seen better years, pointed out the Aherne cabin. 'Shall you be going in, sir?' inquired Bowler, his breath whitening on the sunny but still cold air.

Sandes raised a pained eyebrow. 'In there, Bowler?' He pointed disdainfully with his riding crop. 'Indeed not. Call the women out '

Finn Bowler sidled his horse as near to the doorway as he could and, bending in the saddle, shouted into the cabin. 'Mistress Aherne. Tis Bowler here. I have Master Sandes with me. Will you be coming out now, woman?'

The two men heard a sudden chatter of female voices. A few moments later the sacking across the doorway was pulled aside and Mrs Aherne appeared, a black shawl over her head. She stood, her arms folded across her, gazing up at the men high on their horses. She'd been expecting this call ever since she'd told Finn Bowler that she was unable to pay the next quarter's rent. One by one, her daughters stepped through the doorway behind her, all muffled against the cold, their faces pinched and grey from lack of food and warmth. Jonathan Sandes surveyed them with distaste.

'Well, Mistress Aherne,' he said coldly, 'And what are we going to do about this rent you're owing?'

'I don't know, sir,' she replied quietly, after a moment's hesitation. 'It has been terrible hard since me man was killed last year The girls have done their best . . .'

'But not well enough, I fear,' interrupted Sandes. 'The rent must be paid, you know, if you're to stay on. Sir James is most clear on that point.'

'Sir, things will be better when the winter is over. We'll plant the patch and have a few things to sell at market.'

'Perhaps so, Mrs Aherne. Perhaps. But until then, what? How's the rent coming?'

'Can't you wait until next quarter, sir?' Mistress Aherne asked desperately.

Sandes smiled without the least warmth in his expression. 'If it was me, Mistress Aherne . . . if it was only me . . . but Sir James would have my hide. Let you off with the rent and they'd all want the same. You must see my position.'

'I don't know, sir. I just don't know,' she whispered, her eyes lowered. She was near tears as she searched her mind for some way to postpone the inevitable sentence of eviction.

'Can't your daughters find other work?'

'They've tried, sir, but there's none. No one has any money to spare.'

Sandes looked more closely at the girls standing protectively by their mother. Two were too young, two looked old before their time, but the fifth . . . now that's the prize of the litter, he thought, as he noted Brigid's fine beauty. He pointed his crop at her. 'You, girl, step forward.'

Brigid's green eyes flicked up at him defiantly. Mistress Aherne turned and gave her daughter a push. Reluctantly, she moved out of the group and stood by Sandes's horse.

The land agent looked down at her. A pretty one this, he decided, with a good spirit as well. An idea began forming in his mind. 'Can't she find service in a house?' he asked Mistress Aherne looking over Brigid's head.

'But, sir, Brigid's getting wed in the spring.'

'Well? She has a few months to wait. Time enough to work if she wants to keep the cabin.'

Mistress Aherne didn't reply.

Sandes spoke directly to Brigid. 'Do you want to work, girl?'

'Yes, sir,' Brigid said quietly. 'I'll work . . . but where?'

Sandes made up his mind. It would solve the problem. 'There's a girl needed in my kitchens. You'll get food and somewhere to sleep. Work for a full quarter and I'll reckon the rent on the cabin is paid. What do you say?'

She looked round at her mother, a mute appeal on her face. Mistress Aherne dropped her eyes to the ground and shrugged her shoulders. Brigid turned her head slowly and gazed up at the land agent. 'All right, sir,' she said resignedly. 'If working for you is the only way, then I'll work.'

'Good. That's settled then. Come to the kitchens on Monday.'

'Yes, sir.'

'A good girl you've got there, Mistress Aherene,' Sandes called as he took up his horse's reins again. 'She'll do you credit, I'm sure.'

Brigid's mother nodded dumbly. Tears were running down her full cheeks. As Sandes and Finn Bowler trotted away, Brigid ran into her mother's arms. 'Twas the only way,' sobbed Mistress Aherne. 'The only way.'

Brigid Aherne arrived in Listowel just as the first grey January light was breaking the darkness. The streets of the small town were completely deserted. Everywhere there was the eerie silence that preceded a new day.

The castle ruins, picked out in the dull light, looked more fore-boding than usual. It was hard now to imagine that once, near the end of the thirteenth century the castle had been all there was of the town. That'd been when the all-conquering Norman family of Fitz-maurice, the Lords of Kerry, had started the construction to protect the strategic ford across the River Feale.

At her ditch school, Brigid had learned something of the violent history of the North Kerry plain; how it had once been inhabited by a Celtic people called the Alltraighe, later to be known as the O'Connors; how learned monks had built an abbey at Rattoo, nine miles from Listowel, fortified against the Norsemen who raided and plundered from their settlements along the Shannon, until the Normans had arrived and overwhelmed the native populace in their turn.

For the Kerry people, like most Celtic Irish, it had been a history of raid and rape, conquest upon conquest, death and terror at the hands of alien races. And finally, of course, it had been the English who conquered all.

Sir Charles Wilmot, for Queen Elizabeth the First, had besieged Listowel Castle in the winter of 1600, taking it after a month from the rebellious descendants of the Normans. They, and their native Kerry supporters, dozens of them, had been hanged from the para-pets, dangling till their flesh had been picked to the bone by grateful carrion. The thought of that time, the awful images, made Brigid shiver even more in the sharp cold of the morning.

She stood in the market square, gazing round, apprehensive. Her feet in Loipins, soleless stockings, were frozen nearly solid from her two-mile trudge over frost-hardened tracks and fields. She walked down an alley by the side of Jonathan Sandes' house and saw the glow of an oil lamp in a basement window. She went down three steps and knocked at the kitchen door, timidly at first and then harder. After some minutes Brigid heard bare feet padding up to the door, bolts being drawn, and a key turning. The door was opened by a girl with long, dark hair, not much older than herself, dressed only in a white shift that emphasized the plumpness of her body. Her voice was full of sleep.

'So what are you wanting this early in the morning?'

'I'm to work here,' Brigid said nervously.

'Oh, the new girl, is it? Well, come in quickly. Tis perishing I am with no clothes on.' The dark-haired girl beckoned Brigid inside and locked the door behind her.

'What's your name then?'

'Tis Brigid Aherne.'

'Welcome then, Brigid. My name's Finoola Gaughan. I'm thinking you're to work in the kitchens with me.'

'That's what Master Sandes said.' Brigid shivered with cold.

'Here now,' said Finoola. 'Here's me blathering on about being perished and sure you must be real frozen. Come into the warmth. I've just lit the range.'

The sight of the kitchen took Brigid's breath away. She had never seen anything so luxurious before. It was the size of her family's small cabin with a long wooden table and chairs and a cooking range running almost the length of one wall. By the range was a rocking chair filled with cushions.

'Well, sit yourself down and have a warm, Brigid,' said Finoola as she went to the range and dipped her finger in a large bowl of water which was warming over the range.

Brigid moved towards the rocking chair. She'd never sat in such a chair in all her life.

'Not that one,' said Finoola sharply. 'Only the cook, Mistress Stack, sits there. Pull up one of the others.'

'Is Mistress Stack . . . ?'

'No. She's not up yet. She sleeps the sleep of a good widow woman, that she does. And the master and mistress were out hunting with the O'Mahony yesterday so they'll not be rising yet awhile.'

'What is it I have to do, Finoola?' asked Brigid.

'Just warm yourself for now. Mistress Stack will tell you herself. Humping water from the pump in the square, cleaning dishes and pans, carrying food to the dining room, and such like.' Finoola went on, smiling mischievously 'There's one or two other duties but you'll be learning about them soon enough.'

'Where do I sleep? Do you know?'

'There's a room in the attic for us. Tis quite cosy enough. Warmer than the cabin you're coming from, I'm thinking.'

'It couldn't be any colder,' Brigid conceded with a smile.

'Good. Tis glad I am you're smiling. We'll get on well enough, I'm sure.'

Brigid spent her first day in a welter of bewildering activity. Mistress Stack, a tiny, dried-up woman with a sharp tongue, ordered her from this task to that. She watched wide-eyed as meals that were feasts to her were cooked and carried upstairs without any comment. That evening she tasted beef for the first time in her life as Mistress Stack carved at the remains of the joint left at dinner by Jonathan Sandes and his wife. By the time she'd finished eating, she was almost asleep in her chair with exhaustion.

'To bed, girl,' ordered Mistress Stack, a slightly friendlier tone in her voice. 'You've had a hard first day. I made it like that so that you would know that although we have warm beds and full bellies here, we have to work for them. You're a lucky girl being here. And don't you be forgetting it. Now off you go with Finoola.'

The two girls climbed four flights of narrow back stairs to their room with Finoola lighting the way with a smoking candle. The room was tiny with a low, sloping ceiling and a small uncurtained window.

Finoola unbuttoned her skirt, letting it fall carelessly to the floor, and shrugged off her blouse. Then she lifted the hem of her white shift and pulled it over her head. Without a trace of embarrassment she stood naked before Brigid for a moment and then climbed under the blankets. 'Come on then, Brigid,' she said quietly, patting the bed beside her. 'Tis cold here without you.'

Brigid had never undressed before a stranger in her life. She turned her back to Finoola as she quickly pulled off her blouse and dropped her skirt. She blew out the candle on the windowsill before getting into bed. She'd often slept with her sisters but the feel of a strange, warm body against hers was different, somehow exciting. Finoola put her arms round her and pulled her close. Brigid, to her surprise, realized that Finoola's nipples were erect as they pushed against her breasts. She tried to move away but there was little spare room in the narrow bed. Brigid felt Finoola's breath against her cheek.

'A goodnight kiss, little one?' whispered Finoola, pressing her lips against Brigid's, moving her hands caressingly down her back towards her firm buttocks. Brigid could feel her bed companion trembling against her. Finoola's lips pressed insistently on hers and her tongue prised open Brigid's mouth and darted between her teeth. She tried to push Finoola away with her knees, but the dark-haired girl gripped one firmly between her legs and began pressing down on it rhythmically.

Brigid pulled her face away with an effort. 'What are you doing, Finoola?' she gasped.

'Just a cuddle, little one. Just a goodnight cuddle,' Finoola crooned in her ear.

'Well, I'm tired out. Go to sleep,' said Brigid, pulling out of Finoola's grasp and turning her back on her.

'All right,' sulked Finoola. 'But it's sure I am that your pretty body wants a proper cuddle.'

The last thing Brigid heard before sleep overwhelmed her was Finoola's voice speaking to no one in particular. 'And so innocent too. Master Sandes made a proper fine choice in her.'

When Brigid awoke next morning she didn't recognize her new surroundings. She gazed at the ceiling and wondered why it wasn't thatched. And then she remembered where she was.

'I bet you were thinking you were still in your mam's cabin,' whispered Finoola beside her, noticing Brigid's confused expression.

'I was that.' She felt Finoola's arms encircle her, her hands gently squeezing her breasts.

'And isn't this a sight more comfy?' murmured Finoola, her caresses becoming more urgent.

In her half-wakened state, Brigid felt a warmth inside her that she'd never known before. She pressed her back against Finoola and shivered slightly as her companion's hand wandered over her body. She could stay like this for ever, she thought dreamily to herself. Then Finoola's hand slipped between her thighs and tried to push them apart.

'What are you doing?' Brigid asked angrily, pushing the intrusive hands away and sitting upright in the bed.

'Just warming you,' said Finoola softly.

'Well, you can stop it,' cried Brigid angrily, now fully awake.

'Oh, don't say you didn't like it,' muttered Finoola crossly. 'Look at those.' She reached up and tweaked Brigid's firm-pointed breasts.

Brigid blushed in the half-light as she realized that the caresses had excited her. She jumped out of bed and pulled on her skirt and blouse. 'I'll see you in the kitchen,' she muttered to Finoola as she left the attic room in some confusion.

In the days that followed neither girl mentioned the incident again although Brigid took to sleeping fully-clothed, much to

Finoola's annoyance. After the strangeness of her surroundings wore off, Brigid began to enjoy her work. She wasn't allowed to serve meals in the dining room yet but Mistress Stack, recognizing her interest, began to give her little hints about cooking and even allowed her to do simple jobs at the range like par-boiling potatoes or frying eggs. Her relations with Finoola were easy enough outside the confines of their shared room and the two girls discovered they had a deal in common. Finoola, too, was in service because her father had met an untimely death from pneumonia. Her mother and younger brother and sister remained in their cabin at Shanacool, near Listowel, simply because Finoola worked for the land agent. Brigid learned that, like Finoola, she would be allowed one free day each month when she could visit her home. She began counting the days until she would see Jack and her family again.

One morning, three weeks after she'd joined the household she entered the kitchen to find Mistress Stack hard at work on her own. The cook was wrapping cuts of beef and ham, pies and cakes, in muslin cloth and packing them in a large wicker hamper.

'Tis the mistress going away,' she explained to Brigid. 'Her sister in Cork has been brought down ill so the mistress will be off visiting for a few days. You can give me a hand.'

Together they had the hamper of provisions ready in time for Finn Bowler to carry it, puffing and blowing under its weight, to the daily stage coach that trundled the rutted tracks between Limerick, Listowel, and Cork.

After saying goodbye to his wife, Jonathan Sandes worked in his study and ate alone, served, as usual, by Finoola. Brigid was doing the dishes when Finoola told her that she was to serve a meal that evening for the first time.

'Master Sandes wants to know how much you've learned,' Finoola said, a quiet smile playing around her mouth. 'Oh, not to worry, I'll be here to help you. And, by the by, the master says you've got to bathe this afternoon and put on some of my clean clothes before serving him.'

'Why should that be?' asked Brigid.

'He wants you looking your best, I'm thinking.' Finoola put her arm round Brigid's shoulders and squeezed affectionately. 'Twas the same with me when I started here. You'll be all right.'

That afternoon, while Mistress Stack was resting in her room, the two girls filled as many pans as they could with water and heated them on the range. Finoola dragged a tin hip-bath into the kitchen and began filling it with warm water. Brigid watched in amazement.

She'd heard about people bathing in such things but she'd assumed they were only used by the very rich. Until now, washing in cold rain water had been good enough for her and her sisters.

Finoola tested the water with her finger and added a little cold water. 'Now that's about right,' she announced. 'In you get, little one, and I'll be bringing some towels and fresh clothes.'

Brigid undressed and stepped gingerly into the bath. Steaming water slopped over on to the wooden floor as she lowered herself into an awkward and uncomfortable sitting position. Finoola returned to the kitchen with her arms full of clothes and towels.

'Holy Mother of God. You look as though you're being tortured,' she laughed, seeing the worried expression on Brigid's face as she sat stiffly in the bath covering her breasts with her hands. 'Relax, little one. The water won't hurt you. Here, I'll soap your back and then you can wash yourself.'

Finoola leaned over the hip-bath splashing Brigid with the warm water and then rubbed soap over her smooth back, working her hand in a circular motion. Brigid sighed as a delicious feeling of relaxation spread over her. She smiled gratefully up at Finoola.

'Tis nice indeed, this bathing.'

'You look all pink and fresh – like a new-peeled prawn, that you do,' smiled Finoola, standing back and looking admiringly at Brigid. 'Now to make you smell sweet as well.' She produced a small glass vial from a pocket in her skirt, uncorked it, and sprinkled the contents into the bath.

'A touch of the mistress's perfume,' she explained. 'She won't miss it and it'll remind the master of her when he smells it on you.'

'Won't he be angry?'

Finoola looked pityingly at her. 'So beautiful you are and so innocent.' She shrugged as she picked up a towel. 'Still, it's none of my business. Here, out you get and dry yourself.'

That evening Mistress Stack cooked a meal of roast mutton with dumplings and roasted potatoes. Finoola showed Brigid how to lay out the table in the dining room; the way to uncork a bottle of claret; and the correct procedure for serving the meal.

'The master'll do his own carving of the meat but you'll have to give him his vegetables and then wait outside the door while he eats,' she instructed Brigid. 'When he's finished, he'll ring his little bell and you clear away and serve the pudding and then wait outside again. That's all there is to it. Then he'll expect you to take him his brandy and baccy later on.'

Jonathan Sandes greeted Brigid with a long, admiring look when

49

she carried in the covered meat platter. The white blouse she'd borrowed from Finoola emphasized the raven blackness of her hair; the green skirt matched her eyes almost exactly; and a wide, buckled belt showed off her slim roundness.

'Welcome to the dining room, Brigid,' he said, pointing to the space on the table where the platter had to go. 'You're looking a sight better than when I last saw you. It shows you what good food, hard work and a warm bed will do, eh?'

Brigid merely nodded.

'Come along girl. Lost your pretty tongue?'

'No, sir.'

'Good.'

Sandes lifted the cover off the platter and sniffed the aroma rising from the mutton.

'Just the meat to build a man's strength, eh, Brigid?' he smiled.

He didn't speak to her again until he'd finished his meal and was half-way through his second bottle of claret.

'Wait fifteen minutes, Brigid,' he ordered. 'And then serve me in my dressing room upstairs. Finoola will tell you where.'

When Brigid reached the kitchen, she found that Finoola had already prepared a tray carrying a decanter of brandy, a bowl of tobacco, a clay churchwarden pipe, and two crystal glasses.

'Two glasses?' Brigid asked. 'But the mistress is away.'

'The master will probably offer you a glass,' said Finoola, a strained, curt note in her voice. 'He usually gives me one when he's on his own. And it's no good refusing him because he'll be insisting you drink with him.'

Brigid walked carefully up the stairs, balancing the tray, and knocked quietly on the brown mahogany door. Sandes swung it open, looming over her, dressed now in a long, dark green dressing gown with quilted lapels. He stood aside to let Brigid squeeze past him with the tray. The drawing room was lit by two candles, casting flickering shadows over the heavy maroon curtains and the two easy chairs in the room. Through a second door, Brigid glimpsed the bedroom, looking rosy and warm from the wood fire she guessed was burning in the grate. She placed the tray on a low table and turned to leave.

'Not so fast, little Brigid,' said Sandes sharply. 'You have two glasses on the tray so I'm guessing Finoola has told you I like my serving girl to take a drink with me before retiring.' He lifted the stopper off the decanter and poured out two large glasses. He handed one to Brigid. 'Take this and sit down.'

Brigid huddled back in the upholstered chair furthest away from Sandes.

'Have you ever tasted brandy, Brigid?' he asked, trying to inject a trace of gentleness into his normally sharp voice.

'No, sir,' she whispered. 'But I have sipped a little poteen.'

'Well, drink your glass then. This is much better than that cabin-brewed poison.'

She smelled the sweet brandy fumes before she tasted the amber liquid. It warmed her stomach quickly without burning her throat like poteen. 'Tis good, sir,' she agreed.

'Good? That's the finest French brandy, Brigid. Good?' he repeated jocularly. 'Tis the very best.' He hovered over her filling her glass to the brim again. Brigid tried to stop him but he brushed her protesting hand away. He put his glass down and moved his chair nearer to Brigid's.

'I hear good reports of your work, Brigid,' he said expansively. 'From the way you served table tonight you've not been idle. I can always tell a girl who'll learn to her advantage.'

'Thank you, sir,' said Brigid, gulping a large mouthful of brandy in her surprise at the unexpected sincerity in the compliment. Master Sandes could be quite pleasant, she thought. She found his face slipping a little out of focus. The room was terribly hot all of a sudden, she noticed. She wiped her hand across her brow.

'Anything the matter, Brigid?' inquired Sandes, anxiety apparent in his voice.

'Just a little dizzy, sir. 'Tis the heat in this room.'

'Well, come and lie down next door. You'll be better soon.'

'No, sir,' protested Brigid, trying to struggle from the depths of the chair. 'I'll get to my bed.'

'I insist, Brigid. Remember I'm your master. I know best.'

Sandes rose from his chair and lifted Brigid around her waist as if she weighed nothing.

'Put me down,' she cried twisting in his arms. 'Put me down.'

Despite her efforts, he carried her easily into the bedroom and sat on the four-poster bed. Brigid, now thoroughly alarmed, prepared for a further struggle, but, to her surprise, he moved away from her towards the door.

'Now just lie down and have a rest, little Brigid,' he said quietly. 'Don't be alarmed. I'll be next door.'

He left the bedroom, shutting the door behind him. Brigid fell back across the bed and giggled to herself. She'd been prepared for the worst and now she was alone on the most comfortable bed she'd ever lain in. She gazed into the flames of the roaring fire in the grate for a few moments, her head still spinning, then fell into a deep sleep.

Next door, Jonathan Sandes, still smiling, poured himself another brandy.

Soon there came a low knock on the door. It opened slowly and Finoola came into the room. 'Where is she?' she whispered.

Sandes put a finger over his lips and pointed at the closed bedroom door. Finoola nodded and tiptoed over to his chair. She looked down at him for a moment and then bent and kissed him on the lips. Sandes grasped her round her waist pulling her on to his knee.

'Have you . . . ?' Finoola breathed in his ear.

'Not yet. The drink got to her too quickly. She's mighty innocent, is little Brigid.'

'So was I once.'

'But not any more, eh, Finoola?' murmured Sandes, fondling her breasts through the thin blouse and kissing her.

Finoola pulled away and stood up. She unbuttoned her blouse quickly and let it slip off her shoulders. Then she unbuckled the belt round her waist to allow her skirt to fall to the carpet. She stood naked before him caressing her full breasts with her hands, smiling down at him. Sandes half-rose from the chair to untie the sash of his dressing gown. Finoola knelt between his thighs, running her short fingernails over his bare chest. Then, with deft fingers, she opened the waist of his grey breeches, lifting his swollen manhood into the flickering candlelight. She rested her head on his thigh, her long hair falling over his flat stomach, as she caressed and kissed him. He moaned with pleasure.

'Next door,' he gasped. 'Let's go next door.'

Sandes stood up and took off his dressing gown. His open breeches fell to his knees. 'Get her prepared,' he muttered thickly. 'Don't worry, you vixen. There's enough for both of you.'

Brigid was still fast asleep as Finoola entered the bedroom. She scarcely felt practised hands opening her blouse and slipping off her skirt. Brigid murmured once in her dreams and that was all. Sandes stood by the bed as Finoola caressed the sleeping girl. His excitement hardened as he looked at the two young, naked bodies lying close together on the bed. He could bear it no longer.

'Is she ready?' he whispered to Finoola.

Finoola's insistent hands wandered over Brigid's smooth thighs, parting them gently. Brigid began to stir under the pressure, coming out of her sleep. She tried to sit up as she felt her legs jerked firmly apart, but the weight of Jonathan Sandes pinned her to the bed. Her eyes looked wildly into his face, distorted with passion. Her mouth opened to scream but Finoola's hand clamped across her lips. She tried to beat Sandes away with her fists only to find her arms held by the wrists as he began to thrust into her. She tried to twist away but was held fast. Suddenly, she moaned as she felt a sharp pain between her legs and then Sandes was in her and the pain had dulled. His body pushed her thighs achingly wider than they'd ever been. He pumped urgently into her. She moaned in anguish as she saw Finoola next to her watching with wild excitement in her eyes, fingers busy between her own thighs.

Brigid thought she was being torn in half. She could feel Sandes quickening his plunging strokes. Then he stiffened above her, groaning deep in his throat. Brigid's insides flooded with pulsing liquid warmth and then there was only blackness as she fainted.

Brigid regained her senses to find herself still in the four-poster bed. Finoola was cradling her in her arms, an expression of relief mingled with concern on her face. For a moment Brigid couldn't remember what had happened but then the aching soreness of her limbs brought it all back to her. 'Oh, God,' she sobbed. 'He's taken me. The bastard divil has taken me.'

'Hush, Brigid,' crooned Finoola, feeling her companion's tears on her skin. 'Tisn't the end of the world. It happened to me as well . . . '

'You . . . you . . . you helped him, you did,' Brigid complained bitterly, heaving with sobs.

'If I hadn't it would have been even worse for you,' said Finoola matter of factly, no trace of contrition in her voice. 'He was much rougher with me.'

'But you were enjoying it.'

'So will you one day.'

'Never. Never. Help me get dressed and out of this divil's house,' Brigid pleaded, sitting up on the bed.

'And, sure, and what good will that do?'

'I have to get away.'

'If you leave it'll be the worse for your family.'

'But I'm getting wed in a few months to me Jack.'

'Who'd have you as a bride now, little one,' said Finoola coldly. 'I don't want to hurt you but there's no mistaking that.'

'Oh, Holy Mother of God. Why? . . . Why? . . . ' Brigid sobbed into the bed. She turned and looked directly at Finoola. 'Is there nothing I can do? If there's not, I'll kill myself.'

'And, sure, that's a mortal sin. You won't be doing that.'

'But what can I do?'

'Nothing, as I told you. From the minute you stepped into this house you were the master's property, you poor little one,' said Finoola, shaking her head sadly. She put her arms round Brigid to comfort her. 'All that's happened tonight, Brigid, is that Master Sandes has put his brand on you, and that's the truth.'


## Chapter 4 March, 1823


The only sounds in Jack Keane's ears were the beating of his own heart, the burring of the nightjars, and the spluttering of the rush torches that lit the small clearing in the copse of yew trees. He stood alone in the circle of white-shirted men. His eyes still ached from the tight blindfold that his brothers had put on him before leading him the last half mile to the meeting place of the Whiteboys. Jack knew it was to the east of Listowel, somewhere near the township of Duagh, but he didn't know exactly where. He had been warned by Michael and John about the blindfold after he had persuaded them, much against their better judgement, to let him be initiated into the Whiteboys. But Jack was still frightened by the aura of menace in the silent gathering of men. He shivered slightly in the cold night.

Suddenly, a man stepped forward from the circle and walked slowly towards him stopping a few yards away. 'Who brought you here to a meeting of the association, Jack Keane?' he demanded in a clear voice that echoed around the copse.

'My brothers did,' Jack said as loudly as his dry throat allowed.

'Is that so?' said the man, turning back to the circle.

'It is so, Master Whiteboy,' chorused two voices from the circle. Jack recognized them as belonging to his brothers.

The man took another pace towards Jack. 'And is it so that you wish to join this association?'

'Yes, it is so.'

'Tell why then, that we may examine you and judge whether you are suitably fitted.'

Now the man was nearer to him, Jack could see in the twilight that he had a vivid scar across his forehead and a badly misshapen nose that seemed to spread over his entire face.

Jack began to reply, 'I have been done . . . '

'Speak up, I tell you,' interrupted the man. 'All the brothers here gathered will hear you.'

'I have been done harm by Master Jonathan Sandes and wish to be avenged.'

A murmur ran round the circle of men at the mention of the land agent's name.

'What harm, Jack Keane?'

'I was to be married but he took the girl into his service and has so twisted her opinion of me that she will not even meet me anymore. He has cast a spell on her and she is no longer mine. She turns her face from me.'

'And you wish to revenge yourself on this man?'

'I do.'

'What say you, brothers?' called the man, raising his voice. 'Is his cause worthy?'

A low mutter of assent came from the assembled Whiteboys.

'Then, Jack Keane,' said the man, 'You can join the association when you have taken the proper oath.'

A second man moved from the circle. In the flickering half-light, his billowing white shirt made him look like a giant white moth. He walked up to Jack carrying a shallow bowl. He grasped Jack's right hand and pushed the bowl into his left. Then he pulled a knife from his belt and drew it sharply across Jack's palm. Jack winced at the sudden pain. The man held his hand over the bowl, which Jack could see was half-filled with water, letting the blood run into it. He let go of Jack's hand after a minute when the water in the bowl had turned red. The bowl was taken from Jack and handed to Master Whiteboy.

'Jack Keane, this is the oath and article of the association. Be knowing that if you disclose them you will be cast into hell from a high place and your remains, such as they may be, consumed by the swine of the field. Are you knowing this?'

'Yes,' Jack gulped.

'Know this also,' cried Master Whiteboy in ringing tones, 'This secret association shall fight the soldiers of the foreign oppressor. We shall drive the usurpers from the island of our fathers. We shall not bend in subjection nor shall we hold in honour those that most cravenly do. Rather shall we torment them from their ways. We declare that the bones of Erin's martyrs crack under the weight of the foreign repression; that the eyes of Erin's saints weep at the sufferings of their faithful servants. We swear that we shall do our utmost to ease that weight and dry those tears. And we further swear that to do so we shall willingly give up our lives and forego all ties of family and kinship. Do you so swear, Jack Keane?'

'I do.'

Master Whiteboy held up the bowl of bloodied water.

'This is the blood of Erin's martyrs reborn in this most worthy association of Whiteboys. It is the blood of the Fianna, resurgent and scourging this land.'

He handed the bowl to Jack.

'Drink this blood and be born into the association.'

Jack raised the bowl to his lips and sipped the mixture of water and his own blood.

'In your own blood you are baptized a Brother Whiteboy,' said Master Whiteboy, a smile breaking across his mutilated features as he stepped forward and clapped Jack on the shoulder. 'You're one of us now and mighty welcome you are at that.'

He gripped Jack's bleeding hand tightly in his large fist. 'I'm Paddy Quillinan from Knockamoohane. 'Tis good to have you with us. If you're half the fighter your brothers are, Master accursed Sandes will soon be ruing the day he took your girl from you.'

The other men in their white shirts crowded round Jack patting him on the back and shaking his hand.

'Is this all there are?' Jack asked Paddy Quillinan, amazement in his voice.

'That's right, boy. Just forty-two of us now that you've joined.'

'But, I thought . . . well, I thought there'd be many more what with all the raids and that.'

'We don't need any more, Jack. Our weapons are surprise and secrecy,' explained the Whiteboy leader. 'If we had more men then we'd be afeared our secrets would soon reach the likes of Sandes and his cronies.'

'What use can I be? What can I do?' asked Jack eagerly. 'When can I go out on a raid, Master Quillinan?'

'Not so fast, young Jack,' laughed his brother, Michael, punching him affectionately in the chest. 'You're in too much of a hurry to be caught by the soldier boys, I'm thinking.'

'But I want to fight,' Jack persisted.

'And sure if John and I weren't awful certain of that, we wouldn't have brought you here tonight.'

John interrupted. 'But to fight you've to have a cool head, Jack. If you've anger like you have, you're only going to get captured and transported to Botany Bay or even stretched on a rope after the Sessions at Tralee.'

Jack felt deeply disappointed as he trudged home across the fields with his brothers. He had thought that as soon as he had joined the Whiteboys, he would be able to go with them on their raids. He had dreamt of fighting against overwhelming odds and dying romantically, gloriously, with Brigid's name on his lips. They had been comforting dreams and had helped soften the blow of the message he had been given a few weeks before by Theresa Aherne – that her younger sister never wanted to see Jack again.

'But why?' he'd asked Theresa. 'Why, when we're set to marry in the spring?'

'I'm not knowing why,' Theresa had replied. 'Brigid hasn't been home for weeks. But we're all thinking that she's in the power of Jonathan Sandes.'

He had been inconsolable for days afterwards, moping around the cabin hardly speaking to his family. The one thought in his mind was revenge on Jonathan Sandes.

Now, he thought, as he neared Drombeg with his brothers after the initiation ceremony, he would have to wait even longer for his revenge. The sour bile of disappointment was in his throat.

Captain Eugene de Vere Pearson, resplendent in the red and gold uniform of the 12th Dragoons, was quite adamant. 'Gentlemen,' he declared, 'I don't think it matters whether these murderous ruffians are called Whiteboys, Ribbonmen, Carders or Rockites. The simple fact is that they have to be stamped out.'

The men sitting round the table at Gurtinard House, the home of Dr Peter Church, nodded their approval. Jonathan Sandes banged his pewter mug of ale on the table enthusiastically. 'Hear, hear, Captain. You're absolutely correct.'

'Ever since the unsuccessful rebellion and the Act of Union twenty-five years since,' the officer continued, 'these cursed associations have terrorized the countryside. They might have different names depending on where they've sprung from, but they're all repealists at heart.'

'I doubt if the Whiteboys know the word "repeal", dear Captain,' drawled Sandes. 'They're just damned murderers who destroy farms and ruin our revenues, simple as that. Nothing more.'

'Hush, Jonathan,' murmured Dr Church quietly. 'Let the officer finish. After all, he's come all the way from Dublin to address us.'

'The secret of this exercise will be intelligence,' Captain Pearson continued, wearied already at interruptions from men whom he regarded as little more than country bumpkins. 'We can chase around after every raid like your local Volunteers but that, I would hazard, is somewhat without purpose. We've got to discover these ruffians' plans before they're carried out.'

'Easier said than done,' ventured Dr Church mildly.

His friends nodded in agreement. Inspector McMahon, who commanded the police in the Listowel area had nothing to say, preferring to take his lead from others.

'I understand, gentlemen, that you have access to funds denied to me,' Captain Pearson said curtly. 'Your patrons have wrung these monies out of the government to pay informers, I believe.'

'That's correct,' said Sandes.

'What success then?'

'Little, I'm afraid,' replied Dr Church. 'We have placed a man in the association but he's not been made privy yet to any of their plans. We know their leader is called Quillinan of Knockamoohane, and that's about all. We've tried to follow him but he's as slippery as a Shannon eel.'

'Is that all?' Captain Pearson sniffed disdainfully.

'Oh, and another thing,' Sandes broke in, 'Seems they all cut the palms of their hands when they take their blasted oaths. We could look for scars, I'm thinking.'

'Not the quickest solution, I fear,' said Captain Pearson flatly. 'No, the answer is intelligence. And to contain them, an immediate imposition of martial law. Anyone outside their cabins between sunset and sunrise without special reason goes before a drumhead court martial.'

The 120 dragoons drafted into Listowel were split into small units to enforce the imposition of martial law. In the smaller townships, like Drombeg, only two men were needed to make certain that everyone stayed indoors during the night hours. In the larger parishes, like Ballybunnion or Ballylongford, units of ten men commanded by a corporal patrolled the curfew. The remainder – some thirty men – were stationed permanently in Listowel or detailed to set up check points with the Volunteers on the main arteries of north-west Kerry. Large notices threatening transportation or death to anyone breaking the martial law regulations were posted liberally throughout the area and, at first, served as an effective deterrent.

Paddy Quillinan realized immediately that a special watch had been mounted on his cabin on the outskirts of Knockamoohane township. Night raids would be too dangerous. It was a time to wait and plan.

Eventually, Quillinan decided that the Whiteboys would have to risk attacks in daylight. They would strike at more than one target simultaneously, hoping to cause maximum confusion to the military. He travelled to Listowel market to spread his plans by word of mouth. His 'shadows', a pair of dragoons, didn't even try to conceal themselves as Quillinan walked towards Listowel, driving a pig before him and carrying a pigeen under his arm. They were thoroughly bored with their assignment, much preferring to be on ceremonial duties back in Dublin. Quillinan exchanged cheery greetings with the people he passed on the way to market and the soldiers were too far away to hear the occasional order muttered from the corner of his mouth as he met another Whiteboy. Two days later, in the copse near Duagh, about twenty Whiteboys who had heard of the meeting, gathered to receive their orders.

'Master Whiteboy can't be here for reasons that you know well enough, brothers,' said Padraig Broder, the burly and affable second-in-command. 'But his instructions are clear enough. While he's being watched we're to carry out two raids at the same time. The Master thinks tis necessary to give our reply well and clear to this Captain Pearson and his dragoons for putting on this damned curfew.' Broder looked at the expectant faces pressed around him. 'Today, we'll be burning a grand house and helping His Majesty's mails on their way to perdition. Get your weapons and then divide yourself into two groups.'

'Come on, Jack,' said Michael Keane to his younger brother. 'Under this tree. Help me lift this turf,' he called as he knelt on the grass. His brother helped him pull it away and then watched as he scrabbled at the black earth underneath. 'Ah, here we are.'

Michael pulled a long, slim parcel from the ground, dusting the earth from it. Jack saw it contained something wrapped in oilcloth. His brother undid the cloth and carefully lifted out a flintlock pistol.

'There we are,' Michael smiled. 'You see, Jack, tis not only taters that grow in the ground.'

Inside the cloth was another packet, doubly wrapped for protection. Jack undid this to find some lead bullets, firing caps and a small box of gunpowder.

'You carry those, Jack, and I'll take the pistol,' ordered Michael. 'Push them under your shirt.'

Jack pulled up the voluminous white shirt he was wearing and stuffed the ammunition in his breeches. The shirt was much too large for him. It really belonged to his brother John but it had been decided that it would be better for one of the brothers to remain at the cabin in Drombeg in case the dragoons came by and noticed that only their father was working in the fields.

When the Whiteboys had dug out all their weapons and covered up the hiding places again, they split into two groups to receive further instructions.

Padraig Broder pointed at the group containing the Keane brothers. 'You'll be after the afternoon stage to Cork, me boys. I'll be leading you.' He turned to the second group. 'And you'll be making your way to Riversdale and burning the mansion of Samuel Raymond. Master Whiteboy thinks he should be concerning himself with something other than brewing ale and using his profits to support the soldier boys in the Volunteers. You'll be having no trouble, I'm thinking, since there'll only be servants there and they'll be supporting you. But remember to travel there singly and keep off the main tracks to avoid the dragoons.

'Finally, brothers, when we've finished our work, don't come here,' said Broder. 'We're not to use this place again. Take the weapons to your own cabins and listen out for the next orders. Now off you go and God be with you in your enterprises.'

Jack walked with his brother for well over an hour to the rendez-vous. They took the necessary precaution of bundling their white shirts under their waistcoats. The other Whiteboys arrived in ones and twos, until they were all gathered out of sight of the track leading from Listowel to Cork.

Padraig Broder shielded his eyes as he peered at the position of the bright April sun. 'I'm thinking we've got maybe an hour to wait before the stage comes but we can't be too sure, me boys.' He pointed to Jack. 'Now you, young Jack Keane, are going to have a mighty important task here. Give him your pistol, Michael. You needn't bother to load it.'

It was the first time Jack had ever held a weapon. He found it heavier than he had expected.

'Get your shirt and waistcoat off, lad,' ordered Broder. 'You've got some acting to do. You're to lie in the track and pretend you're mortal bad. That'll make the stage stop when the driver sees you lying there.' Broder grinned hugely, 'At least, it'd better make him stop or you're *really* going to be mortal bad.' He laughed out loud as he saw Jack's worried frown. 'Don't be alarmed lad,' he said grip-ping Jack's shoulder. 'We'll be on hand to help.'

Jack walked from the shelter of the wood, and stood alone on the rutted track. He dipped his hand into a drying puddle and smeared mud over his face and chest, then lay down on his stomach with the pistol concealed under his body. Into his mind came distorted images of Brigid, of Sandes kissing her like Brigid and he had kissed. He concentrated on listening to the sounds around him. The birds in the wood whistled their calls of alarm, the long grass rustled in the sighing breeze.

His body felt the approach before the sound reached him. Then the rattling, rumbling sound was upon him. Jack pressed closer to the earth of the track, his face turned away from the approaching coach. Would it ever stop, he wondered? If it didn't would he have time to roll out of its path? He tensed his body as the coach's noise overwhelmed him. Then came an urgent shout, the screeching of wooden brakes on iron-covered wheels, the creaking of leather harnesses, and the protesting neighs of horses as the bits sawed hard into their mouths. Then silence, followed by the clumping of heavy boots towards him.

'What have we here then?' a gruff voice said alarmingly close to him.

'Looks like a sick lad,' a voice called.

A boot prodded into Jack's ribs, trying to turn him over. Then a hand pulled at him and Jack knew he could act no longer. He pushed himself away with all his young strength, rolling over and thrusting the pistol upwards into the startled face of the stagecoach driver, a man of about fifty with reddened, weatherbeaten features. The driver's expression of amazement changed to anger as he grabbed at the pistol stuck in the belt of his thick coat.

'Blast you . . . ' he cried.

'If you move, you're dead,' Jack shouted, pointing the unloaded pistol.

The driver's hand rested on the wooden butt of his weapon. Their eyes locked together for a moment and then a piercing blast from a horn made both Jack and the driver look towards the woods. Broder and the eight other Whiteboys came bounding out of the trees, some waving rusty swords, others carrying muskets and pistols. The driver backed away from Jack, fear in his eyes, as he saw the men in their flapping white shirts. His empty hands shot up into the air. 'Mercy . . . Oh God, mercy,' he stammered in a strangled voice.

Jack got up from the drying mud of the track keeping the pistol trained on the driver who stumbled away from him, hands still raised, until his back was pressed against the heaving flanks of one of the stage's lead horses.

'Keep him, there, lad,' called Broder, waving his musket in the air. 'We'll take care of them in the stage.'

The Whiteboys gathered around the coach while Broder pulled open the door.

'Out, out,' he shouted, poking his weapon menacingly into the coach. 'All of you, me pretties, out for the Whiteboys.'

Four men, dressed in topcoats and high-crowned hats, stumbled from the coach. They huddled together uncertainly in a group, gazing fearfully at the Whiteboys.

'Right, gentlemen, empty your pockets,' ordered Broder. 'Master Whiteboy says no harm should come to you but he says to lighten your loads. I call that mighty considerate, too, thinking on the walking you'll be doing later.'

'This is an outrage,' stormed one of the passengers, a stout, middle-aged man, florid of face from rage and self-indulgence. 'I refuse to hand over anything.'

'Is that so?' murmured Broder, still smiling. 'Now aren't you the brave one?'

Without changing his expression he reversed his musket swiftly and crashed the butt against the man's face, catching him on the bridge of the nose with a sickening crunch. Blood gouted from the man's face as he staggered back against one of the coach's wheels, falling senseless on the track.

'Now, gentlemen, is there anyone else with an argument in him?' said Broder. He walked over to the unconscious man and kicked him casually in the ribs.

As one man, the other three began frantically turning out their pockets, tossing clinking leather bags of money on to the track. One of them pulled his watch off its chain; another tugged at the ring on his index finger.

'Not your jewellery,' said Broder evenly. 'What would the likes of us be doing with such pretty things. No – your money will do.' He stooped and picked up the purses.

'Now, while we attend to the mail, you can all be taking off your fine boots. Master Whiteboy doesn't want you to walk too fast, after all.'

One of the Whiteboys clambered up into the driver's seat and began tossing sacks from the roof of the stagecoach. Broder poked them with his musket until he found the one containing the mail. He gestured to a Whiteboy with a sword to slit open the sack. The letters tumbled into the dust.

'Right, me boys,' he called, 'You know what to do.' Broder looked over at Jack who was still menacing the now-barefoot driver with the empty pistol. 'You all right, lad?' Jack nodded. Three Whiteboys began tearing the letters into little shreds, tossing them up into the air and into the hedges.

'Nothing upsets people more than not having their mail delivered,' Broder observed generally. 'Really makes them mad, so it does. And that's the truth.'

When all the letters had been destroyed, Broder ordered his men to unhitch the horses. He lifted the driver's long whip off the stagecoach and cracked it over the lead horses's withers making them bolt. 'Off you go then,' he said flicking the whip at the feet of the stage's erstwhile passengers. 'And take the driver with you. You've a fair step to the next township.'

'What about him?' asked one of the passengers, pointing at the unconscious man.

'No matter to me, gentlemen,' smiled Broder. 'You can either carry him with you or leave him where he's resting. But if he stays there, he'll be stripped as naked as he was born. Such fine clothes are a mighty rare sight for the people hereabouts. They'll probably slit his throat from ear to ear for good measure.'

The passengers looked at each other, shrugged their shoulders, and began walking off down the track in their stocking feet, picking their way gingerly between the sharp stones. The driver, feeling a twinge of duty, hesitated for a moment and then hurried off to catch up with the others.

'That's fine gentlemen you are,' Padraig Broder taunted their retreating backs. 'Leave him to be murdered, would you . . . and him the bravest of you all?'

Broder turned to his men. 'That's the sort who are bleeding us dry. Mark them well, the cowardly swine. They're not so high and mighty when it's their miserable skins they're after saving.'

He went over to the bleeding and unconscious man and began lifting him under the shoulders. 'Give me a hand, one of you,' he called. 'We'll put your man back in the stage. It'll be more comforting for him when he wakes from his sleep I'm thinking. He'll be found soon enough, if he's lucky.'

The man was eased on to the coach floor. He started to groan as he began to regain consciousness.

Broder surveyed the torn up letters all round the coach with a satisfied smile. 'That'll show them soldier boys. Now let's be off through the woods before anyone claps a sight on us.'

Once the party of Whiteboys were well away from the coach, deep into the safety of the woods, Broder called a halt.

'So you won't be needing any more instructions, boys, let me tell you what Master Whiteboy has decided. Two days from now we're to raid one of the Palatine farmers over at Knockanure. We'll meet by the cross there, three hours before dusk.'

'What about the others? Will they be coming?' asked Michael Keane.

'No, they'll be away burning another big house. Master Whiteboy wants to keep the soldiers hopping around. For the next few raids we'll be in two groups. That way the soldiers won't know how many we are or where to guard. We'll learn them to leave Dublin and hunt for us, that we will.'

The Whiteboys split up as they left the woods to make their way back to their cabins.

'Why the Palatine farmers?' Jack asked his brother when they were well on in their journey to Drombeg.

'Because they don't belong here, that's why. They're on some of the best land round here, paying little enough rent just because they're Germans settled on us by an English king. We're going to make sure that they don't stay.'

'But they don't cause any trouble,' persisted Jack. 'They were persecuted out of their own homes, weren't they?'

'That's as may be. But now they've taken over our land. They help the landlords, they do. We want none of them.'

''Tis strange we should attack other farmers.'

'We'll attack anyone,' said Michael grimly, 'Until Ireland's for the Irish.'

'The farms of the Palatines near Knockanure, eh?' mused Captain Pearson the next evening. 'You sure of that?'

'That's what the informant says,' replied Dr Church. 'He passed the news to me at the apothecary shop.'

'I must confess to some surprise, Doctor. I'd have thought holding up the stage and burning out Raymond would have been enough for them.' He slapped his kid leather gloves in his palm. 'So they want all-out war do they? Well, we'll see. We'll see.'

'You'll occupy the farms then, Captain, and ambush them?'

'I think not, doctor.' The officer rose from his chair in the shabby Listowel police barracks, and looked at the map on the wall behind his desk. 'The farms of these Germans are all to the east of here?'

'A few of them. Most of them are on the Blennerhasset estate near Tralee.'

'But there are some near Knockanure?'

'Two or three, I believe.'

'Well, I don't think I'll move my men there. They'll be too conspicuous and the Whiteboys will change their plans.'

'But . . .' Dr Church started.

'But nothing, Doctor,' said the officer sharply. 'From our information some of them must come from the townships to the west of Listowel. On this map, there are only two tracks they can take. We'll try to surprise them on their attacks at the farms, they'll run in panic, and snap.' Captain Pearson clapped his palms together. 'When I've got 'em, I'll teach 'em a very quick lesson.'

He turned back to Dr Church with a grim smile on his face. 'I just pray your information is correct.'

Jack Keane and his two brothers crouched under the hedge by a wooden farm gate bearing the sign 'Swizer' in rough, Germanic writing. The air was still in the late spring afternoon as if the whole world was holding its breath. Jack held the pistol, loaded now, pointing carefully away from him. John and Michael Keane were carrying ancient muskets which they'd primed during their walk to Knockanure. Jack felt uneasy. He'd been worried ever since the previous evening when the Keane family had been sitting around the peat fire in their cabin. Jack had peered through the gloom and seen a frog leap away from the glowing peat, straight between his brothers and into some straw in a dark corner. He'd jumped up, grabbed his shillelagh and beaten at the place where he'd last seen the frog but it vanished.

'Tis an omen,' he'd told his family who were highly amused by his antics. 'A frog came right out of the fire.'

'Hush, Jack,' his mother had said, patting his arm. 'And what sort of omen is that, pray? Just a hedge frog keeping warm if you ask me.'

'But it came straight out of the fire, I tell you.'

'Sure and you've been thinking on the little people too much,' said his father. 'Tis no omen at all except maybe to a foolish boy like you.'

But nothing could rid Jack of the certainty that it was an omen, and a bad one. He hadn't liked the idea of attacking another farmer simply because he happened to be a foreigner from the start. But if he refused to go on the raid he knew full well that the Whiteboys would have had little further use for him.

The brothers waited for a few minutes while the other Whiteboys got into position and then Padraig Broder's horn signalled the attack. They scrambled over the hedge, guns at the ready, and raced towards the neatly whitewashed cabin. Other Whiteboys held smouldering pieces of turf wrapped in sacking as they ran towards the farm's two outhouses. One howled in anguish as he tripped over a pigeen and fell on to the hot sacking he was clutching.

The door of the cabin flew open and a tall, bearded man, wearing a black wide brimmed hat, emerged with a musket at his shoulder. He aimed carefully at the Whiteboy rolling on the ground, trying to disentangle himself from the lump of burning turf at the same time as beating away the squealing pigeen trapped between his legs. The gun went off in a cloud of smoke with a thunderous clap. The Whiteboy heaved into the air like a hooked fish, reaching for his shattered breastbone, blood already spattering his white shirt, and then fell back, dead.

For a moment there was a silence then, with shouts of rage, the Whiteboys flung themselves at the farmer. He showed not a trace of fear as he whirled his empty musket around his head like a club. Two Whiteboys toppled to the ground under its blows before Padraig Broder managed to get a sword thrust into the farmer's body, catching him high up on his right shoulder. He dropped the musket with a cry of pain but still closed with his attackers. He gripped Jack and John Keane round their necks, pulling their heads across his broad chest. John dropped his musket as he tried to punch the farmer away but Jack's pistol was trapped between himself and Hans Swizer. 'Ihr mordenden schweinehunde,' shouted the farmer.

The blood running down his arm and chest made them so slippery that Jack's head pulled out of the farmer's grip. But as he backed away the farmer grabbed at his pistol. Jack's index finger tightened involuntarily on the trigger and the pistol exploded into the farmer's face at point-blank range. The lead ball smashed upwards through his brain and out through the crown of his skull. The air was filled with a pink mist of blood, brains and skull fragments. He fell away from Jack and lay on the ground, his legs twitching. Then he was still, eyes staring blankly upwards at the sky.

'Oh God,' Jack moaned as he stumbled away vomiting over the ground. 'Oh God, I've killed him.'

The Whiteboys gathered round the body, stunned and silent at this grotesque act of violence. Suddenly, they were pushed apart with demonic force by a woman who ran shrieking from the cabin. She flung herself across the body, looking wildly up at the men standing above her. Tears ran down her round, plump face.

'What have you done? Me man, you've killed him. Me man,' she kept shrieking. 'Me man. Me poor man.'

The Whiteboys turned away, shame and pity in their hearts. John Keane comforted his younger brother who was kneeling on the ground, heaving and retching.

'Come away, boys,' called Padraig Broder. 'Twas an accident. Nothing more. Let's finish the job we came to do.' He tore one of the glowing sods away from a Whiteboy and hurled it high into the rush thatch of the cabin. 'Come on, boys,' he urged. 'The soldiers will be here with all the shooting. Hurry up.'

More lumps of burning turf were flung into the thatches of the cabin and the outhouses. Tiny licks of flame spread around them and the thatch crackled fully alight. The flames engulfed the roofs sending plumes of dark grey smoke into the sky. Then with a roar the roofs collapsed and the screams of burning pigs, chickens, and a horse filled the farmyard, joining with the sobbing shrieks of the farmer's widow in a cacophony of horror. The Whiteboys looked dully at the awful scene, fascinated yet totally dismayed by the devastation they had caused. Their eyes and ears were so numbed by the dreadful sounds all around them that it was some moments before any of them realized that their look-out was standing by the farm gate, shouting and waving frantically.

'Horses are coming,' he bellowed. 'For Holy Mary's sake, tis the soldiers. Get away. Tis the soldiers.'

'Quickly, boys!' shouted Padraig Broder. 'Make for the woods. Quickly now.'

Without apparent effort, he heaved the dead Whiteboy across his shoulders and, bowed under the weight, ran towards the gate. The other Whiteboys scrambled through the hedges, pulling their shirts over their heads as they went and disappeared into the nearest cover. The three Keane brothers hid in a ditch, pressing deep into the undergrowth as the sound of galloping horses grew nearer and then passed. John peered cautiously out and saw four dragoons, their sabres drawn, jump down from their mounts and run into the farm which was now almost totally obscured by a pall of smoke.

'Come on,' he whispered to his brothers, 'Tis clear now.' They left the ditch and ran along the track that led back to Knockanure Cross and Listowel. For a quarter of a mile they kept to the track before crossing fields and copses towards the lower track leading westwards. Only when they reached it did they begin to relax.

'What about the guns?' asked Jack breathlessly. 'We surely can't carry them all the way back to Drombeg.'

'Tis right he is, Michael,' agreed John. 'Let's bury them.'

'They'll get rusty.'

'We can wrap them in our shirts. That'll protect them a little and get rid of our shirts at the same time.'

The brothers looked for a suitable place and chose a ditch under a broken dry-stone wall. They pulled away tussocks of grass to make a large enough hole to bury the pistol and the two muskets. Then they marked the spot with a small cairn of stones from the wall.

'We'd better hurry,' said Michael. 'We don't want to be caught in the curfew after getting away by the skin of our teeth.'

They began running again, their bare feet pattering on the hard earth. Then they rounded a sharp bend in the track to find a farm cart and horse barred their way.

'Halt, in the King's name,' came a gruff shout as the sergeant of dragoons stepped from behind the cart, the bayonet on his musket pointing at the brothers.

They looked quickly around them for a way of escape but saw two more dragoons clambering out of the ditch behind them.

'And what might you three fine buckos be running from?' asked the sergeant menacingly. More dragoons rose from the ditches on either side of the track and surrounded the brothers. The points of their bayonets pressed lightly against the chests of the three young men.

'Sure and weren't we just running to get home before curfew?' replied Michael, trying hard to appear nonchalant and at ease.

'Sure and weren't we just running to get home before curfew?' mimicked the sergeant. 'So that's your story, is it? Where do you live?'

'Drombeg.'

'And what are you doing so far this side of Listowel?'

'Just visiting a friend, that's all.'

'Shut your gob, farmboy,' snarled the sergeant. 'Search them.'

The dragoons ran their hands roughly over the brothers' clothes. One of them turned to the sergeant and shook his head. 'Nothing on them.'

'So they've got rid of their shirts, have they?' drawled Captain Pearson as he walked from behind the cart. 'And their weapons as well, no doubt.'

The brothers shrank inwardly at the sight of the officer in his resplendent uniform, his height emphasized by his black stovepipe uniform hat with its curved peak.

Michael put on a bold front. 'Sure, and I don't know what you're talking about, your honour.'

The butt of a musket crashed into his stomach, driving the breath from his body. He doubled over gasping for air.

'I said shut your gob,' said the sergeant evenly. 'You speak to the officer when you're told to.'

Captain Pearson strolled up to them. 'You see, lying won't help you now,' he remarked pleasantly. 'We know what happened back at the German's farm. I must say I didn't expect you Whiteboys to go as far as murdering him.'

'Whiteboys? And who's to say . . . ' John started, then went silent as the dragoon who'd hit his elder brother drew back his musket.

'You were going to reply, I think, "who's to say we're Whiteboys",' said Captain Pearson. 'Well, no one is going to say you are until we look at your hands. You see, a friend told us all Whiteboys had a scar across their palms.'

He smiled as he saw the brothers clench their fists. 'Ah, yes,' he murmured. 'That's what's going to say you're Whiteboys. Not your shirts, not your weapons, but your own dirty, stinking bodies.' His tone sharpened. 'Sergeant!'

'Suh.'

'Their hands.'

Strong fingers gripped the brothers' wrists and prised their palms apart, turning them upwards.

Captain Pearson leant forward casually and ran his gloved finger softly along one of the three scars. 'The newest recruit, wouldn't you say, sergeant?' he said, holding up Jack's hand with the red raw scar vividly on it. 'Who are you, Whiteboys?'

'We're the Keanes; Jack, John and Michael Keane,' said Michael defiantly. 'And we're not . . . '

'Not Whiteboys, eh?' the officer interrupted. 'Well, I think you are. Your scars prove it. So there's no use pretending any more, is there?'

Michael dropped his head.

'No, I thought not. The problem is who to make an example of. All of you . . . ? No, I think not. Someone has to tell the Whiteboys what sort of punishment they're going to receive in the future.'

'I shot the farmer,' Jack blurted out. 'I shot him, not the others. 'Twas an accident but I was holding the pistol.'

'Well, well. A volunteer, eh, Sergeant?' remarked Captain Pearson. He looked closely at the three brothers standing sullenly before him. For all the emotion he showed, he could have been appraising cattle at the market. 'I think the eldest should have the honour, Sergeant,' he said quietly. 'The first-born son is a little special after all. And I've little doubt he recruited the other two. Tie him.'

'No, you want me,' protested Jack, struggling in the soldier's grip. 'I'm the one.'

Captain Pearson ignored his cries. 'The rope, Sergeant. Fix the rope.'

The sergeant took a long, thick rope from the back of the cart and flung it over a branch of an elm tree which hung out over the track. The end had been fashioned into a noose.

'Tie him,' ordered the officer.

Two dragoons pulled Michael away from his brothers and, while one held him, the other tied his hands behind his back. They carried him to the cart, pushing him up into it. Michael looked up at the noose dangling above him and ducked away, pressing himself against the dusty floor of the cart.

The sergeant lifted him without any difficulty, pulled down the noose and fitted it around his neck. 'Pull up the slack,' he shouted and two dragoons heaved on the other end of the rope.

Michael twisted his head as the sergeant hung a large card around his neck. He tried to see what was written on it but the rope stopped him. The sergeant jumped down and then the cart jerked forward as the officer slapped the horse across its quarters. Suddenly, there was nothing beneath him. He choked for breath and tried to kick his legs upwards but there was no escape.

His brothers ceased their struggles as the cart pulled away leaving Michael dangling from the rope. Struck rigid and silent by the horror before their eyes, they saw him arch convulsively, kicking his legs wildly, and then swing limply under the tree, his tongue swelling out between his darkening lips. His body turned gently in the twilight breeze, blood oozing from its ears, a stench of human waste filling the sweetness of the air as all muscles relaxed in death.

Tears ran down Jack's face as he looked up at his dead brother. He could hardly make out the sign around his twisted, bent neck. It bore only two words, 'A Whiteboy'. 'British murderers,' he screeched and lashed out with his feet catching a dragoon in the groin. 'British murdering bastards,' he shrieked again, just before the butt of a musket crashed between his shoulders. As he fell forward, diving into unconsciousness, he thought he heard the officer shout, 'Beat them but don't kill them.'

His voice, Jack thought, croaked just like a frog. The frog . . . the frog . . . and then another musket cracked across his skull and he heard no more.

# Chapter 5 April, 1824

The news of Michael Keane's death spread over the district like a rain cloud off the Atlantic. The Kerry people, with little between survival and starvation in their lives, had a close kinship with death. It was not something to be offered a glass of hospitality round their peat fires, but death was more than a nodding acquaintance and so was usually accepted with the minimum of ill grace or resentment. What feeling there was would be blown away by the grief-absorbing rituals of the wake and sooner or later the everyday considerations of living would take over. But the manner of Michael Keane's dying was different. It was not even softened by the procedures of justice, long enough for a man to adjust gradually to the notion of his execution, accepting it finally as a welcome release from the torment of his own uncertainty. Nor was it in hot blood. The treatment of Michael Keane's body, too, repelled them. After the deed, whispered the Kerry folk in the darkness of their cabins, it should have been returned to the sorrowing family for a proper wake and burial, not left hanging under guard of the dragoons until the crows and ravens had pecked out its eyes and eaten its tongue; until the flesh, muscles and bones had given way and the body had toppled out of the noose, not even then to be buried but only flung carelessly into the ferns for the carrion eaters to finish their work.

'They shall pay for this foul deed,' vowed Paddy Quillinan, as he sat in the Keane cabin at Drombeg. He'd denied all caution in his rage at Michael's death and had joined the dozens of others who'd called on the family to try to ease their grief.

Master and Mistress Keane sat close by the fire, their hands clasped as they huddled together in their shock. Near them, on a pile of straw and sacks, lay John and Jack recovering from their beating by the dragoons, their faces and bodies swollen and mottled with bruises.

'I swore eternal vengeance when the soldiers beat me nigh to death and left me with this scarred and misshapen face,' said

Quillinan grimly, running his hand over his battered, bristly features. 'For Michael Keane, they will pay double. And for the sufferings of his brothers and parents, they will pay threefold.'

'And what about the person who told the soldiers so that they could lay their trap?' John asked, raising himself on his elbows with difficulty.

'Tis true. He is the foulest and blackest of all for didn't he betray his solemn oath?' Quillinan agreed gravely. 'He is the first to be rooted out else none of us is safe. Padraig Broder and meself have already been thinking on it.'

'Who is the traitor?' asked Jack eagerly.

'We're not sure yet but have a plan to reveal him. You're not to worry about him yet. I promise you the satisfaction of meeting your brother's Judas.'

As John and Jack slowly recovered from their beatings and time began to numb the pain in their memories, Quillinan and Broder went ahead with their plan. They had reduced the possible informants to two.

'It's either Paddy Stack or Jimmy McElligott,' said Broder.

'And both of them recent members, too,' Quillinan observed. 'Tell both of them that the Whiteboys are going to raid the police barracks at Ballylongford. Then we'll watch for the one who tells the dragoons.'

Broder passed on the false information to the men after arranging for two trusted Whiteboys to watch their cabins and follow them wherever they went. Within a day, they had the identity of the informer. Stack had remained in his fields, but McElligott had hurried off to Listowel and entered Dr Church's apothecary shop in the market square. If confirmation was needed, it came when McElligott immediately repaired to the Listowel Arms coaching house and began spending lavishly on whiskey and porter.

'A foolish man as well as a cursed one,' was Quillinan's satisfied reaction when he heard the news. 'Since the blasted Captain Pearson saw fit to make an example of Michael Keane, bless his tortured soul, then the Whiteboys shall do similar to his spy.'

'How many men shall we be needing?' asked Broder. The two Whiteboy leaders mingled with the crowds at Listowel market, keeping a wary eye open for constables or the soldiers who ineffectively followed Quillinan.

'One thing is certain, Padraig,' said Quillinan. 'I shall be there, soldiers or not. I'll give them the slip somehow. You come too and bring the Keane brothers. Tis their right to be present.'

Three afternoons later, Jimmy McElligott, a thin faced, scrawny man, was in the fields about two hundred yards from his cabin at Coolagowan, desultorily hoeing the weeds along the rows of potatoes. He didn't regard himself as a traitor to his own people. What he was doing was born out of necessity. He felt sorrow for what had happened to Michael Keane but, after all, the money helped pay for a few delicacies for his sickly wife and guaranteed him security of tenure at his poor farm. Some of the money was put by in what he called his 'travelling fund' so that one day he could take his family away from Kerry, perhaps to England, maybe even to the Americas. The thought of capture and exposure didn't trouble his mind too much since he believed implicitly in Dr Church's guarantee of his safety.

'Hello there, Jimmy.'

He looked up from his work and saw Padraig Broder alone by the hedge, leaning on the shafts of a hand cart. McElligott waved and began tramping across the field towards the visitor. This must be the instructions about the next raid, he thought.

'Padraig, tis nice to see you. Tis fine weather is it not, thanks be to God?'

'It is that, Jimmy,' replied Broder, a wide smile across his face. 'I've brought something for you.'

'And sure, what would that be?'

'Come over the hedge and have a look. Tis in the cart.'

McElligott scrambled over the stone and turf hedge and went up to the cart.

'Tis under the sacking,' said Broder, standing away from the shaft.

'Now what could this be?' puzzled McElligott as he leaned over to pull the sacking aside. Broder's shillelagh caught him twice squarely on the back of his head before he slumped unconscious over the side of the cart.

McElligott came to under the pile of sacking as the cart was being pushed along a rough track, its wheels squeaking and grinding. He tried to sit up but found he was bound hand and foot. A gag was fastened over his mouth.

'Your man's awake,' he heard a familiar voice say. It sounded like Broder.

'And just in time too. We're nearly there and I'd have been hating for him to miss our little surprise, Padraig.'

Oh God, thought McElligott, the voice of Master Whiteboy. He realized it could mean only one thing; his spying activities had been discovered. He moved his mouth trying to shout an alarm, an explanation, a plea, but the gag was too tight. He could only lie there and shiver with terror.

Soon the sounds of the Atlantic rollers grew louder. Suddenly, the cart stopped and the sacking over him was pulled away.

McElligott blinked his eyes, adjusting them to the still bright and clear light of the late afternoon. He raised his throbbing head and saw Quillinan, Broder, and to his deepening horror, John and Jack Keane. They stared down at him grimly.

'So there's your spy,' growled Quillinan. 'There's your man who broke his oath and put the noose around your poor brother's neck. Look on him and see the abject terror of him.'

The prisoner shook his head from side to side, attempting to dislodge his gag.

'He wants to speak, does he?' said Broder. 'Well I'm thinking he's talked too much all his life. Let's sit him up so he can see where he's going.'

Rough hands grasped McElligott and propped him up against the side of the cart. He stared wildly round him and realized he was by the ruins of Doon Castle, high up on a green promontory jutting into the sea.

Quillinan leaned over the cart and spat into his face. One by one, the others did the same.

'Curse you to hell,' cried John Keane, slapping him across the eyes. 'May you rot just as our brother did.'

'Amen to that,' muttered Quillinan, lifting the shafts of the cart. The others helped him push it to the edge of the cliff. McElligott's eyes widened in terror as he realized what was about to happen. A strangled, gurgling noise came from behind the gag.

The four Whiteboys pulled the cart around so that McElligott could look down over the cliff to the rocks and stones far below, washed by the angry sea.

'Now,' grunted Quillinan. The cart swayed and tipped. With his last effort, McElligott somehow pushed himself over the side of the cart but it was too late. It fell away from him over the cliff tumbling downwards. McElligott rolled a little way down a gentle slope and then pitched forward. His body twisted and turned several times before it hit the rocks with a thudding crash which could just be heard above the breaking waves. It lay there for a moment before being lifted gently by a wave which began drawing it out to join the rest of the flotsam in the breakers. The body rolled over and, just for a second, it seemed that the pale face of Jimmy McElligott gazed upwards at his executioners peering down over the cliff.

'An eye for an eye, eh, Doctor?' remarked Captain Pearson as he reclined on a chair in Jonathan Sandes' drawing room. 'So much for your spy, what?'

'It's an outrage!' spluttered Dr Church. 'You take it too lightly, sir. That you do.'

'If you'd hanged the other two Whiteboys you caught, this might not have happened,' agreed Sandes. 'I thought you were being too lenient.'

'Gentlemen,' protested the dragoons officer, 'You must expect casualties in a war. This man McElligott was bound to have been discovered and killed sooner or later. In his unhappy case, it happened to be sooner.'

The three men stopped talking as the door opened and Brigid Aherne came into the room carrying a silver tray of glasses and a decanter of wine. She curtseyed slightly to Sandes before placing the tray on a side table for him. Her figure had filled out with the months of regular food from Sandes' table. Her hair shone blackly under the white, frilled mop cap that framed her oval face. Only the dark rings under her eyes betrayed the fact that Brigid was unhappy. Sandes smiled up at her with real warmth. For weeks now he had mistaken her dull submission as real enthusiasm for his increasing desires.

'Thank you, Brigid. You may leave us.'

She bobbed again before him and left the room. Captain Pearson followed her with his eyes radiating open admiration and desire.

Sandes noticed his look. 'Kindness and perseverence,' he said. 'That's what makes a good servant, eh, Captain? Who would have thought that that girl was a dirty, ragged, starving little wretch only a few months back?'

'And what did you do for her, Master Sandes?' asked the officer with an easy smile on his lips.

'Taught her how to serve.'

'Deuced if I'm not wondering who's been serving who by the rings under her eyes and the look on your face, Master Sandes,' replied Captain Pearson, laughing out loud.

'See what you mean, Pearson,' Dr Church cackled venally. 'Who's serving who . . . very good . . . very good indeed.'

'Gentlemen, gentlemen,' said Sandes, joining in the laughter. 'No more, I pray. All I will say to your sallies is that I find Brigid's service a pleasure to us both.'

The three men laughed together as Sandes filled glasses with wine and handed them round.

'Enough, enough, of all this tittle-tattle,' said Dr Church, wiping his eyes with a red silk handkerchief. 'We were discussing more serious business?'

'Right enough, Doctor,' agreed Captain Pearson. 'The Whiteboys.'

'Well then, Captain, what's your next plan? Do you think they will continue with their plan to raid the police barracks at Ballylongford?'

'I doubt if such a plan ever existed. I feel that it was simply the sprat to catch the mackerel, but it's an interesting thought . . . attacking a police barracks. They haven't done it before and it's very boldness might tempt them.'

'But not Ballylongford, surely?' interrupted Sandes.

'No, I think not. That would be hoping for too much. Bluff and counter-bluff isn't their strongest suit.'

'So?' said Dr Church.

'So, my dear Doctor, I am reinforcing all the police barracks except at Ballylongford and here in Listowel. I haven't enough men to go round and thus I'll have to gamble a little.'

'I pray you gamble correctly, this time, Captain,' remarked Sandes sourly. 'Your previous wager in letting those two scoundrels go free cost dear to us. Dublin wouldn't like any more failures, I'm thinking.'

The police barracks at Lixnaw, a few miles to the south west of Listowel, was a squat, single storey building standing greyly on the edge of the village of poor cabins. It was manned by three constables and a sergeant whose standards of living were scarcely better than those of the local population. This brought a feeling of ease between the police and the policed, so that there was rarely any trouble in the village. There were the drunks and the wife beaters to admonish; the disputes about land and creeping hedges to sort out; the occasional eviction. But in all these duties the police managed to retain a friendly relationship with the peasant farmers. This changed when, in early June, 1824, six dragoons were drafted unwillingly to Lixnaw to be received with equal ill grace by the villagers and the incumbent policemen. For a start, there simply wasn't enough room in the barracks for all ten men to sleep in comfort.

'If one turns over, we all have to turn over,' grumbled Corporal Hogg, who was in charge of the dragoons. 'Ever since we left Royal Barracks in Dublin we've had to live in pig styes or worse.'

'Tis a poor nation we are, Corporal,' agreed the police sergeant, Michael Sheehy, sadly. 'But then I'm wondering if it's not all the people who've ruled us who have made us so.'

'Now careful, Sergeant,' warned Corporal Hogg. 'That's the sort of talk these blasted Whiteboys are putting about.'

'Maybe there's a bit of Whiteboy in all us Kerrymen. Maybe most of us are too afeared to know it.'

'If you're all so poor then, why don't you go and work in England?'

Sergeant Sheehy managed to snort with disgust at the same time as sucking his clay pipe alight. 'Wouldn't you know, Corporal, that that's already the curse of Ireland? All the men of spirit are going away, leaving just the women and children and old men to look after the land. What there is of it after your English landlords have had their way.'

'On my oath, that's all I need. A hutch to live in and a constable who supports the Whiteboys.'

'A sergeant, Corporal,' said Sheehy quietly. 'Remember that . . .a sergeant, whatever I may believe.'

The police and the soldiers lived together in an uneasy and uncomfortable truce for the next two weeks. Each day, the police went out on patrol while the dragoons stayed at the barracks. At first, Corporal Hogg tried to keep them occupied with drill but soon gave this up under the derisory comments of the local children who took to apeing the drill movements. Finally, the dragoons simply lolled around the barracks, guarding them against something none of them believed would happen.

All they heard as they sat in the June sunshine outside the barracks after a lunch of dried beef and lumpers, was a blast on a horn. As they began scrambling to their feet, a fusillade of shots came from behind the nearest cabins thirty yards away. One dragoon fell, cursing, with a ball in his thigh but the rest of the shots thudded harmlessly into the barracks, sending chips of brick flying in all directions.

'Inside,' shouted Corporal Hogg. 'For Christ's sake, back inside.'

The dragoons pulled the injured soldier inside, then slammed and bolted the stout wooden door of the barracks before knocking out the glass windows at the front and sides of the building with the butts of their muskets. After the first noise of the attack, an unreal silence fell on Lixnaw as the Whiteboys reloaded their weapons and the dragoons searched for targets.

'There! By the cabin!' called the corporal as he saw a musket appear round a wall. A dragoon loosed off a shot, raising a puff of dust near the cabin. The Whiteboy musket fired and a ball crashed into the wood of the barracks door.

'Christ, they can shoot at that,' said Corporal Hogg in grudging admiration, still cursing himself for the dragoons' unpreparedness for the attack. 'There's another one,' he cried, spying a young man in a billowing white shirt run from behind a cabin holding something wrapped in sacking. The muskets cracked out and dirt flew up around the man's feet but he vanished out of sight behind the barracks without a shot apparently hitting him.

'Where the devil are the constables?' muttered the corporal. Then he heard another fusillade of shots and realized the constables were under attack elsewhere in Lixnaw. In fact, the Whiteboys had chosen the time for their attack after watching the constables' movements closely for more than a week. They had deliberately taken up positions between the troops and the police, reckoning that to divide was to conquer.

The Keane brothers were in the contingent of Whiteboys ordered to concentrate their attack on the barracks. Jack had watched fearfully as his brother ran into the open under the sights of the dragoons' muskets. Now he saw him crawling around the side of the barracks out of sight of the troops who peered from the windows above him. John reached the door and unwrapped two lumps of smoking peat from the sacking he carried. He piled them carefully against the door, then waved back at his companions. The dragoons ducked back from the windows as the Whiteboys' volley smashed into the barracks and John ran, crouching low, towards the shelter of the cabins. Jack could see a grin of triumph on his brother's face as he neared safety. Suddenly, it changed to a grimace of pain as a ball from a dragoon's musket caught him in the small of the back. He stumbled but his momentum carried him behind the cabin wall where he collapsed headlong into Jack's arms.

'Oh, God,' he cried. 'They've done for me. Oh, Holy Mother of God.'

Jack clasped him, turning him gently so that he rested in a sitting position against the cabin wall. John's face was grey with pain, sweat dripping from his forehead. As he held him, Jack could feel the wetness of blood seeping under his palms.

'Rest there, John. Rest there,' he mouthed into his brother's ear. 'We'll get you safe away. You'll be safe.'

The excitement of the battle, the thirst for revenge filled Jack. Without thinking of his safety, he moved out from cover and took careful aim at the police barracks. The musket thumped into his shoulder as it exploded. Smoke was now billowing about the front of the barracks with flames curling around the door.

Inside, the dragoons coughed and rubbed their smarting eyes, hardly able to see through the windows. One began to sob with panic.

'Shut your noise,' bawled Corporal Hogg, desperation now beginning to press in on him.

'We'll be burned alive,' shouted a dragoon, throwing down his musket and clawing at the heavy wooden beam across the blackening door. 'We've got to get out.'

'Steady men,' cried the corporal. 'If we run out there we'll be cut to pieces. Don't panic.'

He looked around the barracks. 'Grab hold of that,' he ordered pointing at the rough table which had been thrust back against a wall. 'We'll use it as a shield.'

Two of the dragoons, coughing deep in their chests with the suffocating smoke, pulled the table upright.

'Right,' exclaimed Corporal Hogg. 'Move away from the door all of you. When I open it, you two get the table through.'

He pulled at the beam securing the door, feeling the heat of the flames burning on the other side. The door swung open and the corporal staggered back from the flames. For a second, he presented a perfect target to the Whiteboys. A musket ball thudded into his chest hurtling him back across the barracks. He cannoned off the table and crashed to the floor, dead. His men hesitated for a moment, shocked by his death, before their training and instinct for self-preservation took over again.

'Come on, lads,' called one of the older dragoons. 'Let's do what poor old Hogg said. Through the door with the table.'

Shots thudded into the table as it was thrust outside, splintering the wood, but it proved an effective enough shield for the two dragoons. They carried it away from the flames that were now threatening to engulf the entire barracks, knelt behind it and started giving covering fire to enable their two unhurt companions to crawl from the cabin pulling the wounded soldier between them. Corporal Hogg was left where he had fallen.

By now, the Whiteboys attacking the barracks had begun to look uneasily over their shoulders as the firing from the other side of Lixnaw came closer. They realized their other group was being forced back by the advancing constables. Paddy Quillinan, ducking low as he ran between the cabins, slumped breathlessly beside Jack Keane.

'Tis looking like we'll have to leave here, lad,' he panted. 'The constables are getting too close.' Then he noticed John Keane leaning against the wall, his breath coming in wrenching gasps that shook his entire body.

'A dragoon got him,' explained Jack. 'But he set the barracks alight first. I'm thinking we shot two of the dragoons, too. There are only four still fighting that we can count.'

Quillinan peered quickly round the wall. Before a ball spattered the whitewash of the cabin above his head, he saw that the roof of the barracks was now alight. The dragoons were firing from a kneeling position protected by the table. The Whiteboys' leader could see that there would be casualties amongst his men if they tried to close with the dragoons across the open ground. He had no alternative.

'We're going now before it's too late. Start moving away one by one so the soldiers don't rush us.' He turned to Jack. 'I'll help you with your brother. We'll get him to your cabin all right.'

Quillinan pulled John Keane upright. 'Put an arm round my shoulder, boy, and the other round your brother. You'll have to try to walk out of here. We can carry you later.'

With the gravely injured man between them, frothy blood dribbling from the corner of his mouth, they stumbled away from the cabins of Lixnaw under the Whiteboys' covering fire that effectively kept the dragoons cowering behind their makeshift barricade. Once, a bullet from a musket thudded into the trunk of a tree a dozen feet from them but soon the sounds of battle faded behind them. John began coughing up gouts of blood and phlegm and they were forced to rest until his paroxysms were over.

'The ball's pierced a lung,' Quillinan muttered to Jack. 'That's why he's bringing up all this blood.'

'Is there nothing we can do?'

'Just get him to his cabin and then it's up to Father O'Sullivan and God, though I'm guessing the priest can do little except ease your man's passing.'

'Hush, John might hear you.'

'He's too far gone to be making any sense of what I'm saying,' Quillinan replied.

John tried to gasp a few words. 'Michael . . . Michael,' he spluttered before lolling into unconsciousness.

'Come on,' urged Quillinan. 'We'll take turns to carry him across our backs. It'll make little difference now.'

It took them nearly two hours to reach the Keanes' cabin at Drombeg. As they neared the cabin in the gathering dusk, Jack saw his mother waiting anxiously outside. As soon as she saw the burden Quillinan carried, Mary Keane began hurrying towards them across the field. Jack ran forward to meet her.

'Tis John, Mam,' he blurted. 'A soldier's ball got him. He's awful hurt.'

An expression of pain crossed Mary Keane's face but she said nothing. She moved behind Quillinan and lifted her son's head, smoothing his black hair from his eyes and brushing away the blood that was still coming from his mouth.

'Tis awful sorry I am,' muttered Quillinan. 'I'd rather it was your son carrying me with what happened to Michael and all.'

'Oh, son,' murmured Mary Keane. 'Oh, son. Carry him gentle.'

They laid John on some sacking and straw in the cabin, turning him on his side to allow his mother to staunch his wound. She ripped off part of her petticoat and thrust it into the gaping hole in his back.

'We should get Father O'Sullivan,' advised Quillinan. 'If you'd like, I'll run for him.'

'Would you, Master Quillinan?' said Mary Keane. 'That's a good man you are. And while you're at it, would you see me man in the fields and tell him what's gone on?'

'Tis my duty, lady. Your lad bleeding there was doing my bidding after all.'

'No – don't be putting the blame on yourself, Master Quillinan. My sons fight for your Whiteboys because they believe in what you stand for.'

She knelt by her son, a tear trickling down her cheek. 'If Ireland has to take them, then let it be so.'

Less than two hours later, Father O'Sullivan knelt by John inspecting his wound. John was breathing shallowly and with great effort. The priest shook his head sadly as he turned to the family standing anxiously around him in the small cabin.

'Tis in God's hands, I fear,' he said quietly. 'There's little man can do for him.' He took a purple sash from inside his cassock, arranged it around his neck, and began administering the last rites, bending close to the mortally wounded man.

'He is at peace and in a perfect state of grace with his Maker,' the priest declared finally, rising from his knees. Mary Keane held her son's hand, crooning a lullaby. Her husband knelt by her, his arm comfortingly around her shoulders as her sweet voice filled the room.

Jack stood by them remembering in vivid flashes times long past. How John had taught him to swim in the shallows of Ballybunnion amid much ducking and splashing and laughter; how they'd hunted for birds' nests in the hedgerows; how they'd learned together at the itinerant teacher's school in the ditch. As he remembered, a great sadness filled him.

Towards the end, as the dusk lit the cabin with a gentle, grey light, John awoke from his unconsciousness for a moment. His eyes were soft and free from pain as he gazed up at his family. 'Tis Michael there,' he whispered. 'There . . . in the shadows by the door. The soldiers didn't . . . ' His voice faltered and then choked. 'Oh, Mam,' he cried once, his eyes staring wildly at that instant. Then his head fell back.

'He's gone. God take him and bless him,' said Father O'Sullivan. 'He made a good death, that he did.'

Joe Keane leaned forward and pulled some sacking over his dead son's face. Then he turned to Quillinan who was standing away from the family at the back of the cabin.

'And what happens now, Master Whiteboy?' he asked bitterly. 'That's two of me boys you've had. Will you be wanting the youngest now? And what about me? And will you be taking this poor woman, too?'

Quillinan shifted uneasily, for once at a loss to find the right words to say.

'Well?' said Joe Keane, rising menacingly to his feet.

'Now, Joe,' said Father O'Sullivan gently. 'Sure and can't you see that Master Quillinan shares your grief? God knows, I've preached often enough against the Whiteboys and I feel like you do that two young lives have been wasted. But isn't it time we thought on the living? God is seeing to Michael and John now.'

'Amen to that,' added Quillinan.

'Will the soldiers be coming for Jack, do you think?' asked the priest sharply.

'I fear so, Father,' said Quillinan. 'They know that Jack is a Whiteboy. We'll have to get the lad away.'

'Oh, no. Not Jack,' cried Mary Keane. 'Not Jack now.'

'But where to,' asked Jack. 'England?'

'You'll find no friends nor safety there,' said Quillinan. 'Tis the

Americas that'll be best for you.'

'That's true,' Father O'Sullivan agreed.

'But how?' said Jack, bewilderment in his voice. 'There's no money for a passage and the soldiers will be watching the ports.'

'The only way will be a boat from the Shannon,' said his father. 'One of the timber ships lying off Tarbert Island. You'll be able to work your passage.'

'Do I have to go?' Jack pleaded.

'Sure, and your mam and me don't want you to go but it'd kill us if you were taken by the soldiers. Much better if we know you're safe somewhere. Anywhere.'

'When?'

'The sooner the better,' said Quillinan. 'The soldiers will be coming on their horses at first light.'

'Not so soon, please God,' sobbed Mary Keane, burying her face in her husband's shoulder.

''Tis for the best,' said Joe Keane, his voice gruff with emotion.

'Wait till it's fully dark in an hour or so, then Jack can walk as far as Ballylongford with me,' said Father O'Sullivan. 'He'll be safe from the soldiers. They'll not question anyone with me.'

An hour later, Jack clasped his mother to him as he said goodbye. 'I'll be back, Mam,' he whispered into her hair. 'I'll be back some time.'

'Be safe, son. You're taking my heart with you.'

'Will you get a message to Brigid for me? Tell her what's happened. Tell her I'll be back.'

'I will, son.'

Jack moved gently from her arms. He knelt in front of his father with head bowed. Quillinan turned away, unable to bear the sight of the farewell.

'Take the blessing of your father,' said Joe Keane, placing his hand on Jack's head. 'And the blessing of this home which will always be yours. And the blessing of your dead brothers, resting with the merciful God.'

'Amen,' said Father O'Sullivan, making the sign of the Cross with his right hand.

Quillinan took Jack's hand in his gnarled fist. 'God be with you, lad. Be sure your sacrifices won't be wasted. The Whiteboys will keep fighting till this land is free and safe for you to return.'

Jack nodded, unable to speak. He took half-a-dozen potatoes wrapped in his father's best green handkerchief. In his pocket were two gold sovereigns from the family's meagre savings, and the wooden crucifix from the tiny shrine to the Virgin Mary fixed to the wall.

He had one last look around the cabin, then ducked through the doorway into the night. As he waited for Father O'Sullivan to join him, he snapped a twig of hawthorn from the hedge outside and slipped it into the pocket of his waistcoat. He gazed up at the dark sky, seeing the stars gleaming in the breaks between the high, flat clouds. He concentrated hard on the sky, trying to blot from his mind any thoughts of what might lie ahead. The stars would be his map for the journey home to Kerry that he was certain he would make one day. 'Michael . . . John . . . Brigid,' he whispered to the night.

'Aye, lad, never forget them,' said Father O'Sullivan, who'd emerged quietly from the cabin to stand by him. 'Your brothers have joined the others who've fought for this land, giving their most precious gift of all to Ireland. May they be blessed for that, because they died for their beliefs, whatever priests like me may think of the terrible waste of it all.' He put his bony hand on Jack's shoulder.

As they moved away from the cabin, Jack looked back once. His mother and father stood in the doorway, their arms around each other.

'Don't look back, son,' the priest said quietly. 'Never look back again. Remember what was but think now on what will be.'

## Chapter 6 July, 1824

The cawing of rooks in the trees woke Jack Keane from his deep sleep. The night before he had walked with Father O'Sullivan to Ballylongford without encountering any army patrols and then had continued his journey alone until reaching the River Shannon. The moon had painted the wide river in dancing silver. Jack had sat for a long while listening to the waves lapping quietly on the shore and almost fell asleep at the water's edge, lulled by its insistent, hypnotic motion. But he had shaken himself awake again, realizing that he needed to be under cover when first light came. He had found a hiding place in the deep undergrowth of a thick wood along the shore. When dawn came, Jack ate one of the lumpers in his hand-kerchief and continued along the riverbank. He kept to the edge of the wood as much as possible, always ready to duck into it if he sighted any soldiers or other early-morning travellers. He had no clear plan except to reach Tarbert where the ships that crossed the Atlantic discharged and took on cargoes.

By mid-morning Jack had reached some cabins on the outskirts of the small port. He could travel no further under cover. His clothes were grubby and stained from sleeping the night in the open; his legs and hands were dirty, his chin rough with fine stubble. He realized he painted a suspicious picture. Jack summoned up all his nerve as he approached a cabin outside which a grizzled old man sat mending a fishing net.

When he was still a few yards away, the fisherman looked up. 'Been travelling long, lad?' he asked gruffly.

'Some . . . some distance,' Jack stammered.

'Rest a while here,' said the fisherman. He gestured at the water-barrel by the cabin door. 'Wash and freshen yourself. A stranger shouldn't be looking like a running man in these parts, not with soldiers and militia as thick as fleas on a mangy dog.'

Jack's heart jumped in alarm but he hid his nervousness as he splashed water over himself.

'Need a razor, lad?'

'I have a few bristles.'

'There's one on the window ledge inside the doorway. Use it carefully. Tis sharp.'

Jack went into the neat little cabin and shaved without a mirror, feeling the blade pull at his soft bristles.

'I'm not a man to be pushing his nose into any man's business,' said the fisherman. 'When you're as old as I am you've learned to keep your silence. But tis sometimes better to share a problem.'

Jack felt that he could trust the old man. 'I must find a ship to get me to the Americas.'

'And what would a young lad be wanting to be away for?' asked the fisherman, his fingers still busy at his net.

Jack hesitated.

'Have the little people got your tongue then? Or is it something that might be shaming you?' the old man persisted.

'Tis nothing to be ashamed of to fight the English soldiers,' Jack said hotly. 'Me brothers have died fighting and now the soldiers are after me.'

'So tis a fighting man you are then. Well, that's a surprise for one with so few bristles. Well, if I was a few years younger I'd be there helping you fight the soldier boys.' The fisherman laid down his net. 'Now, that's tight enough to catch the salmon.' He smiled conspiratorially at Jack, peering at him from beneath his eyebrows. 'Can you be paying your passage?'

'I've only a little money. Two sovereigns in all.'

'Ah, then , tis a fine problem,' said the fisherman, rubbing his chin thoughtfully. 'That's not enough for a passage. You'll have to stow away and then throw yourself on the mercy of the captain. There's the *Grannia* of Captain Higgins making ready to sail tonight to fetch some timber from the Americas. She's lying just where I was thinking of laying my nets.' The fisherman winked at Jack, and clapped him on the shoulder. 'Well, if we're to be shipmates you'd better be knowing I'm called Sean McManus.'

'My name is . . . '

'No, better not be saying, lad. Though you remind me of me own boy who's a long time away working in England.'

The fisherman took a stub of a pipe from his pocket and filled it with shag tobacco. 'You rest the day with me, lad, and I'll be seeing if any of me boy's clothes will be fitting you. If you're to cross the Atlantic, you'll be needing stouter clothes than you have now.'

When the heat of the day had passed, Jack and the fisherman made their way down to Tarbert Harbour. A patrol of soldiers in red and black uniforms lounged by the quayside watching the activity in the small port. A number of tiny one-masted fishing smacks were being prepared for their nightly expeditions to the mouth of the Shannon where the fish were plentiful. Jack was prepared for the shout of discovery at any moment, but in fact, he was indistinguishable from any of the dozens of fishing folk making ready for sea. He was now wearing a thick blue sweater, heavy canvas trousers, and boots that reached nearly to his knees. With a net swung across his shoulders, he looked every inch a seafaring man as he walked alongside Sean McManus.

After stowing the nets, the old fisherman pushed his boat off from the quay and began rowing out of the narrow harbour. 'You just be sitting there and look busy, lad,' he told Jack. 'I'm thinking you're a country boy who might not be too much at ease pulling a pair of oars.'

When they were clear of the harbour, the fisherman shipped his oars and hauled up the boat's single sail. The soft summer breeze pushed them out into the river. Ahead, Jack could see the low, grey shape of Tarbert Island rising from the Shannon, its outline tinged with the sun's orange, and the tall masts of the ocean-going ships lying safely at anchor in its lee.

Sean McManus pointed to a two-master. 'See, the one with the red deckhouse?'

Jack nodded, peering through the haze.

'Well, lad, that's the *Grannia* bound for North America. A fine ship that'll carry you safely across the Atlantic.'

Jack helped him throw out the nets as the fisherman steered his boat out in a circle. The corks on top of the nets bobbed in the gentle swell out in the river. The fiery sun sinking beneath the horizon transformed the Shannon into a scarlet carpet.

After drifting for an hour, hardly speaking, content with nature, they pulled in the net and a dozen silver, wriggling salmon tumbled into the bottom of the boat. The fisherman was delighted. 'You brought luck with you tonight, lad. Tis a fine catch.'

But Jack's thoughts and eyes were firmly on the *Grannia*, looming hugely over the small fishing boat as it drifted, seemingly without purpose, closer to her hull.

'See those ropes hanging from her rails?' said Sean McManus. 'When we get closer, you slip over the side and swim to one of them. Pull yourself up and slide into one of the ports. After that tis up to you to stay out of the way until the *Grannia*'s well into the Atlantic. If Captain Higgins discovers you before he clears the river, he might put you ashore with a few lashes across your back.'

Jack nodded apprehensively. The fishing boat slid under the bow of the timber ship. Jack stood up, ready to clamber overboard.

'Best be taking those boots off, lad,' called the fisherman. 'They'll fill with water and send you straight to the bottom of the river. Put them between your teeth.'

Jack did as he was told. Then he slipped quietly over the side of the boat.

'Thank you for your help, Sean McManus,' he said, holding on to the side for a moment. 'One day I'll return and pay you back.'

'Don't be thinking on it, lad. May God go with you in your travels.'

Jack raised a hand in salute and swam into the shadow of the timber ship as she swung gently on the rising tide. He grasped one of the ropes hanging down nearly to the water and started to haul himself up, hand over hand. The first port he reached was securely battened down. The second was open and he swung through it.

He was in a hold stacked high with barrels lashed together to stop them rolling around when the ship met the open sea. Jack concealed himself behind the barrels in a corner of the hold and peeled off his sodden sweater, shivering slightly as the night air played over his body. Above him he could hear orders being shouted, feet running on the deck, the creaking of ropes, and then the rattle of the sails being hoisted. Away from him, towards the bow, he heard the heavy clanking of the anchor chain as it was pulled up. Almost imperceptibly, the motion of the ship changed as she began to make headway towards the mouth of the Shannon. A slurping noise came from the barrels around Jack. He guessed they must be filled with drinking water for the voyage.

He took a last look out of the open port. Tears formed in his eyes as he watched the river banks, hardly more than a smudge against the sky slipping by. He thought about his dead brothers; the gentleness of his mother; the reassuring strength of his father; the happiness that had always seemed to fill the cabin at Drombeg. Jack was suddenly filled with a terrible loneliness, and the tears rolled down his cheeks. Then he felt in his trouser pocket and pulled out a package wrapped in oil cloth by the old fisherman. Inside were the crucifix and the twig of hawthorn from the hedge by the cabin. Somehow they comforted him. 'I'll be back,' he murmured. 'One day. One day.'

Then, he heard a noise directly above him. He scuttled back to his hiding place just as the hatch was pulled back and a seaman began clumping down the ladder into the hold. Jack shrank back into the darkness of his corner.

'Tis right you are, Captain,' the seaman bawled. 'Some lazy beggar didn't close the port.'

Jack heard the seaman move to the port, only a few feet from him, and slam it shut before securing it with an iron bar.

'Now that would have been a nice state of things if the sea had got to the barrels,' the seaman muttered. 'All battened down, sir,' he called up through the open hold and, satisfied, climbed the ladder and pulled the hatch back over the entrance to the hold.

Jonathan Sandes was in exultant mood as he dined with his wife that evening. Everything seemed to have worked out to his advantage. The battle at Lixnaw had ended in a bloody draw. One Whiteboy and one soldier killed, a few on each side wounded, a police barracks razed to the ground; but most important, the leading Whiteboys had scattered into hiding and Captain Eugene de Vere Pearson had been ordered to return to Dublin to explain his actions. The troops in North Kerry had been left under the command of Robert Leslie, the head of the local militia, a man whom Sandes knew he could easily dominate.

'You look happy, dear,' remarked his wife, helping herself to two slices of roast beef.

'Not happy,' replied Sandes. 'Just thoughtful. With that Dragoon popinjay on his way back to Dublin we've got to consider our next actions against these accursed Whiteboys.'

'From what you were saying before dinner, dear, they don't seem to pose much of a threat now.'

'Far from it. They're slippery and cunning. They'll lie low for a few weeks and then they'll strike again. We must tighten the curfew and go on searching the cabins for weapons, that sort of thing.'

'I know I shouldn't feel sorry for them but I can't help but feel a little sympathy for that Drombeg family who've lost two of their sons.'

'All three of them, by all accounts,' snorted Sandes. 'The youngest is well away in hiding by now, I'm thinking. If we find him he'll be the first to dance on a rope at Tralee. There's ample proof he was at Linxaw. He and his brothers went everywhere together.'

'I'm sure you know best, dear.'

'Well, that may be so,' said Sandes expansively, stretching across the table to ring the tiny bell. 'Certainly I know better than that fool Pearson with his soft tactics. Things are going to be harder from now on. And that's the truth.'

Brigid Aherne came into the room to clear the table. Her eyes still showed the signs of the tears she had wept after hearing in the market square about John Keane's death and Jack's flight.

Sandes barely glanced at her. 'I have some late work to do tonight,' he told his wife. 'So I'll be wanting some brandy and a pipe in my sitting room after you retire.'

'As you wish, dear.'

'Did you hear that, Brigid?' asked Sandes, smiling at her. He was in such an expansive mood that he'd decided to risk an hour or so with Brigid even with his wife in the house.

'Yes, sir,' said Brigid dully. 'Whatever you say.' Her mind was so numb with grief and shock that she didn't even experience her usual feeling of self-disgust at Sandes' command and all it would mean. 'In your sitting room later, sir.'

When Jack Keane awoke, the ship was yawing and pitching as it ploughed through the heavy swell of the Atlantic. He stood up, stretching his cramped, aching limbs, and looked round the hold. Slivers of light filtered through the port and the hatch above him. He paced up and down for a few minutes, trying to adjust to the motion of the ship. If he could put up with hunger perhaps he could remain undetected for the whole voyage. Then a queasiness began to fill his throat. A sudden cramp in his stomach bent him double and he retched up bile. He slumped to the deck, clutching his stomach and moaning in agony. Fresh air, he must have fresh air, he thought. Jack crawled over to the closed port. He pulled the iron bolt from the port and pushed it open. A rush of sea spray spanked into his face as he gulped air into his lungs. He felt as if he was going to die as he retched again and again, bringing up almost colourless liquid. He swayed and slipped in his own stench and misery for hour after hour as the ship, with little ballast in her holds, continued its rolling. He was barely conscious when the hatch was pulled open above him. He moaned and turned his head away from the shaft of bright light.

'Ye Gods and what have we here?' a voice shouted. Rough hands grasped him and pulled him upright. 'A stowaway, eh, and won't the Captain be right glad to see you.'

A hard face swam into Jack's vision and he moaned again as his body was racked by another bout of retching.

'You're learning the hard way about the sea, and that's the truth,' said the seaman. He hauled Jack upright pushing him towards the ladder. 'Up you go, lad. The captain will be wanting to meet you.'

Jack crawled up the ladder on his hands and knees, until a final shove sent him sprawling on the deck. He lay there unable to move.

'Well, well, Flannery,' a gruff voice said above him. 'So you found a hidden piece of cargo, did you?' A heavy sea boot crashed into Jack's ribs lifting him almost off the deck and thrusting him on to his back.

'Belay that, sailor,' a voice roared. 'Can't you see your man's half-dead already? What are you kicking him into hell for?'

'Aye, aye, Captain,' the man standing above Jack replied. 'Flannery found him in the water hold.'

'We won't be getting any sense out of him yet awhile, Flannery.'

'I'm guessing not, Captain.'

'Well, strap him to the mast for his own safety and let him suffer his sickness until it's out of him. He'll be better before the day's out and then maybe we can be teaching him what happens to stowaways.'

'Aye, aye, sir.'

After six hours on the open deck, Jack felt weak and empty but, at least, the motion of the ship wasn't making him dizzy anymore. He began to take an interest in his surroundings, watching the crew climbing the rigging to adjust the sails which billowed and cracked in the strong wind driving the *Grannia* westwards. By twisting his head he could just see the coxswain straining at the wheel on the raised afterdeck, trying to give the ship every advantage of the prevailing wind. By the wheel, Jack could see the man he presumed to be Captain Higgins; a tall, gaunt man with a dark beard shot through with grey, wearing a navy blue reefer jacket and a peaked cap. A shiny brass hailing tube for shouting commands was tucked under one arm. Jack noticed that the captain's spade beard was divided in half with each side cut at a different length. The captain saw Jack watching him and approached the mast.

'Feeling better now, laddie?' he said.

Jack nodded, a weak and guilty smile on his pallid face.

'Aye, well I think we can be unstrapping you since you won't be falling overboard now in your sickness.'

Jack stood up, rubbing his arms where the rope had bitten tightly.

'Now, laddie,' said Captain Higgins. 'You've got some reckoning to give about how you came to be in my ship.'

'I . . . I . . . ' Jack coughed as he tried to speak.

'Get some water for the boy,' ordered the captain.

When Jack had supped two mouthfuls of brackish water from a mug he tried to speak again. 'I came aboard from Tarbert,' he began.

'I'm aware of that,' snapped the captain. 'From one of those fishing smacks that were skipping around like mosquitoes on a stagnant pond.'

Jack nodded agreement. 'I had to be away from Ireland and your ship was the only one ready to sail. Tis sorry I am for any trouble I've caused you.'

'You've caused me no trouble at all, laddie,' said Captain Higgins grimly. 'But I'm wondering if you know how much trouble and pain you're going to cause yourself.'

Jack looked puzzled. 'I feel better now,' he said.

'Not your seasickness, you bilge rat,' roared the captain. 'Stowaways have to be punished or we'd have every guttersnipe sneaking aboard. Since you've suffered a mite already, I'm not going to be harsh on you. But you have to be punished.'

The captain turned to a burly seaman standing by him. 'Tie the stowaway to the rails.'

'Aye, aye, Captain.'

The seaman deftly slipped a rope around Jack's wrists and pulled him towards the rails on the after deck. Jack was too weak to resist. The seaman looped the rope around the rails above his head and tugged on it so that Jack's arms were jerked high into the air. He was forced to stand on tiptoe to ease the excruciating pressure on his arms. His face was pressed against the timbers of the ladder leading to the afterdeck.

'Right,' he heard the captain bellow. 'Administer the punishment, if you please.'

'How many, Captain?'

'Six will be enough, I'm thinking.'

'Aye, aye, sir.'

Jack heard a whistling sound behind him and then an agonizing blow laid his back bare. He screeched in his agony as he felt the hot blood running down his back. Jack rocked his head from side to side, screaming all the time, as the lash tore into his flesh five more times, ripping and cutting.

'That's enough,' shouted Captain Higgins. 'Cut him down and take him below. And swab down the deck. The lad's bled like a stuck pig.'

Jack slumped to the deck and lay moaning and writhing in a spreading pool of his own blood. Another sailor picked up a bucket of seawater and flung it over him making him sob with renewed pain as the brine bit into the open wounds. Two sailors lifted him under the arms and dragged him across the deck to the ladder leading to the crew's quarters.

'You either walk down, lad, or you fall down,' one of them muttered in Jack's ear. He summoned all his remaining strength to stumble down the ladder. At the foot of it he collapsed in a heap. The sailors picked him up effortlessly and laid him face down across the wooden slats of a bunk.

'Let him rest there,' said one of them. 'He's near done in.'

'No, tis better if we get it over with now,' said the other. 'He's as near senseless as makes no difference.'

'Hold him then.'

Jack felt the weight of a body press across his lower back, while other hands grasped his arms and held his head in a vice-like grip. A rough gag of sail cloth was thrust between Jack's teeth and a sailor began rubbing salt in the long stripes of his wounds. The gag turned his screams into agonized groans. The sailors needed all their combined strength to hold Jack down as he quivered and bucked. His mind filled with the glowing redness of his suffering. Finally, mercifully, he slipped into unconsciousness.

For the next two days Jack hovered in and out of delirium as he lay on the rough bunk. Occasionally he was aware of someone lifting his head and pouring cooling water between his lips but for the rest of the time he was in a deep sleep. On the third day he awoke, his head clear, aware of the creaking and swaying of the ship. He raised his head slowly and looked at his surroundings.

The crew's quarters were long and low and narrow. On either side of a rough table were bunks filled with lumpy-looking sacks. A candle in a lantern swung from one of the beams, bringing some light to the gloom below decks. Jack saw two sailors sitting on a bench by the table. They were carving slices off what appeared to be a leg of pork and eating them with square biscuits. He tried to speak but only a croak came from his parched throat.

One of the sailors looked up from his eating and gestured towards Jack with his knife. 'Sounds as if the stowaway's come to his senses,' he said. He stabbed the knife into the top of the table and walked over to Jack's bunk, bending to peer closely into his face. 'Are you better then?' he asked.

Jack tried to speak again but the effort was too much. He nodded weakly.

'Right then, tis best we get you out of there or else you'll be permanent stiff. Can you move at all?'

Jack pushed himself up a little on his arms and rested on his elbows.

'Come on, Martin,' the sailor called to his companion. 'Give us a hand.'

The two of them lifted Jack off the bunk with surprising gentleness. His whole back ached dully but the hurt was no longer jaggedly painful. The sailors supported him as he limped to the table, his arms around the sailor for support. He sat gingerly on the bench and rested his head in his hands. The sailors watched him with concern until Jack lifted his head and smiled gratefully at them.

'Thanks be to God,' he muttered hoarsely.

One of the sailors banged his fist on the table and roared with laughter. 'You be all right now, stowaway. Just awake and already giving thanks.'

The other thrust a lump of meat in front of Jack but he pushed it aside. 'Water,' he whispered. 'Any water?'

A mug of water was put on the table. Jack picked it up with shaking hands and gulped it down. He wiped his mouth with the back of his hand. Then, painfully, he began to eat.

'How long?' he asked eventually, his voice still low and thick.

'Two days, lad, you've been laying there since your lashing,' said the sailor who'd given him the water. 'The carpenter was getting all set to sew you in canvas and slide you twelve fathoms deep. Twould have been unsettling not knowing what name to bury you under.'

'Tis Jack Keane.'

'Well, I be Patrick Deane,' said the friendly sailor, a huge man, well over six feet tall with a round, moon face. He gestured at his companion. 'And this mate of mine be Martin Flannery. Twas Martin that found you baulking your belly up with seasickness.'

Flannery smiled apologetically at Jack. He was as tall as Deane but as thin as a begging priest. 'Sorry, Jack, but if it hadn't been me, twould have been someone else.'

Jack nodded understandably. 'What happens next?'

'Well, by rights,' said Flannery, 'We should be taking you to Captain Higgins right away but just you be resting a bit and find your strength, shipmate.'

Jack began walking unsteadily around the crew's quarters knocking himself painfully against the bunks, but soon he had adjusted to the roll and life of the ship. Surprisingly, he found, he no longer felt any sickness. The two sailors watched him carefully as he eased the stiffness and soreness out of his limbs.

'You'd better be cleaning yourself up before you meet the Captain,' said Patrick Deane. 'You can use my razor on your bristles but be preparing yourself for a shock when you look in the glass.'

Jack took the broken piece of mirror from Deane and looked blearily into it. A face he hardly recognized stared back at him. It was no longer the face of a young, untried man. The cheekbones were more prominent in the thinner, gaunter features. The eyes were gleaming hard, reflecting the extreme pain he had suffered. But, most apparent of all, there was now a streak of snow white hair on his head, about an inch in thickness, running back from his widow's peak.

Jack brushed his hand back through his hair, and studied his new face as he tugged at the bristles with Deane's blunt razor. It wasn't unpleasing, he thought; definitely the face of a man to be reckoned with.

When he'd finished, Deane handed him a thick red shirt woven out of soft wool. 'That comes from the Frenchie trappers along the St Lawrence River,' he explained. 'Twill keep you warm and be gentle on your back until the scars harden.'

'I'll take you to the Captain now,' Flannery volunteered. 'He can be a hard man, Captain Higgins, but I'm telling you he'll be mighty glad to see you up and around.'

He led the way up on to the deck. The sky was grey and sullen but it was one of the most welcome sights Jack had ever seen, and he breathed the spray-filled air deep into his lungs. Captain Higgins was by the wheel of the afterdeck. As he approached him, Flannery raised a knuckle to his forehead.

'The stowaway, Captain. He tells us he's named Jack Keane.'

'So, Jack Keane,' remarked the captain with a welcoming smile, 'you're up and about again.' He offered Jack his hand. 'No hard feelings, I hope. A captain dare not be making an exception to the rules on stowaways.'

Jack shook the calloused hand. 'I didn't understand at the time, Captain.'

Captain Higgins laughed throatily. 'No, I reckon you didn't. But there be very few men at sea without some scars on their backs.'

Jack looked around him. All he could see was water; foam flecked green waves to every horizon, pounding under the bow of the *Grannia* as she rolled and bobbed like a cork in and out of the troughs. ''Tis green, not blue,' he observed. 'The sea's green.'

'Aye, lad, out here and under this sort of sky, tis green. I can tell you've never been on an ocean before.'

'Nor have I, Captain. I'm a farmer if anything.'

'So, lad, what are you running away from to come to sea?'

Jack gripped the rail to steady himself as he told Captain Higgins the story of how he had been forced to flee from Ireland. The captain listened in silence, merely grunting with disgust when he heard of the hanging of Michael Keane.

'So, you're a bit of a rebel, are you, lad?' he said when Jack had finished.

'Sometimes you've got to fight,' Jack replied simply.

'Aye, and isn't that just the truth? Twas what me dad used to say when I was a youngster. He was hung in Wexford in the '98. But that was a proper rebellion that was. Not like your Whiteboys dashing around the countryside.'

'You've got to start somewhere,' Jack said lamely.

Captain Higgins laughed and slapped him on the shoulder. Jack winced at the sudden pain. 'Sorry, lad, I'm forgetting,' the captain apologized, still chuckling to himself. 'So now you want to go to the Americas?'

'I can pay, Captain,' Jack fumbled in the pockets of his canvas trousers and pulled out the two gold sovereigns.

Captain Higgins looked at the money in Jack's hand with a surprised expression. 'Still got them, have you? I must have a more honest crew than I was thinking,' he said, smiling broadly. 'Put them away, lad. True they'd help towards a passage but you'll be needing them when you reach the Americas. You can work your passage. Put some muscle on you, so it will, and the more hands I have crossing this ocean the better I like it.'

'Where are you bound?'

'Boston town, lad. That's where we'll be taking on some more provisions and then we sail up the coast to Canada picking up timber. You can leave the ship where you will, but I'm guessing Boston's as good a place as any. There be quite a few Irish settled there, although I hear tell most of them are from Ulster rather than Munster like you.'

At first, Jack was put to scrubbing decks and polishing the brass, but his new friends, Deane and Flannery, began teaching him how to splice ropes and tie knots and soon he was allowed to climb dizzily into the rigging of the ship to help reef the sails. The work was hard and unremitting, as the *Grannia* ploughed ever westwards. Jack enjoyed it, although at first he hardly had the energy left at the end of the day to climb into his bunk. Later on, as his muscles hardened and he became used to the work, he stayed some nights on deck with the rest of the crew, watching the gamblers playing pitch and toss, throwing coins into the air and guessing which side up they would fall, or joining in the shanties sung to the accompaniment of Flannery's mouth organ. Sometimes he would listen entranced as one of the sailors told of the far distant lands he had visited and the exotic women he'd known. Jack blushed at first at some of the bawdier tales and was glad the night hid his innocence from his shipmates. Occasionally he would stand by himself at the ship's rail looking up at the stars and thinking of his home. It was then he would feel totally alone in the world, alone with the sea, and yet very close to his family and to Brigid Aherne. The harsh thoughts about Brigid and Jonathan Sandes had faded from his memory to be replaced by a deep, warm longing to hold her again as he had the first evening they'd met.

Once Flannery came up to him as he stood gazing up at the stars pinpricking the dark blue coverlet of a clear sky. 'Sure, Jack,' he'd said 'and doesn't it make you wonder? Looking up there at all those tiny lights, you sometimes think you're the only person in creation, so you do. And then you wonder if there might be sailors on a sea up there looking down on you and wondering the same.'

'Tis true, Martin.'

'Aye, Jack, and that's why the men who go to sea are very different. They see things others don't. Out here on the ocean you're terrible close to the secret of life. And because you are, you live happier and harder than most others, I'm thinking. You belong to no one but you belong to everyone. You've no home but everywhere is home.'

'Is that why you go to sea?'

'Didn't me dad go to sea and his dad afore him? We Flannerys have been putting to sea ever since Grannia was Queen of the West.'

'Queen of the West?'

'Of course, you wouldn't be knowing about the greatest she pirate of them all. A handsome woman she was, by all tell, but she could fight down any man or three. Hundreds of years ago Grannia was the terror of the West coast, raiding and plundering all the Dagoes and Frenchies and Portugee who traded into Cork and Limerick. She even took on Turkish merchantmen, and made them haul down their flags to her. And wasn't she a true queen as well? Didn't Elizabeth of England, that cursed Protestant, receive her as an equal when Grannia sailed into London to offer her help to beat the Armada? And didn't Grannia chase all the Dagoes on to the rocks clear around Ireland? Sure, and tis lucky you are to be crossing the ocean in a ship named after her. Tis a lucky charm.'

Jack was fascinated by Flannery's tales and his cavalier approach to life. Flannery sensed this admiration and tried to persuade his young friend to stay with the ship.

'Tis a good life, Jack, and you'd be enjoying it,' he urged.

It was tempting for Jack but he had the feeling that if he became a seaman, he would never see his home again. That was the driving thought in his mind; to return eventually and claim Brigid Aherne. He was explaining this to Flannery one day, the forty-second of the voyage, while they were busy on deck coiling ropes.

'Tis probably true, Jack,' conceded Flannery. 'Once a sailor, always a sailor, and once a landsman, always a landsman. Tis weaned into you at your mam's breast.'

Just then, from high up the main mast, came a shout, 'Land ho! Land ho! Two points on the port bow.'

With the other sailors on deck, Jack and Martin Flannery rushed to the port rail and peered into the distance. At first they could see nothing but then, as the *Grannia* rose on the crest of a wave, there, running along the horizon, was a grey smudge.

'Where are we?' asked Jack excitedly. 'What land?'

'Tis too early to know,' said Flannery. 'But Captain Higgins being the navigator he is, it won't be too far off Boston town. Somewhere along the New England coast, to be sure. It has been a good voyage for charting the stars, even if the wind's been against us a deal of the way.'

Jack noticed that even the most experienced sailors were excited at the prospect of land. They went about their routine work with a new bounce in their step, talking among themselves like womenfolk at market.

In another two hours, the coastline was clearly in sight. Occasionally, a flash of white was visible as a wave broke upon the rocks along the low, featureless shore.

'Tis New England without a doubt,' observed Flannery. 'I be reckoning we're just a mite south of Massachusetts Bay, just as we should be. The Captain'll want to run up into Boston around Cape Cod rather than beat down past Salem from the north.'

'You'd be right, Martin,' said Patrick Deane. 'The last time I made fall at Boston, the Captain found the coast north of Salem Harbour and had the divil's own job coming down the shore. The wind was howling from every point of the compass, so it was.'

For three hours, the *Grannia* stood well off the coast as she ran north west with the prevailing wind. Then the coast fell away, as the ship rounded a rocky headland and entered a wide bay. By now, dusk was beginning to fall.

'We'll be staying out another night,' Flannery explained to Jack. 'There be islands between us and Boston Harbour and the Captain won't be risking them at night. He'll lie well off until first light. You be ready to get into the rigging to shorten sail.'

Sure enough the order came to reef back all sails until the *Grannia* was wearing only enough canvas to maintain the slightest headway. From high in the swaying rigging, Jack could see small, twinkling lights along the shore, and above them one steady, stronger light.

'The lights of Boston town,' said Flannery, hanging in the rigging beside him. 'The light above them all is what's called "Bullfinch's Pillar". In the old days it was called the Beacon Light till the Yankees renamed it.'

Hardly anyone slept for more than a few hours that night. At dawn, the *Grannia* took on more sail and under a brightening sky began moving towards Boston harbour. She slid past large, wooded islands on her port side before Jack got his first real sight of the town. From the buildings along the quays, bristling with the masts of ships, Boston rose, undulating on hills, along a promontory, clearly separated from the mainland by a wide river. As the *Grannia* nosed into harbour, she was taken in tow by three rowing boats which pulled her to a berth. Even at this early hour, the quays were thronged with men, loading and unloading other vessels in the port, moving cargoes between wooden warehouses that stood only a few yards back from the cobbled quayside. Lines were thrown from the *Grannia* and tied to bollards. When she was secured, her anchor dropped into the murky water of the harbour with a loud splash and a rattle of iron links. As gulls mewed and swooped above, the crew was assembled by the bosun on the quarterdeck.

'We have a day before we take on provisions,' Captain Higgins told them. 'Apart from one watch, you can go ashore, but be back aboard at first light tomorrow. I need not be reminding you that those who go adrift forfeit all their pay under the ship's articles.' He pointed his telescope at Jack. 'You . . . report to me before you go ashore.'

'Right, Jack, since you've determined not to be a seaman,' said Flannery, 'at least you can see your new home for one day in the company of your old shipmates.' He winked at Deane. 'We'll be showing you some sights, I'm thinking, that you didn't see in Kerry. Now off with you and talk to the Captain.'

Jack clambered up the ladder to the afterdeck. Captain Higgins was standing by the rail watching the activity on the quayside. He swung round at Jack's approach.

'Ah, the fighting man, eh?' he smiled. 'All ready to be starting your new life?'

'Aye, Captain.'

'Well, in the absence of your father, let me be giving you a little advice, lad.'

'Captain?'

'This is a new country you're coming to. The Yankees threw off the English yoke just as the men of '98 tried to do. But that doesn't mean it's all that different here. There's them that serve and them that are served. Just like anywhere else. Keep to your kind, work hard and curb your spirit. They've had enough rebellion here to fill their stomachs for a lifetime.' He smiled warmly. 'But I'm guessing you'll adapt. You've learned to be a passable seaman quick enough. It might have given you some white hairs but it's also built you some useful muscles.'

Captain Higgins reached inside his waistcoat pocket and pulled out a gold sovereign. 'Here's your wages for the crossing. I'm reckoning you deserve them.'

Jack took the coin and shook the Captain's outstretched hand. He didn't know quite what to say in the face of such kindly generosity. 'I'll never forget you, Captain, and that's the truth.'

'No, lad, I doubt if you will. Every time you undress, you'll have the scars on your back to remind you.' The Captain guffawed. 'Now be off with you and God watch over you.'

Jack Keane strode down the bouncing gang plank behind the tall figures of Flannery and Deane, his three gold sovereigns jingling in his pocket. He felt ready for anything that Boston had to offer.

## Chapter 7 August, 1824

A definite odour came to Jack's nostrils as he walked along the quayside with Martin Flannery and Patrick Deane. Later, he was to recognize sewerage and mud from the marshes of Back Bay, the oxides belching from the iron works and the smell of raw cotton from the textile mills. The smell suggested people and industry on a scale he had never encountered before. There was a bustle among the people that was strange to him. They scurried about their work purposefully, speaking in a burring accent with an indefinable nasal harshness. They dressed more sturdily than the Irish but not as finely as the land agents like Doctor Church and Master Sandes. There were some men in high crowned hats, men obviously of high station, but many still wore the tricorn hats which even Jack knew had passed out of fashion on the other side of the Atlantic. The buildings too were immediately different to his eyes: constructed more of wood than stone, two storeys high with narrow, latticed windows. Such large, brick buildings as there were, clearly great centres of commerce or worship, dominated the cobbled streets and alleys that rose and fell, higgledy-piggledy, behind the quayside.

Flannery and Deane seemed familiar with the town, and pushed past people, bumping shoulders, in a way that was quite new to their young companion. Down one street, up an alley, under an archway, they made their way to a two-storey, wooden building in a narrow cobbled street which was divided by an open gutter.

'Now, Jack,' said Flannery, 'This is the most important place for you in all Boston town. If you're a wise lad, this is where you'll make your life for tis here you'll meet all the people you should be knowing.'

He unlatched the wooden door and flung it open. 'Mother McCarthy's groggery!' he announced loudly.

A torrent of noise flooded out of the low-beamed room to greet the three men as they stood in the doorway. It ceased for a moment as the men and women inside, seated at rough tables, turned to look at the newcomers and then it swelled again as they settled back to their chattering and drinking. Jack coughed as the fetid smell of spilt drink and rough tobacco hit him. Flannery laughed sympathetically and gave Jack a push towards a wide plank set on two upturned barrels. It was covered with bottles and empty mugs and clearly served as the bar. Jack stumbled over someone's feet and nearly fell to the sawdust strewn floor. He gripped the bar to save himself and stared directly into the leer of a dried pig's face, the colour of a mouldy lemon with salt caked in its ears, which lay morosely on the end of the plank.

'Flannery and Deane!' a voice shouted raucously above the din. 'Tis me favourite sailor boys back to see their old Mother McCarthy.'

A large, lumpy figure in black with a grimy, once-white mop cap, swept past Jack and gripped Flannery and Deane round their shoulders in a tight hug, planting smacking kisses full on their lips. Jack's two companions whooped with joy and, together, lifted the woman off her feet, swinging her high into the air. Her stained petticoats fluttered up revealing a pair of thick, knobbly legs encased in black stockings.

'Tis not for long, mother,' exclaimed Flannery. 'We've only a bit of a day and a night here so we've to be getting down to serious business straight away.'

Deane caught Jack's eye and winked. 'Mother,' he cried, 'We've brought a new friend for you, fresh from the old country he is too.'

The woman turned round and looked up at Jack.

'His name's Jack Keane and he'll be staying on in Boston town, that he will.'

'Welcome then, Jack Keane,' shouted Mother McCarthy. She was at least fifty years old, thought Jack; thin, grey hair straggled from under the mop cap; tiny broken veins in her nose and cheeks betrayed her taste for hard liquor. 'My, my . . . and tis a handsome young friend you've brought me, boys,' she said, her voice punching loudly through the hubbub in the room. Her arms reached up and encircled Jack's neck, pulling down his face to her own level. Her lips devoured his.

Flannery and Deane guffawed at his squirming unease. They patted the woman on her ample shoulders.

'Come on, mother. Tis cradle snatching you are. Let the lad be.'

Mother McCarthy released Jack and stepped back, a broad grin on her face. She gestured towards the bar. 'Come on, now, and get some grog down you. You've had a mighty long voyage to build up a thirst that you have.'

Flannery reached out and picked up a dusty bottle lying by the pig's head. He slopped the contents into three earthenware mugs.

'Come on, lads. Let's join the party!'

Jack and Patrick Deane lifted their mugs. Deane drained his in one gulp and Jack, still embarrassed from Mother McCarthy's embrace, did the same. The undiluted alcohol, oily and sweet tasting, coursed down his throat like a stream of red-hot lava. He gagged on it and was almost sick on the floor. 'By the Holy Saints,' he spluttered, red in the face once more, 'What's this concoction?'

'The juice of the juniper,' said Flannery calmly, picking up the bottle and pouring another mugful for each of them. 'Mother McCarthy's gin brewed by her own sweet hands.'

Jack followed his friend's example in draining the second mug. This time the room took on a cheerier, less sordid, atmosphere. Everyone gave the appearance of enjoying themselves. The women at the tables laughed vivaciously, attractively. Many of them, Jack saw, wore paint on their faces, emphasizing their eyes and lips. Occasionally a man and a woman would get up from a table and walk towards the stairway at the back of the room with their arms around each other's waists. He nodded towards the wooden stairway as Flannery filled his mug again. 'Where does that lead to, Martin?'

'Paradise, lad. But get in the proper mood first or you'll be thinking it's more like hell when you climb them stairs.'

Jack looked puzzled.

'Women, lad,' explained Deane with a lop-sided smile. 'There's more to this groggery than gin. You can find anything you want at Mother McCarthy's from a business deal to a sturdy wench.'

'Have you any friends for us?' Flannery called over to Mother McCarthy who was now deep in conversation with a tall, well dressed man in a stovepipe hat.

She waved over at Flannery. 'The best, lads. Only the best.' She hurried around the tables with surprising agility, whispering in the ears of three young women and nodding over at Jack, Flannery and Deane who had by now seated themselves at an empty table by the stairway.

The girls walked over to the table, mugs in hand, swaying a little. Two of them were flaxen haired; the third was very dark, her hair the shade of a raven's wing. Jack, now sipping his third mug of gin, felt a pang of memory, and thought how similar her hair was to Brigid's.

'Sit you down, girls,' invited Flannery, grabbing one of the fair haired girls round the waist and pulling her on to his lap. 'Which one do you want, lad?' He noticed Jack's eyes flick towards the dark haired girl. 'Right Patrick, tis you for the other then.' he told Deane. 'Tis only right the lad should be having his choice on his first visit to Mother McCarthy's.'

Without hesitation, the dark haired girl sat down next to Jack. 'And would you be getting a girl a drink, Irisher?' she said, putting her hand on his forearm.

Close to her, Jack could see that the paint on her face helped conceal the fine lines around her eyes and at each corner of her mouth. Her eyes sparkled; her features were pleasant, if not beautiful, her perfume was fresh and light. There was a sense of vulnerability about her, an eagerness to please, that attracted Jack.

'Sure I will,' he said. 'But first be telling me your name.'

'Meg.'

'I'm Jack Keane.'

'Hush with your name giving,' the girl said. 'You're my Irisher with the white streak of hair.'

She reached up and touched his hair. 'They say a man with a streak like that has fortune on his side.'

Jack laughed. 'You wouldn't think that if I was telling you how I got it.' He drained his mug and pulled the pitcher of gin on the table towards him. By now, he was feeling relaxed and happy. Flannery and Deane were whispering into their companion's ears, making them giggle. Jack leaned closer to his girl. 'And what would you be doing in this groggery, Meg?'

Her eyes widened a little. 'Tis your first time here, Irisher?'

'Tis indeed. I was leaving Ireland only a month back.'

Meg hesitated for a moment. 'Then I guess you weren't being the sarcastic one. I work here, earning a living – such as it is. Twas this or the mills.'

'Don't your mam and dad mind?' asked Jack.

Meg giggled into her mug. 'Aren't you the innocent one with the questions? I come from a farm up in Maine, a way from here. There wasn't enough to support us all so I had to make my own way.'

Jack suddenly felt protective towards her. His head was beginning to feel a little muzzy, but he decided it was because of the smoky air in the room. He swigged another mouthful of gin, peered over at Flannery and noted, with surprisingly detached interest, that he was now kissing his companion, passionately. One hand had disappeared under the folds of her skirt. Deane, too, was embracing his girl. Somehow, such private behaviour didn't appear out of place in the free and easy atmosphere of the groggery. Flannery stood up, lifting his girl off his lap.

'And who's for the stairway to dreams?' he asked.

Deane broke away from his girl. 'Why not, shipmate? We've not that long before the captain will be wanting us back aboard. What say you, young Jack? Ready for a taste of Paradise?'

Jack, still slightly puzzled, looked at Meg. She nodded. 'If you like, Irisher,' she said softly.

Flannery overheard her reply. 'If he likes . . . ' he guffawed. 'I doubt, lass, if he knows what he likes yet.' He leaned over the table and pinched her cheek. 'But you'll be teaching him, won't you?'

Meg took Jack's hand and led him towards the stairway. The floor of the groggery tilted and swayed just like the deck of the *Grannia*. He stumbled on the stairs and would have fallen but for Meg's support. 'Just a few steps more, Irisher,' she said, encouragingly. 'Then you can lie down.'

Jack smiled at her blearily and nodded, feeling queasier with every moment.

It was dark at the top of the stairs. A long corridor lit by only two dim oil lamps stretched the length of the groggery's upper floor. A dozen or so cubicles led off the corridor. Jack could still hear the sound of the drinkers below but now there were other noises as well; low rustlings, creakings and soft moans came from the occupied cubicles. Flannery and Deane disappeared with their girls into the first two empty cubicles but Meg led Jack further along the corridor. The curtain was pulled aside and through the narrow entrance Jack saw that the cubicle contained a narrow bed and a wicker chair. Nothing more. Meg gave him a slight push and he tumbled gratefully on to the bed. He lay on his front, his head spinning and then looked round over his shoulder.

Meg had drawn the curtain across the doorway but enough light filtered through from the oil lamp outside for Jack to see her beginning to undress. She pulled her brown blouse over her head letting her full breasts tumble free, and then she slipped her black skirt down over her hips and stood naked at the foot of the bed. Jack blinked as his eyes were drawn to the triangle of dark, tight curls in the shadow of her plump belly. It was the first time he'd ever seen a woman so brazenly naked and, even in his inebriated state, felt a stirring in his loins. He rolled over on the bed and tried to prop himself up on his elbows but they slid away from him. He fell back on the blankets, smiling up at Meg.

'Too much gin for such a young lad,' whispered Meg, half to herself. She knelt on the bed and unbuckled the thick belt around Jack's waist. Her fingers opened the trousers and pulled them down to his knees. 'But perhaps then not too much gin, eh?' she added as she grasped Jack's thickening, lengthening maleness for a moment. She pulled off his sea boots, dropping them on the floor with a thud, and slipped his trousers off completely. Then she unbuttoned his shirt and ran her fingernails over his hairless chest.

Jack reached up and squeezed her soft, bare shoulders, pulling her down to him. Her lips met his in a long, fierce kiss. He felt her belly grinding gently from side to side and tried to raise himself, but as soon as his head left the blankets the cubicle began to spin round him.

Meg pushed him back, shaking her head. 'You rest there, Irisher, or I'm thinking you'll be awful sick and Mother McCarthy wouldn't be pleased with little Meg if that happened. She told me to gentle you and I'm guessing tis the first time you've been with a woman. Am I right? Now tell the truth?'

Jack nodded, not daring to speak.

A smile of delight crossed Meg's face. 'And aren't I a lucky one? They say a man never forgets the first woman he beds.' She bent forward and kissed him again. Then she knelt back and straddled his body. Jack could feel her warmth and wetness against him. She pushed a hand between her legs, grasping him again and guiding him into her as she lowered herself on to him.

Jack threw back his head and gasped. Meg supported herself on her arms and began moving up and down on him, slowly at first, savouring every sensation as he filled her, then faster, moving her hips from side to side. A mist of pleasure closed over Jack as he lay passively beneath her but then he reached out to hold Meg's waist to steady himself as he began thrusting upwards into her. There was nothing except the sensation welling up inside him until, finally, he exploded into her. Meg groaned as she felt her insides dissolve in a torrent of burning liquid and collapsed across Jack. They lay close together, panting, slippery with perspiration.

Meg looked directly into Jack's face. 'And was that nice, Irisher?' she whispered. 'Was it worth crossing the Atlantic for?'

Jack nodded and impulsively gave her an affectionate kiss on the cheek. ''Twas like nothing before nor since,' he mumbled. His head fell back and he was fast asleep.

He was still asleep. hours later, snoring gently, when the curtain of the cubicle was pulled back. Flannery and Deane, both fully dressed, stood in the entrance gazing down on the couple intertwined on the bed. They grinned at each other.

'Well, the lad seems to have broadened his education, and that's the truth,' said Flannery with a wink. He squeezed into the narrow cubicle and shook Meg by the shoulder. She murmured protestingly in her sleep, then awoke.

'What do you want?' she asked, looking up at Flannery, not in the least embarrassed by her nakedness.

'Just this, pretty one – and don't you look sweet enough lying there to tempt a saint? – just tell the lad goodbye from Flannery and Deane. We're off back to our ship now. Tell the lad we'll go to his folks and say he's safe. And tell him also to see Mother McCarthy when he's fit because she has something that might be interesting him.'

Meg nodded sleepily before turning back and burying her head in Jack's shoulder.

When Jack awoke some hours later, his head ached and his mouth tasted foul. He groaned as he lifted his head off the bed and looked round the cubicle. In the light of day he could see just how shabby his surroundings were. He gazed at Meg with distaste and remorse. No longer was she the alluring person of the night. Her mouth hung open slackly as she snored loudly. Her body appeared white and slug-like to Jack as it curled around him. A vivid image of the clear, unsullied beauty of Brigid Aherne flashed into his mind. He felt ashamed of himself. He rolled quietly off the bed and began pulling on his clothes. The first thing to do, he thought, was to find Flannery and Deane and get away from this place.

He was just leaving the cubicle to search for them when Meg, who'd been watching him dress, noting the scars on his back, spoke.

'They've gone. Your friends are gone some hour back, Irisher. They told me to tell you their goodbyes.'

Jack was bewildered. What was he going to do without their

guidance and support? His head was hurting so much that it was difficult even to think.

'But you're to see Mother McCarthy before you go,' Meg continued, swinging her legs over the side of the bed and reaching for her clothes. 'That's what your friends said. Something that might interest you, they said.'

Jack swayed slightly in the doorway, wiping cold sweat from his forehead. 'Where . . . where is she?' he asked in a voice still thick with drink.

''Tis a bit early for her yet,' replied Meg, buttoning her skirt and pulling her blouse over her head. She fluffed and patted her dark hair into some order. 'I'll be cooking some breakfast while you wait. You can wash up in the kitchen as well.'

She led the way down the dark corridor. Sounds of snoring and coughing came from the curtained cubicles. A half-naked girl appeared at the entrance of one of the cubicles by the stairway, and smiled at Meg as she stretched sleepily. 'How was your young Irisher?' she asked, ignoring Jack completely.

'Well enough,' muttered Meg, grabbing Jack's hand and pulling him past the girl.

All the customers had left the groggery. The door to the street was open while an old man swept up the sawdust and cigar butts. Jack coughed as the pungent dust caught the back of his throat. The man with the broom glanced up at them, winked slyly, and continued his work. Meg led Jack into a small room behind the bar. Inside was a cooking range, a long table, and half-a-dozen stools.

Meg busied herself cooking bacon and beans as Jack washed himself. He felt slightly steadier after he'd splashed cold water from a wooden bucket over his face and chest.

'Sit yourself down,' said Meg briskly, putting two filled plates on the table alongside a round loaf of bread. 'You'll feel better with something inside you to soak up all that gin you guzzled.' She smiled at Jack and patted his hand. 'I'm guessing how you feel, Irisher. Not too proud of yourself, eh?'

Jack shook his head as he chewed on a thick rasher of bacon.

'Bet you left a girl behind in the bogs,' Meg chattered on between mouthfuls of food. 'Bet you think she'd be proper ashamed of you if she could see you now. That's what I thought me mother would be feeling after my first time. Well, what the eye doesn't see, the heart doesn't grieve at. That's what I say.'

Jack smiled gratefully at her, touched by her desire to put him at ease. She was clearly a woman of kindness and understanding.

As they were mopping up the fat and juices from their plates with hunks of bread, Mother McCarthy swept into the kitchen.

'Me pretty little Meg and her handsome Irish boy,' she boomed. 'Very nice. Very domestic-like.' She went over to the range and poured herself a steaming cup of black coffee. 'Did you get the message from those two rascal shipmates of yours, Jack Keane?'

Jack nodded.

'A good head for names, that's what you need in this business. And a good head for figures, as well.' She sat down beside Jack with a loud sigh. 'Trouble is I'm not getting any younger and running a business like this is becoming a might difficult for a poor old woman like me.'

Meg giggled behind her hand.

'Now, none of your cheek, young lady,' said Mother McCarthy sternly. 'Didn't I take you from the streets and treat you just like me daughter? Shame on you. Now off you go and help the other girls tidy upstairs while I have a little chat with young Jack here.'

Meg flounced out of the kitchen. Jack watched her with an affectionate smile.

Mother McCarthy drained her mug of coffee and thumped it down on the table. 'Now, lad, to business. So you're going to stay on in Boston, are you?'

'I can't go back to Ireland.'

'You can tell me all about that later,' interrupted Mother McCarthy, brushing a straying lock of grey hair under her cap. 'You'll be needing a job that's for sure, and since Flannery and Deane reckon you're a good shipmate, that's enough. Will you be working here for me?'

Jack looked doubtful. The groggery was so unlike anything in his previous experience that it frightened and overpowered him.

Mother McCarthy sensed his hesitation. 'You'll be helping me in the business, Jack Keane, not drinking and wenching all night and day. I need someone young like you to help me make the gin and keep order in the house. I'll be teaching you the tricks of the trade and a lot besides. You'll learn about keeping the books and banking the cash and paying our dues. Why, if you're half as smart as I'm thinking you are you'll be a proper businessman in no time, and that's the truth.'

'But what about the girls? What about them?'

Mother McCarthy began to laugh. 'So that's it, is it?' she cackled loudly. 'I should have known too, what with you being fresh from the old country. The priest's teaching still in you, eh?'

She leaned forward and ruffled his hair affectionately. 'Holy Mother, if only I'd had a son like you to keep me in my old age . . . Tell you what, young Jack, you can have a cubicle upstairs all to yourself, then it's up to you what you do about the girls, though from the way little Meg was looking at you you'll have a problem keeping to yourself.'

'Well,' Jack said. 'Well, I'm not sure . . .'

'I'll be paying you five dollars a week and all you can eat,' Mother McCarthy continued quickly, sensing that Jack was weakening.

'How much is five dollars?' asked Jack.

'More than you'd be getting in a month back in the bogs.'

'Tis settled then,' said Jack. 'What would you be wanting me to do first?'

'Well, seeing as you had such a hard night, by the look of your eyeballs,' Mother McCarthy smiled, 'you can have the day off. Take Meg and have her show you Boston. That way you won't be getting lost when you venture out on your own.'

When Meg heard the news, she rushed back upstairs to put on a brown bonnet and borrow a black shawl from one of the other girls. As they went through the door of the groggery, she thrust her arm through Jack's. She smiled up into his face, 'Now we'll be looking like any other couple taking the air. I'm thinking we'll walk to the Common. The sight of the cows will make you feel at home.'

'You've got to show me Boston town,' insisted Jack.

'Well, we'll see it on our way. I'll take you the roundabout route.'

They stood in the narrow street outside, just by the open gutter.

'Now see behind the groggery,' Meg pointed. 'That's called Fort Hill and we're in Bread Street. So if ever you're lost you can always head for the hill and you'll fetch up not far away from the groggery.'

They strolled along a network of narrow, cobbled streets, standing aside to let men on horseback trot past them. Jack peered down each turning, trying to memorize its name scrawled on the corner of a house. He kept looking back towards Fort Hill to fix his position.

'They're all black people down there,' he exclaimed in amazement as he crossed the entrance to one street. Jack stood for a minute looking at the first Negroes he'd ever seen as they sat on the stoops of their tall and narrow houses.

'Aye,' said Meg. 'That's where them Nigras live. Southac and Belknap Streets. The old Boston people have taken to calling Fort Hill "Nigra Hill". Still, they don't treat them like they do in Virginia and the other states. They don't have bond slaves here. Nobody owns anybody else in Boston.'

'Not like back in Ireland,' Jack muttered. 'The landlords own everybody there. That's why I had to leave.'

'Is that how you came by those wicked scars on your back?' asked Meg.

As they walked along, Jack told her briefly of how and why he'd come to Boston. Meg squeezed his arm sympathetically when he'd finished his account. 'Well, that's all behind you now, Irisher. Here, you're free.'

'Now look here,' she said as they approached a squat, handsome, three-storey brick building with a balcony opening out from tall windows on the second floor. 'That's the old State House where the Britishers used to have their headquarters. When we'd beaten them, the Declaration of Independence was read from that balcony up there.'

'One day,' said Jack grimly, 'we'll read our own declaration of independence in Dublin.'

'Of course, you will, Jack,' said Meg soothingly, sensing the bitterness within him.

By the time they reached the Common other couples were enjoying the warm early autumn sunshine strolling on the open land. Barely a mile from the groggery and the congested heart of town families sat in leafy glades just off the cow trails or watched the cattle grazing on the fenced pastures. Meg led him through a thicket. 'There you are . . . water!'

Before them stretched the marshy fens of Back Bay. In the distance the sun glinted off the River Charles and the windows of the homes and farmhouses across the river.

They sat down on the shore of the bay. ''Tis different from the shore in Kerry. 'Tis much wilder there,' said Jack.

The sickly-sweet smell he'd noticed the day before when he'd left the ship came to his nostrils again.

'Phew!' he sniffed. 'It smells like the dungheap back of our cabin.'

'You get used to it,' said Meg, amused at the expression on his face. 'After a time you don't notice it at all. There's talk of filling in the bay with other than dung. Some of the work has started, too. But I don't reckon they can fill in the whole bay. It's too big.'

'Where's this place you come from? Maine, didn't you call it?' asked Jack.

Meg pointed back over her head. 'About thirty miles to the north. A little place called Kittery, or just outside it.'

'All farmland is it?'

'Oh, no. They build ships up there and what farms there are have been hacked out of the forests. It's rough land. Not so many years back, me pa kept his rifle by him in the fields in case the Redskins attacked.'

Meg led him along the shore of Back Bay until they could see a high column of grey stone rising above the trees. 'That looks familiar,' Jack said.

'Well, you would have seen it out at sea, I'm thinking. That's Bulfinch's Pillar on Beacon Hill.'

'Oh, yes,' Jack remembered. 'The light that guides ships into harbour.'

They came to the edge of the Common. Before them was a wide cobbled roadway with tall, elegant houses standing in spacious grounds on the far side. Women in pretty bonnets, carrying parasols to protect them from the sun, clattered past in gleaming open carriages. Their coachmen, usually Negroes, wore uniform livery with high crowned hats brightened by feathers stuck in their sides.

'Them's the ladies of the swells,' said Meg, jerking her thumb at the carriages. 'Anyone who's anyone lives round Beacon Hill.'

Jack looked wonderingly at such outward signs of wealth. He caught the eye of one young woman in a carriage, sitting opposite an older, bearded man wearing a high stovepipe hat. For a second, her cornflower blue eyes appraised Jack before she turned away. The carriage stopped further up the roadway outside a four-storey house built of brick and fronted with wood. As the man got out of the carriage, Jack thought for a moment that he recognized him.

Meg, who had been watching Jack's face, broke into his thoughts. 'High and mighty he is up here. But you should see him upstairs at the groggery.'

Then Jack realized he was the man he'd seen the previous evening talking with Mother McCarthy.

'That's Master John Patrick Kilfedder,' said Meg, a contemptuous note in her voice. 'The richest Irisher in Boston, and didn't I carry his marks for weeks? To look at his prissy wife, you'd think butter wouldn't melt in his mouth.'

'He lives in grand style . . .'

'On the interest he charges his own countrymen,' said Meg bitterly. 'None of the banks will give loans to Irishers when they arrive here so they have to bend the knee to J. P. Kilfedder for the money.'

'Did Mother McCarthy . . . ?'

'Aye. That's why none of the girls dare complain about his treatment of them. He all but owns the groggery. If he snapped his fingers, Mother McCarthy would have to close down or hand the business over to him. Not that he'd want it. Wouldn't do for someone living on Beacon Hill to be seen connected with a groggery in Bread Street. Wouldn't do at all.'

They passed the domed Massachusetts State House before heading back towards the crowded alleys and streets of Boston. High above the reddish brown roofs of the houses, the steeples of half a dozen churches poked upwards. Meg pointed out one. 'That's the cathedral for you Irishers; the Holy Cross in Franklin Square. All good Catholic girls get their learning at the nun's convent next door to it. Even Mother McCarthy goes to hear Bishop Fenwick preach sometimes, not that he's Irish, but she says he's nearly as good as the priests you've got back in the bogs.'

At the corner of Ann Street, Meg stopped to admire the bow window of a shop selling bonnet ribbons and pieces of lace.

'Would you like one?' asked Jack.

'Oh, yes, they're so pretty. Can I?'

'Sure and you can. I'm thinking you're deserving a present from me.'

Meg blushed. ''Twas a pleasure, Jack Keane. Every moment.'

Inside the shop Meg behaved like an excited schoolgirl as she picked her way through the ribbons and lace. Eventually, she chose two lengths of silk ribbon – and a strip of finely worked lace. Jack grandly handed over one of his gold sovereigns and received a handful of dollars and cents in change.

'Now what about something for you to wear Jack Keane,' said Meg. 'You can't stay dressed like a sailor just down from the rigging. Remember, you're going to be an important man at the groggery.'

Jack looked down at his red shirt, canvas trousers, and heavy sea boots. ''Tis right you are, Meg.'

Further along Ann Street, they spied a shop selling men's clothes. Jack broke into his second gold sovereign to buy a white shirt, brown breeches and stockings, an emerald green waistcoat, and the first pair of shoes he'd ever owned in his life. He told the shopkeeper to set his trousers and seaboots against the bill for his new clothes but insisted on keeping the red shirt he'd been given by Patrick Deane.

''Tis a keepsake,' he explained to Meg as they left the outfitter's shop. 'Its redness will remind me of the lashing on the ship long after the scars have faded. 'Tis something I shouldn't be forgetting.'

They stopped to eat at a tavern a few streets away from the groggery, and used their fingers to dip into a large earthenware pot of corned beef stew with potatoes, turnips, carrots, and cabbage.

112

'Tis a dish we eat all the time here,' said Meg, licking her fingers with relish.

Jack who'd been careful to pick out as much meat as possible, was amazed. 'All the time?' he exclaimed. 'Sure and back in Kerry, it would be a feast even for St Stephen's day. All this meat . . . you live like lords here.'

'We haven't finished yet. There's "heaven and hell" still to come.'

'What?'

' "Heaven and hell", tis very sweet, made with molasses, corn meal and milk.'

'Tis delicious whatever its name,' exclaimed Jack after finishing a large portion of the pudding. 'Sure and I feel bloated out like a cow in calf, that I do.'

'We'd better be going,' said Meg anxiously. 'Mother McCarthy will be thinking I carried you off.'

The groggery was busy even in mid afternoon, the air thick with tobacco and Irish voices. Mother McCarthy greeted them in a booming voice like her own long lost children. 'My, you look smart, Jack Keane. That you do. And have you been shown Boston properly?'

'Sure and it's a fine town,' said Jack, successfully side-stepping her attempted embrace. 'Only a day here and I'm feeling at home already.'

With a sense of well-being from his full stomach and new set of clothes, he looked round the groggery with something of a proprietorial air.

## Chapter 8 December, 1824

As Boston's autumn gave way to the fierceness of winter, Jack Keane worked long hours under the tutelage of Mother McCarthy. He learned how to deal with fighting drunks – how to use a shillelagh to knock them unconscious rather than risk a brawl by accepting an invitation to fight. Down in the cellars he was taught how to distil gin from juniper berries, watching the clear alcohol drip from the maze of pipes that made up the still. He learned a crude form of book-keeping and paid in the takings once a week at the Massachusetts Bank, where as much as sixteen per cent interest was paid on deposits. He came to recognize which of the town's constables were sympathetic towards the small Irish community, who could be treated with confidence and a mug of gin and who should receive the deferential approach. Similarly, he came to know which selectmen from the town's council liked to spend an occasional day's drinking and whoring away from the prying eyes of their voters.

'Discretion and hard work make a successful groggery,' Mother McCarthy would tell him. 'But most of all discretion. See all, hear all, but say nothing.'

As the months passed, Mother McCarthy spent more and more time drinking with her cronies, leaving Jack a virtually free hand to run the business. The groggery's customers gave Jack the respect due to someone who held sway in an important Irish meeting place. He was called on to arbitrate in disputes about rates of pay, about rent levels and about who should be the ganger in a team of labourers.

Many of the Irish who'd settled in Boston during the early nineteenth century found it easier to earn a wage by laying aside their skills and relying on labouring jobs, either along the harbour wharves or in the public construction works beginning to spring up all around Boston, which tried to link the town more securely to the mainland with better and bigger toll roads, or to expand the area of the town by filling in the fens and marshes on the outskirts. This work was shunned by the native Bostonians as being too menial and so gave an opportunity to Negroes and settlers from Europe. Much of the money earned by the Irish labourers found its way into Mother McCarthy's coffers. As Boston grew, so did the credit balance of the groggery at Massachusetts Bank.

The one problem which caused Jack headaches was controlling the dozen or so girls who used the groggery as a place of business. He went on sleeping with Meg when she didn't have a customer but soon discovered the other girls saw this as unwarranted favouritism. The dilemma was clear to Jack; either he had to sleep with all the girls in turn or else he had to end his relationship with Meg.

'Tis a terrible problem, to be sure,' he told Mother McCarthy when he confided in her. 'I'm very fond of Meg and getting used to her ways. But tis mighty clear it cannot go on like this.'

'You've another choice if that's the case, Jack. You could always marry her and then the other girls would have no cause for complaining.'

Jack shook his head emphatically. 'No. My word is given to a girl back home and I shall return one day and claim her.'

'Well then, Jack,' said Mother McCarthy, gulping down the last of a mug of gin, 'Tis certain what you've got to do. You must find a friend outside the groggery.'

The first thing Jack did after accepting her advice was to pay a carpenter to fit a wooden door to his upstairs cubicle. Then he had an uncomfortable half an hour breaking the news to Meg.

'Let's still be the best of friends,' he urged as he saw tears welling into her eyes. 'But no more can we be sharing a cubicle when you've no business. We can still walk out together but nothing else.'

Meg sulked for a few days and some of the other girls, thinking Jack was looking for a new friend, began calling on him in his cubicle in various states of undress to make it clear that they were his for the asking. But at last it became accepted that Jack wanted to be on his own. Not that he didn't regret his decision. Many nights he lay behind his secure door listening to the sounds of love making in the cubicles adjoining his, wishing he had Meg beside him to slake his lust. But his self imposed celibacy gave him an added inner strength that enabled him to deal successfully with men and women older and more experienced than himself.

It was that strength he needed when Mother McCarthy fell ill during the early spring of 1825. Her considerable constitution had been weakened by her increasing drinking and by a troublesome cold which had failed to respond to any remedy.

Her physician, Samuel Dillon, who was called to the groggery, shook his head sadly as he came down the stairs after seeing Mother McCarthy in her room. 'Tis her tubes,' he told Jack. 'They're awful congested. Over the years the atmosphere in here can't have helped, nor her liking for her own gin.'

'What's to be done then, Master Dillon?'

'Tis a rest she needs well away from this place. She says she can stay with friends on a farm at Dorchester and that would be the best thing, to be sure. If she spends the spring in good, clean air it'll aid her a deal, but she's not a young woman. She'll have to take care if she's to survive many more winters.'

But Jack found Mother McCarthy in ebullient spirits when he went upstairs to see her. She was propped up on pillows, grey hair fluffed out, a pink shawl across a nightgown that failed to hide the outlines of her pendulous breasts.

'Ah, Jack,' she wheezed. 'Did that quack tell you I had to be going away a wee while?'

'He did that. He said you were needing some good air.'

''Tis a mug of gin I'm needing. Send one up to me, will you?'

'He says you're to take care.'

'And sure I will.' She began to cough. 'By the saints,' she spluttered, thumping herself on the chest. ''Tis the dampness of the winter that's brought me low. Get me the gin, lad, for Holy Mary's sake.'

When Jack returned with the gin, she sipped at the mug as if it contained the foulest of medicines. 'Sure and you can lose your taste for this without regular practice,' she smiled. 'But I can feel it easing me already.'

She put down the mug on a bedside table. 'I'm thinking I can leave here without worrying about it. You'll take charge, lad, and to show my confidence in you I'm set to make you my partner. I've been thinking on this for a time so while I'm resting up for my journey the lawyer can draw the proper papers.'

'Is that necessary?' asked Jack, overwhelmed at the offer.

''Tis fair. Only fair. You've been running the groggery for six months past while I've been in my dotage.' Mother McCarthy grinned. 'And besides it'll be mighty galling to Master J.P. Kilfedder, so it will. I'm surprised he's not already perched on my bed waiting to pick the groggery clean when I'm out of the way. He'll be surprised to find a spalpeen like you in control.'

Two days later, Jack and Mother McCarthy signed their partnership agreement and a day after that she set off for Dorchester.

As she sat in the carriage, well wrapped in blankets and rugs, she gave Jack some last words of advice. 'Remember what I was telling you before, lad. Discretion is the word. Be discreet, watch Kilfedder close and don't be drinking too much of our own gin.' She winked at Jack, 'After all, look what it's done for me.' She gave a last wave to Jack and the girls standing outside the groggery before settling back into the seat as the carriage rattled away over the cobbles of Bread Street.

That night the groggery was full to the doors. Jack and his three potmen were run off their feet trying to serve all the customers. Two men – one with a fiddle, the other with a tin whistle – added to the hubbub by playing lively jigs and reels. Eventually Jack cleared a space in the middle of the floor so that the girls could dance with the customers. He was standing beside some drinkers who were avidly watching the girls' skirts swirling up their thighs when he felt a tap on the shoulder. He looked round and found himself staring directly at a man's chest, matted with dark, curly hair. He raised his eyes and saw an unshaven face split by a large, hooked nose, its right eye covered by a black patch.

'Master Keane?' The man looming over him by some six or seven inches spoke in a high, squeaky voice.

'Yes, who's wanting him?'

'This is for you.' The man handed over a note sealed with wax.

'And who are you?'

'I'm called Hawk. I'm Master Kilfedder's man.'

Jack moved away from the men watching the dancers and slid open the note with his thumbnail. The message was to the point. Would Master Keane call on J. P. Kilfedder in his office in State Street at ten o'clock the next morning?'

'Tell him I'll be there.'

'Then I bid you good night, Master Keane.'

Jack watched Hawk thread his way through the customers to the door. He walked with a lightness of foot uncommon in such large men. Jack could see the muscles bulging under his black shirt.

When most of the evening's customers had gone, Jack left the potmen to deal with the remaining few and went to sit in the kitchen. He took with him the box of business papers handed to his care by Mother McCarthy. He searched through them for the agreement with J. P. Kilfedder. As he read the document, drawn up several years previously in 1818, he began to realize the extent of the hold Kilfedder had over the business. Jack began jotting down figures on a scrap of paper.

The document showed that Kilfedder had loaned Mother McCarthy 3,000 dollars at an interest rate of thirty per cent per annum, payable every quarter. In default of payment, ownership of the groggery would pass automatically to Kilfedder. Only in the last year had Mother McCarthy managed to begin repaying the capital of the loan in addition to the quarterly interest of 225 dollars. The amount of the loan still outstanding was 2,600 dollars.

Jack felt anger as he studied the figures. J. P. Kilfedder, he decided, was nothing more than a thief who battened on other people's desires to build their own businesses. 'A leech,' he muttered furiously to himself. 'Nothing but a blood-sucking leech.'

What made him even angrier was the knowledge that Kilfedder was as Irish as the overwhelming majority of his customers, yet still he exploited mercilessly their lack of capital.

At nine o'clock the next morning he stood on the whitewashed steps of the Massachusetts Bank as its doors opened for business. He advanced to the cashier's grille and asked to see one of the bank's partners. Five minutes later he was in the sombre office of Oliver P. Dunwoody.

The banker, a small middle-aged man, peered benevolently over his half moon glasses at the agitated young man standing before his desk. 'Master Keane,' he said, rising to shake Jack's hand. 'And how is Mistress McCarthy? Is she recovering?'

Jack's surprise showed in his face.

'Boston is really only a small village,' said Dunwoody by way of explanation. 'Mistress McCarthy is one of its better-known characters. I am told she is planning a convalescence in the country.'

'She's gone,' said Jack shortly. 'I'm running the business as her full partner.'

'Congratulations, sir,' said the banker. 'You're making your mark swiftly in the community. What service can I be to you?'

'Are we in good standing with this bank?' Jack asked, settling back into the upholstered chair by Dunwoody's large desk.

'Indeed, sir. Oh, indeed.' The banker looked down at a document on his desk. 'A credit balance of more than four hundred dollars. Regular payments in, a healthy balance. Most commendable.'

'Then Master Dunwoody, look on these documents.' Jack pushed the agreement with J. P. Kilfedder on to the banker's desk.

Dunwoody studied it for a few minutes and then leaned back in his chair and coughed. 'I fear this sort of thing is not unknown Master Keane,' he said, fingering the agreement with an expression of distaste. 'Master Kilfedder's methods of business are known only too well to me.'

'Well, I want no more of him,' Jack stood up and bent over the desk, looking directly at the banker. 'Will you help me? Will you loan me the money to settle his agreement?'

Dunwoody put the tips of his fingers together and looked thoughtful. 'Security, Master Keane. There must be security, you know.'

'What about my share of the business? I'll sign it over to you.'

'But without you, sir, there is no business. That's not particularly good security . . . But you'll have your money. In this particular situation, an honest face will suffice, sir . . . and your share of the business assigned to the bank till the debt is paid.'

'At what interest?' asked Jack suspiciously.

Dunwoody laughed drily. 'We pay you 16 per cent on your balance, Master Keane, so I fear it will be 18 per cent interest on the loan. That sir, is banking.'

'I'm to see Kilfedder at ten o'clock this very morning, and would like to pay him off then.'

'I understand.' The banker adjusted his glasses, a half-smile playing round his mouth. 'Then you can have it now and return here to sign the agreement.' He scribbled on a piece of paper with a scratchy quill pen. 'Take this to the cashier and he will give you 2,600 dollars.'

Jack shook hands with Dunwoody. 'I cannot thank you enough.'

'It's business, Master Keane. But a word of advice before you leave. Master Kilfedder will be far from pleased at losing his hold on your business. I'm advised he can be an ugly man if he's crossed.'

Twenty minutes later, Jack was being ushered into J. P. Kilfedder's office on the first floor of a tall, narrow building on State Street. Kilfedder had his back to the door when Jack was shown in. He was standing with his hands clasped behind him gazing up at a portrait of the woman Jack had seen in the carriage on Beacon Hill.

Without turning round, Kilfedder spoke. 'A woman, Master Keane, is the most important attribute in a man's success.' He swung round. 'Don't you agree?'

'I . . . I . . . I'm not sure,' Jack stammered nonplussed at this approach.

'Not sure, Master Keane?' said Kilfedder sternly. 'Why, you should know as well as I do. Without Mother McCarthy, you'd be carrying a shovel on your back. Without my Elizabeth, I'd probably be down there digging with you.'

Kilfedder carefully parted the tails of his dark grey jacket and sat in the high-backed chair behind his desk, gesturing to Jack to sit down at the same time.

'When I arrived here ten years ago, Master Keane, I was as penniless as you are. Until I met Elizabeth I had no ambition but to survive. Certainly her father's chandlery business was prosperous enough but it was she who showed me how to make money work. Without her inspiration and my desire to give her the best of lives, why there would be no J. P. Kilfedder of any standing in Boston today.' Kilfedder stroked his beard, evidently well satisfied with himself. 'Let that be a cautionary tale for you, Master Keane. Stay close to Mother McCarthy and you will not go far wrong.'

'I intend to, Master Kilfedder.'

'Good.' He smiled thinly at Jack. 'I asked you here simply to ascertain that that was the case.' His tone sharpened. 'You are aware, of course, of my place in Mother McCarthy's business affairs.'

'I've read the agreement,' Jack replied simply.

'Excellent – so there'll be no need for me to be worrying myself about the payment while Mother McCarthy is regaining her full health with God's help.

Jack stood up. 'None at all, Master Kilfedder. Twill be no worry at all.' He reached inside his shirt and pulled out the wad of notes he'd been given at the bank. 'Tis your money, Master Kilfedder. All of it. All 2,600 dollars.' He placed the notes carefully on the desk, pulled the agreement from his pocket, tore it in half, and put both halves beside the bank notes. 'You've no hold over the groggery any more.'

Kilfedder's lean jaw slackened in amazement. 'But how . . . the money? . . . '

'Tis not your concern. Check your accounts and you'll find it is the correct amount.'

Kilfedder gazed balefully at Jack for a moment, then rose from behind his desk and strode quickly to the office door. He flung it open and shouted into the outer office, 'Find me Hawk.'

He turned to Jack. 'Before it's too late, you upstart bog-trotter, it would be better if certain facts were made clear to you.'

Hawk knocked on the door and came lightly into the office. His presence, towering over both Jack and J. P. Kilfedder, made the room seem overcrowded.

'You've met Hawk, haven't you?'

'Yes.'

'Well, Hawk plays a very important part in my organization. You could say he protects my investments. He helps persuade people that they should stick to the letter of their agreements with the House of J. P. Kilfedder. Don't you Hawk?'

'That's right, sir,' came the answering squeak.

'Good,' said Kilfedder. 'Well, let me explain, Master Keane, my fine young friend. Apart from financing the establishment at which you work, I take it upon myself to offer it my protection. Fort Hill is notorious, is it not, for containing some of the rough elements of our fine citizenry?'

'We've never had any trouble at the groggery,' said Jack firmly, beginning to catch the drift of Kilfedder's words.

'Precisely. And I suggest tis because anyone who causes trouble knows they would have to explain their actions to Hawk here.'

'But . . . '

'Please not to interrupt, Master Keane, while I'm instructing you in the ways of business. If you terminate our agreement, then I fear I shall have to withdraw my protection from your business. You

120

already have enough white hairs for such a young man. You wouldn't want more, would you? I urge you to reconsider your hasty action.'

Kilfedder walked to the desk and picked up the bank notes and torn-up agreement. He offered them to Jack, an ingratiating smile on his face.

'Here, take them and let's forget all about what's happened this morning.'

Jack shook his head. 'No, Master Kilfedder. Our agreement is at an end, paid up, finished. I shall bid you good day.'

Jack walked back to the groggery deep in thought. He stood on the corner of Bread Street and looked up at the cinder coloured sky. Some time soon, he knew, he could expect a visit from Hawk and his friends. But how to protect himself and the groggery? He couldn't rely on his customers, he realized, and anyway it was hardly fair to involve them in a private battle.

When he reached the groggery, he was delighted to find Martin Flannery and Patrick Deane waiting for him.

''Tis a mighty auspicious day you've picked to sail back into Boston,' he told them, signalling a potman to bring over a fresh jug of gin.

'Well, we're only here for a day and a night again,' said Flannery, 'But weren't we agreed that we had to see how our old shipmate was faring?'

Jack brought them up to date with the happenings at the groggery.

'Now, didn't Captain Higgins spot you aright,' exclaimed Deane. 'He said you were a man with a future. We'll have a proper tale to tell your mother when we reach the Shannon again in the summer.'

'You've seen her?' asked Jack eagerly.

'Aye, Jack, we passed on the news about your reaching here and finding a good berth.'

'How are me mam and dad?'

'Just fine. Fine. Though missing you a deal, I'm thinking.' Flannery reached inside his shirt and produced a stained, crumpled letter. 'Your mam bade the priest to write you.'

Jack seized the letter and opened it. Flannery and Deane kept silent as he read.

'Dear son,' the letter began, 'Your friends from the sea brought us the news of your safe arrival and your start in Boston, for which we thank God. Your dad and me are well, considering all. John had a proper funeral and the neighbours were mighty good. Your dad is managing the extra work and we have enough to live on and some over to sell at market. Before St Stephen's Day we saw your Brigid in Listowel and passed her the news. She works still for Master Sandes and sent her kindest felicitations and thoughts to you. All your other friends are safe and have come out of hiding. The militia is mighty busy searching and patrolling but there's been little trouble hereabouts, thanks be to the Holy Mother. Must end now as your friends are waiting to return to Tarbert. You have our love and blessing, Jack. Remember all your teachings and your mam and dad. With kisses from your loving mam.'

At the bottom of the letter was a note. 'Think not on returning yet, my son, since Master Sandes has rewards out for you. God's blessing and comfort on you.' The note was signed simply 'O'S' – from Father O'Sullivan, Jack presumed.

He put the letter down with a smile. 'Tis as you said, Paddy. The folks seem well enough. Before you go, I'll give you a letter for them. That's presuming you intend to spend your time in Boston as my guests here.'

'Where else? Tis you have the finest gin and the prettiest girls in the whole of this town. What more can a body want after a month at sea?'

'Then I shall give the day to you,' Jack laughed. 'Though you'll have to be taking care of the night yourselves.'

'Is that dark-haired friend of yours still here?' asked Flannery, his eyes shining in anticipation.

'Meg, you mean? Meg Griffiths? Aye, she's still here and no doubt glad to entertain you.'

Deane lowered his voice. 'Tis true you could be in trouble with this gombeen man Kilfedder you were mentioning?'

'Looks likely, Patrick. Tis a call his bully-boys will be making before long, I'm thinking. And wouldn't it have been nice to have had all Captain Higgins' crew here to meet them?'

'Twould be a true brawl, that it would,' agreed Deane. 'But why don't you find a crew of your own?'

'And haven't I been wracking my brains about just how to do that?'

'I remember once in New York someone having the same problem,' volunteered Flannery. 'He found his own crew, he did.'

'How?'

'Well, he organized a money tournament to find the best bare-knuckle fighter in the town. And didn't he hire on all the best fighters. Strange to tell, not only did he get a crew of men but the fights were so popular that he's still holding them to this day.'

'Tis a grand idea,' said Jack excitedly. 'We could hold the fights here and charge money to see them. That way we'd win both ways.'

'And isn't he just the man of business?' said Deane. 'Making his fortune while his friends sit here with empty mugs.'

That day Jack first took the precaution of writing a note to Father O'Sullivan for his parents before getting drunker with Flannery and Deane than he had on his first day in Boston. He had to be carried off to bed by two potmen while his two friends stumbled behind him up the stairs, Deane with a fair haired girl and Flannery clutching on to Meg. Jack awoke with a blinding headache but with the conviction that Flannery's idea was the solution to his problem of defending himself against any action by J. P. Kilfedder. He hurried round to O'Hanlon's the printers to order one hundred posters advertising a forthcoming tournament. When the posters were delivered a day later he distributed them to the staff and the girls at the groggery with instructions for them to be placed all over Boston. He himself took some into the Negro district. Jack approached Southac Street with some trepidation. At first everyone pointedly ignored him as he stuck a poster to a wall using flour and water paste. But as soon as the poster was up, crowds gathered round to read it.

GRAND PUGILISTIC CONTEST
AT MOTHER McCARTHY'S
IN BREAD STREET
SATURDAY SATURDAY
ALL WELCOME TO FIGHT
PRIZES FOR ALL FROM
$10 TO $100
SPECTATORS $1
PROMOTER AND REFEREE
MASTER JACK KEANE
SATURDAY SATURDAY

'Hey, white man,' a tall, husky Negro called to Jack. 'Does that "all welcome" on your poster include us Nigras?'

'Sure and it does. And isn't that why I'm putting the posters down this street?'

'You'd let an Irisher fight a Nigra?'

'Why not?'

'Well, Irisher, that ain't usual even in this town,' said the Negro, shaking his head. 'Why, I ain't never heard of it before nowhere,

123

nohow.'

'You a pugilist then?'

'That I ain't, mister. But I reckon I can lick most anyone hereabouts.'

'Enter the contest then. You might win.'

'I will that. Tell your man he'll be hearing from Homer Virgil Socrates Penquick.'

'Is that really your name?' Jack asked with a wide smile.

'My given name by the slave master. I know you white folk find it right amusing so I ain't taking any offence at your humour.'

'Nor should you. Tis a fine name; a name surely to remember, Master Penquick.'

With a wave, the Negro sauntered off down the street. Jack watched him thoughtfully. Now, he reckoned, half a dozen men like that would certainly give Hawk and his thugs more than a bloody nose if they dared to call at the groggery

The tournament was held that Saturday evening. Even by late afternoon, the groggery was crowded with more than three hundred people who'd paid their dollars to watch. Two of Jack's regular customers, Timmy Brehoney and Padraig Costelloe, both Irishmen who worked along the wharves, had decided to enter the tournament and three Bostonians had also announced their intention of taking part. Jack had cleared the tables and benches in the middle of the bar and roughly roped off a ring, covering the floor liberally with sawdust. As the time of the tournament grew closer, Jack started to get a little anxious about having only five contestants. Then he saw the black face of Homer Penquick appear in the doorway. The Negro spotted Jack and pushed his way through the packed bar. Another Negro, thin and barely five feet tall, was with him.

'A good evening to you, Irisher.'

'Master Penquick.'

'Where be this Master Jack Keane who's running this here tournament?'

'And aren't you just looking at him?'

'Well, well, so all along you were the boss man.'

'That's right Master Penquick, and tis mighty glad I am to see you.'

'When do we start then?'

'We?'

Penquick gestured to his under-sized companion. 'He's entering the tournament too. His given name is Horace Archimedes Plato Penquick.'

124

'A relation?'

'Nope. We come from the same plantation in Viginia run by . . . '

' . . . Master Penquick, I'm guessing,' interrupted Jack.

'Ain't you catching on then?' smiled Homer Penquick. 'He was a devil for them Greek and Roman folk was Master Penquick. Even spoke their languages, or said he did.'

Jack looked doubtfully at Homer's companion. 'Isn't he a bit small?'

'Small he might be but he's as quick and wriggly as s swamp snake.'

'He'll be tangling with bigger men.'

'That ain't never worried him, Master Keane. Nope, never had.'

'Right then, we'll get started.'

Jack took the shillelagh from behind the bar and banged it repeatedly on the floor. 'Silence! Quiet!' he shouted. The hubbub in the groggery declined. 'The draw for the tournament is about to take place. Are there any more wanting to take part?' There was no response. 'For the last time, is there anyone else who fancies himself as a fighter?'

There was a commotion at the back of the crowd and a squat, sun-burned man, wearing a coon-skin cap and clothes made from leather, jumped up on a table.

'Look here for a fighting man,' he cried, slapping his broad chest. 'I've fought with redskins, swum with alligators, wrassled with bears . . . ' The crowd around him began guffawing.

'If that be so, friend,' Jack shouted across the room, 'Then you be mighty welcome, though there be no alligators or bears in this groggery. Only a few bilge rats . . . ' The room exploded with laughter.

The man jumped off the table and stuck out his hand. 'Augustus Hawkins, sir, at your service.'

'Well Master Hawkins, we shall put your name in for the first bouts of the tournament,'

The draw matched Hawkins against one of the Bostonians; Homer Penquick against Padraig Costelloe; Horace Penquick against the second Bostonian, with the third fighting Timmy Brehoney.

'Come to scratch,' shouted Jack, standing inside the ring, when the first two men were stripped to the waist and ready to begin.

The first fight was over almost as soon as it had begun. Augustus Hawkins, four long white scars running vertically down his back, rushed at his opponent, gripped him in a bear hug, and squeezed

125

him for almost a minute. The Bostonian struggled unsuccessfully to free himself, growing redder in the face every second before Hawkins the trapper disposed of him by throwing him on the floor and jumping on his stomach. Even those who had wagered on the Bostonian realized the fight was over when they heard the breath whoosh out of their favourite's body.

The second fight didn't take much longer. Costelloe swung huge roundhouse punches at Homer Penquick's head but the Negro ducked easily out of their way and hit the Irishman two fierce blows to his overhanging belly. When Costelloe bent over, gasping for breath, Penquick brought both his hands together and clubbed him on the back of the neck, smashing his knee upwards into the Irishman's face. He slumped unconscious to the floor, blood pouring from a broken nose.

Tiny Horace Penquick turned the third bout into more of a running race. His opponent lumbered after him swinging blows but the Negro took to his heels and ran round and round the ring. The crowd in the groggery shouted derisively at the Bostonian and cheered wildly when Penquick suddenly turned and tripped the larger man to end the first round. When the two men came to scratch for the second time, the Bostonian was so out of breath that he merely stood still swatting blows at Penquick who continued to run round him. The bout ended suddenly when Penquick jumped on to his opponent's back like a little monkey and throttled him into submission with his forearm wrapped round his wind pipe.

The last fight was more conventional, with Timmy Brehoney eventually pounding the Bostonian unconscious after both men had knocked each other down at least a dozen times.

After a short break to enable everyone to refill their mugs, another draw was held. Jack breathed a sigh of relief when the two Penquicks were drawn against separate opponents. He had feared that the Negroes would have refused to fight each other and he wanted another opportunity to watch them both in action.

Augustus Hawkins had as great difficulty as the defeated Bostonian in getting to grips with Horace Penquick. Again the tiny Negro ended the first round by tripping his opponent, but when he tried to climb on to the trapper's back he was thrown right across the ring by Hawkins, who shrugged him off with a heave of his broad shoulders. The fall badly winded the Negro and when the men came to scratch for the third time Hawkins was able to slow him down even further with a solid blow to the side of the head that knocked him to the floor. It was clear to the jostling crowd in the groggery that, this time, Horace Penquick was outmatched. He struggled back to scratch but quickly succumbed when the trapper caught him in another bear hug. The Negro lay panting on the floor for more than a minute trying to get the breath back into his crushed ribs, but, after recovering, seemed little the worse for wear. He was cheered resoundingly from the ring.

The sixth fight of the evening was again a battle of attrition with Homer Penquick swapping blows with Timmy Brehoney. At one stage, it appeared that the Irishman had the Negro beaten, when a particularly vicious punch knocked him senseless. But a spectator bent through the ropes and emptied a mug of gin over him. The alcohol stinging into the bruises and cuts on his face brought Penquick round before Jack called the fighters to scratch again. Somehow he absorbed more blows from the Irishman before butting him across the bridge of the nose. As Brehoney staggered back, roaring in agony, Homer Penquick kneed him in the groin with all his remaining strength. It seemed that all the spectators winced. The Irishman writhed in the sawdust, moaning loudly, one hand between his legs, the other clutching his face. Jack didn't even bother with the formality of calling both men to scratch. It was obvious that Brehoney wouldn't be fit to fight again that evening.

To give Augustus Hawkins and Homer Penquick time to recover from their earlier bouts, Jack announced that there would be an hour's delay before the final contest. He had never seen such scenes in the groggery before. Clutching handfuls of dollar bills, the customers were striking bets with about a dozen spectators who'd set themselves up as bookmakers. The given odds seemed to favour the trapper, who was surrounded by his cronies in one corner of the bar. Hawkins was unmarked in contrast to the big Negro, who had left the groggery telling Jack he wanted to breathe some fresh air and get some balm for his cuts and bruises.

'You'll default, Master Penquick, if you're not back when I call you to scratch,' Jack warned.

'Even that trapper's alligators won't be keeping me away, Master Keane,' Penquick replied through swollen lips. 'He might have wrassled bears but he ain't yet tangled with the likes of me.'

'Whoever wins, Master Penquick, I'll be wanting to talk business with you and your little friend after the fights are done.'

An hour later, the yellow light from the oil lamps on the walls flickered over the gleaming torsoes of the two men on either side of Jack in the middle of the ring. It was impossible to see from one wall of the groggery to the other through the cigar and pipe smoke. Jack tried to introduce the fighters but the noise was so great that only the spectators pressed around the ropes could hear him. He shrugged his shoulders helplessly and began to give instructions to Penquick and Hawkins.

'By now, you should know what the rules are. Just fight clean and fair.'

'How's that?' interrupted the trapper.

'I'm thinking you're not to kill each other or tear each other's limbs off or gouge the eyes.'

'That be fine with me,' exclaimed Penquick, spitting on his palms.

'The loser be the one who can't come to scratch after a knockdown,' said Jack finally. 'Go to it on my cry and good luck to you both.'

The noise in the groggery rose to a crescendo as the two men squared up to each other. They began circling each other warily and Jack called for the fight to begin.

The Negro was the first to strike, rapping a blow into Hawkins face that sent the trapper staggering back, almost colliding with Jack. A trickle of blood began running down Hawkins' nose. He shook his head and brushed the blood across his face with the back of his hand. Suddenly he rushed at Penquick trying to grasp him around the body, but the Negro stepped nimbly out of the way and clubbed Hawkins on the back of the neck. The blow carried the trapper into the rope around the ring. His head caught a spectator under the jaw. The man fell back into the crowd while Hawkins rebounded straight into a vicious punch to the kidneys from Homer Penquick. He dropped, groaning, to his knees and Jack stepped quickly between the fighters. Hawkins crawled into a corner where a spectator tossed a bucket of water over him, then painfully pulled himself upright on the rope.

'To scratch,' shouted Jack above the excited clamour.

Hawkins, obviously in considerable pain, tried to keep away from Penquick but the Negro pursued him throwing out straight punches that cracked into his face, drawing more blood. The trapper turned his head after one blow and spat two teeth on to the sawdust. Under the barrage of blows he sank slowly to his knees again. The second round was over. His face and shoulders were now covered with smears of blood. He groped his way into a corner and gulped down a mug of gin handed him by one of his supporters. Penquick stood nonchalantly in the other corner blowing on his bruised knuckles and talking through the uproar to his diminutive friend, Horace Penquick.

When Jack called the men to scratch for the third time, Hawkins staggered towards the centre of the ring. Penquick, perhaps over confident, strode forward, hands at his side, ready to settle the fight quickly. He was totally unprepared when the trapper, summoning his last strength, launched himself backwards into the air with a shout and kicked out with his bare feet. The blow caught the Negro squarely in the stomach. He reeled back, bounced off the rope, and crashed to the floor. Hawkins flung himself down on him, snarling with rage and pain. He gripped the Negro round the throat, squeezing with both hands, at the same time banging Penquick's head up and down on the wooden floor. Jack leapt forward and gripped the trapper round the waist, trying to pull him off. Hawkins, maddened with blood lust, butted his head backwards catching Jack on the forehead and knocking him to the floor. Horace Penquick was under the rope in an instant. He pounded Hawkins on the top of his head to try to make him release his friend but to no avail. Other spectators who'd bet on Hawkins began clambering under the rope to reach the tiny Negro. Jack scrambled up again in time to see Horace Penquick jab his first and index fingers into Hawkins' eyes. The trapper reared upwards, hands across his eyes, and began staggering around the ring colliding with the invading spectators. Within seconds the ring was a mass of people swapping punches with each other. Jack stood above Homer Penquick to protect him as the Negro retched and heaved some air back into his lungs. He desperately sought some way to end the fighting which had now spread all over the groggery. Suddenly, a shot rang out. The noise of the explosion reverberated under the low beams. The men stopped fighting; some dropped to the floor not knowing where the shot came from.

'Haven't you seen enough broken heads tonight?' shrilled a female voice above them. They looked up and saw Meg Griffiths standing on the stairway, a smoking flintlock pistol still pointed above her head. She lowered the pistol, beginning to blush as she realized that she was now the centre of attention.

'And didn't me mam say I should only use a pistol to protect my virtue against a man?' she said, dropping her eyes in embarrassment.

The silence in the groggery was broken first by a titter from Jack. 'Your virtue, Meg?' he laughed aloud. 'You'd need a musket and a blunderbuss to protect that!'

The men near Jack began laughing, slapping each other on the back. The laughter spread throughout the groggery. Jack saw his chance and moved quickly to the bar.

'The gin's on Jack Keane,' he bellowed. 'A free mug for everyone.'

There was a shout of jubilation as the spectators surged towards the bar. Jack pushed through them to reach the Penquicks and Augustus Hawkins. They were all sitting dazedly in the tangle of rope that was all that remained of the ring. Horace Penquick was massaging his friend's neck gently while Hawkins tried to prise open his swollen eyelids. Jack helped them to their feet.

'Gentlemen,' he shouted. 'Your attention, if you please.'

The crowd packed near the bar turned round clutching their refilled mugs.

''Tis the result of the fight I have to announce,' Jack called. 'Since neither man was able to come to scratch for the very reason that the referee was on the floor with them the contest is declared a draw. They each win fifty dollars, as much gin as they can drink, and the girl of their choice. That's if they've the strength left.'

A roar of approval greeted Jack's decision.

'Don't I deserve them both?' whispered Meg Griffiths, sidling up behind Jack with the pistol still in her hand.

'You deserve almost anything you want, lass, for stopping that brawl,' Jack replied. 'Murder would have been done, I'm thinking.'

'Almost anything?' asked Meg, with a pout.

'That's right. Now find me Brehoney and Costelloe and bring them to the kitchen.'

Jack guided Hawkins and the two Negroes to the kitchen behind the bar, trying as best he could to protect them from back-slapping customers.

In the comparative quiet of the kitchen, the fighters slumped exhaustedly on the benches around the table, streaks of blood and sweat across their shoulders and chests. Meg ushered in the two Irishmen and then began washing the men's bruises and cuts. Jack produced a bottle of rum and poured them all generous tots. Then he went round the table placing the men's winnings in front of them, peeling the bills off a large wad of notes.

'Meg,' he said, handing her thirty dollars and another bottle of rum, 'Go and find them Boston men and pay them off with my compliments. Then tell the potmen to make sure no one comes in here while I have a quiet talk with these gentlemen.'

When she had gone, he stood at the head of the table and surveyed the men around him. All of them displayed signs of their recent fights – black eyes, swollen lips, cut and bruised knuckles. 'Friends,' he began. 'First I'd like to thank you for taking part in the contest tonight. All of you showed that you're fighting men out of the ordinary.' Then he explained about the threat from J. P. Kilfedder and the reason why he had organized the contest. 'And I'm guessing I've found the right men to help me,' he concluded. 'I'll be paying each of you two dollars to come here every day. You get your food, as much as you can drink without losing your senses, and the pick of the girls if they're willing, and I'm betting they won't mind pleasuring such fighting men as you.'

'How long for, Jack?' asked Timmy Brehoney.

'Till Kilfedder's men pay us a call or I'm satisfied that your man was just blathering. What say you?'

The five men nodded their agreement wearily.

'Sure and it'd be a pleasure,' smiled Brehoney. 'Wouldn't it, Padraig?'

His friend grinned. 'Twill be the easiest money I've earned, Timmy, since we pinched that man's pig and then sold it back to him.'

Jack poured another tot of rum for each man. 'A toast,' he said.

'Who to?' asked Hawkins.

'Why, who else but your man, J. P. Kilfedder? He's found each of you a job and given me the five best fighting men in Boston town.'


## Chapter 9 July, 1825


The half-filled glass of claret sang as Jack Keane tapped his finger against it. He held it up to the light from the candelabrum in the middle of the table, admiring the rich red of the wine through the sparkling lead crystal glass.

'Pretty, isn't it, Master Keane?' said Elizabeth Kilfedder across the table from Jack. 'You should be flattered. It's the best crystal in the world and it comes all the way from Dublin.'

'Sure, and don't you live in fine style?'

'Master Kilfedder has worked hard,' his wife said simply. 'Not that you haven't benefited as well from your short time in the Americas.'

Jack looked down at his maroon coat, white stock, lace ruffled shirt, and grey breeches. Yes, he thought, his new outfit, chosen with Meg Griffith's help, was a far cry from his ragged clothes of nearly a year before.

Her low, husky voice broke into his thoughts. ' . . . and everything was going so well until you came to Boston and chose to defy us.'

'Defy, is it?' said Jack, gazing directly at her. He felt for the yellowing bruise under his left eye. 'The word I would be using would be defend . . . not defy.'

'My husband said you were a stubborn man.'

'I'm thinking he might also have called me other things after the wee fight last week.'

Elizabeth Kilfedder laughed, her ringlets of blonde hair dancing in the candlelight, but there was little humour in her voice. 'A wee fight, you call it? If that was a wee fight then I understand all the tales I hear about Ireland.'

Jack sipped his wine, not replying immediately. She was right, of course, he thought to himself. By any standards, it had been a memorable brawl while it had lasted . . .

Jack had been sitting with the Penquicks and Augustus Hawkins at a table near the bar, listening with fascination to their tales of life in the less civilized parts of America.

At first, it seemed just like any other drunken brawl among four men at a table. Voices began to be raised, mugs clattered on the table and, suddenly, fists began whirling. One of Jack's potmen hurdled over the bar, shillelagh in hand, ready to settle the fracas with a few sharp cracks around the head. Jack watched with idle amusement. It was a scene often witnessed in the groggery. But this time the apparently drunken men didn't scatter before the shillelagh. One of them calmly slid a knife from his jacket sleeve and slashed it across the potman's face. The potman dropped the shillelagh and staggered back with a scream of agony, clutching a gaping wound that ran from his cheekbone to the corner of his mouth. As Jack and his three companions jumped up the brawlers lifted their table and hurled it through the leaded window opening on to Bread Street. As the glass crashed on to the cobblestones outside, the wooden front door splinterred off its hinges and half a dozen men, led by the giant figure of Hawk, poured into the groggery. At the same time, three more strangers, until then seated quietly by the stairway, pushed their table over and produced shillelaghs from under their coats.

'Lord Almighty,' muttered Homer Penquick. 'There be enough of them varmints!'

'Like Redskins from the bushes,' whooped Augustus Hawkins, slipping a large-bladed hunting knife from its sheath inside one of his tasselled boots.

One of the girls in the groggery screamed. The other customers scattered away from the three groups of men advancing on Jack and his three friends, who retreated into the corner between the bar and the door to the kitchen. That way no one could get behind them.

Little Horace Penquick began picking up empty mugs and hurling them at the advancing mob. One caught a man next to Hawk square on the forehead and he dropped to the floor without a sound, but most of the mugs missed their targets, bouncing harmlessly off the walls.

'Throw at their legs, Horace,' urged Jack, remembering the faction fight in Listowel. The tiny Negro needed no second bidding. The mugs were soon landing on unprotected shins, and Hawk's men began to hop and shout with pain.

Hawk himself was squeaking with excitement as he brandished a thick wooden club, its end bristling with nails. He twirled it around his head as he advanced on Jack's party, his one good eye glittering with enjoyment. But his height and bulk were disadvantages in such a restricted space. The men around him were unable to get in any blows or even approach within striking distance. Roaring and shouting, two of them began picking up benches and stools and smashing them to pieces on the floor.

Suddenly, Hawkins darted forward under Hawk's swinging club. His knife stabbed upwards in a silvery blur catching Hawk along the ribs. A wide sweep of red welled up through the rip in the black shirt. The knife thrust must have cut through muscle as well as skin because Hawk's arm dropped helplessly to his side. The club impaled itself in the shoulder of a man beside him who fell away, shrieking in pain, pulling frantically at the shaft of the club to try to dislodge the nails from his flesh. As he cannoned into the others behind Hawk, Jack and Homer Penquick saw their chance. Penquick lowered his head and charged forward. His skull cracked into Hawk's damaged ribs sending him reeling back into the already disorganized mob behind him. Squealing like a pig, Hawk tried to keep his balance but his feet slipped on pieces of broken pottery. He fell sideways making the floor shudder with his impact. Jack moved swiftly forward and kicked him twice in the head, his heavy shoes smashing into Hawk's long, matted hair. The high-pitched squeals changed to groans and then silence.

With the fall of their leader, Kilfedder's thugs retreated into the centre of the groggery smashing everything within reach. Hawkins dashed around them, like a circling sheepdog, occasionally slashing out with his knife at an arm or leg which came within reach. One man, holding a stool above his head, dropped it with an oath as Hawkin's knife caught him across the forearm. Little Horace Penquick curled himself into a ball and dived at knee height into Kilfedder's men sending two of them to the floor.

The tide was turning: only seven of Kilfedder's men remained in the fight and they were quickly losing any stomach for it as Jack, Homer Penquick, and Augustus Hawkins began landing solid blows with their fists. But they fought on, trading blow for bow, until they were set on from above by Jimmy Brehoney and Padraig Costelloe. After being roused from their pleasures by the sounds of breaking furniture and the howls and shouts of the injured, they had quickly dressed and vaulted over the stairway, crashing down into the middle of Kilfedder's men. Jack and his two friends dived into the pile of struggling, cursing bodies on the floor striking out with fist and foot. Two of Kilfedder's men began yowling with pain and shock when Augustus Hawkins bit through the lobes of their ears. Others staggered upright, hands clutched to their eyes, after being jabbed by the fingers of Horace Penquick who, somehow, had managed to continue fighting even while pressed under the combined weights of a dozen big men.

As it became obvious that Jack's men were gaining the upper hand, the groggery's customers began to join in. They pulled Kilfedder's men from the mess of bodies on the floor, stood them upright against the walls, and then battered them unconscious with pieces of broken furniture, mugs, fists, indeed anything they could lay their hands on. Two of the thugs managed to break free and made a run for the door only to bounce off an incoming patrol of constables who promptly knocked them to the floor with their truncheons. As soon as they saw the blue uniforms of the town constables, the rest of Kilfedder's men gave up the fight.

'Jesus, we've had enough,' one shouted. 'No more,' pleaded another as he lay on the floor under a threatening truncheon.

Gradually the defenders began sorting themselves out and taking stock of their injuries. Jack's left eye was closing rapidly where he'd been struck in the face by an elbow; Homer Penquick's face was covered with blood, some of it his own from a bleeding nose. Augustus Hawkins clutched his right side, muttering that he thought he'd cracked a rib; Horace Penquick nursed a hand broken by someone stepping on him during the fight; Brehoney and Costelloe were unmarked except for bruised knuckles.

'You're a fine pair,' Jack chided them. 'You were almost missing the fight altogether.'

'And weren't we busy when it started?' replied Brehoney.

'Well, you could have stopped what you were doing sooner,' Jack continued, pretending anger.

'And maimed ourselves for life?' said Costelloe. 'The women had too close a hold on us, and that's the truth. Indeed, we couldn't have stopped what we were at even if the Angel Gabriel had tapped us on our shoulders.'

As the constables carried or led Kilfedder's men out of the groggery, Jack surveyed the damage caused by the brawl. Nearly every piece of furniture was smashed; the floor was littered with broken bottles, mugs, and pitchers; the bar was overturned and splintered; every window was smashed; the door hung off its hinges.

'Well, they succeeded in wrecking the place, that they did,' said Meg Griffiths, who had watched the fighting from the stairs.

'Aye, but we certainly damaged them somewhat as well. I'm doubting if Master Kilfedder will be sending his men down Bread Street again.'

'What about that son of a whore mother?' demanded Costelloe, keen to continue fighting now his blood had been roused. 'Sure and wouldn't it be the proper thing to give him a taste of his own medicine? Why should it just be us left to pick up the broken bits?'

''Tis right he is,' agreed Brehoney. 'Let's be paying him a call, Jack.'

'Aye, let's settle it once and for all,' said Augustus Hawkins. 'When you've wounded an animal, it's only fair to track him to his lair and put him out of his misery.'

'You're right,' Jack conceded finally. 'Your man Kilfedder has to be settled.'

The six of them were joined by a dozen customers as they strode through the streets and alleys towards Kilfedder's office on State Street. The flames of the oil lamps cast grotesque images on the cobbles and on the walls of shuttered houses that were soundly, and, in the main, respectably asleep; the flickering shadows of giant, elongated men carrying shillelaghs and table legs.

'Will he be at his office? Let's go to his home instead,' said Costelloe as they tramped along.

Jack shook his head. 'Knowing Master Kilfedder, he'll be behind his desk awaiting news of how we were battered in the fight. He won't want his brawlers calling at his high and mighty house on Beacon Hill.'

His judgement proved correct. From the street below they saw a light shining palely through the windows of Kilfedder's office on the first floor. Jack put his finger to his lips. The door to the office building was unlocked. They doused their lamps before going in. Even on tiptoe, the stairs creaked as they crept upwards to the office. The glass door stood ajar. It squeaked open at Jack's push.

'Would that be you, Hawk?' Kilfedder called from his inner office. 'Come in and tell me the news.'

Jack said nothing. He was standing with his men around him outside Kilfedder's inner sanctum. Hawkins bent down and slipped his hunting knife from his boot. It glinted in the yellow half light.

'I said come in, Hawk,' called Kilfedder again. 'Damn you, man, have you no ears?'

The men outside the office heard the sound of a desk drawer slamming shut and then footsteps.

'Hawk, Hawk,' shouted Kilfedder, flinging open his door. 'What the divil is the . . . ?' His voice died as he saw Jack and the men around him. 'Holy Mother of God . . . ' he muttered, beginning to back away.

As Jack advanced towards him, Kilfedder overcame his shock and tried to slam the door. Homer Penquick took two steps forward and effortlessly leaned into the door with his shoulder sending Kilfedder staggering back across his office.

Jack moved into the room. 'Good evening, Master Kilfedder,' he said pleasantly. ''Tis obvious you weren't expecting me, but I won't apologize for coming. I'm afraid,' Jack continued quietly, 'that your gang of thugs won't be helping you for some time. They weren't as good fighting men as you were thinking.'

Kilfedder stumbled round the desk until it stood between him and Jack, then sat down in his heavy chair. A muscle began twitching high up on his right cheek. 'How much?' he croaked. 'Money . . .how much?'

Jack moved round the desk. Kilfedder cowered before him, holding both hands in front of his face.

'Come along, Master Kilfedder,' said Jack. 'No one's going to hurt you.'

Kilfedder slumped in his chair. 'How much?' he repeated his dark beard contrasting with the shocked whiteness of his features.

Jack sat on top of the desk swinging his legs nonchalantly. 'The damage at the groggery, you mean? Well, tis hard to tell but I'm thinking two hundred dollars would put it right.'

'Here,' said Kilfedder, reaching forward towards a drawer low in the desk. Jack raised his leg and pushed him firmly back into the chair.

'Homer, see what our man wants to show us.'

Penquick, a broad grin across his battered features, knelt by the drawer. He pulled out a small polished wooden box and placed it on the desk.

'There,' muttered Kilfedder. 'Take what you want.' He unlocked the box and spilled some notes onto the desk. Jack carefully counted out two hundred dollars and then slammed the box shut again.

'Witness that, friends,' he said. 'No more, no less than he owes us. I wouldn't want your man telling the constables that we came here to rob him.'

Kilfedder shook his head. 'Just take what you want and leave,' he said wearily.

'Not so quick,' Jack replied. 'You sent your men to wreck me so I'm thinking you should be taught a lesson.'

The men standing around the desk murmured in agreement.

'Go to it, boys,' ordered Jack, not taking his eyes off Kilfedder. He saw the eager flare in his eyes as the men began smashing up the furniture, tearing open cupboards, ripping and scattering business papers all over the floor. Then the anger was replaced by dull despair as Jack slid off the desk to allow Homer Penquick and Hawkins to pick it up and carry it over to the window.

'One, two, three . . . ' chanted Hawkins, ' . . . and away!'

The desk sailed through the window with a splintering of wood and a crashing of glass to smash on to the cobbles below.

'That's enough,' exclaimed Jack. 'By the saints, that must have woken the whole town. Let's be going before the constables arrive.'

Jack stood in front of J. P. Kilfedder and pulled his hands away from his face.

'We've finished now, Master Kilfedder,' he said, staring into the despairing eyes. 'You might be thinking twould be healthier for you to leave Boston for a while. Some of my men might not be as soft hearted as meself.'

'. . . a wee fight?' Elizabeth Kilfedder went on, awaking Jack from his reverie. 'With the constables called, five men in hospital beds, a mob rampaging down State Street to ransack my husband's office . . . is that a wee fight, Master Keane?'

Jack shrugged. 'If tis so bitter you are, mistress, why ask me to Beacon Hill for supper?'

'Ever since I was a small girl I have been versed in the ways of business, and now you have ruined my husband I must salvage what I can from those ruins.' She smiled disarmingly. 'Quite frankly, Master Keane, you and I have to reach an accommodation.'

'An accommodation?' asked Jack in a puzzled tone.

'Yes, in short, you must manage my husband's business.'

Elizabeth Kilfedder raised her glass of wine. 'To the victor, the spoils, Master Keane. We must ensure that some good comes out of it, otherwise all that blood will have been spilt in vain.'

Jack sipped his wine, responding to her toast. 'I'm not sure I would be wanting to run Master Kilfedder's business,' he said, placing his glass carefully on the white linen table cloth. He looked across at Elizabeth Kilfedder, admiring the smooth shoulders revealed by her low cut, powder blue silk gown.

'Oh, come now, Master Keane,' she smiled. 'Everyone says that you have ambitions. Surely you want to be as powerful as my husband?' She looked at him from under her eyelashes, a half smile playing round her mouth. 'Now you wouldn't refuse me such a small thing? A woman would be hard put to run an enterprise such as Kilfedder's. Surely you'll help me?'

Before, Jack had been needed for his physical strength, his honesty, his good nature. Now, a mature and beautiful woman – a woman who attracted him – was virtually begging him as an equal to join her in a business which had held him in its hands a few weeks before. And, as he felt his own power, he also began to feel stirrings of anger at the way Elizabeth Kilfedder was using her femininity.

She persisted. 'Think of what we two could achieve, Master Keane.' She reached across the table as if to touch his hand. Until that moment, she'd employed her wiles purely to persuade him into the business. She had no qualms whatsoever about doing so. Elizabeth Kilfedder had enjoyed her luxuries for too long. She had no intention of reducing her standards because of her husband's flight. Although she'd enjoyed a relatively comfortable upbringing among Boston's middle class families, her life on Beacon Hill, the privileges of real wealth, had become very precious to her. And, undoubtedly, she'd decided, Jack Keane was the person to help sustain those privileges.

She'd been quite cold blooded in her efforts to enmesh him. But during the dinner, she'd begun to sense within herself a growing physical attraction for the young Irishman, particularly when she sensed his depth of feeling.

'God's teeth, mistress, do you know what you're asking?' he muttered. 'Your man hardly away and you already making plans without him. What happens when he returns?'

'He won't. Not ever,' she snapped back at him.

'But why? I gave him a warning. He only has to keep clear for a few weeks.'

'He won't be back,' Elizabeth Kilfedder said flatly. 'You might merely have warned him, but it was I who told him to go. He's weak and beaten and finished. Oh yes . . . a mighty strong man with the likes of Hawk around him, but a snivelling cur on his own. And do you think I don't know about his nights at Mother McCarthy's with your trollops? Coming to me all grogged up and smelling of cheap scent . . . '

'Enough,' Jack cried, pushing his chair back from the table and standing up. 'What sort of wife is it who says these things? Have you no modesty, no shame?'

Elizabeth Kilfedder's eyes hardened. She rose from her chair and walked swiftly to the dining room door. As she opened it, a plump Negress, listening at the key hole, almost fell on to the rug. 'Clear the table, Naomi,' she snapped. 'And if I catch you eavesdropping again I'll cut your ears off.'

'Yes'm,' muttered the Negress as she scrambled to her feet.

'And show Master Keane to the door. He's leaving.'

'Not so fast, Mistress Kilfedder. I have some more to say.' Jack took four steps to her side and gripped her waist, 'I haven't . . . '

She shook his hand away. 'If you have further insults, at least have the decency not to utter them in front of a servant,' she exclaimed not turning her head to look at him. Jack followed her as she moved stiffly into the hallway and then into the salon at the front of the house. She walked to the mantelpiece and stood for a moment with her back to him, both hands clenched to her mouth. 'Well,' she said, swinging round to face him. 'What else does the big brave Irisher have to say of my virtues?'

''Tis clear that I misjudged your . . . '

Jack stopped as he noticed tears running silently down her cheeks, streaking the powder on her face.

'Go on,' she said furiously, brushing the back of her hand across her eyes. 'Spare nothing. Damn you.' A sob escaped from between her lips. 'Say what you will and leave. Get out!'

Jack stepped forward and she was in his arms, sobbing wildly, her head pressed against his chest. He felt her body shake and her tears wetting his shirt. He heard himself crooning words of comfort into her sweet smelling hair. 'Hush now. Hush, Elizabeth. Dry your tears now.'

She looked up at him with wet eyes. 'Oh, Jack Keane,' she sobbed. 'Tell me you'll help me. Don't leave me now.'

'No, I'll stay.'

She raised herself on tiptoe, closing her eyes, offering her lips to him. He bent his head and kissed her. Her mouth tasted salty from her tears, sweet from the wine at supper. At first, her lips were pressed firmly together but then they opened and their breaths mingled. Their tongues touched delicately, tentatively.

Elizabeth Kilfedder shivered in his arms and pulled her head slightly away from his. 'Truly I have no shame nor modesty,' she whispered. Then she smiled. 'But then I suppose I never did have.'

'What now, Elizabeth?' said Jack, cupping her face in his hands and gazing into her eyes. The tears drying on her cheeks made her seem more vulnerable, more childlike. Her eyes shone up at him.

'Let me show you.'

She led him by the hand to an ornately carved bureau in a corner of the salon. From a drawer she took out a ledger bound in red leather. 'This contains the real secrets of Kilfedder's business. Everything is written in here – the loans, the bribes . . . everything. It was too important to too many people for it to be left in the office.' She handed the ledger to Jack. 'What is in there will make you one of the most feared men in Boston. Let me show you.' She opened the ledger at the first page. It was covered with spidery writing. 'Now this is the index,' she explained. She ran her finger down the page. Her nails were long and finely manicured. 'Look here – "Bread Street", page 29. We turn to the page and here's your business.'

She handed Jack the open ledger. He read the details of Kilfedder's agreement with Mother McCarthy and saw that all the repayments were entered neatly column by column. At the bottom of the page, scribbled in the margin and encircled, were the initials 'D.P.' 'What does that stand for, Elizabeth?' he asked.

'That's what will make you powerful. Look back at the index.'

Jack did as she suggested and found the initials again with 'Page 75' written against them. He turned to this page. On it were dates and figures, ranging from fifty to five hundred. He looked quizzically at Elizabeth.

'I've no idea what it can mean,' Jack said.

'Well, it's a record of payments made by Kilfedder . . . '

'To D.P. whoever he is,' Jack interrupted.

'Well, only Kilfedder and I know who D.P. is . . . '

'And who might he be?' Jack asked, a note of impatience entering his voice.

'Daniel Proudlane. The selectman whose ward includes your groggery.'

'Why should he be paid?'

'You silly . . . If he wasn't paid, why he'd have been on his feet in the town meetings telling the world and his wife what a sink of iniquity the groggery was. And then the constables would close the business and if that happened a fat chance Kilfedder would have had of making you pay him his interest.'

Jack whistled through his teeth, shaking his head in amazement. 'So that's how tis done.'

For the next half hour, Elizabeth, pressing close to him, explained the full extent of Kilfedder's business. There were seven groggeries under his control, two bakeries, a tailor's shop, and three coffee and eating houses. On the payroll were four selectmen, all responsible for wards bordering the harbour and Fort Hill, and twelve constables.

When they had finished examining the ledger, Jack leaned back in his chair, rubbing his chin thoughtfully.

'I can see now how you can live in a style like this and why Kilfedder held such sway in Boston.'

'Oh, I knew you would understand, Jack. But you see why you must help me with the business. Kilfedder took all the money before he fled and there's all this money still owing.'

'Tis as I said before, Elizabeth. I don't care for such a business and now you've told me about the bribes and all, I care for it even less.' He shrugged his shoulders, 'But I did say I'd help . . . '

'You have to Jack,' Elizabeth pleaded. 'If we don't carry on collecting the money, then we can't pay the bribes, and then the groggeries would be shut down.'

'But bribing selectmen? Thy should know better than to be taking money. The people who voted for them would be mighty angry to hear it.'

'It's the way it's done,' Elizabeth said simply. 'No one gets hurt by it and everyone profits in some way. And anyway it's only Daniel Proudlane who matters. The others are very small fish.'

'Well, I don't like it at all. I shall think on it for a day or so and then decide what to do.' He stood up, reached inside his waistcoat pocket and pulled out a small roll of dollar bills. 'In the meantime, take these to see you through.'

Elizabeth waved them away. 'My credit is well enough for a few more days.' She smiled mischievously. 'It's other than money I need from you.'

Jack moved towards her, put his hands around her narrow waist and pulled her to him. He looked down into her face. Her lips were slightly parted. Her tongue flicked out and moistened them.

'Truly shameless,' she murmured. 'And to think I hardly know you.'

They kissed deeply, standing together in the middle of the salon. Jack could feel himself becoming excited by her warm, perfumed softness.

'So long,' she whispered, her eyes shining up at him. 'So very, very long, my sweet Irisher.' She moved from his embrace and walked to the door. 'Just wait a few minutes and then come to me,' she said quietly as she opened the doors of the salon.

Jack picked up Kilfedder's ledger from the chair and leafed through it. He suddenly shivered despite the warmth of the room, realizing what power lay in its carefully annotated contents; what an extensive web of intrigue and greed was revealed by the spidery names, dates and figures. He shook his head sadly. How could he use it? He placed the ledger carefully back inside the bureau and then strode into the hallway.

A single oil lamp was burning on a table. He took the stairs slowly enjoying the richness of the paintings hanging on the walls and the feel of the polished wood of the banisters under his hand. Everything around him spoke of money and influence. He drew strength from it, knowing that such things were now within his grasp. At the top he saw a slightly open door and flickering candlelight in the room beyond.

'Sweet Jack in the dark.' Elizabeth Kilfedder spoke from a dim pool of light at the far end of the room.

Jack closed the door behind him and pressed his back against it. The smell of her perfume was everywhere. As his eyes adjusted to the darkness, he saw her standing beside a large four poster bed, its curtains drawn on three sides. The candle on the table reflected in the highlights of her blonde hair. She had unpinned it and let it fall across her shoulders and down the front of her long white negligee. She took one pace towards him. Jack's breath caught in his throat as the candlelight shone through the lacy material and outlined the

142

curves of her body. 'Dear God,' he muttered, half to himself, wondering at her loveliness.

'Dear Jack,' she replied dreamily. She held her arms out towards him, palms raised upwards, offering herself. The next moment her arms were around him and his face was buried in the curve of her neck. She pushed him gently away and stood against the side of the bed. Without taking her eyes from his, she raised her hands slowly to the front of the negligee. He watched, mesmerized, as she undid a large silk bow. With the slightest whisper, the negligee fell apart, the candlelight catching and playing on the fullness and roundness of her pink tipped breasts. She shrugged her shoulders and the negligee drifted filmily to the floor. He grabbed for her but she pushed her hands flat against his chest, restraining him. 'So ardent, my Irisher,' she smiled. 'But let me enjoy you first.'

She stood on tiptoe, her breasts rising tautly, and slipped his coat from his shoulders. She untied the stock from around his throat, tossing it to one side, then began unbuttoning his shirt, at the same time pulling it free from his breeches. Jack groaned deep in his throat as she ran her fingernails lightly down his chest. She bent her head and kissed both his nipples in turn. Then she unbuttoned his breeches and slipped her hands inside to grasp his hard maleness. She gasped as she felt its warmth and strength. His breeches fell to his knees and there was no longer any pretence nor softness in their desire for each other. He felt her pulling him backwards and allowed himself to fall with her on to the bed. Her thighs opened beneath him, her knees rose to grip him round the waist, and, instantly, he slid into her velvety, sucking warmth. Her nails bit into his lean buttocks, urging him ever closer and deeper as their bodies began moving rhythmically together. Their desire for each other was so strong, so urgent, that their climaxes were quickly upon them. Jack's body arched upwards as he felt himself flow into her. Elizabeth's eyes opened wide, staring unseeing upwards into his face, and then she moaned and thrashed her head from side to side until the overwhelming paroxysms had passed. Jack knelt by her to lift her into the centre of the bed. In the half-light, her eyes were mauve rather than blue.

'Oh, my Irisher,' she whispered, her lips a few inches away from his still erect, shining hardness.

'Pull the curtain,' she said, rolling away from him. He gazed lovingly at the smooth twin muscles running down her back and bent forward to kiss her between her two dimples. Then he drew the curtain that shut them snugly away from the rest of the world in their own cocoon of desire.

Towards morning, as they lay quietly content, hands clasped, Elizabeth Kilfedder turned her head on the pillow. Her eyes, bruised now with fatigue, looked softly at Jack. 'Oh, it's so beautiful to be loved,' she said.


## Chapter 10 September, 1825


Jack Keane paused outside the State House and looked up at its massive round dome. It always raised a sense of wonder when he saw it on his way to Elizabeth Kilfedder's house on Beacon Hill. For him, it was the one building which summed up the spirit of his adopted country. Everything about the building spoke of ordered democracy where the cries of ordinary supplicants would be equal to the voices of the rich and influential.

The outer lobby of the State House was thronged with people; some scurrying here and there, others talking or arguing in groups. Jack stood bewildered in the entrance for a moment, trying to take his bearings. One or two people looked round at him casually and, not recognizing him, turned back to their conversations.

He swung on his heel and collided with an elderly man who was hurrying past. The man staggered back a few paces and would have fallen if Jack hadn't reached out to steady him.

'My apologies, sir,' Jack blurted out.

'That's the trouble with this place, isn't it,' said the elderly man, slightly winded by the collision. 'Everyone in a hurry to catch the eye or ear of someone or other.'

'Indeed I wish it were so, sir.'

'I beg your pardon?'

'Well, I'm trying to talk to Master Daniel Proudlane on most urgent business but I don't know where to find him.'

'Proudlane, eh . . . a friend of his? A supporter, perhaps?'

'No, sir. My name's Jack Keane and I simply have business with him.'

144

The man, plump and bald but for a few whisps of white hair fluffing out behind his ears, smiled and held out his hand. 'I am Josiah Longman, sir. By your accent I presume you're an Irisher not so long on these shores . . .'

''Tis right you are, Master Longman,' Jack said.

'Well, Master Keane, let me help. Follow me, if you will.'

He set off with twinkling steps, hands clasped under the tails of his green jacket, nodding to his left and right at those who sought to greet him. The elderly man, Jack realized, was someone of importance at State House. He led Jack across the lobby towards a group of six men who were deep in conversation, standing under a large canvas depicting a scene from the War of Independence. He addressed a small, weasel faced man at the centre of the group. 'A young Irisher to see you, Proudlane,' he said curtly. From his tone, he was no friend of the selectman for the Fort Hill district. But he turned to Jack with a smile. 'A pleasure to bump into you, Master Keane, as it were. Perhaps we'll meet again one day under more formal circumstances.' Without waiting for Jack's thanks he scurried off again back across the lobby.

'Well?' said a voice behind Jack. He faced the man spoken to by Josiah Longman.

'Master Proudlane?'

'Indeed . . . and I don't see any of my constituents without an appointment. You are a constituent?'

'I come from Fort Hill, sir . . .'

'Write to me of your troubles then, though I fear you Irishers bring so many problems on your own heads that I can be of little help.'

One of the group behind Proudlane tittered. Jack flushed at the studied insult. The selectman was turning back to the group as Jack gripped his arm. He bent slightly to whisper in his ear. 'I come from Kilfedder's, Master Proudlane.'

Jack felt the selectman's muscles tighten under his grip. He let go of his arm as Proudlane turned to him again. His narrow eyes bored into Jack's face.

'Not here, you fool,' he hissed.

'Here,' Jack insisted in a loud voice.

Proudlane stared at him for a moment and then nodded. 'A moment, my friends,' he said over his shoulder to the group behind him. 'This Irisher does have an urgent problem indeed.'

He guided Jack into an unoccupied part of the lobby, well out of anyone's hearing. 'Damn you,' he said furiously. 'What do you mean by coming here? And, anyway, who are you? I've never met you before.'

'I'm Jack Keane.'

'Keane?' Proudlane looked thoughtful for a moment. 'The spalpeen from the groggery in Bread Street?'

'You know your people, Master Proudlane,' Jack said sarcastically.

'What's all this about Kilfedder? From what I hear your cronies sent him packing from Boston. What concern is it of mine?'

Jack smiled. 'I would have thought you were worried about where your funds were coming from.'

'Funds?' Proudlane snapped. 'What funds? You're mad like all the other Irishers. I bid you . . . '

'I have a ledger, Master Proudlane, which lays out all the kindnesses shown to you by J.P. Kilfedder.'

'A ledger? How . . . ? What ledger?' Proudlane spluttered, his bleak eyes flickering around the lobby to make sure he couldn't be overheard. 'I know nothing of it. It's a ruse by my opponents. I should have known that you're a friend of Longman.'

'So be it, Master Proudlane,' said Jack, turning away from him. 'Your opponents, as you call them, can have the ledger then . . . '

'No . . . wait . . . wait . . . come to my house in Salem Street before dusk this evening.'

Jack walked down the steps of the State House feeling less than proud of himself. His meeting with Daniel Proudlane had confirmed everything that Elizabeth Kilfedder and the entries in the red ledger said about him. Every word, every gesture from Proudlane had been those of a conniving, corrupt politician. Jack glanced back at the State House as he strode briskly up Beacon Hill. He wondered how many more politicians like Proudlane defiled the building's proud architecture with their shabby dealings.

'They have to be stopped,' he declared to Elizabeth Kilfedder as he sat in her salon an hour later.

'Stopped? Why stopped, dearest Jack?' said Elizabeth perching on a small stool at his knee gazing up at him. 'In every barrel of apples there are always some rotten ones – and always will be. You can never change that.'

'I know, Elizabeth. But when you find the rotten ones you don't leave them in the barrel to ruin the others. You throw them away.'

'If you stop Proudlane – as you term it – then what of your business? And what of Kilfedder's? You'll be bringing them both crashing down. If you expose Proudlane and the others, then you expose us as well. Yourself for running a disorderly house and myself as the wife of a criminal who bribed public servants and officials.'

Jack bent down and gently kissed her warm lips. 'I promise I'll do nothing that will harm you, and that's the truth. You know that.'

Her arms encircled his neck, pulling him from the chair to kneel beside her. They embraced, their kisses becoming more ardent.

'You'll stay for lunch and then we can spend the afternoon together?' she whispered.

'Doing what?' he replied, feigning innocence.

'Anything you like . . . ' she breathed.

Jack was tempted. Ever since that first night together, their passion for each other had grown wilder and more abandoned than he had ever thought possible. In Elizabeth's arms he forgot everything, even Brigid Aherne. But he found he felt no remorse for this. Elizabeth's sophisticated voluptuousness – and his matching desire for her – did not mean he was in love with her. He knew that. Between them was a flame that would burn itself out eventually. Until then he was determined to enjoy the affair in all its fullness. But not that afternoon. He had people to consult before his meeting with Daniel Proudlane: an idea was taking shape in his mind.

Although Jack was not particularly religious – indeed he had not been to Mass since leaving Ireland – he was well aware of the growing influence of the Roman Catholic Church in Boston. As yet it had no resonant voice, but it was spreading its roots deep among the families arriving from Europe, building on its support among the old French families who had lived in America for generations past. Its influence stretched down the eastern seaboard of the United States among all the arrivals from the Old World. Sooner or later, the Church, Jack realized, would have a great say in the law-making process of the new country.

Father O'Flaherty gazed at Jack curiously as he was shown into the priest's small office next door to the Church of the Holy Cross in Franklyn Square.

'Do I know you?' he asked directly.

'I think not, Father,' said Jack, standing awkwardly before the priest's desk.

'And yet you're Irish from your voice, my son, and thus I presume a member of the Church. But I cannot recollect you at Mass. Perhaps you're newly arrived, although I'm doubting that from the appearance of your fine clothes.'

''Tis a long story, Father, and not one you'd be caring to hear, I'm

147

thinking.'

'Sit you down then and jaw, young man.'

The priest smiled at him – amused at his visitor's unease – and settled back in his chair. Jack hesitated for a moment, wondering where to begin. He looked at Father O'Flaherty's austere, high-boned features and was reminded of Father O'Sullivan back in Listowel. There was the same twinkle lurking behind the cold, light blue eyes which suggested a man with an understanding of worldly matters which transcended his calling. Haltingly at first, and then with more urgency and fluency, Jack told the priest what had happened to bring him to Boston and all that had occurred since his arrival. He went into detail omitting only his relationship with Meg Griffiths and Elizabeth Kilfedder. These, he decided to reserve for the confessional.

'A tale fit for a bishop,' said the priest when Jack had finished. 'Indeed yes, Master Keane. You have supped with a mighty short spoon so you have. And now you want advice on how best to exercise this hold you appear to have over Daniel Proudlane.' He looked at Jack with obvious distaste. 'Tis a matter for your conscience, such as it is, and I have far weightier matters to consider than easing your problems.'

'You don't understand, Father,' said Jack desperately. 'I intend to have no part of this at all. What I want is advice on how best to help us . . . you . . . Boston town in bringing this corruption to an end.'

Father O'Flaherty eased himself back into his chair, an expression of surprise on his face. 'So,' he grunted reflectively. 'Well, the Church has been known to take an interest in such secular matters; Church and State, you realize . . . Church and State.'

'Twould be in the Church's plan to rid Boston of Master Proudlane and his gang?'

'Indeed . . .'

'And have selectmen who were beholden to the Church and the Irish,' Jack went on eagerly.

The priest pursed his lips and nodded approvingly. 'The matter has exercised us, tis true, since so few of our countrymen have the qualifications to vote as yet.'

'Then I know what I shall be doing. I'll hand the ammunition to Master Proudlane's opponents on condition that they look well on our interests.'

'If you do that, I'm sure they will, Master Keane, but tell me . . . what of your enterprises? Won't they be at an end?'

Jack looked straight at him. 'Not with the support of the Church,' he said evenly.

Father O'Flaherty started in his chair. 'The support of the Church in running a jilt shop, a place of assignation, a house of the divil? Master Keane, I fear you are either mighty naive, a rogue, or insane.'

'None of those things, I'm hoping, Father, although you're the second today to suggest I was leaving my senses. When I help Master Proudlane's enemies, the women of the house will be gone and so will the still in the cellar. Mother McCarthy's will become a business where only the best spirits are sold, all properly purchased from Master Felton's distillery, and where the finest foods are served. Twill become an establishment which even yourself, begging your pardon, would be happy to patronize.'

Father O'Flaherty shook his head sadly. 'A commendable idea, Master Keane, but I fear you would soon be bankrupt. You flourish now in your fine clothes because of your women and your illegal still. Such a new establishment as you envisage, worthy as it maybe, would lose you money.'

'Not if I had seven such establishments all around the North End and Fort Hill.'

'Such schemes, Master Keane . . . an empire so soon . . . ' The priest shook his head doubtfully again.

'There are six other groggeries like Mother McCathy's mentioned in the ledger. I'm thinking their proprietors will be ready to sell up when they hear of the coming change in their circumstances.'

A smile, almost beatific, spread over Father O'Flaherty's thin features. 'Master Keane, I congratulate you.' He leaned over his desk to shake Jack's hand. 'God and Mammon satisfied. Sir, you have a young body but an old head.'

'Then I have your support, Father?'

'Support and blessing. Indeed you have. Perhaps even my occasional custom.'

'You'll help me tell Master Proudlane's opponents what we want in exchange for his downfall.'

'Master Keane, tis true what the Lord said about better the sinner who repented,' the priest said warmly, moving from his desk to pour two glasses of wine from a decanter on a side table.

The two men silently toasted each other. Father O'Flaherty sat down in a chair by Jack, his earlier reserve and suspicion replaced by interested concern for the young man. He asked Jack about his home and family in Ireland and whether it was his intention to bring his bride back to Boston town.

'Tis in the future, Father, but twill be a difficult decision I'll be having to make, so it will. I want to help Ireland.'

'Amen to that . . . ' the priest murmured.

'But here I am sensing a future and opportunity. At home, I fear there'll be a mighty long struggle before the English set us free to build our own country as we would want.'

'Aye, tis true, young man. Not only in Ireland, though, will there be a struggle, I'm thinking. What happened in France is just the beginning I fear.'

The priest leaned forward and gripped Jack's arm. 'And that's why it's important to establish the Church firmly here, my son.' Father O'Flaherty continued. 'Here will come the poor and oppressed from the old world. God knows, the Church has made mistakes in the past – though don't be telling the Bishop I've been saying that – but here is our chance to build again. Perhaps that's why this country attracts us all. It's writing its own history day by day on clean, blank pages, so it is, and that is why the Church must go out into your world if she is to survive and prosper.'

The priest insisted on giving Jack a blessing before he left to put his plan into action. He checked the stock of gin to ensure that there was enough for at least a week, then ordered two of his potmen to dismantle the still in the cellar. He would have liked to consult Mother McCarthy but there was no time. He promised himself he would write to her the next day with a full account of what he was planning. His next move was to ask Meg Griffiths to call the girls together in the kitchen, and invite Padraig Costelloe and Homer Penquick to listen to what he was going to tell them.

'Whatever you hear me say don't be surprised, Padraig,' he said. 'What I'm about to do will be the making all our fortunes, I'm praying.'

But for all his apparent confidence, Jack was at a loss how to begin as he saw the dozen faces looking expectantly at him in the kitchen.

'I have some news for you all,' he started. Then he paused. 'Hell's teeth, Padraig,' he exclaimed. 'Pour some drink for everyone else I'll never get it out.' The faces around the table became apprehensive. 'Oh, tis nothing terrible,' he reassured them. 'You're all going to have to change your jobs.'

There was silence around the table. One girl began to laugh. Meg rounded on her angrily. 'Can't you see Jack's serious? And all you can do is bray like a donkey.'

'Tis not that serious, Meg,' said Jack, trying to calm her. 'It does not mean you'll be without work. In fact, I'm reckoning you'll have to work harder than ever.'

Jack explained how and why he was changing the groggery. Dismay crept across the girls' faces as Jack outlined his plans, making it clear that they were no longer to ply their trade with the customers.

'Where are we going to go?' Meg wailed. 'You're going to throw us back on the streets.'

'No so. Tis not so,' Jack replied. 'You're still going to serve the men . . . but not as ladies of the town. You're going to be cooks and waitresses.'

'Give up the men!' said the girl sitting next to Meg, a defiant tone in her voice. 'Never. Give up the men . . . you'll be just as well making us nuns.'

'You can still have as many men as you like,' said Jack curtly. 'But twill be on other premises and in your own time. If you stay here you'll do honest work for honest wages. You can keep your cubicles to live in but you'll not be having men up there.'

'There be too many of us just to serve this groggery,' sniffed Meg. 'Most times you'll be having more waitresses than customers in this hoity-toity establishment of yours.'

'That may be true at first,' Jack agreed. 'But I have ideas of acquiring other groggeries where you can all find work. If you measure well enough, you might be running an establishment of your own before long.'

'That's fine talk,' complained the girl next to Meg. 'But I'm thinking we should stick to the trade that we know best.'

'Suit yourself,' snapped Meg. 'I'm knowing which side of the loaf is crusty.'

Jack nodded at her approvingly. 'Tis the right attitude, Meg. This way you'll be after building something for the future.'

'And what of us?' interrupted Costelloe, gesturing at himself and Homer Penquick. 'You won't be needing our fists any more when you become all proper and legal.'

'You and Timmy Brehoney can give up your humping on the wharves and join the enterprise, if you want. The same goes for the Penquicks. As for Augustus Hawkins . . . well, I'm reckoning he'll be back to his mountain traps soon enough.'

'But we ain't knowing nothing about it, Jack,' said Homer Penquick. 'They ain't learning us how to be waitresses and cooks down on the plantation.' He rolled his eyes. 'We ain't nothing but Nigra trash, you be forgetting, Mister White Man.'

Jack joined in the general laughter at the sorrowful expression on the big Negro's face. 'What you're forgetting, Homer, is your own people will be wanting to use proper eating and drinking houses as well. They'd be mighty easier if one of their own folk was running it for them.'

'You mean that?'

'Why not, indeed? Nigra money spends as well as white money, doesn't it? And as for being cooks and waitresses . . . well, you'll learn as quick as I did. There's not much to it.' He tried to imitate Homer Penquick rolling his eyes. 'Why down in the bogs, they didn't teach us Irish trash much either.'

Most of those in the kitchen seemed to approve of Jack's plan. They chattered their way excitedly back into the groggery. Two or three of the girls, though, still wore sullen looks. Jack called Meg to one side.

'Them that don't approve . . . see them off the premises by tonight. Give them five dollars from the monies behind the bar and send them on their way with a square meal inside themselves and a bottle of gin.'

'And that'll make this place respectable?' said Meg, sceptically.

'Get a sign made to go on the bottom of the stairway. Something like "No customers allowed upstairs" should be enough.'

'And where be you while all this respectablizing is going on?'

'Well, I reckon I'll be buying some proper liquor from Master Felton and then giving a certain gentleman some mighty disagreeable news. When I return tonight, I want the groggery fit to entertain Bishop Fenwick himself.'

Meg pulled a sour face. 'It'll be terrible dull and no mistake.'

'The duller the better,' said Jack cheerfully. 'Tomorrow we start painting the house in pretty colours so twill be better if you all get a night's sleep without your usual exertions.'

'And yourself?' Meg asked slyly. 'Will you be learning how to serve proper ladies up on Beacon Hill tonight?'

'You're above your station, waitress,' laughed Jack, slapping her behind playfully.

'And are you sure that you're not, Irisher?' said Meg shrewdly. 'I'm remembering the scars on your back and how you got them scarce a year since and here you are all high and mighty with society and political folk. Mind you're not scarred some more.'

Meg's warning returned to Jack's mind as he strode towards Daniel Proudlane's house in Salem Street. His business in Felton's distillery had gone well although there had been raised eyebrows at first when he'd said he wanted wines, whisky, gin, and rum delivered to Mother McCarthy's.

'And has the still broken?' Master Felton inquired.

Jack looked at the large, jolly man, well padded with fat, his appearance advertising his wares. 'You could say that, sir, and it won't be getting repaired again, I can assure you.'

'Then, Master Keane, we can conduct business at a proper discount,' the distiller had replied.

Was he indeed rising dangerously above his station in life, Jack wondered? He remembered dancing at the crossroads at Ballybunnion when Brigid Aherne had declared her love so openly. He remembered the silence and space of Kerry, the dew-fresh mornings, the vividly wild sunsets, as he moved through Boston's narrow, busy streets. He listened to the sound of his shoes striking the cobbles and thought of how his parents had used their own footwear so sparingly. A pang of home-sickness wrenched at him. Wouldn't it have been a better life in Ireland despite the poverty and disease and hide-bound class system? Wouldn't he have been happier in a small cabin with Brigid, rather than wearing fine clothes and intriguing against men of high education and low cunning? Jack shook his doubts from him. No, Ireland and all it meant had passed for the moment. It was there to be savoured, but in the future. He squared his shoulders as he approached Daniel Proudlane's wooden framed house.

The selectman awaited Jack in his neat front parlour. Two copper bedwarmers hung, gleaming, each side of the wide, empty fireplace. The furniture was dark and well polished, the chairs were deep and upholstered. It was a room which spoke of secure affluence. Jack was impressed.

'Well, Master Keane, I cannot say it is a pleasure to welcome you to my home,' said Proudlane sourly after the servant had left them together. 'I have been pondering all day on whether to give you to the constables for threatening me as you did at the State House.'

'Threatening, Master Proudlane? How so?'

'All this nonsense about funds and kindnesses from Kilfedder. Your tone implied you have a hold on me.'

'There is a ledger . . .'

'Showing proper business transactions, no doubt.'

'As far as Kilfedder was concerned they were proper,' said Jack, somewhat taken aback by Proudlane's confident attack.

'And so they were, young man,' Proudlane said, putting an avuncular arm on Jack's shoulder to guide him to a chair. 'Kilfedder and myself had a business arrangement, that's true, but it was for the best of motives. He helped finance my elections and my work in the ward.'

They sat on opposite sides of the fireplace. Proudlane offered him a churchwarden pipe of tobacco but Jack refused politely.

'Tis not a habit I have.'

'Seems to me, though, Master Keane, you have other habits equally addictive,' said Proudlane, smiling tightly. He puffed at the long clay stem of the pipe. 'Like the habit of honesty; the habit of curiosity, or call it meddling; and the peculiarly Irish habit of blind naivety.'

'Sir?'

'I've explained what it was between Kilfedder and myself and why it was thus. I'm not sure whether you understand yet.'

'I do understand. The practice of politics, it seems to me, is merely a way for those with the most money to have the biggest say. If I'm not mistaken, the system you approve of is very much like that at home where the biggest landowner either goes to Parliament as of his right or pays someone else to do his work for him.'

'Exactly,' purred the selectman, relaxing a little in his chair. 'You see most events most clearly, Master Keane.'

'Perhaps I do, sir. And that's why I'm concerned at the payments shown in the ledger I'm holding. They're clearly illustrating that the old system of doing things still applies to the Americas. And I'm thinking that that isn't right at all.'

Proudlane hunched forward in his chair again. 'And, pray, why not, my young Irisher?'

'Because you fought to have it otherwise,' Jack replied calmly. 'The Yankees who died fighting the English this century and the last died because they wanted a different way. They wanted a say in the running of their lives. They wanted their voting at elections to mean something.'

'I don't want to sound a cynic, Master Keane, but there have always been those who want and those who get. Those who want live in a world of dreams. I state that those who get deal in the real world. The true reason we fought the English was because we didn't like paying our taxes to them and then having no say over how they were spent. Talk not of glorious revolutions nor wars of independence. The man in the real world knows that they're only squabbles between those that have money and power and those that don't. Sometimes those without money and power win the squabbles by force of arms, by superior numbers. But, when they do win – and this

154

is the truth, Master Keane despite the distaste on your face – they quickly make sure to re-establish the old order. They elect themselves leaders to gain power and with that power comes money, and out of money comes power and out of power comes money and so on and so on until the next squabble.'

'In your case, Master Proudlane, you had the power and J.P. Kilfedder had the money. Or was it the other way around?'

'It matters not. They're interchangeable.'

'But not unchanging, I'm thinking,' said Jack quietly.

This time the selectman looked puzzled. 'I don't . . . '

'Well, it seems that I have the power now. And it appears you don't have enough money. So you're out of your real world, as you put it. You have neither power nor money.'

'You are threatening me again, Keane.' The politician's voice began to rise in anger.

'No. I'm telling you,' said Jack calmly. 'Sure and I don't live in your real world because what I'm going to do is give away my power to someone else. I'm going to hand it back to the people who voted for you by opening the ledger to them so they can see your real world and how it operates. Then I won't have the power, nor will you.' He leaned forward in his chair, jabbing his finger at Proudlane to emphasize the point. 'The people who will have the power will be simple people, ordinary people who should have had it all this time while you and Kilfedder have been running things the way you want.'

'Then, sir,' Proudlane snapped, 'you will be nothing. I shall show you who has the power. The elections are two months away and by that time you shall have no business.'

The selectman stood up, his face white with anger. 'I've tried to be reasonable, but you are as ignorant as your background suggests. You Irishers will never succeed in this country until you empty your heads of your dreams. There is only one place for your heaven and it isn't on this earth.'

Jack shrugged. 'That may be . . . ' He rose from his chair and walked towards the door.

'May be . . . may be . . . ' Proudlane flung after him. 'Even your precious Church knows where power lies in this life.'

After Jack left the house, he stood outside in Salem Street for a moment, breathing deeply. He could understand Proudlane's anger. Jesus, he thought, I must have sounded a proper prig with all that talk about simple, ordinary people. But Jack knew he had reacted to the politician's gross cynicism. He knew that some of what Proudlane had said was probably correct. But the selectman's total contempt for the voters and his naked greed for power had sickened him. Other politicians, he believed, lived in the real world, as Proudlane kept calling it, but still managed to reconcile it with an honest desire to serve their voters. Josiah Longman, he was certain, was such a man.

The next morning, Jack woke early and roused everyone. By the time he'd finished a quick breakfast of bread smeared with pork dripping, the girls had come downstairs and were sitting in various states of undress at the tables around the bar. They looked at him blearily as he repeated his instructions of the previous afternoon. Some of them groaned as he announced that he wanted them to begin painting the establishment that morning.

'The groggery will be closed for two days for the work to be done,' he said. 'That should be enough time for the customers to realize that Mother McCarthy's is on the change.'

'They realized that last night,' Meg complained. 'Dozens of them left when we told them there was no service upstairs any more.'

'They'll get used to the new ways soon enough,' Jack replied with as much confidence as he could muster. In truth, by the light of the new day he was wondering if he had not made a series of grave errors. Had he committed himself too firmly to too many people? He cursed himself inwardly for not leaving himself more room for manoeuvre. If his plans failed, if he was rejected by Longman, then he knew he had lost the business. And then there was still the problem of unseating Proudlane; perhaps the voters would prefer the morals of a corrupt politician to those of a reformed proprietor of a former jilt shop!

Those doubts persisted as he paced nervously at the foot of the steps leading to the State House. He had decided to waylay Josiah Longman rather than risk another confrontation with Proudlane in the lobby of the State House. The sun was almost directly overhead by the time Jack saw Longman arrive in a carriage.

'Be you back at four o'clock, Joshua,' Jack heard Longman instruct the Negro coachman before he turned to hurry up the steps.

'Master Longman,' Jack called after him. 'Master Longman . . . a moment if you please.'

The politician turned and saw Jack. A flicker of recognition crossed his face followed by a friendly smile.

'When I said yesterday that I hoped we would meet again, young sir, I little realized it would be so soon.'

'The truth, Master Longman, is that everything is happening to me sooner than I anticipated.'

'I have yet to meet a young man not in a hurry, sir, either to make his fortune or to fall in love. Of what service can I be to you now? I trust it will be of more pleasant a nature than an introduction to Daniel Proudlane.' He placed a hand under Jack's elbow to urge him up the steps.

Jack shook his head. 'Twould be better if we talked outside the State House, Master Longman. Too many years to listen, and that's the truth . . .'

'Well then, where shall we go? A stroll on the Common perhaps? Fresh air would do me more good than all the stale words I'd have to listen to in there.' He jabbed his thumb at the State House behind him.

Jack nodded in agreement. 'Twould be fine, Master Longman. And then perhaps tis I can offer you a glass of refreshment at a friend's house along Beacon Hill.'

'Capital, sir.'

As the two men strolled in the summer sunshine through the glades and along the paths of the Common, Jack explained his predicament for the second time in two days. Josiah Longman interrupted him rarely, but from time to time, glanced sideways and upwards at his companion, assessing and weighing his words.

'A pretty tale, indeed,' he grunted when Jack had ended his story. He smacked one fist into his other and repeated, 'A very pretty tale indeed. 'Pon my word it is.'

'You don't seem surprised, Master Longman, at the assocation between J. P. Kilfedder and some of your colleagues?'

'Surprised? Surprised? Not in the least, sir. There have been rumours for some time that Proudlane and the lesser denizens of his party were not all they seemed. Not that I don't suspect some of my own colleagues of soiling their hands in similar manner. It is a common ailment in politics, sad as that may be.'

'But you'll help me, won't you?' Jack asked, slightly worried at the politician's apparent cynicism over his allegations of corruption.

Josiah Longman stopped for a moment. He looked Jack up and down. 'Are you sure you wish to proceed on this course? It's hard enough for a newcomer to survive in this town. If we fight an election using your evidence, you might go under in the storm that will blow.'

'The hatches are battened down to weather the storm. You forget my experience at sea.'

Longman laughed. He reached up and patted Jack on the

shoulder. 'Indeed I do. Why, any man who has sailed the Atlantic, outrun the English army, and done as well as you have, must have an instinct for survival. Such an instinct is possibly the most valuable weapon in life's battle. People talk more of heroes than survivors but then heroes tend to be with us for less time. Heroes are useful but not half as useful as survivors. That, my boy, was even the considered opinion of General Washington. Why, I remember . . .'

'Master Longman,' Jack interrupted. 'You will talk with Father O'Flaherty about choosing a candidate to fight Proudlane?'

'I'm sorry. I was digressing. Of course I shall, sir. I already have someone in mind who is not only totally trustworthy but of Irish descent. He might be an admirable choice to satisfy yourself, the Church, and my colleagues.' Again he chuckled. ''Pon my word, Proudlane will never stand a chance against such holy opposition. With this ledger of yours . . .'

'Will you be wanting to peruse it?'

'Of course, my boy. As soon as possible. And we must satisfy ourselves that it is in safe keeping.'

''Tis not far away, at my friend's house.'

Longman patted Jack on the shoulder again. 'Lead on.' He gazed up at the sky. 'Every moment with you in this fresh air is making me feel quite young again. You did a great service in insisting on walking with me.'

By the time they had arrived at Elizabeth Kilfedder's house, the two men had slipped quite easily into first name terms.

Jack rapped at the front door. After a short wait it was opened by Naomi, Elizabeth Kilfedder's maid. Her eyes brightened as she saw Jack standing on the step.

'Why, Master Jack, we were expecting you last evening,' she said as the two men stepped into the hallway. 'Why, Mistress Elizabeth was so worried that she was almost sending me on a message to you.'

'Naomi, who is calling?' Elizabeth's voice came from the salon.

'Master Jack,' the maid called. 'I done tell you there was nothing to . . .'

'Hush your chattering, Naomi,' said Elizabeth as she hurried into the hallway. She ran towards Jack, her arms outstretched. Then she noticed Josiah Longman. She dropped her arms, and a blush appeared high on her cheekbones. Longman's twinkling eyes missed nothing. He looked at the beautiful young woman and then glanced at his new friend.

'Elizabeth,' said Jack, 'May I present Josiah Longman, a friend of mine who is here to help us.'

158

She curtseyed, immediately recognizing Longman's name. 'You are most welcome to my home, sir,' she said.

'The pleasure is mine, dear lady,' Longman replied.

''Tis Elizabeth Kilfedder, Josiah,' Jack explained. 'The wife of J. P. Kilfedder who saw fit to desert her.'

'My commiserations, madam,' said Longman. Then he added slyly, 'But how nice to know that Jack here is affording you his protection in your difficulty.' He looked sideways at Jack. 'Your circle of acquaintances continues to amaze me. It does indeed.'

'Naomi,' Elizabeth ordered, 'let us have some wine.'

When the claret had been poured, Jack explained to Elizabeth about his arrangement with Longman. At first she seemed alarmed but gained confidence quickly as she heard of the precautions taken by Jack.

'And now for the famous ledger, dear,' said Jack. 'Will you fetch it for Josiah?'

The politician put on half-moon spectacles to study the heavy book. Elizabeth explained the index to him in the same way she had done for Jack. Longman's face darkened as he read the pages that indicated the extent of the corruption.

'A public disgrace,' he muttered. 'These men are nothing but villains, pure and simple.' He slammed the ledger shut and handed it to Jack.

'It must be kept safe and its existence must not be revealed to any more people than already are aware of it. Thus, when we do expose its contents nearer the election, its effect will be heightened.'

## Chapter 11 March, 1826

Paper lamps with candles burning inside them hung from the whitewashed ceiling of Mother McCarthy's. Their light shone blue, red, yellow and green on the faces of the two hundred or so people packed into the bar. They swayed and turned, throwing their colours in every direction, in the currents of warm air rising from the noisy chattering crowd. The lamps danced in time to the reels and

159

jigs and the musicians stamping their feet on the floor. The sounds from the groggery – now officially re-named 'Mother McCarthy's House of Refreshment' – reached out into the warm night air of late summer in Bread Street and dragged more and more people inside. Potmen, trays held high above their heads, thrust their way through to deliver bottles and mugs to tables. Six girls, supervised by Meg Griffiths, darted back and forth behind the bar, green silk bows bobbing in their hair, trying to keep pace with the orders. People kept looking expectantly at the long trestle table, covered with a gleaming white linen cloth, which stood empty at the end of the groggery by the stairway. Then, those with sharp enough ears picked out the sound of a drum beating steadily and the cheers of a crowd approaching, closer and closer to the groggery.

'They're here,' shouted someone by the door. 'They're here!'

People surged to the windows and through the door to watch the procession burst noisily into the narrow, cobbled street. At its head Padraig Costelloe and Homer Penquick held the poles of a long canvas banner proclaiming simply 'Vote Finucane'. Under the banner a single drummer rapped out the marching pace. A crowd of about one hundred followed, most of them with burning, smoking torches held high. In the middle of this crowd a youngish man swayed uneasily on the broad shoulders of Jack Keane and Timmy Brehoney, waving at the people who leaned from the upper windows of the houses on either side of the street. Their cheers and those from the procession almost drowned the staccato drum beat. The banner was dipped and thrust into the entrance of the groggery, forcing the crowds to move aside and make a pathway. Inside, it was unfurled again and the drummer led it around the bar. Jack Keane leapt up the stairs, becoming visible to all in the room, and signalled with his arms for silence. The hubbub grudgingly subsided.

'Friends,' he shouted. 'Friends, the vote went as follows . . .' Jack plucked a small piece of paper from his waistcoat pocket and read from it. 'Daniel Proudlane . . . one thousand and ten votes.'

There was silence now.

'Matthew Finucane . . . one thousand, six hundred, and . . .'

A great cheer erupted drowning the rest of his words. People hugged each other, jumped up and down, kissed the nearest woman, and hurled their hats into the air. Little Horace Penquick turned a cartwheel of joy on the floor.

Jack allowed the wild celebration to continue for more than a minute and then shouted and gestured for silence again.

'And so I present you with your new selectman . . Matthew

Finucane.'

There was another roar as he stepped back and the man who'd been chaired into the groggery jumped up the stairway, hands clasped above his head. He stood alone for a moment and then grabbed Jack's arm and raised it so that both men acknowleged the delirious shouts from the crowd. From the groggery door a chant began, reinforced by the stamping of feet which made the paper lamps dance and sway even more.

'Speech! Speech! Speech!'

The chant and the stamping spread throughout the groggery.

'My friends,' Finucane began, shouting against the noise reverberating around the room. 'Me mam and dad came to this town nigh on thirty years back from County Clare . . .'

Another roar went up. Finucane waited for it to die away before continuing.

' . . . so that makes me as Irish as any of you. But I was born here so I speak to you as one of the first Irish-Americans. What happened tonight is just the beginning. At last you will have a voice in the running of this town; a voice that understands your needs and problems; a voice that will listen to the counsel of our Church. It says a deal for this new country of ours that this should be so. We bring to this land many cultures and legends. Let us not forget them, rather let us treasure them, but we must not forget that we are now Yankees first and Irishers second. There will be many who will resent us coming here; there will be many like my unlamented opponent, Daniel Proudlane, who will try to exploit us; there will be many who will pour scorn on our beliefs and our customs. Let them, because, in time, they will become the strangers in this land; their voices will be the ones crying from the wilderness of ignorance and prejudice and bigotry. Not ours. Ours will be the voices giving thanks for this new land where we can ensure that the wrongs of the old world are not repeated. Friends, I thank you, and particularly I thank my friend, Jack Keane. Bless you all.'

For a moment there was silence and then another gust of cheering swept through the groggery. Some of the crowd, moved by Finucane's rhetoric, were crying openly; crying and smiling at the same time.

The politician pushed Jack forward against the banister of the stairway. 'Go on. It's your turn now. Say something, Jack,' he urged.

'Come on, Jack,' came a shout from the front of the crowd. 'Let's be hearing you.'

Jack raised his hand for silence. 'I'm not a man for speechifying,' he began, his hands nervously clutching the banister. 'And hasn't Matt Finucane said all there is to be said, and that's the truth.' He looked desperately around him for inspiration. At the top of the stairway, hidden from the crowd below, he saw Elizabeth Kilfedder, her eyes shining with excitement. At her side was the dumpy figure of Mother McCarthy, who'd insisted on returning for the election party, dressed in a voluminous beige silk gown, her hair neatly combed, a strand of Elizabeth's jewellery around her throat. The effect was only slightly spoiled by the inevitable mug of gin in her gloved hand. Jack smiled at them and then turned back to the crowd that waited expectantly for his next words.

At that moment, Padraig Costelloe thrust a mug through the rails of the stairway. Jack bent down to take it and then raised it, turning to salute the two women at the top of the stairs. 'Friends,' he called, 'the toast is "The Ladies". God bless 'em!'

The building shook with the response from the hundreds crammed inside and from those still outside in Bread Street unable to force their way through the door.

'Now that's enough talk,' Jack shouted. 'Let's have a proper hooley.' He bounded up the stairs and hugged Mother McCarthy and Elizabeth Kilfedder in turn.

'Come on down now and join the party,' he said, slipping his hand into Elizabeth's.

'Am I looking in fashion enough?' asked Mother McCarthy anxiously. 'Why, I've never been dressed as such since I wed McCarthy. Not that he noticed with the drink in him . . .'

'You look fine,' Jack reassured her. 'All the country air has brought colour back to your cheeks. If you're not careful you'll be finding yourself in front of a priest again with another man at your side.'

Mother McCarthy laughed throatily. 'At least the next time I'll be knowing what to do with him on the wedding night.'

Jack felt happier that evening than ever in his life. He felt a twinge of guilt at clasping such happiness to him. Images of his parents, his dead brothers, and Brigid Aherne came briefly to his mind but he deliberately pushed them away as he gazed down the table at his guests.

At the head of the table, opposite him, was Matthew Finucane, a man in his early thirties, already becoming successful in his co-operage business. Jack had taken to him immediately, realizing that

162

Longman had chosen the ideal candidate; transparently honest, solidly respectable; in all, the perfect contrast to Daniel Proudlane. If Proudlane and his friends hadn't spent so much money buying votes then Finucane's victory would have been even more decisive. But then, Jack reflected, Proudlane had been forced to spend money desperately to try and offset the damning evidence in the ledger. Throughout the election, which had been surprisingly free of trouble, the ledger had lain open, available for anyone's inspection, on a table at the groggery in Bread Street. Hundreds had come to see it, not only helping Jack's business, but decisively undermining Proudlane's campaign.

On his right was Matt Finucane's wife, Alice, complementing her husband with her charm and fresh looks. 'And what plans are you hatching now, Master Keane, so deep in dreams that you are?' she asked.

Jack started out of his thoughts. 'Plans, Mistress Finucane? What plans now?' He glanced at Elizabeth Kilfedder to his left and saw that she was watching his reaction closely. He smiled to himself. Women together, he knew now, would always attempt to harry an unmarried man to the altar. It was as if the state of bachelorhood was a personal affront to them.

'Well, you've achieved so much so quickly that I was thinking you would have further ambitions.'

'My ambitions are to enjoy the company of my good friends around this table. And as for achieving what you call so much, so quickly, why, I've had the luck of the Irish, and that's the truth. No. No more ambitions on this side of the ocean except to dance this night away.' He turned to Elizabeth. 'And will you help me realize that ambition, too?'

'Of course, Master Jack Keane,' she smiled brightly. 'Yours is to ask and mine to accept.'

By midnight, the crowd in Mother McCarthy's had thinned out. Most of Jack's guests had left. Padraig Costelloe was asleep at the table, head buried in his arms, snoring loudly. Meg Griffiths had helped Mother McCarthy to bed and then returned to the establishment she managed four streets away. Josiah Longman had given Father O'Flaherty a lift in his carriage and the Finucanes had hurried home to their family. Timmy Brehoney and the Penquicks had joined some cronies at another table and were clearly set on drinking and yarning into the small hours.

'Well, Elizabeth,' Jack said, holding her at arm's length, 'are you

163

going to spend the night here in my room?'

She looked around the groggery, noting the people still present, and shook her head.

'Twould be too public, dear Jack. I have little enough reputation already in the eyes of the town without that. My carriage should have been outside for an hour since. Come back to Beacon Hill.'

'Yours is to ask,' he said gently, echoing her earlier words. She smiled softly at him and inclined her head.

Jack escorted Elizabeth towards the door.

'Don't be up all night,' he called to Timmy Brehoney and the Penquicks.

They waved to him and then, almost as an afterthought, Brehoney hurried to his side. 'Here, take this, Jack,' he muttered, pulling a shillelagh from under his coat and thrusting it into Jack's hand. 'You can't be too careful; not with Proudlane's men around. They're still mighty upset at his defeat.'

Jack tried to push it away. 'There's no need, Timmy. We're not going on foot.'

'Take it, for God's sake, and don't be so foolish, man,' urged Brehoney.

'For peace's sake,' said Jack, reluctantly putting the thick stick under his coat. 'But you're fussing about nothing.'

Ouside, he helped Elizabeth into her carriage, letting his hands hold her slim waist longer than was strictly necessary.

'What was Timmy giving you that stick for?' she asked as the carriage clattered over the cobblestones.

'The drink had made him fearful,' Jack explained lightly. 'He thinks Proudlane's men will want to crack my skull.'

'And will they?'

'Not at all. Proudlane, whatever he may be, is no fool. He'll be spending his time plotting to get back his position, not chasing Irishers for revenge.'

'Are you sure?'

'I'm sure,' he said, putting his arm round her shoulders and pulling her closer to him.

The carriage passed hardly anyone on its journey to Beacon Hill.

'There,' he said as it pulled up outside her house. 'Nothing at all to worry about. Brehoney's worse than an old woman, that he is.'

They stood for a moment on the footpath as the carriage moved away towards the stables at the back of the house. Then they turned, arm in arm, to go indoors.

Suddenly, from the darkness behind him, Jack heard footsteps. A voice shouted hoarsely, 'At last, you bastard spalpeen!'

Sensing mortal danger, half-recognizing the voice, he pushed Elizabeth away from him, at the same time spinning round in a crouched position. His hand darted towards the shillelagh under his coat. He caught a glimpse of a white, demented face, full bearded, and two flintlock pistols pointed at him. Before he could move any further Jack felt a smashing blow in his chest followed by the flash and roar of a pistol. He staggered and began to fall. Dimly, before he spun into blackness, he heard Elizabeth scream wildly and then another roar from a pistol.

An eternity later, he opened his eyes and groaned. The anxious face of Naomi the maid swam fuzzily into view. He tried to move but groaned again with pain. The left side of his chest felt as if it was on fire. I've been whipped again, he thought weakly. Then the memory of the man with the pistols flooded back to him.

'Kilfedder,' he muttered. 'J. P. Kilfedder. He came back.'

'Hush now, Master Jack,' Naomi murmured. 'Just you rest. You been injured.'

He lifted his head slightly and saw that he was lying on cushions spread on the floor of the salon. His shirt had been removed and white bandages bound tightly around his chest. As Naomi bent solicitously over him he felt spots of water falling on his bare shoulders. He blinked his eyes, making another effort to focus them. He looked into the Negress's face. She was crying silently, tears running down her cheeks. He shook his head slightly and blinked his eyes again.

'Your mistress?' he whispered. 'Elizabeth? Where is she?'

Naomi sobbed loudly. She turned her head away and wiped her hand across her eyes. 'Don't worry, Master Jack,' she said quietly. 'Mistress Elizabeth is just fine. Just fine.'

'Where is she?' Jack demanded, his voice becoming stronger. He forced himself to sit up, choking back a shout of agony. 'Where's Mistress Elizabeth?'

'She's resting, Master Jack,' Naomi said gently. 'She is in good hands. You just lie back until your men come. I send the coachman to Bread Street for them near an hour back.'

Despite his pain, Jack shivered. From Naomi's tears and words he suddenly knew. 'She's dead, isn't she, Naomi?' he said evenly. Then more fiercely. 'She's dead, isn't she. Tell me.'

Naomi nodded her head and began crying openly. 'She done gone with her Maker, Master Jack. She done gone.'

'I want to see her,' he demanded, his own pain now totally

forgotten. It seemed as if his whole body was filling with a clammy emptiness.

'No, Master. You lie and rest. You been hurt bad.'

'Pull me up,' he shouted. 'Pull me up or I'll crawl.'

Reluctantly, Naomi helped him to his feet. He put his right arm around her strong shoulders and stumbled into the hallway. He gripped the banister somehow and hauled himself up the stairs, wincing in his agony. Naomi supported him as best she could as he limped towards the closed door of the bedroom where he and Elizabeth had shared so many hours of love. Naomi pushed the door open. Jack leaned against the door jamb and looked inside. A candle burned on each side of the bed. Elizabeth lay there, her blonde hair spread on the pillow, a single sheet covering all but her face. Jack moved to the side of the bed and looked down at her. Her face was pale and in the soft, flickering light, she seemed asleep, her eyes gently closed. Then, with a sudden movement, Jack grasped the edge of the sheet and wrenched it aside. Elizabeth's hands were folded over her naked breasts. Just below her left breast there was a small hole, tinged with a blue-grey bruise. There was no blood. Just that obscene hole. Jack's eyes travelled the length of the perfect, empty body.

'We done cleaned her, Master Jack,' Naomi said beside him. 'We dress her later to make her proper.'

He groaned and tried to speak. But the room began swimming around him. With a low moan he fell forward across Elizabeth, his arms stretching around her.

The next three days for Jack were spent in long periods of unconsciousness and brief spells of lucidity when he was aware of being back in his room at Mother McCarthy's tended by Dillon the physician or being watched over by Meg Griffiths, Padraig Costelloe, or Timmy Brehoney. Their faces would swim out of the blackness. He would hear comforting, murmured words or feel gentle hands soothing him before the room slipped away from him again. On the fourth day he awoke just after dawn. He moved his head on the pillow and saw Meg Griffiths in a chair by the bed. Her head was sunk on to her chest, her breath coming in light snores. Jack stretched out his right hand and plucked at her skirt. She wakened instantly, tossing her head up. He smiled at her weakly.

'Water, for the saints' sake, Meg.'

She rose quickly from her chair to pour him a mug from a pitcher set on the floor. She lifted him gently and helped him sip the liquid. He sank back on to the pillow.

'How long?' he whispered.

'Four days,' Meg replied quietly.

'And Elizabeth?'

A worried expression crossed Meg's face.

'I remember what happened Meg. I know she's dead.'

Meg took his hand. 'She was buried yesterday.'

Jack nodded. 'It had to end,' he murmured. 'One day.'

Meg lifted his hand, kissed the palm lightly, and then laid it against her cheek.

''Twas Kilfedder, you know. He came back.'

'We know. The coachman glimpsed him running off on to the Common, but it seems he's clear away.'

He glanced down at his own body covered by blankets.

'Why not me, Meg? How did he miss?'

'He didn't, dear Jack. The ball hit Timmy's shillelagh under your coat and went round your ribs. Master Dillon said if it hadn't been for the shillelagh it would have pierced your heart for sure.

'Dear God. Saved by Timmy's stick. And there was I after not carrying it.'

'Now rest, Jack. No more talking. I'll be making you some gruel soon for your strength.'

'You're a fine girl, Meg.'

'Hush now. Just rest.'

She patted his hand and slipped it back under the blankets. Jack's eyes closed and he fell deeply asleep.

It was another week before he was strong enough to get up. He no longer felt keen pain at Elizabeth's death. There was an emptiness but not deep grief. She had died at her loveliest and happiest knowing that he adored her. Perhaps, he thought, she would have wished it like that, realizing, as he had done, that the affair would eventually have come to nothing. Now, he would never forget her: he would always remember her as warm and vibrant and passionate, as full of life and love.

The first day he was allowed to go out, he walked stiffly, his ribs still bandaged, with Costelloe and Brehoney to the church in Park Street to visit Elizabeth's grave. It was covered with flowers but had no headstone as yet. It looked tiny in the shadow of the church's four-tiered spire pointing thinly into the sky. He stood by the grave for a few minutes thinking of the laughing, sensuous warmth of the four-poster bed. He knelt to place a large spray of red roses at the foot of the grave. He tried to think of a prayer but none came to mind.

'Be happy, mavourneen,' he said in a low voice. And then he rose and walked away without a backward glance.

Jack never visited the grave again, but every year he sent one of his friends to place flowers there.

During the months after her murder he drew closer to Matt Finucane and his family, taking comfort from the tranquillity and happiness of their settled home life.

Twice more he helped Finucane in election campaigns and twice more they beat off challenges from Daniel Proudlane. Jack never told Finucane but in the second election he had to resort to Proudlane's tactics of buying votes to ensure that the Irish people's candidate was elected. Indeed, during these elections, a relationship of grudging admiration grew up between Jack and Proudlane. They came to recognize and appreciate each other's cunning.

'Politics makes the strangest of bedfellows,' Proudlane observed to him during the second election as they waited for the votes to be counted. 'I remember talking to you, Master Keane, about power and money and here you are using my former strengths against me.'

'I've never claimed cleverness,' Jack said cheerfully. 'Only a willingness to learn, Master Proudlane.'

'If only we had met under different circumstances. You could well have been my campaign manager.'

'But then tis I would have been supporting a loser.'

Proudlane shook his head ruefully. 'A bad mistake not to realize the dangers in an Irisher's open face, his way of spinning words into dreams, and his totally ruthless cunning. A mistake, I believe, many others will make after me.'

'Perhaps so, Master Proudlane. Perhaps so. Better maybe to join us than fight us.'

The politician laughed shortly. 'How many years, I wonder, before there comes a brood of you Irishers strong enough to be Presidents of the United States, all proudly proclaiming their heritages and all having to use maps to find their ways back to Ireland.'

'Twill not be in my lifetime, I fear, Master Proudlane. At present we hang on by our fingernails, so we do.'

'And not in my lifetime either, I hope, because another political truth is that men with dreams are the most dangerous of this profession. Realists, pragmatic men, are safer than any dreamer. Take that as another free lesson to be learned, Master Keane.'

A year after Elizabeth's death, Mother McCarthy's health began to decline sharply. A winter of early snow and icy winds from the

Atlantic brought her to her bed and her friends realized that this was one winter she was unlikely to survive. In the strange way that dying people have, Mother McCarthy herself knew that her time had nearly come. She sent for her lawyer and drew up a will which made Jack her sole beneficiary. She explained this to him as she lay, weak and drawn, in her room during the second month of her illness.

'You'll have everything, Jack Keane, when I've gone,' she wheezed.

'Talk not like that. Tis you'll see the spring buds,' said Jack trying to comfort her.

She smiled at him wearily. 'Tis you always had a sweet tongue but then I'm hearing McCarthy himself calling me away. I'm terrible tired of this life so I'm not being afeared of the next. You must remember to make provisions yourself for all those that are working for us. As I've tried to watch over you, so you must care for them.'

Mother McCarthy died in her sleep two days after the bells of Boston's churches had rung in the year of 1828. Her funeral was probably the biggest ever seen by the growing Irish community. Her wake beforehand lasted for a full two days, aided by the five hundred dollars left in her will for drink to be given to the customers of the seven establishments. The hearse was drawn from Bread Street by four black horses with plumes of black feathers nodding on their heads, their hooves slipping and sliding on the icy, snow-covered cobbles. A fiddler walked in front playing laments, and behind a crowd of about four hundred proceeded to the Church of the Holy Cross for a funeral Mass conducted by Bishop Fenwick.

Afterwards, Jack invited his closest friends back to Bread Street for food and drink. Ever since Mother McCarthy's death he had been thinking of a scheme to protect them in the event of anything happening to himself. The occasional twinges from the scar tissue along his ribs reminded him how near he had already been to death.

'Tis you're going to become owners of the establishments you've been running,' he told them. 'Twould have been Mother McCarthy's wish.'

'But we can't afford that,' said Meg Griffiths, 'The money needed is beyond us all.'

'Women!' muttered Homer Penquick contemptuously. 'Ain't you ever learning just to listen?'

Jack looked at Meg with affection mingled with irritation. 'As Homer said, just listen for a moment. I'm going to give you the establishments at values suggested by my banker, Master Dunwoody. If you disagree with the values then Matt Finucane will hold the ring, and I promise I'll accept his decisions.'

'There's still money to be found,' grumbled Meg. Jack ignored her.

'You'll pay me the values at so much a quarter out of your profits over as long a time as you can afford. That way you won't be noticing it so much. And with the money you give me, I'll be paying off the loans I needed from Master Dunwoody to buy the establishments in the first place.'

'As simple as that?' asked Padraig Costelloe.

'Just one condition . . .'

'Ah!' said Meg triumphantly, her suspicion apparently vindicated.

' . . . You have to keep your present signs outside. They must all stay as "Mother McCarthy's". Tis a fitting memorial to her.'

'Is that all?' asked Meg, somewhat disappointed in tone.

'Tis so, you shrew. By the heavens, you be making a fine, grasping businesswoman and that's the truth. I'll be trusting you all to run the establishments as they are now. You'll not be wanting to besmirch Mother McCarthy after a bishop conducted her funeral, I'm sure.'

And so it was settled. Jack kept the original establishment in Bread Street, now free of all debts with the help of the bequest from Mother McCarthy. The business continued to prosper, the people of Boston coming to realize that he offered honest food and drink and honest prices. His boast to Father O'Flaherty even came to fruition when Bishop Fenwick and a party of priests set the seal on his new respectability by dining at Bread Street.

But as his standing in Boston grew, so did his loneliness. After Elizabeth, he couldn't bring himself to form another attachment with a woman. There were plenty of opportunities, many of them engineered by Matt Finucane and his wife, but Jack's memories were too powerful to allow him to be deeply interested in any of the young women he escorted to supper parties or formal dances.

'You're really breaking Alice's heart,' Matt Finucane remarked to him one day. 'One of the most eligible bachelors in all Boston and she can't find a suitable girl for you. You could have your pick, you know, Jack.'

'Maybe so, Matt, but I'm finding my heart is turning more and more to Ireland again. With Elizabeth still alive, I might have settled here happily enough with all my resolves about going back. As it is, with her and Mother McCarthy gone it does seem a terrible empty life.'

'But you've many friends. Alice and I . . . '

'I know that. Many good friends, and true they are. And all wanting to see me happy, I know. Yet inside me there's a mighty yearning to visit home again.'

Jack's homesickness grew with each letter brought to him by his old shipmates, Martin Flannery and Patrick Deane, on their annual visits to Boston. The letters were now written in a different hand. The one that reached him in 1829 informed him that Father O'Sullivan had died and that the writer, Father Jeremiah O'Mahony, was the new parish priest.

'A nice young fellow,' Flannery commented. 'From Killarney, your mam tells us. Most concerned he was when he learned of how you'd been driven out of the district.'

'Said he'd be happy to do all he can to settle the matter with the police and the army,' Deane added, filling up the mugs again with Master Felton's best rum.

'Much chance of that,' Jack said glumly. 'Here I'm sitting with all the money a man could be wanting and not able to visit my home.'

'No, Jack. Don't be disheartened,' said Flannery as optimistic as ever. 'This new priest's a real spinner of words and no mistake.'

'We told him what you'd done here and he was mighty impressed,' Deane continued. 'Things haven't been quiet in Kerry over the past year or so, not since that Captain O'Hare got himself elected to Parliament, so Father O'Mahony does reckon his words about you will be listened to.'

'Listened to maybe,' said Jack. 'But acted upon? Tis a very different mare. Jonathan Sandes is still high in the saddle as Watson's agent so what can have changed?'

'What's changed, Jack – don't you realize it? – is that you're now a man to match Sandes. Your clothes are as fine as his; your pockets are just as full; your name's as powerful.'

'Maybe here, my friends, but not there.'

'Doesn't do to underestimate the word of the Church,' said Flannery. 'There's word in Kerry that some cleric in Boston has been writing mighty pretty letters about you to the priests back home.'

'Tis not as if your mam and dad have kept silent either,' Deane broke in. 'The word is around the Shannon that the bilge rat of a stowaway we brought to the Americas has become a powerful strong man in this town.'

Jack looked at both of them. They wore smiles of smug self-satisfaction as they raised their mugs and clinked them together.

'I'm thinking I don't have to look far to see those people who've made my reputation such,' said Jack. 'Tis the two of you who've been blathering, I'm not doubting.'

'Us, Jack?' said Flannery with an air of hurt innocence. 'Us blathering?'

Deane nudged him in the ribs and all three men began laughing.

'Just you be remembering us now you've turned that respectable,' said Deane with a wink. 'Take us where that Meg girl works and we'll still be regarding you as a friend and putting the proper word in for you.'

As the years passed, the visits of Deane and Flannery became more and more eagerly awaited by Jack. With them, he could reminisce without feeling embarrassed; he could get drunk and forget his deep loneliness; he could breathe through them even for a day and a night the peat-fresh air of Kerry.

The letters they brought from his parents were always cheerful, although the one that came in 1831, contained for the first time no mention of Brigid Aherne. Jack's parents seemed to be coping well and enjoying a few luxuries with the money he had been sending back across the Atlantic. The cabin had glass windows now, and his parents had a proper wooden bed, raised from the floor. Although his mother still insisted on keeping fresh straw underneath the bed in case it might collapse.

In June of 1833, the two seamen again came to Boston and immediately made for Mother McCarthy's in Bread Street. By now, after so many years, Jack had a warning system from his customers on the wharves about the arrival of the *Grannia*, still plying across the Atlantic on the timber trade. A steaming pot of rabbit stew awaited Flannery and Deane as they came through the door in Bread Street together with, by custom, two flagons of the best rum.

But this time Jack noticed they seemed ill at ease after he had greeted them and sat them down at the table.

'A bad voyage, friends?' he inquired. 'Captain Higgins driving you harder with the years?'

'Tis not that, Jack,' said Flannery, pushing away the plate of stew served by a waitress. He took a long pull at his mug of rum.

Jack looked across the table at Deane and saw that he was equally ill at ease. Jack lowered his head.

'Tis the news, isn't it?' His dealing with people over the years, and his own experiences, had taught him to recognize those bearing bad news which they were reluctant to impart.

'Tis only life, Jack,' said Flannery quietly, handing Jack a letter addressed as usual in the spidery hand of Father O'Mahony. Jack

172

opened the letter, smoothed it out on the table, took a gulp of rum, and began to read.

Father O'Mahony regretted to inform him that his father had passed away in the spring of that year, peacefully, after a sudden attack of the chest ailment.

'Twas sudden,' said Flannery softly. 'Knew nothing of it says the tell.'

'A blessed way,' echoed Deane.

Jack said nothing. He continued reading. 'Your mother took the event well,' the letter said, 'Although it is I must be informing you that there is much opinion that she is ailing herself. Certainly from this writer's observation, it is doubtful how she can sustain the farm during the coming winter. This writer must express concern whether she can plant, let alone gather, the crops necessary for the farm's or her survival.'

Jack gazed at his two friends. It was obvious to him from their glum expressions that they knew the import, if not the exact contents of the letter.

'Read on, Jack,' said Deane. 'Your dad brought a lot of good for you even in his dying.'

Jack blinked his eyes, finding it difficult to focus on the writing.

'Your father's untimely death has caused much genuine concern in this district, and happily, I am able to inform you, on a word satisfactory to myself, that your presence at your home to care for your mother would not lead to unusual harrassment, attention or action from the authorities.'

Jack smoothed the letter again and reread the paragraph.

'Tis so?' he asked his friend.

'Aye. Tis so,' Flannery replied. 'The word is given in the district. You can return.'

# Chapter 12 July, 1833

The hooves of the dapple-grey horse raised puffs of dust as it eased into a gentle canter along the track leading from Tarbert in North Kerry. Jack Keane looked neither left nor right as he clung grimly to the reins and bumped along in the saddle, gripping the sides of the horse tightly with his knees. The dealer who'd sold him the horse had assured him that it was the mildest of creatures but its rhythm was still strange to its new rider. The two bags of gold sovereigns he'd obtained from Master Dunwoody's bank before his hasty departure from Boston banged comfortably against his thighs, safe in the deep pockets of the heavy brown top coat he was wearing. Two pistols, loaded and primed, nestled in leather holsters slung across the horse in front of the saddle. The rest of the possessions he'd brought were in a chest back in Tarbert awaiting more leisurely delivery by a carter to the family cabin in Drombeg townland.

Master Dunwoody and Matt Finucane could be trusted to wind up his business affairs in Boston and transfer the remainder of the proceeds across the Atlantic to him. He'd wanted the ownership of the establishment in Bread Street to pass jointly to his friends and was surprised when Finucane made a firm offer for it. But after Finucane had explained that it was a natural diversification from his cooperage business, Jack was happy to accept the offer with proper guarantees about the futures of the other businesses. It had happened so quickly, that there had only been time for perfunctory farewells, although everyone had come down to the Long Wharf to wave goodbye as the *Grannia* had slipped her mooring.

During the voyage Jack had many doubts about his decision to leave Boston but as soon as he glimpsed the coast of Ireland, just north of the Shannon Estuary, he knew there had been really no choice. It was inevitable and right that he should return to his home.

The countryside south of Tarbert seemed to have changed little in the nine years he'd been away. Everywhere and everything was the same; the tiny cabins dotted here and there with the occupants working the rough fields around them; the sense of space and permanence under the clouds scudding off the Atlantic, the dampness of autumn in the air changing to a light drizzle as he trotted through Ballylongford, every stride of the horse taking him nearer and nearer to his home, his mother and Brigid Aherne. He thought fondly of his mother, remembering her strength and hoping that she hadn't changed too much, that the years hadn't taken too much of a toll. He imagined Brigid as he had last seen her, fresh, loving, her black hair framing her beautiful face. He wondered why the last letters from his parents had not mentioned her. As soon as possible, he resolved, she would leave the service of Jonathan Sandes and marry him. He would build the best cabin money could buy, not too far away from his mother's, and then purchase a score of cows and pigs so that they would never again have to rely on the fickle harvest.

Along the way, as he turned east towards Listowel, he exchanged greetings with other travellers. There seemed little movement in the countryside but then he remembered that it had always been quiet on market days. He would have to stop comparing everything with the bustle and prosperity of Boston town. Now he remembered just how poor and deserted Kerry was. His memories and reminiscences had blurred the edges of the truth that was all around him.

As he passed the first cabins of Drombeg townland, he looked in vain for familiar faces: the people outside their cabins simply gazed dully back at him. One woman, a shawl on her head, a pipe stub in her mouth, actually curtseyed to him as he went by. He was puzzled and embarrassed until he realized that, of course, any person dressed as he was, riding a horse, displaying pistols, would naturally be taken as someone in authority. He wanted to shout aloud, 'I'm only your Jack Keane, back from the Americas. I'm no different from you. No different at all.' But he didn't and felt guilty that he didn't. And then, a hundred yards away, there was the cabin where he'd been born and raised.

The only sign of life was a thin trickle of smoke rising from the thatch. There were no animals outside; the fields were untilled; the walls in obvious disrepair, covered with large bare patches where the whitewash had flaked away. He reined in the horse and looked at the cabin with dismay. Suddenly, all the cheerful words from his parents' letters came back to him and he knew they had been a proud sham, a pretence to ease his own worries.

Jack dismounted from the horse, deep shame filling his heart, and then called out. 'Mam, are you there? Mam?'

He heard a chair pushed back inside the cabin. A thin voice

replied, 'Who is it there?'

Jack walked to the rough wooden door and pushed it squeakily open. 'Tis me, Mam. Your Jack. Tis your Jack.' His eyes peered into the darkness inside.

'Jack?' the voice quavered.

And then he saw her standing by a table in the middle of the cabin, a shawl over her shoulders, grey hair falling over her begrimed face; a bent, old woman.

'Oh, Mam,' he muttered quietly. 'Oh, Mam, you should have said.' He took two paces and gathered her into his arms. She had no weight to her. He could feel her bones through her clothes.

'Tis really you, Jack?'

'Aye, I'm home, Mam.'

She pulled away from him and looked up into his face. Her eyes once so strong and enquiring, were dull and rheumy. But they brightened as they gazed up at him and began misting with tears. Soon her whole body shook with sobs.

'There now, Mam. Tis all right now,' he said softly, guiding her back to the chair and helping her sit down. He pulled a second chair around the table and sat close to her holding both her hands. Her fingers were thin, the nails broken and dirty.

'Oh, Jack,' his mother kept repeating between sobs. 'Tis really you.' After a few minutes, she pulled one hand away from his, picked up a corner of the apron she was wearing, and wiped her eyes. 'You must think me a silly old woman, squealing like this,' she said, smiling tearfully at him. 'Twas the shock of you. Here was I sitting and thinking on you and your brothers – the Lord keep them – and suddenly there you were as if conjured from my dreams.'

'I know, Mam.'

'And why, haven't you changed, son? You're the build of your dad without his belly yet.' She reached out and touched his hair. 'And what's all this? Your sailor friends never said you'd white in your head.'

'They never said a lot of things, Mam, so I'm thinking,' said Jack, at that moment silently cursing Flannery and Deane for keeping the truth about his parents' condition from him.

He looked round the cabin. The chicken coops and pig pens were empty. The earthen floor was littered with dirty straw, the bed in the corner covered with stained sacking. The glass windows were so filthy that light hardly penetrated them. The peat fire was small and giving out little heat.

His mother saw the dismay growing on his face. 'Since your dad went, there's been little to live for,' she said quietly.

'But what about the money I sent? Didn't that help?'

'Did keep us alive and in the cabin for the last two years. Your dad couldn't work the fields much so we sold the chickens and the pigs gradually to keep going and pay the rent.'

'Why, in God's name, didn't you say? Why didn't you ask?'

'Your dad, his pride . . . and fearful proud of you he was until the end.'

Jack shook his head in bewilderment. 'You should have told me.'

'Oh, well, tis over now. You're home and that's the blessing. Now tell me all you've been doing.'

'No, Mam, not yet. When did you last eat?'

'The other day or so . . . yesterday, I'm thinking . . . but I'm not feeling the hunger as I used to.'

'What food have you?'

'Some lumpers and some bacon fat I was keeping for a wee treat.'

'Right then, we'll make a feast of them now. You start preparing them while I'll be building up the fire. And then when we've tidied a bit and filled our bellies we can jaw . . . but not until then.'

By the time they'd finished their meal, the cabin was glowing with heat. The flickering flames and shadows from the fire played around the cabin investing it with the kind of cosy homeliness he had always remembered. He'd brushed the floor, wiped down the windows, changed the sacking on the bed, taken the straw from under it to spread outside for the horse.

He produced a bottle of Master Felton's rum from the saddlebag, poured himself and his mother a mugful and settled back in his chair.

'Now then, Mam,' he said, stretching his legs out towards the fire. 'Tis I who'll be asking the most questions I'm reckoning.'

'How long are you staying, son?'

'For good, Mam. I've sold up in the Americas. We'll be needing the money to put this farm on its feet again. Tomorrow I'll be taking you to Listowel to buy all the provisions we'll be wanting and a few more besides. We'll be buying some animals and maybe even a good trap so that the horse can be taking you on your calls. An then I'll hire myself a man to help get the fields back from the weeds and then we'll paint . . .'

His mother held up her hands to interrupt him. 'So many plans you're having, Jack. You always were the one with plans to change the world, but tis an awful lot of money in one gobful of words.'

'Don't be worrying about the money, Mam. There be enough

177

even to make Master Jonathan Sandes pull on his boots with envy.'

His mother lowered her eyes when he mentioned Sandes' name.

'And how has the fine land agent to the mighty Sir James Watson been these years past, Mam?' he asked sarcastically.

'He hasn't harmed us. He called after your dad went and was right gracious. He was asking after you and your affairs in the Americas and saying that he'd told Father O'Mahony that the price was off your head.'

'How fine of him after so many years!' Jack's tone was bitter. 'I'll be paying a call on him soon enough to sort out the rent so I'll be giving him the thanks due, and that's the truth.'

'He's no better, no worse than the others,' his mother said. The warmth of the fire and the rum was putting the colour back into her cheeks. Her voice sounded stronger already.

'And how of Brigid Aherne? Why haven't you been mentioning her to the priest for the letters to me?'

His mother stood up and poked at the fire, sending showers of sparks into the air. 'She be in the district,' she said noncommittally.

'But how is she?'

'Like all of us, I'm guessing.'

'Does she still work for Sandes?'

'No. No more.'

'You're not saying she's off and married?' he asked anxiously.

'No. Not married. Not her.'

'Thanks be,' he said, relief flooding through him. 'Then where is she? Why won't you be telling me more?'

'She's at Gortacrossane as always and I'm thinking you should find out yourself how she is.'

'I will. I will that. As soon as we've been to Listowel for the provisions.'

They talked for hours: Jack telling her about some of his experiences in Boston; she telling him about his father's last years. Eventually, the combined effects of the fire and the rum made them both sleepy. Jack damped down the fire while his mother stumbled into her bed and then settled down on the hard-packed earth. One of his first purchases he decided would be another bed.

Jack woke early after a fitful night's sleep. He looked round the cabin in the greying light of dawn and smiled ruefully to himself. So this was the home he'd been dreaming of for so long. He rose and washed in the stingingly cold water in the butt by the front door. The sun was just peeking redly over the hills to the east, lighting the mists on the fields. For the first time since he'd left Ireland, Jack listened to the silence and felt peace; not contentment because he knew a great deal of work lay before him, but peace. This truly was the land of the saints, he thought. Harsh, unremitting, violent, yet with a deep reservoir of peace. He went back into the cabin, and then roused his mother. 'Let's away to Listowel. We'll breakfast at the inn before doing our purchasing.'

'At the inn?'

A breakfast you've not seen the likes of. You'll be needing flesh on your bones for all the work we've to be doing.'

Before they left the cabin, Jack hung up the wooden crucifix he'd taken with him to Boston, and beneath it he tucked the dried and brittle sprig of hawthorn he'd carried on his journey those many years before.

'Now doesn't that look like home again?' he said, standing back to admire his handiwork. 'They'll be in the family forever, and that's a promise.'

They arrived in Listowel as it was beginning to come to life. People looked strangely at them, the old lady high on the horse, the handsome, well-dressed man at her side. A couple of women outside a shop in Tay Lane muttered to themselves, seemingly recognizing Mary Keane and wondering about her sudden change of fortune.

At the coaching inn in the market square, Jack helped his mother down and instructed a boy to take the horse to the stables at the rear. The potman inside looked at him deferentially and then more curiously as he seated his mother at a table. She was clearly a poor woman and yet was being treated courteously by a man of means and quality.

'You have some eggs and meat?' Jack demanded.

'Tis the very finest beef, your honour, and sure aren't the eggs just dropped from the hen,' said the potman.

'Well then, we shall be having two best cuts of your beef, six eggs to lay alongside them, a loaf, and some butter,' ordered Jack. 'And a bottle or two of your best claret to wash them down.'

'Indeed, sir. Oh, indeed, sir. As quick as the cook can prepare them.'

'Tis a lively man you are.' Jack took a sovereign from his pocket and placed it on the counter. 'And be taking the care of my horse out back from the change.'

The potman sprang into action around Jack like a moth near a flame. 'And have you been coming far, your honour?'

Jack smiled into his face. 'Me mam and I have just ridden in from our cabin at Drombeg and mortal hungry we are.'

The potman's face fell. 'From Drombeg, sir? Tis I was thinking I was knowing most people hereabouts, but I cannot be recalling serving you before.'

'You might have a way back but I'm thinking you would have known me dad, Joe Keane.'

'Joe Keane, the fighting man who went this springtime, God rest him?'

'The very same.'

'Well, bless me, sir, then you must be Jack Keane from the Americas.'

'Fresh back yesterday.'

The potman almost danced with delight. 'And isn't that the news then? Isn't that just the news? The town will really be on its ear about this, and that's the truth.'

After the meal, Jack escorted his mother around the shops to order provisions and the materials he would need to transform the cabin: timber and nails, whitewash and brushes. He haggled with some drovers who had brought cows, pigs and chickens into the market square on the chance of a sale and eventually selected the livestock he wanted. The drovers were only too happy to promise to bring the animals to Drombeg when they realized he was ready to pay hard cash. Everywhere Jack and his mother went, they received curious glances and whenever he turned there seemed to be a crowd of people watching him, virtually following from shop to shop. But their innate sense of courtesy prevented them from approaching and asking all the questions they were bursting to put. Indeed, so intense was the scrutiny that Jack was glad to finish his buying and return to the coaching inn to collect the horse for the journey home.

'And is it really yourself then, Jack Keane?' a voice calld from outside the inn as he led the horse from the stables and into the bustle of the market square. He instantly recognized the barrel-chested man advancing towards him. There could be no mistaking the scars on his face.

'Quillinan! Paddy Quillinan!' Jack shouted.

'Aye, tis so, but the truth is I wouldn't be recognizing you, Jack, if it hadn't been for the prattling potman in the inn here.'

The two men embraced, slapping each other on the back, and then stood apart, delight on their faces.

'You're back for good?'

'Aye.'

'Then we must talk. There's much to tell . . .'

'You're right, Paddy, but not now. Me mam . . .' Jack gestured up at his mother who was holding tightly on to the pommel of the saddle at the same time as balancing two sacks full of provisions.

'And wasn't I forgetting?' said Quillinan. 'You must be a mighty happy woman this day, Mistress Keane.'

'That I am, Master Quillinan. That I am.'

'Let me walk with you, Jack. Give me down those sacks, mistress. Does seem you're having enough to do staying on this fine animal.'

'But tis out of your way, Paddy,' Jack protested.

'Sure and I'd be walking home through Galway today just to have a jaw with you. You cannot be imagining how glad I am to see you. The Keanes have been weighing mighty heavy on my mind these last years.'

As they made their way out of Listowel, Quillinan chattered excitedly away. 'And sure you should have returned years back,' he said. 'The Whiteboys have all but disbanded. Things are awful quiet in these parts nowadays. Isn't that so, Mistress?'

'Father O'Sullivan, the saints preserve him, saw to that, Master Quillinan.'

'He did that, mistress. He did us more harm than any of the soldier boys.'

'More harm, Paddy?'

'Aye, Jack. After your John died and you left for the Americas, he preached stronger than ever against us and raised petitions all over the district. The people were awful hurt by what happened to your brothers. And to tell the truth, the association lost a deal of its heart for the fight what with the people turning against us.'

'So Sandes and his like won again, Paddy,' said Jack bitterly. 'Michael and John died for nothing, eh?'

'Oh, no, Jack,' Quillinan tried to reassure him. 'The days of the bad landlords are numbered what with Daniel O'Connell winning support everywhere for the repeal of the Union. Your brothers were martyrs to the cause, so they were.'

'O'Connell? I heard some tell of him in Boston town.'

'He's the man we follow now. Didn't we give him a powerful welcome when he came to Listowel a few years back. He'll be getting us our rights through the Parliament, just you see.'

'Tis true, Jack,' his mother interrupted. 'As the Father said before he was taken, your brothers and the other martyrs before them had to die to get the politicians talking. Master O'Connell will be getting us our dues.'

'We'll see, Mam. I'm just hoping your man O'Connell isn't just all words. Spinners of words and dreamers is what this politician in Boston thought of us Irishers. We fight one minute and talk the next as though no blood had been spilt. Talking and fighting and dreaming, that's us. Now isn't that the truth of it?'

'And is that bad?' Quillinan said, recognizing the cynicism in Jack's word 'Isn't that the way it has always been?'

'And will always be, eh, Paddy?' said Jack. Before he'd fled the district he'd always reckoned Quillinan as the fount of all wisdom. Now he saw him as a man of simple beliefs, ready to fight or not to fight, ready to listen or not to listen, according to what the people around him believed. He remembered Daniel Proudlane's strictures about those who shaped the world and those who were shaped. Quillinan was undoubtedly not a shaper. And as he realized that, Jack felt guilty about his patronizing re-assessment. He gripped Quillinan's shoulder and smiled at him. 'Daniel O'Connell is sure to succeed with men like you behind him, Paddy.'

'Aye, tis true, Jack,' said Quillinan, visibly brightening. 'We'll be ruling ourselves and worshipping how we choose without any interference from the English, when O'Connell has his way.'

'But until then, Paddy, tis a powerful amount of work I've to do to set the cabin and the fields properly as they should be . . .'

'I'll help, so I will, Jack. And so will the rest of the boys.'

'That's what I was wanting to hear.'

Jack pointed to the family cabin as they approached it. 'Me mam's cabin needs a new thatch, some paint, the walls want rebuilding . . . and won't I be paying a fair wage for the labour as well?'

'There's no need for that, Jack.'

'No, Paddy. I can't ask you to neglect your own fields without payment. And twill be a way of sharing my good fortune with my old friends. And then there'll be the building of my own cabin for Brigid and . . .'

'Brigid?'

'Brigid Aherne. Don't you remember her, Paddy? Now I've my fortune and she's stopped working for Sandes, we'll marry.'

He noticed Quillinan look quizzically up at his mother. She shook her head slightly.

'What's this between you?' he asked. 'Me mam's close-mouthed about her and here's you seeming to have forgotten her.'

'Tis nothing, Jack,' said Quillinan hastily. 'Have you seen her since coming back?'

'No, not yet. When we've stowed the provisions at the cabin I'll be riding over to Gortacrossane to pay a call.'

'Things change, Jack,' said Quillinan quietly. 'Now let's be setting these provisions down. Where will you be wanting them?'

After Quillinan had left, Jack built up the fire before telling his mother he was leaving for Gortacrossane.

'So be it, son,' she sighed wearily. 'I'll be waiting for your return.'

If anything, Gortacrossane looked more miserable and poverty-stricken than Drombeg. Most of the cabins had gaping holes in their thatches. A few people were working in the fields but many more were simply sitting, shoulders hunched outside their cabins, smoking stubs of pipes and gossiping. Their clothes were ragged – their faces smeared with dirt, their expressions sullen and uncaring. There was an air of despondency; a feeling everywhere of listlessness and acceptance of defeat. Jack dismounted outside the Aherne cabin and called inside.

'Is anyone there?'

He heard the chatter of children and then a man he didn't recognize came to the cabin entrance. He looked at Jack's clothes, his boots and then at the horse.

'If you're from Master Sandes, you can be telling him there's no more rent to be squeezed from here,' the man said defiantly. Jack judged him to be in his early thirties but he was bent and thin; older, much older than his years.

'Rent? Master Sandes?' Jack replied, a sinking feeling beginning to grip his heart. 'Why say you this?'

'You're from Sandes, aren't you? And wasn't I telling that divil Finn Bowler he'll have to be waiting for the money or else be putting us in the ditch along with five wee ones.'

'No, not from Sandes or his man Bowler . . . '

'Well, what do you be wanting?'

'Brigid Aherne. This is the Aherne cabin?'

'Was . . . was their cabin until the typhoid took them nigh on six years ago. Now it's mine for all the good it does.'

'But I was told Brigid Aherne lived in the townland.'

'That she does, your honour, but not here. The cabin on the outskirts is hers.' He pointed in the direction of Listowel. 'Just keep heading that way and tis the last cabin before the fields.'

Jack felt in his pocket for a coin.

'Here. Take this for your trouble,' he said, handing the man a shilling piece.

The man held the coin up before his eyes as if disbelieving his fortune. Then he bent in mockery of a bow. His thin features twisted into an obsequious smile. He put a knuckle to his forehead. 'Bless you, your honour, for your charity,' he muttered.

The cabin to which he was directed was simply four stone walls with a small amount of thatching over one corner to protect its interior from the weather. Jack felt as if he was living in a nightmare. Surely no one could live here? Surely not his Brigid?'

'Brigid,' he called. 'Brigid Aherne. Is it you there?'

A woman's muffled voice came from beneath the thatch.

'Who be wanting her?'

'Jack Keane. Your friend Jack.'

'Jack Keane? Is it you there?'

'Brigid?'

'Wait a moment,' said the voice, excited now. Jack heard sounds of movement before a shawled head peered round the doorway.

'Jack?'

He looked into the face, framed by the dark red shawl. The skin was stretched tight over high cheekbones, the green eyes seemed hugely luminous, ringed with dark lines of fatigue. Jack jumped down from the horse and walked slowly up to her as she moved fully into the doorway. He saw that her brown skirt was torn and ragged and stained; her feet bare and dirty. He gazed into her eyes so deeply green, and knew that he had found her.

'Brigid,' he said softly, holding open his arms. 'Oh, Brigid.'

She hesitated for a moment and then ran towards him. She threw her arms around his neck. He lifted her up, feeling how light she was, and whirled her round before putting her carefully to the ground again.

'Tis you, Brigid.'

'Aye, tis me, Jack Keane.'

He held her at arm's length. 'And how, in God's name, did you come to this?'

She moved close to him, burying her head in his chest. 'You were away a long time, Jack,' she whispered. 'An awful long time.'

He looked over her shoulders and saw a small child, no more than three years old, standing in the doorway. The child, a boy, by the cut of his jet black hair, sucked his thumb as he looked curiously at them. He was dressed in sacking with a piece of string pulling in the waist. Jack watched the child toddle forward on thin, stick-like legs and tug at Brigid's skirt.

'Mam,' the child sniffled. 'Mam, I'm cold.'

Brigid bent down and picked him up, tucking his head under her shawl. 'Hush, babbie,' she murmured. 'Hush, avourneen.'

She kept her eyes averted from Jack as she comforted the child. Then she stared directly into his face.

Jack nodded at the child snuggling against her for warmth. She shrugged her shoulders and smiled ruefully.

'You can't keep a babbie secret, Jack Keane. Tis mine. You're right, tis mine.'

He began to speak but she interrupted him fiercely. 'He's mine and no one else's. One day perhaps you'll be knowing more but not now . . . not now, Jack. Please.'

'His name, Brigid?' asked Jack softly, reaching out to brush the child's soft cheek.

'Matt. Matt Aherne. That's all.'

'A fine boy.'

'He is that. Aren't you then?' She smiled down at the child in her arms. 'They say he has my looks.'

'Your family? The girls? Your mother?' Jack said, still speaking softly, standing close to Brigid.

'Gone. Dead.'

'All of them from the typhoid?'

'Aye. You heard tell then?'

'Just now . . . from a man at the old cabin.'

'And was he telling you else about me?' she asked slyly.

'No. that's all.'

Brigid sighed. 'Well then, you're knowing most of what you should know.'

'How, Brigid?'

'I said not now, Jack.'

'No, not that. I meant how do you manage, the two of you in this place?'

'We have a small fire and each other to keep the other warm.'

'But food?'

'What the Cooleens give me . . . what I scratch from the fields when no one is watching.'

'But why didn't you go to my people?'

'With you away and them Mulvihills? The Cooleen men wouldn't have helped me then.'

Jack raised his arms and looked to the sky in a hopeless gesture. 'Cooleens . . . Mulvihills . . . and you near starving with a child in this . . . this . . . this hovel. Tis true, we're a race of madmen.'

'Jack?'

'Oh, it matters not now. The main thing is to get you away to

185

warmth and shelter.'

'And where might that be? I heard tell of your fortune in the Americas but are you a magician as well?'

'Gather whatever you have. Matt and you are coming home with me.'

'But . . .'

'But nothing. There's me mam to care for and now you two. You can all be putting flesh on your bones and some warmth in your bellies together.'

Brigid looked up at the low, grey sky, sniffing the approaching bitterness of winter in the air, and shook her head reluctantly.

'I'm not sure you know what you are asking, Jack. The Cooleen men have been good in their way to me. They won't be liking me taking Mulvihill protection.'

'Think on the child here. He's as skinny faced as a gombeen man when his money's due. And, anyway, weren't you spoken for before I had to flee to Boston town? You have no one to care for you but me. Can't you be seeing that?'

She hugged the child closer to her. Jack could see that beneath the shawl she wore a rough blouse made of the same sort of sacking that covered the toddler. He remembered suddenly the bright-coloured blouses that Brigid used to wear. He put his hand on her shoulder thinking that she was still beautiful, even as thin and worn as she was now.

Brigid bent her head. 'For the babbie, then, Jack. I'll come with you; not for meself but for the babbie. You hold him while I gather a bundle together.'

'I'll help.'

'No. You stay out here and mind the babbie,' Brigid said firmly, pushing Matt into his arms. He unbuttoned his top coat and wrapped it around the child to give him some warmth. Matt Aherne had his mother's green eyes.

In a few minutes, Brigid came out of the cabin dragging a sack behind her.

'You ride on the horse with Matt,' said Jack. 'I'll carry the sack.' He lifted her into the saddle and handed the child up to her. Brigid smiled down at him.

'Not what you were expecting, eh?' she said quietly.

Jack shook his head. 'Twould have been better if someone had warned me. But what's done is done.'

'And that's the truth, dear Jack.'

'Me mam'll have a shock, so I'm thinking.'

'I doubt that if you're meaning the babbie. The district's fallen woman, that I am, and well known for being so. But I've prayed to the Virgin and can find little shame in my heart for what happened.'

Brigid began protesting when she realized that Jack was leading the horse back through Gortacrossane.

'For pity's sake, don't be passing the cabins. They'll be anger enough when it's discovered I've gone with you. Don't be flaunting it in the Cooleen faces.'

Jack shrugged. 'So be it, woman. We'll take the long way round the townland though I'm thinking the sooner everyone knows the matter, the sooner we can settle it.'

'Time enough then, I say.'

'As you like, woman.'

'You've changed in the years, Jack,' Brigid remarked as they skirted the cabins and headed for Drombeg.

'Changed? And haven't we all?'

'Not the lines on my face or your white hairs, silly . . . '

' . . . lummock, you used to say,' Jack interrupted. 'Remember?'

'Only too well. But I cannot be calling you that now. The years have made you a fine man, that they have.'

'There have been many things to forget in those years,' Jack replied, looking back at her over his shoulder as he plodded along in front of the horse.

'For both of us, I'm thinking. But when I wanted to forget, I always thought on us in that summer we had.'

'We'll have others, Brigid.'

'Perhaps so. Perhaps not. You can't go back in time, though. If me mam hadn't forced me into service . . . if you hadn't gone with the Whiteboys . . . '

Jack stopped the horse. 'You're talking with melancholy, Brigid Aherne,' he said sternly. 'Be forgetting the things that have hurt us both. There's a deal in the past that was fine and warm and worth thinking on, and there's more in the future that'll be the same. Think on that.'

Brigid paused for a moment before replying. 'Pray it be so,' she said quietly. 'Pray that it be so, Jack, but in the Americas you made your future in a place which had one. You forget that here there's none for the likes of me, or for the likes of you as you were.'

'Well, I changed my future, then,' Jack grunted. 'And I'll be changing yours if you stop being so gloomy.'

'And sure and divil you will,' Brigid laughed. 'Jack Keane, you always had your dreams.'

They travelled on in silence, both locked in their own thoughts, until the cabin at Drombeg came into sight. By now the light was leaving the sky with early evening settling over the fields, painting them and everything around them with greyness.

'Oh, Jack,' Brigid cried suddenly when they were less than fifty yards from the cabin. 'I'm scared, Jack. Take me back for God's sake.'

'Don't be so silly,' he said shortly. 'You can't be going back ever again.'

'But your mam, Jack . . . what'll she say?'

'A mighty lot if I'm knowing her. But nothing that should be worrying you.'

He tied the horse outside the cabin and lifted Brigid and her child down from the saddle. The cabin door squeaked open and his mother stood watching them, framed in candlelight and the rosiness of the peat fire. Brigid hung back until Jack put his arm round her shoulders. They walked forward towards his mother. She didn't move from the doorway. Her face was without expression.

'Mam,' Jack said in a quiet, firm voice. 'We're back.'

His mother looked at Brigid for a moment and then her mouth softened. She smiled as she saw Matt's head peeping out from under the shawl. 'Twill be good to have a child in the cabin again,' she murmured. She stood aside to let them enter the warmth. As Brigid passed her, her eyes fixed firmly on the floor, Jack's mother leaned forward and kisssed her on the cheek. 'Welcome, again, Brigid Aherne,' she whispered.

'We're cold and we're hungry, Mam,' Jack said, suddenly embarrassed, not quite knowing how to fend off what he thought would be the inevitable questions.

'Well, be warming yourselves. There's lumpers and bacon for your meal. Plenty for all, I'm thinking,' said his mother.

'I'm sorry, Mistress Keane . . . ' Brigid began.

'Hush, girl. And wasn't I expecting you all along? I knew Jack would be bringing you. My son wouldn't be leaving you where you were. And no more of this Mistress Keane, if you please, Brigid Aherne. In this cabin, I'm mam and that's all. And let's be looking at the babbie then.'

Brigid handed Matt to her. Jack's mother felt his bare legs as she pressed him close.

'So thin and cold, you wee man. But we'll be feeding you up now, just you see. You'll be as big as your dad in no time.' Then she realized what she'd said. 'I'm sorry, Brigid. Sorry . . . ' she stumbled. 'An old woman's tongue . . .'

Brigid smiled gently. 'No need to be sorry, Mam. In time he'll know his dad and so will you all. But as I said to Jack . . . not now, please.'

'In the district there's tell . . .'

'I know,' Brigid said wearily. 'There's tell . . . if you're believing all the tell then every man's his dad, particularly every Cooleen man.'

She sat down heavily in one of the chairs at the table and sunk her head into her arms. Her back began heaving with sobs.

'Hush, child,' said Jack's mother. 'I said I was sorry. I'll not be mentioning . . .'

Brigid raised her tear-stained face. 'Tis not that, Mam. Not that. Tis not that. Tis Jack. Why didn't you tell him I was the Cooleen woman?'

'I knew you were Cooleen . . .' Jack broke in.

'Yes, you knew that,' Brigid said bitterly. 'But you didn't know how they took payment for all their kindnesses to me, did you?' Her voice rose shrilly. 'I'm the Cooleen whore. That's what. When they want a woman they come to me. Any Cooleen. Any time. Just for a penny, or a lumper. Anything. Didn't matter. Anything to keep alive.' She looked pleadingly at him. 'Don't you understand. There was nothing else to give. That's why you should have left me where I was. Don't you see?'

Jack sat down in the chair next to her. He put out his hand and cupped her wet cheek, smoothing the tears away with his thumb. His whirling thoughts went back to Meg Griffiths and all the girls he'd known in Boston; all the girls who'd nothing to sell but themselves. He remembered their compassion and how much he owed them.

'Brigid,' he started. 'Brigid, I understand. I do, truly. As I said before, be forgetting the past. Think on the future.'

He heard his mother sniff and stifle a sob behind him. 'Now look on this,' he said. 'All the women sobbing away and I'm back only a day.'

Brigid smiled at him through her tears.

'That's right, mavourneen. Smile. You're here and that's all that matters. You're to stay here for as long as you like. Perhaps for always. But that's to be your choice. Not mine. I've made mine.'

# Chapter 13 June, 1834

Hundreds of small fires built from driftwood spattered and crackled their glowing sparks into the warm summer night among the dunes. At both ends of the wide beach at Ballyeagh, a few miles south of Ballybunnion on the coast of Kerry, the fires danced their reflections and shadows on to the faces of more than two thousand people who had built makeshift shelters along the beach to protect themselves from the chill that would come in the night. Here and there, the tune from a fiddle rose above the sibilant slapping of water on the sands. A shriek of laughter punctuated the low murmur of conversation climbing into the clear sky pricked with stars. Occasionally, people camped at one end of the beach would glance at the fires burning at the other end, make a remark to their companions and another burst of ribald laughter would be heard. But there was little hilarity in the buzz of talk along the beach, a definite tension reached into the darkness dividing the two camps.

'And aren't you feeling honoured, mavourneen, that all these people have come here because of you?' Jack Keane asked Brigid Aherne jokingly as they lay in the soft sand and looked across the beach.

'Honoured? More like mortal scared . . . so many of them. Where have they all come from?' said Brigid, leaning up on one elbow and trying to count the number of fires. 'Oh, they're too many even to guess at.'

'Well, this had been a long time arranging so I'm thinking the word reached out to every faction man in the west.'

Brigid touched his hand. 'Couldn't we just be stealing away now, the two of us?'

Jack laughed, reaching out to ruffle her shining hair. 'Tis a bit late for that. You were the one saying we should try to make everything proper. And didn't I do just that? Didn't I jaw with your Cooleens till me teeth near dropped out? And now you're mortal scared . . . women!'

190

The first approach from the Cooleens had come only two weeks after Brigid and Matt Aherne had moved into the cabin at Drombeg. Jack and Paddy Quillinan had been working in the fields, restoring the dry-stone walls, when they had been hailed from the nearby track by a man seated on a donkey.

'Is Jack Keane there?' the man shouted.

Jack waved and walked over to him. Paddy followed on a few yards behind.

'You're calling my name?'

'A fine day, Master Keane, is it not, thanks be to God.'

'It is that,' Jack replied, wiping his forearm across the sweat on his brow. 'And who might be calling here?'

'Flaherty's the name. Sean Flaherty . . . '

'Well, welcome . . . '

' . . . from Gortacrossane, and from the Cooleen men.'

Quillinan advanced menacingly on the man. 'I'll crack him one, Jack, and send him back asleep on the donkey.'

The man began pulling the animal's head around, ready to try to make his escape.

'Whoa there, Sean Flaherty. No need to be hurrying off. Leave him be, Paddy. I expected a call from the Cooleen men sooner or later.'

Flaherty smiled with relief. He dismounted from the donkey and led it up to the wall. He was a tall man, as big as Jack, with curly hair flapping from under a battered felt hat.

'You're a wise man, Master Keane. There be no need for unpleasantness between us,' he said with a grin that displayed a mouthful of broken, blackened teeth. 'There's talk we must have about Brigid Aherne.'

Jack heaved a sigh.

'The Cooleen men have sent me here in great respect,' said Flaherty. 'They knew your dad well, Jack Keane, many of them to their personal cost.' He laughed shortly. 'And haven't I felt the weight of his stick meself? A fighting man so he was, a credit to any faction. And we be knowing of your history as well how you suffered under the soldier boys; how you made your fortune in the Americas and then returned here to care for your mam. 'Tis a fine man you are, Master Keane, but the Cooleen men are thinking you're forgetting the ways of the factions during your travels.'

'I did that, thanks be,' Jack grunted. 'Go on.'

'Well, the Cooleens cared for Brigid Aherne out of memory for her dad when she was alone and with child. Without our protection, she and the babbie would have been frozen in a ditch these winters past.'

'You call it protection to keep her in a hovel and treat her as your whore?' Jack said bitterly. 'Is that your protection?'

'Twas more than the Mulvihills offered. Twas more than you could offer, Master Keane,' Flaherty replied with a disarming smile. 'Now isn't that the truth of the matter'

'That's not fair,' Quillinan protested. 'Jack was away . . . '

'Fair or not,' Flaherty continued, 'tis a fact that only the Cooleens helped. We're as poor as anyone else in the district. We couldn't be offering much but the fact is they survived in their fashion, so they did. And then Master Keane here comes tripping back from the Americas, ordering banquets at the inn, buying animals from every drover in sight and, without a by your leave, takes it upon himself to carry this Cooleen woman away. Can't you be imagining how the men feel? To tell the truth, they're mighty angry with you, Master Keane. They're wanting some satisfaction.'

'Satisfaction, Flaherty?' asked Jack. 'What sort of satisfaction?'

''Tis the Cooleen men are wanting her back,' said Flaherty quietly. 'And they're demanding an acknowledgement from you that you did them wrong. That's the message I'm bringing, so I am.'

Jack stared at him for a moment. Truly, he thought, I've forgotten the ways of Ireland where men barter over a woman as if she was prize livestock.

'Sean Flaherty,' he said in an icy voice. 'I'll talk to you if it's a matter of paying you money for all the troubles you've taken over Brigid and I'll talk to you in the proper old way about arranging a marriage but you can go to the divil if you ever expect me to return her to being your whore.'

Flaherty tried to deflect Jack's obvious anger. 'Master Keane, your views come as no surprise to me, no surprise at all,' he said in a conciliatory tone. 'I'm only the message boy but I can be telling you the Cooleens, out of respect for you and your family, are willing to talk to your man about any arrangements you may be offering. Tis the custom after all and the Cooleens are not denying that.'

'Quillinan here will talk for me,' said Jack. 'You be telling him where and when and he'll do the talking.'

'Twill be as you say, Master Keane,' Flaherty replied, rising to his feet. 'I'll bid you good day and thank you. But may I be reminding you that under the custom you should tell Brigid Aherne of what's being proposed.'

'Aye,' Jack agreed. ''Tis the custom and she's the right to know.'

That night after they'd finished their supper Jack told Brigid and his mother of his talk with the Cooleen messenger. Neither of them expressed the slightest surprise at the news.

'I told you there'd be trouble, Jack,' said Brigid. 'Wasn't I telling Mam the very same only this day?'

'Why trouble, mavourneen? They simply want to talk. I'll pay them some money for their trouble, call it a wedding dowry if you must, and that'll be the end of the matter.'

'I doubt that,' his mother said, now almost her bustling self again after a fortnight of proper food and warmth. 'Your dad always said the Cooleens needed little enough excuse to call for a fight and here they are thinking they've every reason in the world now.'

'You're right, Mam,' Brigid echoed. 'That's just what they'll be wanting . . . a fight. They've had little enough cause for years past so they're losing a deal of support whenever they've sent out the word for their men to be joining in some head-whacking.'

'You women are always seeing the dark side of the moon,' Jack laughed. 'We'll go through the old customs about a marriage, sweeten them with a handful of gold, and that'll be that, so it will. It'll all seem different in the morning,' he continued as he got up from his chair and began setting up a curtain of sacking to divide the cabin. 'Young Matt there's got the proper notion, bless him,' he said, gesturing at the child asleep in Brigid's arms. She rose slowly and carried Matt over to Jack's sea chest, which now doubled as his cot.

From her first night at the cabin, Brigid had shared the bed with Jack's mother while he had to content himself with a pile of straw as a resting place. But, within a few days, the bed he'd ordered in Listowel had arrived and been placed in the further corner. As he'd lain back comfortably during his first night for weeks in a bed, the sacking had whispered apart and Brigid had slipped into his half of the cabin. She stood by the side of his bed for a moment looking down at him, her black hair, grown long, hanging down over a well patched shift she'd been given by Jack's mother. He smiled up at her and lifted the covers as he moved over in the bed. Brigid put a finger to her lips as she clambered in beside him.

'No noise,' she whispered. 'Mam's fast asleep and we wouldn't be wanting to wake her.' He felt her breath against his cheek. They snuggled against each other. Jack could feel every outline of her body against him through the thin material of the shift. He shivered as an overwhelming tenderness flooded through him.

'Are we cold?' Brigid murmured, a giggle in her voice. 'Well, I'll warm you but no more till the priest has said his words. It must be proper between us, don't you see that?'

'Aye, mavourneen,' Jack replied, disappointed and pleased at the same time. 'I want you awful bad but let it be in the marriage bed. Then we can truly make a fresh start, both of us.'

'Not that fresh,' Brigid said softly. 'I want to know what sort of man I'm getting, and isn't that my proper due?' Her hand slipped under his long shirt and began caressing his strong body. They lingered, wondering, over the scars on his back and along his ribs and then moved lower to stroke and grasp his stiffening nakedness. He twitched as she touched him and they smiled broadly at each other in the darkness. There was a confidence between them now that the pact had been sealed, a confidence born out of experience and their mutual desire to give pleasure to each other. His hands caressed the smoothness of her back and played around her buttocks. They kissed deeply and soon the silence of the cabin was broken by their low sighs and moans.

Suddenly, Brigid pushed her hands flat against his chest. 'No more, Jack. No more, avourneen,' she panted against his mouth. 'Else our resolutions will have vanished as soon as we are making them.' She kissed him once more before she returned to the other bed behind the sacking.

She came to him most nights but now they knew how far to allow their love-making to go. The joked sometimes with each other about their frustrations when his mother was out of earshot, but both agreed that the final consummation of their love should wait until all the obstacles to marriage had been removed.

In the meantime, Quillinan had a series of meetings with the Cooleen leaders. He put to them Jack's proposals but they remained adamant that Jack should acknowledge publicly that he'd offended against the unwritten code of the factions.

'I won't do it,' Jack declared. 'They won't be getting that humbling from me, and that's my final word, Paddy. They know I did no wrong except to show everyone their shame at the way they'd been treating Brigid. That's what hurts them, and so it should.'

The negotiations were virtually suspended for the winter since neither party was willing to travel far in the biting weather. Jack spent the months transforming the cabin at Drombeg into one of the cosiest and neatest for miles around. He built a small, thatched stable on to the side where all the livestock wintered together, and employed a carpenter to lay a wooden floor in the cabin. The women, now restored to full health and vigour, busied themselves making pretty curtains and colourful bedspreads and soon the cabin's interior was as bright and attractive as the outside. When the warmth of an early spring came to the district, the Cooleens agreed reluctantly to a formal meeting where a marriage contract could be considered.

Brigid dressed herself in the new clothes Jack had bought her for the meeting at the cabin of one of the Cooleen leaders, Thomas Sheehan.

'Tis not too dazzling for them?' she asked nervously as she twirled around in front of Jack and his mother to show off the deep red skirt and the lace-edged white petticoat underneath.

'Oh, tis lovely, sweet one,' breathed Jack's mother.

'They'll think you a princess from the little people, so they will,' Jack smiled. 'They won't be daring to refuse you anything.'

'Would that my head told me what my heart was wanting to hear,' Brigid replied with a wry grin.

Some of her fears vanished when Jack, Quillinan, and herself arrived at the Sheehan cabin. They were greeted outside with solemn courtesy and respect by Sean Flaherty. He, too, was clearly dressed in his best clothes. His eyes widened as he saw Jack help Brigid down from the horse. Her skin shone with health. Her eyes were bright and clear. Her round face was framed by gleaming black hair. Flaherty could hardly recognize the bedraggled, half-starved woman he'd known only a few months before.

Inside the cabin, they were met by three other Cooleen leaders who offered them each a mug of poteen. After the introductions, Sheehan a small, wizened man past middle age, invited Quillinan and Jack to sit at the table.

'As is the custom, the woman being the subject of the meeting will wait outside with those who are not the principals,' he announced firmly. 'The door will be left open so she can hear the matters discussed but she is not to be present.'

Jack glanced at Quillinan. 'Paddy will wait outside with you, Brigid,' he said.

'Suspicious, Master Keane?' asked Sheehan. 'Fearing a trick, are you?'

'No, Master Sheehan. The poor girl's nervous as it is. Can't you be seeing that? She'll be happier with Paddy here to keep her company.' Jack lied with little conviction. The fact was that he feared the Cooleens might try to abduct Brigid if the negotiations proved unsuccessful.

When the cabin had been cleared, Jack sat down at the table

195

opposite Sheehan and Flaherty.

'Well, let's be beginning this custom of yours,' he said curtly.

''Tis your custom as well, Master Keane. Be remembering that,' Sheehan replied.

'Was my custom, perhaps. But I find it distasteful now, mighty distasteful.'

'The tell is you're finding many things distasteful about the old customs since your returning from the Americas,' Flaherty said.

'You know my feelings well enough, but still I'm here at this meeting to dicuss the marriage, aren't I?'

'Not only a marriage,' Sheehan broke in. 'There's also the matter of stealing this Cooleen woman away from her people who'd been giving her their best protection . . . '

'Protection!' Jack snorted.

'Protection,' Sheehan repeated. 'The best that could be afforded. So before any marriage contract can be arranged, there has to be an acknowledgement of the wrong else the Cooleens will have lost a deal of face.'

'That cannot be,' said Jack, crossing his arms across his chest and leaning back in the chair. 'I'll recompense the Cooleens . . . '

'How much?' Flaherty asked eagerly.

'Twenty sovereigns.'

Sheehan's eyes narrowed. 'An awful amount of money, Master Keane,' he muttered. 'An awful amount . . . '

''Tis on the table if you're wanting it.'

'We could be saying it was payment for the wrong caused?' Flaherty asked tentatively.

'You can call it what you want but I'm calling it a repayment for the protection you say you gave to Brigid. Twill settle all debts.'

'And an acknowledgement of the wrong to the Cooleens?' Sheehan pressed, mistakenly believing that Jack was weakening.

'To the divil with an acknowledgement,' Jack said fiercely. 'I made that clear to Flaherty. There'll be no acknowledgement from me and each time you be mentioning it I'm thinking I'll reduce my offer by one sovereign.'

'You're a hard man,' said Flaherty loath to lose the offer of such money. 'A hard man, just like your dad.'

'And as pig-headed as him as well,' Sheehan added angrily. 'You have little rights in this matter at all. Brigid Aherne is Cooleen and is beholden to us. After Tom Aherne died tis we helped the family; when her mother and sisters were taken, we paid for their burial; when Brigid was with child, our women delivered her; when she was

196

starving, we gave her the means of surviving; when she was shunned by all the district for having a babbie with no husband, we gave her companionship . . . '

'Companionship?' Jack's anger was showing in his face now. 'You used her as a whore.'

'She didn't have to accept the men who called. There was no force, believe me Keane, and . . . '

'And no choice either. You sicken me. She's a grown woman. She belongs to no one but herself. Not to me and certainly not to the Cooleens. She is herself, not the chattel of one faction or the other.'

Sheehan jumped to his feet, sending his chair clattering to the floor. 'By the saints, tis enough,' he shouted, almost hopping with rage. 'You're piling insult upon insult, Keane. There'll be no marriage here blessed by the Cooleens, and that's my word. You've wronged us; you're tried to buy off our rightful grievance with your American gold; and now you abuse us. Tis enough, I say.'

'But the money, Mick . . . the money,' Flaherty interrupted.

'To the divil with the money, Sean. We'll be taking our satisfaction in a fight, so we will.'

Jack began to laugh as he realized that Brigid and his mother had been correct all the time. The formal meeting, short as it had been, was nothing more than a sham. The Cooleens had never had any intention of settling the matter peaceably.

His amusement enraged the Cooleen leader even more. Sheehan banged the table with his hand. 'In my cabin, he insults us . . . ' he sputtered. He leaned across the table, fists raised, face distorted with anger. Jack pushed out his arm and shoved Sheehan gently, almost lazily, away from the table. The small man stumbled back, caught his legs in the upturned chair behind him, and, with a howl of surprised rage, fell heavily on the floor. As Flaherty went to help his leader, Jack rose from the table and was at the door in three strides.

Quillinan, already alerted by the shouting and clattering, had pulled Brigid away from the two Cooleens who were now peering anxiously into the cabin. Jack shouldered his way past them, quickly lifted Brigid up on to the horse and began leading it away at a jog.

'You watch the rear, Paddy,' he called. 'They're awful upset, those Cooleens. They might be wanting to start the fight here and now.'

He glanced up at Brigid. 'And don't you be saying you told me so, mavourneen.'

'There'll be a fight?' she asked.

'I'm guessing so.'

Angry shouts pursued them until they were about a hundred yards away but the Cooleens made no attempt to follow. Jack slowed the horse down to a walk and turned towards Drombeg.

'What happens now, Paddy?'

'A proper challenge to the Mulvihills,' Quillinan replied shortly. He was still slightly puffed by their hasty retreat.

'How long?'

'Oh, it'll be taking some weeks to arrange. All the factions will have to be told. They won't be waiting for the Tralee Fair so I'm thinking they'll want it to be at the Ballyeagh Races.'

'And will we be having enough people?'

'What with the boys from the association who'll be supporting you, I'd say more than a thousand.'

Jack whistled through his teeth. 'A thousand? That's a terrible lot, Paddy, just for a cudgel fight.'

'Not with the Cooleens as angry as they are. They'll muster all they can and that'll be not much less than a thousand, perhaps even more. Tis an important matter of face this.'

'As everyone keeps saying . . . '

'What'll be the outcome of it all?' Brigid said, anxiety clearly in her voice.

'The Mulvihills will pulp them as usual,' Jack said confidently. 'And that'll be the last we'll be hearing from the Cooleens about you.'

'But what if they win?'

'Don't be worrying your pretty head, mavourneen. In the case of that miracle, we'll still be together even if I have to be taking the pistols out of their holsters for a while to show I really mean to keep you. The fight is all about face, as Paddy says. Tis ridiculous, but then wasn't it ever so?'

He had no reason to change that opinion, Jack reflected, as he looked down on the gathering of the factions at Ballyeagh. All these people, he thought, had travelled miles from all over Kerry to hammer at each other with shillelaghs. At least three quarters of them, he reckoned would not know the fine points of the dispute that had brought them there to huddle round their camp fires. They had simply answered their traditional rallying call like so many sheep.

Jack lay back on the sand, hands behind his head, and gazed up at the stars. Brigid leaned over and kissed him softly on the lips. 'Tis I remember, mavourneen, a time when I looked at the stars long ago and a sailor friend of mine said he wondered if there were people up there looking back down at us. Twas long ago but I've never forgotten that.'

'And what would they be thinking, those wee people up in the stars?'

'I'm thinking they'd be mighty puzzled.'

Brigid kissed him again, more deeply, her tongue slipping between his lips.

'Does make me feel embarrassed thinking they might be watching us,' she whispered against his ear. 'But at least tonight we won't be having to worry about mam hearing us.'

He reached up and gripped her shoulders.

'And what would you be saying?' he grinned. 'Don't be forgetting our pact, you hussy.'

'I will if you will, avourneen,' she murmured. 'You've said that whatever happens tomorrow we'll be wed soon. It's an awful wasting of time.'

They stared at each other for a long moment, smiling gently. Without a word, they crawled into the small tent rigged by Jack with blankets and wooden poles carried from Drombeg. He closed the entrance carefully and looked round at Brigid as she lay on the blanket on the sand. Brigid unbuttoned her blouse, slowly, tantalizingly, and shrugged it from her shoulders. Next, she unfastened her skirt and kicked it from her. He experienced a feeling of sudden loving, lusting wonder as he gazed on her perfect nakedness.

He lay down beside her, kissing her smooth throat, moving his hands slowly over her body. She opened his shirt deftly, her breath fast against his skin, and helped him wriggle out of his breeches. They hugged against each other, caressing and kissing, until, at last, he moved over her. Jack gasped as he slid into her. He paused and looked down at her. Her face was turned to one side on the blanket, her eyes closed, a smile playing around her lips. He moved gently at first, in rhythm with the water breaking on the sands below them, and then more fiercely as her calves and ankles tightened around his thighs, urging him closer and deeper.

'Dearest, oh, dearest,' she moaned as she moved her hips under him in unison with his quickening thrusts. Her hands moved urgently on his buttocks, the nails pressing into his skin, and finally tightened and clutched convulsively as she felt him shuddering inside her, matching her own climax. He lay, panting on her for a few moments before pulling slowly away. They kissed staring closely into each other's eyes.

'Mavourneen,' he whispered. 'Oh, Brigid, you're really mine.'

'I always was from that first day at Ballybunnion. No one has ever meant anything to me except yourself. I've never felt a man's loving before until you. Nothing has ever counted until now.'

'I love you, Brigid.'

'And I you, dearest, dearest Jack.'

They held each other close throughout the night, laying contentedly together, caressing and kissing, langorously, idly, or locked together in overwhelming passion. At times they dozed but then one would wake the other and the loving would start again. As the dawn light began to sneak into the tent, they dressed and embraced kneeling on the blanket.

'We'll never forget this night, Brigid.'

'No, not ever. It was ours, only ours, so it was.'

Jack pulled aside the blanket and peered outside. A sea fret was covering the beach with misty dampness – a sign that the day would be fine and warm. He could only see for twenty or thirty yards as he went searching for some wood to rekindle the fire. As he moved among the dunes, he greeted the other early risers who were crawling from their shelters and tents to yawn and stretch the sleep from them.

'A good night, Jack?' called Quillinan from his tent about ten yards away.

''Twas so, Paddy, thanks be to God,' Jack answered cheerfully. 'Does promise to be a fair day for the fight. Let's be meeting in an hour or so to talk some tactics.'

He lit the fire again with some difficulty and thrust four lumpers into the burning wood to cook for breakfast. Brigid emerged from the tent almost shyly to sit beside him. Hands clasped they looked into the flames, both thinking about the night that had just passed. Jack gazed at her profile and felt a surge of possessive pride.

'Tonight, avourneen, tis I'll be telling you all you should know about Matt and what went on while you were away,' Brigid said quietly, talking into the darting flames. 'There can be no secrets between us now.'

'You're wanting confessions, woman?' Jack smiled, putting an arm round her shoulders and drawing her close. 'Well tis I have a few to tell and no mistake.'

Jack knew that the exchanging of confidences would be the final link in the chain binding Brigid and himself. He would never tell her that his own discreet inquiries had already satisfied him about the identity of Matt Aherne's father. The final confirmation, he knew, would have to come from Brigid herself and at a time of her own choosing.

The sea fret was already lifting from the beach by the time they'd finished breakfast, juggling the hot potatoes in their hands to bite into the succulent flesh. Paddy Quillinan wandered over to join them and together they studied the lay-out of the beach. The mouth of the Shannon was to the west and the waters that washed Ballyeagh strand were those of the River Chasen, a hundred yards and more wide at this point with fast, treacherous currents. The river, leading off the Atlantic and the mouth of the Shannon, divided further inland into the rivers Feale, Brick and Galey. The Mulvihills were gathered at the west end of the beach, nearest the Atlantic, with the Cooleens to the east, near to the landing point for the boats which ferried people from the south bank of the Cashen. Already the boats were busy carrying people over to Ballyeagh.

'Bound to be Cooleens,' Quillinan observed. 'There's a deal of them south of the river.'

'Tis right you are, Paddy,' said Jack. 'And look there . . . by the fill of the pockets and sacks they're bringing over their ammunition with them.'

'So they're planning to be hurling stones,' Quillinan muttered.

'Seems so. Let's be watching where they store them.'

'I'll be sending one of the boys to travel the ferry. He'll be finding out.'

They discussed other tactics before Jack sent Quillinan hurrying around the Mulvihill supporters with their instructions. For the next couple of hours, he strolled with Brigid among the dunes as preparations were made for the race meeting to begin when the tide was out, about midday. Dozens of tinkers were setting up stalls selling everything from pots and pans to straw hats to keep the sun off the women's faces; from hot lumpers stuffed with bacon fat to bottles of poteen and cheap whiskey. Music from the fiddlers drifted along the sands to mingle with the sounds of a fife and a bodhran, a large tambourine, being played by two old soldiers, with a felt hat before them to collect any offerings. Everywhere there was colour and noise and music; mothers shrieked at their children as they dashed into the wavelets for a swift paddle; men, already in drink, called bets to each other about the forthcoming races; officers and soldiers of the 69th Regiment in their tall black caps and red, white and yellow uniforms shouted at the crowd, ordering them behind the rope to keep them off the sands when the races started; a dozen or so constables wandered among the throng watching for any pickpockets; the 'quality' – the nobility, their land agents, doctors and lawyers – sat in their carriages with their ladies, picnicking on cold chicken and hams washed down with claret.

A great roar went up from the crowd as five stewards walked out on to the glistening sands to set out the poles which would mark the course for the riders. It would run from the west end of the beach to a pole half-a-mile away. The riders would go round the course twice, a total distance of two miles. But above the mounting excitement and joy and fun of that St John's Day meet at Ballyeagh in 1834, there was the brooding presence of the two factions at either end of the beach, gathered beyond the furthest poles of the racecourse. They sneered at the soldiers who'd been detailed to stand in front of them. To most of the crowd it looked a vain hope that no more than sixty soldiers would be able to contain upwards of two thousand men intent on cracking one another's skulls.

There was a great roar from the watching crowd as the stewards flagged away the first seven riders, coloured scarves tied to their arms for identification. Clods of still-wet sand flew into the air as the horses thundered along the flat beach, their manes flying in the breeze. One horse charged through the surf sending sprays of water over its jockey. The horses were hunched close together at the first turn but a rider wearing a yellow scarf just managed to reach the pole first. The speed of his horse meant that he had to round the pole in a wide sweep but he escaped the bumping and boring which went on among the riders and horses a few yards behind him. One rider pulled his horse round too violently, and his mount slipped in the sand. In falling, it took the legs away from another horse. They tumbled on to the sand whinnying and kicking. One jockey rolled away from his mount in time but the other received a flailing hoof in the small of his back. He tried to rise but fell back with a loud groan. Two constables dashed forward from the ropes and pulled him clear. The five horses still in the race were at full stretch as they approached the starting line again but the rider with the yellow scarf retained a narrow lead. On the second lap he was overhauled by a big grey horse whose rider sported green favours. These two rounded the far pole together but the grey made a smaller turn and was a head in front as the two horses pounded towards the finishing line. Both jockeys were now using whips on their horses, occasionally slashing at each other. The noise from the thousands watching was at a crescendo as the two animals strained for the line, ears flattened, nostrils flaring, hardly an inch between them. With a dozen or so strides to go, the jockey on the grey caught his opponent across the face with a particularly vicious swipe of his whip. The rider lost his grip momentarily and the grey swept past the finishing line a clear head in front. From the wild applause of the crowd, he was a popular winner.

Quillinan, who'd watched the race with Brigid and Jack, was beside himself with delight. 'Well, the rent money's safe,' he roared before pushing through the crowd to find the man with whom he'd struck his bet.

'Paddy doesn't seem to be worrying about the Cooleens,' Brigid laughed, her face glowing with excitement.

'Not he,' said Jack. 'To Paddy, a horse race and a fight are all part of a day's enjoyment. Are you wanting to strike a bet on the next race?'

'No, I'm preferring just to watch with you.' She clasped his arm tightly. 'When is it the fighting will start?' she asked anxiously.

'Mighty soon, I'm thinking,' Jack replied. 'Look at those Cooleens. They're so much in drink they're scuffling amongst themselves already.'

He pointed towards the further end of the beach. Brigid stood on tiptoe and saw a swirling movement in the men penned behind the rank of soldiers. Four Cooleens were struggling together on the sand, punching each other around the body.

'Tis someone not paying a bet, I'm guessing,' Jack grunted. 'Let them be wasting their energy on themselves, the animals.'

Six more horses cantered on to the sands, their jockeys standing high in their stirrups and the crowd settled down to watch the next race. But, suddenly, as the horses lined up at the start, there were screams of alarm from the women in the crowd nearest to the Cooleens. In an instant Jack saw what had happened. The small fight had been merely a diversion. The soldiers had been lured into the Cooleen crowd to drag the four men apart and as soon as a gap appeared in the soldiers' ranks the Cooleens had burst through. Now hundreds of them were running across the sands towards the horses and the Mulvihills. As they advanced, they pulled shillelaghs from under their coats and shirts and began fastening green ribbons around them.

'Coolee . . . coolee . . . coolee . . . cooleeee . . . '

Their chant swelled and grew to blot out all other noise along the beach. The crowd began scattering back from their positions along the rope towards the safety of the dunes. Six constables, arms linked, tried to form a line to stop the advancing mob but were brushed aside and swallowed in the crowd.

Quillinan ran towards Jack, pushing his way through the families who were struggling in panic to leave the beach.

'Get the men on the strand as we planned, Paddy. I'll lead the others.'

'Good luck,' Quillinan cried as he raced through the dunes, urging the Mulvihills to follow him. As they ran they fixed white ribbons to their sticks and began their own chant.

'Mmulvi . . . mmulvi . . . mmulvi . . . mmulvi . . . '

Jack turned to the hundred or so men who had stayed behind according to plan.

'Hide yourself in the dunes,' he ordered. 'We'll be biding our time.' The men fell on their stomachs, keeping their shillelaghs close by them. Jack pushed Brigid down beside him.

'Now when we move, you stay here, mavourneen, and keep out of sight. I'm afeared the Cooleens may come looking for you.' He gave her a quick kiss. 'And don't be worrying yourself. Paddy and I have a fine plan.'

'Oh, I'm so scared for you, Jack,' Brigid cried, trying to put her arms around his neck. He pushed them away and smiled reassuringly at her.

'In less than an hour, it'll be all over, and we'll be together for always.' He kissed her again and then peeked over the dunes to watch the battle beginning on the sands below.

The first Mulvihills to reach the beach were already engaged in running battles with the Cooleens, swinging their sticks and hitting empty air more often than not, as the main body of Mulvihills took up their positions.

Instead of meeting the Cooleens head on, the Mulvihills formed themselves quickly into a square. At first, the result was total confusion as the Cooleens, advancing in disordered ranks, found no one to fight except the close knit Mulvihill formation. The Cooleens swirled around the square not knowing where to press their attack. The Mulvihills stood firm in their square, not moving out of position until a Cooleen came into easy range.

'Tis working,' Jack cried excitedly as he watched the uncertainty in the Cooleen ranks. Instead of the individual combat they had expected, the Cooleens were faced with a solid phalanx of opponents standing their ground and responding only to the most suicidal of attacks. But soon the Mulvihill square was surrounded by Cooleens pressing in from all sides and the combat became sterner. Curses and groans mingled with the sharp cracking sound of shillelaghs striking bones as the factions closed together. And then, on a shouted order, the Cooleens withdrew a few yards as the men behind them lobbed a hail of stones into the Mulvihill ranks. The first barrage caused many injuries; Mulvihills in the middle of the square staggered and fell; scalps were split apart by the stones. Then Quillinan's shouted orders began to be obeyed. The Mulvihills inside the square knelt as the stones rained down and warded them off by spreading their coats and shirts tautly above their heads. The flying stones continued to take their toll but most of them bounced harmlessly off the improvised Mulvihill shields.

The factions closed together again as the Cooleens' supply of stones ran low. Jack watched as the men joined in combat, punching, kicking, hitting out with their cudgels. Only the keen eye could see that the square of men with white ribbons on their shillelaghs was standing firm.

By now, thousands who had come to watch the Ballyeagh races were spectators to another event, taking the best vantage points overlooking the beach to watch the faction fight. One or two of the braver tinkers were still trying to rescue their wares but, in the main, the beach had been given over to the men with ribbons on their sticks.

The battle went on for more than half an hour before Jack was satisfied that the Cooleens had committed all their forces. The casualties from both sides were crawling away from the fighting, trying to find any refuge from the flailing sticks, staunching bleeding wounds with anything they could find. But still the battle was even. The Cooleens had not managed to break into the Mulvihills' ranks. It was clearly a stalemate.

Jack motioned to the men lying in the dunes around him.

'Keep down,' he shouted. 'We'll keep low till we're on them.'

Jack crouched, waving his arm in the direction he wanted the remaining Mulvihills to follow. Before he started moving, he ran his hand gently down Brigid's back.

'Stay here, mavourneen,' he said. 'Be out of sight.'

Brigid nodded, her eyes wide with fear from the sounds and sights of the battle. She said nothing, only mouthed the words, 'Take care, avourneen.'

For nearly half a mile, Jack crept away through the dunes with the rest of the Mulvihills. His legs and back ached from the crouching position they had adopted. They had almost reached the end of their cover in the dunes before they came across the cache of stones that Quillinan's spy had found earlier. Young Cooleen men were filling wicker baskets from the pile and carrying them two hundred yards to their elders to hurl into the hard-pressed Mulvihill formation. For a few minutes, Jack watched them before signalling his men forward. The Mulvihills rushed from their hiding places in the dunes and clubbed the Cooleen youngsters unconscious with hardly a sound except that of wood meeting bone.

The Mulvihills stuffed their pockets and shirts and coats from the pile of stones and on Jack's command moved forward towards the fighting. As they reached the Cooleens, now pressing closer than ever against the sorely-tried Mulvihill square, they were greeted with smiles and shouts of encouragement. To the Cooleens there was no way of distinguishing their enemies since Jack's contingent of Mulvihill reinforcements wore no ribbons. But, suddenly, awfully, the Cooleens realized their mistake, as stone upon stone ripped into their backs, slashing open legs, arms, and heads. Jack concentrated his attack on one section of the Cooleens and as they fell away, confused and hurt, the Mulvihill ranks opposite them advanced. In a few minutes, the battle of Ballyeagh sands was transformed as the Mulvihills switched their formation from a square to a wedge, splitting the Cooleen ranks and cutting them off from any retreat into the dunes. The effect was dramatic. At one moment the Cooleens were surrounding and seemingly pounding the Mulvhills, the next they were split into small groups fleeing for their safety under a hail of stones they themselves had brought to the battle. Jack directed his men but so sudden was the collapse of the Cooleens that he hardly had time to strike out at any individual. The beach was filled with men running wildly through an avenue of cracking shillelaghs, trying desperately to reach the rowing boats which would take them out of range across the river Cashen. But even those who were in the boats suffered under the barrage of stones.

Paddy Quillinan, a small cut on his forehead, shouted his men on as he came towards Jack. 'Tis a rout,' he exclaimed. 'Just as you said, Jack. Them Cooleens will fall for any trick.'

Jack threw his arms around his friend. 'And wasn't that just a fight, Paddy. I thought you were nearly done for till we crept up behind them.'

Quillinan's battered features split into a huge grin. 'A fight? Twas a massacre so it was . . . and with their own stones they'd carted all the way across the river.'

'How was it though, Paddy?' Jack asked, his voice quiet and serious.

Quillinan's reply was in an equally serious tone. 'To tell the truth,

Jack, we couldn't have held out much longer. They'd nearly broken a side of the square and that would have been that.'

'No fear, Paddy. They didn't and that's what matters. Just see them running now.'

The two men looked over the beach as the Cooleens scattered in all directions, pursued by Mulvihills. Many of the Cooleens had taken to the boats and were frantically trying to row across the river. Jack watched, laughing, as the Mulvihills stood on the shore hurling stones at the boats, seeing the splashes as the missiles fell near or the Cooleens clutch at their bodies as a stone hit them.

'Oh, Jesus, Paddy,' he suddenly cried as he caught a glimpse of a woman in a red skirt in one of the boats crossing the river. ''Tis Brigid. They took Brigid. She's out there.'

Quillinan followed his pointing finger. 'You're right, Jack. But where . . . ?'

'I told her to stay down. They must have been after taking her all the time.'

Jack could see her more clearly now. She was in a boat being rowed by Sean Flaherty. On either side of her were two Cooleens holding her arms. She was struggling wildly to escape but to no avail.

Flaherty was bent over the oars, pulling strongly for the far side of the river, when a fusillade of stones smashed down on him from Mulvihills who'd waded knee-deep into the river. For a moment, it seemed as if they'd all missed him but suddenly he clutched the back of his head, half stood up in the boat, and then tumbled overboard. As he went into the water, the boat capsized throwing everyone into the river.

'For God's sake, stop them,' Jack screamed as he saw more and more stones splashing into the water around the upturned boat. He began running towards the water's edge, tearing off his shirt as he went. Quillinan began shouting orders at the Mulvihills who were standing in the surf throwing stones.

Jack saw Brigid struggling in the water, breaking free from the men around her and striking for the shore. And then, as in a nightmare, a slow dream, a ghastly dream, he saw a stone smash her forehead. Her hands reached up for the wound, her head vanished under the water, a hand surfaced briefly, and she was gone.

Jack swam thirty yards into the river and trod water frantically as he looked for her. Despite Quillinan's orders, stones were still raining down on the Cooleens in the river. One of them struck Jack on the shoulder but he scarcely felt the blow. All around him were the screams and groans and cries of drowning people but nowhere could he spot Brigid. And then he saw her. She was floating face downwards twenty yards from him, moving away with the tide, her red skirt billowing voluminously on the surface. Jack's arms clawed at the water as he surged towards her. He reached her and turned her face upwards, dragging her by the shoulders back towards the beach. But as he looked into her face, eyes glazed open, jaw sagging wide, hair straggling over the gaping wound, he knew it was too late. He pulled her into the shallows, callously pushing aside the bodies of drowned Cooleens, and picked her up in his arms. Her green eyes, reddened by the water, stared sightlessly at the sky.

He carried her over to Paddy Quillinan and lowered her gently on to the sand before him. Quillinan was crying openly.

'Call them off, Paddy,' said Jack quietly. 'There's nothing to fight over any more.' He looked down at Brigid's body at his feet. 'We won, Paddy, didn't we?' he asked. And then in a voice that carried across the beach, 'Oh, Jesus, we won, didn't we?'

The report of the official government inquiry into the Battle of Ballyeagh reached its inconclusive findings and the people of Kerry read of them in their rudely-printed newspaper, Master Chute's *Western Herald*.

Who was to blame, had asked the lawyers, for the deaths of perhaps twenty people? The final toll was never known. Everyone and no one, the inquiry decided. It was just faction fighting and that, all agreed, had to be stopped. And so it was on any large scale. There were spats between the factions but only involving two or three dozen men and then infrequently and well away from the eyes of the authorities.

Thin blades of grass soon began to grow on Brigid Aherne's grave next to those of Joe and John Keane at the bottom of the far field near the cabin at Drombeg. Each Sunday, whatever the weather, Jack and Matt Aherne walked hand in hand to Brigid's grave to replace the sprigs of hawthorn or sprays of wild roses.

Matt, now a sturdy-growing little boy, knew for certain that his mother was with the angels, because Father O'Mahony had said so and for sure she wasn't around any more to comfort him when he fell over or was pecked by a chicken. Sometimes Matt remembered his mother vividly, her smell, her eyes, her black hair, but he was well content in the arms of the grey haired old woman he knew as Mam Keane. Gradually, the memories of his mother faded although, for some reason he always told people otherwise. It was clearly what they wanted to hear, because he was invariably rewarded with a pat on the head or a hug.

But he did remember – or later told his children that he did – a day, not long after his mother died, when a tall man on a big horse rode up to the cabin. The person he always called Jack-Da lifted him up to the man on his horse. The man held him at arm's length, examining his features closely, then hugged him before pressing a shiny gold sovereign into his tiny palm and handing him back.

'This won't be forgotten, Master Keane,' the man on the horse said.

'And that's the truth,' Jack-Da said shortly.

'You have truly shamed me.'

''Tis your shame.'

'But don't you understand?' the man on the horse added, almost a begging note in his voice. 'My position . . . in my position it was impossible to do anything . . . to acknowledge this.'

'No man would want to be ignoring his own son,' Jack-Da replied.

'I offered money but she refused.'

'Aye, she would be doing that, I'm thinking. She had a pride too full to be taking your money.'

'We both loved her you know,' the man on the horse pleaded.

'Aye, to our likes,' Jack-Da said contemptuously, glancing over his shoulder as he led the small boy back into the cabin. 'To our very different likes, Master Sandes.'

*BOOK TWO*

# Chapter 1 July, 1845

It was a warm, lazy summer day. The earth threw up a fecund smell of contentment. The crops of corn and wheat moved gently, serenely, in the soft breezes whispering over the North Kerry plain from the Atlantic. The black dairy cattle sought what shade there was between yielding pails of rich, frothing milk. The pigs in their sties fattened steadily, nosing somnolently into their feeds of maize. The chickens, almost stunned by the heat, stayed out of the midday sun, saving their clucking energies for early morning and late afternoon. Even the flies, inevitably gathered around the dung pit at the rear of the cabin, swarmed only in the coolness of sunset, seeming to ignore humans and animals alike during the day.

By any standards, June and early July that year had been particularly dry and hot in the west of Ireland. The fields were still green from the water stored during the wet season but on the mountains east of Listowel the heather was becoming parched.

Despite the heat, Jack Keane and Matt Aherne worked steadily alongside their five labourers in the neat fields surrounding their cabin at Drombeg townland.

Ever since he had returned from Boston twelve years since, Jack had worked to expand the farm until it had become one of the most prosperous in the district. As adjoining fields had become vacant through eviction, death or emigration, he had systematically acquired them, paying rent in advance to Sir James Watson through his agent, Jonathan Sandes. At first, Jack had had to dip into the reserve of money he'd brought back from America but by the time his mother had died in 1837 the farm was making enough to pay the annual rent of £12 an acre, on all its eighty acres.

Sandes made numerous gestures in an attempt to curry favour, but Jack had only to look at Matt Aherne for his heart to harden once more against the land agent. The young man grew to resemble his mother more during each passing year. He had her green eyes, shaded with brown, her oval face, her jet-black hair. From his father, Jonathan Sandes, he had acquired only a tall, wiry build, unlike his guardian's which had thickened with years of good eating and drinking despite all the hard work. By the time he was fifteen years old, this hot summer, Matt Aherne stood a head above his guardian. He still called him Jack-Da, although he knew who his actual father was.

Jack had agonized for years about when – indeed whether – to tell the youngster of all that had gone before. Finally, he had decided the boy should know the truth, if only to protect him from any vicious, childish gossip he might hear during his years at the ditch school set along the main track between Listowel and Ballybunnion.

Matt had listened intently, wide-eyed, as Jack told him the story surrounding Brigid Aherne's life.

'So there you are, Matt,' Jack finished. 'Your real father is the land agent Sandes. I'm thinking he'll not want you with him but I'm sure he'd give you a preferment in Sir James's service if you want to leave here.'

'Do you want me to, Jack-Da?' Matt asked, a suspicion of a tear trembling in the corner of one eye.

'Want you to leave? Never, Matt. This farm is your home and your birthright if you wish it.'

This July day they worked the fields as father and son. With the sun at its fullest, they slumped gratefully into the shade of a wall to share a snack of lumpers and milk.

'Has it ever been so hot a day, Jack-Da?' Matt asked, wiping his shining brow with the tail of the shirt tied round his waist.

'Be not complaining, lad,' Jack grunted. 'Tis the weather for farmers like you and me and, pray God, it stays till September. Rain then and we'll be lifting the tatties from soft enough soil.'

'When you look at the other folk in the district, you don't know how they survive.' It was more of a question than a statement from the youngster.

'Aye, that's true. There be too many people and not enough land to work. But tis the tradition to divide the land among the children. Over the years, it has been cut up so much there are families trying to find a living from half an acre. This'll be a good year for them though, and the hanging gales are likely to be paid.'

'The rents?'

'They're near twice as high as in England because of too many people sharing too little land. They take a field, build a cabin on it, and then pray mightily for a good first harvest. The landlord's agent is forced to let the rent hang over until the harvest to collect his money, unless the farmer goes borrowing against his crops from the gombeen man.'

'And if it's a bad harvest?'

'Evictions like you've seen, lad, and someone else takes the land.'

'Tisn't fair.'

'Fair? You want fairness from landlords? Know this . . . if I failed with my rent I'd be thrown off these fields without one penny compensation, not even for all we've been building to the cabin or how we've improved and cleared the farm. Up in Ulster, they'd be getting some compensation but nowhere else in this country.'

Jack took another swig from the tin can filled with milk, held out to him by Matt.

'You won't be remembering the monster meetings held by Daniel O'Connell and his Repealers but you've seen his lawyer man, Mahony, who's living on the Feale at Kilmorna. Until the Repealers get a parliament again in Dublin, Ireland run by Irishmen, then the landlords will be riding high over us.'

'But the Repealers are a force in the English parliament, aren't they?'

Jack snorted contemptuously. 'Anything they be getting through that Parliament is soon stamped on by the lords above them and they're the parasites who live off our backs. God forgive them, many of them were born in Ireland themselves, not that they speak our language or worship at our Church. But Irish they are. Now think on that, lad. Irish against Irish. Be thinking on that while we get back to the fields.'

Jack Keane had resisted considerable temptation to take part in politics.

On many occasions he'd met Daniel O'Connell's lawyer, Pierce Mahony, at Listowel market. They'd drunk wine together at the Listowel Arms while Mahony had urged Jack to fight for a parliament in Dublin, once even suggesting he stand for election in Cork. The slight, thin-faced lawyer was full of assurances that Jack could become a member of parliament if he wanted to. His forceful arguments led Jack to promise he would consider the matter seriously. He talked for many hours with Father O'Mahony, now his trusted confidant, and even travelled with the priest to Limerick, spanning the Shannon, to attend one of O'Connell's self-proclaimed 'monster meetings'. He'd been impressed by the oratory of the fat, balding politician but the open adulation of the huge crowd had disturbed him. The banners fluttering everywhere acclaimed O'Connell as 'The Liberator' or 'The Great Liberator' or 'England's Scourge' yet the politician still spoke of a parliament in Dublin giving loyalty to the British monarchy.

'Tis strange that, Father,' Jack remarked to the priest as they journeyed back together to Listowel. 'The mob call him Liberator yet he would still tie us to the English.'

The priest smiled gently. 'A good politician – and O'Connell is certainly that – is akin to a parish priest, Jack. Haven't I drunks enough come to confession? Now how would it be if I told them they'd find eternal damnation if they kept on with the bottle. They'd think me a fool; they'd not cease the drink; and, likely as not, they'd not be confessing again . . . '

'So . . . ?' Jack interrupted, rather impatiently.

'So, my friend, I chide them gently, remind them that money spent on drink doesn't fill the bellies of their children, and pray to God that their natural goodness – and don't all men have that? – will bring them moderation.'

'With respect, what's that to do with O'Connell?'

'Don't you see, Jack. Like me, he's only interested in the possible. Why, he knows that the English will never let Ireland go while memories are still fresh of the '98 rising and the offers of Ireland to Bonaparte as a base to fight, even to invade, England. So O'Connell tells the English – you find us so troublesome to govern, why not let us govern ourselves under your control?'

'O'Connell promises the mobs what he can't give them, then?'

'Oh, no. He tells them the truth, but so that they believe he is promising more than he is. Tis politics, old friend.'

'Tis cynical,' Jack retorted, recalling another conversation in another country when a politician had attempted to explain what he regarded as the realities of the world. In that moment he decided against accepting the offer of a safe entry into politics.

'Politics should be about beliefs, Father,' he explained later when he told the priest that he was going to remain a farmer. 'Tis my belief that if the people of Ireland want freedom, then they should grasp it, wrest it from the English, die for it if necessary. The Yankes did it. Why can't we if we crave it so much?'

'But you're forgetting that there's no Atlantic ocean between us and the English,' Father O'Mahony said quietly. 'We're in each others pockets, so we are.'

'No, you're wrong,' Jack insisted. 'The poorness of land, our poverty of belief in ourselves, make it so. Nothing else.'

And so Jack Keane was pleased this fine summer to work his farm with Matt Aherne, certain of his skills, sure in his political beliefs, settled in his mind. He sat the nights in the comfortable cabin at Drombeg, talked with Matt until the lad went to bed, then thought his thoughts alone, taking occasional mugs of rum.

He had toyed with the idea of marriage, thinking that Matt would need a woman's help and influence, particularly after Jack's own mother died. He'd discussed the matter at length with Father O'Mahony and the priest had agreed that a woman's presence in the cabin might help Matt during his formative years. He'd even gone as far as introducing Jack to eligible young women. A couple of girls had been pretty and intelligent enough to send a stir of longing through Jack Keane. But as he continued his acquaintanceships with them, subtly pressed on all sides to begin a formal courtship, fierce memories of Brigid Aherne, fond thoughts of Meg Griffiths, dark remembrances of Elizabth Kilfedder, continued to haunt him. He measured the local girls against the previous women in his life and found them wanting. The memories kept him from loneliness. They were always fresh in his mind. Sometimes, as he sat by candlelight, he wondered if he was living too much in the past. Then he would think of Matt and realize he was living for the youngster's future. He was content in his small world, perhaps even a trifle smug, that glorious summer of 1845.

But one morning towards the end of July, Jack awoke, the light in the cabin still grey, feeling cold. He'd been sleeping uncovered during the past weeks of summer heat. No he was shivering with cold. He tiptoed to the window, and rubbed away the condensation on the glass. There was nothing outside but the clinging, grey cottonwool of fog. 'In July,' he thought. 'Fog?'

'What is it, Jack-Da?' Matt was standing by his shoulder, his white shirt reaching to mid-thigh.

'Fog, lad. Tis fog.'

'Now?'

'Aye, in July.'

'But it was steaming yesterday.'

'So it was. A real burner but now tis fog. And cold it is, as well.'

'Shall I be getting the rugs from the chest?' Matt said.

'No, lad. Tis nearly dawn or past it. We'll dress and take a meal.'

The two of them struggled into their breeches and tucked in their shirts. 'We'll be tending the animals before getting to the fields when this murk clears,' said Jack.

Sudden mists and fogs were not uncommon in a Kerry summer as layers of cold air met warmer vapour from the night sea.

But Jack and Matt couldn't work the fields that day, nor for the next three weeks, as the appalling weather continued. It was as if the North Kerry plain had been robbed of all natural light during those long days. The nights merged into dusk-like, chill days when there should have been bright sunshine and lively breezes. The fog and rain hovered, unmoving, over the entire country and, from newspaper reports, over many neighbouring counties. The initial sullen acceptance of the weather began to change into panic by the middle of the second week. A few more days and the farmers were despairing of their crops.

At Listowel market that third week, the farmers stood around in small groups openly forecasting their own and everyone else's ruin. Jack, with Matt at his side, moved from group to group, commiserating, listening.

'Tis fine for you, Jack,' one of the neighbours told him. 'You've the animals to tide you through.'

'And what to feed them on if nothing grows?'

'At least you'll be eating them . . . me? . . . well, you know I've scarce two acres of lumpers with a woman and four wee ones to feed. What if that crop dies? What then?'

Jack realized that it was precisely that question which was causing so much worry. All the farmers knew that there'd been at least a dozen failures of the potato crop in various parts of Ireland during the last fifty years or so.

'This time it's our turn,' they moaned. 'Tis Kerry's turn now.'

Jack, in a position of comparative safety with his spread of crops and livestock, tried to cheer them up. He'd gesture towards the stalls lining the gentle slope of the market square.

'Be seeing the bags of new tatties for sale alongside the old lumpers. There's plenty for all still.'

'And what of those in the trenches, Jack?'

'They're looking well enough if you can see them in the fog and I'm reading in the newspaper from Dublin how the tattie crop has never been so large or abundant.'

By the middle of August the farmers' depression and panic dispersed along with the fog.

In September, Jack took a good harvest of wheat from his fields, milled it in Listowel, and stored the bags of flour in one of the three outhouses he'd added to the cabin. He planned to use these along with turnips lifted from one field to help feed the livestock through the winter, make the rough, unleaven bread he and Matt liked so much, and then sell the remainder at market the next year when the prices should have risen. The last job of the season, before the late autumn ploughing, would be to lift the potato crop from the five fields. By common agreement, he and his neighbours decided that the second week in October provided the ideal weather, the soil damp but not clinging, the skies cloudy but not threatening. Any lingering doubts they had vanished as they dug the tubers from the ground. The potatoes were firm, large and unmarked, as they were laid on straw by their trenches to dry off for a couple of days.

'We'll be eating well this winter, young Matt,' Jack said, open delight on his face. 'The lumpers are better than some years past, the flour's bagged, the pigs are fattened . . .'

' . . . the hens are laying, the cows are milking,' Matt chimed in, mischievously.

Jack laughed, recognizing his own self-satisfied pomposity. 'You gosseen! Don't be cheeking your elders and betters,' he roared in mock anger. 'Run to our neighbours and find how their lumpers are. Be off with you.'

Matt raced off across the fields, black hair streaming, hurdling the stone walls without effort. Jack knew that at each cabin Matt visited, he would be pressed to eat a little something, perhaps a scone cake fresh from the griddle, and then given a mug to drink. One or two of the farmers would delight in slipping the youngster a nip of poteen to send him light-headed on his way. Jack would do the same to their sons who'd soon be calling out of breath at his cabin. It was a ritual, this swapping of news about the most important crop of the year. As he sat at the table in his cabin, waiting for the first caller, Jack uncorked a bottle of rum, poured himself a generous measure, and buttered slices of new-made bread. He reflected that, if there was a luckier or more content man in the west of Ireland, then Jack Keane didn't know him.

Jonathan Sandes moved uncomfortably in the chair by the front window of his drawing room as a spasm of rheumatism stabbed his right hip.

'Always in October,' he thought bitterly. 'Cursed weather.'

He was getting old. His body told him so every day. His stomach revolted at large meals. His liver complained at an excess of wine. His legs trembled in protest at too long a walk. The knowledge hurt him every bit as much as the symptoms of his physical decline.

The land agent looked out on the milling crowds in Listowel market square. He'd heard as soon as anyone that the potato crop lifted in the last two days was good. That meant rents would be paid, yet Sandes was still unhappy.

'God, they all look as if they've found the crock,' he muttered to himself. He scanned the crowd, trying to see his wife, who was out among the stalls with their son, George, the child who'd arrived when he and his wife had virtually abandoned all hope of having a fruitful marriage. The boy was now ten years old, nearly eleven, and much loved. 'The apple of my eye,' Sandes told his friends when he was feeling expansive in company, which was very rare these days.

'Tis the crab apple of his eye,' the people of Listowel joked to themselves, noting that young Master Sandes showed most of the traits of a spoiled, indulged child, and promised to be as unlovable as his father.

It was not a good day to have rheumatism, to feel old, to gaze through a window at such a happy throng.

Sandes craned forward and peered at the smiling guffawing, crowd outside the inn. 'Just like cattle,' he thought grumpily. 'Feed 'em, milk 'em, slaughter 'em. They'd still be happy.'

Anyway, there was some consolation. The agent's commissions from Sir James Watson for collecting the landlowner's rents would be assured.

Jonathan Sandes decided to risk a glass of sherry before lunch. It might help to ease the pain.

He rang the tiny silver bell on the table beside him to summon his new maid.

As she entered the room and curtseyed before him, young breasts thrusting against her dress, another twinge of pain shot through Sandes. He clenched his teeth in a vain attempt to keep a groan from escaping.

The girl rose, began to move to his side, concern in her soft eyes.

'Sherry,' snapped Sandes, trying to control the pain with his mind. 'The sherry, Brigid.'

The girl paused, then turned hesitantly and went to the door.

'Sir,' she said quietly.

'Sherry. Bring the sherry!'

'Sir, I'm Bernadette. Not Brigid.'

Another spasm of rheumatism surged through Jonathan Sandes. He looked determinedly through the window but his eyes saw nothing.

The smell, rank and clinging, spread over the townlands around Listowel during the next two days. It crept through windows and under doors, clung to clothes, assailed the nostrils of animals and people alike, and poisoned the air and soul of north Kerry.

Jack Keane stood in the middle of his largest potato field, a wet cloth pressed to his nose and mouth, and looked slowly along the long rows of potatoes lying on straw. He bent to pick one up. Its skin was slippery. The flesh inside felt soft and mushy. It's putrid smell sank deep into Jack's lungs. He began to cough and, as he did so, tears started to run down his cheeks

'Oh, Mary, Holy Mother of Jesus,' he choked. 'Oh, Holy God. The whole field . . . all of them . . . they're done for . . . they're rotten.'

His streaming eyes looked over his fields and the fields beyond. He turned slowly around to take in every part of the landscape. A watery October sun played among the fast-moving clouds. Everywhere seemed bleak, forbidding, and harsh.

Jack walked down each row of potatoes, stooping now and again to pick one up. They were all the same, rotten or rotting.

'Matt!' he shouted. 'Anything there?'

The youngster threw a lumper away from himself, wiped his hands disgustedly, shook his head.

'Nothing, Jack-Da,' he called. 'They're all lost. A stinking mess.'

'Holy Mother, what's to be done with us now?' Jack whispered. 'Without the lumpers, we're done for. Holy God!'

The extent of the disaster became clear as farmer after farmer came to call at Jack Keane's cabin seeking to share their misery, their hopelessness. The potato crop of 1845 was a total failure throughout the area, and, from reading Mr Chute's journal, throughout Ireland, it seemed.

'Why have we been visited so?' the farmers would ask.

Jack would shake his head, run his fingers through his streak of white hair, and shake his head again.

'They were good when they were lifted, weren't they? Now they're nothing but pulp!

'Tis that stuff they're calling electricity from all that smoke and steam of those new locomotive things,' one farmer would say.

'No, tis the vapours of the volcanoes under the earth,' another would contradict. 'Sure and wasn't Ireland thrown up from the sea by a volcano? Tis those vapours.'

Everything was to blame, and, indeed, was blamed. Confusion, panic and doubt were rife. And when all had been said in those first awful days of the crop's failure, a dullness spread through the townland as it was finally accepted that many faced ruin and hunger, perhaps even starvation and death.

Suddenly, though, leaping hopes were raised by the government's

221

scientific commissioners who published in every newspaper in the land their solution for saving the precious potatoes.

Jack Keane shook his head in disbelief as he read it aloud to Matt while they sat by candlelight in the cabin. 'Tis what they're saying so we'll be trying it, lad, but tis mighty strange. Listen to this . . . first, dry the potatoes in the sun, then mark out on the ground a space six feet wide and as long as you please. Dig a shallow trench two feet wide all around, and throw the moulding potatoes upon the space then level it and cover it with a floor of turf sods set on their edges. Sift on to this packing stuff comprising of materials made by mixing a barrel of freshly burnt unslaked lime . . . '

'What?' Matt interrupted.

' . . . unslaked lime, it says here. Now don't be interrupting.' Jack peered again at the small, uneven print in Chute's *Western Herald* '. . . unslaked lime, broken into pieces as large as marbles, with two barrels of sand or earth, or by mixing equal parts of burnt turf and dry sawdust.'

He put down the newspaper and rubbed his eyes wearily.

'Tis all, Jack-Da?'

'Well, them scientists are saying that if we're not understanding it, then we should be asking the landlord or the clergyman to explain its meaning, but tis my opinion that Father O'Mahony nor Sir James Watson won't be helping much.'

But, dubious as they were, Jack and Matt, like many of their neighbours, followed the scientists' advice to the letter. It offered hope and raised them from apathy as they worked in the fields again.

At the end of the month, they lifted the potatoes from the specially-prepared pits but, if anything, they were more rotten than before.

But the scientists published more advice and the constables pasted it to walls throughout North Kerry. They admitted defeat in saving the crops but tried to salvage something from the disaster.

For two days, Jack followed the learned advice and transformed the cabin into a smelly, steaming kitchen. First, he grated the rotten potatoes with a jagged piece of metal so that the slimy flakes filled the large tub normally used for collecting rainwater. He washed the resulting pulp, strained it through a muslin cloth, washed it again, and then dried it on the griddle warmed by a low fire. When it was dried through, the substance set like a rough lump of grey stone.

Jack scratched his head in bewilderment. 'What in God's name do we do with this?' he wondered aloud.

'Try it on the pigs?' suggested Matt.

'Are you sure? Those scientists say we can be eating it.'

'Not me, Jack-Da.'

'Well, they say what's left in the tub should be starch which'll make bread when it's mixed with this dried stuff.'

They both peered over the edge of the tub at the sticky, noxious liquid inside. They glanced at each other, noted their similar expression of pained disgust, and broke into laughter.

'Tis pure nonsense, so help me,' spluttered Jack, as they rushed outside to breathe some fresh air. 'We'll be losing even our pigs if we feed them it.'

'So, Jack-Da?'

'So, my lad, let's get the whole mess out of the cabin and into the dung pit else we'll be suffocating ourselves with the smell.'

Some of Jack's neighbours without his reserves of turnips, maize and flour as animal feedstuff, were forced to use the rotten potatoes, however. They boiled them into a mash, mixed in bran and salt and fed their pigs and cattle. The livestock survived on this feed long enough to be sold at market to raise rents or to be slaughtered to provide food for families deprived of their normal diet of potatoes and milk.

As the smaller farmers began to kill the animals, they were left without any means to pay their long overdue rents. The inevitable happened. Eviction notices began being pinned to cabin doors through North Kerry. Most families gave in meekly, standing dumbly by as the bailiffs, accompanied by constables and soldiers, pulled down the thatches and smashed the cabin walls. Their hunger and despair robbed them of any defiance. Once the eviction party had left, some returned to the ruins of their homes and tried to rig up temporary shelter to help them through the winter. Others dug holes in the side of ditches, covered them with tree branches layered with sods of turf, and called this 'scalp' their new home.

A few summoned anger from their anguish and resisted the bailiffs. They barricaded their windows and doors against the expected onslaught. Crowds, sullen, jeering, gathered around the cabin to try to obstruct the bailiff's small army of paid thugs. But it was to no avail. A magistrate was quickly summoned. The troops fixed bayonets, the constables drew truncheons and the crowds were moved away from the cabin to allow the bailiff's men into action. With practised ease, they rigged a battering ram. Even under a hail of stones from the family inside the cabin, sometimes dodging tubfuls of boiling water, the bailiff's men needed only a few swings of the ram to smash aside the flimsy defences and shatter the mud and stone walls. Then personal scores would be settled while the troops and police held back the crowds. The men of the family who had resisted, including the youngsters, were pummelled and thwacked with clubs. Then the troops and police would leave followed by the crowd, angered yet guilty at its own inability to help. The family, with perhaps five or six children, were left standing amid the ruins in their ragged, inadequate clothing, wailing and weeping, nothing between themselves and the fast-approaching winter. The grim workhouse at Listowel might take the mother and the younger children, but there was no hope for the father and his elder sons or daughters.

As the number of evictions increased, a group of farmers, threatened with the same fate, approached Jack Keane to ask him to intercede with Jonathan Sandes on their behalf.

It was a difficult meeting between the two men that morning in mid-November 1845. They sat on opposite sides of the drawing room looking out on to Listowel market square. Jack was dressed in his newest chocolate brown coat and breeches, and a white silk stock. Sandes, visibly ailing, wore a long, heavily brocaded dressing gown. Jack declined the land agent's offer of wine, nervously clearing his throat as he tried to find the right weight of words with which to begin the conversation. During his ride to Listowel, he had determined to ask the favours with all the force at his command but he was equally determined not to beg.

'Sad days, are they not, Mr Keane?' Sandes interrupted his thoughts. 'A few days ago, all seemed well but now . . . ' He spread his hands and raised his eyes as if appealing to Heaven.

'Now, tis disaster, Mr Sandes.'

'Quite so. A disaster for many. But I trust not for you.'

'Not quite. Matt and I shall be surviving since we're not dependent on the potato. You shall be having your rent, have no fear.'

'My dear Keane,' Sandes said effusively, 'I had no concern on that matter. None at all. You are a man of substance, not like those feckless peasants I normally have business with. Your progress has pleased me, as has the way in which you have cared for that young man . . . ' Sandes paused, unable for a moment to find the correct phrase.

'Of Brigid Aherne's,' Jack broke in, harshness in his voice.

Sandes coughed nervously. 'Quite so,' he added hurriedly. 'Quite so, but I'm sure you've not come to talk of such matters.'

'No, tis the plight of some of my neighbours that concerns me . . . the Deanes, the Stacks, the . . . '

The land agent held up his hand. 'The names are known to me, Master Keane. All that you may care to mention. Their troubles are known to me. They exercise me. They exercise us all.'

'Can't you be holding over their rents? They have nothing.'

Sandes smiled wearily. 'Would that I could, but Sir James has heavy financial responsibilities to bear in England. He needs the rents.'

'But they have nothing to pay with,' Jack persisted. 'Cannot you be reducing the rents at least so they have a chance to pay? Next harvest will be better. Plenty always follows scarcity, Mr Sandes. You know that adage.'

'Indeed, Mr Keane. But the people you speak of fail to think of the bad times. When they have money, they pour it down their throats. When they have none, they expect charity.'

'Can you be reducing the rents, though?' Jack's voice was beginning to rise in anger at Sandes' unfeeling stubbornness.

'Sir James has been asked — I anticipated such requests, you realize — but he is firm in his intentions. If rents cannot be met, then evictions must follow. Those are his instructions. Lord Listowel has given similar orders, I am told.'

'Have they no mercy?' Jack cried. 'These people will starve.'

Sandes leaned forward in his chair. 'Oh, I think not,' he said, trying to calm the atmosphere. 'Relief is on the way, you know.'

'Relief!' Jack snorted.

'The Prime Minister has authorized £100,000 to be spent on buying Indian corn from the Americas.'

'I read of that. A generous man that Peel,' Jack went on, sarcasm heavy in his voice.

'Some will be stored in Limerick for distribution here,' Sandes said quickly. 'And there'll be local people on the Relief Committees to ensure that the needy will be helped.'

'Like who?'

'Well, two of them will be Dr Church and myself.'

'Land agents both. Landlords' men,' Jack said disgustedly.

'Who better to know those in true need?'

'So you and Church will put these people in the ditch, in the scalp, and then hand out someone else's charity. Tis roguery of the worst kind.' Jack pushed his chair back, walked over to Sandes and stood menacingly above him.

'People like you are the curse of the Irish.' The farmer spoke slowly and deliberately. 'And the time will come . . . '

'Threats change nothing, Keane.' The land agent flicked his eyes away, avoiding Jack's challenging stare. 'You are safe and will be safe because of my word years back. Be thankful for that. And now I think we've spoken enough.'

'We shall never say enough, Sandes,' Jack replied. ''Tis what is in my heart will make that so. Your kind and mine will speak words again until the time comes when your words are seen for what they are. And then no one will listen again. God, may I live to that day!'

Unknown to both men that day, one of the greatest of the Catholic peers in the House of Lords had just had an inspiration for helping the stricken farmers of Ireland. As Jack Keane broke the bad news to his neighbours in the bar of the Listowel Arms and Jonathan Sandes thought darkly on the future, the Duke of Norfolk was rising to expound his new idea to his peers at Westminster.

'If the Irish cannot eat the potato because of the murrain,' the Duke intoned, 'then let them eat curry powder mixed with water. It is cheap and plentiful and undoubtedly sustains the millions in India.'

The Duke sat down again to a few murmured calls of 'Hear, hear.' He smiled to himself with a properly modest sense of self-satisfaction.

## Chapter 2 November, 1846

'Pon my soul, there are thousands of the creatures,' remarked Lieutenant Peter Markison of the 5th Regiment of Foot, a distinct note of worry in his thoroughly English voice. He stood at a second floor window of Listowel workhouse looking down at the mob converging on the building from three sides. 'Sergeant,' he called. 'Position twenty men outside, bayonets fixed, muskets loaded with ball. But on no account are they to open fire without a direct order from myself.'

The sergeant saluted then hitched his pack more comfortably around his shoulders before hurrying off to execute the order.

'What do you make of it all?' the British officer asked, turning to the older man beside him.

'A rabble, Lieutenant. Just a rabble,' snapped Jonathan Sandes, hunched over a thick cane. 'A few constables could deal with them, let alone a platoon of the British Army.'

'They're chanting something, sir. Shall I open the window?'

Without waiting for an answer, the officer pushed up the sash window. The land agent stepped unsteadily backwards as a blast of icy November air enveloped him.

Through the open window, carried by the wind, came a roaring sound, indistinct at first in its cacophony, but soon clearer as the chanting mob approached.

'Bread or blood . . . bread or blood . . . bread or blood . . . bread or blood . . . '

Sandes permitted himself a half smile. 'There's no bread here but there might be a deal of blood, eh, Lieutenant?'

'But, sir,' the officer protested, 'We've more than ten score sacks of Indian meal here and a similar amount in the store near the castle.'

Their chant continued. 'Bread or blood . . . bread or blood . . . bread or blood . . . '

Sandes was forced to raise his voice in order to be heard. 'If you allow even one sack out, those peasants will tear down these walls to steal the rest.'

'But, sir . . . ' Lieutenant Markison began.

'Anyway, my gallant young officer of the line,' Sandes continued, brushing aside the interruption. 'We have firm instructions from Charles Trevelyan at the Treasury in London not to give away any relief supplied. They have to be sold. Market conditions must prevail. Those are Trevelyan's firm instructions. Sell the corn at market prices and let the charity people, like the Society of Friends, give anything away free they wish. But not us. Not us.'

'If that is the situation, sir,' the lieutenant replied heavily, 'I think I should join my men outside. With your permission, of course, Mr Sandes.'

'I fear you're doing little good here, young man, with your ill-informed prattling.' Sandes made little, if any, attempt these days to mask his impatience with the methods used to alleviate the disaster which had befallen Ireland in the past year.

As he had prophesied, the Irish farmer had just survived the winter of 1845 after the failure of the potato crop. The government had set up public works, mainly road building, and paid the farmers who turned labourers between sixpence and tuppence a day to work on them. A man might have to walk seven miles to work and back in a day but his wages enabled him to keep his family from total starvation, with perhaps, a meal of turnips one day, a portion of oatmeal the next. Some of the more foolish and desperate, Sandes reflected, had even eaten seed potatoes, seed corn and seed oats, but nevertheless the weather in May and June of 1846 had been good, raising hopes of plentiful and early crops. In August, the potato fields had been in full bloom but by the end of the month, as mysteriously as before to the farmers, the leaves were scorched black and the stench of diseased tubers covered the townlands once more.

Even Jonathan Sandes had been shocked by this second total failure of the main crop. There was little he could do for his most important patron, Sir James Watson. He realized the small farmers had no money. There was little point in evicting any more families because no one wanted to work the blighted land. The people were starving. He told London so in despatches in his capacity as a Relief Commissioner. But the unwavering reply that came from Charles Trevelyan, the Assistant Secretary at the Treasury, was that market conditions must prevail. It wasn't as if there was no food in Ireland. The wealthier farmers still grew corn and maize, continued to raise cattle and pigs, but no one could afford to buy them at local markets and they were forced to export to England. The troops and constables had been kept busy as the starving peasants tried to ambush the convoys of food and livestock on the way to the docks.

Now it had come to this, Sandes thought, as he surveyed the milling throng outside the workhouse door. The public works programme had ground virtually to a halt. The relief inspectors, hidebound by the rigid rules, were unable to pay even those with employment tickets allowing them to work on the existing projects. And when they were paid they could only afford to buy small amounts of Indian corn because of the high prices of vegetables like peas and cabbages.

Beggars lined every corner of Listowel. But few had money to spare for them. The people had started eating grass, weeds, and nettles. The march on the workhouse had been inevitable. Jonathan Sandes, aching with cold and rheumatism, was surprised that it had come later rather than sooner.

At close quarters, the sight of the mob filled Lieutenant Markison, late of Rugby School and his father's gentle estates in Gloucestershire, with overwhelming horror. He had arrived that July for service in Ireland with his regiment. Since then, everything had been a cameo to be thrust into the recesses of his mind, hopefully forgotten except in moments of half-sleep. Before him now was a gigantic canvas filled with the suffering of the people of the north Kerry plain – of all Ireland.

Families huddled together for protection from the shrivelling wind. Around the men's heads were hats fashioned of old sacking: some completely covered the head except for jagged holes for the eyes. All the faces which Lieutenant Markison could distinguish were pinched, almost opaque, skin stretched tight over cheekbones, the eyes dull with dark rings, sunk deep into their sockets. Women were swathed in shawls, sacks, cast off petticoats; their feet wrapped in the ubiquitous sacking; their legs protected with old newspapers stuffed with straw. Children leeched on to their parents for any warmth, faces lined and gaunt from hunger. Their constant condition of near starvation had caused clumps of hair to fall from their scalps – some were totally bald – but, strangely, horrifyingly, downy hair grew on their foreheads and their cheeks. Many resembled wizened monkeys. In every hand was a mug or a bowl thrust towards the soldiers. One young soldier was crying at the sight before him, tears running silently down his face, but still his musket and gleaming bayonet were steady, pointing upwards and outwards towards the encircling wraiths.

A low murmur ran through the crowd as the impressive figure of Lieutenant Markison came into view. A hum of expectant conversation swept through the waiting thousands until a group towards the back took up the chant again.

'Bread or blood . . . bread or blood . . . bread or blood . . . '

The sound beat round Lieutenant Markison. Instinctively, he surveyed the tactical position of his men and himself. There was no doubt his platoon was trapped. The only possible help would be from the dozen constables half a mile away at their barracks. The nearest regular troops were at Tralee, nearly a day's march away. At that moment, the lieutenant was certain bloodshed was inevitable. His men might be able to loose two rounds of fire before retreating into the workhouse to defend it. But he also knew that their ammunition stocks were inadequate to hold off such a large mob. Men, women and children would die before the mob broke through the defences but when that happened the lieutenant knew there would be no mercy. Already, he had noticed men, dotted here and there in the crowd, holding shillelaghs with nails driven through the clubs' heads.

Lieutenant Markison looked quickly up at the window where he had been standing, hoping for some sign of guidance from Jonathan

Sandes, but the land agent had retreated to a safer position.

The officer raised his arms. 'Quiet. Quiet,' he shouted against the throbbing tide of the chant. 'Quiet! Listen to me!' And then in a quieter voice to his men, 'Keep steady, lads. Show 'em no fear or we're done for. Steady.'

'Quiet,' he roared again. 'Be silent and listen!'

'Bread or blood . . . bread or blood . . . bread or blood . . . '

The chant drowned his words. The mob started slowly to press forward. The men at the front looked dully, rather than fearfully, at the bayonets bristling in front of them, as they were thrust nearer and nearer the sharp steel by the pressure of the throng. They began pushing their women and children behind them, as if accepting that their fate was to die first. There was no terror in their faces, Markison realized, rather expressions of relief as if it were better to die quickly than to continue in their present sufferings.

There was little choice left to him. He lowered his arms and began moving his hands gingerly towards his pistols. He thought of his father, gruff pride in his voice, presenting him with the finely-chased guns on the day he'd obtained his officer's commission. Such weapons, the lieutenant thought, were not made to be used against the pathetic targets which faced him now. Sadly, there seemed no alternative.

Suddenly he noticed a movement towards the front of the crowd as it parted reluctantly, grudgingly, to allow a tall man through its ranks. At first, Markison could only see that the man had a shock of grey hair and was enveloped in a thick black cloak which swirled about him. Some of the crowd, particularly the women, crossed themselves and bent to their knees in half-curtseys as the man brushed by them. As he came to the front of the crowd, the officer saw he carried a large Bible thrust out in front of him. Lieutenant Markison, although not recognizing him, realized immediately that the man must be the parish priest, Father O'Mahony. His hands moved away from the pistol holsters. He raised his arms again and shouted for quiet. The young officer knew that the next best thing to a troop of dragoons had come to his aid.

The priest walked forward from the front of the crowd until the ring of steel around Lieutenant Markison was only inches from his chest. His face was grim but his deep-set blue eyes looked calmly at the British officer.

'Let the priest through,' Lieutenant Markison ordered. The bayonets lowered, parted, and Father O'Mahoney stepped into the protective semi-circle.

'You have a wise head, sir, on such young shoulders,' he said in a surprisingly resonant voice. 'One shot and this would be a massacre. In the madness, I doubt that even I would be spared.' The priest smiled.

'But what can I do, Father? My clear orders are to stop these . . . these . . . '

'Human beings,' Father O'Mahony interrupted gently.

' . . . these people from entering the workhouse.'

'That is clear from your demeanour, lieutenant, and I'm sure that you would carry out your orders to the letter. This is not of your making, nor of mine, nor of these poor wretches.' The priest gestured towards the crowd which had been silent as it watched the priest and the officer talking but had now begun to chant again.

'Bread or blood . . . bread or blood . . . bread or blood . . . '

The priest leaned close to Lieutenant Markison. 'Have you any bread in the workhouse, sir?' he shouted above the din.

'No, Father. No bread. There is . . . '

'Hush, sir. Tell me no more. If you have no bread, then that is all I need to know. I shall not, nor ever will, lie to my people. Now, if you will, please move your men aside so that the crowd can see that I am unmolested. Let us discover together, lieutenant, the power of the Church and pray that it possesses enough.'

Lieutenant Markison hesitated for a moment, then nodded. 'Part the ranks, Sergeant,' he ordered. 'Move back into the workhouse.'

'A great cheer broke from the crowd as the troops shouldered their muskets before filing back into the building, a few of them looking fearfully over their shoulders as they passed through the doors. The mob surged forward expectantly towards the priest and the young officer, now standing side by side on the workhouse step.

The priest spread his arms, the cloak unfolding like a raven's wing, holding the Bible aloft, allowing all in the crowd to see his cleric's collar and the cross dangling on his chest.

'My people, My poor people,' he began. The chant died away gradually. The crowd stopped and strained to hear the priest.

'You know me. You all know me. Father Darby. Your Father Darby who's received you into the Church, who's danced at your weddings, who's keened at your wakes, who's heard your confessions and eased your mortal souls, who's taken a jar or two more than he should with many of you when times were better . . . '

There was laughter from some in the crowd. Father Jeremiah 'Darby' O'Mahony was known and loved as a man who liked his jar or two as much as he liked collecting rare books.

The priest seized on the laughter. 'And who's confessing now? And to the biggest congregation of his life? Why, anyone could be telling the lord bishop, so I'm thinking I should be asking this young bucko of an officer to be taking round his hat for my last collection!'

He pointed at Lieutenant Markison's tall uniform helmet, an exaggerated expression of pleading on his face.

The crowd broke into general laughter. ''Twould make a mighty fine piss-pot, Father Darby,' someone shouted amid the growing laughter. 'That's all that'd be collected here and that's the truth.'

'And don't I just know that, friends?' the priest shouted. His tone became serious. 'Sure and I'm knowing you have no money and little enough food for your wee ones let alone yourselves.' He shook the Bible in the air. 'Oh, that Lord Jesus was here himself to perform the miracle of the fishes and the loaves, for you cannot be expecting any miracles from your Father Darby. Sure and I pray for one every waking moment, but so many miracles are being asked of Our Lord from this poor land that I'm fearing He hasn't one to spare for us. But twill do no harm, no harm at all, if all of us here joined in prayer now.'

'What about the bread, Father?' a voice cried from the back of the crowd.

'There is none, my friend. I have the word of this young officer beside me that there is no bread in the workhouse. And he wouldn't be lying to me and then standing by men now, defenceless, away from his soldier boys, if that wasn't the truth, now would he?'

Many of the crowd nodded in agreement.

'No, there is no bread here, my people,' Father O'Mahony hurried on, his voice rising as he tried to retain his momentary control over the thousands. 'But let us join in prayer that soon there shall be bread – not only for you, but for the poor wretches lying, starving, inside this workhouse itself. We'll be having no bread by spilling blood this day. Let us pray instead.' He fell to his knees, the Bible clasped between his hands. Lieutenant Markison stood awkwardly above him. 'Get down, sir,' Father O'Mahony muttered from the side of his mouth. 'You've been wanting a miracle to save you and your men, so give thanks you might be having one.' The officer slipped off his black chin-strap, pulled off his helmet, and knelt quickly by the older man. Lieutenant Markison's blond hair ruffled in the biting wind.

'Oh, Lord Jesus, who knows all things . . . ' the priest began. The people in the front of the mob dropped to their knees as they heard the start of a prayer. The remainder quickly joined them. 'Oh, Lord

Jesus, who knows all things,' the priest repeated. 'Look into the hearts of these your people this day and know their love for You who were born of Holy Mary. As You suffered on the Cross, Jesus, look down on our mortal sufferings with mercy. Let not your people's sufferings cause anger in their hearts, Lord, rather let their weakness and hunger bring them closer to You who knew the same weakness and hunger. Oh, Lord Jesus, if You cannot comfort their bodies, then give them the strength to endure, just as you endured the nails and the thrust of the spear.'

Father O'Mahony lifted his face to the sky. A shaft of sunlight daggered through the clouds and lit his features. 'Oh, Lord Jesus, give us the strength to endure for truly Thine is the power and the glory. Amen. Thine is the power and the glory. Amen.'

A rumbling 'Amen' rolled from the crowd. The priest lifted the cross on the chain around his neck and pressed it to his lips. He stood up, watching the people – his people – in their thousands cross themselves before scrambling to their feet again.

'Go to your homes, my friends, and God be with you,' he roared. 'Go to your homes.' The people began dispersing slowly, talking quietly among themselves.

Then the priest realized the young officer was still on his knees by his side, eyes screwed shut, lips moving silently. He put a hand on the gold epaulette on his shoulder. 'Your prayer has been answered, my son,' the priest said softly. 'They are going now. There'll be no bloodshed.'

Lieutenant Markison stood up, brushed the dust from his trousers, and watched the departing thousands, backs bent in weary resignation. 'My prayers might have been heard, Father,' he muttered. 'But what of theirs?'

'God knows, Lieutenant. Only God knows.'

Suddenly a small boy ran up sobbing, past tears streaking his face.

'Come quickly, Father. They've eaten the weed.'

'What weed, boy? Quickly now.'

'Someone said tis called praiseach.'

'Oh, Lord,' the priest cried. 'Show me, boy. Fast now. Show me.'

The priest pushed through the crowd followed by the British officer.

'Oh, Lord,' he repeated. On the ground by the hedgerow lay nine men, seven women and eleven children.

They were writhing in the dirt, legs kicking, backs arching, frothing at the mouth, screaming in agony, hands clutching first at their throats then at their stomachs.

'What is it, Father?' shouted Lieutenant Markison above the awful cries of pain.

The priest said nothing. He just pointed at a luxuriantly green bunch of weeds growing under the hedge. Then he began to administer the last rites of the Church to the people in their death agonies around him.

'What is it?' the lieutenant asked the people in the crowd, bewilderment in his voice.

'Tis praiseach. Poison weed,' one man replied, his eyes transfixed by the scene before him. 'They were so hungry, they ate the weed. Just plucked it and thrust it down their throats. There was no bread so they ate the weed.'

A harsh light filtered through the high arched windows of the Faneuil Hall in Boston. The market on the ground floor had long since ended its day's business leaving the building to fulfil its natural role as the town's public focus. Outside, a fine sleet was falling this February day in 1847, making the cobbles slippery for horses and carriages, yet hundreds had packed into the hall to dicuss the plight of the Irish. Already, hundreds of thousands of dollars had been raised by the town's Catholics and by merchants of all denominations to buy cornmeal to send to the starving millions across the Atlantic. From one church collection alone, Bishop Fitzpatrick had sent provisions worth more than one hundred thousand dollars.

Boston hardly needed reminding by Thomas D'Arcy McGee, the editor of the *Boston Pilot*, that the Irish should not be regarded as foreigners but as an indispensable factor in the growth of the young nation. In an impassioned editorial McGee told Boston 'that Ireland did supply the hands which led Lake Erie to the sea and wedded the strong Chesapeke to the gentle Delaware, and carried the roads of the East to the farthest outposts of the West'.

Alderman Matt Finucane, still the elected representative for the town's Ward 8 district where many of the emigrants had settled, was rightly proud of what had been done. Indeed, much of the support had been at his instigation.

'The conscience of Boston can be clear,' he told the gathering of merchants and their ladies from the podium in Faneuil Hall. 'But something more should be done, must be done. Something that will show the world that not only Boston but all of America extends its generosity, its pity, to those starving nigh unto death.'

A murmur of assent ran through the hall followed by a ripple of applause. Matt Finucane, grey haired and respectably portly as befitted a substantial man of business, waited for the noise to subside. He glanced sideways at his wife, Alice, and his youngest daughter, Mary, sitting on the platform behind the podium, and smiled. He had rightly judged the mood of the meeting.

'The English government might be excused of tardiness in helping our brothers but then think of the enormity of the task,' he went on. 'It is true that that government has given millions but it is also true that some of the high and mighty of England have shamed themselves by their utterances . . . '

'The Duke of Cambridge,' someone shouted from the body of the hall. There was an angry stir mingled with contemptuous laughter.

'Yes, friends, people like the great Duke of Cambridge. Do you remember what he said? That everyone knew Irishmen could live upon anything and that there was plenty of grass in the fields. Yes, that's how the mighty duke will be remembered wherever this sorry episode is told and re-told but . . . '

Finucane paused for effect. He jabbed a finger at the audience.

' . . . but be remembering this also. The ordinary citizens of England have not forgotten the starving ones. They have dug deep into their purses and sent even more charity to Ireland than we have. So today let us decide upon a gesture which will not only help the poor and weak in Ireland but will show them also that their suffering is our suffering.'

The alderman scanned the hall and the sea of high-crowned hats and bonnets in front of him.

'In this town's harbour, under our very noses lies America's messenger to poor Ireland – the sloop of war, *Jamestown*. She lies there, swinging at anchor. Let her be provisioned and sent across the ocean in order that the Stars and Stripes should be seen fluttering off Ireland's coast, thus demonstrating that she is deep in our thoughts and hearts at this time of her awful travail.'

There was silence in Faneuil Hall for a moment before the merchants, politicians, and ordinary Bostonians began cheering, applauding even stamping their feet in approval.

Within weeks, the United States Congress had granted Boston's petition and the sloop *Jamestown* was heading for landfall at Cobh with forty thousand dollars' worth of grain, meal and clothing in her holds.

A few days after her arrival, a dying man caught the eye of the bewigged Speaker in 'the mother of parliaments' by the River Thames, and hobbled painfully the dozen steps towards the large ornate table in the centre of the House of Commons. He paused for a moment, catching his breath, and looked round the debating chamber at his fellow members of Parliament. They were chattering away among themselves, virtually ignoring him, where once they would have been silent, attentively listening to his every word.

Daniel O'Connell, 'The Liberator', gathered his remaining strength and began to speak in a low, halting voice. At times his speech was delivered in a whisper. Even the official reporters were unsure of what he was saying for much of the time as O'Connell criticized the government for not doing enough to help Ireland.

The politicians who were near him shrugged their shoulders as O'Connell rambled on. Hadn't the government spent eight million pounds on aid, they asked themselves? Hadn't the young Queen Victoria personally given £2,000 from her own fortune? What more did the old man want?

O'Connell heard the deprecating comments all around him. He made one more effort to be heard amid the growing chorus of disinterest.

'Ireland is in your hands, in your power,' he tried to declaim with all his former power but his voice hardly rose above a mutter. 'If you do not save Ireland, she cannot save herself.'

He moved slowly back to his seat as another member of Parliament caught the Speaker's eye and raised a point of order.

Daniel O'Connell's final illness had struck when Ireland needed him most. He gazed around the dark panelled chamber for a few minutes before nodding his respects towards the Speaker and leaving the House of Commons for the last time.

Hunger and disease had killed about a million people by the spring of 1847. Jack Keane didn't know whether he and Matt really were lucky to be alive in the middle of such desolation. The agony of living among wholesale suffering was made worse by the knowledge that there was little he could do to help. He was virtually bankrupt, both emotionally and materially. He had worked unceasingly to help his poorer neighbours and his own labourers only to see them disappear one by one, either dying from starvation and disease or joining the ragged thousands in their agonizing march to a new life in the English slums, the industrial cities of North America, even to far off Australia.

Jack couldn't remember how many times he'd stood at the side of a newly dug mass grave at Teampáillin Bán by the track from Listowel to Ballybunnion as his friends had been buried, family by family. Most of the available wood in Listowel had been burned as firewood. There was none left over for coffins. The dead were taken to the grave in a trap coffin and dropped into the earth through its hinged bottom, sometimes two at a time.

He'd sold or slaughtered his livestock to provide fares and provisions for those who chose emigration. Now there was little left. Without help, Jack and Matt found it impossible to work all the farm's eighty acres. The last quarter's rent had been paid only thanks to an unsolicited gift from Alderman Finucane in Boston which had arrived with a letter from his old friend urging him to return to Massachusetts. At first, Jack had dismissed the idea but lately he had given it more and more consideration.

'I can't be seeing a future here anymore for yourself,' he'd told Matt when his mind was finally made up. 'Twill be years before Ireland recovers – if she ever does. And here, in the west, twill be even worse. We were poor to begin with. Now we have less than nothing. Half the people have died or gone across the sea.'

'But if we leave, we'll be giving up all we've worked for,' Matt said defiantly.

Jack smiled. He was pleased to see spirit still in the youngster after everything he'd seen and endured. 'Twice I've started from scratch, lad. They say tis easier the third time. If we go to Boston town, I'm reckoning my old friends will give us a helping hand.'

'But couldn't we survive here, Jack-Da?'

'After a fashion, perhaps, but I'm thinking of opportunities for you. There's nothing here,' Jack insisted. 'And also there's tell of rebellion in the air. They say the Young Irelanders are planning something but I'm guessing twill come to naught as usual. But when it's all done, why the English will have even less reason or desire to help us. Times will be harder, you mark.'

'And in Boston?'

'The world, lad. The whole world,' Jack replied, slapping the table in the cabin for emphasis. 'Tis a young country, what they've explored of it. Half of it isn't yet on the map. Tis not tired like Ireland. There's little past there, just the future.'

Matt was not completely convinced. 'You once said this farm was my birthright. Me mam's here, so are all your folks. Do we just leave them like that? Does someone else take the farm?'

'I'm praying not, Matt. The Keanes have lived in this townland for five generations or more. The family split their nails and cracked their fingers making the farm worthy. That I'll not lose, nor the graves of our own people. You're right to remind me of that and, sure, there's a deal to be struck with Mr Sandes before we'll be making any more plans.'

The next day, Jack rode to Listowel to see the land agent. All along the track half-naked families were crouched in their rude shelters in the ditch and hedgerows, dirty, long haired, grunting to themselves as if they'd become animals of the forest. By the workhouse, more than a hundred women and children were queueing for their free soup. Jack knew that the gruel would pass straight through most of them without providing any nourishment. What was the cost? Less than one penny for four gallons if the soup was made according to the official instructions. An oxhead without the tongue, 28 lbs of turnips, 3 lbs of onions, 7 lbs of carrots, 21 lbs of peameal, 14 lbs of Indian corn meal, all mixed together with 30 gallons of water. The stingiest citizen couldn't object to an increased local rate being levied to make such an economic mixture, yet the bigger landowners, had found it cheaper to encourage their tenants to emigrate than to subsidize aid and work for them. Perhaps, Jack wondered, Jonathan Sandes would prefer Matt and himself to go to America rather than staying to become charges of the parish. Surprisingly, the land agent took the opposite view.

'This is the right time to be staying on the land, Keane, not to be leaving,' he said as he slumped wearily into the recesses of the high-backed chair in his study. 'There are so many acres going begging which you could rent for peppercorns. As you've impressed upon me before, plenty follows scarcity. Well then, now is the time to invest your time.'

'My mind is certain, Mr Sandes. I'm not looking to my future, God knows, but to the youngster's. All I'm wishing to retain of the farm are the fields containing the cabin and the family graves. The remainder can be turned over to a new tenant, if you can find one,' Jack declared.

'A new tenant, eh? It'll be difficult finding one. Are you sure you won't stay?'

'I'm certain.'

'Then, as you like, Keane. As you like,' Sandes muttered almost apathetically. His grey appearance and apparent disinterest bore the hallmarks of a man who knew he had little time left.

''Tis Matt I'm thinking of. That's all.'

Sandes leaned forward. He coughed wheezily. 'The young man has been told of his relationship to me?'

'Aye. Some years past.'

'And he has the preference to be going with you rather than

238

relying on this relationship for any advantage hereabouts?'

'That he does.'

'Spirited, is he?' Sandes interrupted.

'As his mother,' Jack replied shortly.

The land agent smiled wanly, acknowledging the implied rebuke.

''Twas the boy who wanted to keep a hold on the cabin and the graves,' Jack continued. 'So I'm thinking he might be returning one day. The rent will be sent from America to keep those two fields.'

'Fear not, Keane. I shall give instructions that the young man shall have first call on that land.'

'Then, tis a final farewell I'll bid you, Mr Sandes. Whatever happens, I'm sure I'll be spending the years which remain to me in America. Three crossings are enough for one lifetime.'

'As you say, Keane, a final farewell. Even if you return, I shall be in a better place than this benighted land.'

Jonathan Sandes held out his right hand. 'Once, at least, Keane. Just once,' he said quietly.

Jack hesitated for a moment then shook the proffered hand. 'It changes nothing,' he muttered.

'I know. I know,' Sandes replied wearily. 'But then it doesn't matter, does it? At the end nothing matters really except the end itself.'

Two weeks later, Jack and Matt played hosts at a farewell ceilidh. The drinking and dancing went on into the early hours while they entertained the twenty or so friends and neighbours they were leaving behind. During the evening they divided among their guests the cabin's furniture, the four remaining chickens in the run, and the sacks of maize and turnips still stored in the outhouse.

After a few hours sleep, Jack Keane and Matt Aherne woke and washed, before kneeling in silent prayer before the cross and the tattered picture of the Virgin Mary set into the cabin wall.

'Lord, let this be the right way for us,' Jack prayed. 'Let us journey in safety.'

'Lord, let me return one day,' Matt asked.

When the prayers were finished, Jack stowed the cross and the Virgin's picture safely in the bundle of clothes and rugs which were strapped to his horse for the journey to Tarbert where he hoped to find a ship.

'The graves, Jack-Da?' Matt asked as he closed the cabin door behind him.

'Aye, lad, for a moment. Then we must be away.'

The two of them stood in front of the headstones for a few minutes. Jack stooped to snap a sprig of the fresh bunch of hawthorn lying on Brigid Aherne's grave. He handed it to Matt.

'Here . . . carry this with you always, then you can be sure of returning one day if you want.'

Matt nodded, too full of emotion to risk speaking.

'A long time ago,' Jack said gently, 'I was told never to look back. Tis good advice. Carry your memories in your heart, but never look back, lad.'

Matt Aherne smiled gratefully at his guardian, then looked away. He had never seen a grown man crying before.

## Chapter 3 April, 1847

Captain Josiah Swain had converted the *Egypt* to carry passengers only when he had realized the size of the lucrative trade to be had from the Irish who were fleeing from famine and disease. His instructions to the ship converters at Liverpool had been precise: as many bunks as could be fitted into the main hold with a long table and benches down the centre of the deck. Nothing more, nothing less. What could people expect for a £5 passage between the Shannon and Boston, the comfort and speed of Brunel's new iron steamship *Great Britain*? Captain Swain's conscience was untroubled as his passengers – men, women and children – continued to suffer during the fifth day since the *Egypt* with its 258 passengers had left the shelter of the Shannon.

Another spasm of seasickness gripped Matt Aherne as the ship wallowed in the heavy Atlantic swell. He groaned and pressed his face into the foul smelling lump of cloth stuffed with straw which served as a pillow.

The air in the passengers' hold was rank and fetid. The planks of the deck were slippery with vomit and human waste. Babies howled continuously in their distress and fear in the enclosed world between decks. The creaking timbers, vile smells, swinging oil lamps and heaving decks were terrifying to youngsters used to green fields and fast-running skies.

The few passengers who, like Jack Keane, had some familiarity with the sea tried to ease the general suffering.

'Am I dying, Jack-Da?' Matt mumbled, colourless bile dribbling down his chin.

Jack knelt by the bunk and wiped it away. He was confident that Matt would recover shortly but he feared for some of the under-nourished babies and young children. The worst affected lay supine in their bunks, hardly ever crying, their eyes bright and feverish, fixing and staring.

'Have you no medicines aboard?' Jack demanded of one of the crew when he was stumping around with that day's water ration.

'Medicine, mate? This is a blurry sailing ship – not a lying-in hospital. There's no medicine in Cap'n Swain's ships 'cept maybe some rum.'

''Tis for the children,' said Jack. 'Can you not be seeing that the wee ones are dying? They're needing something to help them take nourishment.'

'Is that the truth then?' the seaman replied sarcastically. He dropped his pail heavily by Jack. Some of the water splashed over Matt, who tried to sit up.

Jack rose to his feet, glaring at the seaman. ''Tis your manners need improving, I'm thinking, sailor.'

The seaman, sharp faced and skinny, slid a hand towards the knife sheathed on his belt. Jack stepped forward and lashed out with a roundhouse punch. The seaman staggered back, and slipped on the wet planks. His arms flailed wildly as he crashed backwards and the back of his head struck the edge of a bunk with a sharp crack.

'Jesus,' Jack thought, 'Your man's cracked his skull open.' He bent over the seaman, looking for signs of life. There was still a strong pulse in his wrist. Jack heaved a sigh of relief, picked up the pail of water and emptied it over the prone man.

The seaman's eyes flickered open. 'I'll kill the bastard. I'll kill him.'

'You're lucky, sailor. You've had a bad knock.'

The seaman wrenched himself away from Jack's grasp. His eyes showed his fury as he looked his assailant up and down. They softened slightly when they took in Jack's girth and obvious strength.

'Are you recovered then?' Jack asked, genuine concern in his voice.

The seaman glowered. 'Like a footpad that was. Struck when I wasn't looking,' he declared indignantly to anyone in hearing. The incident, in fact, had happened so quickly that few passengers had noticed it. 'Cap'n Swain'll know of this. Attacking the crew.'

He swayed towards the ladder and began climbing upwards. When he was within a few steps of the main deck, he turned his head. 'Blurry Irish, the lot of you. Best if your brats do die.'

Jack stooped over Matt again when the seaman had vanished from sight. 'Thanks be to God, lad,' he muttered as he bathed his brow. 'I thought that was the second man I'd killed.'

But Jack's relief lasted only a few minutes. He heard heavy sea boots clumping on the deck above him and then begin descending the ladder towards the passengers' quarters.

'That's him,' cried a voice from the top of the ladder. 'There's the rat who attacked me.'

'Stay still or it'll be the worse for you,' another stronger voice commanded. Jack, peering up into the light could make out three men on the ladder. One of them, burly and dark-bearded, carried what appeared to be a blunderbuss. It glinted darkly as it pointed down at Jack.

'Right then. Come up here. Up the ladder and quick about it,' ordered the man with the blunderbuss. Jack presumed this must be Captain Swain, and reluctantly began to clamber up the ladder. The three men retreated before him, but although the captain walked backwards, the blunderbuss never wavered in its aim.

Jack blinked against the strong daylight as he stepped on to the open deck.

'Yes, that's him, Cap'n. Definite.'

'You know who I am?' the man in the cap asked.

'Captain Swain, the master?'

'That's right. And you are . . . ?'

'Keane. Jack Keane from Drombeg in Kerry.'

'Then, Jack Keane, why did you attack one of my crew?'

In a few terse sentences Jack told him what had happened below.

'True, Sims?' the captain barked. 'Did you spill water over him? Did you reach for your knife?'

'Defending myself I was, Cap'n.'

Captain Swain lowered the blunderbuss and let it hang by his side. But his finger stayed on the trigger guard. 'Riled you, did he, Keane?'

'He didn't seem to care for the suffering creatures below, Captain.'

'And should he? They've only the sea sickness. They'll recover.'

'But the wee ones are in a mortal state, Captain.'

'The law says they're to have seven pounds of provisions each week and that's what they're getting.'

'They can't eat, Captain. And what they drink, they can't hold down.'

Captain Swain looked quizzically across at the man wearing the leather jerkin. 'Is that true, Master Mate?'

'No one's told me, cap'n.'

'Haven't you inspected the passengers?'

'Gone below?' the mate said incredulously. 'Not since we slipped Tarbert Island, Cap'n. They're having the food and water, I know that.'

Captain Swain scowled at his mate. 'And what if they're dying on us? Pretty name that'll give this ship.' He heaved a sigh. 'I suppose I'll have to look for myself,' he said, and handed the blunderbuss to the mate. 'Stay here but come running if you hear my shout. And don't be afeared of using the weapon.' He turned to Jack. 'You first . . . and no trouble or your friends will be scraping bits of you from the deck.'

Jack started down the ladder with the captain close behind him. After breathing fresh salt air on deck, the stench of the passengers' quarters was even more oppressive.

Captain Swain coughed and gagged. He pressed a large red handkerchief to his mouth and nostrils.

'Tis your ship, Captain,' Jack said sarcastically. 'Not a pretty smell, is it?'

The captain waved him on. Jack led him round the bunks, pointing to those in most suffering. At one bunk, he stopped to pick up a baby which was scarcely a year old. He held the child out to the captain. The baby's head dropped sideways because of its lack of strength. The wrapping shawl was stained and stiff with dried vomit. Captain Swain pushed Jack aside and hurried back to the ladder leading upwards. Jack placed the baby gently back in the bunk and murmured some comforting words before following him.

'Well, Captain?' he asked. The captain didn't answer for a moment as he gulped in deep breaths of fresh air.

'It's bad, Keane. I'll give you that. And I should have been told earlier.'

'What are you going to do? You cannot just let them die in their own filth like that.'

Captain Swain gestured helplessly. 'There are no physicians out here, Keane, and my crew are no nurses. The provisions and water they've been having are all that we've aboard. They're in God's hands.'

'Have you any opiates?' Jack asked, an idea forming in his mind.

'Opiates?'

'For when any of your crew is hurt . . . '

'Rum?'

'Anything else?'

'Oh, come to reckon it now, my wife did buy some laudanum to ease any ague aboard.'

Jack smiled. ''Tis not much, Captain, but I've heard tell that such an opiate does settle the stomach. What if we made porridge from the oats in the provisions and then laced it with your laudanum? Such a stirabout would help them, I'm thinking.'

'Anything, Keane. Anything,' Captain Swain replied quickly. 'The crew will help but you'll have to feed the sick ones yourself. Seamen don't like being near such people. They know disease and illness can spread on ships. They're mortal frightened of that.'

That afternoon, Jack and the few other passengers who'd found their sea legs began dosing the sick with the mixture of porridge and laudanum. They waited anxiously to see if they could hold down the food and were pleased when most did. The feeding was repeated every three hours and before long most of those who had been sick were able to leave their bunks and get up on deck for fresh air. Inevitably, some of the babies were too ill to respond.

Nine days out of the Shannon, the crew and passengers of the *Egypt* stood bareheaded on the main deck as Captain Swain intoned a prayer over eleven small canvas bundles. The mothers of the dead children sobbed quietly during the brief, makeshift burial service, then began shrieking hysterically as, at a signal from the captain, the pathetic little bundles were sent splashing into the Atlantic. The suddenness of the burial, its harsh irrevocability, stunned most of the passengers.

'Poor wee mites,' murmured Matt Aherne as he stood alongside Jack Keane. 'They survived all the death at home only to die on their way to their new life.'

Jack looked at the youngster closely. He was still weak from his prolonged bout of seasickness but the colour was beginning to return to his cheeks. Jack rubbed at the dark rings of tiredness under his eyes. 'We've a deal of ocean to travel yet in this old ship before we reach Boston town. Think not so much on them who've gone to their Maker. They might be the lucky ones. Think more on us surviving the voyage.'

'You've a seaman's philosophy, Keane,' Captain Swain interrupted as he strode over towards them. 'You've travelled the ocean before?'

'Crossed the Atlantic twice, so I have.'

'Then, Keane,' the captain said, 'I shall be wanting help from you. You can be the go-between between myself and the passengers. I'm sure they'll be happier to be told what's going on by one of their own.'

'If twill help . . . The coffin ships are in their minds all the time. Everyone knows of the ship which left Westport and then sank in sight of land with all the relatives still watching from the shore.'

Captain Swain gave him a sharp look. 'The *Egypt* will carry you to the Americas, that she will. With these winds I'm reckoning on another thirty days or so.'

For the next three weeks, the old sailing ship bucketed and wallowed her way steadily westwards. The passengers became accustomed to shipboard life, even organizing ceilidhs to keep their spirits high. Some of the young children continued to suffer from diarrohea but the general health of the emigrants remained fairly high. Then one day in the middle of the fifth week of the voyage with landfall not another seven days away, Matt was strolling on the main deck with Jack when he pointed to a man sitting alone on the opposite side of the deck.

'Has he the toothache, Jack-Da?' he asked. 'His face is awful swollen, so it is.'

'Aye, lad, it is that. Are you knowing who he is?'

'Murphy, I think. Willie Murphy from Foynes.'

Jack sauntered casually across the deck towards the man. A few feet from him, he stopped and took a closer look at Murphy's face. Not only was it swollen, but the complexion was dark and congested, almost blue in colour.

'How's it going then, Willie?' he asked, still keeping his distance.

'Not too good, friend,' Murphy replied through swollen lips. 'All of a sudden I've this bloated feeling all over me. Strange it is. Like I'm swelling up.'

There was a definite smell coming from Murphy. It reminded Jack of rotting vegetables. Immediately he knew where he had smelt it before. It had been in a cabin at Gortacrossane where an entire family had died from the black fever, typhus.

'Oh, Lord,' Jack murmured under his breath. And then aloud as casually as he could, 'How's the family, then, Willie?'

'Just fine now they've their sealegs.'

'I'm thinking you should be staying away from them for a bit, Willie,' he said quietly, almost apologetically.

Murphy grasped the ship's rail and pulled himself to his feet. 'What are you saying, Mr Keane?' he demanded, concern mounting in his voice.

'Just that, Willie. It might be nothing but from the look of you, you could have caught what's called a spreading illness.'

'Like the black fever?' Murphy was now thoroughly alarmed.

'Aye, like the fever. But that's not saying you've got it. Why, Captain Swain'll probably find you a cabin all to yourself. Just you stay here, breathing all this fine air, and I'll be fixing you up. Don't you be worrying yourself.'

'And the woman and the four wee ones below?'

'Leave them to me, Willie. Sure and I'll be telling them enough to soothe them and yet not enough to frighten them.'

Jack hurried below to Captain Swain's sparse cabin.

'Come to see the latest position, Keane?' the captain asked with a smile. He pointed to a cross on the map. 'There we are. With these southeasterlys as they are, you should be seeing Boston again in four days or so. Ahead of time for once. I told you she was a good old . . . '

'Would that it was tomorrow, Captain,' Jack said.

'Eh? Impatient aren't you?'

''Tis not that. If I'm right then we've real trouble aboard. I'm reckoning one of the passengers is sickening with black fever.'

'Black fever?'

'That's how tis known in Ireland. Typhus is the . . . '

Captain Swain jumped to his feet, knocking his chair over in alarm.

'Typhus! Merciful Christ, not that. We'll all be dead.' He paused and tugged at his beard. 'How many are down?'

'Only one that I know. He's on deck at present. I'm thinking the sooner we put him somewhere on his own the better chance we'll all have.'

'Are you sure, man?'

'Have I not seen enough cases of black fever in the last year?'

'I remember one ship I was in as first mate. Near three-quarters of the crew died, they did. We'll get him below into the mate's cabin and lock him in.'

'I'll check the other passengers.'

'Right. But be careful.' Captain Swain beat his fist against his forehead. 'Oh, Christ, this would happen. Only a few more days . . . only a few . . . '

'There'll be help in Boston, I'm thinking, Captain.'

'If we ever reach there. Pray that the fever doesn't strike the crew or we're all done for.'

Half an hour later, Jack escorted the sick man down to the mate's cabin, ensured that adequate provisions and fresh water had been placed there for him, and then locked him in. He tried to turn the key as quietly as he could but still Willie Murphy heard the click.

'What's this you're doing?' he shouted through the door, pounding on the wood. 'Don't be leaving me here alone, for God's sake.'

'Tis for everyone's good, Willie,' Jack shouted back. 'We're not wanting a person to wander into the cabin by mistake.'

'So tis the fever I've got then,' Murphy half-sobbed. 'Oh, Jesus have mercy on me.'

'Hush there, Willie. Tis just a precaution as I said.' Jack hated himself at that moment.

Murphy began hammering on the door again, crying in rage and fear. 'Have pity, for mercy's sake,' he screamed. 'Don't lock me away like an animal. My woman. The wee ones. Oh, Jesus, you cannot be doing this . . .'

Willie Murphy's screams stayed in Jack's ears even when he was out of hearing. On deck, he explained to Matt what had happened.

'We'll be sleeping topside till we reach Boston, lad, and keeping ourselves to ourselves. Tis our only hope and I'm thinking you'd be better by staying away from me as well.' Jack took a step away from the youngster. 'But don't be worrying,' he said reassuringly. 'I've not survived all these years to be letting the fever get me.'

Matt smiled at his bravado.

Willie Murphy's wife, Mary, was stunned by the news that he had been isolated in the mate's cabin. Her four children, the eldest only eight years old, failed to understand what Jack told them.

'When will we be seeing our da then?' one of them asked.

'Don't be fretting yourself, little one,' Jack answered. 'I'll be looking after you while your da's getting better.'

'Getting better, Mr Keane?' their mother said bitterly, an accusing look on her face. 'Getting better, did you say?'

Jack felt wretched. He could only nod as he moved away from the family whose world had just been destroyed.

'And will we be getting better too?' the woman's shrill voice, edged with hysteria, followed him. 'Or will we be hearing some more of your fine words when you'll be putting us all away?'

The first inspection of the passengers failed to find anyone else with noticeable fever symptoms, but the inspection itself, coupled with rumours about Willie Murphy, spread fear and despondency throughout the *Egypt*. That Willie Murphy had typhus was clear by the evening of that day.

Jack and Captain Swain went to the mate's cabin after supper. They approached the door quietly. Jack slipped the key into the lock and softly turned it. There was little need to enter the cabin to realize that Murphy's condition had deteriorated. The smell was almost intolerable and from inside came the sound of the diseased man's delirious ravings.

Within the next forty-eight hours, as the *Egypt* drew nearer and nearer Boston, the symptoms of typhus appeared in another fourteen passengers, most of them women and children, including the entire Murphy family. There was nowhere else to isolate them so they were kept below in their quarters while the remaining passengers rigged what shelter they could on the main deck. Captain Swain posted an armed guard above the passengers' quarters to ensure the infected ones stayed below. The guard had to be changed hourly because the seamen became upset by the stench and horrendous noises reaching them.

Captain Swain set every square foot of canvas that could be safely carried on the masts of his old ship to urge her towards a quicker landfall. About mid-morning on the 38th day of the voyage, a great cheer swept into the wind as the look-out spied the first grey smudge on the horizon. A few more hours and it became clear that the captain's navigation had been immaculate as the *Egypt* beat her way along the coast of Cape Cod before heading into Massachusetts Bay.

'We'll lay off for the night,' the delighted captain told Jack. 'And then it's Boston harbour in the morning. I don't think I've ever been so pleased to reach port in my life.'

'Not before time, Captain. Not before time. Another few days and I'm guessing we'd all have contracted the fever.'

At dawn the next day, the *Egypt* started to move up the bay towards Boston but when she was still some fifteen miles out the man in the crow's nest sang out, 'Sail three points on the starboard bow.'

Captain Swain peered through his telescope. He could make out the sleek lines of a small cutter flying the Stars and Stripes.

'What course do you make, Cap'n? She's making a signal now.'

The captain steadied his telescope on the rail to read the fluttering, coloured message flags in the cutter's rigging. 'Heave to. Boarding party alongside,' he deciphered.

The captain shouted the orders to reduce sail. The *Egypt* slowed in the water. The passengers crowded the rails as the cutter slipped under the stern of the larger ship into a parallel course fifty yards astern.

A voice came faintly across the water between the vesssls. 'Who are you? Identify yourself.'

Captain Swain pressed his hailing trumpet to his mouth. 'The *Egypt*, 39 days out of the Shannon, bound for Boston. We've more than 200 passengers aboard. Who are you?'

'The *Lexington* carrying the Boston port physician. Have you any sickness aboard, *Egypt*?'

Captain Swain grimaced at Jack. 'So that's it,' he said. 'A sick inspection, is it?' Then he shouted his reply to the cutter, 'A few cases of ship's fever, *Lexington*.'

'Heave to, *Egypt*. The physician will board you.'

The captain bellowed orders for all but a small mizzen sail to be reefed in. The *Egypt* came to a virtual stop, only maintaining steerage way, pitching and rolling in the swell, the sea slapping against her hull.

'What'll be happening now?' Jack asked anxiously as he watched a rowing boat being lowered from the cutter.

'I'm not rightly knowing,' Captain Swain replied, scratching his cheek nervously. 'Could be the physician will take the sick ones off us before we enter harbour. It'd be a blessing, that would.'

The rowing boat, with two seamen at the oars and two passengers in the stern, pulled quickly alongside the *Egypt*. The passengers – one in a frock coat and carrying a small leather bag, the other wearing a blue naval uniform – clambered agilely on to the main deck using the nets and ladders heaved over the side for them. A crewman directed them towards Captain Swain who stood by the wheelhouse, an apprehensive Jack Keane beside him. As far as they both knew, no restrictions had been placed on the entry of Irish immigrants into the United States but they realized that carrying typhus victims might be another matter.

'Good morning, Captain,' the man in the naval uniform called cheerily as he mounted the ladder to the wheelhouse deck. 'A good voyage, I'm trusting.'

'Fair winds, sir. Fair winds.'

'I'm Captain Tucker, sir, from the port cutter *Lexington*.' He turned to his middle-aged companion. 'And this is Doctor Emmanuel Smithers, the official physician for the port of Boston.

He'll be wanting to examine your passengers, Captain . . .Captain?'

'Swain, sir. Josiah Swian.' In turn he introduced Jack and all four men shook hands.

'Some fever aboard, I understand,' said Dr Smithers.

'They're isolated below, sir, after taking sick not three days ago.'

'If I may see them, Captain.' The request was polite but carried the clear note of authority.

'As you wish.'

The four men stood to one side as the hatch to the passengers' quarters was opened. A cloud of foul air rolled upwards and engulfed the inspection party. The doctor looked severely at Captain Swain.

'Ship's fever you said, Captain?'

'Well . . . I'm no physician, sir,' he replied, hesitantly. 'That's what we were thinking . . . ' His explanation tailed off lamely.

'The smell, Captain, hardly makes an inspection necessary but I shall go below.' The physician pulled out a large silk handkerchief and knotted it around his nose and mouth before clambering down the ladder. Less than a minute later, he returned to the open deck.

'As I thought, gentlemen,' he reported grimly as he pulled the handkerchief from his mouth. 'Typhus fever and well advanced at that. I counted fourteen sick, Captain. Are there any more?'

'One, sir. The first to be affected. We placed him in a cabin aft and have kept a close watch on him. I fear he has little hope.'

'Gangrene already,' Jack interrupted.

Dr Smithers shook his head. 'This'll mean quarantine at the very least.'

'Quarantine?' echoed Jack and Captain Swain.

'At Deer Island, some five miles from our present position,' said Captain Tucker. 'Because of the condition of some of the passengers from Ireland, Boston has found it necessary to set up a quarantine station on the island. New York has taken similar precautions.'

'After all, many of your other passengers may be carrying the fever,' Dr Smithers added. He looked round the emigrants gathered on the deck. 'And I see you've some old folk aboard as well. That'll mean bonds being posted if they're to land at Boson after quarantine.'

'A thousand dollars for each old 'un,' explained Captain Tucker. 'Your owners have the money?'

'I'm the owner, sir,' Captain Swain bristled. 'And I've not a sufficiency of funds for . . . '

'When did all this come about?' Jack demanded. 'I know Boston and us Irish have always been welcome. Alderman Finucane wrote only months ago saying that.'

'Finucane? You know Matt Finucane then?' the doctor asked curiously.

'Indeed I know him. Twas I who helped his first election nearly twenty years back. He held his victory party at my groggery, so he did.'

'So you're that Keane, are you?' the doctor said, rubbing his chin thoughtfully. 'To this day, Mr Keane, your name is well known among the Irishers in Boston. I've often had cause to minister to your countrymen who work the docks and wharves.'

'So then, Doctor, what's this quarantine and bonding?'

'The regulations are only a month old. So many sick and old are arriving from Ireland that the town council fears Boston will be swamped by them. There's fear of an epidemic and too heavy a charge on the community in caring for the elderly.'

The doctor shook his head. 'Unfortunate, Mr Keane, but that is the plain truth of the matter. This ship'll have to lie off Deer Island for at least fourteen days and then, if the fever is cleared, there'll still be bonds to be posted for the elderly.'

'We're done for, that's what,' Captain Swain exclaimed, open despair in his voice. 'I've no money for the bonds even if we survive the quarantine and I'm sure neither have the passengers.'

He looked helplessly at Captain Tucker. 'What can I do? We surely can't be the first ship here since your new regulations.'

'Indeed not,' Captain Tucker replied. He gazed down at the deck as he tried to conceal his feeling of embarrassment and shame. 'Since you're sailing under English colours, I suggest you make for the colonies in Canada.'

'That's the advice we're giving all British ships which cannot satisfy the port regulations,' Dr Smithers continued quickly. 'It's not we're against helping the Irish but we must protect the citizens of Boston. Their welfare is the paramount responsibility. Surely you can recognize that?'

Jack sniffed contemptuously. The doctor grasped him by the elbow and led him to the rail. 'You of all people, Mr Keane, should understand our concern. But if you'll come ashore in the cutter I'm sure we can waive any regulations in your case. After all, sir, you're almost as much a Bostonian as . . .'

Jack pulled angrily away from his grip. 'I'll not be wanting any favours. I've been travelling with these wretches and I'll not be leaving them now.'

'But . . . '

'There are no buts, Doctor. Just be telling Matt Finucane what's happened. That's all I'll be asking of you,' Jack said bitterly. 'Just be reminding him of what he said once about people of all races being welcome in Boston.'

Dr Smithers reddened. 'As you choose,' he said stiffly.

'And before you return to the safety of your hospitable town, perhaps you'll be looking at the poor soul locked in the mate's cabin aft.'

The doctor bowed slightly from the waist. Jack led him below decks, leaving the two sea captains to commiserate with each other.

'Now be careful here, Doctor,' Jack warned as he slid the key into the cabin door. 'Poor Willie's been raving and thrashing around for two days now.'

'You have already made clear your opinion of myself and my position,' the doctor said coldly. 'I'd be obliged if you would not question my medical training. Remain outside while I examine the patient.'

Dr Smithers entered the silent cabin as Jack stood outside, trying to avoid inhaling the awful smell. There was a murmuring inside before the doctor returned to the cabin door. His face was ashen. He held a hand over his mouth as if attempting to stop himself being sick.

'Any hope?' Jack asked.

The doctor shook his head. Then, as he stood with his back to the cabin, there was a terrible yell from inside and Willie Murphy burst out of the doorway. His charge hurled Dr Smithers into Jack, knocking the breath out of both of them. By the time they'd recovered, Willie was half-way up the ladder leading to the main deck. Jack leapt after him but was unable to stop him reaching the open air.

Passengers screamed with horror and revulsion as Willie Murphy burst through the hatchway. His naked body was virtually black in colour. His limbs were bloated to almost twice their normal width. Blood dripped from his fingers and toes and from the stumps of the teeth still in his mouth. He was roaring with pain and delirium as he ran towards a group of passengers by the rail. They drew back, terrified and hysterical, as Willie Murphy approached them.

Still screaming, he ran straight through them, bowling aside two children, hit the rail and toppled over the ship's side with a last shriek.

Jack and the doctor ran to the rail and looked down. Willie

252

surfaced for a moment, face convulsed, arms splashing, before he sank again. There were a few ripples, a lungful of bubbles, and then nothing as he disappeared finally beneath the waters of Massachusetts Bay.

'The Lord's mercy upon him,' muttered Dr Smithers.

'You shouldn't be wasting your prayers on Willie, Doctor,' said Jack, suddenly feeling very weary and drained. 'He's the lucky one. He's finished his journey to the promised land.'

# Chapter 4 May, 1847

The small island looked enchanting from the St Lawrence River. Trees and shrubs ambled down to the very edge of the lapping water. Long, low white sheds could be glimpsed through the vegetation. On a grassy knoll covered with wild flowers, a small wooden church poked its white spire into the blue sky. To those in the long line of ships standing off Grosse Island, thirty miles downstream from Quebec, it seemed the unlikeliest of places for the Canadian authorities to have established their official quarantine station.

At least twenty ships filled with emigrants had ventured up the St Lawrence since the winter ice had cleared reluctantly from the river barely a fortnight before. More arrived each day. The passengers from continental Europe, particularly the Germans, were free from disease and, almost without exception were allowed to proceed up river in the two steamers, the *Queen* and the *John Nunn*, which made the three-day voyage to Montreal. As they sailed past Grosse Island, fiddlers playing tunes on the steamers' decks, the smiling, healthy passengers looked curiously at the rowing boats and longboats clustered round the island.

Jack Keane and Matt Aherne panted under their masks as they manoeuvred a stretcher up from the passengers' quarters and onto the ship's main deck. They tried to avoid looking down at the patient strapped to the stretcher, at his grotesquely swollen limbs jerking against the binding ropes in a typhus delirium. They carried the stretcher to the rail before lowering it, as gently as they could, over the side and into a longboat. Jack counted eight typhus victims already aboard, packed tightly into the well of the longboat. After pushing and pulling their diseased bodies enough room was made for the new arrival. The longboats sank lower in the water.

'Watch how you move, Irisher, else you'll capsize us,' the boat-man, a grizzled man of about sixty, called to Jack.

'How are you managing?' Jack asked, pulling down his handker-chief mask and wiping his brow.

'All I can do is take them to the shallow water. That's all. After that they make their own way ashore best they can,' the boatman replied. 'The island's got no landing pier,' he added in explanation.

'But this is the third boat load from the *Egypt*,' Jack protested. 'Have they all been dumped ashore like that?'

'And the rest of them from the fever ships. Near on a thousand of 'em so far.'

'Jesus,' exclaimed Jack. He looked up at Matt who was peering over the rail. 'Stay there, lad, and help all you can,' he shouted. 'I'm going ashore with this boat.'

'Your choice, matey.' The boatman shrugged his wide shoulders as if disclaiming all responsibility for Jack's decision. He picked up an oar and began sculling the longboat the few hundred yards to shore.

'Take care, Jack-Da,' Matt hailed.

Jack waved back before wedging himself into the bow of the boat. 'Are any recovering on the island?' he asked.

The boatman spat into the water. 'In a hospital built for one hundred and fifty? Now they're putting 'em in the church, there're so many of 'em.'

''Tis really that bad?'

The boatman nodded. 'Look behind you, matey. Just clap your eyes on the river.'

Jack craned his neck round and saw that the longboat, only about fifty feet from Grosse Island, was nosing its way through lumps of bloodied straw gummed together with excrement, through lengths of stained bandage, through foul-smelling and discoloured mattress covers, through bobbing barrels which leaked yellow pus and vomit.

The longboat scraped bottom twenty feet from dry land.

'Far as we go, matey,' the boatman called, shipping his oar. He bent down over one of the typhus victims and began lifting him unceremoniously out of the boat and into the water.

'Hold fast. I'll help,' Jack said as he jumped into the knee-deep water. He grasped the sick man around the waist and supported him while he floundered ashore. He turned in time to see the boatman heaving another typhus victim into the cold water.

'Can't you be waiting?' he cried.

'No time,' the boatman repeated. 'Hundreds more of 'em waiting in the ships to come ashore. Hundreds of 'em. Are you coming back with me?'

'I can't be leaving these in the water,' Jack shouted.

'Suit yourself, matey. I'll be back later anyhow.'

Jack looked around helplessly as the sick people flopped and flapped in the muddied shallows like a shoal of exhausted fish. Then two middle-aged priests, shirtsleeves rolled up, ran out of the trees and began carrying them onto firm ground.

'Holy Mother of God,' one kept murmuring.

'There are scores more,' Jack volunteered as he carried an elderly woman into the shade of the island's trees.

''Tis a miracle they've reached here at all,' the priest grunted. 'I'm Father Moylan and him over there is Father McQuirk,' he added, gesturing at his colleague.

'Where do we take the sick anyway?' Jack asked. 'They can't be staying in the open.'

'The hospital's overflowing. The church is full. The sheds we put up not a week ago are packed. They've sent some tents from Montreal so we'll be using those but we haven't had time yet to bang in one peg,' Father McQuirk said.

'Four doctors who volunteered are already down with typhus, God help them. No nurses will come anywhere near this island so there's only us, Father O'Reilly, and the medical officer, Dr Douglas, to look after more than a thousand mortal-stricken people,' sighed Father Moylan.

Jack shook his head in disbelief. 'I've never seen anything like it. Not in all the suffering back home. Jesus, tis not a question of if I can be helping, but where.'

'You're not afeared of the typhus?' Father McQuirk asked curiously.

'I've lived cheek by jowl with it for two weeks or more,' Jack said, banging his chest with his fist. 'See . . . still fit as any bog-trotter so I am.'

Father Moylan laughed and clapped him on the shoulder, 'Then, Master Jack Bog-Trotter, let's be showing you what's to be done before you change your mind.'

Jack spent most of the day pitching the tents and moving the sick into them. When he'd finished he went off in search of some water and nourishment for the sick. The stench of disease and waste increased with every step he took towards the church and the hospital sheds set in the large clearing in the centre of the island.

Jack peeked through the open doors of the pretty little church. Every pew bench and aisle was filled with the sick. A woman lay sprawled across the single step in front of the altar as if in prostrate prayer. The single cross on the altar cast its shadow over her back.

Jack walked down the knoll towards the largest hospital shed, a room of about a hundred and fifty feet by twenty feet filled with more than six hundred fever victims of all ages and both sexes. Father McQuirk stepped gingerly between them offering ladles of water here and there to those who were strong enough to drink. Those who were too weak had a little water dribbled between their swollen lips.

'It's like we're treating the suffering of the entire world,' Father McQuirk said wearily.

Jack shrugged his shoulders. 'Those who can, help. Or rather those who can and who want to.'

'The people of Boston who turned your ship away?'

'The people would help. Left to themselves, people of any country will help each other. But when the politicians have their say, it all happens different, doesn't it?'

The priest looked Jack straight in the eye and asked, 'Will you be staying to help ease them, Jack? We've awful need of able-bodied men like you.'

'What can I be doing, Father? They're all most likely to die, help or no help.'

'Truly so. But even the smallest comfort will be a blessing for them. Anything that reminds them of their dignity as human beings. It's important to face your Maker as a human being not like pigs in a sty full of swinefever or cattle in a slaughterhouse.' Father McQuirk turned and gazed back into the hospital shed. 'This may be a charnel house,' he said quietly, 'But the love of God can be brought to it, the love of being for being.'

Jack sighed. 'I'll stay, father. How could I be leaving after seeing all this? But before I buckle down a boatman has to take a message for my youngster.'

Four times a day, boats brought the dead from the emigrant ships continuing to arrive off the quarantine station. By the end of May, forty vessels waited in a line two miles long for clearance to unload their passengers on to the river steamers. Their dead came ashore wrapped simply in canvas or rudely boxed in coffins made from bunks.

Jack watched one lad, scarcely older than Matt, walk ashore, and slump down with his back against a tree. Jack went over to offer a ladle of water. The youngster, his clothes tattered and dirty, shook his head weakly so Jack left him alone. Twenty minutes later he walked back past the same tree. Father Moylan was kneeling beside him, administering the last rites.

'When I came by I thought he was asleep in the sun,' the priest said when he had finished. 'But when I looked closer I could see he had gone from us.'

'He's only a youngster like Matt, so he is.'

'I think he was simply too weak to manage. He's probably had no proper food nor rest for weeks. He just gave up the ghost.'

Jack swayed slightly as a wave of dizziness passed over him.

'Are you unwell, son?' asked the priest, jumping to his feet in concern.

Jack waved him away. 'Tired, Father. Tis tired I am. Just that.' He steadied himself by holding on to the tree trunk. 'I'm thinking of Matt. If this poor lad can keel over and die like that, then how's my youngster going on?'

'Are you wanting to go back to your ship then?'

'I reckon I must, Father. Tis about time we were free from quarantine and heading up river.'

A boatman rowed Jack back to the *Egypt*, swinging serenely at anchor in the wide river. He wondered how many tens of thousands of Irish people had perished in their attempts to reach America and how many more were waiting to risk the crossing. If only he had known the truth, Jack thought, he would have taken the shorter route to the English slums in Liverpool, Birmingham or London. Matt and he might not have had such opportunities in front of them but at least they would not have faced death at such close quarters.

A shout of welcome pulled him out of his morbid thoughts. He looked up and saw Matt's face grinning down at him as the rowing boat slipped into the shadow of the *Egypt*. Jack jumped for the ladder. Suddenly, his strength left him. He rested for a good minute before he started climbing slowly upwards. When he was nearly at the top, panting with exertion, Matt clambered over the rail to pull him up the last few feet.

Jack staggered when his feet hit the main deck. The familiar faces of Matt and the captain whirled in front of him and he fell into blackness. Matt's voice, anxious, pleading, came from a long way off as he slid back into consciousness. He came round sitting under the ship's rail. He blinked to focus his eyes.

257

'You scared us, Jack-Da,' Matt said, holding out a mug.

Jack took a sip and spluttered. The rum brought him fully to his senses.

'How are you, lad?' he asked, smiling up at Matt.

'He's fine, Keane. Fit as a flea,' Captain Swain said cheerfully. 'More to the point, how are you? Falling aboard like that. You're sure you're well, Keane?'

'Aye, Captain. Just hand me to my feet and give me another sip of rum.' Jack gripped on to the rail as another wave of dizziness struck him. 'That rum's mighty powerful after a time away from it,' he laughed weakly.

'You're back for good?'

'Aye, Captain. We've been doing our best but I'm fearing tis a lost battle. No opiates, no surgical tools, no bedding, no more tents nor sheds, nothing more but prayer and that's running out mighty fast, so it is.' He paused to clear his throat. All of a sudden it felt closed and rough. 'When are you free from quarantine and off-loading your passengers into the river steamers?'

'That's why we were awful glad to see you, Keane. What passengers are left can be leaving tomorrow.'

'How many?'

'Out of the 257 who left the Shannon,' Captain Swain said quietly, 'There are only 89 left here. The rest are in their graves or on that cursed island.'

'That's . . . that's . . .' Jack was unable to think clearly for a moment.

'One hundred and sixty eight dead or wishing they were, God rest 'em.'

Jack sighed then smiled at Matt. 'Still the main thing is you're fine, lad. And so will I be after a night's rest. Then tis off to Montreal in the morning.'

'It's bad there, Keane. The steamer captain who came aboard yesterday said the Irish were dying in their hundreds in the sheds along the old wharves. The fever's everywhere. Even the priests and politicians trying to ease the sick are catching the fever. You'll only be safe when you're in the barges for Kingston and beyond. Reach Lake Ontario, the captain said, and you're half-way safe. But not till then.'

'Does it never end?' Jack asked despairingly. 'Does it never end?'

But he cheered up a little after taking some more rum from the captain's private stock. For the passengers' last night in the *Egypt*, the captain had thrown all his usual financial caution overboard by purchasing a dozen wild turkeys from one of the boatmen. They were devoured voraciously by people who hadn't tasted fresh meat in two months or more but Jack could only pick at his portion.

'You're not sickening, Jack-Da?' Matt asked when they'd rolled themselves into their blankets under the deck awning.

Jack shivered. He didn't feel well, he had to admit, but he didn't want to alarm the lad. 'Go to sleep, you gosseen,' he said as lightly as he could. 'These old bones need some rest after all their slaving on that island, that's all. Don't be worrying yourself.'

Jack slept heavily, dreamlessly, for a few hours before waking. His body was burning, and there was something else, he realized with growing dread. A swelling feeling; a sense of his limbs bloating up, of becoming heavier. 'Holy Mother of God,' he whispered to himself, his eyes closed, his jaw clenched in awful fear. He gulped, unable to put his thoughts into words, even to form them in his brain. 'Jesus, not me. Not me,' he muttered.

Jack kicked his blanket aside and shifted a yard away from Matt who was soundly asleep. He held his hands in the dim light from the four lanterns hung round the deck. Was he imagining it? Were his hands turning darker? And swelling? Jack pressed them together as hard as he could. There was a definite numbness in them. He peered closely at his fingers one by one. Yes, they were rounder and their nails were darker.

There was no doubt in his mind. He had seen the symptoms too often for that. He had typhus fever. How long before he became a helpless, twitching victim, unable to think coherently or talk intelligibly? He had to speak to Matt before that happened. There was so much to tell him with so little time left. He leaned over and shook the youngster awake.

'What . . . what is it?' Matt woke, his eyes wide with alarm.

'I must speak to you, Matt.'

'Now, Jack-Da? Tis the middle of the night. Why now?'

'Because there's not much time, lad. Don't be getting upset now with what I've to tell you.'

Matt peered closely at him in the half light. His eyes reflected the shock of what he saw.

Jack watched the expression on his face. 'There's little doubt, lad,' he whispered hoarsely. 'I've the fever.'

'Oh, God! Jack-Da. Oh no!' Matt sobbed.

'Tis no respecter of age or person, lad. Be remembering that,' he said gently.

Strangely, a weight had been lifted from him by confiding his fear, his certainty, to Matt. He felt calmer as he began to talk of the inevitable.

'When light comes, Matt, be seeing that I'm taken to the island. Make sure that the priests are knowing I'm there. I'm sure they'll do all they can for me.'

'You're stronger than any man alive, Jack-Da. You'll beat the fever.'

Jack smiled at the youngster's attempt to cheer him up. 'Aye, lad, the old faction fighter's strong, so he is. Mighty strong. Twill take more than a rotten old fever to put him in a box, and that's the truth. But I still can't be going up river. Don't you see I'd be infecting the others?'

'Then I won't be leaving, Jack-Da.' Matt spoke firmly.

'And isn't that what I want to speak of, lad? If there's bad fever in Montreal, there's little point in going there or even to Kingston. We've no friends there. No, leave me on the island and strike out for Boston. Tis less than three hundred miles. A strong lad like you will stride it easily in two weeks or so.'

'But how can I leave you alone here?'

Matt went to pat Jack's arm but the older man drew back.

'Don't be touching me, lad,' he warned. 'One of us has to be reaching Boston. You're the last of the Ahernes from Gortacrossane. Be remembering that.' Jack lowered his voice. 'Listen well, Matt. In my chest stowed below . . . you know it . . . there's a secret drawer at the bottom. The catch is one of the nails at the side. In the drawer there are twenty or more sovereigns. Enough for you to hire a boatman to take you to the south bank of the river. More than enough to see you through the journey. But be careful slipping ashore. I'm guessing there'll be Yankee guards posted all along the river and the border to stop any Irish crossing.' Jack paused. He ran his tongue round his mouth to moisten it. His throat was closing fast. 'When you reach Boston, and all trails east lead to it, go near the harbour and ask anyone for Matt Finucane. He'll help, so he will. I'll be joining you as soon as I can so tell Finucane to be saving a position for me.'

Tears welled in Matt's eyes and began to roll down his cheeks.

'I can't be leaving you alone, Jack-Da,' he said fiercely. 'Not on that island. Not alone.'

'Can't you be seeing that I'm not alone, lad.' Jack lay back, his strength dissipating fast. 'When you've had a life like mine, Matt,' he continued, his words becoming slurred, 'when you've seen the things I've seen, then you're not alone . . . when you're older you'll know that . . . you're not alone. Haven't I told you that the only life worth living, worth a fiddler's damn, is in your head? And that's where I'm not alone. So many people . . . so many . . . thoughts . . . memories . . . so many . . . ' His voice tailed away. He was silent for a minute. Then he croaked, 'Can you be getting me some water, lad. I'm awful hot and parched. Can hardly talk.'

Matt hurried over to a pail of water lying on the deck and returned with a ladleful. He held the ladle steady for Jack to take a drink. Even this small effort seemed to exhaust the sick man. He groaned at his own weakness.

'Are you afeared, Jack-Da?' Matt asked tentatively, curiously.

'Afeared lad?' Jack coughed again, his chest heaving painfully. It was now becoming difficult for him to speak. 'No, there's no fear in me. When you're so near . . . maybe you're . . . no, tis not fear . . . only a mighty reluctance.' Jack smiled and repeated, 'Only a mighty reluctance, so it is.' He held his right hand into the light again, looked at it closely, then screwed his eyes shut in his distress.

'Rest, Jack-Da,' Matt implored. 'Don't be speaking on. Rest your strength.'

Jack waved his protests away. 'Not long while I can speak, lad. Then will be the gibbering. Close your ears to that, for I'll be saying words from the fever . . . words that are in the dark parts of me . . . Be ignoring them, lad, while you're remembering what I'm saying now.'

'You're a stubborn one, Jack-Da. You're real stubborn.'

Jack tried to smile at the youngster but the grin was merely a grimace of swollen lips. 'We Irish have to be stubborn, don't we? Else we'll never have our own land again. Once we possessed it but we fought each other and delivered Ireland to the English, so we did.' Jack's eyes were closed now. His voice had become so much of a whisper that Matt was forced to lean closer in order to hear him at all. 'Tis when we learn the value of freedom that we'll be uniting . . . and when that happens we'll be taking our land back from the English. It'll happen one day, lad. I'm praying twill be this suffering, this history, that'll be bringing the Irish together one day . . . Aye, together one day . . . together . . . together, Brigid . . . Brigid . . . '

Jack's voice died away and then, suddenly, he sat up, his eyes staring in alarm. 'What was I saying, lad? Was I seeing your mam? Was she in my mind?'

Matt put an arm around his shoulders and pressed him gently back on to the blanket. The youngster started to cry silently as he realized his guardian's delirium had begun.

By morning, Matt could look quite calmly on Jack's swollen, twitching features and limbs. He felt that Jack had already gone from him. The sick man he and Captain Swain helped load into a boat to be taken to Grosse Island was no longer Jack Keane. Matt didn't want to – he wouldn't – remember him in this condition. He would remember him as he was; a brave, laughing man who had looked life squarely in the face and had regretted nothing.

Despite the pleadings of Captain Swain, Matt insisted on accompanying Jack to the island. There, he helped the priests nurse him through the fever for the next three days. He bathed and cleaned him and sat by his side, restraining him throughout his delirious agony.

On the fourth morning, just as first light crept across the island, Matt woke from a brief sleep on the floor of the church, next to the pew where his guardian lay. His heart leapt when he saw Jack's eyes were suddenly clear. He bent over him, smiling. The eyes smiled back from their ravaged sockets. For a moment they held all their old strength. Then they glazed over and rolled upwards. There were no tears left in Matt Aherne, none at all.

## Chapter 5 June, 1847

The young man, black hair drooping over his forehead, sat on the edge of the bed and scuffed his bare feet in the rich pile of the carpet. He looked around the bedroom, his gaze lingering on the wardrobe, the dressing table, the two chairs, and the curtains half-pulled across the windows. He pushed himself off the bed, walked over to the dressing table and ran his hand gently, almost reverentially, round the neck of the china pitcher in its wide bowl before the mirror. He cocked his head a fraction, listening intently to the faint creaking noises of the house.

Matt Aherne thought that he'd never been so alone before. Being alone in a closed room was different from being alone in the fields or woods. He knew that there were people in the other bedrooms of

Alderman Finucane's Dorchester home, but within his own room it was as if they did not exist. Here he felt master of his own destiny. He liked that. The thought filled him with tingling excitement.

His mind drifted back over the past three weeks or so of his journey from the St Lawrence River to Massachusetts. Matt had little doubt that Jack-Da would have been proud of him. He had kept a wary eye for Yankee border patrols after being landed at a small settlement on the south bank some five miles upstream from Grosse Island. He'd come ashore dressed in the warmest of clothes from Jack-Da's sea chest with two rugs strapped on his back and the pair of pistols round his waist. The sight of only one of his twenty-two gold sovereigns had brought instant, almost overwhelming service and advice from the owner of the log-built store at the little town perched between forest and river. Matt bought dried strips of venison, biscuits, beans and oatmeal and asked, as off-handedly as he could, directions towards the east.

'Just keep to the main tracks and paths, son,' the storekeeper had advised. 'That way you won't be getting lost in the forests and mountains or meeting any Redskins.'

'And how will I be knowing if I'm heading in the right direction then?' Matt had asked, beginning to worry as he realized that he would be journeying through entirely wild territory. He knew that the West of Ireland was considered desolate and under-populated by strangers but his new surroundings had the daunting magnificence peculiar to country virtually untrodden by man.

The storekeeper had laughed at his question. 'Why, son, it's mighty easy to see you're no woodsman. Now all you do is face the sun in the morning — and the birds'll make sure you don't oversleep — then keep it at your right hand during the day and make certain it's on the back of your neck at dusk. That way you'll be heading roughly east. But don't be fretting yourself too much. If you do what I'm saying and stick to the main tracks you're bound to be meeting other travellers more versed than yourself.'

Matt spent the first night of his journey alone, cold and extremely fearful, under a bush about ten miles along the track leading east from the settlement. The sounds of the forest, the night call of the animals, ensured only fitful sleep and he was glad to leave his resting place at first light and chew a breakfast strip of venison as he continued along the main track through the trees. After an hour's trudging along the rutted surface of dried mud Matt heard the unmistakeable creaking of wheels round the next bend. He broke in to a run, pack bumping on his back, to catch up with an uncovered wagon pulled sedately by two large workhorses. A man wearing a broad-brimmed hat held the reins loosely in his hands. A woman in a sun bonnet was beside him on the driving seat, her arm casually around the shoulders of a young boy. The rumblings of the swaying wagon forced Matt to shout to gain their attention. The man immediately dropped the reins and reached behind the driving box. Matt found himself staring into the shining barrel of a flintlock musket. He skidded to a halt. Still panting from his dash, he moved his arms away from his own weapons. The middle-aged man on the wagon studied him for interminable moments, squinting through the crude musket sight.

'And where might you have sprung from, youngster?' the man asked finally, his voice low and determined.

'Back there. Just back there, sir,' Matt replied. 'I heard the wagon . . . '

'Squawking like a Redskin, you were,' the man said accusingly. 'Near scared me britches off. What you be wanting anyway?'

'Well, I was just thinking . . . ' Matt began lamely.

'Thinking was it?'

' . . . you're heading east, aren't you?'

'So?'

'Well I was just reckoning we . . . I'm going your way.'

'We?' The man's tone was still suspicious but he'd lowered his musket. He glanced at the woman and child beside him. They in turn gazed rather more sympathetically at Matt.

'Don't bully so, Jebediah Wren,' the woman said sternly. 'The lad's only looking for company. Aren't you, young man?'

'Tis so, ma'am.' Matt looked gratefully at her.

'How long on the road then?' The man put down his musket with studied reluctance.

'A day, sir.'

Jebediah Wren snorted. 'From the boats in the St Lawrence then. An Irisher, I'm betting.'

Matt nodded.

'And heading for your friends in Boston or New York.'

'Boston, sir.'

'Well, we're only travelling as far as Concord in New Hampshire but that's nearer Boston than you'd be reaching on your own with all that hollering. If you want you can tag along. But, mind you, no more screeching.'

'I've food,' said Matt but Jebediah Wren picked up the reins and nudged his horses into motion.

Matt walked behind the wagon as it jolted along the forest track. He was disconcerted by the man's suspicious attitude. An Irishman, he thought, would have been much friendlier than this Yankee.

After about an hour, he was invited to clamber up on to the wagon. 'You'll be doing enough pushing and heaving over the mountains, youngster,' the wagon-owner explained with a half-smile.

As the day's shadows lengthened, Matt and the Wren family swapped tales of their background and their travels. By nightfall, with a stew bubbling over the fire, they had become good companions.

'You can't afford to take a man on face value out here, Matt,' confided Jebediah Wren. 'This here ain't civilization. No, sir. Why a man'd shoot the kid, my woman and me just to get the wagon and team. And what them Redskins would do, don't bear thinking about. Always sleep with a firearm at your hand and one ear to the night. That way you won't be waking up and finding you ain't gotten no hair on your head to comb.'

In the weeks that followed, Matt learned a deal from the hardy frontier family. He saw the virtues of self-discipline, of self-denial, of self-reliance. He compared them with the often feckless behaviour of his old neighbours back in North Kerry and found himself agreeing with the Wren family that no person was owed a living. Jebediah Wren was particularly hard on the Irish when Matt described the way of life he'd left behind.

'A man has two choices, youngster,' he'd said. 'Either he uses his brains and muscles to change what he don't like or he uses them to up and go somewhere better. Them that do neither have no right to complain. And, begging your particular pardon, that's how many Yankees look on you Irishers as you'll find when you're reaching Boston.'

Matt saw many practical examples of that New World philosophy in his long journey. He passed through communities of a few houses carved out of mountainside forest where everyone seemed so busy that the wagon hardly merited a glance. He marvelled at the calm and prosperity of the small towns in the valleys and on the plains, their neat white-painted houses always built around a steepled church.

When he had left the Wrens at their new home in Concord and travelled alone the last miles to Boston, the small towns and villages seemed to get closer to one another. There were sizeable civic buildings and increasingly busy streets. Matt's anticipation grew with every stride, but his expectations were dwarfed by his first impressions of Boston itself. Everywhere there were people – dashing people, scurrying people – all apparently moving with a firm purpose in mind. Any one of the buildings, Matt thought, would have been regarded as a wonder back in the stony flatness of the West of Ireland. And after the buildings, the noise: from the horses, the carts, the carriages, the factories, the people themselves. They didn't talk but shouted. They didn't smile gently but laughed uproariously. They didn't weep but cried aloud. They appeared to have no inhibitions. Matt felt so cowed by everything around him that he had to pluck up all his courage to approach any of the people brushing past him on the rude sidewalks.

Then he saw the burly, uniformed figures of two constables ambling towards him, sticks twirling on their fingers and amiable smiles and greetings for all they passed. Matt ran up to them eagerly.

'I'm a stranger here . . . ' he began.

'And wouldn't we be knowing that?' one of the constables interrupted. 'What with your pack and your pistols and your dust even a man with his lanterns out would be seeing that.'

'I'm trying to ask the way,' Matt explained.

'And what way would that be?'

'To Alderman Matt Finucane.'

'The alderman, eh? . . . a friend of his?'

'My da . . . I mean, my guardian was.'

'Well, my friend and associate here and myself happen to be heading the way you're wanting so you'd better just come along.'

The constables shepherded Matt through busy streets and alleys pointing out places of interest to him while they asked questions to elicit the youngster's background. After quarter of an hour they turned down yet another side alley. There, in a courtyard, Matt saw the gates of a small factory with a sign hung above them – 'Finucane-Cooper'. The constables hammered on the gates with their sticks until a fresh-faced boy pulled them squeakily open.

'The alderman here, lad?' the older constable demanded.

'In his office, sir.'

Matt thanked the constables for their help before being led through the yard, littered with half-built casks, and up a narrow wooden staircase to a small office on the first floor of the building. His guide knocked on the grimy window set into the door, turned the handle without waiting for an answer and motioned for Matt to enter. To his surprise, he found himself looking down at the crown of a young woman's head. Her long fair hair almost totally obscured her face as she bent over a ledger on the desk. In another corner of the small office, Matt saw a man sitting with his back to him, also hunched over a desk.

'What is it?' the young woman asked without raising her head.

'I am wanting Alderman Finucane,' Matt replied hesitantly. 'They said he was here.'

'Oh, you are, are you?' She looked up. Her clear green eyes took in Matt's dishevelled countenance and clothing, the pistols at his waist, the uncertainty in his expression. 'You're wanting the foreman in the cooperage below if you're seeking work. The alderman doesn't hire labour.'

The dismissiveness of the reply disconcerted Matt. He was about to turn and leave the office when he heard a half-suppressed guffaw from the man at the far desk.

'I'm from Jack Keane of Drombeg townland,' he blurted out, suddenly finding a growing anger within him at the off-handedness of the Bostonians. 'And I'll not be leaving here until I see the alderman. I'm no workman wanting hire.'

The young woman's eyes showed her surprise. The middle-aged man at the desk swung round in his chair, laughter on his face.

'And who might you be, you cheeky spalpeen?'

'Mr Keane's ward . . . '

'Matthew Aherne?' the man asked, the amusement leaving his expression.

'The same.'

The man jumped from his chair, crossed the floor in two strides and grippd Matt's arm below the elbow. 'And Jack?' he continued urgently.

'Dead these three weeks or more.'

'Dead?'

'And buried on an island in the St Lawrence along with thousands of other poor souls.'

The man turned away. He pressed a hand across his mouth. 'God rest him. Holy Mary, he was the truest friend a man could have,' he muttered.

'You're Alderman Finucane?' Matt asked quietly, recognizing the man's genuine emotion. Matt Finucane shrugged his shouldesrs as if throwing off his grief. When he turned again to his young visitor a broad smile of welcome pointed up a sudden bleakness in his eyes.

'Two days running her da's office and she thinks she's the head man already. That's the female for you, lad,' he said in a mock serious tone. 'Welcome, Matthew Aherne. *Cead mille failte.*' They shook hands firmly. The young woman rose gracefully from behind her desk and offered her hand. Matt was aware of its softness, of its fine bones, as he held it for a second.

'My youngest, Mary,' explained the Alderman, brushing a hand through the grey hair at his temples. 'And was any hard-working man so cursed with a girl-child?'

Mary pouted, then laughed.

'That's it, daughter, mock me, will you? Now lock up the office and call the trap. It's straight home for us or your mam'll be giving me her tongue for holding him here and him exhausted from his travels.'

Despite his protests that he wasn't tired, Matt was ushered from the office, helped into the trap and almost rushed to the Finucanes spacious, airy home at Dorchester. In fact, Matt felt so excited by the sights of his short journey across the Boston Neck – the sea on one side, the Charles river on the other – that he forgot the deep fatigue within him. But, within an hour of his rapturous welcome by the alderman's wife, Alice, he felt his eyelids beginning to droop. He sat in a high-backed chair, his stomach full from a huge plate of cold cuts, and tried desperately to stay awake as the family fired question after question at him. Eventually, he was unable to suppress a wide yawn much as he attempted to disguise it with a fit of coughing.

'Bless me, Father,' exclaimed Alice Finucane, 'You're blathering away and all that Matt's wanting is his bed. The talking can wait till morning.'

Matt smiled to himself as he dressed for breakfast the next morning, remembering the family's solicitude. Jack-Da, he thought, had been wise in his choice of friends. He felt thoroughly at home with them.

He was aware of darting, curious glances from Mary Finucane during the family's breakfast, and reddened perceptibly under the girl's inspection. He sighed almost audibly with relief when the alderman drained his third cup of coffee and announced that Matt and himself would retire to the drawing room.

The alderman settled back in his favourite cushioned rocking chair, twined his fingers over his thickening paunch, and smiled reassuringly at Matt. 'When you're well settled in, lad, I'll be wanting to hear all about the last days of my old friend, Jack, but right now I'm more exercised about your future. If I'm a mite impertinent just tell me so but starting from now I'm regarding myself as filling Jack's shoes. You can clearly look after yourself and

I guess you know where you're headed, but I feel duty bound to help you along the path. We Irish aren't the novelty we were when Jack or my folks came here. Indeed, there are Boston people who'd be quite happy to dump us all back in the sea. The Irish who've arrived over the past year or so haven't exactly been the pick of the crop – and that's this Irishman's opinion. So however tough you are, Matt, you'll still be needing all the help I can give you.'

Matt lowered his eyes, embarrassed for a moment at the older man's obvious sincerity.

'Come on, lad,' the alderman urged. 'The little people haven't got your tongue, have they?'

'Well, for a start, before we left Kerry Jack-Da arranged for me to keep the cabin and fields at Drombeg in case I ever wanted to return to them. I'm sure I'll want to one day.'

'Then I'll be contacting the landlord's agent. Who is he?'

'Well, that's one problem. His name is Sandes . . . '

The alderman held up a hand to interrupt Matt. 'I know of him from Jack's letters . . . and of your kinship with him. Have no fear lad. We'll arrange to keep your cabin and land safe. But what's puzzling me is why you should want to return. There's so much opportunity here for a youngster like you and, of course, I'd be insisting on giving you a start in business.'

'Tis hard to explain, but I know I shall be going back. I don't know when or why precisely but I'm sure Ireland can't be helped by people like me leaving her for good.'

Alderman Finucane nodded. 'I reckon Jack talked of politics and such with you.'

'He did that. Aye, he did. The ways of landlords and their agents like Mr Sandes have to change if Ireland is ever to be more than a cat's paw for the English.'

'And you'll be wanting to help?'

'Aye, I shall. Although I've no idea yet about how.'

'Well, then, young Matt, how's this for a proposal? Be my assistant, my secretary if you like, in the business and in the politicking. You'll find out how Boston town works and maybe you'll discover a way to help Ireland. You'll get a wage. You'll live here with us. You'll be one of us.'

Matt's face shone with excitement at the offer, and before he could speak, the older man said, 'I see you're liking the idea. We'll take it as settled then. And what better time to be starting than now, today?'

Matt nodded quickly in agreement, then frowned. 'One thing's worrying me.'

'What's that?'

'How do I call you?'

The alderman slapped his thigh and laughed. 'And now isn't that a problem. You can't be calling me da, can you? And two Matts together will confuse everyone. And Alderman's a bit high-falutin' . . .'

He thought for a moment before announcing, 'You'll call me Finny. That's what. That's how I'm known to my cronies and you've just signed on with them.'

Alderman Finucane stood up and held his hand out to Matt. 'A deal then, Matt Aherne?'

'A deal. Aye, a deal, Alder . . . I mean, Finny,' replied Matt.

The two women next door looked round in surprise, then smiled at each other, as they heard the burst of laughter from the drawing room.

The owner of the boarding house in Oliver Street shifted his feet uneasily under the remorseless questioning of the visiting committee's chairman, Lemuel Shattuck.

'Only three to a room, Cahill?'

'At the very most, your honour, the very most.'

'But we counted six straw sacks in the small room. Presumably they pass as mattresses.'

'Just storing them, your worship.'

'Mr Cahill, you are prevaricating. In all the ten rooms you let to those brought here by your runners this committee found sixty-eight mattresses of palliasses or what you will. Surely you couldn't have been simply storing all of them?'

The boarding house keeper didn't reply. He stared sullenly at the six men confronting him in the small entrance hall of his rickety three-storey premises which had been converted from a warehouse only a few months before. Although he tried not to show it, Paddy Cahill was thoroughly overawed and frightened by the gentlemen in their tall hats and sombre clothes.

Shattuck paused for a moment. 'Very well, Cahill, this committee shall merely record the facts about your establishment in its report. Now, how much do you charge the poor wretches here?'

Paddy Cahill fingered his broken nose thoughtfully. 'Fifty cents per person per room?' he offered tentatively.

Matt Aherne, standing behind the committee's members, found this so ridiculous that he laughed openly. The committee swung round, wondering at his impertinence and levity.

'It's no laughing matter, Matt,' Alderman Finucane warned sternly. Matt stepped away from the wall revealing two notices hanging there.

One was headed simply 'Rules'. In large, uneven print it warned occupants of the room that they faced instant eviction and forfeiture of their baggage if they were the slightest tardy with payments of their rents of two dollars.

Lemuel Shattuck turned back to the hapless Cahill. 'I think a constable posted outside these doors to warn any of your would-be guests will cramp your business enough, Cahill. There are already too many of you living off the miseries of your less fortunate country-men. You should be ashamed of your vile trade. Ashamed, sir.'

As the committee members murmured assent and the boarding house keeper began to protest, Matt peered closely at the second notice on the wall. It hung beneath small etched portraits of Daniel O'Connell and George Washington.

Robert Emmet's last words from the scaffold: ' . . . Let no man write my epitaph; for as no man who knows my motives dare now vindicate them, let not prejudice or ignorance asperse them. Let them rest in obscurity and peace, my memory be left in oblivion and my tomb remain uninscribed, until other times and other men can do justice to my character. When my country takes her place among the nations of the earth then and not till then, let my epitaph be written.'

The exploitation was pathetic, Matt thought, but typical of the Irish in Boston in this year of 1848, forty-six years since Emmet had been hung and then beheaded.

Alderman Finucane had insisted that he accompany the state legislature's committee during their investigation, which had interrupted his training in book-keeping at the cooperage factory. The youngster, now eighteen years old, supposed the alderman had wanted to make clear to him how fortunate he was to be in a privileged position among Boston's middle class. Certainly, Matt had been shocked and disturbed by the awful conditions of most of the sixty to seventy thousand Irish who'd arrived in Boston during the previous two years.

To leave the city for the small towns on the mainland you had to cross bridges, paying tolls of up to ten cents in each direction. The wretched emigrants with little enough money and hardly any spirit left were stranded in the districts near the docks, particularly Matt Finucane's Ward 8, Fort Hill, and in the North End. As the human

271

flood increased so Boston's old families moved inland across the peninsula. The gardens and courtyards of once-fine houses became covered with shacks; backyards and alleyways were built over; rooms were divided and divided again. Disused warehouses, lacking water and drainage, were leased by get-rich-quick speculators, mainly Bostonians, and split with flimsy partitions into living compartments, most without windows.

Each new address visited by Lemuel Shattuck's committee provided a new insight into the hellish conditions. After the third week of the investigation, the commitee had still not grown used to the cramped rooms, to the cellars barely 100 feet square inhabited by twenty people, to the smells of excrement and stale urine, to the foul-running open drains. In such conditions the newly-arrived Irish sank into apathetic despair: they had little strength to resist the New World's rape of their consciences and sensibilities. Each day, the investigating committee found new evidence of their almost total moral disintegration.

In Hamilton Street, one crisp March day, the committee, with Matt tagging along to take notes as usual, pushed their way through at least a dozen child beggars before they could enter one house. From the outside it still bore the decorative fineries and fripperies which had marked it as the residence of a prosperous merchant family.

A woman, eyes bleary with drink, swayed against the doorway of the first tiny room along the dim and dirty hallway.

'Have you children inside?' Alderman Finucane asked her courteously.

The woman patted her long dark hair, knotted with filth. She smiled coquettishly . Her mouth was filled with brown stumps of teeth, where teeth there were.

'Why . . . a fine gentleman like you wanting such things . . . '

Before the alderman could explain she continued, winking at Matt at the same time, 'And wouldn't you prefer a woman of experience like me, sir? Your lad there can be having the girl at the same price of a dollar.'

Without turning her head, leering grotesquely, the woman shouted back into the dark recesses of the tiny box of a room, 'Bernadette, Bernadette, get your pretty self out here. Some fine gentlemen have come calling.'

A girl of about twelve years appeared at her side, smiling shyly. Her thin body, grimed with dirt, showed through a tear in the grubby shift she was wearing. Matt saw the pink tip of a budding breast. He looked away in shame.

'Madam, I do protest,' the alderman said sternly when he had recovered his composure. 'Your husband, madam. Where's your husband? Get your husband! Find the man this instant!'

'Him?' The woman spat contemptuously. The spittle dribbled down the flaking plaster on the wall. 'He's so bottled in the groggery below that he won't be disturbing your pleasures.'

She lunged drunkenly at the alderman, trying to grab his arm and pull him inside the room. Matt, who saw what was happening, stuck out a foot. The woman tripped and slid to the floor in an ungainly flurry of stained petticoats.

The committee voted with their feet and headed down the hallway towards the first upward flight of stairs. Alderman Finucane and Matt were pursued by a stream of obscenities, much of them in the piping voice of the little girl.

The upper three floors of the house were much as they'd seen elsewhere; airless, windowless rooms crowded with young children, many of them visibly sick. Some were on their own, screaming in their distress, others were being cared for by their older brothers and sisters. The absence of grown ups puzzled the committee. The invariable answer from the children was that their parents were 'down below'.

'The groggery?' Matt suggested.

Lemuel Shattuck nodded grimly. 'I fear so, young man. This is the first time I've heard of a groggery in the cellars catering just for the occupants of one of these hell holes.'

'And what else can the wretches do?' Alderman Finucane interrupted, shaking his head resignedly. 'They sell their children's bodies or put them on the streets to beg to raise some money, then spend it on drink to dull their consciences at what they're doing.'

The committee were silent for a moment. There was little to say.

'Do we go below, Finny?' Matt asked.

'Aye, lad. We do,' the alderman replied with a weary sigh. 'But you go first and keep a weather eye for that harridan and her she-child. Lord above, I've had some offers in my time but that one's enough to turn me away from the ladies for life.'

Matt couldn't stop himself guffawing at the expression of total dismay and distaste on the alderman's face. In return he received a helfty shove in the small of the back which sent him stumbling down the stairs. He grabbed the banisters to ease his descent and poked his head round the stairwell to see if the hallway was clear. There was no sign of the woman or the girl. The committee members, some on tiptoe, descended the stairs quietly, turned a bend and then with more boldness, started down some more steps towards the cellar.

The first thing they noticed were the keening, ill-played notes of a fiddle coming from somewhere below, rising above a peal of men's drunken laughter and a shriek of female mirth. They stood on the top steps until their eyes became accustomed to the flickering yellow light thrown by the oil lamp hung on the wall.

Matt heard a grunting, panting sound from under the stairway beneath his feet. He craned over the rail and, to his astonishment, looked straight down on to a man's naked buttocks, rising and falling, thrusting and twisting. For a moment, the youngster was completely nonplussed. Then he noticed the slimmer legs wrapped, ankles interlocked, around the man's thighs. He'd heard of it. He'd dreamed of it. Now he was seeing it at close quarters. Matt watched, fascinated, as the man's thrusting became quicker and more vigorous. The woman's ankles beat a frenzied tattoo as his movements juddered to a halt.

'So that was it,' Matt thought. 'That was what it's about.'

There was no doubt that the love-making had excited him. He ran one hand quickly, surreptitiously, over the front of his breeches to feel the bulging proof of his arousal. As he straightened up, Matt found himself looking into the flushed features of Lemuel Shattuck and, above him on the stairs, the narrowed eyes of Alderman Finucane.

'Herrumph . . . gentlemen, let us proceed.'

When they reached the foot of the stairs a couple staggered past them, their clothes still in disarray. Matt thought he recognized the woman as the one they'd met earlier.

They followed the couple along a short passageway into a large room lit by two smoky oil lamps. The lights threw long shadows across the cellar. A plank had been placed on two upturned barrels across the angle of one corner. It was covered with stone bottles, some lying on their side and dripping the last of their contents on to the dirty straw on the ground. About fifty men and women sat on the cellar floor with their backs to the walls, most drinking from broken cups and mugs, some fast asleep and snoring in their drunken stupors, heads resting on their neighbours' shoulders. Three couples were on their feet attempting to dance a reel to the discordant tune of a fiddler who was as drunk as they were. They kept slipping and sliding on drying pools of vomit on the hard packed earth floor, screeching with laughter.

In another corner, Matt saw a middle aged man, face blotched with drink, fondling Bernadette, the young girl he'd seen upstairs. Her shift was bunched around her waist, her head tossing, as the man's thick fingers sawed back and forth between her thighs.

The man and the woman whom Matt had seen under the stairs looked round the cellar room before walking over towards the girl. They slumped against the wall beside her. The woman – her mother, Matt presumed – looked up at her once, dully, before accepting the stone bottle offered by her companion.

As she took her first swig, the girl was lifted by the man until she hung monkey-like around his neck, her legs almost encircling him. He fumbled with his breeches, adjusted Bernadette's position, and began moving upwards and inwards against her. The girl whimpered thinly. Her moans hardly carried against the cacophony of noise in the cellar. Those nearest her glanced up once then looked away or busied themselves with their drinking.

The stench in the cellar of unwashed bodies, vomit and rot-gut alcohol bit into Matt's throat. He stumbled out of the room, retching bile deep from his stomach. Alderman Finucane followed him and put a comforting arm around the youngster's shoulders as he leaned, shaking helplessly, against the stairway upwards.

'Come on, lad,' the alderman urged. 'Hold on till we leave here. Don't let them see. Never let them see weakness.'

'How can it be?' whispered Matt. 'They're our people, Finny. They're Irish. Our people.'

'I know, Matt. Whatever they might be now, they're still our people.'

'How can it be?' Matt repeated. 'Oh, Mother of God, how can it be?'

A roar of laughter and applause came from the makeshift groggery. Matt looked up just in time to see the little girl disappearing naked up the stairs.

275

# Chapter 6 July, 1848

The good people of Boston were properly shocked by the report of the Committee of Internal Health. It was explicit in its descriptions of how the Irish were living. It spared few details of how they had been exploited, deserted, brutalized. Many Bostonians had known about their condition but had preferred to ignore it. As they said to themselves with no little self-satisfaction, the state of affairs seemed much worse in New York. The report was a heavy blow to their civic pride.

Matt Aherne and Alderman Finucane were particularly pleased with the report's concluding paragraph about the emigrants lives. 'Under such circumstances, self-respect, forethought, all the high and noble virtues soon die out, and sullen indifference and despair or disorder, intemperance and utter degradation reign supreme.'

The 'utter degradation' was left to the imagination but the phrase had been written with the scenes in the Hamilton Street groggery firmly in mind.

Newspaper editorials and charity organizations urged the emigrants to uproot their families from the slums and strike out for the opportunities further to the west. The Irish preferred to hug the stink and misery of their existence in Boston.

Their obstinacy began to sour any sympathy aroused on their behalf by the efforts of Alderman Finucane and his friends. Other official reports which followed soon transformed any remaining sympathy into resentment against the Irish.

Every citizen knew that violence and crime had increased in Boston since the mass arrival of the Irish. The Clerk of Boston Police Court disclosed that in the five years since 1843, the number of murders had nearly trebled; cases of attempted murder had increased 170 times; assaults on constables had quadrupled, as had aggravated assaults with weapons ranging from knives, dirks, pistols, slingshots, razors, pokers and clubs to flat irons and bricks.

'Trouble's coming, Matt. There'll be trouble, mark my words,'

Alderman Finucane said gloomily as he perused the columns of the *Boston Pilot*. 'Word's already reaching me of some night hawks ganging up to attack our people. If they retaliate . . . well, we'll be having riots in the streets and the work of years'll be undone.'

'Do you think we'll ever be accepted, Finny? Will we never belong here?' Matt asked earnestly.

'Oh, there's no fear of that, boy. No fear at all. The Yankees might have the high ideals but they haven't our native cunning or ruthlessness.' The alderman smiled suddenly. 'They haven't our sense of belonging to each other either. One thing we Irish do well is stick together. Oh no, we'll survive here. The next generation or so will have hard times, make no mistake. They'll take a buffeting but in the final day the Yankees will need us. They'll appreciate our muscles and our like of a fight, you see.'

Matt laughed at his optimism, his lightening of spirit. 'You're almost talking like a Yankee, Finny.'

'And isn't that the truth?' The alderman joined in the amusement. 'And what young spalpeen, may I ask, is learning the Yankees' talk mighty quick? Why I've hardly heard a tis or a twas out of you for weeks. And that's the truth as well.'

'Twas Mary . . . ' Matt stopped, smiled and began again. 'Mary said I'd soon lose the habit if I thought of what I was going to say before I opened my gob.'

'She did, did she?' The alderman had a broad grin on his homely face. 'And what else has she been saying, young man, while you've been walking out together?'

Matt lowered his eyes, embarrassed for a moment. 'Oh, not much, Finny. Just this and that. Really, she's only been showing me around the town when we've finished at the cooperage.' He tried to steer the conversation into more political avenues, anxious not to discuss his deepening friendship with Mary Finucane. 'One thing she did say, though, was that the only matter uniting the Irish and the old Boston Yankees was our hating of the English.'

'Dislike them, maybe. Distrust them, certainly. Not hate though. There's too much between us in history for that. But you know Matt, I often think, with the world as it is, that God made the English first, looked at them, examined them, turned them this way and that and then changed his mind for the rest of us.'

The yellow light of the single oil lamp reflected back into the office from the windows which were covered with specks of sawdust and glue. The late autumn sun had disappeared long since and the half moon was too busy dodging in and out of the ragged clouds to shed much light.

Matt Aherne shivered suddenly in the chilly office. He glanced across at the desk where Mary Finucane was still poring over the account books and saw that she had tucked a heavy shawl around her shoulders. His eyes softened as he gazed on her. The cold seemed to lift from him. His thoughts drifted from the pile of invoices in front of him to warmer times spent with Mary, particularly the day a week before when their hands brushed as they walked together across Boston Common. He could swear that she momentarily ran her little finger across the back of his hand. Matt was certain that it had been deliberate. Why else had she not looked directly at him for the next minute or so but walked on with head demurely bent, a slight blush spreading on her cheeks? He smiled to himself as the side of her mouth flicked up a little in a grimace of impatience caused, no doubt, by the columns of figures she was trying to add up. She rubbed her hand wearily across her eyes. Soon, Matt thought, her father would return from his weekly tour of the six 'Mother McCarthy' bars and restaurants. Then, the two youngsters could finish their tiresome work on the accounts of the cooperage factory. He cupped his chin in his hands, preferring to surrender his thoughts to Mary. There had been no formal courtship, he realized. How could there be when their closeness had pushed them into a relationship near to that of brother and sister? He had sensed a definite tension in recent months. It was as if there was a barrier between them which neither had the experience nor confidence to attempt to cross. There was also a rough mateyness in their conduct together which Matt, a least, used to disguise his increasingly romantic feelings for the alderman's daughter.

But Matt's state of mind hadn't been helped by the deep humiliation he'd felt at the debacle of William Smith O'Brien's uprising in Ireland in late July. Mary had been particularly caustic about that.

'Can you Irishers never do anything right?' she'd asked cuttingly. 'You blow your tin trumpets hard enough, wave your flags and pistols in the air, then run for your lives when the English say "boo" to you.'

Matt hadn't replied. Indeed, he didn't know what to say. Even the *Boston Pilot* had been markedly unenthusiastic about the uprising although it had uttered, for its readership's sake, the usual condemnations of the English rule in Ireland.

The final humiliation for Matt had been the news that the English, learning from earlier mistakes, had not even created martyrs from the rebel leaders they'd captured. Try as they might even the most rabid among the new Irish-Americans could raise little indignation that William Smith O'Brien, Thomas Meagher, and Tom McManus had been transported to Tasmania after their trials. Unpleasant as that fate was, it was not the stuff of martyrdom. The later news that some of the others, including James Stephens, had escaped successfully to France went almost unreported as everyone with an Irish background tried to draw a veil over the bungled affair. Unhappily, they were not allowed to do so. The rising's failure had given added impetus to anti-Irish feeling throughout the Eastern States of Amrica.

As Alderman Finucane had feared, gangs of thugs now regarded the Irish as legitimate targets for their drunken attacks. The Irish had retaliated and already there had been two full-scale riots in Boston. The town's constables had been ordered to keep special watch on any Irish business premises but many of the constables were only too happy to nip down an alley for a quick smoke while the gangs smashed up Irish-owned shops and warehouses. The outbreaks of violence, although sporadic, were increasing in number. That was why this evening Matt Aherne and Mary Finucane had not ventured home on their own from the cooperage factory but had waited for Alderman Finucane and his carriage driver, newly employed for his brawn as well as his skill with horses.

'Back in the mists again, Matthew?'

Mary's voice cut low into the young man's thoughts. He jerked his head out of his hands and looked round at her.

'What, Mary?'

'Thinking again, then? Away back in Kerry?'

'No, but twas of Ireland I was thinking.'

'It was of Ireland,' she corrected.

He smiled at her. 'It was . . .'

'Aren't you happy here?'

'Oh, yes. But . . .'

'You're doing so well,' she interrupted. 'Father's extremely pleased with your advancement.'

Matt stood up, stretching himself. His shoes echoed on the office's wooden floor as he walked over to Mary's desk. He face glowed in the light from the oil lamp. He gazed down at her. 'Sometimes I'm knowing clearly what I want to do, what I have to do with my life. Then . . .' he spread his arms. 'Then it all becomes confused and I'm not sure.'

Mary lowered her eyes to the ledger on her desk. 'Mother says you've always to do what's in your heart and there's so much to be done here for the Irish. You and Father both say that.'

'We do and there is. Sure there is. But I'm thinking we'll maybe never really succeed here until Ireland's a free nation again. Until then the Irish'll always be refugees, always be looked down on. And isn't that what's happening here and now in Boston. After the uprising . . .'

'That again. That silly nonsense,' Mary said scornfully. 'I knew we'd return to that.'

Matt shrugged his shoulders. 'How can you forget it?' he asked. 'It happened so it did. And made us the laughing stock again. And ruined a deal of the alderman's work.'

'It did that,' said Mary as she stood up and adjusted the shawl around her shoulders.

'I wish Father would hurry up,' she declared rather petulantly. 'It's a mite cold in this office.'

She moved out from behind her desk and brushed past Matt as she went to the window. For a moment, Matt thought of clasping her in his arms. He cursed inwardly at his timidity.

Mary rubbed the window with her hand and peered out. Then she cocked her head slightly. 'I can hear something,' she said.

'Your father's carriage?' Matt asked.

'No, it's not that. More like a parade. A deal of people by the sound of it.'

Matt took two paces to the window. Mary was right. He could hear the tramp of feet, the low grumble of voices. The sounds were still some distance away, perhaps two or three streets, but they seemed to be coming nearer.

'What is it Matt?' There was anxiety in her voice.

'A crowd of some kind, that's for sure, but what kind is anyone's guess.' Matt was puzzled but unconcerned.

He was more concerned by his closeness to Mary. They were barely six inches apart as they pressed their ears to the window, then tried to peer through the encrusted grime on the outside of the glass.

Her green eyes were huge, luminous, at such a distance. Suddenly, they flicked upwards and gazed directly into Matt's. The approaching sounds of the crowd, whatever it was, seemed to vanish. He was aware only of the stillness in the office and the warmth flowing from Mary. It was as if he and she were cocooned together in a world of infinite, unspoken yearning. The feeling of wonder, a definite physical feeling clutching at his chest, grew inside him like a bubble. Matt could smell her sweet breath on his face. Her eyes, serious, wondering, drew him still closer until they filled his vision. Their lips touched, then pressed fleetingly against each other. Matt lifted his arms to encircle Mary, to hold her closer, but after an instant, she turned away, her head bowed.

'Mary . . . Mary . . . ' Matt whispered. 'Oh, Mary.'

She didn't reply. Her right hand groped backwards searching for his. Their fingers met and entwined, softly at first, then more fiercely. Mary turned and pushed her face against Matt's chest as though listening to his heart. Matt smelt the freshness of her hair, felt the softness of her body, marvelled at the cool smoothness of her hand in his.

They stood profiled against the window for long seconds, wrapped in each other's warmth and love.

Distantly, as if from another time and place, Matt heard a rough hammering mingled with harsh, raised voices. He wanted them to go away, to leave him in the peace of newly-declared love, but they persisted, even grew stronger. He shook his head, attempting to make the sounds vanish, trying to remain in his and Mary's tender world. She looked up at him as she felt his movement and heard the noises too. The spell binding them was broken. They stepped slightly apart and peered through the window again.

'Holy Mother of God!' Matt breathed.

Below them, outside the factory gates, was a large semi-circle of torches flickering in the night. The noises they'd heard was a crowd trying to break through the stout gates.

The baying of the mob flooded into the upstairs office.

'Irisher scum . . . Irisher scum . . . Irisher scum . . . '

Matt and Mary could see the gates bending and swaying under the pressure of the men outside. They heard, rather than saw, a fusillade of bricks and stones hurtle over the factory walls, clattering into the courtyard below, smashing into the wooden building.

Matt pulled Mary away from the window and fell with her to the floor.

As they did, a brick crashed through the office window, showering them with shards of glass.

Mary screamed shrilly.

# Chapter 7 August, 1848

The drunken mob attacking the Finucane cooperage was out for blood. Each brick hurled against the slatted wooden walls was a protest against the Irish influx and against the spreading slums. Every wave of a flaming torch was angry defiance against the authoritarian meddling by the Roman Catholic hierarchy in the traditionally liberal politics of Massachusetts. Every curse and chant was a cry of fear that one day the alien minority might hold the balance of political power, might even become the majority. The fact that Alderman Finucane was a prime mover in attempting to reconcile the two cultures made his factory a target. Reconciliation meant compromise and the mob was in no mood for that.

The constable manning the factory gates had run the other way as soon as the mob had flooded into the narrow street. Now he watched from a safe distance while a group of men rammed a cart repeatedly against the factory gates. The rest either threw bricks and stones or vainly tried to scale the high walls topped with sharp, pointed flints. The constable noticed a flicker of flame on the first floor of the factory and decided he ought to hurry off to alert the nearest fire brigade. The thought that any people might still be in the factory so late in the evening simply did not occur to him.

Matt Aherne pulled Mary into the corner of the upstairs office furthest away from the spreading pool of burning oil spilt from the lamp which had toppled off the desk when the youngsters fell to the floor.

Mary was sobbing more from shock than from fright. Matt tried to comfort her, holding her close, patting her hair, while he surveyed their desperate situation. The flaming oil licked hungrily at the cane seats of the office chairs and devoured the pieces of paper in the waste bin. Within seconds, it threw a leaping barrier of heat and fire across the office in front of the door. Matt realized their only route to safety would have to take them through the flames.

'Quickly, Mary!' he gasped, acrid smoke already beginning to bite into his lungs. 'The door . . . the door . . . we must reach it or we're done for!'

Mary shrank back into the corner, panic in her wide eyes.

'Holy Mother . . . Holy Mother . . . ' she kept repeating as she clung to Matt.

He forced himself away from her. He realized they had only seconds in which to save themselves. Matt shrugged off his coat. He flung it over Mary's head covering her face and long hair. ''Tis the only way . . . through the flames,' he shouted, his voice hoarse with smoke and fear. 'Come on . . . come on now!'

He gripped Mary's wrist tightly to heave her to her feet. She hung back, coughing and sobbing, one arm flung upwards as if warding off the heat of the flames.

'Come on!' Matt implored. He wrenched harder but she would not budge from the corner, immobilized by panic.

There was only one thing for Matt to do. He bent down, circled his arms round Mary's thighs and lifted her bodily over his shoulder.

With one arm gripping Mary and the other across his eyes, he plunged towards the flames, now waist high.

For a moment, his world was one of unbearable heat. The rays of a thousand suns pierced his body. He felt as if his very blood would boil, as if molten lead was being poured into his nostrils and down his throat. His scalp and skull seemed to shrivel and tighten, squeezing his brain in a vice.

The fleeting parts of a second were more like hours. And then he and Mary were through the flames and by the door. Matt fumbled for the catch and thrust it upwards. As the door flew open under his frenzied strength, the inrushing air bellowed the flames behind him The heat flared terrifyingly on his back before he managed to negotiate two or three steps down the rough staircase to the factory yard. He turned his head to look back just as a ball of fire exploded from the shattered window of the office. Jagged flames shot upwards and outwards in the night, curling round the outside of the upper floor of the factory, searching voraciously for the sloping roof timbers.

Matt stumbled under another engulfing wave of intense heat. He put Mary down, holding tightly on to her until he was certain that she had a steady footing on the stairway and slipped the coat from over her head.

'Oh, Matt!' she gasped. 'Are we safe now?' Long strands of hair covered her features. She brushed them aside impatiently. An expression of horror mingled with disbelief grew on her face when she saw how fast the fire had spread.

The inside of the office they'd escaped from only seconds before was a mass of whirling, crackling fire. Fingers of flame were even now reaching for the first step of the stairway.

'Oh, no,' Mary whispered. 'Oh, no, Holy Mother.' The factory was doomed.

'Quickly!' Matt urged. 'Before these steps go.'

The youngsters hurried down the staircase, hand in hand, oblivious to the stones and bricks still smashing around them into the walls of the factory. It was only when they reached the courtyard they became aware again of the baying sound of the men outside. The factory gates were starting to give way under the continuous battering.

'This way,' Matt ordered, pulling Mary away from the gates and towards the end of the wide courtyard. He realized the mob would soon break through. The cries and shouts from beyond the walls already contained a note of exultation, of triumph, as the men saw that their work of destruction was well under way. Like the constable, they too thought the factory was unoccupied and assumed one of their own number had started the fire with a torch flung over the walls.

Matt searched his mind desperately for a way out of the courtyard while they cowered in a corner of the wall. Mary held Matt's coat above their heads to protect them from the fiery clouds of sparks and glowing splinters of wood billowing from the factory. The flames were well on to the roof and had spread already to the lower floor. The pile of barrels stacked outside the main door to the factory were coloured a dull red in the fierce light of the blaze.

Matt looked at the barrels and realized there was a chance, a slim one, but still a chance if he was quick enough. 'Stay there,' he shouted to Mary over his shoulder as he sprinted across the yard towards the barrels. They were stacked according to their different sizes. First, Matt flipped one of the largest on to its side and rolled it back towards the wall, its metal bands clattering on the cobblestones. He levered it upright before hurrying back again to the stack. This time he selected a taller but narrower barrel to roll back to the wall. He clambered on to the first, larger barrel. 'Quick. Hand me the other,' he called to Mary.

She nodded, her shock replaced by her usual resourcefulness and understanding.

It was a strain for her to lift the narrower barrel but she managed to raise it high enough for Matt's groping fingers to fasten on the rim. He pulled it on the larger, wider barrel, before scrambling gingerly on to it. Now he could reach the top of the wall with his hands.

'Tis I shall go first, then pull you up. But quick for they're coming.'

Mary caught her breath as Matt teetered on the barrels, searching for a hold on the wall away from the jagged flints. She looked anxiously round at the factory gates. Already one of the panels had been smashed. Through it, she could see the waving torches of the mob. Her lips moved in a silent prayer for their safety while she watched Matt haul himself painfully onto the top of the wall.

'My coat,' he called down, his voice cracking with pain. The flints cut into the inside of his thighs as his legs straddled the wall. 'Hand up the coat, then on to the barrels.'

Mary peered at him, silhouetted by the dancing glare of the burning factory. The height frightened her but she knew there was no alternative. She handed up the coat before managing to crouch first on the large barrel and then pull herself up again. She winced with pain from the raised rims of the barrels cutting into her knees.

Matt folded the coat into a pad. He groaned from the pain of the flints gashing his legs. Eventually, after more painful manoeuvring, he succeeded in balancing himself on top of the wall. He lay flat on his stomach, partially protected by the coat beneath him. He leaned over as far as he dared, his legs dangling into empty space acting as a balance. His hands searched for those stretched upwards by Mary. He caught her wrists, holding them gently at first. Matt felt their small, fine bones. His grip tightened. Mary gasped with pain.

'A moment, mavourneen,' he whispered, using his first word of endearment towards Mary. 'Twill only be a moment.'

She smiled up at him although the strength of his grip was almost unbearable.

Matt looked quickly down the yard. One of the mob was squeezing through the widening hole in the gates. His arm was reaching to lift the stout wooden plank which held the gates shut.

He began to pull Mary upwards. As he took the strain, the flints in the wall pressed, jagged, into his stomach through the protection of the coat. Mary's shoes scrabbled at the wall, trying for a foothold, the smallest ledge, to help lift herself.

Matt gave a convulsive heave, almost toppling over in the effort, and then Mary's face was level with his. He couldn't resist brushing his lips across hers before starting the agonizing manoeuvre to help lift her firmly on to the wall.

'Ooh! . . . . Ouch!' Mary complained, the flints bruising into her through her skirt and petticoats. But there was a lightness in her voice. She realized she was safe.

With Mary perched safely on the wall, Matt took a deep breath before pushing himself into the darkness on the other side of the high wall.

He was ready for a jarring fall on hard ground but instead landed squelchily up to his knees in a pile of rotting straw. The immediately overpowering stench of horse dung flared into his nostrils, making him cough and retch.

'What is it? Are you safe?' Mary called down, concerned and alarmed by the noises from below.

'Jump now,' Matt spluttered. 'I'll catch you.'

Mary hesitated. She couldn't see into the dark shadows under the wall.

'Is it safe?' she asked tremulously, shutting her eyes and pushing herself off the wall.

'For horses, at least, mavourneen,' Matt laughed, catching Mary around the waist to stop her falling headlong on to the pile of well-rotted manure.

'Oh, no!' Mary shrieked. 'Horse dung! My shoes . . . my dress! You've ruined them, Matthew Aherne. You've ruined them . . . you . . . you ignorant spalpeen!' Her protests died and were re-born as chuckles, then peals of laughter when the ridiculousness of their plight dawned on her.

They clung to each other, arms around waists, still laughing.

The street outside the factory had quietened when they looked round the corner of the alley. Some men were still entering the gates but their shouting was drowned by the crackling of the giant bonfire that was the once-thriving cooperage. A red glow was reflected in the windows of the houses and warehouses opposite. As the youngsters watched, a dozen constables ran into the street, truncheons drawn. They were followed by two horse-drawn insurance company fire wagons, flanked by men whose efforts would clearly be in vain.

Emboldened by the constables' presence, Matt and Mary ventured out into the street, walking nearer to the factory entrance. The mob were pressed into the courtyard and around the shattered gates.

The crowd cheered when the factory collapsed upon itself with a grinding explosion, but those near the front yelped as large splinters of burning wood whirled among them.

The youngsters began to walk away, unable to watch any more, and were just turning the corner when they heard a commotion behind them.

Alderman Finucane had been enjoying his weekly tour of the 'Mother McCarthy's' bars and restaurants when news of the fire had reached him. He had been taking a few glasses with two particularly old friends, Padraig Costelloe and Timmy Brehoney, and the three of them had run nearly a mile to reach the scene.

'Where are they?' the alderman shouted at one of the constables, nearly hysterical with anxiety.

'Who, sir?' The constable had immediately recognized the distraught politician and businessman.

'Mary and Matt, they were inside. Are they here? Are they safe?'

'Inside there, sir?' The constable, horror spreading on his face, nodded towards the twisted, broken factory, still covered with dancing flames. 'In there?'

'Yes, in there, you gobbeen. In there . . . '

'No one came out as far as we know. This mob were everywhere, just everywhere around the building . . . oh my God . . . in there . . . '

Alderman Finucane staggered fractionally as if he'd been punched in the chest. Costelloe moved to his side, ready to comfort him, while Brehoney began shouldering his way through the mob. Many of them were turning away, leaving for their homes, content with their night's work.

'Have any of you swabs seen the youngsters from the factory? Have you seen them?' he kept bellowing. Nobody answered him or even attempted to. They looked at him dully, sated by the destruction they had wrought.

'Father! Father!' cried Mary, pushing her way against the tide of men ebbing from the street.

'Over here, Alderman!' Matt shouted. ''Tis safe we are.' He held Mary's hand tightly as they struggled through the crowd.

The alderman's face told of his delight at their safety. He hugged them closely and then stepped back, sniffing the air. 'By the saints!' he exclaimed, a quizzical smile on his face. 'And what have you two been grovelling in?'

''Twas out of the fire, Finny, and into the horse sh—'

'Manure,' Mary interrupted sharply. 'And there's that "twas" again, Matthew Aherne.'

The alderman and his companions roared with laughter.

'That's the female for you, Matt. You'll learn, lad. You'll learn.

Even in the state she is, she won't be letting you be.'

'State, Father?'

'Just look at the pair of you, lass.'

Matt gazed at Mary. Her face was streaked with black, the ends of her long hair were singed, her dress was soaking and covered with evil smelling straw up to her thighs.

'And you're a pretty sight too, Matthew Aherne,' she snapped. 'Filthy, smelly, and with hardly an eyebrow left.' Then her tone softened. 'But you saved my life, so you did, with all your tis and twas . . .'

She stretched up, put her arms round Matt's neck, and kissed him firmly on the mouth. She wasn't able to see her father wink broadly at Costelloe and Brehoney.

The next morning there was a feeling of subdued tension around the breakfast table at the Finucane household. The alderman was worried about meeting his insurance company; whether they would pay his claim in full and whether that amount would be sufficient to rebuild the factory. His wife was more concerned with the previous night's public show of affection between Mary and Matt.

The alderman pushed aside his business worries when his wife, with a shrewd nod, drew his attention to the young people's evident preoccupation with each other. 'Mother,' he announced, 'I'm thinking before we consider the question of a new factory, we should be looking at some matters closer to home, don't you?'

'As you decide, dear.'

Matt and Mary exchanged quick glances. Two small red spots appeared high on Mary's cheeks.

'Then, when the table's finished, perhaps you'll talk with your daughter here, while I take this young man into the drawing room. I've a liking to know his intentions.'

When they were seated in the drawing room, the alderman began speaking his voice as soft and concerned as he could manage.

'The question, Matt, is quite simple. What's there between you and Mary? Was last night's display just in the heat of the moment?' He began laughing. The tension eased. 'What a gobbeen way to put it, eh? In the heat of the . . . well, was it anyway? Or is there something deeper?'

'Deeper, I think,' Matt replied quietly.

'You think?'

'Well, for me, tis knowing I am.'

The alderman tut-tutted.

Matt smiled. 'I know it's deeper on my side, Finny.'

'Then, your intentions?'

'Marriage, if she'll have me. And if you're approving, of course.'

Matt looked appealingly at the older man, who hesitated deliberately. The tension grew. Then the alderman smiled broadly, pushed himself out of his chair and crossed the room to shake Matt's hand.

'Of course, I'm approving lad. Fact is, I was guessing this would happen for some time back.'

'But what of Mary?'

'We'll be knowing soon enough, I'm thinking. But, what if she does say "Yes". What then? You'll not marry yet, will you? Eighteen is young, so it is. Wait till you're twenty, eh? The years'll help you be certain in your minds.'

'They will?'

'Aye, they will. And we'll be wanting to rebuild the business, won't we?' The alderman guffawed, 'And I'll be needing all your strength and concentration for that, I'll be bound.'

Matt reddened and changed the subject. 'As you like then, Finny. I'll be waiting if she'll have me. But I'm wondering if the factory's worth rebuilding. Won't they burn it again?'

'They might, lad, but that's hardly the point. The Ursuline nuns didn't leave town, when the mob burned down the convent a few years back, did they?'

'No.'

'Well, then, neither shall we. If we're to stay and grow in this town, we've got to fight back. The factory's of no matter in itself. It's our determination that counts. As I've told you time and time again, if we stay together, we'll survive and prosper.'

The door opened behind him. His wife came into the room with Mary hovering behind her.

'Ah, Mother!' the alderman exclaimed, moving to her side. 'And what does the daughter say?'

'More to the point,' his wife replied, nodding at Matt, 'What's he saying?'

'His intentions are perfectly honourable.'

Mary's mother beamed. 'Then, father, I'm sure we can leave them to discuss the future themselves.' She turned back to the door. 'Don't you agree?' she added pointedly.

'Oh, yes, dear.' The alderman hurried to join her, pausing only to give Mary a light kiss on her forehead.

The young people stood at opposite ends of the room, looking serious and slightly embarrassed. There was silence for long seconds. Then they began speaking at the same time.

'Mary, what . . . ?'

'Matthew Aherne, did you . . . ?'

They laughed, their eyes softening towards each other. Matt walked up to Mary and took her hands in his.

She spoke softly without looking up at him. 'So your intentions are perfectly honourable are they, Matt?'

'You know they are, mavourneen,' he replied quietly, smelling her freshly-washed hair.

'And what are they then?'

'To marry, if you'll have me.'

'Then you'd better ask, hadn't you?'

'Will you?'

'Will I what?'

Matt sighed. 'Mary Finucane . . . mavourneen . . . will you be accepting my hand in marriage?'

'Of course, Matthew Aherne. I will,' she said simply. She lifted her face towards his. They kissed without embracing. It was a chaste kiss, the sealing of a bargain rather than a passionate avowal.

Two years later, in the autumn of 1850, Matt and Alderman Finucane stood beside a grave in the Granary Burying Ground alongside the church in Park Street.

The grass on the slight rectangular mound was well clipped. The grave stone was free from the moss that disfigured some of its neighbours. Matt could read the inscription easily: 'Elisabeth Kilfedder – 1797–1826' and underneath the single word 'Beloved'.

'Jack-Da said there'd been someone else apart from my mam, Finny,' the young man said. 'Just before the fever took him, it was.'

'Theirs was a mighty love, lad.'

The alderman stood on the opposite side of the grave to Matt. They spoke in hushed tones although there was no one else in the yard.

'Strange to think but I'm doubting if you'd be here today, Matt, if Elisabeth hadn't died. I'm guessing Jack would have stayed his time in Boston and never returned home.'

'And I would still be in poverty with them Cooleens.'

'Or worse.'

'Aye.'

Matt bent down to place a spray of red roses at the head of the grave.

'Did they ever catch him, Finny?'

'J.P.? Not that we ever heard. There was tell though that he'd been sighted in Natchez and then later that he'd been tumbled off one of them riverboats after being caught with one too many aces up his sleeve. That divil deserved an end like that after all the misery he brought on people. And yet if it hadn't been for all his conniving I might never have been elected.'

'So it didn't end here,' Matt replied, pointing at the grave.

The alderman nodded. 'Everyone's dying alters life here and now. Elizabeth's altered Jack's and yours, now didn't it? And that means it's going to change the lives of mother and me when you marry Mary. There'll be a new family in the world. The Ahernes. Not the Finucanes. That's what the churching means this afternoon. You'll have to build your own life as a family just as we Finucanes did ours, just as Jack Keane did his. It won't be easy. It doesn't happen natural. There'll be times when you and Mary'll gladly strangle each other. But you'll stay as one if you never forget you're building your own piece of history.'

Later that evening, it was as bridegroom and father of the bride that they stood beside each other toasting themselves and the two hundred wedding guests in the ballroom of the United States Hotel in Beach Street, just across from the depot of the Worcester Railroad.

Matt's head was in a whirl. The champagne, the dancing, the strangers to be greeted and hopefully committed to memory, the wedding ceremony itself, had all conspired to draw a veil over his mind. Even words of a moment before seemed to have been heard in the distant past. The only clear image was of Mary approaching him along the aisle on the arm of her father, her face covered by the tucks of a white veil. The short, tulle train of her dress had been carried by the small daughter of her only sister, Kathleen, who, as matron of honour, assumed the proprietorial air of someone who'd seen it all before.

She'd arrived from her home in Philadelphia three days before the wedding and had set to gleefully helping her mother in all those last minute panics of a family marriage so beloved of women. Her husband, a physician and budding surgeon, had offered to be best man but Matt had preferred, as a gesture in memory of Jack Keane, to ask Padraig Costelloe. And to give Costelloe full credit, he'd avoided becoming too drunk until after his speech at the crowded reception.

Now the toasts and speeches were done, the relatives and guests began to relax. The jigs became wilder, the drink stronger and the songs more fervently Irish or tearfully sentimental as the evening wore on.

Matt glanced sideways at Mary sitting beside him. Her face was slightly flushed from the heat and the champagne. Her eyes were following the whirling dancers. Matt nudged her under the table with his knee. He leaned closer to her.

'I'm thinking they wouldn't be missing us, mavourneen,' he breathed into her ear.

Mary didn't reply. Her tongue flicked out once and moistened her lips. Her eyes turned towards his. She nodded almost imperceptibly.

Alderman Finucane had been watching the exchange of glances. He tried not to smile, remembering his own feelings on his wedding night. He tapped Matt lightly on the forearm.

'Slip away now, lad,' he whispered. 'They're too addled to be noticing much. Use the serving door behind you, eh?'

'But there are many to thank. Is it being right?' Matt protested, looking about him to ensure that he wasn't overheard.

'Just go, lad. Don't be worrying about them. Be off and God bless you both!'

Matt took Mary's hand. They rose quickly together and disappeared through the kitchen door without daring even a backward look to see if any of their guests had seen their leaving.

A plump, middle aged waitress, stacking dishes, started with surprise as the newly-weds burst into the kitchen. Then her face broke into a large, welcoming grin. Having served at many weddings before, she instinctively understood the young people's predicament. 'This way, my loves,' she giggled, beckoning them through another door. 'The suite is it?' she asked over her shoulder as she scurried on.

After climbing three flights of stairs the waitress stopped outside a door. She pressed her ear against it, listening. She opened the door only when she was satisfied that no one was passing along the corridor outside. 'There it is,' she reported in a conspiratorial whisper. 'It's unlocked with the key inside. We always do that so you poor loves won't be having to stand around the night-clerk's desk.'

'Thanks for that,' Matt muttered.

Mary gave the waitress a quick peck on the cheek before she and Matt slipped across the corridor and into the bridal suite reserved for them.

The red velvet curtains were drawn. They threw back the light from the oil lamp bathing the large room in a pinkish glow. A silver ice bucket containing an unopened bottle of champagne stood shinily by the side of the high double bed. Across the rich coverlet lay two nightgowns.

Matt turned to Mary, his arms circling her slim waist.

'Well, Mrs Aherne?' he said softly.

'Well, Mr Aherne,' she whispered in reply. She lifted her lips to his. They kissed, softly at first then more fiercely. Their breaths, sweet with champagne, mingled. They clung to each other for a second until Mary pushed Matt lightly away.

'I'll change in the bathroom,' she said matter-of-factly. She smiled up at him. There was no hint of nervousness in her voice or expression.

While Matt stayed near the door, Mary lit another lamp on the dressing table and carried it into the adjoining bathroom. She left the door ajar. Matt quickly stripped off his clothes, kicking them under the bed, pulled his fine linen nightgown over his head, and sat down on the side of the bed. He was uncertain what happened next.

Suddenly, he realized Mary had left her nightdress, all lace and frills, lying across the bed. He picked it up, wondering what to do.

'Matt?' Her voice came softly from the bathroom.

'Mavourneen?'

'Blow out the lamp will you, avourneen.'

Matt crossed the room, doused the light and felt his way back towards the bed in the dark.

The door of the bathroom opened wide. Mary stood in the entrance, her long hair flowing over her shoulders, the slim curves of her body outlined in the light of the lamp she'd left burning behind her.

Matt stood up, still clutching her nightdress. He stepped towards her, offering it to her, but Mary waved it away.

'Have you ever been with a woman?' she asked, her voice breathy and slightly hoarse.

'No. Never.'

She took a step towards him. Her arms were raised a little, palms turned towards Matt in a compliant gesture.

He gasped audibly as his eyes took in the roundness of her raised hard-tipped breasts, the slimness of her waist, the dark triangle beneath her flat stomach.

Mary allowed him to gaze on her for breathless seconds before she moved towards him.

'Then we'll have to learn how to make babies together, won't we?'

she said with an almost joyous lilt in her voice as Matt swept her into his arms and on to the bed.

There were no more words for a while, nor any need for them.


## Chapter 8 February, 1858


The atmosphere seemed to grow colder in the master bedroom of the Aherne household in South Boston.

'Do you really have to go?'

The concern was apparent in Mary Aherne's voice.

Matt stirred slightly on the pillow beside her. He'd pretended to be dozing when Mary had come to bed. He knew too well what her tactics would be. 'Uh-huh,' he murmured.

'You're leaving us then?' Mary Aherne's tone sharpened.

'Just for a month or so,' Matt answered sleepily.

It was no good, he thought. There was no escape. He turned to look at his wife. She stared straight up at the ceiling, her hair spread like a brown halo on the white bed linen of the pillow. Her profile was as beautiful as ever. Her body still excited him even after eight years of marriage and three children. A candle flickered on the bedside table. In its light, Matt could see that his wife's mouth was set in a firm line.

'You'll do us the honour of coming back?'

'Of course, darling.'

'But why you? Why do you have to go?' she persisted.

'Because I was asked, that's why. Because the association wanted Joe Denieffe and me to go to Dublin.'

Mary sniffed. 'It's all right for him. He's no responsibilities. You've a family to look after and a business to run.'

'You and Finny can manage, dearest. You've been fine before when I've had to go to New York or Philadelphia on business.'

'That was only a week or two. Not months.'

'Won't make a mite of difference, you'll see.' Matt tried to keep his temper under control. It was the third time in as many days that Mary had mounted a campaign to dissuade him from going to

Ireland on behalf of the Emmet Monument Association. He regarded the invitation to meet James Stephens as a singular honour.

After taking part in the failed uprising of 1848, James Stephens had spent years in exile in Paris. There he had learned a great deal from continental revolutionaries, and had accepted many of their views. John O'Mahony, another rebel, had fought alongside him on the barricades during Louis-Napoleon's *coup d'état* of 1851.

When memories of the '48 fiasco had had time to dim, Stephens had set off for Ireland once more. O'Mahony had gone to the United States with their comrade Michael Doheny.

Stephens had travelled the length and breadth of Ireland, assessing the state of nationalist sentiment, and planning a secret rebel organization, to be divided into cells for the sake of security, with himself at the head. This was the man Matt and Joe were going to see. What Matt saw as an honour, Mary saw as an imposition.

'It'll be dangerous mixing with all those revolutionaries . . . that Stephens.' Mary switched her attack.

'Why should it be? All we're doing is taking messages to him.'

'Messages pledging support if he starts his revolt.'

'Yes, but . . .'

'And money, I guess. You've been holding enough money-on-the-plate dinners, haven't you?'

'Not a deal. Only £80. The very minimum he wanted.'

Mary sniffed again. 'Fat lot that'll do. If the English get hold of you, it'll mean prison more than likely.'

'They won't.' Exasperation was creeping into Matt's voice. Mary sensed it. She turned to him and buried her head against his chest.

'Please, darling. Just for me.' She begged like a little girl denied her favourite doll. Then she started to sob. Matt could feel the damp tears seeping through his nightgown. He raised his eyes to the ceiling in silent prayer.

'It has to be, Mary love,' he said quietly.

Her sobs grew. He put his arms around her and was instantly aroused.

'Hush dearest. You'll be waking the wee ones.'

'Oh, damn them!' Mary said fiercely. 'I'm married to you, not them.'

Matt bent his head and nuzzled her cheek before kissing her gently on the lips. Her mouth, wet and salty with tears, opened under his. Their tongues flicked together.

'Please, Matt,' she whispered.

'I have to, dear one. You know that.'

He silenced her reply with another kiss. His hand slid down her back to caress her buttocks. His fingers gripped the folds of her nightgown and pulled it upwards. She lifted herself slightly to allow it to slide around her waist. Matt did the same. Their lower bodies pressed nakedly against each other. Her hand moving gently to and fro, gripped his stiffness.

'It's always your solution, Matthew Aherne, isn't it?'

'What is?'

Her sobbing had ceased. Their voices were low and husky with passion.

'This.' She squeezed softly.

'So?'

'Well, it is, isn't it?'

'Do you mind?'

'No.'

'Is it safe?'

'Should be.'

Their caresses became more urgent until he lifted himself on his arms and moved over her. The silk-smooth inside of her legs gripped his hips tightly and he entered her, smoothly, warmly.

'Do you really love me?' Her breath was coming in short gasps.

'You know I do.'

'You never say it.'

'I love you.'

'Won't you miss me?'

'Mavourneen . . .'

'Will you miss . . . this?' The last word was an effort. The slow, deep, deeper rhythm quickened. He didn't, couldn't answer.

Mary's head tossed from side to side on the pillow. Matt's lips were fastened to the smooth skin between her neck and her shoulder. The moans grew low in her throat. Her heels tattooed on his buttocks. Matt felt the contractions inside her, her liquid flooding, before, moments later, climaxing himself.

His weight pressed down on her as the strength went from his arms. They lay together, warm, close, while he softened and shrank inside her. Then he pulled back and shifted sideways off her. He put an arm across to ease her nearer to him. His mouth was buried in the pillow. He could feel a few beads of sweat on his forehead.

'Love you,' he murmured.

'Love you,' Mary replied, running her nails down the small of his back to the crease in his buttocks. The muscles under his skin twitched. She giggled and repeated the caress. Matt turned back to her. She felt his new tumescence press against her thighs.

'No . . . no,' she protested softly, pushing him away. 'Do you ever have enough?'

'Do you?'

'That's quite enough, Matthew Aherne,' she scolded, though without any rancour. 'Else you'll be coming home to another babbie when you've finished your gallivanting across the Atlantic.'

He continued to hold her close. 'You don't mind then?'

'Mind? Of course I mind. But you're set on it and you're as stubborn as only the shanty-Irish can be, so what's the point?'

'As stubborn as you.'

'Go to sleep, lummock,' she whispered affectionately. Mary twisted away but still thrust her nudity into the angle of his body and his thighs. 'Go to sleep.' She had conceded as gracefully as she could. Matt knew that and loved her even more.

Usually he fell asleep quickly after love-making, but this night early in February, 1858, he lay awake for a long time, his mind still whirling at the prospect of his return to Ireland.

Would it be as dangerous as Mary feared, he wondered? How far ahead in his planning for revolution had Stephens got? What would Dublin be like? Would he have time to journey to Kerry? What help would the Irish-Americans provide in any rebellion?

Nationalism had been rekindled among the emigrant Irish living in the Eastern States. The living conditions for the vast majority of them had not improved overly in the past ten years. And, try as they might, he and Alderman Finucane hadn't found great success in their attempts to reconcile the two cultures. Under the influence of the Catholic Church, the Irish settlers had opposed almost every liberal policy put forward in Massachusetts. They'd upheld Negro slavery, opposed temperance laws, voted for the Democrat Party, clamoured for more places of worship, and generally made themselves an object of dislike to the native Bostonians. Resentment had shown itself in a flood of vicious, nearly obscene, anti-Papist pamphlets and books, then more violently, in riots and attacks against Catholic churches. Finally, for four years until 1857, Massachusetts had been run by the Order of the Star-Spangled Banner, a secret society opposed to the emigrants and whose members were commonly called Know-Nothings. Under their administration, the Irish were fired from jobs on the police force and in state agencies; Irish military clubs – although more social than military – were officially disbanded; laws were passed affecting Irish voting rights; and, as a final blow to many Irish, the temperance laws were strengthened.

In the face of such determined and organized opposition the Irish had turned in on themselves. The emigrants began devoting their energies to the common enemy across the Atlantic and away from their entrenched opponents who were making their lives such a misery in their new home. Ironically, Matt thought in his half-dozing state, the resurgence of Irish nationalism had sprung directly from the anti-Irish campaign in Massachusetts.

The Irish Emigrant Aid Society, along with its Massachusetts Lodge, had been formed initially to combat the Know-Nothings before that organization was absorbed into the stripling Republican Party. But within months, a society convention, attended by Matt and Alderman Finucane, was discussing a resolution to decide 'the speediest and most effective means of promoting action leading to ensure the success of the cause of liberty in our native land'.

Matt had looked round the faces of the people at the convention. Most were those of white-faced groggery owners, frightened small businessmen, avaricious lawyers, itinerant journalists, and young, genuflecting priests. None of them, Matt had thought, at all capable of aiding the success of any project, let alone a rebellion against the mighty British Empire. In fact, he'd stood up and said so. He smiled to himself in the dark of the bedroom as he recalled the stony, outraged silence which had greeted his remarks.

The very next day, he was contacted at the cooperage by an Irishman called Joseph Denieffe, who'd apparently been at the same convention and had listened to Matt's withering comments.

Denieffe had sounded Matt out about the strength of his nationalist views then, satisfied, had invited him to join an organization recently founded in New York called the Emmet Monument Association, in memory of that disastrously misled rebel, Robert Emmet. It wasn't until two months later that Matt discovered the driving forces behind this vehemently anti-English society were John O'Mahony and Michael Doheny, the companions in exile of James Stephens, who had fled to Paris after the '48. By then, though, the inflammatory words of O'Mahony and Doheny had filled his brain. It was as if his guardian, his beloved Jack-Da, was speaking directly to him. The association's secret meetings drew upon the well of revolt dug deep within him long before. He looked upon his mission to Dublin with Denieffe almost in terms of a pilgrimage.

This spiritual longing for nationalistic fulfilment added to the emotions of his farewells a fortnight later. His family gathered in the spacious entrance hall to say their goodbyes while Alderman Finucane's best carriage waited outside. Matt clasped each of his children to him in turn.

Firstly, there was seven-year-old Brigid, long black hair tumbling down her back. She, being the eldest, had sensed the tensions and misgivings between her parents about this journey. Once, she'd discovered her mother crying to herself as she sat in front of her vanity mirror. Brigid was determined not to cry but the tears still moistened her wide, green eyes when her father hugged her.

'You and your mam are in charge now, little one,' Matt whispered to her before turning to her sister, Bernadette, just eighteen months younger. She looked up at him with solemn, unblinking eyes. To lighten the moment, Matt swirled the folds of his heavy travelling cape around her and pulled her to him. He uncovered her, hair all tousled, then knelt to be at a level with her face.

'You be good, mind,' he warned in a mock-serious tone.

'Yes, da,' she piped, her voice a little unsteady.

'That's the girl.' He began to rise from his knees.

'Da . . . you won't be gone for ever, will you?'

Matt laughed. 'Before you know, I'll be back to read you the bedtime story.'

He ruffled her hair as he moved towards Mary. She was holding their little boy, born three years before. He pushed his face between theirs. His embrace pulled them close.

'Goodbye, Mother. Don't be worrying too much. All will be well.'

He felt a tear slide down Mary's cheek. Little Jack's lips fastened on the lobe of his ear in a misdirected kiss.

'Be careful, dearest, and the Holy Mother bless you and watch over you,' Mary murmured.

Matt felt the emotion rising in his throat. He turned to leave, unwilling for his family to witness his tears. He was passing through the door when Mary called to him.

'Take this as your talisman, Matthew Aherne.'

She held out to him the dried sprig of hawthorn that, so many years before had grown on a hedge in Drombeg townland. Matt took it without a word, a tight, forced smile on his features.

The last sight of his family on the front steps of his home, grouped protectively around Mary, stayed with him during the long days of the winter crossing of the Atlantic. The comparative comfort of his own cabin did little to ease Matt's misery at being without their love and support. It was not until the Irish coast was sighted that his imagination became fired again at the prospect of the mission before him.

He and Denieffe stood at the ship's rail, fine spray billowing around them, while the grey smudge on the horizon gradually took on the distinct image of a coastline.

Two days later, Matt looked apprehensively down on the bustling crowds along Customs House Quay in the centre of Dublin. From Dublin Bay, the Irish capital had appeared small and rather flat. From the River Liffey, stabbing through Dublin's heart, he had noticed the perfect, almost model-like proportions of the public buildings. Now close up, he had the immediate feeling of being in a great capital city, an important outpost of a thriving empire. There was a sense of assurance, of self-confidence, among the people on the quay.

Much to Matt's relief, the customs officers showed little interest in himself and Denieffe and, within the hour, their baggage had been loaded on to carts to follow them to Buswell's Hotel. Despite his companion's entreaties to behave like the well-off Irish-American businessman that he was, Matt still flinched inwardly whenever he caught sight of a constable's blue uniform or the red jacket and black helmet of an Army officer. Indeed, it was a full twenty-four hours before he was entirely convinced that nobody was paying any undue attention to him. Denieffe had been watching him closely, waiting for Matt to relax and behave normally, before suggesting they make contact with James Stephens at his lodgings behind Lombard Street, not far from the centre of the Irish capital.

Matt saw another side of Dublin's life in their walk through the damp March evening. Groups of child beggars, ragged and shivering, pulled at his clothes. Prostitutes, half-drunk and predatory, advertised their blowsy wares openly, vocally. Human filth and waste ran in the gutters from the breeding pens for degradation which were the dilapidated tenement buildings. Well-dressed Dubliners walked past these scenes without a second glance. It was an everyday part of their lives.

The welcome from James Stephens was as warm as the brandy punch he poured for them as soon as they'd settled in the comfortable, if small, sitting room at his lodgings.

'I'd heard the ship had arrived,' he told Matt and Denieffe, hands thrust deep into the pockets of a silk smoking jacket. 'I'd an awful temptation to come down and meet you but that would have been breaking my own rules, wouldn't it? A commander should never do that, should he?'

Stephens tried to make light conversation inquiring about their voyage and their health. It was obvious to Matt, though, that his host was bursting for news and messages from America. Eventually, after about ten minutes, he could contain himself no longer.

'Well, Joe,' Stephens said as casually as he could. 'What's for me then? What have you brought?'

'Messages from all your friends in the New World, James.'

The sides of Stephen's mouth creased in disappointment.

'And this,' Denieffe added with a smile, reaching into his jacket pocket and pulling out a large chamois leather purse the contents of which clinked as he handed it over. Stephens tore at its neck and spilled a cascade of gold sovereigns into his lap.

'How much?' he asked eagerly.

'What you asked, James. £80. A month's funding from your supporters. A sign of their faith in you, their belief.'

'Oh, very good. Very good. Well done!' Stephens exclaimed gleefully, tinkling the money through his fingers. 'And easily raised?'

'Without trying,' Matt interrupted. 'Well, not very hard.'

'And the remainder?'

'The remainder?' Matt didn't understand.

Denieffe nodded reassuringly almost patronizingly, in his direction before speaking. 'Matt here is something of a newcomer to the association but we've great hopes for him,' he told Stephens. 'That's why he came. A blooding, as it were. But he hasn't been fully involved in the councils yet.'

'Admirable, admirable,' Stephens commented. 'Discretion. Secrecy. Very worthy. Very.'

'Well, he doesn't know what you're asking and wanting, James.'

Stephens grunted to himself before speaking. 'As I told you last time we met, Joe, give me five hundred Irish patriots from the States, fully armed with those Lee-Enfield rifles, and I'll undertake to have an army of ten thousand men organized here within three months. Most will have pikes but I guaranteed at least fifteen hundred will have firing pieces of some kind. And didn't I pledge that when I have them, they'll be ready to rise and fight at a day's notice?'

'You did, James. You did.'

'Well?'

Denieffe spread his hands and shrugged his shoulders. Stephens sank back into his chair. Matt looked at each of them in turn. His mind was still trying to absorb all this sudden talk of arms and armies.

'There's support, James,' Denieffe said deliberately, stroking his dark beard. 'There's support all right but there's no proper organization yet in America. There's the clubs, the societies, the association, but no organization. So we can't give you the men for certain. O'Mahony and Doheny think you should form the organization here in secret and then we'll found a similar body over there.'

'Why so?' Stephens replied shortly, disappointed at the obvious lack of material pledges.

'Well, they're thinking – and I agree with them – that we'll find a stronger response if the Irish-Americans can be told of a secret, suppressed organization over here. They'll give themselves and their monies more readily if they think they're supporting the actual men at the barricades, as it were. The men doing the stern work, as you put it yourself, James. Anything founded in America must be rather nebulous while here – why you're under threat of exposure and arrest all the time.'

'Makes an awful sense,' Matt interrupted.

'Well, I do have a detailed plan for an organization,' Stephens laughed. He leaned forward in his chair, warming his hands against the heat of the coal fire in the grate, while he began to explain his ideas. Matt and Denieffe listened with silent approval.

'That's it!' Denieffe exclaimed when Stephens had finished. 'Every unit watertight from the other. The police agents'll never penetrate us.'

'Precisely. They won't know who are the men and who the officers.'

'It'll survive, Matt. You'll see.'

'What are you calling it then, James?' asked Denieffe, his face glowing with fervour.

Stephens waved a hand deprecatingly. 'I'm just thinking of it as "Our Organization" or "Our Movement". I've nothing firm in mind.'

'Didn't O'Mahony have an idea for a name?' asked Matt. 'I remember it from one of his speeches.'

'And isn't he the Gaelic scholar?' Stephens broke in.

Denieffe ignored the implied sarcasm. 'Matt's right. O'Mahony talked of the warrior Fiona MacCumhail and his legion of Fianna.'

'The Knights,' Matt murmured.

'I have the Gaelic,' Stephens said testily.

'Well, from the Fianna, O'Mahony took the name, Fenians,' Denieffe continued. 'He reckons the organization should be called The Fenian Society, or perhaps The Fenian Brotherhood.'

Stephens thought for a few moments, looking deeply into the fire. Then he nodded enthusiastically.

'It sounds right. The Fenians.' He rolled the name around his tongue several times. 'Yes, the Fenians.' He paused for a second before going on. His voice was quiet and determined. 'Two things, though. Or perhaps three. I'm absolutely certain that what I'm called, the Head Centre or Chief Organizer, if you like, should be utterly free, totally unshackled in making decisions. He'll have to be a sort of provisional dictator of Ireland. Definitely a provisional dictator.'

Denieffe nodded. 'I think O'Mahony and Doheny'll accept that. Discipline is needed.'

'Then, there'll have to be the same oath both here and in America.'

'Agreed!'

'And thirdly, I want one of you two to become vice-centres or centres over here in Ireland. It'll be a gesture of faith from America. It'll inspire our men. It'll cement the link between us. And it'll help me in my approaches to our friends on the Continent.'

Matt and Denieffe looked at each other in bewilderment. They began speaking at the same time, their voices rising.

'But I'm too well-known as an agitator,' said Denieffe.

'My family . . . my business,' Matt protested.

Stephens sat calmly back in his chair. 'I can yield nothing on this point. It must be agreed or there'll be no Fenians – or what you will – formed here. From the very start, you Irish-Americans must supply more than fine words.'

'I'll be a danger, James. They'll spot me for sure. Can't you see that?'

'Perhaps, Joe. Perhaps. What about Matt?'

'No one knows him,' Denieffe continued quickly. 'And you do have land in the West to settle, don't you Matt?' You told me yourself.'

'But my family, the wee ones.' Matt was becoming angry and flustered. He realized he was being forced into an impossible situation. 'They're born and bred in Boston. They're Americans.'

'Of an Irish father and a half-Irish mother,' Denieffe snapped.

'Gentlemen, gentlemen,' murmured Stephens, scenting eventual victory. 'There is a solution.'

'What?' Matt and Denieffe echoed.

'A coin, of course. The toss of a coin.'

'No!' exclaimed Matt.

Stephens shrugged. 'Then there'll be no . . . '

'Come on Matt,' pleaded Denieffe. 'I don't like it any more than you do. But it'll be the fairest way.'

'Well, gentlemen?'

It seemed to Matt as if the dark walls of the sitting room were closing in on him. Stephens took a cigar from a pocket in his waistcoat and started preparing it for lighting. Denieffe appeared to be studying the heavy, faded velvet curtains. Matt knew he was trapped, and that whatever his call, the outcome would be equally inevitable.

Stephens flipped a sovereign into the air.

Denieffe called, 'Royal.'

The coin slapped back on to Stephen's palm with Queen Victoria's profile upwards.

Denieffe was quick to try to alleviate Matt's discomfort.

'Are you sure, Matt?' he asked.

Matt nodded. He felt numb all over.

'It'll be my duty to help you bring Mary round, for I'm sure she'll be having misgivings.'

'You're too proper, Joe,' Matt said sourly. 'Misgivings? Her? Mary? Leaving Boston to live in Ireland with a man committed to rebellion? She'll be as pleased as when I jumped her into a pile of horse shit.'

'Horse shit?' Stephens tried not to laugh but the amusement was in his voice.

'Doesn't matter,' Matt replied disconsolately. 'Matters not at all.'

Denieffe couldn't keep the elation he felt out of his remarks. 'Well, now that's settled, James. What now? What's halting the Fenians? You've your first vice-centre.'

Stephens stretched up from his chair, satisfied with the evening's work. He leaned over Matt to pat his shoulder. 'Don't be worrying,' he said reassuringly. 'I'll help explain to your good lady the need for your return to the old country. Don't be worrying about that.' He straightened, walked to the narrow mantelpiece, turned and clapped his hands decisively. 'Well, the next matter of moment is the oath taking. Tomorrow would be propitious. Yes, tomorrow would indeed be entirely propitious.' Clearly, James Stephens would brook no argument.

The next evening, Matt Aherne stood opposite him across a

dining table covered with a ragged piece of green cloth. A rusty-looking flintlock pistol lay diagonally on the table.

'Place your right hand on the firearm,' intoned Stephens, remembering the way of the oaths of the Phoenix Literary Society of Skibbereen. 'And recite after me . . . '

Matt gazed round the room. He saw Joe Denieffe standing stiffly to attention, beard bristling, alongside two other men whom Stephens had introduced only a few minutes before as Tom Luby and Owen Considine. They were looking at him with an expression Matt had seen before on the faces of women about to take Holy Communion, one of great expectancy, of untried belief. Matt spoke automatically in a low voice.

'I, Matthew Aherne, do solemnly swear in the presence of Almighty God, that I will do my utmost, at every risk, while life lasts, to make Ireland an independent Democratic Republic; that I will yield implicit obedience, in all things not contrary to the laws of God, to the commands of my superior officers, and that I shall preserve inviolable secrecy regarding all transactions of the society that may be confided in me. So help me God. Amen.'

The Fenian Society, the Irish Republican Brotherhood, was in being. It was March 17th, 1858. St Patrick's Day.

## Chapter 9 December, 1866

'Come on, me boyos. Smarten yourselves.'

Matt Aherne's voice carried into the biting Atlantic wind blowing across the sands at the mouth of the River Cashen on the north Kerry coast.

He was perched on one of the dunes towering over the beach. His vantage point enabled him, even in the fast-fading winter dusk, to watch and judge the drilling of the Listowel Company of the Fenian Brotherhood.

Lookouts were posted on top of the dunes to warn of any strangers, of any nosy constables, but Matt wasn't worried in the least about that particular danger. The authorities hadn't stumbled across the secret drilling ground in all its years of use by the Fenians. The high dunes protected it from the gaze of anyone wandering along the nearest track and the slapping waves forcing their way through the narrow mouth of the river drowned most noises.

The men below him on the smooth beach marched and wheeled and halted to the commands of a former private in the British Army. He was one of nearly twenty regular soldiers who had deserted the ranks to become Fenian drillmasters for the sum of one shilling and sixpence a day, twopence more than they received for serving the Colours.

As he watched his men go through their paces, Matt had to admit that they did not look anything like fierce rebels against Queen Victoria's Empire, even under the drillmaster's professional tuition. Their clothes were ragged, their step uneven, and their pikes at every angle except the correct one. Their 'pikes' consisted of staves cut from tree branches with any piece of metal sharpened and lashed to the end. They were adequate instruments of death and mutilation in a racetrack brawl or an old fashioned faction fight, Matt thought, but he dreaded to think what would happen against properly armed soldiers or police. Surprisingly, though, the ordinary Fenian's keenness and appetite for drill hadn't diminished during the long years of waiting for the call to action.

'Let's have a song then, drillmaster,' Matt bawled, his voice echoing off the wall of the dunes. The men heard his shout. Their faces brightened as they broke into the Fenian marching song. The words, slightly out of tune, mingled with the gurgling, choppy waves of the river.

'See who comes over the red-blossomed heather,
'Their green banners kissing the pure mountain air,
'Heads erect! Eyes to the front! Stepping proudly together,
'Out and make way for the bold Fenian men.
'Side by side for the cause have our forefathers battled,
'On our hills never echoed the tread of a slave,
'In many a field where the leaden hail rattled,
'Through the red gap of glory they marched to the grave.
'All those who inherit their name and their spirit
'Will march with the banners of liberty then.
'All who love foreign law, native or Sassenach,
'Must out and make way for the bold Fenian men.'

Matt found the words stirring, although he realized only too well that the history of the Fenian Brotherhood had scarcely been one of glorious revolution in the eight years since its founding. Indeed, it had nearly sunk into total obscurity at times. But, by this December afternoon in 1866, the movement was in the ascendancy once more. There had been a power struggle among the hierarchy which had diverted attention from the Fenians' main aims.

During the American Civil War, both sides had sported Irish Brigades. Sometimes Irishmen had fought against Irishman gaining, at least, grudging acceptance from the native Americans as well as a deal of much-needed experience in modern warfare. The Civil War also increased the Irish-American thirst for action against the British, a thirst that James Stephens was unable to quench. He urged caution and preparation while the war-hardened Fenians across the Atlantic wanted immediate revolution in Ireland.

The previous year, the American Fenians had strained at the leash when they met for their annual convention in Cincinatti. Stephens' old friend, John O'Mahony, didn't even have to disguise his fiery intentions since the Fenians had been declared a legal organization in the United States.

'This brotherhood,' O'Mahony had told the wildly enthusiastic delegates, 'is virtually at war with the oligarchy of Great Britain. The Fenian Congress acts the part of a national assembly of an Irish Republic. Our organized friends in Ireland constitute its army!'

The leaders of Irish society began packing their silver and gold into boxes and sending it to banks in London. Reports from boatmen along the Shannon spoke of large boatloads of Fenians crossing to the Limerick side of the river from County Clare. The country grew tense, expecting the long-anticipated rebellion at any moment.

James Stephens sent a letter to the Fenian cell in Clonmel telling his volunteers that the uprising would come in a few months, in the autumn of 1865. His messenger got drunk before leaving Dublin and decided to sleep it off in the offices of the pro-Fenian newspaper, the *Irish Post*. While he was relieving himself into a chamber pot the next morning, the letter was stolen from his coat pocket by a police informer who'd been working undercover at the newspaper for more than eighteen months.

The *Irish Post* was suppressed and, in a carefully coordinated operation, the police arrested dozens of Fenians. Stephens himself was picked up nearly two months later but managed to escape from gaol with the help of Fenian prison warders. Cheekily, he went into hiding in the centre of Dublin, in lodgings almost directly opposite the staunchly Unionist gentlemen's club in Kildare Street. His actions were as bold as his future strategy was timid.

A meeting was held at Stephens' secret address, which Matt attended, and the Irish-American Fenians pressed for immediate action.

'No! No! It would be wrong,' Stephens argued. 'It would seem as if we were striking out of desperation, that we were in a corner after the arrests.'

'But you've the men, haven't you, James?' persisted Michael Kelly, the Irish-American who'd been lately titled 'Colonel' and voted Fenian chief of staff.

'We have that, sir. Almost two hundred thousand of them in Ireland alone,' Stephens replied, banging the table enthusiastically in an effort to appear more confident and decisive than he himself felt. 'Fifty thousand of them are thoroughly armed and add to that my intelligence reports which say a third of the British garrison here are on our side. Oh yes, colonel, we have the men alright.'

'Then, strike now, dammit,' urged Kelly, furiously stubbing a half-smoked cigar into an ash tray. 'Let the rising begin!'

Stephens leapt to his feet, realizing that Kelly carried support around the table. He leaned over, fingertips spread on the brocade cloth. 'And how many times have risings failed just because of that attitude?' he exclaimed. 'When we rise against the British, we must be certain of our organization. I don't believe Ireland can stomach another bungled affair. There have been too many, draining the resolve and spirit of the people. We must be sure of success this time.'

Kelly wagged his beard in dismay. His argument with Stephens continued throughout the two days of the meeting. Eventually, more from weariness than conviction, he conceded the point. The rising would be postponed. Kelly and his supporters returned to America with doubts growing in their minds about Stephens' qualities of leadership.

The truth, if the Fenian founder would recognize it, was that Stephens was besotted with the concept of revolution but his years in the wilderness had almost completely blunted his desire for action. If his rebellion failed, then he knew his power was over. While the revolt was still theoretical, he remained in command. Or so his mind instinctively worked. But he was driven out of his ivory tower by a further move by the authorities against the Fenians in February 1866. It forced Stephens to flee Ireland and seek sanctuary with Colonel Kelly in New York. Kelly lost little time in demonstrating his influence over the Irish-American Fenians and their desire for swift action.

On May 31st, about two hundred armed Fenians rowed across the Niagara River and took over the small Canadian village of Fort Erie. The inhabitants were quite bemused when the Fenians paraded with rifles along the hard-packed mud of their one and only street, a green flag with an embroidered yellow harp fluttering before their columns. That was all the Fenians could do since the only representative of the British Empire's far flung authority was the part-time village constable who promptly surrendered and insisted on buying liquor for his captors.

Within forty-eight hours, though, a company of Canadian volunteers, mainly students, moved against the Fenians. Both sides' experience in such matters led to a circumspect battle fought at rifle range at a local landmark called Lime Ridge. The marksmanship was of a surprising quality. After three hours, the Canadians had lost twelve killed and forty wounded; the Fenians, eight dead and twenty wounded. The Fenian leaders decided they'd had the best of the day and withdrew, fearing they might not do so well against regular troops if they were cut off from the river and their route back into the United States.

Colonel Kelly, from his campaign headquarters at Buffalo, issued a triumphant statement to the gathered newspaper representatives. 'The Irish Republican Army has been in action for the first time,' he announced. 'Arise Irishmen, a glorious career has opened for you. The Green Flag has waved once more in triumph over England's hated emblem.'

The success of the invasion of British soil meant the virtual end of James Stephens's influence over the Fenian movement. His counsels of caution were ridiculed as Kelly was voted head of the Fenians' 'military' sector with the grandiose title of Acting Chief Executive of the Irish Republic. In an hysterical attempt to regain favour, Stephens even offered to return to Ireland 'to get hung'. There were no takers. The leaders of the self-styled Irish Republican Army were firmly in control of any future revolution in Ireland.

'Perhaps there'll be action at last,' Matt remarked to his wife late that summer as he read of Stephens' eclipse in a letter sent from Boston by Joe Denieffe.

Mary gave him a sour look.

'And how long have you been waiting? Eight years, is it?' she said, complaint in her voice. 'An awful lot of parading up and down the sands with your long sticks that is.'

'You know there've been problems, dear,' Matt said soothingly.

'Problems, is it?' Mary put her sewing down in her lap and removed her glasses. 'Problems . . . So now they've got rid of your precious James Stephens, have they? The friend who deceived you into leaving our future behind in Boston. Fine friend, he was!'

Matt sighed inwardly. He really had thought that, at long last, the subject had been closed. But then, Mary had been increasingly tetchy recently.

'You know it wasn't like that, dear.'

'And what was it like then, Matthew Aherne?'

He looked round the sitting room of the house in Church Street. It was a solid-stoned, high-ceilinged concession to Mary's aversion to living in the old cabin at Drombeg townland. It was a concession he'd felt bound to make in the trauma of moving her and their children from the comfortable Boston suburbs to what Mary still regarded as the most backward part of a backward country. He sighed again, audibly this time.

'It had to be. You know that.'

He thought Mary had realized that inevitability those years ago when he'd returned to Boston to tell her of his oath-taking with the Fenian Brotherhood. Strangely and surprisingly, she'd said very little. No violent tantrum of objection had occurred. The sea voyage had been like a second honeymoon with Mary's sexual passions undoubtedly aroused by her journey into the unknown. They had explored each other's minds and bodies as if for the first time. The doubts had set in, though, within a few days of arriving in Kerry.

Alderman Finucane had been as good as his word in ensuring that the Ahernes could return to the cabin and two fields where the Keanes had lived and where Matt's mother was buried.

Matt's first meeting with the land agent, George Sandes, had been agreeable enough despite the awkwardness between the two men as they tried not to mention – or even acknowledge – the fact that they were half-brothers.

They were not dissimilar in build, both lean and tall, but there was a weakness around Sandes' almost feminine mouth and chin. His eyes were watery and bloodshot, the pupils coloured an unusually pale blue. His voice, as he greeted Matt, bore little trace of an Irish accent.

'My dear fellow,' he said, shaking Matt's outstretched hand and guiding him at the same time to an armchair next to the desk in his study. 'My very dear fellow,' he repeated. 'On his deathbed, my father . . . ' He smiled faintly to himself. 'Jonathan Sandes told me of you. Oh, indeed he did. He said you might return here one day and then, lo and behold, your letter of last month announcing your intentions. So unexpected. So very pleasurable.'

Sandes rubbed his hands together as if washing them. His eyes flicked to some documents on his desk.

'Your family?' he inquired. 'Are they with you?'

'In the hostelry next door.'

'Ah, the dear old Listowel Arms. Many an evening in their private room . . . ' Sandes laughed. Matt sensed his nervousness, his unease. 'Are you comfortable?'

'Well enough for the present.'

'Wanting to take possession of the Keane cabin again?'

'Indeed.'

'Well, everything's in order, of course. The rents were properly remitted by your patron, Finucane, and so you can go in directly. But I must warn you the years have taken a toll. The roof . . . the outhouses . . . the fields. Plenty of work there, Mr Aherne, a sufficiency indeed . . . now that's silly, isn't it? . . . Mr Aherne. . . Matthew, I meant . . . or is it Matt?'

'Matt.'

'Matt, then. You don't mind?'

'No.'

'Good. Capital. Well, as I was remarking, there's work a-plenty there but I'm sure you're used to that. Have to be tough to survive in the colonies, or rather the former colonies, what? And we're just approaching our prime, aren't we?'

'Not yet thirty.'

'Of course.'

'And you?' Matt asked curiously.

Sandes' eyes flicked again to the table. 'Some five years after you, I believe. Can't be precise, I think . . . about you, I mean.'

'No. I think not, George.'

Matt placed a heavy emphasis on his half-brother's given name.

'The documents, Matt,' Sandes said quickly, seeming to wish a change of subject.

'Yes.'

'I've had them put in order. A proper agreement is needed now. Not like the old days.'

'Security of tenure?'

'Not quite. But having everything in writing is a step in the right direction, isn't it?'

'You can still put us in the ditch when you like,' Matt made a flat statement of fact.

Sandes looked sideways at him, not sure how to take the remark. Then he laughed.

'Come now. How could I do that? Hardly with you. Hardly.'

It became clear, though, at the family's first sight of the cabin that to live there was out of the question. The property was overgrown and almost completely tumbledown. The Ahernes' natural excitement at being in a strange country, of returning to their father's birthplace, long told on in bedtime stories, vanished in a torrent of dismay. Even Matt felt abject with disappointment.

The long silence of the journey back to Listowel in a cramped jaunty cart remained in Matt's memory for years afterwards.

Within weeks, he'd moved the family into 36 Church Street, Listowel. The next problem had been to make a living.

He and Mary took stock of their experience with the Finucane cooperage and tavern business and eventually settled on opening a hostelry further up Church Street, just opposite Forge Lane and the police barracks. It was named, 'The Boston Tavern' although people were soon calling it simply 'Aherne's'. The customers were attracted by Mary's New England cooking and Matt's brainwave of making the hostelry the clearing house of any news and gossip about all those Kerry families who'd sought a new life as emigrants.

Soon, the establishment became a necessary port of call for anyone whose relatives had left the district as well as the 'local' for the police constables of the town. Matt knew he would never make his fortune there but, then again, he was certain the business would always provide a comfortable, sociable existence. He also realized that the hostelry gave him an ideal cover for his Fenian activities. Who would, after all, suspect someone who was on such good terms with so many police constables? From their alcoholically indiscreet comments, Matt was able to glean many snippets of information which were invaluable in establishing a Fenian network in Kerry. And by observing his customers in their unguarded moments of relaxation he was in a good position to weigh up who were potential recruits. Once they had been recruited, though, the firm rule was that they should stop drinking in 'Aherne's' and take their custom to another of Listowel's many hostelries. Only his two most trusted lieutenants who passed all orders to the rank and file members, Paddy Sugrue and Bryan Stack, were allowed near his home or the tavern. Indeed, Matt attempted to keep his involvement with the Fenian cause as far as possible from his home and business lives. He knew only too well that Mary's dislike of it was never far below the surface. That it should emerge again with the news of the hawkish elements assuming control of the Fenians was unfortunate but, with hindsight, not unexpected.

'So when's all this action you're braying about going to commence?' Mary's questions remained sour and pointed. 'Is it tomorrow you'll be picking up your pointed sticks and beginning the war against the English?'

'What war, mama?' Brigid Aherne, now a burgeoning fifteen year old, caught her mother's last remark as she entered the sitting room. 'Mama, you said war against the English,' the girl persisted.

'Mama was only joking,' Matt interrupted. He and Mary exchanged frosty glances.

'Run along, dear,' said Mary. 'Your father and I are talking of matters not for your ears. You were supposed to be making tomorrow's pig's pudding, weren't you?'

'Yes, mama but I'm thinking the blood isn't smelling fresh.'

'The pig was fresh killed yesterday, Brigid,' her mother replied. 'It'll be fresh enough. Be off with you now, will you?'

Brigid, suitably chastened, returned to the kitchen to set about mixing the blood with grated pig's liver, bread, wheatmeal, oatmeal, lard, and onion. The smell of the pudding as it steamed would fill the house for hours. So would the acrimonious words between Matt and Mary.

The Fenians began to drill in earnest again, three times a week at Ballyeagh Strand, whatever the weather. Matt knew that with Kelly in charge of the movement action would not be far away.

The call came shortly after Stephen's Day that year. Matt was woken at home by a banging on the kitchen door. He opened it, grumbling audibly, to be confronted by an apparent stranger, a tall clean-shaven man.

'I'm sorry to be rousing the house, Matt.' The man smiled, clearly not sorry at all.

'It won't be helping me back into Mary's good books, I'm reckoning.'

Matt peered closely at him in the grey, early morning light. There was a familiar smile in the caller's eyes but surely it wasn't . . . ?

The stranger's smile broadened as he noticed Matt's bewilderment. 'Put some weight on me, Matt, a fair weight, and then a beard.'

'Joe. Good Lord, Joe Denieffe, by all that's holy. But why?

When?'

Denieffe looked quickly over his shoulder. 'Hush, Matt.' He pressed a finger to his lips. 'Don't be spoiling the disguise by telling the town who I am.'

Matt pulled him into the kitchen and swiftly bolted the door again. 'It's mad you are, Joe, coming here yourself. Mad!' he exclaimed. 'And us just opposite the police.'

'Had to, old friend. Orders for me and orders for you. And anyway even yourself wasn't knowing me without the whiskers.'

'But still a risk, Joe. Are you straight here from Boston?'

'Not directly. I've been in London making arrangements, then in Liverpool, and finally a few stops over here.'

'With the orders?'

'Aye.'

Matt looked at Denieffe across the kitchen table, excitement growing within him. 'Then it's really happening?'

'It is that. You've some travelling to do in the next weeks, so you have, Matt.'

The next morning, after strained family farewells, Matt and Denieffe set off to visit Fenian cells in Limerick, Cork, Tipperary and Waterford, before journeying to the North West of England and North Wales. They spent a week there together before Matt broke away. He took a train from Crewe to London, arriving in the heart of the great Victorian empire late on January 25th.

He took temporary lodgings off Bloomsbury Square. For the first time in his life, he had seen his sworn enemies at close quarters, in their natural surroundings, and had recognized them as human beings like himself with similar aspirations and emotions. The experience unnerved him so much that he hardly slept that night. But the next morning, January 26th, 1867, he was at the rendezvous at the appointed time to meet the Irish-Americans who were to lead the revolt.

He stood outside the entrance to the Langham Hotel in Portland Place with its lofty statues dotted along the wide thoroughfare towards Regents Park. Matt felt unnaturally conspicuous in his heavy tweed suit, cloak and long green muffler beside the elegantly dressed men and women entering and leaving the hotel. He waited on the edge of the pavement for ten or more minutes, pretending to be absorbed in the study of Christopher Wren's small masterpiece of church building, All Souls, just across the busy road. Light flurries of snow stung his cheek and dampened his hair.

'The day is coming.'

A drawling voice beside him dragged Matt out of his thoughts.

'When Ireland's woes are done,' he replied automatically, smiling into the heavily bearded face of the man who'd stolen up behind him. They shook hands, introducing themselves.

'Aherne. Matt Aherne from Kerry.'

'I know, Matt. I'm Gordon Massey from New York.'

'Joe Denieffe told me of you.'

'Good. Well, let's be off and meet the others. You haven't been watched, have you?'

'Not that I've seen.'

'No, I think not as well. I was watching from across the street and no one was paying too much attention.'

'Where are the rest?'

'Just a cock's stride from here. No 137, Great Portland Street. At least, that's where Cliseret is. The colonel's been staying near Tottenham Court Road. General Halpin and Dick Burke and myself are in Tavistock Square. Spread all over the area we are under a variety of names. Safer that way. But this address we're going to is our main headquarters, as it were.'

It took them less than five minutes to reach the house, as tall and imposing as its neighbours along the fashionable street in the heart of London. The Irish-Americans, who'd apparently rented the entire premises, were gathered in a drawing room downstairs when Matt arrived. Some he remembered from past meetings in America and Ireland. The others clearly had been recruited into the Fenians during the American Civil War. Most of them were introduced to him with military titles but Matt had no way of knowing if the titles had been assumed or awarded in other armies.

'... Colonel Kelly you know, of course ... General Halpin... Captain O'Sullivan Burke ... Brigadier-General Cliseret... Major Fariola ... Major Vifquain ... Captain McCafferty... Captain O'Brien ... and finally, last but not least, Mr Corydon ...'

Matt shook hands or merely nodded at the men gathered around the large table, strewn with maps, railway timetables and piles of paper.

'And my rank is general,' said Massey rather self-consciously when he'd finished the introductions. 'I'm to be senior commander of our forces on Irish soil.' He gestured for Matt to be seated.

'You know the plan, Aherne?' asked Kelly at the head of the table.

'Aye. Denieffe acquainted me, Colonel.'

'What chances of it in your estimation?'

'Good, I hazard. Joe and I have studied the terrain and there's no reason why we shouldn't have success . . . that is, if . . . '

'What?'

'If there's complete surprise, and that means total secrecy.'

'There has been and there is,' interjected Massey. 'I'll stake my life on that.'

'You might have to,' Kelly added with a harsh, throaty laugh. 'We all might have to.'

He turned back to Matt.

'Your men are ready?'

'Not only mine but all those you've called for.'

'Excellent. Excellent.'

Massey broke in again. 'Can we move on, Colonel, to the proclamation?'

'But the plan?'

'Can't we return to that in detail later?'

'Indeed, yes. Perhaps it would be more advantageous. There has to be final discussion and approval and better that it should be as the last item on the agenda. It will remain fresh with us that way.'

Kelly riffled through a stack of papers in front of him then began passing them around the table.

'Gentlemen,' he explained. 'This is a draft of what will be delivered to the newspapers within the next few days. As you will see, it has had careful consideration.'

Matt read the three pages handed to him. He felt distinctly uncomfortable on reading the appeal from the Fenians to the British public at large. Where were the grand phrases of previous proclamations? Where was the disinterested note of scholarship? These words in front of him seemed to be demand for total revolution in social thinking and attitudes, rather than a simple explanation of Fenian aims.

Certainly, the first part of the proclamation from what was termed 'The Provisional Government of the Irish Republic' was conventional enough. 'We have suffered centuries of outrage, enforced poverty and bitter misery,' it read. 'Our rights and liberties have been trampled on by an alien aristocracy who, treating us as foes, usurped our lands and drew away from an unfortunate country all material riches.'

But it was the concluding paragraph which worried Matt.

'As for you, workmen of England, it is not your hearts we wish but your arms. Remember the starvation and degradation brought to your firesides by the oppression of labour. Remember the past, look well to the future, and avenge yourselves by giving liberty to your children in the coming struggle for human freedom.'

The draft statement ended, 'Herewith we proclaim the Irish Republic.'

'Well, gentlemen?' Kelly inquired after a few minutes.

A variety of approving remarks spread around the table.

'Everyone in agreement, then?' the colonel asked.

Matt looked at his companions, seeking some moral support for his doubts. By the smiles on their faces, it seemed he was in a minority of one. He raised his hand reluctantly.

'Aherne?'

'It's these phrases about the workmen of England and the oppression of labour.'

'Yes?'

'We're after the freedom of Ireland yet here we're talking about English workers, urging them to rise against their masters.'

'So?'

'Are we not confusing the issues?'

Kelly's pitying look added to Matt's discomfort.

'The issues are indivisible, my dear sir. One and the same. Ireland can never be free until the peasants are, until the people are.'

'I can understand that, but the proclamation mentions English workmen as well.'

'The struggle in Ireland is but part of the greater struggle for freedom among working men and women in all the countries in Europe. Surely you know that?'

'But . . . '

'But nothing, sir.' Kelly's voice held traces of frustration and anger. 'You are a friend of Stephens, aren't you? A good friend?'

'Yes.'

'Then you should know his philosophy. Dammit, Aherne, he founded the movement even if he did lose his resolve. His principles remain. They predominate. All he learned during those years on the Continent. The match to our flame. The steel to our sword arm. Oh yes, sir. His are our principles. They are why we shall succeed. Have no doubt. None at all. The Fenians are in the vanguard of a great historical movement sweeping across the civilized world. Established orders must be overthrown before there is real freedom.'

'Isn't that the belief of the anarchists?'

Matt continued his questions although he saw a growing restlessness and resentment from his companions. Kelly's face began to whiten with anger.

'Anarchists?' he boomed. 'Anarchists?'

Massey tried to mediate.

'Matt,' he said soothingly, 'That's just a name the authorities give to anyone or anything they see as a threat to the traditional ways. We are patriots, nationalists if you like, whatever label others might attach to us.'

'That's correct, Matt,' McCafferty murmured beside him. 'Let the matter rest.'

'Colonel, I propose we move on,' Massey urged. The slapping of hands on the table drowned any question on Matt's lips. He bowed to the inevitable and sat back in his chair, his doubts unresolved.


## Chapter 10 February, 1867


Down the centuries, more than one invader bent on plunder had come to the town of Chester in north west England. The Romans had recognized the site's strategic importance as far back as AD79, sending the XX Legion to establish a camp where the broad River Dee narrowed to a fordable stream. From there, they dominated the valuable salt mines in central Cheshire and protected the rich farmland of the plain against the marauders from Wales and Yorkshire. When the legion moved on after two hundred years, the Saxons re-named the settlement 'Chester' from the Roman word for camp. The town could not fail to prosper with its direct access to the Irish Sea, the rich agricultural lands and the lusty industrial towns further to the north. And being such a prize, it had been properly fortified over the years with stout, red sandstone walls and a fine castle high on the banks of the salmon-rich river.

Matt Aherne and John McCafferty stood on the side of the bridge over the river on the morning of February 11th 1867, pretending to study the layout of the racetrack set in the meadows below. Their vantage point also gave them a good view of the sentries at the castle entrance on the other side of the bridge. They stood in huts by the wrought iron gates leading to the cobbled square in front of the castle.

'The most action they've seen is someone dropping their musket on Sunday church parade!' muttered McCafferty.

'And isn't that just why we're here?' Matt replied, leaning on his elbows over the balustrade of the bridge.

'Sure and they'll be in for a fine surprise when the boys come calling. They'll be dropping more than their guns then, I'm guessing.'

Both men laughed and began strolling back over the bridge into the maze of the town's narrow streets. Chester wore that air of well-ordered gentility common to most towns steeped in history and benign feudalism. The citizens instinctively knew their place in the order of things. The soldiers and constables were to remind and reassure the gentry of their own superiority, the outward proof that Victoria was on the throne and all was well with the world.

It was one of the reasons why the Fenians had chosen the town; that and Chester's importance as a railway junction with tracks running along the Welsh bank of the Dee to Holyhead on the Isle of Anglesey, the departure point for mailboats bound for Ireland.

The plan was so breathtakingly bold that, even at first hearing, Matt had been convinced of its chances of success.

First, the Fenians would overpower the castle sentries and seize all the available arms and ammunition in the barracks. Then, at gunpoint, they would commandeer trains to carry the weapons to Holyhead having cut all telegraphic links to and from Chester and the Welsh sea port. Once there, the Fenians would capture the mailboat and set sail for Kingstown, just south of Dublin. Simultaneously, the uprising would begin on Irish soil.

Matt had arrived in Chester two nights previously, taking cheap lodgings near the station. McCafferty had joined him the next morning. They had checked all the back alleys for the most unobtrusive routes to the castle entrance, and for possible escape routes. Their confidence grew. The town was clearly going about its business as usual. Surprise, the plan's supreme element, seemed to remain with them.

Despite his warm tweed clothes, Matt shivered suddenly just as they'd completed their tour of the town's centre and had retraced their steps in Lower Bridge Street.

McCafferty noticed Matt rubbing his hands together and felt the frosty nip in the air himself. 'A last jar then?' he asked, pointing to the long rows of casement windows of the Bear and Billet Inn further down the street.

The two hundred-year-old inn had a dozen customers scattered about its gloomy bar when the two Irishmen entered. They ordered a jug of porter with two large glasses of cognac and took their drinks to a well scrubbed bench table.

'Nervous then?' McCafferty asked after they had their first mouthfuls.

'Not much, John. There's too much in my mind at present for nervousness to slip in.'

McCafferty peered closely into Matt's face. 'Well, you can say better than I can. The porter's jumping round my insides like it's alive.'

'Take the cognac.'

'I will that but I'm thinking now of what can go wrong, Matt.'

'Nothing, friend.'

'I'm trusting so, but last night an awful strange feeling took me. For want of a better word, Matt, I had a foreboding.'

'That it wouldn't go well? Oh come on, man,' Matt urged. 'Isn't it your plan and haven't we discussed it often enough?'

'We have.'

'And could we see a weakness?'

'Not one.'

'There you are, John,' Matt said cheeringly. 'A bad dream. That's all you had.'

McCafferty brightened slightly. 'Aye, you're right. Didn't I have the feeling enough during the war between the states and aren't I still here to be blathering away?'

'You are that.'

Although he tried not to show it, Matt felt some of his companion's unease begin to creep over him. But he tried to reassure himself. The Fenians would start arriving in town within an hour or so and wasn't Chester quiet enough? He slipped his hand into his jacket pocket to feel the comforting weight of the small Remington revolver McCafferty had given him the day before.

'Not long now.' McCafferty spoke suddenly, breaking into Matt's thoughts. Automatically, they both pulled out their fob watches. McCafferty's was inscribed inside.

'An hour,' Matt said quietly.

'Aye.'

'A last cognac?'

'To settle my nerves, eh?'

'No,' Matt smiled. 'To settle the ones I've been catching from you.'

Matt called his order to a rotund, jolly faced man in a stained apron.

'Busier now,' he remarked casually as the man started filling the glasses on the counter.

'It is, sir. Always around this time before midday.'

Matt nodded.

'But you'll be seeing it busier later,' the man continued.

'I expect so.'

'Yes, them manoeuvres are always good for trade.'

'Manoeuvres?' Matt said, not thinking for a moment.

'A little early this year. They're usually in the spring. The soldier boys from London or wherever bring their camp followers with 'em more often than not. Trollops but good for trade. You'll see. Just you wait and see. Like bees round the honey, my regulars are. All wanting a dip, if you'll pardon the expression.'

A pang of alarm gripped Matt. 'You mean military manoeuvres? Here?' He tried to sound as casual as he could.

'That's what Constable Skidmore reckoned when he came for his breakfast. The Volunteers are called out and the Welsh Guards entrained from London. That's what the constable said.'

'Why?' Matt realized the question was too urgent. He softened his tone. 'Did the constable say why?'

'That's the strange thing, sir. He didn't know. Leastways he said he didn't. Special manoeuvres at the castle. That's all he knew. That's fourpence, sir.'

Matt fumbled in his pocket and handed over the coins before striding across to McCafferty with the glasses.

'There's trouble, John,' he whispered urgently. 'Sink this quick and outside. Hurry now!'

They gulped their glasses and walked swiftly outside. Matt glanced up and down the cobbled street.

'What the devil is it, man?' McCafferty demanded.

In three clipped sentences, Matt repeated what he'd been told in the Bear and Billet. Although the street was virtually deserted his voice was so low that McCafferty strained to hear.

'Oh God, no!' he muttered. 'They're on to us then . . . Holy Mother!'

Matt pulled him by the arm away from the inn.

'We don't know that yet, John. It could be coincidence.'

'You think so,' McCafferty said bitterly. 'You really think so.

Someone's talked, that's what. We're dished right and proper, that's what.'

The Irish-American seemed stunned by the news. His complexion had turned ashen, muscles working high on his cheek-bones, eyes blinking rapidly. Matt saw that he was scarcely capable of thought.

'The castle!' Matt exclaimed. 'That's where we'll see.'

McCafferty stood motionless. 'Dished . . . dished . . . dished,' he kept murmuring.

'Come on, John.' Matt almost dragged him down the street. 'The others'll be here soon. We must get to the castle.'

'But the boys . . . ' McCafferty protested, apparently still in a daze.

'The boys are coming in now,' Matt half-screamed at him through clenched teeth. His companion's panic was beginning to affect him. 'That's why we must go to the castle. To see what's happening there. We must find if the game's up.'

'It's too late.'

''Tis not. Come on, for God's sake. We'll still be having time for the others.'

Matt put his hand under McCafferty's elbow to force him into a stumbling walk. After a few yards, the Irish-American seemed to regain his composure. He began to stride out through the narrow streets, now busier, up and down the alleys and narrow flights of stairs, his pace keeping up with Matt. Neither spoke. Here and there, they noticed small groups of constables where before, hardly an hour before, there had been none.

Their deepest fears were realized when they burst out of a side street and came in sight of Chester Castle. Instead of just two soldiers guarding the entrance, there was now a cordon of troops spaced a yard apart inside the perimeter railings, fixed bayonets twinkling in the watery sunlight. Four gleaming pieces of artillery were positioned by the castle building itself, muzzles pointing across the parade square towards the now-padlocked gates. The men stood at ease. They looked impassively through the railings but the constant pacing to and fro of the officers and sergeants behind them gave little doubt about their state of preparedness.

Curious crowds had gathered to watch this unexpected and, as yet, unexplained show of strength by the military. Dozens of constables and what looked like part-time volunteer soldiers were pushing them back away from the railings and gates. The Union Jack fluttered limply from the flagpole on the castle's gently sloping roof. Its presence seemed to warn any would-be attackers of the garrison's strength under the flag of empire.

Matt's first instinct was to turn tail immediately. McCafferty skidded to a halt on the cobbles, his feet nearly going from under him, spun round and started back the way he'd come. But Matt realized instinctively that this would be a mistake, would draw attention to both of them. He grabbed McCafferty by the arm again and almost forced him to saunter to the edge of the milling crowd. The snatches of conversation were enough to discover what was happening.

'Where's the guards then?'

'There . . . behind the railings.'

'No, not them. I mean the Welsh Guards.'

'Oh, them . . . they're nearly here. Our Albert says they're past Crewe.'

'Your Albert?'

'Him with the moustache and rifle down by the gates.'

'They've all moustaches and . . . '

'The tall 'un . . . '

'Oh, I see 'im . . . when's the navvies coming then?'

'Navvies?'

'Them Irish your Albert told you.'

'They're not navvies.'

'What are they when they're at home then? Irish are navvies, ain't they?'

'Maybe, but these are rebels so Albert says.'

'Rum sort of rebels, if you ask me: navvies.'

'They might be navvies but Albert says they're rebels and they're planning to raid the castle . . . '

'Raid the castle? They must be off their chump. Proper mad, they must be. What they want to do that for anyway?'

'Dunno. Albert didn't say.'

Matt and McCafferty turned away, despairing. They hurried back down a side street and stood, backs pressed against the wall of a house.

'What now then?' McCafferty spoke first, his voice strangely even and calm.

'We must warn the others.'

'And in Ireland. Not only warn them but call off the whole rising.'

'But how?'

'I'll telegraph them and head there straight off. I've the escape route. You know that.'

'They'll be waiting for Irishers.'

'They will that. But I've my American papers. They'll not be harming me too much. Catch you and you'll be doing the rope dance, more than likely.'

'Nothing's happened though.'

McCafferty snorted derisively. 'You think that'll stop them. We're rebels, Matt, whether there's a rebellion or not. And I'm reckoning we haven't even that now. No, you warn the boys here and I'll signal the rest. We've to be quick though.'

Matt glanced at the Irish-American. 'You've not the nerves now, have you?' he asked curiously.

'Friend,' McCafferty smiled wanly, 'When the worst you've feared happens, there's nought to be feared about. Believe me.'

The two men shook hands, their grips strong as if trying to reassure and strengthen each other, before parting in opposite directions.

'For Ireland,' McCafferty whispered.

'Aye,' said Matt. 'The blessed saints save her. And us.'

He ran down the streets towards the inns where meeting places had been previously arranged, slowing to a walk only when he spied the knots of constables dotted round Chester. Some inns were still empty but in others small groups of men, fellow Fenians, mostly young, stood expectantly in small groups.

Swiftly and in lowered tones, Matt told them what had happened, that the action at the castle was cancelled, before rushing off to the next rendezvous point. The rank and file were urged to dump what weapons they possessed and disperse discreetly on foot to make their way home as best they could. All but a few of them needed no second bidding. Some objected.

'I've not been coming from Manchester to be scared off now,' one protested. 'The women'll not let me in the house. And the boys'll be thinking what a fine da they've got after all the big words.'

'How can I be going home without one shot fired?' another remonstrated. 'We'll take a crack and the divil have the soldier boys!'

But a few minutes' muttered argument – and the departures of their friends – soon convinced them that nothing but hopeless bloodshed would come of any attack on the castle.

Matt enlisted the aid of their 'captains' to contact as many as possible of the Fenians who'd arrived in the town that morning from all over Lancashire. He decided himself to make for the railway station to see if others could be stopped in time but it quickly became apparent that it was an impossible task.

He saw dozens of what he knew from his previous visit to the area to be young Fenians scurrying down the streets leading from the station. One looked round to check if any police were watching before he dropped a handful of bullets down an open drain. Another tossed a revolver surreptitiously into an untended brewer's dray. Matt wondered if McCafferty had had time to warn them. There were so many of them that even the large numbers of police on the streets had little chance of stopping and questioning more than a few. But when Matt came in sight of the station he realized immediately what had alerted them. The train from London had arrived with the reinforcements from the Welsh Guards. The elite soldiers, immaculate in their red and black uniforms even after their journey, were drawn up in ranks on the station forecourt ready to parade through Chester to the castle.

'By the left, quick march!' bawled a sergeant and the men moved off as one, rifles sloped precisely over their shoulders, a line of constables on each side of them.

Matt shrank into a side alley. His eyes darted round for any way of escape. There was none. The small alley ended in a high wall topped with iron spikes. The sound of boots tramping on cobbles came nearer and nearer. Matt was trapped. Instinctively, without a conscious thought, he did the only thing he could. He stepped boldly out of the alley and stood in full view. He swept off his tweed cap and waved it enthusiastically above his head.

'Hurrah!' he cried, trying to sound as English as possible. And again, 'Hurrah!'

His cheers mingled with those of the citizens of Chester who watched the impressive progress of the two hundred or so guardsmen.

The crowd began drifting away when the troops had wheeled out of sight into the next street. Matt realized suddenly that he was almost alone and under the surveillance of the half dozen constables remaining on the station forecourt. He feared that any moment one of them would walk over and ask a routine question which might lead to inevitable exposure and arrest. The revolver in his pocket felt like a ton weight. Again his instincts took over.

Matt strode out firmly towards the constables. 'Could any of you gentlemen tell me the next train to London and which platform I need?' he asked.

The constables looked at each other.

'You're lucky, sir,' one said. 'I think there's one in fifteen minutes

325

but the conductor in the station'll tell you better.'

Matt touched the peak of his cap. 'Thank you for that.'

'You're welcome, sir. Been watching the Guards, have you?'

'Indeed I have.'

'Thought I saw you there. Fine body of men, aren't they?'

'They are that. The finest. We're fortunate to have them.'

'We are that.'

Matt decided to risk a question. 'But why were they here today? They weren't due, were they?'

'Oh, no, sir. There were rumours of some trouble coming at the castle.'

'Trouble? Really?'

'Some hotheads from Ireland, they say, but it's scotched now and no mistake what with the troops and all.'

Matt nodded, forcing himself to smile agreeably at the constables. 'Well then,' he said, 'I can go about my business without worry, thanks to the Guards and you gentlemen.'

As he settled back into his empty carriage he wondered how McCafferty had fared and whether many of the Fenians had been arrested after that morning's debacle. Most, he reckoned, would have been safe unless they'd been caught red-handed, carrying firearms. The Irish population in the north west of England was so large – after successive famines – that the police would have been hard pressed to choose between a law-abiding Irishman and a Fenian.

The longer the journey went on, the more depressed Matt became, swearing at himself for ever becoming involved with the Fenians. How could they hope to overthrow the British in Ireland? How on earth had he been persuaded to endanger Mary's and the children's futures in Boston by joining such a hare-brained enterprise? He felt ashamed and angry with himself. When he reached London, he decided, he'd go directly to Kelly and the others in Great Portland Street and tell them he was finished with the brotherhood.

London was still busy, despite the chill evening, when the train pulled in. Matt welcomed the anonymity of the crowds on the pavements as he walked out of Euston Station. Here, he thought, not many people, if any at all, had heard of the day's events in Chester. He turned into the tavern nearest the station, drawn by its beckoning lights, and ordered a plate of cold beef and porter with cognac. His meal was served well away from the bar and the energetically out-of-tune pianist. Matt signalled for more drink. He closed his eyes for a moment, leaning his head against the alcove's greasy upholstery, shutting his mind to the tensions of the day.

''Ullo, sir. All on your own?'

It happened so quickly. One moment, Matt was alone, his thoughts far away. The next, a young woman had slid into the alcove on the opposite side of the narrow table. A dark green straw hat, sporting a white flower, was perched on top of her mop of curly blonde hair. She shrugged a black shawl off her shoulders and settled into the seat. Her painted lips smiled glisteningly. Blue eyes looked straight into his, challenging and assessing at the same time.

Matt stared blankly at her for a second, then opened his mouth to protest, to sent her away.

'Just a port and lemon, sir,' she continued quickly, anticipating his rejection. 'And another slosh of brandy for you?'

Before he could speak, her right arm shot above the back of the alcove and waved.

'Nellie, Nellie Shaw, that's me.'

'But . . . '

'I saw you on your own, sir, and thought to myself, Nellie, I thought, that gentleman's on his own and needing some cheering up.'

'I'm not . . . '

But before Matt could continue, a barman appeared carrying a tray.

'Port and lemon, Nellie, and a brandy for your gentleman friend?'

'Ta, Alf.'

The glasses were slapped on the table before Matt could object.

'He'll pay later, Alf,' the girl said. 'Won't you dear?'

Her manner oozed brisk confidence with, perhaps, a slight note of pleading. Matt smiled resignedly at the barman, shrugging his shoulders. He'd had enough experience of tavern life in the various Finucane establishments in Boston to realize he'd been accosted by what polite society termed a lady of the night. Looking more closely at her, he saw that she was rather pretty with delicate features beneath the mandatory rouge and paint. Probably, he thought, she wasn't much older than seventeen or eighteen. They each raised their glasses at the same moment, their eyes meeting over the rims. The idea struck Matt that it was ludicrous that such a supposedly epoch-making day in his and Ireland's history should end with him drinking in a London tavern with a whore, and an attractive one at that.

The girl mistook the bitter laugh as a sign of friendliness, of acceptance, of a bargain sealed even before negotiation.

'Far from home after a busy day, then . . . you're?'

Matt waved at the barman. Another two glasses arrived.

'Matt.'

'Irish?'

'Uh-huh.'

'And a bit of a toff from your duds.'

'Not really.'

'Anywhere to stay?' She looked shrewdly at him, a tiny smile playing at the corner of her mouth.

'No,' Matt replied. He paused for what seemed long seconds. His mind, beginning to fume with brandy and the acrid tobacco smoke clouding the bar, was tired of trying to think rationally any more. It didn't matter after all, did it? he thought. Nothing much mattered now, he decided, not even Mary and the children. They were in another world, nothing to do with this girl or this tavern. The rising had failed. He had failed. Or so it appeared to him in his deep depression. 'No,' he repeated. 'Tis I've nowhere to stay.'

He drained his glass again.

'Well now, fancy that, duckie,' she giggled triumphantly. 'And there's me with a cosy little gaff just round the corner.'

'Fancy that.' Matt signalled for another two drinks, then leaned across the table and lightly touched the girl's left hand.

By the time he left the tavern, nearly two hours later, his legs were so unsteady that he was forced to lean on the girl for support while they weaved the fifty yards to her room. His nostrils were filled with the smell of cheap brandy and her even cheaper scent. He tumbled on to her squeaky brass bed and watched through bleary eyes as she shrugged off her clothes. Her body, he was to recall later, was slim and pink in the light of the bedside candle. He was to remember her pushing one finger deep into the downy triangle between her legs before holding it, moist, out to him in offering. He was not to remember, though, how tears dripped down his cheeks to fall on to her soft-spread nipples while she writhed beneath his thrusting, twisting hips or how he cried out Mary's name when he eventually climaxed deep inside her.

The next morning, he left the small room as soon as light shone through the begrimed curtains. The girl protested, kicking back the stained sheets to offer her gleaming sex to him. Matt merely shook his head, not speaking, and placed a single gold sovereign between her wide stretched thighs. As he went through the door, he looked back once. The girl's scrabbling fingers had closed round the coin.

A wave of nausea and self-disgust gripped him when he reached the street below. He wandered through the early-morning crowds not caring where he was headed and swore at himself for his weakness, his infidelity.

He saw a red and white striped barber's pole poking out of a narrow alley, rubbed the stubble on his face and decided a shave with hot towels would ease his feeling of wretchedness. The chatter in the barber's was mainly of steeplechasing and the murder of a whore near Fleet Street. Presumably the news of the previous day's events in Chester had not yet reached London. From his greeting an hour later at 137 Great Portland Street, though, it was clear that the Fenian leadership had heard. Richard O'Sullivan Burke, the armaments organizer, opened the front door, starting with surprise when he saw Matt.

'Good God, Aherne! You! What the devil . . . ?'Burke leaned out of the doorway and looked swiftly up and down the street. 'You're not followed?'

'No. No as far as . . . '

'Come in quickly, then, man.'

Burke called up the stairs before ushering Matt into the drawing room, its table covered with maps and papers as before.

'You look done in,' Burke's tone was concerned.

'A hard journey and a long night,' Matt said shortly. 'Where are the others?'

'All over the place, frankly, but the colonel's here. He'll be with you in a trice.'

Kelly's greeting seemed genuinely effusive. 'My dear chap,' he exclaimed. 'We were fearing you'd suffered the same fate as poor McCafferty.'

Matt's face showed his dismay.

'You hadn't heard? No, that's silly of me. Of course, you wouldn't have. Nabbed good and proper, I'm afraid,' Kelly went on, pulling at his beard. 'Picked up off a collier from the Dee—Connah's Quay, I think. His false papers were good, mind you . . . in the name of William Jackson, I recall . . .but he would insist on carrying his ring everywhere. The police found it in the lining of his coat.'

'His ring?'

'The one inscribed by our circle in Detroit. Quite damning, I fear. Straight into the hoosegow for him.'

'And the others?'

'McCafferty's warning was in time, thank the Lord. None took to the field except in Kerry — Cahirciveen, wasn't it? — but the few hundred there dispersed quickly enough when they realized they were alone.'

'In Chester?'

Kelly gave a short laugh.

'Thanks to your presence of mind, only a few arrests compared to what there could have been. But the police'll have to search the ponds and canals for quite a time, I'm guessing, if they want to find all the guns and bullets that were abandoned.'

Matt had to smile, despite his grim mood. 'I know. I saw some being tossed away myself. A mighty panic that was when the Welsh Guards arrived.'

'But how did you escape?' Burke interrupted.

In a few sentences, Matt offered a censored version of his movements. ' . . . it was a total fiasco,' he ended bitterly. 'Total and utter.'

'Come along now, Matt,' Kelly said, putting a hand on his shoulder. 'It could have been much worse, you know.'

'Worse. What could be worse? The entire rising is finished. The government is alerted. We've lost weapons and men for nothing. And what about the informer amongst us? What about . . . '

Kelly's face whitened during the angry tirade. His voice rose above Matt's to interrupt. 'No, sir. Definitely not. No informer,' he roared. 'Idle chatter from the men over a jar of porter maybe, but no informer.'

'But they knew the very day, the very time . . . '

'Coincidence, my dear sir. I can understand your feelings but pray remember whom you are addressing.'

Burke went to put a conciliatory hand on Matt's forearm but he brushed it away. 'There's no point in continuing, Colonel. You're blind to the facts. I want no more of it.'

Kelly looked him directly in the face, eyes staring with rage. 'No more, sir! No more! What do you mean, sir? Here I greet you as a hero of the brotherhood and you throw this at me. Explain yourself, sir. Now!'

'I mean I'm leaving the brotherhood, Colonel,' Matt said, trying to make his voice as firm as possible although it rasped in his brandy-dry throat. 'I cannot go on. I've sacrificed enough, transporting my family from Boston, working these long years, and for what? There's no point any more in the brotherhood. It's as hollow as all the other so-called secret societies which have failed Ireland time after time.

'Be careful, Matt,' Burke warned quietly, moving to his shoulder.

'You're tired and disappointed. We know that. But think of what you're saying.'

'I know what I'm at.'

'Do you, sir? Do you?' Kelly swung round, his piercing gaze reaching out across the room. 'When you took your oath to the brotherhood, Aherne, you made a vow of loyalty, a vow to be broken on pain of punishment.' The colonel took three steps towards Matt before flinging out his right arm and pointing dramatically into his face. 'Punishment, sir, I said, and punishment I mean. You might have heard of how informers in New York have disappeared to be found in the Hudson River. Let me inform you that the punishment didn't end with them. Their families suffered too. They became virtual pariahs, outcasts in their own communities. They didn't bless the names of their dead believe me. Rather they cursed them and spat on their headstones. That, sir, is the Fenian punishment for disloyalty. It is swift and terrible.'

Matt tried not to flinch under Kelly's vicious words and stern gaze but, after a moment, his eyes flicked downwards towards the carpet. He attempted to clear his parched throat. 'I cannot be going on, Colonel, whatever you're threatening,' he said quietly, hesitantly.

Kelly's tone softened. He took another three paces and thrust out his hand, taking Matt's in his. 'Now Aherne, you've had a bad time. We all realize that. I'm not wanting to be too hard on you, you should know that.'

Matt looked up in some bewilderment as the colonel continued.

'Loyalty cuts two ways. As you must be loyal to the brotherhood, so we must be loyal to you. That's only fair. I'm certain you'd never desert us just as I'm certain we must find you a role here at headquarters. You're too valuable to risk in the field, don't you agree, Burke?'

'I do indeed, Colonel.'

'Well, let's be forgetting our hasty words and settle down to our unfinished business.'

'Unfinished?' The surprise was clear in Matt's voice.

'Oh, yes, Aherne,' the colonel replied confidently. 'Chester was a mere hiccup in the rising. The rebellion will still go ahead and will be even more deserving of success if we learn the lessons of yesterday's unfortunate episode.'

'The main one must be secrecy.'

'You're correct, of course, Matt,' Burke cut in hastily. 'We've already decided that only the inner council will discuss strategy and timing. The vice-centres and centres will be told only the general outlines until the actual day.'

'It's a beginning,' Matt sniffed.

'That's so, Aherne. I look forward to having you work alongside us here. Your advice will be invaluable.'

'Thank you, Colonel. I'll be waiting a few days in London before going home to tell my family what's transpired. Then I'll return.'

Kelly's features hardened. 'I really don't think that would be wise. Better to write to them, I'm sure. They'll understand, you'll see.'

'I must . . . ' Matt interrupted.

'No, Aherne. You stay here. And you, Burke, become our friend's closest companion. Day and night.'

'You're making me a prisoner, Colonel?' Matt felt a lump coming in his throat.

'Just ensuring that nothing goes amiss. My words about punishment were not light ones, sir.'

Matt shook his head, hardly believing what was happening to him. The set expression on Kelly's face left him in little doubt, however, that his loyalty was in question after his threats to leave the Fenians.

'Have you your revolver still?' Burke asked quietly, almost apologetically.

'Yes,' Matt muttered, anticipating what was to happen next.

'I think it would be better if I took it.' Burke was obviously embarrassed about his new role as, in effect, Matt's gaoler.

Without a word, Matt lifted the Remington from his pocket and handed it to Burke.

Kelly clapped his hands, rubbing them together, as if washing away the unpleasant, strained atmosphere. 'Good. Capital. I'm sure that in the fullness of time you'll come to accept my decision as the correct one. But, now, to business. The inner council meets this afternoon. It'll want a full report from you about Chester.'

To Matt's amazement, the council did, indeed, regard the previous day's events as no more than an unfortunate setback. The leading Fenians went on to discuss mobilizing their members again. No exact date was mentioned but Matt gained the firm impression that it would be within a matter of weeks.

During the meeting, he looked continually around the table at the members of the council, wondering which one could be an informer. Massey? Cliseret? Vifquain? Which one? He was convinced that one of the men in that room was a government spy. Joe Denieffe even?

Why hadn't he been in Chester after working so closely on the plan? And Corydon? He was out of the ordinary all right, almost disinterested in the meeting but not so disinterested as not to listen.

The next two weeks were miserable. Matt's letter to Mary eventually brought a cool reply filled with complaints and veiled threats about the future of their marriage. He could only leave the house with Burke as an escort, invariably to walk in Regent's Park. Council meetings were held daily and, more often than not, his attendance wasn't even requested. He spent many hours sitting in his attic room sharing bottles of cognac with Burke. At least the drink numbed his despair and made the hours appear to pass more quickly. Although his friendship with Burke grew quite naturally in their enforced proximity, his escort never once relaxed his vigilance. Even if Burke had, Matt mused, it wouldn't have made much difference. He felt completely drained and apathetic. In his moments of lucidity, usually filled with self-recrimination, Matt wondered if he had become what he described to himself as a 'broken man'. But, after a few glasses, he didn't really care one way or the other.

In the first week in March, the arrival and departures increased at Great Portland Street. A fever of activity and expectancy was everywhere. On the afternoon of March 3rd, Matt was summoned at last with Richard O'Sullivan Burke to the drawing room. Only three members of the inner council were seated around the table.

Colonel Kelly appeared, for him, light-hearted as he handed Burke an envelope. 'The moment has come, Richard,' he said with an all-embracing smile. 'You know what to do and where to go, don't you?'

Burke nodded.

'Take Aherne with you. Of necessity he's had a trying time. He deserves to be part of this time of destiny.'

Outside the house, Burke hailed a cab and directed it to Ludgate Circus.

'What is it, Richard?' Matt murmured. 'What's happening?'

Burke held up the envelope, tapping it in the palm of his hand. 'For *The Times* and the English government. Tomorrow, when it's printed, the Irish Republic is in being.'

'The proclamation?'

'Aye. You know the wording?'

'I read a draft. And the rising?'

'The day after tomorrow. All Ireland will be on the march, thanks be to God!'

'Thanks be,' Matt responded dispiritedly.

# Chapter 11 March, 1867

From the crest of the hill not two hundred yards away, the Fenian pickets could see the smoking chimneys of Tipperary. The townland of Ballyhurst had been chosen as the rendezvous point and the battleground for the one thousand Fenians in the district. Here, on March 5th, they would confront the British troops garrisoned in Tipperary.

The news had not yet reached Tipperary – or anywhere else for that matter – that Massey and John Corydon had been detained by the police the night before at Limerick Junction nor that the entire battle plan was in the hands of the authorities.

The motley Fenian ranks were silent except for nervous coughing and feet-stamping here and there. They watched the precise wheeling and flanking of the professional soldiers before them. As if by magic, with hardly a spoken command, their files fanned out into long ranks. The soldiers marched steadily towards the Fenians, spotless rifles at the port, bayonets fixed.

Suddenly, from the front rank of Fenians a cloud of smoke puffed upwards, followed by the crash of a musket discharge.

'Wait till they're in range!' screamed an officer.

His voice was drowned by the rippling crash of a ragged volley. Tiny pieces of earth and grass flicked up twenty yards in front of the British soldiers. One soldier on the right flank leapt visibly off the ground. His rifle fell at his feet. He clapped a hand to his shoulder, stung, perhaps even bruised by a piece of shot which had somehow outdistanced the rest. With hardly a break in their stride, the soldiers continued their advance.

A light drizzle began to blanket the scene. The Fenians swore aloud, trying to reload their weapons, hands slipping on wet metal. They could hear now as well as see, the measured tread of the troops. It was a relentless sound, grass and divot crushed under boot. It came on and on.

An unexpected silence made the Fenians straighten up. The first of the two ranks of troops had knelt, rifles now pressed into shoulders. The second rank's weapons pointed straight ahead over the heads of the first rank.

Some of the Fenians redoubled their efforts to prime their ancient guns, fumbling in desperation. Others shuffled around so that their backs were towards the troops. The movement spread through the ranks.

It wasn't an accurate volley. Perhaps the soldiers were more excited than their ordered drill suggested. Some bullets hit targets, thudding soggily into body flesh, or shattering bones, the dry, echoing snaps mingling with agonized cries.

It was too much for the Fenians. This wasn't the glorious death depicted in paintings and legend. This was slaughter of the untrained by the skilled.

Who broke rank first didn't really matter. Within a minute, most of the thousand Fenians were fleeing in every direction away from the soldiers.

The British troops, confident of the rout before them, resumed their measured advance, not even attempting to chase their fleeing enemy. That, their officers knew, could be left to the Royal Irish Constabulary.

The disaster at Ballyhurst was just one of many. At Drogheda, a thousand rebels were routed by thirty-seven constables. Worse, at Tallagh, seven hundred Fenians fled after the first volley from just fourteen constables. Only around Cork did the rebels acquit themselves with anything approaching honour.

The gloom of the Fenian headquarters in Great Portland Street deepened perceptibly with news of each successive disaster. Colonel Kelly locked himself in the drawing room, refusing to talk to any of his aides for the whole afternoon.

'You go where you like, when you like, from now on, friend,' Richard O'Sullivan Burke told Matt as the day wore on.

'It's over, isn't it, Richard?'

'All over. Finished. Perhaps for ever.'

Although he'd opposed the Fenian plans, Matt couldn't help but feel sadness for them. After all, he still agreed with their aspirations. He tried to comfort Burke. 'The Fenians will never die. It's not all over, you know.'

'It is for many years.'

'Possibly. But if we remember the oath, we can stay together. We must go underground, become a secret society again.'

'You were the one who wanted to cut and run,' Burke reminded him sourly.

'Not from the ideals of Fenianism,' said Matt. 'I was against precipitant action. There have been too many bungled rebellions already.'

'And now this . . . '

'Yes, and now this. We must wait for a proper cause we can make our own. Something that the people can understand, something that affects their very lives. If we can unite them in such a cause, then we can lead them into the greater fight against the English.'

'All very fine, Matt,' said Burke, slumped disconsolately in his chair. 'But what are we to do in the meantime?'

'We must stay close to the people, identify with them. We've overestimated their resolve, their stomach for fighting. We must never lead from in front again. We must guide the people to do what we want them to do. Allow them to think that rebellion is their idea, not ours. When there's an issue, a dispute, which concerns them, angers them even, we can turn it to our advantage.'

'Mislead them, you mean?'

'Of course. Our fight now should be one of stealth, not of standing and waving flags before a British Army. That's never worked and probably never will.'

'Have you been listening to James Stephens recently? Is that what you're about?' asked Burke suspiciously.

'Well, Stephens was right, wasn't he? He counselled against open revolt. England's struggle will be Ireland's opportunity. That's what he said. But no one listened and now we've failed.'

'Tell that to Kelly,' Burke said flippantly.

'No, you tell him, Richard, if you want to. There are other bridges for me to build.'

'Mrs Aherne?'

'Uh-huh. I should have said fences to mend, really,' Matt smiled. He felt his depression lifting for the first time since that day in Chester more than three weeks before.

When he arrived back in Ireland two days later, Matt found little or no sign that the country had just undergone a major attempt at rebellion, however inept. None of his travelling companions spoke about it and, in Ireland herself, the people seemed too ashamed to mention it. The newspapers he read during the train journey from Dublin were still praising the authorities for their swift action and castigating the Fenians as being unrepresentative of the Irish. Only one editorial noted that the Fenians would have had no support if there were not still discriminatory laws against the Irish in Ireland. In general, the newspapers expressed total satisfaction at the outcome. They welcomed the authorities' policy of charging captured Fenian leaders with treason but dealing with the small fry more leniently. The government was clearly determined not to create any more martyrs.

In the last few miles of his journey, Matt wondered continually what sort of welcome he would receive in Listowel. He prepared for a cheery one from the town and a frosty one from Mary. In the event, it was almost exactly the reverse.

During his walk from the station to Church Street, he passed several Fenian colleagues, among them Tom Luby, Jim Bunyan and Mike Quille. He started to greet them, to ask what had happened around Listowel, but they seemed embarrassed to meet him. After a few stilted words, they hurried on their way, promising to see him later at the tavern.

Matt was still perplexed by their attitudes when he flung open his own front door. 'I'm home, everyone,' he called, trying to sound more cheerful and confident than he felt. 'Mary. Children. I'm home!'

The door to the kitchen burst wide. Mary ran out, wiping her hands on an apron, followed by Brigid, Bernadette and Jack. 'Dearest husband, you're back,' she cried, throwing her arms round his neck. 'You're safe. Oh, you're safe.'

Matt felt a wetness on his cheek as Mary pressed her face against his. It took him a moment to realize that the tears were his own.

Much later, in the hushed warmth of the bedroom, Mary asked only one question when he had finished recounting his adventures. 'Your heart is here?' she whispered.

'Aye. With you and ours. It was madness but I'm thinking it's over. Oh God, I hope it is!'

Mary placed a finger gently on his lips. 'And didn't I realize that in these last weeks? Sure and I was awful upset when you didn't come home but I knew it wouldn't be your doing.'

He nodded, then gathered her to him.

In the months that followed, Matt slipped back into the quiet, ordered life of the small market town. It was as if the rebellion had never happened. The only outward sign of it was the company of infantry still garrisoned in Listowel. The soldiers had arrived at the magistrate's request following the Chester fiasco when the local Fenians, not receiving the news of the rising's postponement, had mobilized at Cahirciveen. The actual day of the rebellion had passed off in Listowel virtually unnoticed. Some Fenians had congregated but the overwhelming presence of troops and two hundred and fifty armed constables had persuaded them that discretion was the better part of valour. Those who had been arrested were merely charged under the law dating from the Whiteboys troubles. Most were bound over in their own assurances of future good behaviour.

Matt's only source of information now was the occasional letter from Joe Denieffe, still hiding out in London. It seemed that the Fenian leadership had decided to adopt, after all, the policy of James Stephens and regroup as a smaller secret society comprising only the most fanatical, the most dedicated, members. The final blow to any lingering hopes of open revolution was the lack of effective support from the Fenians in America.

They'd chartered a ship, optimistically renamed *Erin's Hope*, which sailed from New York with five thousand repeating rifles and one and a half million rounds of ammunition. The ship didn't arrive off Sligo until two months after the abortive rising.

'Too much, too late,' Denieffe wrote sarcastically.

A subsequent letter from him saying that, at long last, the informer had been identified as John Corydon served only to strengthen Matt's opinion of the brotherhood's incompetent leadership. Corydon had steadily fed the authorities in New York and London with every twist and turn of Fenian planning. He was now, according to Denieffe, under heavy guard, available to identify and give evidence against captured Fenians. His arrest earlier with General Massey had merely been a subterfuge.

The final confirmation for Matt that he was well out of it was the news that Colonel Kelly had been arrested in Manchester along with Captain Deasey, his diehard commander in Cork during the rising. They'd been trying to reorganize their units in the north west of England. They gave their names as Wright and Williams but soon, thanks to information from John Corydon, their real names were known. It was in this ignominious capture that Kelly, named chief executive of the Irish Republic by the Fenians, was to serve his cause best.

A week later, September 18th, 1867, a horsedrawn prison van rattled and jolted its way through the Ardwick district of Manchester, an area of grimy little streets and small workshops, traditionally one of the main homes of the Irish who'd settled in the city closest to Britain's industrial revolution. In the back of the van, a police sergeant watched over the crude cells containing the two handcuffed Fenian leaders and some common criminals, including women, while they were returned from police court to Belle Vue Prison.

Suddenly, as the unescorted van passed under a sooty railway bridge, thirty Fenians leapt, whooping and yelling, from the side streets.

Brandishing revolvers, they held back passersby and ordered two constables down from the driving seat. Then they began battering the vans with heavy stones in an attempt to break it open. The police sergeant drew his wooden truncheon and stood by the doors, prepared to fight off the attackers if they should break through.

One Fenian, Peter Rice, pointed his revolver through the ventilator and jerked the trigger. The bullet smashed through the thin metal slats and into the police sergeant's temple. With only a sob of surprise, he fell back, blood and brains jetting upwards, spraying the walls of the van. A few seconds later, the van door swung open. The Fenians pulled Kelly and Deasey, still handcuffed, into the street, over a wall and across a railway line on the start of a long journey which eventually took them – and Peter Rice – to freedom in the United States.

The police action was immediate and draconian. Hundreds of Irishmen were picked up for questioning before five were charged with the police sergeant's murder. One was later to be granted a free pardon when it was admitted that he was nowhere near the scene of the rescue at all. Edward Condon, of Irish descent but an American citizen, was reprieved after diplomatic pressure, although he was, in fact, the person who planned the rescue. The remaining three were destined for the scaffold. None of them had fired the fatal shot but legally they were all accessories to murder.

Matt Aherne read the reports of the trial in his copy of *Freeman's Journal* while he stood behind his tavern bar. His first reaction was of cold anger. The few customers at that time in the morning had read the statements from the dock as well. The feelings of pride and anger and shame and resentment were, perhaps, too strong to be expressed. Matt, within his heart, rededicated himself to Ireland's fight, to the Fenian Brotherhood. So did thousands of others. Three Fenians, William Allen, Philip Larkin and Michael O'Brien, were executed before the people of Manchester on November 24th. Larkin and O'Brien jumped and twisted for ghastly, agonizing minutes at the end of the hemp rope because of the executioner's incompetence. Matt had no doubt – nor had many in Ireland – that they had died not because they were involved in the death of a

339

gallant policeman but simply because they were rebels against British rule. They were martyrs, of that Matt was certain. He cursed his inability to express his feelings. His depression was all too clear to Mary.

'You shouldn't be taking it so hard, Matt,' she said one late November night after the bar had closed and they sat alone by the glowing peat fire in their front room. 'There's nothing you could have done.'

'I could have believed like they believed,' Matt said. 'I could have done that, at least. All of us carry blame for their deaths. We're fine ones for talking and plotting but not many of us are good at dying. That takes something special in a man.'

Mary rose from her chair and knelt by Matt's knee, resting her head on his thigh, gazing into the fire, shadows flickering across her face. 'You tried at Chester, didn't you?' she said soothingly.

'Yes,' Matt conceded. 'I was ready then. For an hour I was prepared for anything that came. But after that, resolve went from me. Perhaps a man has only one chance, a certain time, to offer himself. And when that moment's gone . . . well, he's only left with a lifetime of regrets. Isn't most of living, anyway, an apology for not having done something or regretting what was done?'

He traced a finger gently through the fine hairs at the nape of her neck.

'Women have a truer notion,' he continued. 'They have the way of living for the present, for knowing what's important and what's so much dross. They regret very little. They know there's little enough time for that when there's all life to be savoured, to be fought for.'

'I wouldn't stop you. You know that,' Mary said quietly. 'If you want to go on with the brotherhood, well, that's fine.'

'A little late, isn't it?' Matt said bitterly. 'More than a little late, I'd say. The dying's done and that's that.'

Mary tried to comfort him. She had seen how his feelings were gnawing at him, his increased drinking, his growing irritability with his customers and the children. He had been so certain of himself once. Now he seemed unsure and questioning.

Matt's depression deepened when the newspapers reported that Richard O'Sullivan Burke had been arrested and was being held, pending trial, in Clerkenwell Prison in London.

Then, three days after his friend's arrest, Matt's spirits soared with the arrival of a cryptic message from Joe Denieffe. 'Help needed to open locked door,' it read. 'Come to usual place.'

Matt showed it immediately to Mary, his hands trembling

slightly with excitement. Her expression didn't alter. 'Burke?' she asked calmly, quietly.

He nodded, eyes pleading.

'Well, you'll have to go, won't you,' she decided briskly, turning away from him.

'Sure and it'll only be a few days, Mary.' He stood behind her, folding her into his arms and pulling her close. She rested her head back on his shoulder.

'Will it?'

'I know things have been wrong between us,' he said softly. 'But nothing will keep me away from you and the children longer than necessary. Helping Joe is something I must do.'

'I know that.'

'And when it's over, there'll be no more, I promise. Just here and the tavern. But this time it's awful important to me.'

'I know that, Matt,' she repeated.

'More than . . .' he went on, then stopped.

'I know,' she repeated before tearing herself out of his embrace and rushing into the kitchen, hands clasped across her face.

Two days later, December 11th, 1867, Matt stood under light falling snow outside the Langham Hotel in London. After an hour's wait, stamping his boots in the slush, he began to wonder if he'd chosen the correct rendezvous. He was just considering whether to chance the house in Great Portland Street when a cab jangled up to the hotel entrance. Denieffe leaned through the window and beckoned Matt to get in.

'No words now, friend,' he said. 'We'll talk at the lodgings.'

The cab clattered its way east towards the oldest part of London. Here, poverty existed within spitting distance of the great financial institutions which extracted the maximum wealth from the new colonies claimed in the name of Queen Victoria. Denieffe halted and paid off the cab within sight of the dome of St Paul's.

'We'll walk a bit now,' Denieffe grunted. The pavements were crowded with people in spite of the chilling flurries of snow.

'You're well?' Matt inquired.

'As can be, what with all the changing of lodgings I've had since the affair at Manchester.'

'You weren't there?'

'No, but the way the police are out looking for me, I might jut as well have been. That bastard Corydon gave them most descriptions.'

'Mine?'

'They haven't been to see you?'

'No.'

'Well then, I'm reckoning he thought you weren't important enough to bother with.'

'We'll be rectifying that, won't we, Joe?' Matt said grimly.

'Aye. We will that.'

After twenty minutes of brisk walking, occasionally checking to see if anyone was behind them, they rounded a corner into a depressing row of terraced houses called Warner Street. Half-way down, Denieffe stopped at a door, looked round once more, and then entered using his own key. Matt followed him up the rickety stairs into a small room furnished only with a cot bed and an armchair.

'Not much, is it?' commented Denieffe, sensing Matt's dismay. 'But it's cheap and the landlord doesn't ask questions.'

'Do I stay here?'

'You have the armchair. It's more comfortable than that damned bed. It's only for a night anyway. We strike tomorrow.'

'So soon?'

'The planning's been done. Our man, a fella called Mick Barret, has been to see Burke in prison. And he's arranged the explosives from our friends in the gravel quarries in Middlesex. Everything's ready. All I've been wanting was someone I could trust and now you're here. So why not tomorrow?'

'Why not indeed?'

Denieffe pulled a large street map from under the straw palliasse on the bed and spread it on the floor. For the next two hours, he led Matt through the plan. In the late afternoon, when they'd finished, both men changed into ragged and stained sets of clothes which Denieffe had bought off a stall in Club Row market.

'That's what you are now, Matt, my boy,' Denieffe said cheerfully, jamming a cap with a torn peak on to the side of his head. 'An honest Irish navvie working on the underground railway.'

He bent down, rubbed his palm in the dust on the bare floorboards, then wiped it across Matt's cheek.

'With that and a night's stubble even your Mary wouldn't be knowing you. Or wanting to,' he laughed.

Before they went to a hostelry nearby for some food and drink, Denieffe showed Matt a large wooden barrel full of gunpowder – firing powder, he called it – which had been securely locked and padlocked into a small shed beside the earth privy in the backyard of the house. He'd also purchased a cart from the same market where he'd acquired their clothes.

The next afternoon, they manoeuvred the cart out of the yard in Warner Street, the barrel of gunpowder safely roped down, and pushed it the quarter of a mile to the cobbled lane behind the granite walls and towers of Clerkenwell Prison. It was set in the middle of a small common, within range of the sweet fumes coming from the gin distillery just opposite.

Matt and Denieffe pretended to be exhausted and half-drunk, leaning over the shafts of the cart while they waited for the agreed signal from Richard O'Sullivan Burke.

They strained to listen for any sound coming from behind the high walls but all they could hear was the sound of men's tramping feet, presumably the prisoners exercising, and an occasional shout from a prison guard.

'There it is!' Denieffe exclaimed all of a sudden. 'That's the signal!'

Something hollow, perhaps wooden, banged against the wall about ten yards from them.

'That's it!' Denieffe said excitedly. 'The signal. It is. He's knocking with his shoe.'

Both men looked round. The only person within thirty yards was standing outside a stable building ignoring the couple of drunks apparently struggling with their cart.

'Now?' asked Matt.

'For God's sake hurry. Burke's only got a minute.'

Matt leaned under the tarpaulin covering the gunpowder, struck a safety match and held it to the length of fuse. It spluttered for a second, then went out. He struck a second match. The same thing happened. It wouldn't ignite.

'Joe . . . for Christ's sake.' His muffled voice was urgent from beneath the tarpaulin.

'What?'

The question echoed into Matt's ear as Denieffe's face, surprised and worried, appeared next to his under the covering.

'It won't light, dammit!'

'It must. Give me the lucifers.'

Denieffe took the matches and struck one. It blew out and he swore and struck another one. The fuse smoked for a second before going out. There was no doubt now. It hadn't been properly prepared. It wouldn't light.

'On the back arse of a whore!' Denieffe stormed.

'There's not time,' Matt said, his voice surprisingly matter of fact.

'And don't I know that?' Denieffe shouted, pulling his head from

343

under the tarpaulin. 'Get the bloody thing away.'

As Matt frantically pushed the cart down the lane, he saw Denieffe pull a small white ball from his pocket, lean back and toss it over the prison wall.

'What the devil was that?' he asked breathlessly when Denieffe had caught up with him.

'A signal, you ignorant spalpeen. Burke'll know it's off till tomorrow.'

'But won't the guards . . . ?'

'Not they. They've rotting cats and rats and pigeons over those walls all the time. It's the children's way of having a wee bit of fun in this neighbourhood.'

Denieffe spent most of that evening preparing a new fuse in the seclusion of the room in Warner Street. Matt watched him from the armchair, occasionally sipping from the bottle of cognac they'd bought the night before. It was strange, he thought, how detached he felt about everything. He knew the enterprise was extremely dangerous, yet he had no fear, no excitement. Perhaps, he wondered, it had been pre-ordained. Matt slept well and dreamlessly that night despite the uncomfortable armchair.

The area around the prison was slightly busier than it had been the previous day. Some children were playing about forty yards away at the end of the lane. By them, a woman was chatting to a milkman. The two men rested the cart in exactly the same position as before and waited. This time, however, they could hear no sound from beyond the walls.

They waited, nerves beginning to tighten, for a good five minutes. There was still no sound nor any signal.

Matt and Denieffe exchanged uneasy glances.

'Do we call it off again?' Matt asked.

Denieffe scratched the stubble on his chin.

'Twice we haven't been spotted,' he grunted. 'A third time would be asking too much. No, we'll do it now. Burke'll be ready.'

Matt shrugged his shoulders, starting to lift the tarpaulin which covered the barrel of gunpowder. He looked casually up the lane to check that the children had come no nearer. To his horror, he saw that a patrolling constable had joined the woman and the milkman.

'Joe!' he called, almost shouting. 'Joe . . . behind you. Trouble!'

Suddenly, the constable started towards them, breaking into a run, obviously suspicious.

'Oh, Jesus!' yelped Denieffe. He tore the tarpaulin off the cart.

344

'The matches, for God's sake.'

Instinctively, Matt tossed them to him, his eyes remaining fixed on the advancing constable. Everything seemed to be in slow motion.

The sound of Denieffe striking matches desperately jerked him out of his revery.

Matt saw that the fuse had started to splutter and smoke. His eyes switched to the constable and, beyond him, the children down the lane.

'No!' he cried. 'No!'

He ran round the cart almost colliding with Denieffe who was haring off in the opposite direction.

Matt waved his arms, urging the constable away from the cart, trying to attract the children's attention to warn them.

He opened his mouth to shout again but whatever words came out were drowned by the massive explosion.

Matt Aherne was engulfed by the blast and the roaring fireball. He ceased to exist.

Pitch torches and candle lamps threw smoking, grotesquely jagged shadows across the rubble of the slums near Clerkenwell Prison while the police searched throughout the night of December 13th, 1867 for any further survivors from the Fenian bomb.

It was grim work. Many a young constable turned pale and vomited his horror over the shattered bricks as he uncovered the leg of a child, a woman's arm or in one instance a policeman's helmet containing the upper half of a human head, bloodied eyes still open and staring.

The explosion had, as intended, blown a large gap in the prison wall but the blast had also demolished most of the houses in the immediate vicinity and taken the roof slates of others within a radius of a quarter of a mile.

When the final count was done, the authorities announced to an aghast capital that twelve of its citizens had died and thirty-one had been blinded, disfigured or permanently crippled by the loss of limb.

Matt Aherne was not included among the number of dead for the simple reason that nothing tangible remained of him except a few splashes of drying blood on some pieces of shattered prison wall. The fragments and lumps of his body discovered at varying distances from the seat of the explosion were presumed to belong to other victims. Thus Matt was buried in at least half a dozen coffins.

By a fluke of the blast wave, Joe Denieffe was unscathed. He lived with the knowledge that the devastating bomb had been completely purposeless.

A security alert the night before had caused the governor of Clerkenwell Prison to change the prisoner's routine. Richard O'Sullivan Burke had heard the explosion from the locked confines of his cell.

But the deaths of Matt Aherne and his innocent victims brought the discontents of Ireland searingly into the consciousness of the British public.

At first, all over England, thousands enrolled into the special constabulary to guard against what was seen as the hideous threat from the Fenians. Five thousand or so joined in the City of London alone. Even the sleepy Channel Island of Jersey established a force to take on the Irish at a signal from the guns of Fort Regent above St Helier.

One of the instigators of the Clerkenwell outrage, Michael 'Mick' Barrett, apprehended later by chance, faced a jeering, partisan crowd when he was allowed the dubious historical footnote of being the last person publicly executed in Britain.

The shrewder politicians, like William Ewart Gladstone, saw these reactions as the chance to focus public opinion on the Irish problem.

In 1868, when he became Prime Minister, Mr Gladstone made an unequivocal statement on assuming office. 'My mission,' he proclaimed, 'is to pacify Ireland.'

Within months, his government disestablished the Protestant Church throughout Ireland, and, in 1870, enacted a Land Bill which provided legal recourse against landlords who arbitrarily evicted their tenants, although the three 'Fs' – fair rent, freedom of sale and fixity of tenure – were not to become law for another eleven years.

Mr Gladstone's ability to manoeuvre laws concerning Ireland through the Westminster Parliament, however, was certainly helped by the understanding now clear in the British mind that something had to be done about the Irish if further terrorist outrages like Clerkenwell were to be avoided.

The often misguided and inept Fenians had achieved something, not that it was of the slightest comfort to Mary Aherne.

She read of the bomb attack the day afterwards and knew that her husband was dead. Outwardly she tried to pretend that he was still alive, possibly in hiding and unable to write, and was partly aided by the newspaper reports which naturally failed to list Matt among the casualities. The worst part, she found, was her inability to confide in anyone during her torment.

To inquiries, Mary could only say that her husband was away on business.

The letter from Joe Denieffe was a blessing of sorts when it arrived six days after the explosion, less than a week before St Stephen's Day.

Mary scanned the first few lines, giving the barest details, uttered a heart-wracking cry and swooned. She recovered her senses to find herself being comforted by the town's priest, Father Michael McDonnell, who'd been summoned by Bernadette after she'd read her mother's letter and understood its harsh message.

The sorrow deepened though the pain lessened as Mary confided in the priest. They went through the letter together seeking any comfort in the words.

'He couldn't have suffered or known a thing of this, Mary,' Father McConnell said softly, his hands folded over hers.

'No,' she replied dully. 'No pain for him.'

'He believed in what he was at?'

'Oh, yes, Father. Sometimes, I think he wanted to die for Ireland rather than live with all his dreams and ambitions gone.'

'Many men have desired that. Who's to blame them or say they're wrong? Not I, Mary, nor the blessed Church. He was a brave man and you can be proud of him.'

'You really think so?'

'You must think so and you must tell your children so.'

A thought struck Mary. 'But how can we bury him or give him the sacraments? He'd want that, I'm sure. And how do we tell the town he died?'

The priest nodded, understanding her dilemma. 'The Almighty will hear our prayers, will accept my blessing on the departed, I'm certain. And He'll forgive us if we don't tell all the truth. Your Matt died just in an accident while he was away in England and his remains couldn't be got home. That's what I know and that's what I'll say. You must counsel your own family in their answers.'

'You'll bless him in death despite all those poor people dying?'

The priest shifted uncomfortably in his chair. 'I'll commend his soul to Our Lord for being the loving husband and father that he was. But I cannot be condoning what he seems to have been involved in because I'm not knowing what was in his mind at the very time. Only the Almighty can know that. But I'm sure, Mary, that Matt wouldn't have been wanting those deaths.'

'No, I don't think so,' she said quietly, then more strongly, 'No, I'm certain he wouldn't!'

'Then the Lord will know and understand too.'

Four days later, Mary and the children stood in a biting wind off the Atlantic as Father McDonnell blessed the small headstone set next to Brigid Aherne's grave – and the three others – near the tumbledown cabin at Drombeg townland.

Since no one had known exactly when he was born, the inscription simply read: 'Matthew Aherne – 1867 – Beloved of his Family'. Underneath were two words: 'For Ireland'.

*BOOK THREE*

# Chapter 1 December, 1913

The men crowded into the meeting room in Convent Street were of every age and size. Their faces shone with zeal, sweat, and enough porter to carry a man through such an important evening in Listowel's history as this.

Those near the front of the room pressed closer to the small, raised platform. The younger ones chattered away excitedly, speculating or boasting, while the older men tended to remain silent except for perfunctory greetings. The light from the new electric bulbs hanging from the ceiling left pools of dark shadow near the walls and corners.

Jack Aherne had carefully positioned himself in one of these darker places. In his sixtieth year, Jack found himself becoming more and more detached from the people closest to him. Perhaps, he reckoned, it was nature's preparation for the final, loneliest event in anyone's life. When he was more cheerful, he blamed it on a lifetime spent teaching history and geography to the children of Listowel. Jack gazed round with a rueful smile: he was surprised that the reaction to the protests in north-east Ireland against the Home Rule Bill had been so long coming.

Demonstrations had begun in Ulster even before the Bill had been introduced into Parliament more than two years earlier in 1911. The Unionists had gathered in their tens of thousands to march past their leader, Sir Edward Carson. A year later, nearly 450,000 Ulster people signed a Covenant opposing any change in the links between Ireland and England. They were not in the least concerned that the majority of the Ulster members of Parliament were in favour of an Irish legislature for Irish affairs. When the bill passed the Commons in 1914, they formed the Ulster Volunteer Force.

Jack Aherne knew that the rest of Ireland would form a body equivalent to the UVF with its many dummy wooden guns for public drilling, its real weapons for private target practice, its implicit threat of military action if Home Rule became a reality. It was

351

the oldest natural law: every action had a reaction.

He wondered how many of the men at the meeting had sized up what was happening in Ireland and how many were simply being borne along on the emotions raised by the police brutality in Dublin a month before, when one man had died and hundreds of others, including women and children had been injured in baton charges during a transport strike. The call for the formation of the Irish National Volunteers had started in Athlone, spread to the Dublin strikers who called themselves the Irish Citizens Army, and now had reached even a remote market town like Listowel.

The schoolmaster had read the names of the Provisional Committee running the Volunteers in the nationalist *Freeman's Journal*. From his own guesswork and knowledge, almost half the committee were sworn members of the Fenians, the secret Irish Republican Brotherhood.

Jack had long ago declined to join the Fenians. He talked politics only with his family or closest friends. People usually attributed his reticence to the childhood trauma of his father's untimely death. Jack liked to think and observe, not to participate. The town regarded his scholarly idiosyncrasies fondly. Those standing close to him at the meeting nodded their greetings and received a nod in return. That was all they normally got from 'Old Jack', as he was nicknamed by hundreds of schoolchildren.

'To order, gentlemen!' a voice called from the platform. 'To order, please!'

A man stood up behind the trestle table on the platform, removed a homburg hat and unbuttoned a thick overcoat.

It was Jack McKenna, the chairman of the county council. Aherne raised his bushy, grey eyebrows in some surprise. He hadn't expected the man to come out into the open. Surely everyone knew McKenna had been sworn into the IRB in 1910? He'd expected the Fenians to be a little more circumspect in their efforts to infiltrate this new organization.

McKenna waited for a hush to settle over the room.

'We're all aware of the object for which we're assembled here tonight. It's for the purpose of what I consider doing a good night's work for the good old land that bore us.

'We have before us at the present time what I regard as a very good example set by the North. And that is that the best way to insist on having our rights observed by an alien government is to take the rod into our own hands. Carson has been going round preaching what some call sedition, urging people of the North to defend their rights by might, in the way God intended.

'Now, we're going to take the names of every man and boy tonight who wants to join the Volunteers. We're not having any informers, no cadgers, no cads. We want true, manly men and we want nothing to do with any other kind.'

The spindly schoolteacher at the back of the hall snorted contemptuously at the poor rhetoric, and headed for the door. He'd heard and seen enough. As he left, the rest of the crowd in the hall started to queue at the foot of the stairs leading to the platform. One by one they walked up to the trestle table, placed their right hand on an old Lee-Enfield rifle and signed their names on a large sheet of paper. McKenna's beam embraced each volunteer, including Jack Aherne's fourteen-year-old grandson, Bryan, who, unknown to his grandfather, signed his name along with four of his schoolfriends.

Jack Aherne walked home slowly, savouring the ceiling of stars in the sharp night air. To his right, the steeple of St Mary's Church announced the presence of the Catholic faith to the dark mass of St John's Anglican Church, set in the middle of the square not forty yards away.

It was a symbolic juxtaposition, Jack decided, that couldn't have been mere coincidence. First the centuries of Protestant ascendancy; now, the growing, perhaps overwhelming, demands of the native Catholic majority.

Catholic and Protestant, a singularly petty and stupid way of deciding Ireland's future. It gave the extremists of both persuasions the chance to obscure their true motives under the cloak of religion. Now, Jack was certain, the battle lines were being drawn up.

From this night, Catholic volunteers in Listowel were prepared to face Protestant volunteers. And few could see the wider storm signals in Europe. He felt resigned. His life's studies had taught him that men could shape history but never control it. History had a way of making up its own mind, of playing its own hand. So far, he thought, history had dealt Ireland's cards from the bottom of the pack. Why should it be different in the years to come?

Slowly Jack paced round the square, musing that events in Listowel during his lifetime had reflected fairly accurately those in Ireland as a whole. Here, he'd seen the glorious, heady years of Parnell, revered like no Irish politician since Daniel O'Connell, who had often visited Listowel during his times of influence. He'd also come there when he was ruined by his love for another man's wife.

Jack remembered when Parnell, a sick man, had spoken last from the front window of the Listowel Arms Hotel in the corner of the square. 1891, wasn't it? Well, if he wasn't sure of the date, his memory of that evening was crystal clear.

There'd been brass bands to welcome the great man. Dozens of policemen were drafted in, most taking notes in case Parnell uttered seditious words. And the crowd . . . the huge crowd . . . and the heckling led by Father O'Callaghan from Duagh, protesting at Parnell's adulterous relationship with Mrs Kitty O'Shea, now the politician's wife but for too long his mistress during another marriage.

Parnell had refused to accept that his career had been destroyed by the Catholic Church's abhorrence of his private morals. Defiantly he had battled on, his voice with its clear English accent growing hoarser, weaker, against the continuous shouts of 'How's Kitty?' and 'Sinner' and 'Adulterer' and 'Whoremonger'.

Parnell had died within weeks, and his party had begun to decline. When the second Home Rule Bill failed in 1893, the vacuum had been created for a new political party.

They called it, in Gaelic, Sinn Fein. 'We Ourselves' Jack translated literally as he strolled out of the square and northwards up Church Street, but Sinn Fein accepted that foreign policy and defence should be left to the Imperial Parliament in London. Distasteful as some of its leaders found the concept, Sinn Fein said publicly that it didn't want to sever Ireland's links with the British Crown.

In that, Jack believed, they represented the views of most Irish people. But Jack also knew that within Sinn Fein there was the hidden enclave of Fenians, the Irish Republican Brotherhood, which wanted complete independence as a republic and believed that this would come about only through violence. The Fenians lived within Sinn Fein like a dormant, yet malignant, growth, retaining links with the American organization, Clan-na- Gael.

Jack realized that his hatred of Fenianism stemmed from the circumstances of his father's death and his mother's reaction to it.

The day after Matt Aherne's headstone had been blessed at Drombeg, his widow had called the children together. Her black mourning dress emphasized the paleness of her complexion. Her eyes were pools of grief.

'Children,' she said quietly, 'You know how and why Daddy died.'

Bernadette snivelled into a handkerchief edged with black lace.

'No, dearest,' her mother chided, 'No more tears. There should be no more crying. Daddy wouldn't have that, I'm sure.'

Mary looked down at her hands, pressed into her lap, knuckles whitened.

'It was a brave thing he was trying to do for a friend, brave but very foolish. I shall say that once more but then never again. It was foolish. But that doesn't mean your daddy was foolish. He was misled by wicked men he thought were his friends. They used him for their evil work because they knew he loved Ireland, that he would die for his country. They weren't interested in him or our land: they only wanted power for themselves. They tricked Daddy like they tricked all the others who were killed or put in prison during the uprising. They're called Fenians and you must promise me that you'll never have anything to do with them. Do you promise?'

Mary asked the question of each of the children in turn. The girls nodded, both with tears glistening on their cheeks.

'I promise, Mama,' Jack piped up, realizing that this was quite one of the most solemn moments of his young life. He ran to his mother and pressed himself against her bosom. Mary smoothed his hair gently while she went on talking.

'Now we've agreed, haven't we, that the town shouldn't know how Daddy died. So we've to be very careful in what we say. One day, perhaps, there'll come a time when we can tell the whole story but you must allow me to judge when and if that time arrives.'

And so it had been. His two sisters had worked with their mother at 'Aherne's' while Jack pursued his studies. He was reminded constantly that he was the hope of the family. Jack didn't mind studying. The men who drank in the tavern opposite the barracks were too like his father with their changeable moods, sometimes cheery, often morose. His memories were too precious, too few, to be risked. He preferred the unchanging world of his books and immersed himself between their covers.

His mother always wore black, a woollen shawl usually drawn tightly about her head; otherwise life seemed almost unchanged. There was still enough money to satisfy most childish whims and fancies. Jack realized from envious remarks that he was regarded as well-off although the Ahernes never employed servants nor owned a horse carriage like the wealthier farmers and shopkeepers in North Kerry. In adulthood, he learned that his comfortable upbringing and university education in Dublin were not only due to the tavern's income, reasonable as that was, but also to money drafts which arrived every quarter with unfailing regularity from Alderman

Finucane, his grandfather, in Boston. After the alderman died in 1870, a well-loved and respected man throughout New England, the drafts continued. Not long after, when Jack's grandmother was laid to rest the responsibility was taken over by his mother's sister, Aunt Kathleen.

She inherited the Finucane cooperage factory and the taverns-cum-eating houses, but sold them in favour of railroad shares. Her husband, Edwin Aicheson, had become one of Boston's leading and most sought-after surgeons.

With the money draft, invariably came a detailed, gossipy letter describing the increasing stature of Mary Aherne's relatives in America. She insisted on reading these to her children, sometimes more than once. There was never any trace of envy in her voice or comments.

Sometimes when she was alone, Mary thought wistfully of Boston and what might have been. She was never tempted though from the decision she reached after Matt's death. The children would make their lives in Ireland. He would have wanted that, she was sure. As the years went by and her children married and produced grand-children, she began to treasure the cosy intimacies of life in the small Kerry town. She had to concede that she truly felt at home.

Mary took a delight in continuing the tavern's tradition of being the clearing-house for news of Kerry people who'd gone away. She became the acknowledged expert on Listowel's genealogy, often sorting out whose third cousin, once removed, had married into which family and what that relationship entailed. She never con-templated marrying again herself: the tavern and the closeness of her family ensured that she never felt really lonely. Even when Bernadette married a farmer and moved to just outside Ballylong-ford, visiting her mother once a week at best, Mary still had Brigid to confide in.

There had always been Brigid, Jack reflected, as he strolled along Church Street. He looked across the road at the lights burning in the family home, and wondered whether to call on his elder sister. Brigid had never married, preferring to stay with her mother. She still worked a few hours a day at the tavern with Jack's son, Sean, now the licensee, and spent the rest of her time helping Sean's wife, Finoola, look after the children. Bryan was the eldest, followed by Sinead, May, Kevin and the late arrival baby Michael. Sean cheerily called him the froth on the porter.

In was a happy, close family. Sometimes Jack wished that he and his wife Maude had been able to have more than one child. After a day with his beloved grandchildren, however, he was all too glad to escape to the solitude of his books and his thoughts.

No, he decided, he'd go straight home tonight. He'd only wake the children if he dropped in at the house and he guessed it would be a late night if he stopped at the tavern further up Church Street. Everyone in the bar would be excited by the formation of the Volunteers, plenty enough excuse for a hooley.

The old schoolmaster turned off Church Street, a few yards past the police barracks, and into his neat, terraced house in Forge Lane. From its front window, he could look across to the town's imposing, square-built courthouse, set amid wide lawns. Some visitors dismissed the town's regular architecture as boring and uninteresting, but Jack found it reassuring. It was a town with a place for everything and everything in its place, he'd say.

Jack recounted the evening's events while he ate his supper.

'Is it serious, you're thinking?' his wife asked when he'd finished and placed the tray carefully on the floor beside him. He filled his pipe before replying. He and Maude had always been able to talk together, which was a great satisfaction and comfort to Jack.

'What are you meaning by serious?' Jack replied at last, for a moment forgetting that he was not addressing schoolchildren. 'I'm sorry, dear,' he continued, tapping the stem of his pipe against his nose. 'Of course, it must be serious. It's the old, old story of the unstoppable preparing to meet the immovable.' He ran a hand back through his wiry, grey hair, scratching his scalp. 'Mother used to tell the tales she'd heard about the faction fighting round here, how the Cooleens used to go against the Mulvihills.'

'Even in Listowel itself,' Maude Aherne agreed, her fingers busy with her needle.

'And at the races,' Jack went on. 'Oh, yes, they used to beat each other to death for a name or a coloured piece of ribbon. Remember Mother's tales about the last great faction fight at Ballyeagh. Half of them didn't know why they were fighting. Well, that's how I'm reckoning it is now. They're picking sides for another faction fight and, blow me, Maude, I'm thinking most are being led by the politicians like bulls with rings in their noses.'

'Do even the politicians know?' she asked shrewdly.

'Know? Know?' Jack echoed, peering deep into the fire. 'They are like steeplechase jockeys who can only see the next fence. When you get two sets of people in the same country arming themselves against each other, it doesn't take much to reckon that they want a fight and they're determined to have a fight.'

Maude was silent. She knew better than to interrupt when Jack was in one of his pessimistic moods.

'You would think their love of Ireland would bind them together, wouldn't you? A love to win independence together and then build the country to our ways. Now they're squaring up like they've nothing in common except for a love of their own religions. I don't know Maude, I really don't. Whom the gods wish to destroy . . .'

The next Sunday, Jack and Maude Aherne had a grandstand view of the first parade of the local Volunteers from their bedroom window. More than a hundred gathered on the lawns outside the courthouse to march off in columns of three behind the stirring music of the town's fife and drum band.

'Don't they look brave and smart in their Sunday best?' Maude commented, tapping her feet in time to the music.

'Daft more like,' Jack replied grouchily. 'On the march with no guns and nowhere to go. The little people have stolen their brains.'

'Oh, you!' Maude laughed, as they leaned out of the window. 'I do declare you're becoming a crabby old man, Jack Aherne.'

Her husband merely grunted. Inwardly, though, he had to admit to a slight stirring of pride.

'Oh, look, Jack!' his wife cried, pointing down at a youngster carrying a crudely made green flag with a golden harp at its centre. 'Isn't that our Bryan?'

All Jack could see was the top of the boy's large cap. 'Nothing like him,' he muttered. 'Nothing like him at all. Anyway, Sean wouldn't let him join this rabble.'

It was a good four months before they discovered that their grandson was indeed a Volunteer. By then, Bryan had persuaded his father, who'd also experienced a hot flush of nationalism, that there was no harm in being simply the flag-bearer and, anyway, weren't a lot of his schoolfriends in the Volunteers as well?

Jack Aherne, who knew that some of his pupils had even been sworn into the IRB, expressed his displeasure forcibly. He realized, however, that it would be wrong to interfere too much with his son Sean's family. He did toy with the idea of revealing to Bryan how Matt Aherne met his end, joining an organization he didn't understand. But then he remembered his pledge to his mother – a pledge from which he'd never been released – and stayed silent. Nevertheless, he remained deeply worried about his grandson because he recognized how ominously the events in Ireland were drifting.

In March of 1914, sixty British officers at the Curragh Camp signified that they would rather resign their commissions than put down any rebellion by Ulstermen. This further weakened the resolve of Asquith's Liberal Government to force through an unchanged Home Rule Bill. They no longer needed the assent of the House of Lords, but the thought of an uprising in Ulster horrified the Cabinet. Back and forth went the proposals for compromise, but it was deadlock. And in the deadlock, those persuaded that violence was the only solution took action.

A month after what was popularly termed 'The Curragh Mutiny', the Ulstermen managed to land nearly twenty-five thousand rifles and three million rounds of ammunition at Larne, north of Belfast. There was now hard muscle behind the threats of those who totally opposed relinquishing any of their ties with the British Crown. After all, they told themselves, hadn't their Protestant ancestors been settled in the North nearly four centuries ago precisely to provide a bastion against the recalcitrance of the native Celts, the Irish?

The Irish National Volunteers, responded in late July by bringing ashore two thousand rifles at Howth, just south of Dublin. Later the same day, four people died and nearly forty were wounded at Bachelor's Walk, by the River Liffey in Dublin, when troops of the King's Own Scottish Borderers, tired of hunting the gun-runners, fired on a jeering, jubilant mob.

Jack Aherne studied these events in the quiet backwater that was Listowel.

He thought it inevitable that the conference about Ireland, held at Buckingham Palace, would fail. Neither side was happy with the suggestion that any Home Rule Bill should exclude the Ulster area. The proposal was that these counties could, if they so wished, later vote themselves under control of an Irish Parliament in Dublin. Such a proposal would be an Amending Bill to the Home Rule Bill. Since no one could even agree on what time scale should be used such a move inevitably would have brought intersectarian strife to Ireland.

Ironically, the certainty of war in Europe helped heal the breach. The Conservative leader, Andrew Bonar Law, and his staunch ally, Sir Edward Carson, suggested that a united front had to be presented against the German threat; that, in the best interest of all, the Home Rule Bill, which they both opposed so vehemently, should become law but should be suspended until a new Amending Bill could be introduced when the greater European crisis was over.

The Nationalist leader, James Redmond, seized the moment. As the first World War formally began he declared that the British government could remove its troops from Ireland and that Ireland would be defended by the Irish National Volunteers combined with, he hoped, the Ulster Volunteer Force.

Support for Redmond's pledge flooded in from all over Ireland except, not surprisingly, from members of the Irish Republican Brotherhood hidden in the ranks of the Volunteers and the Sinn Fein Party.

The last hurdle had been cleared in a blaze of patriotism, not only for Ireland but for the British Empire.

On September 18th, 1914, the Royal Assent was given to the Home Rule Act, providing once again a government for Ireland, by the Irish, in Ireland. A second law suspended Home Rule for a year or until the end of the war. This was to allow the Ulster argument to be heard again. After the Allies' victory at the Battle of the Marne, no one doubted that the war would be over in months.

Sparks shot hundreds of feet into the air from the bonfire in the middle of Listowel market square. The fife and drum band played their hearts out. People cheered and danced and kissed each other, tossing copies of newspapers into the air or on to the leaping flames. The headlines proclaimed, 'Ireland's Day of Triumph' and 'At Last! Our Own Again!'

Very few people in Listowel doubted that Ireland was again – or very soon would be – her own mistress. Jack Aherne was one, so were members of the local cell of the IRB. They thought the flames might be prophetic.

In Belfast and Derry, there were bonfires too. The youngsters stood round them echoing the words of their elders who drank gloomily in their Orange Lodges.

'No surrender!' they shrieked. 'No Pope! No surrender!'


## Chapter 2 April, 1916


'So what are you thinking of all this in Dublin then?' Sean Aherne asked his father, pouring him a glass of porter.

Jack Aherne looked carefully round the tavern bar half-way up Church Street in Listowel. There were only two old women sitting in the far corner that early in the morning. He glanced sideways at his son and sipped his drink before answering.

'I'm thinking that it's the maddest enterprise since the rising of '48. And it's probably even madder than that. Trying to hold the Post Office against the entire British Army.'

'Aye, Dad, that's what most of the boys in here were reckoning last night.'

Jack nodded ruefully. 'Sheer madness, so it is. But I'm hearing that even a couple of the local boys are up there as well.'

'O'Rahilly's there from Ballylongford.'

'And wouldn't he just be . . . '

'And Mickey Mulvihill and Paddy Shortis from Ballybunnion.' Sean Aherne pulled himself a glass of porter.

'Just as well the rest of the boys got stood down or else Father O'Riordan would be awful busy comforting a lot of fresh widow women,' muttered his father. And then he hesitated for a moment before continuing: 'Perhaps he'd have been calling here with his soft words if young Bryan had taken the Dublin road.'

'Thanks be to Go that he didn't.'

'Thanks indeed. And wasn't I warning you when he joined these Volunteers? And did you pay heed? You did not, Sean, you did not.'

'Now, Dad, that's not fair and you know it.' Although quiet, Sean's voice bore a note of angry protest: 'Not one of us knew the Volunteers would turn to this.'

'If you'd listened to your betters.'

'Like you.'

'Yes, like me, you would have known. If you'd opened your ears and kept your gob shut you'd have . . . '

'You're not in the classroom now, Jacko,' a cheerful voice interrupted. It was their friend, Davy Lawlor, the parish clerk and bell ringer at St Mary's. His use of Jack's nickname broke the tension. Father and son exchanged guilty glances.

'The usual, Davy?' Sean asked quickly.

'Aye, and one for yourselves now. Help you to cool down maybe.'

Lawlor, a thin, wiry man, was known, like the Ahernes, as a person with strongly independent will whose opinion was widely respected.

'The rising?' he went on, passing some money over the counter. 'That's what you're blathering about?'

'Aye,' Jack replied, smiling. 'Enough they should be destroying the fair city without causing trouble in this house.'

'It is that. Blasted fools, so they are.'

'They seem so at the moment,' Sean interrupted. 'But I've been wondering what folk'll be saying of them when it's over.'

'Now you're thinking, son!' Jack exclaimed draining his glass. 'If these are the boys I'm guessing they are then they've a deeper game on than anyone's seeing.'

'Fenians, you mean?' asked Lawlor. 'Are you seeing their hand in this business?'

'Whose else?' Jack replied, gesturing to his son to refill the three glasses. 'They've been planning for this since the war started, I reckon.'

As usual, there was a kernel of truth in what he said. Within a year of the outbreak of war, more than 130,000 Irishmen – well over half of them Catholics – had joined the ranks on behalf of the British Crown.

The vast majority of those who didn't actually join up served in the National Volunteers. Out of the 190,000 of 1913, less than 15,000 split away to form the 'Sinn Fein Volunteers' sometimes called the 'Irish Volunteers'. Most people laughed at the activities of the diehard nationalists as they went about their drill, still dreaming of an independent Irish Republic. They were jeered and abused, stoned and spat upon. They were considered disloyal by the great proportion of Irish people, a fringe of extremists not worth bothering about.

There were about sixty 'Sinn Feiners' in Listowel, drilling secretly with their own shotguns and some of the forty Martini-Henry rifles obtained locally after the gun-running exploit in Howth. Most townspeople knew who they and their leaders were. To Jack Aherne's deepest chagrin, his grandson Bryan remained one of them.

Although the youngster maintained he was still only the flag-bearer Jack had heard enough whispers that Bryan had progressed to carrying a gun. It frightened and appalled Jack. He could see his own father's mistake repeating itself. He talked often to Bryan, attempting to make him realize the danger he was running. The lad listened seriously to his grandfather but always rejected his arguments emphatically.

'What harm are we doing?' he'd ask. 'We only drill and march and talk,' he'd protest. 'The Sinn Feiners are as patriotic as anyone.'

The arguments would invariably peter out in the sad, baffled silence which often occurs when equally sincere but different generations are unable to communicate with each other.

Bryan had picked up enough hints from the conversations of his older colleagues to know that the Sinn Feiners were not dedicated to a peaceful solution to Ireland's future. He didn't mind. It added spice to his otherwise orderly routine of school and home. He admired his leaders: the town's doctor, Michael O'Connor, and Paddy Landers, the genial, huge-muscled blacksmith. To him they were men of action. They appealed to a romantic imagination fed on tales of legendary heroes. There was just enough of a whiff of danger in their company to stimulate him without feeling the slightest fear for his own safety. Life with the Sinn Feiners was a glorious adventure.

In the months that followed, Jack smelt rebellion in the air. He read accounts of the Sinn Fein Volunteers drilling and even practising mock attacks on public buildings in Dublin and other large towns. According to the Volunteers, such exercises were preparation in case Germany invaded Ireland. The organization went its commonplace way despite the hostility of many Irish people who had relatives and friends fighting in the Flanders trenches. And very few noticed the orders, printed in all newspapers, instructing the Volunteers how to spend their Easter days off in 1916.

Following the lines of last year, every unit of the Irish Volunteers will hold Manoeuvres during the Easter Holidays. The object of the manoeuvres is to test MOBILIZATION WITH EQUIPMENT.

Young Bryan spent days cleaning and pressing his suit and shining his belt and badges. He was almost in tears on Easter Saturday when the Volunteers' Chief of Staff, Eoin MacNeill, suddenly cancelled all the manoeuvres, marches and parades.

What Bryan didn't know was that at last MacNeill had tumbled to the active presence of the Irish Republican Brotherhood within the organization's inner sanctums.

MacNeill had known there were extremists who thought insurrection was the only course, but he hadn't realized until a few days before Easter that they already had the uprising planned and poised. When he did, MacNeill agreed reluctantly that it should go ahead in the belief that the British intelligence officers in Dublin Castle already had wind of the rising He feared that the Volunteers might be officially disarmed and disbanded at any moment whether there was an uprising or not. And the hard-line Fenians, the inner members of the IRB, led by Patrick Pearse, told him confidently that help was on its way from Germany in the form of twenty thousand rifles and millions of rounds of ammunition. These were in addition to the weapons already purchased secretly with the tens of thousands of dollars send for that purpose by sympathizers in America, members of Clan-na-Gael. To MacNeill, it was a *fait accompli* whether he liked it or not. He agreed to the plan going ahead. His change of mind came with the news that the arms from Germany were at the bottom of Queenstown Harbour after the gun-running ship had scuttled itself following capture by the Royal Navy. The even later news that Sir Roger Casement, a career diplomat who'd been negotiating in Germany on behalf of the IRB, had been captured after landing from a submarine a dozen or so miles from Listowel only served to confirm MacNeill's opinion. The planned rising was doomed and he knew it. He issued the cancellation orders for the manoeuvres which were to be the cover for rebellion.

To Patrick Pearse and the Fenians under his control, mainly around Dublin, the cancellation was irrelevant. Pearse believed wholeheartedly in the power of myths to become reality. When he led a hundred or so Volunteers through the entrance of the General Post Office in O'Connell Street, Dublin, a few minutes after midday on Monday April 24th, 1916, he knew their rebellion had no chance of success. Whether the rank and file men knew it was doubtful.

Pearse announced the new 'Republic' from the steps of the building's portico to passing crowds who thought him, at best, an eccentric. Then he read a proclamation from 'the Provisional Government' under a fluttering tricolour and, within an hour, the newly-titled Irish Republican Army was busy fighting off units of the British Army, which, ironically, was comprised mainly of Irishmen. The Dublin tenement dwellers welcomed the uprising. It took the police off the streets, allowing them to loot the shops.

In Listowel, each communique from Army headquarters was discussed avidly. They described how the British Army's artillery gradually reduced the rebel positions – and large tracts of Dublin – while innocent people were being shot and killed by both sides. When Pearse surrendered in mid afternoon of Saturday April 29th, sixty-four rebels had been killed out of the fifteen hundred who had eventually taken up arms, one hundred and thirty-four soldiers and policemen were dead or dying, and at least two hundred and twenty civilians had been sacrificed. The captured Volunteers were reviled by the Dubliners as they were led away to prison. Women screamed, 'You deserve to be shot.'

Bryan Aherne was inconsolable. He refused to talk to his family, preferring to remain alone in his room. His father tried to comfort him after breakfast on the morning following the surrender, understanding his deep hurt and humiliation, but Bryan would have none of it.

'Well, I've done my damnedest,' Sean remarked gloomily when he'd stumped downstairs after his fruitless attempt. 'Time's the only healer.'

'He'll get over it, son. He's too young to understand,' replied Jack Aherne.

'No, you're wrong in that. Bryan can understand well enough what's happened. It's his youth that makes it so hard for him to forgive. He feels betrayed.'

Sean gratefully accepted a cup of tea and glanced at his watch. There was an hour before Mass. 'Your grandmother often talked of how confused and angry Father was after that fiasco of a rising in '67. I'm supposing our Bryan feels much the same way.'

'Will they deport the leaders again this time?'

'They'll be fools if they don't or, at least, take them to gaol over the water. But, perhaps, it's different now.'

Sean rubbed the stubble round his chin. He never shaved until minutes before going to the tavern in the morning or, on Sundays like this, to Mass. That way, he reckoned, he spared himself from having to shave again in the evening.

"I see what you're driving at, Dad,' he said reflectively. 'England's at war with Germany.'

'The Irish are at war with Germany as well,' Jack pointed out.

'Aye, and that means Pearse and his friends are traitors in wartime. And there's been the gun-running too.'

'There could be court martials not trials, Sean.'

'And then?'

Jack shook his head despairingly.

'I pray they don't but the English are fools enough to shoot them. Maybe that's what some of them want anyway. Pearse certainly thinks that everything is reborn in sacrifice. I'm trusting, for all our sakes, that the English understand that.'

'They haven't before,' Sean replied gloomily.

'And that's the truth.'

Jack looked at his watch again. 'Are the women ready?'

'Just about, I'm thinking.'

'We'll walk down together. I'll just collect your mother.'

'Right there. And we'll leave Bryan be?'

'Aye. That'd be best, I reckon. And you get yourself shaved now.'

'In the shake of a donkey's tail.'

Jack stretched up from the sofa and walked the few paces to the front door. Suddenly, just as he was about to open it, there was a squealing of brakes outside, loud shouting and the pounding of heavy boots on pavement cobbles.

'What the devil?' he exclaimed when the butt of a rifle splintered through a panel in the door a few inches above his head.

'Open up in there!' a gruff voice cried. 'Open up! It's the Army!'

The door shivered under another blow. Jack stepped back quickly, alarm pumping through him. He felt his thigh muscles tremble.

Sean leapt out of his chair but the door burst open, crashing back on its hinges, before he could reach it. Two soldiers erupted into the sitting room, rifles swivelling round to cover Jack and Sean.

'Back! Back!' they screamed, pushing the muzzles hard against Jack and Sean's chests, forcing them to the nearest wall. Two small side tables swayed and fell, throwing china figurines on to the rug. One of the soldiers kicked them out of his way, shattering them into a dozen pieces.

An officer ran, half-crouching, into the room, his revolver outstretched. Upstairs, a woman screamed then began to sob hysterically.

Two more soldiers followed the officer, their dull khaki uniforms contrasting with his shiny belt and jodhpur leggings. They charged through the sitting room, knocking aside the chairs and hammered open the door to the back kitchen with their shoulders. They knelt at the bottom of the stairway, rifles pointing upwards.

'Where's the rebel sod?' the officer demanded, thrusting his face close to Jack's. His breath smelt of stale brandy and fresh peppermint.

'Rebel? Rebel?' the old man stammered. A rifle butt slammed into his ribs. He gasped and fell to his knees, aware through the pain that the room was filling with even more soldiers. In the distance, church bells began to ring, calling the townsfolk to worship. There was noise everywhere. Shouted orders, splintering chinaware, screaming women, and the bells.

'Where's Aherne?' the officer shouted.

'Which Aherne?' Sean shouted back, forcing himself between his father and the officer.

'The rebel one, you turd!' The officer's voice was high and petulant. He swung the barrel of his revolver at Sean's head.

Sean staggered back, blood flowing from a cut as the metal sliced across his forehead.

'The rebel . . . Bryan Aherne,' the officer stormed, lifting his arm as if to strike again.

'Upstairs,' Jack mumbled, pointing at the ceiling, fearing that Sean would be hit again. 'He's upstairs, but don't harm him. For God's sake, don't harm him. He's only a boy.'

'Get him!' the officer barked. He spun away from the two men.

The soldiers took the stairs two at a time. There were more screams, another door banging open, thuds on the floor above. Sean, guessing what was happening, started towards the officer who now had his back turned. Jack saw it all in slow motion.

'No!' he cried. 'No, son! Don't make it worse.'

The officer whirled round, almost colliding with Sean. He stuck his revolver deep into the tavern-keeper's ample belly. The two men stood there for a moment like a waxworks tableau. Then, Sean lowered his fist slowly, shrugged and turned back to help his father unsteadily to his feet.

The soldiers clattered down the stairs pushing Bryan in front of them. The youngster cannoned into the wall at the bottom and literally rebounded into his escort. They shoved him in the small of the back, sending him tottering into the sitting room. Blood was trickling from his nostrils and lips, staining the front of his collarless white shirt. His face was chalky, shocked, making the blood seem more claret than it was. He staggered towards his father and tried to speak. Sean tried to step forward but was held back by a rifle barrel thrust across his body.

'Holy Mother!' he exclaimed angrily. 'What've you done to the boy?'

'Fell off his bed, suh, then down the stairs,' one of the soldiers called to the officer, pushing Bryan towards the open front door.

'Get him in the truck,' the officer ordered.

'Dad . . . Dad . . . ' Bryan sobbed, twisting his head round to look fearfully back at his father as he was frog-marched into the street.

The soldiers retreated slowly, warily from the bottom of the stairway and the sitting room, rifle barrels still pointing at the two men. When they reached the street, the soldiers broke away suddenly and ran towards the trucks.

Sean and Jack stumbled to the shattered door. They were just in time to see Bryan lifted off the ground by the soldiers and flung bodily through the air and into the back of the leading truck. They recognized some of the strained white faces peering over the tailgate. Dr O'Connor bent down out of view, obviously to help the youngster. Paddy Landers gave a wan smile through swollen lips. It was clear then that the Army had arrested most of the Listowel Company of the Irish Volunteers.

'Where are you taking the boy?' Sean shouted. 'Where's he going?'

'Tralee,' the officer called back, jumping into the front passenger seat of his open staff car. 'You'll find him there with the rest of the rebels!'

He pulled a whistle from his breast pocket and blew three times. The convoy began to rattle off down Church Street. The officer waved his gloved hand at Sean and Jack as he sped away.

Jack leaned on his son's shoulder, coughing deeply and painfully. The screaming of the women still inside the house filled his ears.

Deep hatred enveloped him for probably the first time in his life. 'Oh, the bastards!' he mumbled. 'The bastards!'

His eyes focussed on drips of blood falling on to the cobblestones. They formed a tiny pool between the raised stones. Blood kept dripping and spreading. He could see specks of dust and struggling insects being carried on the spidery, red rivulets. His mind was flooded with the image. He shook his head and gazed into the clear, blue sky. The colours, blue and red, red and blue, mixed together in his brain. Suddenly he realized where the blood was coming from. Sean's face was masked with blood from the cut on his forehead.

'Are you all right?' he asked.

Sean wiped a hand across his face. 'A scratch, Dad,' he grunted. 'Nothing more.'

He was still peering down the long, straight street into the slowly settling cloud of dust left by the Army convoy. The trucks had gone. Sean put his arm around his father's waist and started to help him back into the house.

By now, the women had ventured into the front room with the children. Brigid Aherne, with the experience of an elderly aunt, was the calmest. She soothed Sean's wife, Finoola, whose hysterical crying gradually subsided into a bout of hiccups. Her children gazed in amazement at the overturned chairs, the door hanging on its hinges, the lumps of broken china strewn over the usually neat room. Their eyes widened even more when they saw the two beaten men stumble over the threshold. Finoola ran to her husband, wiping the remaining tears off her cheeks with the back of her forearm.

'Water and – hic – rags, Kevin,' she called. 'Quick now – hic – in the kitchen – hic!'

Brigid quickly placed the chairs upright again and guided Jack and Sean to them.

'The bastards! Oh, the bastards!' Jack continued to mutter.

'Hush, dear,' his sister murmured, stroking his brow. 'Sit quiet and I'll be sending for your Maude. Sit quiet and it'll soon be better.'

A little colour returned to Jack's ashen face. He hobbled round the room gripping his bruised ribs and roundly denouncing the arrest of his grandson. 'It wasn't necessary,' he repeated. 'Not necessary to take the boy like that. Not at all.'

'So what are we to do about this?' Brigid asked.

'Do?' Jack snorted. 'There's not much we can do, is there?'

'But surely they've made a mistake?' his sister persisted.

'Oh, there's no mistake, Aunty,' Sean replied bitterly. 'The British were after rebels and that's that. They'd take a babbie in swaddling clothes if they thought he was a rebel. That they would.'

'And who's fault is that?' Jack demanded, switching the target for his simmering anger.

'Not again, Dad . . . ' Sean began to protest.

'Headstrong, that's what you are, Sean,' said Jack firmly, ignoring the interruption. 'Always headstrong and as thick as . . . '

Then he stopped, noticing properly for the first time the hurt expression in his son's eyes and the white bandage round his temples.

His voice softened. He put his hand on Sean's shoulder, gently kneading the flesh. 'Headstrong you are, and there's no doubt of that, but perhaps not so strong right now, eh? Anyway, not strong enough to bear this silly old curmudgeon.'

Sean smiled. He understood.

'Right then,' Jack decided. 'Let's be dressed and tidied and off to Tralee. We'll have this settled soon enough when we're seeing the proper officer in charge.'

But when the family, crowded into Sean's jaunty cart, reached the gates of Tralee Prison nearly four hours later, Jack realized immediately that there were bound to be difficulties. His earlier bravado had been meaningless.

Three ranks of soldiers, bayonets fixed, stood outside the prison gates holding back a crowd of about sixty people, mainly relatives clamouring for information about the arrested men.

'What are they saying,' Jack asked someone on the edge of the crowd.

'Nothing. Nothing at all. That's what.'

'Is there an officer there?'

'They've sent for one, the much good it'll do us.'

Ten minutes passed before a small door set into the gates swung open. An officer stepped through, hardly glancing at the crowd. Jack recognized him as the one who'd arrested Bryan and the other Listowel Volunteers. A barrage of questions rose from the crowd, all sweaty and dust-streaked in their Sunday-best clothes.

The officer held up his arms, ordering, rather than requesting, silence. The hubbub died away.

'That's better,' the officer said. His words carried throughout the crowd. 'Now, listen well because I'll be saying this once only.'

Jack cupped a hand to his right ear.

'All the men arrested today through North Kerry are here,' the officer went on, his voice ringing and clear. 'They're being questioned about their activities, their rebel activities, mark you, and that'll take a number of days. Then it'll be up to the Army Commander in Dublin to decide what's to be done with them. Their names will be posted in your newspaper and police barracks and you'll be told if they're due to come to trial. There'll be no visits, not even from priests, so you all might as well return to your homes. Understand? Good, that's all then.'

Before any more questions could be shouted, the officer saluted, turned briskly and stepped back through the small door.

Momentarily, the crowd was silent, stunned by the uncompromising baldness of the announcement. Then the protests began. Women started to wail noisily, a few dropping to their knees, crossing themselves, sobbing out prayers. The soldiers stood impassively.

Jack shook his head in disbelief. He'd always supported the force of law and order, never believing wild tales of their brutality and callousness. He felt disorientated, physically and mentally. He knew that later, when he was alone, he would have to think through his values again.

A terrible despair descended like a rain cloud over Listowel, making normal life virtually impossible. People stood on corners, swapping rumours, recounting again and again how their men had been taken. The town had dismissed the Sinn Feiners as foolish, possibly dangerous, extremists. Now, no one dared to criticize them.

Three days after the mass arrests, Ireland was shocked by the news that Patrick Pearse, Thomas MacDonagh and Thomas Clarke had been shot at dawn in the yard of Kilmainham Prison in Dublin. That the rebels had been refused the comfort of a priest made people shiver with disgust and horror.

People flocked again to Tralee Prison, fearing that their menfolk could face the firing squad as well. So tense was the situation that the Army relented and allowed a deputation of priests inside to be assured that the local prisoners were still only being held for questioning.

The Aherne family stayed close together in Church Street, hardly trusting their emotions to others. Their anguish deepened with the news of more executions in Dublin – on Thursday, Joseph Plunkett, Edward Daly, Michael O'Hanrahan and William Pearse, brother of the rebel leader; on Friday, Sean McBride; the following Monday, Cornelius Colbert, Eamonn Ceannt, Michael Mallin and Sean Heuston; the next day in Cork, Thomas Kent and then the cruel wait until Friday May 12th, when James Connolly was lifted from a stretcher, strapped to a chair and shot along with Sean McDermott.

The government, which had bowed reluctantly to Army pressure to allow the executions, announced that the killings were over.

During the next six weeks, nearly nineteen hundred of the Sinn Feiners, the Irish Volunteers, who'd been arrested, were transported to internment camps in Britain, particularly in Wales and the North West. The others, a thousand or more, were put into trucks one early morning and driven back to their villages and towns.

The first the Ahernes knew that Bryan was free was a banging on the front door while they were at breakfast.

Sinead went to answer it. There was silence for a second or two, then girlish whoops of joy. At once the house was in an uproar of laughter and tears.

Bryan was embraced by all the family in turn before his father, who'd been hopping around the edges of the welcome, could reach him.

'Son! Son! Oh, my son!' Sean exclaimed, gripping him tightly by the shoulders.

'I'm home, Dad,' Bryan replied, his voice dull with tiredness. 'They've let most of the Listowel Company home.'

'That's good. That's fine,' Sean went on, excited sweat beading on his cheeks.

'Sinead, get your grandad,' Brigid ordered, pulling Sean away. 'Leave the boy, will you?' she demanded. 'Can't you be seeing he's near worn out. And you jumping and hollering like a lunatic.'

The room went silent as they saw Bryan still wore the clothes in which he'd been arrested, the white shirt encrusted with grime and dried blood. His face was lumped with yellow and purple bruises, one eye half closed and puffed.

'Oh God,' Sean breathed. 'They've proper smacked you, haven't they?'

'They did us all, Dad,' Bryan said simply, swaying a little. Brigid pushed a chair under his knees. He sat down heavily.

'What in Holy Mary's name, did they do?' Sean asked, anger swelling within him. 'Tell me, son.'

'Later, Sean. Later,' Brigid insisted, taking charge as usual. 'Can't you be waiting for the boy to get his breath and strength.'

'He's no longer a boy.'

Jack Aherne spoke quietly from the doorway. He'd stood there unnoticed, looked at his grandson slumped in the chair surrounded by his family.

'Look at him, can't you? He's a man now, not a boy,' Jack insisted.

Indeed, as they looked closer at Bryan, those around him could perceive that the soft features of adolescence had sharpened and set.

'Aye, you're a man now, son,' Sean said, a note of pride and wonder in his voice.

Bryan smiled wanly, nodded, then looked towards the door.

'And a rebel, too, grandad? Am I a rebel?'

Jack smiled broadly, remembering all their arguments about the Volunteers.

'A rebel? Bryan I'm not knowing about you, of course, being that you're your own man now, but I'm thinking they've turned us all into rebels.'

## Chapter 3 July, 1917

They'd been gathering throughout the afternoon on the large common above the beaches of Ballybunnion. The warm sun persuaded the bolder spirits to go down to the sands and paddle in the rippling shallows. There was hardly enough breeze off the Atlantic to fluff the crests of the ocean rollers tumbling through the tunnel in

Virgin's Rock offshore and into the caves worn out of the cliffs.

Curious children gathered outside the entrance to Cassidy's Health Emporium, tucked below the steep sandy track leading from the top of the cliffs to the beaches. Here, the tourists could soothe their aches and hangovers in a seaweed bath or take an invigorating saltwater shower. The former entailed dunking yourself in a tub of smelly, slippery kelp, then trying to avoid the voracious sand flies until the curious after-smell wore off. The latter involved standing naked in a wooden stall and being sluiced down with seawater through a hole in the roof.

The children delighted in hearing – and imitating – the shrieks of unknowing women who thought the shower was mechanical until Cassidy himself, beaming innocently, peered over the top of the stall to instruct them where to stand so that he could be certain of drenching their nudity with the contents of his bucket.

Many families, including the Ahernes, had decided to make the most of the afternoon, travelling in their hundreds to the tiny seaside resort on the Lartigue monorail train which ran the nine miles from Listowel. The women and children could enjoy a few hours on the beach before returning home, leaving their menfolk to the serious business of celebrating Eamon de Valera's win for Sinn Fein in the East Clare parliamentary by-election.

The sun was poised, sinking hugely orange behind Loop Head across the mouth of the Shannon to the west, before the men – Jack, Sean and Bryan – accompanied their families to the small station. They said their goodbyes, watched them depart on the strange train running on its raised track shaped like an inverted 'V', and started back towards the common.

By now, a makeshift platform had been erected there with trestle tables borrowed from Scanlan's Hotel. The Listowel fife and drum band, attracted by promises of free drink, was starting to play, drawing the crowd to the platform, luring the men from the taverns along the pot-holed track which was Ballybunnion's main, and only, street.

There was a feeling of expectation everywhere which didn't appeal to Jack Aherne, a grim, threatening resolve beneath the drink-inspired revelry. He glanced sideways at Bryan and saw a glint of excitement in the youngster's eyes. The old man prayed inwardly that, on this lovely evening, there wouldn't be any trouble like a week before. Then, the police barracks and some shops in Listowel had been stoned by a gang, purporting to be Sinn Feiners, after the win for Sinn Fein in Longford. The fact that Joe

MacGuiness had been in Lewes Jail, in the South of England, throughout the campaign had probably helped his narrow victory, as did the election slogan, 'Put Him In to Get Him Out'.

'There's too many bottles around for my liking,' Jack remarked sourly to no one in particular.

'Bound to be a wee bit of a hooley,' Sean said lightly.

'I know these young ruffians' hooleys,' his father went on darkly. 'They start laughing and end up crying. And, anyway, I thought all Sinn Feiners believed in discipline and proper behaviour.'

'They're not all Volunteers,' Bryan replied, pushing urgently through the crowd, waving now and again to friends. 'They might boast they are but they're not really.'

'And isn't that just the truth?' Jack sighed. 'To hear them tell it, the whole of Kerry mached into the Post Office behind Pearse.'

Bryan laughed, flicking his narrow-peaked cap on to the back of his head.

'At least some of us were prepared to, Grandad,' he called over his shoulder, adding with heavy, though affectionate sarcasm, 'And isn't that just the truth as well?'

'Get on you lummock,' Jack grunted, prodding him in the backside with his walking stick. 'Stop your told-you-so blathering and find my old bones somewhere to rest while I listen to the brayings from the platform.'

'Aren't you afeared of what you'll be hearing?' teased Bryan.

'Don't be cheeking your elders, young man,' Sean laughed. 'Do what grandad says and clear a space for us old 'uns among your rebel friends. I've a wee bottle in my back pocket that's getting awful heavy.'

'A bottle?' Jack gazed balefully at his son, shaking his head in mock reproof.

'The very best of medicine!'

'Is that so? Well, if it's medicine maybe I'll be taking a quiet sip for my legs. Mind you, it'll be just for my legs. I won't be enjoying it.'

The three generations of the Ahernes laughed aloud as they flopped on to the grass by the edge of the cliff, to the side of the platform.

'We won't be hearing too much from here,' Bryan complained without too much rancour.

'Enough, son, enough,' Sean muttered, pulling the cork from a half bottle of Jameson's whiskey. 'If it was de Valera I might be listening closer, but it'll be all the puffed up local gee-gaws spouting away or else I'm Brian Boru's brother.'

'And you're not that,' Jack interrupted, pulling the bottle out of Sean's grasp, sniffing it and tipping back a quick mouthful.

'Won't your pupils be seeing you?' Bryan asked, still teasing.

'A mouthful never hurt a nun,' Jack growled. 'And don't all the boys know my preferences well enough by now, having a gobbeen like you as a tittle-tattle in the family?'

The good humoured rebuke made Bryan redden with embarrassment. He should have known that his grandfather never missed anything at school, that he would have guessed that a deal of Bryan's popularity in the classroom had come from his intimate knowledge of 'Old Jack's' habits.

For all his brutal experiences in Tralee Prison, Bryan retained an adolescent sensitivity, although he tried to mask it with man-to-man banter. Like the others who'd been arrested after the Easter Rising the previous year, he was still held in some awe in North Kerry. Jack and Sean knew that he played up to the role of 'the hard man' with those of his age, the school-leavers entering the humdrum world of menial jobs, if any job at all. Neither of the older men believed that Bryan had been changed much. He hated the soldiers who'd beaten him but not all soldiers. He abhorred the British institutions and systems and policies which had caused so much pain and terror, not the British themselves. His feelings for his fellow Volunteers and Sinn Fein had deepened. They were no longer those of a starry-eyed romantic. They were more mature, more purposeful, mirroring, to a great extent, the change in Sinn Fein itself.

The suicidal uprising, centred in Dublin, had given Sinn Fein and its supporters in the Volunteers, now becoming known as the Irish Republican Army, a clear identity.

In the rebellion's aftermath, Unionists in Ulster agreed that the rest of Ireland could have Home Rule if their counties of influence were excluded. Redmond's Nationalists conceded the principle of exclusion, but only for a limited time. The convention wrangled itself into deadlock over which counties should be excluded before finally sinking into oblivion, helped by leading Conservatives in the wartime cabinet, who said openly that any part of Ireland excluded from Home Rule would remain so permanently.

Even Dublin's leading Unionist newspaper, the *Irish Times*, thought this was nonsense. 'In the first place, the country is too small to be divided between two systems of government,' its editorial column declared. 'In the next place, the political, social and economic qualities of North and South complement one another; one without the other must be miserably incomplete.'

The position of James Redmond and, thus, his Nationalist MPs, started to become untenable.

Even moderate nationalists realized that Remond was unlikely to produce Home Rule for all of Ireland, that his negotiations could lead only to partition.

That view was reinforced when Lloyd George succeeded as Prime Minister and promptly brought Sir Edward Carson, the Unionist leader, into his Cabinet. Ironically, the Westminster government helped to fill it by releasing in a Christmas amnesty five hundred rebels who had been held without trial in Britain since the rising.

Among them was a young man from West Cork named Michael Collins, a member of the London Centre of the IRB, who'd been in the Post Office during the week's fighting. Collins believed the rebellion's failure was due to poor organization. With the star of the moderate nationalists apparently on the wane, he saw the opportunity for Sinn Fein to establish political respectability. He used the Volunteers to build a professional election machine to campaign in a by-election in Roscommon. On February 17th, 1917, Count Plunkett, a Papal Count, father of Joseph Plunkett, executed after the Easter Rising, was elected on an anti-Redmond Home Rule ticket.

Plunkett declined to take his seat as an MP at Westminster, convening instead an 'Irish Assembly' – Dail Eireann – in Dublin. Twelve hundred delegates affirmed that Ireland was a separate nation and called for freedom from all foreign control.

The public's attitude towards Sinn Fein had already become apparent. During the Easter holiday, the IRB flew the orange, white and green tricolour from the ruins of the Post Office with little hindrance. Passers-by raised their hats or waved handkerchiefs at the flag and at what was fast becoming a national shrine. All over Dublin, posters appeared on walls with the message: 'The Irish Republic still lives!'

Easter also brought a further bonus for Sinn Fein, the release of another 117 rebels from prisons and internment camps, including the lanky, ascetic Eamonn de Valera, who'd been serving a twenty-year sentence after the death penalty was commuted. Michael Collins threw his well-tuned organization behind de Valera in East Clare and the result, with the implicit support of the hierarchy of the Catholic Church, was a third parliamentary win for Sinn Fein.

Roscommon, Longford, and now East Clare, reflected Jack Aherne, his eyes wandering over the crowd on the clifftop. He had to concede that, within less than eighteen months, Sinn Fein had achieved a miracle. Here, before him, was the proof.

The people gathered round the platform were of every age and class. Their headwear, Jack mused, showed that – panamas, straw boaters, homburgs, derbys, common or garden caps – worn by labourers and landowners, shopkeepers and solicitors, potmen and priests. Not all of them, of course, were active Sinn Fein supporters but nor were they opponents. Many, like Jack and Sean, were impressed by the movement's growth, its grip on the public's imagination. Now they wanted proof that Sinn Fein might be able to deliver its promise of coming to some sort of deal about Home Rule.

The band broke into a ragged fanfare as the main speaker scrambled untidily on hands and knees up on to the platform. It was Jack McKenna, the chairman of the county council, who'd led the victory celebrations in Listowel the week before. His speech hadn't improved in the days between, Jack quickly decided. McKenna rambled on, extolling the virtues of de Valera and Collins in particular, and Sinn Fein in general. His audience listened tolerantly, clapping and cheering at appropriate intervals.

'They'd clap if he read them *Alice in Wonderland*,' Jack murmured disparagingly. 'Sinn Fein'll have to do better than your man here if it's to get my vote.'

'Aye, Dad,' Sean replied, chewing on a blade of grass. 'He's as dry as stale soda bread, so he is.'

McKenna could see dozens in the crowd beginning to drift away, some towards the bars, others to the beach. In an effort to hold them, the politician's statements became more wild and inflammatory.

'Those who are not with us are agin us,' he shrieked, lifting his arms above his head. 'When Sinn Fein takes power, as we surely will, then names will be remembered. Those who've stood astride the progress of Ireland's march to freedom shall be called to account in this life as well as before the Supreme Judge.'

'Holy Mary!' Sean muttered. 'Your man's going it a bit strong.'

'Blathering windbag,' Jack remarked. 'But some are liking it as fighting talk.'

He nodded towards a group of about twenty youngsters at the back of the crowd. They were beginning to argue with some older, better-dressed men near them who apparently shared the Ahernes' opinion of the speech.

Two constables noticed the slight disturbance as well. They'd been standing well away from the meeting, arms folded, enjoying the tranquility of the early evening. As fists began to wave, they started in the direction of the arguing group at a measured, unhurried pace, thumbs in belts, confident that their mere presence would calm matters. They reckoned without being spotted by McKenna.

'And those who grovel for their Judas silver from the British Crown,' he declaimed, pointing at the constables, 'will be thrice judged and condemned. By the people, by Sinn Fein, and by their Maker. There are some among us even now who profess to be God-fearing Irishmen yet glory in their wearing of the oppressor's chosen uniform. They are no more fit to claim their Irish manhood than . . . than . . .'

The politician hesitated, searching for words.

' . . . than . . . than the porkers in the field,' McKenna ended lamely. But his words had their effect, desired or otherwise.

The group of young men, all about Bryan's age, gleefully turned their attentions to the hapless constables. Any of their usual inhibitions had been drowned by too many pints of porter.

They encircled the constables, jeering and jostling them.

'Porkers . . . porkers . . . porkers . . .' they chanted. Two or three began oinking like pigs.

Even from a distance, Jack and Sean, now standing up to get a better view, could see the constables' embarrassment turn to anger.

'The ruffians!' Jack exclaimed. 'They'll be in trouble.'

The first blow was struck before he finished speaking. The older constable, grey sideburns visible under his uniform cap, pushed one of his tormentors in the chest, trying to clear a pathway. The youngster retaliated with a wild swing which missed its intended target completely but caught the second constable on the side of the face. Suddenly, everyone started punching and kicking at the policemen. They nearly fell under the onslaught until one managed to clear his truncheon from his belt and began to strike out. The sharp crack-crack-crack of wood on bone sang into the greying dusk.

Instinctively, the people not involved in the fracas surged away from the area, some slipping and falling on the grass in their haste, crying out in alarm. Both police truncheons were whirling, forcing a gap in the crowd. The constables shouldered their way through, both bloodied about the face, and ran bare headed across the green, heading for the police barracks some two hundred yards away. Their attackers paused for a moment and then set off in pursuit, open waistcoats flapping, screaming their hatred.

'After 'em lads,' McKenna shouted, jumping up and down on the platform, once almost tumbling over the edge in his excitement.

'Give 'em a pummelin' for de Valera himself! After 'em! Quick now!'

Jack threw his cap on the ground in disgust and frustration.

'The doltards!' he exclaimed. 'Just what they shouldn't be doing, the clods!'

'I'll be stopping it, Grandad,' Bryan cried. 'I'll get them off.'

He raced off across the springy turf, arms and legs pumping.

Sean called once, vainly attempting to stop his son, shrugged despairingly and watched him weave through the panicked crowd before disappearing between the first cabins of the village.

By the time Bryan had caught up with the mob outside the two-storey police barracks, it had doubled in size with more inebriated young men anxious to join the police baiting. He battled his way to the front, searching for any familiar faces. Chanting broke out.

'Come out, porkers! Come on out, you porkers, or we'll fry you where you are! Come out and fight!'

There was no particularly vicious intent behind the shouts. Bryan knew they were simply drunken bravado, designed to impress friends rather than scare the trapped police. A small stone lobbed out of the crowd and clattered on to the slate tiles of the roof. A dozen more followed.

'For God's sake, boys!' Bryan bawled, facing directly into the milling crowd. 'Go to your homes before there's more trouble. Go to . . .'

'And why should we?' a stocky, fresh-faced youngster protested. 'It's fun we're having. Just fun.'

Bryan recognized him as Simon Mulvihill, a Volunteer about his own age, a relative of the Mulvihill killed in the Easter Rising.

'There'll be broken heads this night if you don't, Simon,' he called.

'A baton charge? With only six of the bastards in there? They'd not be so foolish, Bryan Aherne. Come on and take a shy at the porkers.'

'They said we're to cause no trouble.'

'Who said?'

'Michael Collins did.'

'And where's he?'

'In Dublin, I suppose.'

'You suppose . . . well, he's not here then to give his orders, is he?'

Simon Mulvihill ended the shouting match by picking up another stone from the hard-packed earth which made up the village's only street. He waved it defiantly at Bryan before tossing it at the police barracks. This time there was the crash of broken glass in an upper window. The mob cheered and began stoning the building in earnest.

Bryan moved away in despair. He had seen their slack mouths, their wild eyes, their staggering gait. He knew the young men, hardly any of them more than twenty years old, were out of control. What was happening was specifically against the orders of the Sinn Fein leadership. Such rioting could only harm the carefully constructed image of a respectable political organization. It would frighten away the moderate nationalists, the vast bulk of the people who were essential to Sinn Fein's success.

The people of Ballybunnion stood watching from their doorways or their window-sills. The thudding and splintering of stones on brick and slate, the jeering and shouting followed Bryan as he walked sadly back to the clifftop. He was so deep in thought that he paid little heed to the sudden, flatter crack echoing along the row of small houses and cabins. A woman shrieked. Bryan turned in surprise.

'Jesus, they're shooting!' someone shouted.

Bryan saw orange muzzle flashes at the first-storey windows of the barracks. The constables, panicking and vengeful, were firing a volley at the youngsters, trying to scare them off. The front two rows dropped to the ground, screaming, covering their heads with their arms. The others, sobbing aloud with fear, scattered every which way, bumping and bowling into each other in the confusion.

The noise died away with the last echoes of hastily slammed doors and windows and the startled cries of wheeling starlings. The silence. was filled with terror and bewilderment and shock. And then it was no longer silence. A scream of excruciating agony pierced upwards from among the piles of young men lying in the street. Bryan rose from his crouching position by a wall and ran towards the sound.

He stepped over people who were just beginning to sit up, some groaning, winded by their falls. Only one lay on his back, hands between thighs, rocking from side to side with pain, mouth wide open in a continuous, high-pitched scream. Simon Mulvihill knelt beside him on one knee, looking down, his fingers stuck into his ears, trying to cut out the horrendous sound.

'Is he hit?' Bryan demanded. 'For God's sake, where's he hit?'

Simon didn't reply, just nodded his head, retching bile which dribbled between his lips.

Byran's eyes slid over the gawky young man lying on the ground.

There was no apparent wound in his head, his chest, his arms, his . . .

'Oh, God!' Bryan gasped. 'Oh, Holy Mother! Oh, Jesus!' He felt his throat tighten and dry, his back shiver.

Blood welled up through the wounded man's hands, cupped round his genitals. There was no wound to see, just the blood, pulsing, unending like the scream.

Bryan put a hand out, edging it towards the blood. The man's eyes, staring out of their sockets, saw the movement. He tried to roll his lower body away. His head thrashed from side to side in protest. The scream trailed away, replaced by a single word which had no ending itself.

'Noooooo . . . !'

'It's his cock!' choked Simon Mulvihill, wiping the vomit from his mouth. 'That's what the bastard police did. Shot him in the cock. My best friend shot in the cock. The bastard divils!'

'Where's the doctor here?'

'In the bar.'

'The bar?'

'At Scanlan's. That's where he was before the meeting, the drunken soak.'

'We'll carry your man. Get some others.'

Six were needed to carry the wounded man, each step making him jerk and cry with agony. Blood dripped steadily, marking their progress.

Someone ran ahead to warn the doctor. By the time the bearing party arrived, he'd hastily covered a sofa in the hotel's small front lounge with a white sheet.

The taproom customers lined the narrow corridor to the lounge, clutching their bottles and glasses.

'Who is it?' they asked blearily with the concern that only drunks can muster. 'Who's the poor wee fellow?'

'It's young Danny Scanlon,' someone answered. 'Send word for his ma, will you?'

'Hurry!' urged Simon Mulvihill. 'He's hurt something awful. Hurry! There mayn't be too much time.'

His prognosis was tacitly confirmed by the doctor's expression after he'd uncovered the wound.

'Bandages . . . sheets . . . anything . . . ' the doctor muttered. He was a man of late middle age whose mauve veined nose betrayed his weakness. 'Helped him into the world myself I did,' he went on, as he improvised a thick pad to cover the wound. 'It's a terrible sin this. Terrible.'

Within minutes, the pad was soaked through, scarlet. The doctor waved chloroform under his patient's nostrils and tried to make him swallow sips of laudanum. Gradually, Danny Scanlon grew quieter. Fresh pads were continually pressed to the wound between the legs. They simply soaked up his life-blood.

'Is he to live?' Simon Mulvhill asked.

The doctor shrugged helplessly, gesturing at the ever reddening bandages.

'Time,' he murmured. 'Just time.'

'There's no . . . nothing?' Bryan interrupted.

'The bleeding, you see, son,' the doctor said confidentially. 'Not the wound, though that's bad enough. It's the bleeding.'

'Perhaps a mercy what with his . . . his . . . shot away.'

'Aye, perhaps so. The Lord knows best.'

Bryan moved away from the sofa and stood by the door. A glass was thrust into his hand. He gulped neat whiskey and felt little effect. His brain focused on small details; a patch of discoloured wallpaper, the fraying edge on the faded rug, a circle of grease on the back of one of the chairs. Some time during the next hours, he was aware of his father and grandfather coming to his shoulder.

'Not yet,' Bryan whispered, thinking they had come to take him home.

Sean Aherne patted his forearm reassuringly.

'No, son. Not yet. When you're ready we'll be in the bar.'

Bryan nodded his thanks.

It took Danny Scanlon hours to bleed to death. Towards four o'clock in the morning his eyes opened. They drifted round the faces before him; the priest, the doctor, his mother, his friends. He smiled slightly. 'Oh, Jesus and Mary come against me,' he murmured before his eyes closed. He didn't stir again.

The only sign that he had finally died was the doctor straightening up from beside the sofa and stroking a finger and thumb over the young man's almost transparent eyelids, closing them forever.

Bryan crossed himself and pushed his way into the taproom to find his family. It was light outside the hotel when they set off in Charlie Walsh's jaunty cart for home. Knots of people stood around on the grass by the clifftop talking quietly about the night's tragedy. The stones of the castle ruins glinted wet with dew. The houses in the village were curtained and shut. Breaking glass tinkled again and again further down the track leading out of Ballybunnion.

Simon Mulvihill didn't look up at the cart as it swayed and clattered past him. He was too intent, tears streaming down his face, on smashing every window in the deserted police barracks.

'He said he was his best friend,' Bryan explained, his voice dull with tiredness.

'Aye,' Jack grunted. 'It hurts to see someone close die.'

'But why him? He wasn't much older nor younger than me. All he was doing was having some fun. A bit in drink, maybe, but not deserving of that.'

'No, not that. Not there,' Charley Walsh called back from the driving seat. 'No one deserves that. He's a martyr, so he is. The first martyr since the Easter Rising.'

'He'll appreciate that, Charley. He really will,' Jack said with heavy sarcasm. 'So will his mam. We must have martyrs, mustn't we? Martyrs and saints. The land's littered with them, to be sure.'

'Do you think they'll remember him?' Bryan asked, jerking a thumb at an old man on the roadside with a donkey laden with two wicker baskets of cut turf.

'Who?'

'Ballybunnion.'

'Oh, they will that,' his grandfather replied, wiping his dark ringed eyes. 'In a few years, there'll be tell of the lad attacking the police barracks single-handed and falling in glorious battle. Martyrs have to be heroes, Bryan, not beardless boys who die terrified and hurting something awful. If martyrs died like people really do die, why no one would want to be a martyr.'

## Chapter 4 November, 1917

Bryan Aherne waited an hour after the last goodnights had been called before lifting himself gently off his bed. He pulled his night shirt over his head, buttoned up the outdoor clothes he was still wearing underneath, and slid a hand under the mattress for his revolver. He tiptoed gingerly down the two flights of stairs from his room, laced up his boots by the front door and slipped noiselessly out into the street. The lamps had been shut off an hour earlier, at midnight, leaving enough patches of dark shadow under the bright winter moon to conceal his progress for the couple of hundred yards past the darkened police barracks to the gates of St Michael's College.

The wrought iron gates squeaked gratingly. He paused before going through them, looking round to check that no one was watching. The windows of the college facing him down the drive were dark. The priests, the teachers, were asleep like the rest of Listowel. Bryan leaned against the brick wall by the gates, regained his breath and whistled low the opening bars of *Danny Boy*.

A voice interrupted throatily from the shrubbery on the opposite side of the drive.

'Over here. We're over here!'

He darted across the drive just as three figures emerged, crouched, from their hiding place.

'You're late,' Jimmy Sugrue muttered.

'My dad didn't come from the bar till late.'

Paddy Costelloe, one of the few teetotallers in the Volunteers, if not the whole of Kerry, sniffed disapprovingly.

'Stop the blathering and let's get on,' snapped Davy Lanigan. 'Your man'll be too fast asleep for us to wake him if we don't move.'

Crestfallen by his reception, Bryan nodded and followed his three older companions as they ran quickly across Upper Church Street and into the curving drive of the rectangular Victorian villa directly opposite the college gates. They moved stealthily down the drive, keeping to the edge of the lawn, until they were about twenty yards from the front porch.

'Time for the masks, I'm thinking,' Sugrue whispered.

The four Volunteers pulled handkerchiefs from their pockets and tied them across their mouths and nostrils.

Sugrue pointed towards the middle of the lawn in front of the house.

'There,' he told Lanigan. 'Dig there and make it the proper shape. We don't want just a bloody great hole, remember.'

'But . . . but . . . ' Lanigan protested. 'It's in full sight of the street!'

Costelloe sniffed again.

'Folk'll have to see what's done,' he mumbled. 'Or there's no gain is there?'

Lanigan shrugged, hoisted a spade on to his shoulder, and walked on to the grass. He cut through the turf, blessing the fact that frost hadn't yet gripped the earth – it was soft and yielding. The spade bit into the earth as he dug, his breath clouding on the cold air.

The other three walked swiftly to the front door. Sugrue rapped on the glass and banged the knocker while Bryan and Costelloe stood behind him, revolvers in hand. The feel of the cold metal eased Bryan's nerves.

He shivered slightly and wondered whether it was coldness, nervousness or excitement. Although this night's work wasn't exactly blessed by the Volunteers' commanders, he thought, they were bound to be impressed if it went off successfully. Nobody had yet dared to move against Lord Listowel in any way at all so an attack on his right hand man, his land agent, Marshall Hill, was certain to cause a stir. It was just the sort of action to bring the young men to the attention of their officers. And that was precisely their purpose. Until now, the four inseperable friends had obeyed orders to the letter, attracting no particular praise while other Volunteers had undertaken unofficial freelance operations, winning swaggering notoriety.

Bryan's grip on his revolver tightened when he heard the bolts being drawn on the other side of the door.

'Who is it?' a man's voice asked.

'From his lordship, Mr Hill,' Sugrue replied, turning to Costelloe and winking. 'We've a message from his lordship.'

A wedge of light broke into their faces. Instinctively, Bryan checked that his mask was pulled up.

'Yes?' a short bewhiskered man inquired, poking his face round the door.

Sugrue didn't reply. He simply barged his shoulder into the door, thrusting it open, sending the middle-aged man reeling back down the hallway. Surprise flitted across his face, then anger, and finally terror as he saw the three young men walk into his house, each with their revolver pointing at him. Bryan felt almost sorry for the land agent.

'In there,' Sugrue ordered, waving his gun in the direction of the drawing room. Costelloe grabbed Marshall Hill under one arm. Bryan took the other, pushing their captive into a high-backed chair near the still-glowing fire.

The land agent's spirit began to return.

'Rogues and vagabonds!' he kept spluttering while Costelloe tied him to the chair. 'His lordship will have your hides. You'll rot in prison for this!'

'Shut your gob or it'll be shut for you!'

385

Costelloe's voice, though muffled by his handkerchief, was laconic, threatening. It ensured a tense silence broken only when Sugrue ushered Marshall Hill's wife into the room after rousing her from bed. She held the front of her dressing gown tightly round her neck. Her hair was spiky with grips and ribbons. Her face glistened with night cream and fearful perspiration.

'Swine! Oh, you swine!' Hill exclaimed when he saw her. He wriggled and strained so vigorously at the ropes binding him that the chair wobbled, then toppled to the floor. The land agent lay on the thick rug, gasping. His wife ran to him, beginning to sob. She tried to lift him but his weight was too much. He thudded back on to the rug, winding himself again.

'Here, missus,' said Bryan, hating to see the couple in so much distress. 'Leave him to me.'

He heaved the chair upright and stood back to allow Mrs Hill to embrace and comfort the bound man.

'Does bring tears to the eyes,' Costelloe remarked without a trace of genuine sentiment or pity.

'Shut up,' Sugrue ordered. 'We're not here to hurt them.'

'Of course, we're not,' Bryan chimed in. He realized immediately that he might have sounded too glad that violence wasn't contemplated so he added, as menacingly as he could, 'Well, leastways not if you give us what we want.'

'My jewels are upstairs,' Mrs Hill volunteered quickly, eagerly. 'Take them and be off with you. Mr Hill's heart won't . . .'

'We're not wanting your jewels, missus,' Sugrue stated flatly.

'What then?' muttered Hill, ashen grey and running with sweat.

'We were thinking you'd like to be contributing to the Volunteers,' Bryan said helpfully.

'What! What!' Hill exclaimed, indignation and rage overcoming fear. 'Contributing to you Sinn Feiners? Help you rebels? You're nothing more than ruffians, just rogues, just . . .'

The words strangled in his throat as Costelloe thrust the muzzle of his revolver against the land agent's left ear and clicked back the hammer.

'Your guns,' Bryan interrupted urgently, worried that Costelloe might pull the trigger. 'That's all we're wanting. Just your hunting guns.'

'In the gun room,' Mrs Hill cried, wringing her hands anxiously.

Sugrue nodded and left the room, returning a few minutes later with a rifle and four shotguns clapped in both arms and with his pockets bulging with boxes of cartridges and bullets.

'Right, boys,' he called from the doorway. 'Let's away now.'

'What about them?' Costelloe asked, waving his revolver at Marshall Hill and his wife. 'We don't want them raising the chase.'

'They won't be so foolish, what with our man waiting outside till we're away.'

Beneath his mask, Bryan smiled at the bluff. He grabbed Costelloe's arm and urged him from the room. But Costelloe wasn't satisfied. His obvious desire to hurt began to frighten Bryan.

'And no doubt these high-and-mightys will have a telephone.' Costelloe went on, shaking off Bryan's hand. 'Have you thought of that?'

Sugrue laughed. 'They have that, but somehow the wires aren't working since I cut them.'

Costelloe grunted his satisfaction.

'And by the by,' Sugrue continued to the Hills, 'I wouldn't be too hasty about telling the police too much. When you draw your curtains in the morning, you'll be seeing a reminder of what could happen if you open your gobs too wide.'

'Swine!' the land agent exclaimed again, his anger returning now he sensed his ordeal was nearly over.

'Shush, dearest,' murmured his wife, who wasn't as confident.

'Untie him in fifteen minutes, missus. No sooner, mind. Remember our man outside,' Sugrue said, backing towards the front door.

The three young Volunteers ran on to the front lawn where Lanigan, by now was up to his hips in the hole.

'Leave on, now, Davy,' Bryan called. 'That's deep enough.'

Lanigan clambered up on to the grass and vanished into the night with his friends, all of them, even the dour Costelloe, laughing with relief and self-admiration.

Bryan lay awake for almost an hour when he reached home, remembering every detail of the raid. Just before he went to sleep, the thought came to him about whether it was right that he should have felt so good, so alive, when his revolver had been in his hand and pointing at defenceless people. His mind was too tired to provide an answer.

A few hours later, Marshall Hill parted the curtains of the drawing room.

There, in the centre of the prize camomile lawn, was a hole, a grave dug in the shape of a coffin. Mrs Hill seemed transfixed by the sight.

'Oh, the bastards. The young bastards,' Marshall Hill cursed, comforting his wife. The message was clear to him.

The townsfolk of Listowel, walking along Upper Church Street, saw the grave as well. The warning needed no explanations. It was, in fact, becoming all too common.

It needed the detailed view of older men, such as Jack Aherne, to fully comprehend the rising tide of violence and intimidation that autumn and during the winter months leading into the year of 1918.

The youngsters like his grandson, could only think of those days as a series of incidents, each more hilarious and daring than the one before. Imperceptibly they were growing used to violence, embracing it as a way of life, as a philosophy. Those of naturally violent natures gloried in the ripening lawlessness. The others, the great majority, came gradually to accept it as nothing out of the ordinary.

The Volunteers were now drilling openly again, better equipped and disciplined than before, usually in the market square or in the grounds of St Michael's College. Often, when the parades were over, half a dozen of them would toss bricks at the police barracks in Upper Church Street, shout insults, then hare away before any constables dared emerge to give chase.

Farms and houses were raided for weapons. Unpopular landlords had their crops ploughed up and their best stock lamed. They would wake in the morning, as Lord Listowel's agent had done, to find a warning grave on their land.

Tit-for-tat reprisals began from those opposed to Sinn Fein. They called themselves 'The Black Hand Gang' and burned down halls used for meetings by the Volunteers or sent threatening letters to their leaders.

The authorities retaliated by banning all meetings and parades.

Soon, thirty Volunteers of all ranks were on hunger strike in Mountjoy Prison after being sentenced for drilling or making seditious speeches. They demanded the status of prisoners of war, refused to wear uniform and smashed up their cells.

On April 9th, the British Government announced that military conscription would be extended to Ireland. Lloyd George forgot all his earlier prevarication and offered Ireland immediate Home Rule, although with the partition of Ulster.

He declared ringingly, 'When the young men of Ireland are brought into the firing line, it's imperative that they should feel they are not fighting for establishing a principle abroad which is denied to them at home.'

The Irish people remembered the tens of thousands who'd already given their lives voluntarily. They united in their opposition to conscription and, this time, united behind Sinn Fein. On April 18th, political leaders of every persuasion met in Dublin to condemn the British Government.

Their condemnation was echoed at meetings in towns and cities throughout the country. In Listowel, there hadn't been such a gathering since the heyday of Parnell and the Land Leaguers.

The Ahernes rushed their Sunday lunch wanting to be early in the market square to obtain a good position. To their dismay, they found dozens already clustered around the platform outside the Arms Hotel decorated with tricolours and a large banner stretching overhead which proclaimed, 'No Conscription – Stand United'.

Maude Aherne looked anxiously at her husband, Aunt Brigid and her grandchildren. She worried how they would endure the crush in the warm spring afternoon. Her son noticed the expression on her face and understood.

'Wait here,' Sean said. 'I'll be seeing what I can do about a better place.'

Ten minutes later, Jack, Maude and Brigid sat by one of the windows on the first floor of the Arms Hotel with four of the grandchildren grouped around. Sean and Finoola stood just outside the hotel entrance behind the platform, while Bryan insisted on going off on his own, saying he wanted to stand in front of the speakers.

Bryan had another reason for wandering off, a girl with hair the colour of ripened wheat. He prayed she would come as she said she would. It would be too much to hope that she would be alone. He caught sight of her, pressed against the railing of St Mary's Church, right at the back of the throng. Her long straight tresses were instantly recognizable at a distance and even when partially hidden by a wide-brimmed straw hat tied with red ribbons. It had been the colour of her hair, so unusual in this part of Kerry, that had caught his attention first during a Volunteers' route march to Ballylongford. She'd watched the ranks of men swing by from behind the wall of her parents' small dairy farm by Galey Bridge, three miles from Listowel. She'd smiled shyly at the young man. All of them ogled her. Only Bryan had cycled back the very next day. Then, in his own shyness, he'd forgotten to ask her name until he was on the point of leaving, when her mother had called her back into the farmhouse for tea.

'It's Hannah,' she'd called after Bryan had cycled away, his machine wobbling. 'Hannah Wilmot.'

He needed all his strength and height to shove his way out of the crowd to where Hannah stood. She, and presumably her parents, were too intent watching the speakers gather on the platform to notice his approach.

Bryan coughed, exhaling a deep breath.

'So . . . so you came,' he spluttered, pulling off his cap.

'I said we probably would,' she replied demurely.

Her mother, small and round and neat, turned when she heard her daughter's voice. Mrs Wilmot's gaze was friendly yet appraising.

'Mother,' Hannah said coolly, 'This is the young man I told you about. Bryan Aherne.'

'Mr Aherne. A pleasure, I'm sure.'

'Mr Aherne's a Volunteer,' Hannah said by way of an introduction to her father.

'Are you young man? Are you indeed? And what might you be volunteering for?' Hannah's father smiled, winking.

Bryan liked Mr Wilmot immediately. His eyes were, at the same time, shrewd and twinkling, set deep in a ruddy-hued face.

'Well, Mr Wilmot, anything you might care to suggest,' he responded, quickly put at ease by their obvious friendliness. 'I'll be volunteering for anything except that,' he continued, pointing at the anti-conscription banner high above the platform.

'We'll be discussing that maybe, Mr Aherne, some other time, but for now I'm thinking the speechifying is about to start.'

'Then may I join you to listen?' he asked, hoping that he didn't sound too formal.

'Note the young man's manners, mother,' Hannah's father said drily, winking at Bryan again. 'A town boy for sure.'

Bryan realized that he was having his leg pulled but, before he could think of a suitable reply, clapping rippled through the crowd. The main speaker stepped forward to the rail at the edge of the platform, arms upraised for silence. The crowd went quiet, recognizing the town's curate, Father Charles O'Sullivan.

'Fellow citizens,' he began, his deep voice reaching easily to every section of the crowd. 'Fellow citizens, with all my soul I say it is good to be here, it is good to be alive today when the hour of national redemption is nearer at hand than any of us could have hoped for.'

A huge, approving cry rose into the air, lifting the rooks out of their crannies in the ruined keep of Listowel Castle.

' . . . Mankind has reason to remember that day when a money-tax imposed by England led to the birth of a nation and the uprising of the American constitution. Mankind shall have as much reason to bless this day when a blood-tax imposed by England has called forth this declaration which, with God's help and an even more sacred human right, shall carry Ireland along the same glorious way of salvation.'

Father O'Sullivan's right hand, holding the Bible, shot into the air. The crowd cheered and clapped. Bryan looked quickly at Hannah. She smiled back. The young man felt suddenly very possessive towards her. He was elated at the priest's powerful words. He felt part of Ireland, part of its history, simply being in the market square this warm April afternoon. His attention was dragged back to the platform.

'We accept the passing of this conscription law,' Father O'Sullivan roared, 'as a declaration of war on the part of England upon the Irish nation!'

The priest waited for fresh cheers to subside before leaning forward confidentially over the platform's single wooden railing. His voice began again softly but grew in pitch and power, until it boomed and battered at the bricks of the surrounding houses and shops and taverns. A horse tethered behind St John's Church in the centre of the square threw up its head, shaking its mane, scared by the noise. The crowd, some open-mouthed, stood transfixed by the oratory.

'I will tell you plainly what the issue is – whether Irish women, the mothers of our blood, the Irish men, the guardians of our manhood, whose sires have proved in many a bloody battle that they were the owners of their own souls – whether Irish women and Irish men are the owners of their own lives and bodies and blood or whether these things are the property of the Cromwellian breed whose names have often been written in blood over the graves and corpses of small people.

'In God's truth, this is the issue – whether we are freemen in our blessed land given to us by God, or chattels to be disposed of by barter; whether we are freemen or pawns to be played off in a game of political strategy; whether we are freemen or a mere human crop to be seized and mown down by military incompetence; whether we are freemen or slaves to be led to the slaughter by hungry capitalists and greedy traffickers. This is the issue which the people of Ireland are preparing themselves today to fight out to the end.'

The shout of acclaim from the people of Listowel was so overwhelming, so rousing, that Hannah and her mother pressed their hands to their ears.

'Listen!' Bryan shouted, his lips close to Hannah's ear. 'Listen!

Have you ever heard such words? They'll have to take heed of us now. Surely they will!'

Hannah nodded her head up and down, eyes laughing, still trying to block out the noise.

Her father leaned over and tapped Bryan on the shoulder.

'Did you hear him? Did you just hear the curate, Bryan? War, he said! A declaration of war!'

'And war he meant if they force us into the army,' Bryan shouted back.

All around, people were laughing and hugging each other. The hysteria lasted a full five minutes before the crowd began to regain control of itself. Women patted their hair back into place, men fiddled with their ties and cuffs, a few clearly regretting such open displays of emotion. Family groups started to drift away.

'Come on, Father,' said Mrs Wilmot, 'There's the cows to be milked and Hannah has the chickens to feed.'

Her husband seemed disappointed at being dragged back to reality. He grinned lopsidedly at Bryan.

'Young man, exposed for all the world to see are the burdens of being a poor farmer. Women and animals wait for no man. You see that? Well, you better be remembering it.'

Bryan smiled, shrugging, unsure if he was meant to reply. He'd hoped for more time with Hannah, perhaps a stroll around the town.

'You have to go then?'

'We do that,' Mrs Wilmot replied, firmly, offering her arm to her husband. Hannah stayed silent but the downcast expression on her face told Bryan that she would have preferred to remain a while.

'Well,' he said lamely. 'Well, it's been . . . '

'We're at home on Sunday afternoons usually,' Mrs Wilmot interrupted, seeing his glum expression. 'That's if you'd care to call sometime.'

'May I?' Bryan asked eagerly. 'May I . . . next Sunday perhaps?'

Hannah grinned delightedly. Her hair shimmered as it caught the sun. Her father smiled his agreement.

Bryan called the next Sunday at the farm at Galey Bridge and on the following two Sundays before deciding that he'd better tell his family about Hannah. Nervously, he broached the subject only to be met with suppressed giggles: they had known about her ever since the anti-conscription meeting. His grandfather's sharp eyes had spotted them together from his vantage point in the Arms Hotel.

'You're not minding?' he asked defensively.

'Mind? Mind? Why should we?' his mother replied, eyes brimming with amusement and love. 'We're looking forward to meeting her . . . if you choose . . . when you're ready, of course.'

And so, during that summer and autumn, Bryan and Hannah became accepted in and around Listowel as a couple whose families had visited each other and had properly approved the courtship. Not that there was any question yet of becoming formally engaged. They were simply walking together. There didn't seem the time for much more, as events around them moved with increasing momentum.

The groundswell of protest against the conscription law was all that the more militant Volunteer companies needed to step up their campaign of raids and intimidation. Farmers opposed to Sinn Fein, fearing attack, mounted all night guards over their property, but that didn't prevent their animals being mutilated, their barns being burned, nor the macabre warning graves being dug.

Bryan found himself so involved in the planning and execution of these raids that he scarcely had time for his work, albeit casual, at his father's tavern. His rows with his family grew more frequent as their anxiety increased about his activities, but they were powerless to stop him. He didn't even bother to hide his prized revolver from them.

It was as if he were a person split in two. He loved and respected his family, but in the company of the Volunteers, he was as dedicated as any to spreading fear and chaos. Like thousands of young men that spring and summer of 1918, both in the trenches of France and the countryside of Ireland, Bryan Aherne was being moulded by events totally outside his control. There was no going back.

Ironically, the threat of conscription, which had handed so many political cards to Sinn Fein, was shelved as an exhausted German army fell back before the Allies' counter-offensive. But the Government in London quickly provided another *cause célèbre* for the hard-line nationalists.

On May 17th, seventy-three Sinn Fein leaders were arrested, including Eamon de Valera. Within months, more than five hundred people in Ireland were in prison. The charges ranged from concealing weapons to offences such as answering policemen in Irish, and singing songs like 'Wrap the Green Flag round me Boys' Each arrest was another victory for Sinn Fein.

A voluntary recruiting campaign during these months of arrests and repression still produced more than ten thousand Irishmen willing to fight for the British Crown. But that mattered little during the General Election called for December, 1918, weeks after the

Great War ended. Most of the soldiers, loyal to the Crown, never received voting papers because of maladministration. Their absence from the ballot added to Sinn Fein's resounding victory. The Ulster Unionists were badly mauled, gaining a majority in only four of the nine counties to which they laid claim.

For the first time in Irish history, a political party pledged to total independence from Britain had won power. It was swift to capitalize on its supremacy, despite the number of its leaders still in prison.

On January 21st, 1919, Sinn Fein called Dail Eireann, the national assembly, into session at the Mansion House in Dublin. It issued a Declaration of Independence, announced an official constitution, and appointed ministers.

Yet no agreement had been reached with the British Government and British troops effectively controlled the country with the help of British-controlled policemen.

What concerned the Irish more were the killings, a few days after Dail Eireann began sitting, of two constables, shot at point-blank range by four masked Volunteers, acting on their own initiative, at Soloheadbeg in County Tipperary.

There was little else to discuss when the newspapers printed the gory details side by side with the frantic condemnations of the Catholic hierarchy. No one could believe that Sinn Fein would order such a deed. No one could distinguish, not even the learned churchmen, between the public voices of Michael Collins and Cathal Brugha, urging moderation, and their private advice and instructions to the Volunteers firmly under their control. It was no different in Listowel.

'Wasn't it dreadful? Those poor constables . . .' Hannah Wilmot remarked, sitting next to Bryan Aherne on the narrow, lumpy sofa in the front room of the farmhouse at Galey Bridge.

Bryan glanced at the rain pelting against the small, quartered windows. He'd have to borrow a coat from Hannah's father for his return home. It had been clear and cold when he'd set out on his bicycle.

'Hum,' he grunted, not really listening. His eyes darted towards the wooden door leading to the kitchen. As always, it was a few inches ajar. He knew Hannah's parents were sitting in there by the warm range, trying not to listen to the young people's conversation, yet with ears pricked for the tiniest rustle of impropriety. At least, he thought, they were better than some parents who would never let their daughter alone in a room with a young man under any circum-

394

stances. He reckoned it was a fair compromise to leave the door open those few inches.

'I said, wasn't it awful bad about those constables?' Hannah repeated, nudging him gently with her forearm.

'Yes . . . eh, yes . . . terrible sad,' Bryan muttered.

'Their poor wives and children.'

'Yes.'

'Do you think they'll catch them?'

'Who's knowing?'

His hand slid over the shiny leather of the sofa. He touched Hannah's fingers. Their hands twined, squeezing. They didn't look at each other for a moment, savouring the contact of each other's flesh.

'Do you think they were Volunteers like the newspapers say?' Hannah asked, her eyes fixed straight ahead on the fringe of the green cloth hanging from the mantelpice.

'The newspapers say anything,' said Bryan, repeating the message he'd heard so often from his commanders.

'But if they were Volunteers?' Hannah persisted.

'They're not!'

'But if they were, you wouldn't help them, would you?'

Her eyes searched his face. Her lips were so near. He bent his head fractionally closer.

'Help them?'

Their lips were inches apart. He could feel her breath, smell upon it the fresh milk she'd drunk at teatime.

'Do things like they did, if they did . . . with guns . . . shoot . . .kill people.'

Bryan shook his head, his lips brushing hers for an instant before their hands drew apart.

'Still raining,' he remarked, louder, suddenly very conscious of the folded sheets of paper in the inside pocket of his jacket.

Bryan didn't want to show Hannah, her parents, his family, or anyone, the current issue of the Volunteers' secret journal, *An t-Óglach, The Soldier*.

This informed the Volunteers that they were now regarded as the army of Ireland, the Dail Eireann claimed the right of 'every free national government' to inflict death on the enemies of the state.

Cathal Brugha, the son of a Yorkshireman who'd been christened Charles Burgess, presiding in the Dail in the absence in Lincoln Gaol of de Valera, had personally vetted the secret statement.

'Enemies of the state,' it continued, 'are soldiers or policemen of the British Government whom every Volunteer is entitled morally and legally to slay if it is necessary to do so in order to overcome their resistance.'

'Don't worry about the rain,' Hannah said, breaking into his thoughts. 'There must be a spare cape somewhere round the farm.'

She traced her fingernail across the ball of his thumb. Bryan shivered.


## Chapter 5 June, 1920


The small locomotive from Newcastle West and Abbeyfeale, smart in green and black livery, was the obligatory ten minutes late when it puffed and chugged into the station platform at Listowel that sunny June day. If it had been on time it would have upset half the townsfolk who regulated their clocks in the certain knowledge of the noon train's consistently late arrival.

To give him his due, the stationmaster noticed immediately that the locomotive was pulling four carriages, rather than the normal two, and he did wonder why the driver gave three blasts on his whistle instead of just one. His porters were busy opening the first class doors and hunting down tipping customers with the minimum of baggage.

It was the station boy, Billy Mahony, leaning on his broom, who saw them begin disembarking from the last two carriages, kitbags and rifles slung over their shoulders.

'Look at their uniforms!' the lad exclaimed. 'Which regiment would they be from?'

The stationmaster, Henry McGill, did look, face blanching, and then scurried through the ticket gates and off towards the centre of the town. On the way, he told everyone he knew about the arrivals. Finally, considering his duty done and sweating profusely under the midday heat, the stationmaster subsided into his favourite nook in the Castle Bar and gulped down a glass of porter before repeating his news to anyone who cared to listen. His alert ensured a good crowd outside the station to watch the men march away.

People gazed curiously at the unfamiliar uniform, the bottle green jacket of the Royal Irish Constabulary, the khaki trousers of the British Army. They listened to some of the men's rough English voices and saw how hard and fit their bodies were.

'It's the new police,' someone muttered. 'They didn't have enough proper uniforms for all of them.'

'They've been in Cork,' another said, careful not to speak too loudly.

'And Tipperary. They've been in Tipperary.'

'Aye, that's where the name's from . . . '

' . . . after a pack of hounds they called 'em.'

'Aye, that's right . . . a pack of hounds.'

The new police recruits realized they were the centre of attention. They didn't mind. After the horrors of The Great War, the mumblings of some Irish peasants miles from anywhere were of little importance. What was important, however, was to create the right impression, to show these ill-dressed clods who the masters were now.

One of them, young with cropped ginger hair, casually unslung his service issue .303 Lee-Enfield rifle and worked the bolt, thrusting a bullet into the breach as he surveyed his new surroundings. The watching crowd heard him say something to his companions who laughed out loud. The man didn't even seem to aim properly. In one smooth movement, he lifted the rifle to his right shoulder and squeezed the trigger.

Crack!!!

The unexpected shot made some of the crowd literally jump with surprise and a woman's shawl slipped to the dust.

In a field across the railway tracks, a small grey donkey shuddered, gave out a single bellow of shock and pain, and then fell over, kicking and struggling, blood spurting from the fatal wound in its side.

The group of police, already becoming known in Ireland as the Black and Tans, or simply The Tans, were still laughing as they formed up into ranks and marched off towards the barracks in Church Street.

A few minutes later, unaware of what had happened at the railway station, Sean and Bryan Aherne flanked by customers, watched the men's arrival in the street through the dusty windows of the tavern.

'They look hard men for sure,' Bryan commented. 'They know

397

their drill. You can tell that.'

'The sweepings from the English gaols,' a customer broke in. 'At least, that's what they say in Cork.'

'That's all they could find to do the filthy work,' another added.

'You're not surprised at that, are you?' Bryan asked, balancing his half-filled glass carefully on the window sill before rolling himself a cigarette. 'The police hereabouts are scared to move out of their barracks without the soldiers holding their hands.'

'And even if that were true, who's to be thanked?' his father interrupted. 'They wouldn't be here at all but for the shootings and burnings. It's come to a pretty pass when we have English gaolbirds helping the Irish police. I'm thinking the boys'll have to be looking out for themselves now.'

Sean gazed quickly at his son, watching his expression. In public, they never acknowledged Bryan's membership of the Volunteers, the Irish Republican Army. Everyone locally knew as well, of course, but it was never spoken of. Much better, people had decided, not even to mention the organization but just to term its members as 'the boys'.

'Oh, I don't know, Dad,' Bryan said confidently. 'I'm thinking that the boys'll be more than a match for them.' He downed the dregs in his glass. 'The word'll come soon enough how we're to deal with them.'

The tavern door flew open. A railway porter burst in, breathless from running, trembling with suppressed excitement and shock. 'And did you see what those murdering sods just did?' he cried before he was properly through the door.

'The Tans?'

'Yes, them,' the porter continued, pointing dramatically at the men across the street beginning to file into the police barracks.

The shooting of the donkey, described and embellished in horrified tones again and again that day, June 7th, 1920, soon had its desired effect on the people of Listowel. They were now in no doubt that they were caught up in the events which were transforming their country. Like many they'd still been hoping that they could escape from the dreadful reality. Indeed, they were already building myths as a last refuge from reality.

The Black and Tans had already been dubbed as gaolbirds when – and the facts were perfectly well known – they were merely veterans of The Great War, though understandably battle-hardened and undoubtedly cynical. They'd all had to possess a good character reference from their former military units to be able to join

The Royal Irish Constabulary and earn their ten shillings a day. Their reasons for joining might have been more a desire to escape lengthening unemployment queues rather than help preserve the peace in Ireland but their recruitment had been made necessary by the fast-worsening security situation. More and more men were resigning from the RIC as the campaign of terror, ordered and directed by Michael Collins and Cathal Brugha, spread into every village and townland.

Since the killings at Soloheadbeg the previous year, dozens of ordinary policemen, along with magistrates and soldiers, had been callously shot down by the IRA, the majority without even the opportunity to defend themselves. The troops had responded with martial law and curfews but their discipline, like that of the police, had held steady under the utmost provocation. Only in the last few months had it begun to crack.

Politically, there was stalemate. The British Government wouldn't bring in the promised Home Rule Act, promised at the end of The Great War, until the international peace conference was over and went so far as to block the attendance there of an Irish delegation.

Although officially declared illegal at the end of 1919, Sinn Fein progressively filled the vacuum, aided by the sweeping victories of its individual candidates in the local council elections held shortly before the Tans came to Listowel. Michael Collins and Cathal Brugha effectively controlled Dail Eireann, now underground after being suppressed, through supremacy in Sinn Fein and its secret inner circle of dedicated revolutionaries. As the police became powerless, the Volunteers of the IRA took over many of their duties in at least half the country, organizing patrols and even holding courts for common miscreants.

The majority of ordinary people were aghast at this state of anarchy, as appalled and condemnatory as the hierarchy of the Catholic Church which had precipitantly lent its support to the organization behind the chaos. The seeds which had been sown on all sides for so many years were bearing fruit with the arrival of The Tans and the beginning of a backlash from the sore-pressed constables of the regular force.

Sinn Fein clubs and the homes of supporters were being broken up and set on fire just as dozens of police barracks had been previously. The Sinn Fein Lord Mayor of Cork, Tom McCurtain, was murdered in his bed by masked policemen just as their friends and colleagues had been. The forces of authority were striking back.

Acts of terror by the IRA were bringing reprisals. The reprisals spawned further acts of terror.

But, until the arrival of the Black and Tans and the shooting of the donkey, the viciousness of events had seemed remote from Listowel. The small market town was far enough off the beaten track, too much a closed community, to have avoided the worst excesses. There'd been the burnings of police barracks in the area, but, by coincidence or design, the buildings had been unoccupied or evacuated without bloodshed.

The only fatality had been a police sergeant, shot during a gun battle when he'd refused to hand over the police payroll to an ambush party not far from Hannah Wilmot's farm at Galey Bridge. But so bravely had he fought, his family had received donations and condolences from the Volunteers themselves, ashamed and upset at his death.

In this part of North Kerry, the violence had been as ritualistic, impersonal and formal as an old time faction fight. It would soon change. The minuet of death was being danced throughout the land and Listowel would not be allowed to sit it out.

The first indication of what was to come appeared only ten days after the Tans' arrival. Sean and Bryan Aherne were taking a mid-afternoon break from their own bar, leaving Aunt Brigid in charge. Like many other tavern keepers, they preferred to go to another bar for their own refreshment. It gave them an escape from their own, all-too familiar customers as well as the opportunity to see how a rival's business was faring.

This hot summer day, June 18th, they favoured T. D. Sullivan's bar in the middle of William Street, facing on to Market Street, the main road leading west out of town. The streets were quiet, almost deserted, while Listowel basked somnolently in the heat. But to the Aherne's surprise, T. D. Sullivan's was packed and noisy in contrast to the empty establishment they'd left behind.

'What's this?' Sean joked, seeing uniforms all around him. 'Bit early for the policemen's Christmas dance, isn't it?'

Sullivan, busy behind the bar, shook his head worriedly.

'It's no laughing matter, Sean,' he replied. 'There's real trouble on.'

'Trouble? The only trouble they're having is drinking the stuff quick enough. Maybe you're running low . . . is that the trouble?' Sean retorted not taking him at all seriously. He ordered two drinks and leaned his elbow on the bar, surveying the customers. 'Hello, Tommy,' he called to Tommy Carmody, one of the constables

400

packed into the bar. Most were arguing excitedly, hands gesturing. 'The sun got you all off the streets, then? Who's minding the barracks?'

'Bugger the barracks! Bugger the lot of them!' Carmody shouted, eyes angry, voice fierce.

'I'm for us all resigning,' another constable exclaimed in Sean's ear.

'What's all this talk about, Tommy? What's on?' Sean asked.

The constable hesitated for a moment, seeing Bryan standing by his father, knowing full well his connection with the IRA. Then, he shrugged.

'Well, it'll be out soon enough, Sean, so I'm supposing there's no harm in telling you two.'

Carmody paused, looking hard at Bryan.

'Even if the news will have the rebels dancing a jig.'

'Come on, man,' Sean urged, ignoring the barbed remark. 'You've me burning with curiosity so you have.'

'Well . . . well, we've just had a meeting down the barracks with Colonel Smith.'

'The police commissioner for Munster?' Bryan interrupted.

'Himself and Captain Watson from the Army and some big-wigs I'm not knowing.'

'It must have been important,' Bryan interrupted again.

'Shut up, son, and let Tommy talk,' Sean ordered gruffly.

'That's right, son,' the constable agreed. 'Shut up or your rebel friends won't be getting the latest news. The fact of the matter is they wanted us to hand over the barracks to the soldier boys. Said we're to combine totally with them. Said we're to take their orders.'

Sean whistled through his teeth in surprise. Another constable joined the group, his eyes reddened by drink, tobacco and tiredness.

'And what about the pacification, Tommy?' he asked. 'Have you told them?'

'Not yet. Give me time. The colonel said the Crown Forces were going on the offensive.'

He looked hard at Bryan again.

'To beat the rebels at their own game. There's to be martial law and then what he called a ruthless pacification campaign. He said that if any innocent people got killed then he would see that we wouldn't have to answer for it. He reckoned the bloody government needed our help.'

'And what the fuck have we been doing all these months, I'd like to know?' the other constable said vehemently.

'Needed our help to beat the rebels and if anyone didn't want to help then he should get out of the force.'

'Holy Mother of God!' Bryan exclaimed.

'So that's what it's all about,' Sean chimed in. 'I can see why you're talking of resignations. What did you do when he said that, Tommy?'

'Well, we thought something was up so we'd elected Jerry Mee to speak for us. He stepped up bold as brass and said his piece. You should have seen the colonel's face, being talked at like that by a common or garden constable. "By your accent," Jerry said, "I take it you're an Englishman. You forget you're addressing Irishmen." '

'That's telling him,' Sean breathed, his glass of whiskey untouched in his hand.

'That wasn't all, mind. Jerry Mee took off his cap, his belt and his bayonet and flung them on the table in front of the colonel. "These, too are English" he said, standing as straight as the road to Tralee. "Take them as a present from me, and to hell with you, you murderer!" Old Smith went purple. "Arrest that man! Arrest that man!" he screamed.'

'And did you?' Bryan failed to conceal the excitement in his voice.

'Arrest Jerry? Arrest him? Like pig-shit we did. You stand by a man like that, son. In fact we all stood by him. Told the big man that there'd be blood spilled if they laid a hand on Jerry. That finished it there and then.'

'And now you're having the celebration, and quite right too!' Sean exclaimed. 'It'll cost heavy but I'll be after buying a drink for every one of you boys.'

'It's not as simple as that, Sean,' Carmody continued. 'The drink'll be more than welcome but we've a lot of thinking and talking to do. We came across here 'cos we were fearing what might happen if we stayed at the barracks. They might have called the troops to us and clapped us in our own cells.'

'Fat chance,' the other constable snorted. 'They'll be having my resignation papers and that's all. I'm not killing innocent civilians. I'm a policeman, not a bloody murderer.'

'And that's an Ulsterman saying that,' Carmody grinned, jabbing his thumb at his colleague.

'Makes no difference where I'm from. Either we're proper policemen or we're not. And, anyway, an Ulsterman's an Irishman, isn't he?'

The mutiny of the Listowel police – and the resignations of fourteen of the twenty-five constables – meant that the town passed virtually under the control of the troops and The Tans. It meant that martial law, declared three days later, would be doubly unpleasant. It meant too, an immediate dilemma for the Ahernes and all the other families who had relatives in the Sinn Fein Volunteers, the IRA, or Cumann na Mban, the Volunteers' section for women and girls. Should they go into hiding or brazen it out by continuing their normal lives?'

'I've done nothing they can charge me with,' Bryan declared firmly that first day of martial law, sitting in the front room at No 32 Church Street.

'You're sure?' asked his grandfather, leaning back on the narrow sofa, sucking on an empty pipe. 'These people mightn't be too finicky about laws now they're in charge. The regular police are different. Taught some of them myself, so I did. They knew us and we knew them. Bit of respect between them and the boys, I wouldn't be surprised.'

'We never went for them as individuals,' Bryan interrupted. 'Sure I've been at a few barrack burnings but no one got hurt. No one. And I've never been in an ambush yet, never fired a gun in anger.'

'Of course you haven't,' his mother remarked soothingly.

'And I've got rid of the gun,' Bryan continued. 'Buried it at the farm.'

'Hannah's?'

'Uh-huh, but no one, not even her, knows where. I wouldn't let her look.'

There was silence for a moment. The grown-ups suddenly realized that only Bryan could make the decision. The old schoolmaster, still a part-time teacher, peered at his grandson, adjusting his glasses to do so. There were lines on the young man's forehead, not deep yet but unmistakable. Bryan's straight, slightly pinched nose gave his face an appearance of firmness and resolve. A lock of black hair tumbling over the broad forehead suggested vulnerability. His hands were definitely those of a doer, a toiler, not a scholar, large and capable, two long fingers stained a little with nicotine. Was one his trigger finger? Jack shook the question from his mind. But another filled its place. How had the boy, his grandson, the son of his only son, come to this?'

'You think I should go on my keeping, Grandad?'

'Off on your own? Running? Hiding?'

'Yes.'

'Where would you stay, dear?' his mother asked anxiously, reaching out for Sean's hand.

'With friends for a few nights, then move on. Keep moving on. There are plenty of barns around. This weather, it'd be no problem, no hardship.'

'Son,' said Sean, 'Don't you think they'd really start hunting you down if you went missing? They'd really think you'd something to hide, something to be afeared of.'

His grandfather pulled the pipe out of his mouth. 'My opinion is that he should bluff it out. Stay put and not go on his keeping. Keep out of everyone's way for a while. But it's his life, isn't it, Bryan? It's your decision!'

Bryan smiled at him, his eyes reflecting his gratitude. 'I'd never harm the family,' he said quietly. 'You know that, Grandad. If you're troubled because of me, then I'll be away.'

'Aye,' Sean said pessimistically, glancing sideways at his wife. 'If we're troubled . . . ' His voice died away.

That evening, at six o'clock, the streets of the town were empty except for patrols of troops, police and Tans. Gradually, Listowel learned to live under the curfew. Friends who came to spend a social evening, stayed the night. At first, the novelty was welcome. No one really suffered, not even the taverns. Customers seemed to buy the same amount of drink as they did before in spite of the much-shortened licensing hours.

But soon the restrictions started to become irksome. Occasionally, the equally bored Tans livened up the evening and their drinking bouts in barracks by loosing off shots at any lights showing in houses. This forced the townsfolk to barricade their windows.

At No 32 Church Street, Sean procured some oily bales of sheep's wool to block the windows and doors, front and back. The smell, particularly that fine summer, permeated everything in the house. The children grew more fractious, pressing their noses to cracks in the barricades, watching troops stroll down to the river at the end of Tay Lane for a swim in the welcome cool of the early evening.

Their irritability and restlessness naturally transmitted itself to their parents. Throughout the town – and Ireland – resentment increased as martial law showed no sign of coming to an end. House searches became a matter of routine, as routine as the milkman calling. The soldiers were immaculate in their behaviour but unrelenting in their thoroughness. Once Finoola Aherne, panicking like a disturbed chicken, had to unstack every pan, every piece of crockery in her kitchen to satisfy a search party that she had no hidden IRA messages.

A search by the Tans was altogether different. Precious ornaments and family souvenirs were smashed. Small children were shouted at and frightened. Rifle butts somehow dropped painfully on toes and fingers.

The retribution grew more offensive, if that were possible, as summer gave way to a glorious autumn. Members of a new adjunct to the security forces began to spread into North Kerry. These were called officially 'Cadets', part of the Auxiliary Division of the Royal Irish Constabulary. These men were recruited from the ranks of out-of-work British officers. They were paid £1 a day and used mainly for lightning, motorized raids in their Crossley tenders on suspected rebel hideouts. The people of Listowel came to hate the strutting arrogance of the Auxiliaries as much as the physical crudeness of the Tans, marginally preferring the attentions of the regular police constables and the troops.

Their preference became more marginal, however, when District Inspector Tobias 'Toby' O'Sullivan was posted to the town in charge of the Crown Forces throughout the area.

The reputation of this burly, stocky man whose semi-permanent smile never quite reached his bleak eyes, had travelled ahead of him after his surviving an IRA attack on his previous headquarters at Kilmallock, County Limerick. The attackers had set fire to the building during a five-hour siege by breaking open the roof slates and pouring petrol through. O'Sullivan had managed to escape to fight another day, leaving a sergeant and a constable to perish in the flames. That the constable had been a blood relative, his nephew, had added to O'Sullivan's image as an officer with ruthless disregard for human suffering. Not that there was much such regard by either side in those months.

During one weekend at the end of August, seven policemen and one Army officer were killed by IRA gunmen. One was a senior police officer who'd been implicated in the murder of the Lord Mayor of Cork. The officer died in his home town of Lisburn, not far from Belfast, and forty Catholic homes were burned in retaliation.

The flames didn't have to be seen in Belfast for rioting to start there. When order had been restored, twenty people were dead and eighty-seven wounded, most of them from the Catholic minority huddled against the fiercely Protestant majority. Tit-for-tat, it went on.

Soldiers and police were shot. The Tans and Auxiliaries burned entire villages. In some townlands, people slept out in the fields all night for fear of reprisals. But their will didn't evaporate in the way it had in previous rebellions. Terence MacSwiney, the new incumbent as Lord Mayor of Cork, epitomized that freshly-forged spirit following his arrest at a Sinn Fein conference. He chose not to eat for seventy-four days and died in Brixton Gaol in London on October 24th.

Still the terror went on. It increased. Less than a month later on November 21st, Michael Collins's murder gang shot and killed twelve British army officers in Dublin. Most died in their pyjamas, in hotel rooms and lodgings, many in front of their helpless, shrieking wives. Later that same day, twelve civilians, including a woman and a child, died in a hail of bullets when police opened fire on a crowd at Croke Park attending a Gaelic football match between Dublin and Tipperary. That very night, three men, two of them IRA, were shot by Auxiliaries in the guard room at Dublin Castle, the centre of British administration in Ireland. It was said they were riddled with bullets when trying to escape. Not surprisingly the day became known to both sides as 'Bloody Sunday'.

A week later, an entire convoy of Auxiliaries and Tans was wiped out in an ambush near Macroom in County Cork, neighbouring Kerry. The death toll was seventeen of the security forces and three IRA men. The horror was compounded by the fact that many of the Auxiliaries and Tans were shot and bayoneted, terribly mutilated, where they lay dying or dead.

The overwhelming presence of the security forces in Listowel had meant that the Volunteers living there had had to be extremely careful about their actions. In consequence, the town had suffered little by way of reprisals. But now, after such a massacre as Macroom? The worst was feared. The local IRA commander, Paddy Landers, the blacksmith, quickly ordered his men to disperse for a few days and sent messages to the town's tavern-keepers that, on no account, should they allow the singing of the verses glorifying the massacre which were being circulated within hours.

On the 28th day of November
Outside the town of Macroom,
The Tans in their big Crossley tenders
Were hurtling away to their doom.
For the lads of the column were waiting
With hand-grenades primed on the spot,
And the Irish Republican Army
Made shit of the whole fucking lot!

Bryan understood the orders perfectly. Any provocation could only bring more suffering upon the town. He decided, like the others, that he would spend the next week living rough in the countryside.

Early next morning, the day after the massacre when its full impact was beginning to be felt, his mother and Aunt Brigid filled his rucksack with thick brawn sandwiches, two lengths of cooked drisheen and half a cheese.

'You'll be maybe getting a wee bit cold at night,' his father winked, slipping two half-bottles of whiskey in with the food when the women's backs were turned.

'It'll go well, Dad, with the milk I'll be borrowing from the cows,' Bryan smiled back.

'Aye, it will that. Now you're certain you'll be safe on your own keeping? You've your cape and your thickest coat and underwear? As soon as you're gone, son, I'll be barricading the house and the tavern. We'll be safe when you return.'

The whole town seemed to have had the same idea. Bryan cycled away through streets echoing to the sound of nails being driven into planks of wood fitted over windows of shops and homes. There was no sign of any of the security forces, not even outside the police barracks. Their absence from view struck him as somehow ominous. He decided to head for Galey Bridge to explain to Hannah why he wouldn't be seeing her for a few days. Her mother, however, had different ideas when he arrived there.

'I'll hear of no such thing, young Bryan, sleeping in ditches and such like!' Mrs Wilmot exclaimed indignantly, crackling smart in her apron, standing by her gleaming, black-leaded range.

'But there'll be barns to sneak into,' Bryan protested.

'Barns?' Mrs Wilmot sniffed disdainfully. 'Cold and draughty, if I'm knowing anything of most of them in these parts. No more than lean-to sheds, I'm thinking.'

'They'll be all right for a couple of days.'

'They'll not be,' she insisted, waving a stirring spoon at him. 'I can see why you're on your own keeping – and I'm not criticizing you what with those Tans around and awful angry they must be – but if you're to stay in barns, you'll stay here in a proper one. Mr Wilmot's is at least waterproof, and you can be having some blankets.'

'I don't . . . ' he began.

'Can he, mother? Oh, can he?' Hannah asked eagerly.

'Of course he will. That ways, at least we'll be knowing what he's up to . . .'

Bryan shrugged resignedly, smiling.

'But I'll be out cycling during the day,' he said, conceding defeat with some inward gratitude. 'I'll only be coming here at night. The police probably already know about Hannah and me. They've seen us around together, I'm sure. They might come searching if they don't find me at home. I wouldn't want them seeing me on the farm if they drove past.'

'We'll talk about that later,' Mrs Wilmot promised, shaking her head in mock dismay, returning to her pots.

'Come on Bryan!' Hannah urged gaily. 'Let's find a comfortable place for you with the cattle.' She led the way into the farmyard.

The chickens, wandering free in the mud, parted ranks before them, clucking fussily, as the two young people walked towards the two-storey barn, about fifty yards from the house.

Instinctively, Bryan looked across to the other corner of the yard where the pigs were kept. He'd buried his revolver, securely wrapped in oil cloth, close by the entrance to the sty. As far as he could see, the patchy turf there hadn't been disturbed. He assumed it was still safe.

'Will you be having an upstairs or a downstairs room, sir?' Hannah joked once they were inside the barn.

Bryan gazed along the milking stalls in front of him, filled with black cows standing hoof-deep in manure streaked straw. They stared limpidly back.

'Upstairs, I think, miss' he replied.

Both giggling, they clambered up the ladder to the hay loft which ran half the length of the barn. For the next hour, they heaved the bales around creating a hiding place for Bryan in one corner. To reach it, he would have to climb up and over the bales, but once inside he'd be safe from all but the most meticulous search.

He spent the rest of that day in the farmhouse, looking nervously through the windows whenever a very occasional vehicle clattered by. After an early supper with the Wilmots, he returned to the loft with Hannah, this time with blankets. She held an oil lamp above her head, jagged shadows flitting across her face, while Bryan made final adjustments to his sleeping space.

'Right,' he called from behind the bales after a few minutes. 'It's as snug as it will be.'

'You're sure?' Hannah stepped up on to a bale and stood on tiptoe, trying to peer over.

'Aye. You'd better away now.'

His hand waved goodbye above the bales. She leaned forward all she could, just managing to brush her fingers against his. When Bryan felt her hand, he stretched further upwards and clasped it, squeezing for a moment.

'Good night, Hannah,' he said, huskily.

'Sleep tight and God be with you,' she called from the other side of the bales. 'Avourneen,' she added in a whisper, uncertain whether she wanted him to hear the endearment, hoping that he might. Although they'd been meeting for over a year, their romance was still delicate and fragile, their physical intimacy rarely more than an occasional fleeting kiss.

Once, when they were embracing, Bryan's hands had slid down Hannah's back and gently cupped her small, giving buttocks. She'd allowed them to remain there for long moments imprinted on his memory before twisting out of his arms, face lowered, her breath audible. He'd begun to stammer a question, disconcerted, and then had fallen silent, realizing she wouldn't, couldn't, answer. Nor could he ask.

Another time, during that past, marvellous summer, he'd joined the Wilmots in a swimming expedition to the River Gale, alongside their farm. Of course, the river had been reduced by the heat to little more than a trickling brook but it was still delightful to feel water moving against limbs. Hannah had insisted on changing into her mother's bathing costume behind some shrubbery and, as she'd stepped over Bryan, lying on the river bank with her parents, he'd looked up. The sight of the blondish, curly hairs between her thighs, glimpsed through the folds of the overly-large costume, remained with him.

As experienced and hardened as Bryan might have been in other ways, he still possessed the fumbling inexperience with the opposite sex common to most young Irishmen, particularly those brought up outside the larger cities. His courtship of Hannah had progressed steadily, slowly, not dramatically and passionately.

Later that night – how much later – he came awake to the sound of shouting, the slamming of metal doors. He shook his head, not sure whether he was dreaming, confused about where he was.

An angry voice, tinged with defiance, cried out, clearly carrying to him in the blackness of the hayloft.

'And what the hell are you wanting at this time?'

The question, outraged, wasn't answered. There were noises, strange noises at that distance, before a woman began shrieking.

Bryan heaved himself over the bales, feeling his way in the dark, hands outstretched, and started down the ladder. The cows scrambled in the straw, disturbed, rising from their sleep.

'Get out of the way or I'll give you the contents of this!' a man's voice shouted.

'Shoot me!' a woman exclaimed hysterically. Bryan, mind clearing, knew it was Hannah's mother.

'Shoot me!' she repeated. And again, 'Shoot me! I'd sooner die than be living after him!'

'Bring him out or your man's dead,' another man called, his excited voice slightly slurred. The accent was odd to Bryan, his ear pressed against the barn door, unable to find a chink in the wood. It wasn't an Irish voice. Perhaps it was Scots, perhaps English. He wasn't sure. Certainly, the man sounded like he'd had more than a few drinks.

'You've done as much to many a good man!' Mrs Wilmot answered back, desperation yielding defiance.

'You'll take him up in a box!' the same man threatened.

Bryan pushed lightly against the barn door, easing it open a fraction. He could now look out through the tiny gap.

The front of the whitewashed farmhouse was lit yellow and garish by the headlamps of three Crossley tenders.

Eight Tans in uniform, three swaying perceptibly, stood in a wide arc in front of their vehicles, backs towards him, rifles casually at the port position across their chests.

A smaller group stood within the arc. Three Tans were in a line, rifles aimed at Mr Wilmot, who was pressed by his own terror against the wall by the front door. Beside the soldiers was a taller man with badges of rank on his shoulder, his cocked revolver at arm's length. Mrs Wilmot knelt before her husband in the tacky mud, white nightgown rucked and dirt-stained. Hannah stood in the doorway, long hair framed golden by the lamp burning behind her, the outlines of her rounded slimness showing through the thin cotton of her nightdress, the divide between her thighs noticeable. The playing shadows obscured her face. The faces of the Tans were also dark and difficult to see. Bryan realized that the men's features had been deliberately masked with oil or soot or grime,

'Give him to us,' the man with the revolver ordered. 'Give him up or your man'll be shot through.'

'Who? For God's sake, who?' Mr Wilmot shouted.

'The rebel. Give us the rebel or you're dead!'

'I don't know a rebel!'

'You know Aherne, Bryan Aherne. He visits here. And since he's not at home, he's here! Give him up!'

'Bryan? Is he a rebel?' Mr Wilmot pretended surprise without much success.

'He's a rebel as well as the murdering corner-boy who fucks that whore of your daughter!'

Mrs Wilmot screamed. Slowly, she fell on to her side in a faint, nightgown rising above her waist, displaying her nakedness. Her husband knelt quickly beside her. His fingers scrabbled to make her decent. His shocked face, upturned, appealed mutely to the Tans.

'He's not here,' Mr Wilmot said, his tone suddenly flat with resignation. 'I wish to God that he was, that he could face you, but the truth is he's not been here for a week past.'

A Tan, staggering with drink, loomed behind Hannah in the doorway, thrusting her aside.

'No one,' he called. 'No one. It's empty.'

'Sure?' asked the man with the revolver.

'Certain.'

Bryan's mind emptied of everything except the image of his gun lying not ten yards away. He eased the barn door open another six inches, ready to slip through, and then stopped, regaining his senses. What could he do? He'd be shot before he reached the weapon. Even if he did find it in the dark and confusion, how could he use it without causing the deaths of Hannah and her parents?

'You're sure?' the question came again from the man who seemed to be in charge. 'We've none of them yet anywhere. This is the tenth or eleventh fucking call and we've no one.'

'Not one of the rebel bastards here.'

'They'll still pay. Oh, yes, they'll pay or my name's not O'Sull. . . .' The man stopped and laughed to himself. 'They'll pay all right,' he repeated. 'Hold the dirty whore there!'

The Tan in the doorway slung his rifle over his shoulder and pinioned Hannah from behind, hands brutally squeezing her breasts, his lower body jerking against her buttocks as if he was having sex. The other men laughed at the pantomime. One tried to cross his legs and almost fell down.

Sounds of breaking and tearing came from within the farmhouse, wood and china, glass and cloth.

A Tan stepped forward, white teeth grinning across his darkened face. He pushed the muzzle of his rifle hard against Mr Wilmot's forehead, holding him in a kneeling position.

Headlights glinted off the steel blade of a knife, suddenly in the hand of the man who'd held the revolver.

With a lurch and a cry of triumph, he grabbed hold of Hannah's long blonde hair and began sawing at it.

Hannah yelped with pain – Bryan quivered at the sound – but stood straight. The tresses fell round her feet, one by one, until she was cropped like a boy. Jagged clumps of hair stood every which way from her scalp. Tears streamed down her cheeks, glistening in the lights.

Her tormentor stopped, satisfied. Then faster than the eye could follow, he jerked out his free hand, thumb upturned, and thrust it between Hannah's defenceless thighs. She shrieked once and doubled up, sobbing and gulping in her agony.

'No more than she's had from that rebel sod,' the man guffawed triumphantly. 'Maybe thicker and harder though!'

The Tans around him burst into raucous laughter.

'Shall we give it her proper, sir?' one asked. 'Show her what it's like with real men?'

Hannah's violator shook his head, stepping away from her. He sniffed ostentatiously at his thumb.

'They're sweeter smelling in Listowel,' he laughed.

Bryan crouched, retching silently, behind the safety of the barn door. Despite the pain within him, he knew at last that he would be capable of killing another human being.

## Chapter 6 January, 1921

The first time they had tried to murder him, the bullet had missed by feet, spattering harmlessly off a wall, panicking the crowd at Listowel Fair. The second occasion had been even more frustrating. The ambush had been perfect but their damp ammunition had refused to fire. Those selected for the third attempt were more than a trifle nervous as they moved to their positions under the overcast, grey-drizzling January sky.

Con Brosnan, Donalin O'Grady and Bryan Aherne walked singly down Church Street, caps pulled down over their foreheads to keep the rain out of their eyes and to hide as much of their features as possible. The young men kept three or four yards apart, pretending to look into the shop windows or bending down to tighten their bootlaces, eyes alert for the first sign of police or troops. Jackie Sheehan kept pace with them on the other side of the street. The ballot had decreed that he should give the signal. The other three carried the guns.

They paused at the end of Church Street, where it bent back on itself and became William Street. Opposite them were two bars, Kennelly's and Broderick's, flanking the narrow entrance to Tay Lane whose cobbles sloped down to the banks of the River Feale. The clock in the window of McAuliffe's, the boot shop, showed twenty minutes to midday.

'Still plenty of time,' Bryan muttered under his breath. 'Plenty yet.' He slid his hand into the right-hand pocket of his overcoat, letting his fingers caress the barrel of the revolver.

There was no denying he felt on edge. The fluttering stomach muscles, the constant pressure in his bowel, told him that. In fact he was surprised that he didn't feel worse. Of one thing he was certain. He had absolutely no qualms about this mission. Since that night at the farmhouse, nearly two months before, the thought of revenge had burned within him, searing away any conscience he previously had about killing.

His local commanders in the IRA knew this. They were loath, however, to issue the order for execution immediately. The assault on the Wilmots, particularly Hannah, and the sack of their home were terrible, but many similar incidents had occurred the same night in Listowel and the surrounding area as the Tans and Auxiliaries had run amok, infuriated by the massacre of their comrades at Macroom.

The early order to disperse from Paddy Landers had meant that none of the IRA volunteers had suffered, only their families and friends. One by one, the Volunteers had emerged from hiding, apprehensive, only to find that life had returned to normal.

As the weeks passed, Bryan, impatient and deeply angry, often thought of exacting retribution single-handed but an incident on New Year's Eve in William Street made that unnecessary.

A group of Tans, viciously drunk in their seasonal celebrations, set upon a young man as he walked home. They beat and kicked him so severely that he died the next day without recovering consciousness. Their victim was the twenty-year-old son of Davy Lawlor, the parish clerk and bell ringer, a man loved and respected throughout Listowel. Some months before Lawlor had refused to toll the Church bells at a funeral of a Tan who'd died from natural causes. To retain any credibility, the local command of the IRA had to respond to the atrocity. The execution was decided by a unanimous vote. That two unsuccessful attempts had already been made showed just how inexperienced in such matters the local Volunteers were.

Bryan glanced again at the clock in the window of the boot shop. Its hands had hardly moved. There were still more than fifteen minutes before District Inspector Tobias O'Sullivan of the Royal Irish Constabulary, area commander of the Crown Forces in North Kerry, would walk down this street, turn this corner where Bryan stood, on his way home to lunch with his wife and children. He had taken the same route for the last ten days.

Con Brosnan, who was in the lead, nodded his head slightly in the direction of Kennelly's Bar and moved towards its front door. The other two with the guns saw his signal and followed him. Jackie Sheehan stayed on the corner.

The streets were empty except for three women – one in a wide-brimmed, black straw hat, the others covering their hair with thick, dark shawls – and two chestnut horses tethered to the bollard outside Broderick's Bar, nuzzling contentedly into their feedbags.

Bryan had the impression of time almost standing still as he followed the others into Kennelly's. Every house, every shop, was familiar to him, had been since childhood, yet now he seemed in a strange place.

'Morning friends,' said Kennelly's son behind the bar, recognizing each of them. Bryan looked evenly at him, realizing again the impossibility of remaining unknown and unidentified in his own small town. He didn't worry too much about it, though, believing that no one would inform on them, particularly after what they were about to attempt.

O'Grady acknowledged the greeting.

'Half glasses of porter all round,' he ordered. 'And then it might be better if you were attending to the barrels in the back.'

He folded back his overcoat, allowing the barman to see the handle of the revolver stuck into the top of his trousers.

Kennelly's son nodded his understanding, his hands shaking as he poured the drinks. He waved away Bryan's offer of money and disappeared quickly into the bar's back parlour.

'Not long,' said Con Brosnan, moving to a table by the window, swallowing at his glass on the way.

Two elderly men, scarves knotted in place of ties and collars, shuffled to their feet at a neighbouring table and left the bar, their watery eyes registering disapproval of the new customers.

'Long enough,' Bryan said, picking up the conversation. 'But make the drink last.'

'Aye,' said O'Grady. 'Make it last, Connie boy. It could be you won't be having a drink ever again.'

'That's amusing?' said Brosnan, his mouth tightening.

'Not meant to be,' O'Grady muttered. 'There's no joking now.'

'Aye, Bryan agreed. 'No joking now.'

Their eyes swivelled around each other's faces, trying to draw courage and encouragement.

'Remember he'll be wearing the steel vest,' Bryan said quietly.

The three nodded wisely, nursing their drinks. They kept looking through the quartered window at the junction of Church Street and William Street, checking that Jackie Sheehan was still there.

Sheehan himself was literally quivering with nervousness. He'd seen District Inspector O'Sullivan begin walking down Church Street from the police barracks, accompanied, as always, by two Tans, rifles on shoulders. The Inspector's raincoat failed to hide the bulk of the bullet-proof armour underneath covering his chest and stomach.

Now, O'Sullivan had stopped ten yards from Sheehan, chatting animatedly with an elderly man whom the look-out recognized as a retired constable called Dan Farrell. After five minutes, he turned to his escort and waved them away. The two Tans said something – perhaps protesting, Sheehan thought – before returning the way they'd come.

'Well, goodbye then and God be with you,' O'Sullivan said at last. Sheehan, stepping from one foot to the other in his nervousness, heard the words quite plainly.

The police officer resumed his walk home, actually nodding in a friendly fashion at Sheehan, one of the very few people on the street.

As O'Sullivan reached the bend at the bottom of Church Street, Sheehan crossed the road quickly, head pulled down into his shoulders. Opposite Kennelly's, he drew a handkerchief from his pocket, wiping it across his face as if drying away the rain drops, then hurried away into the market square.

The three young men in the bar saw the signal. Bryan suddenly felt an emptiness in his stomach.

Outside, the drizzle had turned into more solid rain. The three fanned out across the narrow street, only five yards wide, in front of O'Sullivan, hands in pockets clasping their revolvers. He didn't even look at them, his attention focussed on a doorway further down William Street. Bryan followed his gaze and saw a woman and a

415

young child, a girl aged about ten, waving. The thought registered that they must have been the police officer's family He felt no emotion about them, only again the emptiness within himself.

They drew their revolvers almost at the same moment, about six feet from their intended victim.

District Inspector O'Sullivan didn't seem to notice their presence until a second or so later, when they were even closer.

He looked into the faces of Con Brosnan, Donalin O'Grady and Bryan Aherne, faces he vaguely knew, the ever-present smile on his face, his cold eyes assessing. They hardly widened when they saw the pointing, aimed, revolvers, only grew more quizzical, perhaps even reproving.

Bryan believed he fired first but he wasn't sure since the three reports were practically simultaneous.

He felt the gun leap in his hand, the muscle spasm akin to that when a freshwater salmon is hooked.

He was so near to O'Sullivan that he thought he saw the flesh opening, tearing, under the impact of the bullets. First, in the side of the neck; then in he middle of the cheek; finally, at the top of the ear, just under the hair line.

The smile didn't leave O'Sullivan's face. In fact, it appeared to widen as his features distorted sideways and his life blood spouted upwards and outwards.

He took one step, still smiling, his eyes emptying of expression, beginning to film over.

Bryan fired again, his revolver by now almost touching the tip of O'Sullivan's nose.

The police officer's head jerked back. His legs shot out behind him, his muscles losing all messages from his shattered brain. He fell to the wet cobblestones, a bubble of air moaning in his throat. His body twitched once, lifting perceptibly off the ground, and then he was still. His uniform cap, bloodied, rolled gently towards the gutter.

'He did forget his head, didn't he?' said Con Brosnan, a note of wonder in his half-whispered remark.

The three young men stood for a second, looking down at the body, revolvers still smoking, in communion with the act of death.

'Toby! Oh, Toby!' a woman shrieked. There was other screaming too. Perhaps a man, probably another woman. Shoes clattered on cobbles, running, slipping in the wet.

Bryan glanced up and saw O'Sullivan's wife rushing towards

them, hair streaming, arms outstretched, her pleasant, round face twisted with anguish.

'Oh, Toby, my Toby!' she repeated, her voice rising to a screech. 'Toby, what have they done?'

'Mama! Mama!' sobbed her little girl, running a few feet behind her mother, terrified by the sound of the shots, the sight of the blood, the crumpled shape of her father.

'Come on, for fuck's sake,' Brosnan grunted. 'Let's away, boys.'

The three turned on their heels and fled towards Church Street, pursued by the shrieks and sobs of Mrs O'Sullivan and her small daughter. Bryan looked back over his shoulder once just before he ducked into a side alley. Mrs O'Sullivan was prostrate over her husband's body, trying to lift his shattered head, blood streaked on her hands and face.

'Jesus! Oh, Jesus!' he panted, the realization of what he'd done beginning to strike him.

'Did you see his head?' O'Grady cried behind him. 'Holy Mother, did you see it?'

The alley twisted and turned before it opened on to the town's sports field. They dashed across the open space and into the comparative safety of Gurtinard Woods on the other side.

Behind them, Listowel was in turmoil. The police had rushed to the scene from their barracks only a hundred yards away. An army patrol was there a minute later. Those few who'd seen the murder had already vanished, leaving the pathetic widow and her child alone in the middle of the street with the body.

Two farmers, who'd witnessed the shooting from the windows of Broderick's Bar, had leapt onto their horses, tethered outside, and galloped pell-mell out of town. At first, the police thought they were the culprits and set off in pursuit. Others ran into the market square, revolvers in hand, cursing and shouting. The townsfolk who saw them coming dashed indoors out of their way.

Then, suddenly, there were schoolchildren all over the centre of town, returning home for lunch from St Michael's College and the National School next door. The police and soldiers swore and cuffed them as they milled and swirled about, making movement of trucks and tenders impossible for vital minutes.

Eventually, the army was able to chase the false trail inadvertently laid by the two farmers and set off along the Tarbert road. By then, though, the farmers were safely at home. The troops' confusion was increased by an old woman with a donkey and cart who'd seen the farmers. She deliberately sent the soldiers in the opposite direction.

In Listowel, businesses closed down, windows and doors were locked and bolted; streets cleared of people. Everyone feared what was to come. They waited fatalistically for two hours. Then the Tans emerged from their barracks in twos and threes, infuriated after viewing the body of their slain commander, inflamed by drink, out for revenge.

They walked along Church Street, smashing windows with their rifle-butts. Some thrust their rifles through the broken glass and loosed off bullets into the houses. Others took aim at people visible behind their makeshift barricades and fired round after round. The town echoed to the crackle of indiscriminate firing. Amazingly, not one person was wounded.

For more than four hours, most of the townsfolk lay huddled, terrified, on the floors of their homes, hiding under beds, even in wardrobes, for protection.

Pet dogs and cats still on the streets were shot or bludgeoned to death.

Shops and bars were looted for drink and cigarettes, food and clothes, before the Tans tired of their orgy of destruction.

That night, Listowel was too afraid to sleep, scared of any knocks on the door which might herald more shooting. Most locked themselves inside rooms, clasping their rosary beads tightly round their fingers.

Bryan and his two companions spent their night among the broken-down walls and under the leaking thatch of the old Aherne cabin at Drombeg. It had taken them nearly five hours to reach it, skirting the town, keeping to the hedgerows and copses, hiding from anyone who passed. The three Volunteers were cold, hungry, wet and tired. In their low state, doubts began to surface.

O'Grady was the first to voice the thought uppermost in their minds.

'The swine deserved to die,' he said quietly. 'He did, didn't he boys?'

'Aye,' Bryan replied wearily. 'He did that.'

'But is it right that we killed him?'

'Who else?' asked Brosnan.

'But was it a mortal sin?'

There was silence. The young men were as religious as any person of their age and upbringing, which meant that the strictures of the

418

Catholic Church were of considerable influence among them, even if they were sometimes loath to admit the fact openly.

'The bishops keep saying all the assassinations are wrong,' Bryan said finally.

'But they supported Sinn Fein.'

'They did that, Con, and Sinn Fein is the government, is Dail Eireann, and we're acting under its orders, aren't we?'

'Through Collins and Brugha.'

'Aye, we're the proper army, they say.'

'They do that,' O'Grady agreed, brightening perceptibly.

'There's the rub, though,' Bryan added shaking his head sadly. 'The people voted for Sinn Fein true enough, but they didn't vote for all this bloodletting. There's been no war declared, has there? And the orders from Collins are secret, aren't they? They're not passed by the Dail, wherever it's meeting, are they?'

The others were forced to agree, gloom returning.

'What would Father O'Connor say?' asked Brosnan, thinking of Listowel's parish priest.

'Grandad talked to him about the killings the other day, so he did,' said Bryan. 'Father O'Connor told him the Church only approved of violence in a rebellion when it was against a tyranny ruling by force against what the people want . . . '

'That's the British, isn't it?' O'Grady interrupted eagerly.

'Oh, yes, it's the British all right,' Bryan went on. 'But the Father also said that the rebellion had to be approved by the whole community if it was to get the Church's blessing as well.'

He drew heavily on a rather limp cigarette before passing it to Brosnan.

'There's the problem. Does the community approve or not? The newspapers don't for sure . . . '

'They'll all approve if we get an Irish government in Dublin,' O'Grady said.

'Oh, yes, they'll do that. We'll be the heroes then, the real boys, not the murdering corner boys they call us now. Oh, yes, they'll be happy then. But I'm thinking most people want the quiet life, Donalin, my boy. They want change without the trouble. They want an omelette without breaking the eggs.'

'Isn't that the truth?' Brosnan echoed.

'But we're sort of doing the right thing?' O'Grady asked tentatively, determined to salve his conscience somehow.

'I reckon,' Bryan sighed. He wasn't sure about anything now that

419

the adrenalin had stopped flowing.

'So, at the worst, it's only half a mortal sin, shooting O'Sullivan?' O'Grady persisted.

'Aye, Donalin,' said Brosnan, suddenly wearying of all the chatter, preferring to seek solace in his own thoughts. 'Only half at the worst!'

'And if your mother wore a moustache, she'd be your father,' Bryan murmured under his breath, angry with himself for trying to ease O'Grady's mind with such futile arguments.

Even while he'd been uttering the words, he'd known the truth within himself. No human being deserved to die in the manner of District Inspector Tobias O'Sullivan, but then no young woman should have been treated like Hannah nor a young man beaten to death like Davy Lawlor's son.

He fell into an uncomfortable, broken sleep, reflecting on how easy it had been to kill, how difficult to justify the killing. He didn't feel especially guilty, only changed, perhaps soiled, certainly older by another man's life. Or should it have been death? And was it true that you killed a bit of yourself when you killed someone? He dozed off, his damp cap under his head.

Shivering with cold, they awoke so early that it was still dark. After a brief discussion they decided to strike out for Ballybunnion hoping for food and shelter during the inevitable hue and cry.

Bryan asked them to wait a few minutes before setting off. He went outside, trying to find the graves he'd often played around as a youngster. The darkness and the thick, matted undergrowth made his task impossible. With a single, regretful glance at the tumble-down cabin, the setting for so many family tales, he followed his friends along the potholed road towards the seaside village.

Their first inquiry on the outskirts of Ballybunnion took them to Simon Mulvihill's cabin where they were welcomed immediately, sat down by a swiftly-revived fire, and plied with hot oatmeal fortified with poteen. The Mulvihills, of course, had a shrewd idea of why the three were on the run but declined to ask questions, preferring the story to be volunteered in time. When it was, they listened in silence, eyes hard and gleaming.

Simon Mulvihill set off that morning with messages for their families and the IRA commanders. In the next ten days, Bryan, Brosnan and O'Grady were moved around the village, spending each night with a different family. It was as if the whole of Bally-bunnion wanted to share the burden and danger of their concealment, realizing that they would share the punishment if the three Volunteers were discovered.

The Army had instituted a policy of official reprisals, burning houses after ambushes, destroying whole townlands after murders and interning suspects without trial, more than a thousand of them so far.

In the circumstances, North Kerry escaped comparatively lightly after O'Sullivan's killing. Three more companies of troops were sent to Listowel with orders to enforce martial law more rigorously. The names of shops written in Irish were defaced. Indeed, shops were only allowed to open from ten o'clock until noon on Mondays, Tuesdays and Wednesdays, and markets and fairs were banned. The life of the town came to a virtual standstill. Even worse, orders were issued and posted throughout Listowel that in future any man, aged between twenty and forty-five years, deemed to be in suspicious circumstances, armed or not, could and would be shot where he stood.

The IRA decided its Volunteers could no longer operate undercover in the town. It was time to establish a permanent fighting force, a flying column modelled on those already in existence elsewhere.

Twenty-nine volunteers from the 3rd and 6th Battalions of the IRA – most of them, like Bryan, already on the run – met at Derk townland, a mile or so from Listowel, on the afternoon of Sunday, January 30th. Their first job was to select a commander. The obvious choice was the only man with experience in the regular British Army, Tom Kennelly, a farm labourer. He was elected by a unanimous show of hands.

Kennelly, tall and powerful, unhurried in speech, stood in the centre of his men as they sat in the grass. Bryan was overjoyed to be with them. The ten days that he, Brosnan and O'Grady had spent in hiding had been the most boring and depressing of his life. There'd been nothing to do except think morbid, fearful thoughts, worrying about his loved ones. Now, he was part of a group again. Companionship and resolve surrounded him, just as the Volunteers surrounded the new leader of the North Kerry Flying Column.

'Men – friends,' Kennelly began, 'Most of you will have heard of the Three Musketeers. They were soldiers too, fighting against greater numbers, great odds. Well, the Musketeers had a motto which we're going to use. You know it. "One for all and all for one". That's how it'll be with us. We've strength in numbers to protect ourselves and to strike at the troops and those bastard Tans. It's not to be an easy life.'

Some Volunteers laughed at the obvious understatement. Kennelly smiled, feeling the sense of unity around him.

'No soft pillows for us. We'll live off the land and we'll stay on the move. They won't know where to find us and, more important, they won't know where we're to attack next.'

He paused before continuing, searching their faces, watching their nods of approval.

'Now, the first job is to pool what resources we've got and then decide where our headquarters are going to be.'

The Volunteers placed what weapons they had on the grass near Kennelly's feet. It was a frighteningly small arsenal with which to start their campaign. There were seven rifles, four revolvers, eight shotguns and just over two hundred rounds of assorted bullets and cartridges, about ten for each weapon.

Kennelly grimaced when the count was done.

'It's a start anyway, boys,' he said, shaking his head ruefully. 'We had to start somewhere. The rest'll come from our own supplies and from the soldier-boys themselves.'

The flying column decided to move south of Listowel, between the town and Tralee, into even more sparsely populated country, into the comparative safety of the Stack Mountains, some rising more than a thousand feet above sea level. Here, the flying column reckoned it was safe from any surprise attack. And so it proved. Alerted by informants, the army followed them to the mountains, but no officer was foolhardy enough to go into the mountain range, to risk ambush among the dark, overhanging crags and the deep valleys, flaming wine-red and yellow with heather and gorse.

From the mountains, the North Kerry Flying Column created a legend of terror.

Those who were believed to be informers were shot and left at the roadside with warning labels pinned to their bodies. Many mistakes were made but none admitted. Not even in the case of a 68-year-old pensioner called Patrick Roche whose only offence was to sell milk and vegetables outside Listowel police barracks.

The flying column stole mailbags, searching for letters from informants. The ripped bags were left in public places so the message was clear.

They attacked police barracks in the dead of night. One simultaneous raid was against those in Ballylongford and Ballybunnion. Usually the Volunteers were driven off in panic, searchlights playing and machine guns hammering. But, in Ballylongford, the column succeeded in fatally wounding a Tan. In reprisal, twenty thatched cabins were burned down in the small village and fifteen men badly beaten.

So it continued week after week, month after month. Attack and reprisal. Reprisal and attack. A Volunteer killed in an ambush that went wrong; a landowner taken out in his dressing gown and shot in revenge. The killings were as merciless as the reprisals. Between the two sides, the ordinary people suffered.

*The Irish Times*, appalled like most newspapers, wrote trenchantly, 'The whole country runs with blood. Unless it is stopped and stopped soon, every prospect of political settlement and material prosperity will perish and our children will inherit a wilderness!'

Such concerned views mattered little to the Volunteers of the North Kerry Column. Their lives were full of romance and adventure, so they thought, with the discomfort and danger providing additional spice. They were swaggering heroes, their otherwise humdrum lives long forgotten. They were the defenders of the people, so they said. They didn't add that the people wouldn't have had to be defended against anything if the Volunteers hadn't begun the campaign of terror in the first place. They were reliving the history of the Fianna, the mythical warriors of Old Ireland.

Sometimes, as it often does, reality intruded. Then, the Volunteers reverted to being simply bewildered youngsters afraid for their lives, unsure of their cause, longing to be home and away from it all.

United, the North Kerry Flying Column was a formidable guerilla group. Fragmented, its members tended to be easy pickings for the security forces. And, in early May, 1921, the column was forced to disperse by an outbreak of scabies, known to locals as 'the IRA itch'. The men were ordered to go their own ways for a week or so since, together they could hardly stop scratching long enough to aim their weapons.

At first, Bryan was tempted to risk a visit to his family in Listowel. They'd kept in contact through intermediaries but he ached to talk to them again, to seek reassurance for what he was doing, perhaps even to receive their blessing.

One night he crept within fifty yards of the bridge over the River Feale leading directly into the town. To his dismay, there were makeshift sentry huts at either end and two soldiers on patrol. He circled the town desperately. Everywhere there seemed to be barbed wire barriers and searchlights. Listowel, in fact, had been effectively sealed off. No doubt there was a way through but he decided the danger of capture was too great.

He laid low for the next few days, living in the dense undergrowth of a copse off the Tarbert road, eating berries when his small supply of bread and drisheen was exhausted. On May 12th, hunger and loneliness forced him into the open again. He set off for the Wilmot farm at Galey Bridge.

It was a warm day with high, gentle clouds as Bryan moved cautiously through the scrub at the side of the road leading east from Listowel. He brushed the back of his hand against his face, feeling the bristles of his beard, hoping he wouldn't appear too disreputable to the Wilmots.

The months away from Hannah had proved to him – if proof were needed – how much he loved and needed her. When he'd joined the flying column, she still hadn't recovered fully from the assault. She'd been quiet and withdrawn, a sadness in her eyes, a bewilderment caused by the brutal realization of how her body could be used by men, a feeling of violation and uncleanliness at the very core of her femininity. Except for her ravaged hair, permanently hidden by a scarf, there'd been few physical after-effects. The main problem was the shock in her mind. Bryan prayed that by now, four months later, she would have returned to her previous laughing, carefree self. He still felt guilty that he'd not been with her during her time of need. That guilt and his desire for her made him hurry on, abandoning most of his caution.

Suddenly, terrifyingly, a voice called from close by.

'Bryan! Hey, Bryan! Here! Over here!'

His body froze, only his eyes moving, darting along the hedgerows and deep into the trees beyond. He was conscious of the beating pulse in his veins. His hand edged towards the revolver in the pockets of his grubby jacket.

'Over here!' the voice repeated. 'On the other side!'

Bryan's head flicked round, his right hand now firmly clasping the butt of the revolver. He saw the face smiling at him over the hedge on the opposite side of the road and relaxed. It was Jerry Lyons, another member of the flying column.

'Jesus!' Bryan exclaimed, relieved, glad to see a friendly face again. 'And that was a helluva shock you gave me, boyo, to be sure!'

Lyons laughed, beckoning. Bryan looked quickly up and down the narrow road, saw that it was deserted and scurried across. The two young men patted each other's shoulders, delighted to have company again.

'You're after going to Gortaglonna then?' Lyons asked.

Bryan was puzzled.

'I'm making for Galey Bridge.'

'Some of the boys are meeting at Gortaglonna.'

'What for?'

'Oh, just a wee chat to see if anyone knows the next chorus,' Lyons shrugged. 'Are you coming?'

'Well . . .'

Bryan was doubtful. Hannah and her family remained uppermost in his thoughts.

'It's not far out of your way. Not far at all,' Lyons urged. 'We won't be long. Just a wee chat. Any more would be mighty dangerous so close to town.'

Bryan shook his head resignedly. He grinned.

'I'll come if you've got a fag, Jerry,' he said. 'I've been out of them for days.'

'Good man you are!' cried Lyons, reaching into his pocket for his battered tobacco tin. He handed it to Bryan and waited until he'd rolled and lit a cigarette before grabbing his arm and pulling him playfully along the side of the field behind the hedgerow.

When they reached the bridge over the gurgling stream just outside Gortaglonna townland, they found three others waiting, concealed at the roadside, the Dee brothers, Con and Paddy, and Paddy Dalton.

Bryan's misgivings disappeared with his pleasure at being with them again after spending so many days and nights alone. They moved into the field next to the bridge, chattering excitedly, quite forgetting all precautions.

They didn't even look up when the lorry rattled over the bridge. And it was too late, much too late, by the time the five young men heard the squeal of brakes.

From the corner of his eye, Bryan Aherne glimpsed the Tans leaping over the side of the lorry, rifles in hand, and starting towards them.

He turned from side to side, searching for an escape. There was none. The Tans had spread far enough across the field to block any retreat.

Dalton flung himself bodily into the prickily hedge. Lyons followed him.

'Take cover!' Paddy Dee shouted, attempting to grab the revolver in his belt, tangling his thumb in his torn waistcoat.

425

Bryan stood still. His hands rose slowly above his head. At least four rifle barrels pointed directly at him.

'Come on out, lads,' he said quietly. 'We're done for. Come on out with your hands up!'

His voice was dull and resigned, empty of emotion.

For a split second, his brain held a vivid image of the shattered head of District Inspector Tobias O'Sullivan.

# Chapter 7 May, 1921

The Tans were almost incoherent with excitement at their capture. They recognized two of the young men in the field, Bryan Aherne and Jerry Lyons, as undoubted members of the North Kerry Flying Column. Hunting the column had become an obsession with the Tans, allowing them no rest, peace nor safety.

'The buggers!' one Tan shouted exultantly. 'We've the buggers at last!'

'Look at the stinking shits!'

'Buggers!'

'Fuckers! Just see the fuckers now!'

Abuse flew from every side.

The five Volunteers, not daring to speak, stood in the middle of the circle of Tans, hands high above their heads, two of them bleeding from bramble scratches. Their faces were grim and set, tearful. Tears ran down Paddy Dalton's cheeks.

A second lorry pulled up. Two inspectors of the Royal Irish Constabulary jumped out of the driving cab and entered the field. They talked briefly to one of the Tans before approaching the prisoners.

When they were about two yards away, they both drew their revolvers from shiny black holsters. The taller inspector was grinning broadly.

He stood in front of Dalton, shaking his head gently like a school teacher who had discovered a naughty pupil. He sucked his teeth in admonition. Dalton turned slightly, seeking support from his friends. As he did, the inspector lashed him across the nose with the barrel of his revolver.

Dalton yelped with pain. Blood poured from his nostrils and into his open mouth. He coughed and choked.

'Search the bastards!' the second inspector, an older, broader man, ordered in a matter-of-fact tone.

'Strip!' the Tan bellowed, jabbing his rifle into Con Dee's stomach. 'Undress. Take your clothes off. Strip or we'll fucking rip 'em off!'

The Tans became even more excited when they found the revolvers in the pile of clothes.

'So it is them indeed,' the taller inspector remarked quietly, almost reflectively.

Suddenly the Tans were all around the naked prisoners, kicking and swearing, punching and spitting, striking out with weapons and fists at the defenceless flesh before them. The frustrations and fears of the past months were vented in their frenzied, vicious attack.

Bryan fell to the ground under the blows, winded, unable to cry out with the pain searing through every limb. He was incapable of defending himself. His arms were wrapped round his lower belly, one hand between his legs guarding his manhood. He felt his flesh jarring and compacting from the blows, sensed an eyebrow tearing open from the side of a boot, slowly almost lost consciousness, drowning under the waves of agony.

'That's enough boys,' someone shouted. 'We've other plans for the murdering bastards.'

The blows stopped as suddenly as they had begun.

'Here,' a voice said from above, throwing his clothes down beside him. 'Put 'em on smartish if you don't want any more of the same.'

He struggled into the garments, still laying on the ground. He knew his limbs would betray him if he tried to stand.

Dalton and Paddy Dee were so hurt that they were unable to do more than wriggle into their vests and shirts. The Tans laughed and picked them up, one to each arm and leg, and tossed them into the back of the second lorry like stooks of corn. The three others limped after them, still groaning, only to be helped into the lorry with kicks and punches.

'Oh, Mary and Joseph!' Lyons muttered, lying next to Bryan. 'We're done for. Oh, Holy Saints come against us!'

Bryan turned towards him, trying to smile through broken, swollen lips. Strangely, he felt very strong and alive although he knew that his body was near to breaking point.

Lyons gathered some of Bryan's apparent inner strength and tried to smile back.

'What now?' he panted. His front teeth had disappeared. Blood spittled from his gums as he spoke, spraying onto the muddy, wooden floor of the lorry.

'Shut your fucking gob,' one of the Tans snarled, lifting his rifle and slamming the butt down.

The lorries cranked into motion, jolting and bumping down the road before turning and heading west back towards Listowel.

Back to the police barracks, Bryan assumed, for a night in the cells, another beating, and then to the interrogation centre in the Ballymullen Barracks at Tralee. Surprisingly, he didn't feel down-hearted. The others seemed in worse shape than he was. He shook his head, trying to clear the singing in his ears. Incongruously, his eyes focussed on Paddy Dalton's penis, not six inches from him. Jesus, he thought, it was a fair size. A bawdy rhyme from his schooldays came into his brain.

'Long and thin, goes right in,
Pleases all the ladies.
Short and thick does the trick,
Out come all the babies.'

He smiled lopsidedly to himself, his mind still spinning. Jesus, he decided, it was a long cock that Paddy had. Bit limp now, but decidedly formidable. He groaned as the lorry jerked to a halt.

'Out you bastards!' the Tan guards shouted. 'Out!'

'Balls,' Bryan muttered, still thinking of Dalton's attributes. 'Big balls . . .'

'What's that?' one Tan demanded, boots planted either side of Bryan's face.

He didn't reply, lifting himself on to all fours before gingerly standing upright, gazing around, opening and shutting his eyes to see properly. To his surprise, they weren't back in Listowel but still in the countryside and, as far as he could judge, only half a mile or so from where they had been captured.

Bryan, prodded in the back by a rifle, jumped down from the lorry first. He stood by the tailgate handing the others down. Lyons helped him support Paddy Dalton as they were pushed and pulled into the field by the road and then roughly shepherded across that field towards another about forty yards from the lorries. The Tans were intent on taking their prisoners as far away from the road as possible, somewhere out of sight and hearing of any passers-by.

With the last kick and shove, the five young men, two of them hardly conscious, held up by their friends, were pushed through a rickety wooden gate into the field.

The Tans didn't follow.

Bryan looked quickly at Jerry Lyons. His face was ashen with fear, his mouth working, trying to speak.

'Oh, Jesus,' Lyons blurted eventually.

Bryan shivered and nodded.

'They're going to do for us!' Lyons went on. His voice rose: 'They're going to do for us here and now!'

Bryan turned and faced the Tans. His mind suddenly cleared and calmed when he saw them leaning over the stone wall surrounding the field, about five yards away. Their rifles rested on the wall, barrels pointing casually. Bryan had seen such expressions before on the faces of his own friends in the flying column just before they had shot a retired policeman accused of being an informer.

'You can't do this,' Bryan shouted. 'There's been no trial.' As he spoke, he realized how futile his plea sounded.

The Tans laughed, genuinely amused. 'Trial?' one of them called back. 'Trial? You fucking murderers expect a trial?'

'They expect a trial,' another echoed mockingly.

'Fucking mad dogs don't get a trial,' a third exclaimed, his voice flat and cold.

'For pity's sake!' Lyons cried.

'Pity?' the tall inspector replied, pushing aside two of his men so that he could be clearly seen. 'You murderers want pity? What pity have you shown? What pity to those you've shot down in the back and in the dark? What pity to Mr O'Sullivan's wife and his wee one? You can be thankful your women won't see you snivelling here, begging for mercy you don't deserve and mercy you're not going to receive!'

Three of the Tans began chanting.

'Murderers! Murderers! Murderers!'

Bryan plucked at Lyons' sleeve, hoping his friend wouldn't protest any more. He knew it was hopeless. All that could be done was to muster as much dignity and defiance as possible.

'Not like this,' Lyons muttered. 'For Holy Mary's sake, not like this!'

'Face the bastards,' Bryan urged. 'Show 'em we're not afraid.'

He gazed quickly along the line of his friends.

Dalton and Paddy Dee were bent almost double, moaning still, pink spittle dribbling from their broken mouths, their bare legs spindly and quivering with weakness. Bryan thought that it was a blessing that they were not fully conscious.

Lyons' head was sunk into his chest. His eyes were screwed shut, his lips moving in prayer.

Con Dee, Bryan discovered, was looking along the line just as he was. Their eyes met. Dee shrugged helplessly and half-winked as if in encouragement.

Bryan's mind began to fill with images of his family, of happy gatherings, of Hannah. He sensed an unbearable sadness, felt his throat closing, tears nearing his eyes.

He blinked rapidly and looked straight ahead into the face of a Tan, his rifle now aimed at his shoulder. A dozen rifles pointed over the wall. The Tan directly in front of him couldn't meet his eyes directly and shifted his aim slightly.

Bryan thought that the man was wanting someone else to fire first, that he didn't want to initiate the killings himself.

The seconds passed like minutes. There seemed silence all around. Bryan tried to think of a prayer. None came to mind. He wanted to say something but couldn't.

And then the rifles exploded.

The crashes and flashes echoed so close that Bryan's ears were deafened. But where was the impact, the tearing and shattering of flesh and bone, the overwhelming pain and the darkness?

Beside him, Lyons moaned. A scream of agony strangled, gurgling, in his throat. Bryan saw his arms fly above his head, the dust puffing from the front of his waistcoat, the redness soaking out through the two holes in the blue serge cloth. Lyons fell back and lay still, eyes and mouth gaping wide to the sky.

Bryan glimpsed Dalton and Paddy Dee spinning backwards.

Dalton clasped the side of his head, trying to touch the hole in his temple. Dee bent his arms in front of him as if embracing and pulling the bullets into his chest and throat.

His brother, Con, was beginning to run, horror mingled with disbelief on his face.

Instinctively, Bryan did the same. He ran like he'd never run before, legs pumping almost to his chest. He ducked and weaved, looking once to his left , seeing Con Dee crouched very low.

Bullets crackled and whizzed past and over him. He thought he heard the sounds of pursuit, some shouting and yelling, but he wasn't sure.

Behind him, the two inspectors were trying frantically to restore some order to the Tans. All of them, when firing, had tried to avoid shooting the prisoners who stood straight and gazed balefully ahead, hoping that someone else would be aiming at them. And when Bryan and Con had started running, some of the Tans had hurdled the wall in pursuit, effectively blocking the aims of the rest. Now, they had stopped their chase and were firing from kneeling or prone positions at the figures fleeing from them, more than eighty yards distant.

Bryan, lungs tightening with exertion, risked another sideways glance. He saw Con Dee stumble momentarily and grab the back of his right thigh. For a second, it seemed he would fall but somehow he continued, limping sideways, dragging his right leg straight behind him.

Ahead of Bryan, twenty yards away, a ditch about four feet deep curved towards a thick copse of trees and overgrown bushes. His stride shortened as he tired. The shooting behind him slackened. He was nearly there, only a few more yards. Bryan wanted to shout in triumph and relief but he'd no breath to spare. He lifted his head in thanks to the sky.

As he did so, a bullet struck him just below his right shoulder blade, tore obliquely through muscles and flesh, skidded off bone and left his body four inches beneath his armpit.

The impact, like a violent shove in the back, sent him tumbling into the ditch.

He tried to move, to lift himself, knowing he couldn't remain where he lay, that he had to reach the copse.

Pain arrowed through his body. His right side was virtually paralysed with shock. Bryan bit into his tongue, attempting to hold back a cry.

Slowly, he dragged himself along the ditch with his left arm. His nails and fingers dug into the earth, hauling him along, until after what seemed an eternity of pain, he reached the copse and slid under the cover of a large bush, a few yards inside the protective greenery.

He lay there, feeling the blood running down his ribs. He pictured in his mind his heart pumping life-blood through the wound, pumping, pumping away till there would be none left.

'God help me,' he whispered, face pressed against the damp soil. 'Please, please help.'

Bryan knew he had to leave his hiding place quickly or else he would have no strength to move at all. He would simply bleed to death where he lay. If the Tans saw him . . . well, it made little difference whether he died under the bush or out in the open with the sun in his eyes and the wind in his hair. Actually, he decided, the latter would be preferable.

He crawled back into the ditch and pushed himself upright, panting with exertion, gritting his teeth and screwing up his eyes with pain.

To his amazement, there were no Tans in the field any more. He clambered out of the ditch, bent over, trying to stem the blood from the exit wound with his left hand. He was unable to reach the wound in his back at all.

The two police lorries were beginning to move off down the road two hundred yards away. Bryan could just make out what looked like three sacks tied behind one of them. They bumped and jolted on the road surface, raising a trail of dust. He looked up at the sun, working out his position, knowing it wasn't too long into the afternoon.

Galey Bridge and the Wilmot farm must be roughly north from where he stood, he thought. He stumbled off with the sun at his back, praying he'd enough strength to walk nearly three miles, hoping that he would recognize the correct road when he reached it. He sensed that his hold on consciousness was only very slight and ebbing fast at that.

Con Dee was watching Bryan as he staggered across the fields. His leg had been shattered by the bullet which struck him in the right thigh. He'd stopped the bleeding with a rude tourniquet but didn't plan to move until darkness. He was still in a state of shock, horrified by what he had seen.

Once Bryan disappeared into the copse, the Tans had given up the chase surprisingly quickly. Probably, Con reckoned, the two inspectors had become worried about being seen at what, after all, had been a cold-blooded massacre. Instead, the Tans had returned to the three crumpled bodies in the field, apparently holding a discussion about them.

Finally, to Con Dee's horror, they'd produced some rope from the lorries, tied it to the legs of the dead Volunteers and pulled them out of the field.

They had secured the bodies to the back of the first lorry and set off, Con presumed, for the mortuary in the old workhouse at Listowel.

He had turned away, sobbing, as his brother's body had bounced bloodily along the road and out of sight.

At least, Con thought, two of them had survived to bear witness to what had happened.

By the time he had walked more than two miles, Bryan was virtually unconscious. He reeled from side to side of the deserted road with little control over his limbs. The pad which he had made to partially staunch the flow of blood had long ago dropped in the dust. His progress was marked by small splashes of red. His eyelids were almost closed. What he could see of his surroundings continually receded and then grew, receded and grew, throbbing and hazy.

He thought he was on the right road. He turned to look up at the sun, eyes flickering. The blinding orb swooped down, searing him with light and darkness. He cried out once with all his remaining strength and fell, swooning, on to the grass verge.

Hannah Wilmot heard the shout while she fed the chickens in the farmyard. It mingled indistinctly with the cluckings of the birds at her feet. She paid little heed to it, assuming it must have come from the gang of boys who liked to play by the stream near the farm.

She finished her chore and started back towards the house. She stopped by the door, listening. There were no sounds of boys at play, no sounds at all except those of the animals.

'Did you hear that cry?' she called to her father, working across the yard near the pig-sty.

'The one a wee while back? Sounded like someone stepping on a thorn.'

'Like someone hurt?'

'Aye. Now you say it, like someone hurt.'

'But no one passed the farm going either way. So if they're hurt they're still out there.'

Her father looked thoughtful. He leaned his mucking out fork carefully against the wall of the sty and waved to Hannah to follow him. She patted the scarf round her hair, checking that it was properly in place, before hurrying into the road after him.

They gazed up and down, shielding their eyes from the sun, before walking fifty yards to the bend in the road, peering carefully into the hedges on either side.

'An animal maybe,' Mr Wilmot remarked, shrugging his shoulders.

Hannah nodded. 'Probably.'

They linked arms affectionately, turning back. They had become very close since their sufferings at the hands of the Tans.

433

'Listen!' Hannah cried suddenly, spinning round, pulling her father with her. 'Listen!'

Both heard the low groans. They ran to the bend in the road and saw the shape forty yards from them. Mr Wilmot's first thought was whether it was even human. The shape, the person, inched along, flat on the road, limbs moving so slowly, like a giant red streaked crayfish.

'Holy Mother of God!' Mr Wilmot exclaimed, breaking into a run.

'Bryan! It's Bryan!' Hannah cried. She knew deep within her that she was right although she was totally unable to recognize him.

In the few seconds they took to reach him, Bryan stopped moving, unconscious again.

One look told Mr Wilmot that the young man was near to death.

'It is him?' Hannah called, a few yards behind her father, not really needing confirmation.

Mr Wilmot nodded grimly. He bent down and lifted Bryan around his shoulders and under the knees. His body was light. A trickle of blood ran from his back, soaking into the dust.

Father and daughter looked into each other's faces, hoping beyond hope, worried beyond concern.

'Quick! Take the horse into town,' Mr Wilmot ordered. 'Bring the doctor and tell your mam to have some bandages. Quick, girl, there's not much time.'

'Can't I stay?' Hannah begged, cupping her hands lightly around Bryan's slack jaw.

'Do what I say, Hannah. Quick, else we'll be burying the boy this night. For God's sake, hurry!'

Hannah ran off, skirts gathered up, weeping silently, leaving her father to carry his burden back to the farmhouse as gently as he could. She clattered past him on horseback before he was into the yard. Their eyes locked for an instant before, without a backward glance, she continued her gallop towards Listowel.

Within an hour, Doctor Maguire's automobile swung through the farm gates with Hannah in the passenger seat.

By then, Mrs Wilmot had cleaned Bryan's superficial wounds and managed to stop the loss of blood with copious bandages torn from old bedsheets.

'There's no bullet there and nothing's touched his lungs,' Doctor Maguire announced after his careful examination. 'Those are the blessings but the poor man's taken an awful beating and lost too much blood for my liking.'

He stretched upright.

'The bandaging's good,' he said, smiling encouragingly at Hannah's mother. 'No worse than I could do . . . and probably better at that. Now tell me, do you know what happened?'

The Wilmots shook their heads, moving closer to each other as if seeking mutual strength.

'No need to tell me anything, I'd guess he escaped from the massacre at Gortaglonna. From where you found him, that makes the best sense.'

By their expressions, the Wilmots clearly didn't know what the middle-aged doctor was talking about.

'The Tans killed three of the boys,' Hannah explained quietly, her face set. 'Shot down in a field this very afternoon.'

'It's all over the town,' said Doctor Maguire. 'Shot while resisting arrest, the Tans say. They're viewing the bodies now to find out who they were.'

'Will he . . . ?' Hannah gestured towards Bryan, unable to complete her question.

Doctor Maguire tucked the stethoscope back in his black bag.

'If there's no infection, no more bleeding, he should pull through. I've stitched him the best I can and now it's simply a matter of rest and quiet. He's in the Almighty's hands, so he is.'

Before returning to Listowel the doctor reluctantly helped move Bryan across the yard and into the barn where Hannah and her mother had prepared the cleanest and cosiest spot possible. They had fashioned a small cubicle in the deepest corner of the barn out of bales of the left-over winter hay and pinned blankets to the hay and the barn walls, shutting out any draughts. They laid two mattresses on a flattened pile of straw. Only four bales had to be stacked to shut the space completely from view. It was to be the limit of Bryan's existence for the next seven weeks.

In the first crucial days, the Wilmots took turns sitting by him. Hannah spent every night in the barn, poised over Bryan, watching every flicker of his face in the light of her oil lamp as he struggled for life.

At times, he was delirious, swearing and cursing, shining with feverish sweat. Hannah would wash him and hold his hand until he lapsed again into fitful unconsciousness. Like anyone who nurses a sick person, she came to know every inch of his body, each of its functions. It didn't disgust her, only made her love him more in his helplessness.

When he was out of danger, his eyes clear but weak, the Wilmots arranged for Bryan's family to visit and nurse him.

Jack Aherne sat with his grandson for hours at a time, twice spending the night with him. The old schoolmaster would re-tell the family legends and, when he judged Bryan to be strong enough, discuss with him the latest political moves and the progress of the IRA campaign.

By now, this late May, Eamon de Valera had returned from America having failed to win recognition for the self-proclaimed Irish Republic following bitter arguments with Irish-American politicians. Once back in Dublin, he was allowed to travel around virtually unmolested on the orders of Lloyd George, the Prime Minister, who knew that he needed the Sinn Fein leader's influence if ever the IRA were to be brought to the conference table.

The campaign of terror, the five hundred soldiers and police killed since the beginning of 1920, had produced the realization in London that only massive repression could end the guerilla warfare. Lloyd George saw that the IRA could not be wiped out without the use of methods which he thought would be wholly unacceptable to the British people.

After all, Lloyd George reasoned, hadn't the recent elections effectively split the country into two, thus dashing the main aim of Sinn Fein and the Irish Republican Brotherhood at its core?

The elections held that May were organized in accordance with the 1920 Government of Ireland Act, introduced as a replacement for the long-promised Home Rule Bill.

Under the Act, there would be parliaments in Belfast and Dublin with clear provision for a Council of Ireland with power to unite both parliaments without reference to the Imperial Parliament at Westminster.

The results of that election had been wholly predictable. Sinn Fein won all but four of the 128 seats in the twenty-six counties of the south. The Unionists won forty of the fifty-two seats in the six counties in the North and North-East, said to comprise Ulster.

In Dublin, Sinn Fein constituted the second Dail but declined to meet in public as the official Southern Parliament, still preferring to move its meetings around secret locations.

In Belfast, it was different. The Northern Parliament convened with majestic ceremony and a moving address by King George the Fifth.

All that the Irish Republican Brotherhood had plotted and fought for – one Ireland, freed from England – was ashes. It had been politically outmanoeuvred. The war, such as it was, might not be lost but it couldn't be won. It was a time for talking, perhaps even a truce.

Such suggestions, reported in the newspapers, made Bryan Aherne doubly frustrated during the tedium of his convalescence. His one aim was to recover his fitness and rejoin the flying column to take revenge on the Tans. That, however, was proving a long process.

He exercised as much as he could, but even seven weeks after the shooting he still became exhausted after little more than an hour's walk round the country roads at nightfall, the only time when it was safe to leave the barn. And all the while he read of the negotiations which were bringing a truce nearer. He felt physically sick at the thought that the war might be over by the time he was fit again. His only consolation was the hours he spent with Hannah. She made no secret though of her delight at the prospect of peace.

One Saturday in July, Bryan was woken from his after-lunch doze in his hiding place by the sound of the barn doors swinging shut.

He peeked over the bales of hay. Hannah stood by the closed doors, her face wreathed in a mischievous grin. She had a newspaper in one hand. The other was hidden behind her back.

'I thought you said you were going into Listowel with your parents,' he called, wiping the sleep from his eyes.

'I was too but I decided to stay behind when the postman brought the newspaper.'

She walked towards him, long green skirt sweeping the floor.

'It's a surprise for you,' she said, handing the paper to him. 'A marvellous, wonderful surprise!'

He looked at her suspiciously, half smiling.

'Go on then,' she urged. 'Look at it.'

Bryan opened the newspaper, the *Irish Independent*, and stared at the front page. His heart fell. The large headlines proclaimed that a truce in hostilities had been agreed the previous day in Dublin. All fighting was to end from noon on Monday, July 11th.

His face registered so much dismay that Hannah had to feel sorry for him despite her own joy.

Bryan turned away from her and threw the paper on the ground. He stamped on it angrily.

'Why?' he exclaimed. 'Why? We were winning. Why give it up now?'

'Because the people are tired of it maybe,' Hannah replied quietly, seating herself on the hay bales and swinging her legs. She placed a hand gently on Bryan's right shoulder. 'You almost died,' she went on. 'And for what? For what the British had offered us all along.'

He struck his clenched palm against his thigh 'We didn't start fighting to finish it like this,' he said. 'We've two Irelands now, not even one, and we're accepting that?'

'They are. Your leaders are. Collins is.'

Bryan turned, arms outstretched, appealing.

'But don't you see? Don't you see that those boys – the two Paddys and Jerry – died for something else? They stood there and took the bullets because they believed that one day there would be a republic for all of Ireland. And now we've a government in Belfast and one in Dublin, believing different things and both still really under the control of the British.'

Hannah looked solemnly up at him.

'I know.' She hesitated before whispering, 'I know dearest, but it means that you're safe . . . that there'll be no more killing . . . no more raids . . . no more Tans.'

A tear slipped down her cheek. She brushed it away, adjusting the scarf round her head at the same time.

Bryan suddenly felt very ungrateful. He sensed the depth of her emotion, knew that she was thinking, caring, about him. He moved closer to her and put his arms round her shoulders. 'And what are you hiding then?' he asked softly, his anger and disappointment vanishing as he looked on her beautiful face. 'What's behind your back? Another surprise?'

She wrinkled her upturned nose.

'Can you smell it?'

'No. Show me.'

'And who's the man of the world then?' She mocked, producing with a flourish, a half-filled bottle of whiskey.

'The hard stuff!' he cried.

'For a celebration of peace.'

'Your da's?'

'He won't be minding.'

'It's been a long time, so it has.'

He took the bottle from her, uncorked it and gulped down a mouthful.

'Hey!' she protested. 'I'm celebrating as well.'

'You don't drink. Girls don't drink whiskey,' he teased, feeling the alcohol warming him already, its fumes filling his nostrils.

'I do.'

'No proper girls do.'

'I do so – and I'm proper!'

He looked at her for a second.

'I know you are,' he said huskily. 'You saved my life, so you did, and that's very proper.'

He handed Hannah the bottle. She took a tiny, apprehensive sip.

'There!' she said, her blue eyes glinting cheekily. 'I told you so.'

'Then, if proper girls can drink the hard stuff,' Bryan interrupted, his voice suddenly serious, 'They can also do something else.'

She looked questioningly at him, not replying.

He smiled gently and began untying the scarf on her head. 'Then proper girls can be forgetting all that happened to them.'

'No, no!' Hannah tried to push him away but it was too late. His hands were touching, caressing her blonde hair, now released from its cover, just reaching down to the nape of her neck.

'It's beautiful,' he said wonderingly, feeling its softness. 'It shouldn't have been covered for so long.'

'It's awful,' she cried. 'The Tans . . . the Tans.'

'I know. I know what they did but that's all gone now,' he said soothingly. 'If it's peace, whether I like it or not, then everything's in the past.'

'It's not like it was.'

'It's still beautiful. Like the colour of ripe wheat.'

He pulled her to him.

'Is it really?' she murmured, her face and hair pressed to his chest, feeling his bare skin against her through his half-opened shirt.

'It is that.'

Bryan moved his hands, clasping her narrow waist to lift her off the bale of hay and into the confines of his hiding place.

'Have they gone?'

'Who?'

'Your mam and da.'

'An hour back. They said they'd be calling on your folks for tea as well.'

During the past seven weeks the two families had become very close, it wasn't uncommon for Hannah's parents to leave the young people unchaperoned.

As Mrs Wilmot had remarked to her husband weeks earlier, 'She's seen him as nature intended when he was half-dead, Cathal, done everything for him, and the Tans . . . well, you know what I mean. She's grown up now, so she has, and they're together and that's that, if you're asking me. He's a good boy and when all this is over . . . well, they're as good as man and wife, so they are.'

Mr Wilmot had to agree. 'He's from a good family, that's true. Mona . . . ah, you're probably right. She's a sensible lass.'

Ironically, the relationship between Bryan and Hannah had grown less easy the more they were left alone. Bryan for one, sensed a growing tension between them.

Perhaps, he sometimes thought, it was because of all she had done for him during those days and nights when he had wavered between life and death, needing total nursing. From the odd, unexplained remarks she had made, he guessed that his body held few secrets or mysteries for her.

During the past few days the tension had become almost unbearable. He seemed to shiver every time any part of their bodies touched accidentally.

They sat next to each other on the mattresses, their backs pressed against the hay. They didn't speak. Bryan felt that the whole barn, the whole world, had shrunk to this tiny space.

She offered him the bottle, tilting it towards him. He took another gulp and watched while she sipped at its neck. He noticed she didn't wipe it after he had drunk. He eased the bottle from her grasp and put it down away from them.

'You've had enough?' she asked.

'For the minute.'

Bryan slid his hand into the space between them, hoping to find her hand. When he did so, he hesitated for a second before actually holding it.

To his surprise, Hannah immediately squeezed his hand, scratching a fingernail across his palm.

'Well, are we celebrating?' she whispered,

'What?'

'The truce . . . you alive . . . us . . . anything?'

'I suppose so.'

'Only suppose so?'

Hannah turned her head towards him, lips slightly parted. The pink tip of her tongue moistened them. They shone in the gloom at the back of the barn. One of the horses whinnied in the stalls a dozen yards away.

Hannah had heard enough of Bryan's feverish ramblings to understand his inexperience with the opposite sex.

She leaned sideways towards him, pressing into him, slightly uncertain herself. Their lips met, softly at first and then harder.

They broke apart, breathing heavily, smelling the sweet whiskey fumes in each other's mouths.

'When I could, I wanted to say . . . ' Bryan stammered.

'Yes . . . ?'

'Well, we'll marry, won't we?'

She nodded, smiling. She offered her mouth to his again, her eyes open until the very last split-second, watching his eyes grow wider and deeper.

As they kissed, her mouth opened under his allowing their tongues to touch.

Bryan's hand shifted towards the front of her white lace blouse, brushing across her nipples. It hovered for a moment, undecided, before moving boldly to her left breast. Hannah moaned deep in her throat. He felt an explosion of her breath in his mouth. She pushed him away from her, twisting, and then relaxed, allowing his hands free passage over her outer clothing.

Their embraces became more frenzied. They tumbled full length on to the mattresses on the straw. Hannah's skirt hitched up above her knees. Bryan's hands became more searching and demanding.

'Careful. Be careful,' she whimpered against his throat as his fingers caught in the opening of her blouse. He stopped for a moment and then tried again to undo the tiny, delicate pearl buttons.

She uttered a deep sigh.

He looked down at her face, framed by her tumbling hair Her eyes were grave, appealing, unsure.

'You do love me?' she asked.

'I do so, mavourneen.'

She paused and sighed once more.

'Then wait,' she said, suddenly decisive. She squeezed from under him and got to her feet.

'No, don't look,' she ordered as she stood behind him. 'No, don't look,' she repeated. 'Don't look! Don't turn round!'

He thought she was leaving, clambering back over the bales. His face pressed against the mattress, sniffing the familiar smells of the barn, waiting to be alone again.

Bryan heard movements behind him and turned his head.

He rolled over onto his back and looked up.

Hannah stood sideways against the wall of hay. The green skirt which she had removed was held shyly up to her neck.

Slowly, she lowered and spread her arms wide. The skirt billowed down on to the pile of clothes already at her feet.

For long seconds, the soft light filtering into the barn played its shadows across her nakedness, touching a pointed nipple, dappling

441

the small triangle of curls, caressing the curve of her buttocks.

Before Bryan could raise himself on to his elbows, Hannah knelt and bent over him, her breasts swaying gently.

'I love you,' she said simply. Her mouth closed over his. His hands slid round her, marvelling at the smoothness and roundness.

Their love-making was swift and fierce. Bryan tried to be considerate but the fact of being inside her, above her, with her, swept everything away. She clung to his neck, panting against his ear.

When it was over, as he began lifting himself away, Hannah's arms circled his back pulling him close again.

He looked down at her, stammering an apology, hoping he hadn't hurt her, hadn't been too rough.

'Don't be sorry. I'm not,' she breathed.

'It was . . . it was all right for you?' he asked tentatively.

Hannah smiled contentedly up at Bryan, her eyes glistening.

'We'll be married . . . ' he began.

'Aye, avourneen . . . '

' . . . as soon as possible.'

'Aye . . . he'll need a da.'

'Who?'

Hannah pointed down between their bodies, her fingers brushing against him, feeling him instantly lengthen and thicken, feeling his seed deep within her.

'He will,' she murmured.


## Chapter 8 February, 1922


The cobblestones in Church Street were so greasy from the overnight rain and the February dampness in the air that Bryan Aherne had difficulty in keeping his feet.

'Are you sure you want to come along?' he asked his wife anxiously, sliding his arm gently round her thickened waist.

'Of course, silly,' Hannah replied, smiling up at him from under her new, pink cloche hat. 'It is a day of history, isn't it?'

'It is that, dear, but just you hang on tight to me. Don't want you slipping up.'

'No dear,' she sighed, wondering why men became so fussy at such times.

Bryan manoeuvred her past the people in the street, nodding greetings here and there, hoping they realized from Hannah's shape that she, as he put it affectionately, carried all before her, now seven months pregnant.

Most of the Listowel folk, of course, knew perfectly well about Hannah's condition. In fact they knew most everything there was to know about the young married couple who had moved into the neat, terraced cottage in Courthouse Road.

After all, they said to themselves, justifying their inquisitiveness, wasn't Bryan Aherne one of the real boyos, the hard men, in the town, if not the whole of Kerry?

Bryan was regarded with considerable awe. His part in the murder of District Inspector O'Sullivan and the escape from the massacre at Gortaglonna were in the repertoires of local ballad singers. Both incidents had been elevated into the realms of myth, glorifying killing and bravado, omitting pain and fear.

'Great morning, Mr Aherne,' a young boy called, brushing past Bryan, touching his cap to Hannah.

'It is that, praise be,' Bryan replied automatically.

'Who's that, dear?' Hannah asked, noticing that the youngster had immaculate puttees wound around the lower half of his trousers.

'Don't recognize him,' Bryan grunted. 'One of Davie Carroll's Fusiliers, I'd bet.'

Hannah said no more on the subject, knowing that Bryan was particularly irked about how many of the town's young men were trying to give the impression that they had been active in the Tan War, as it was now termed.

It had become the vogue to dress in puttees or gaiters and long raincoats, the style of the North Kerry Flying Column.

Davie Carroll, the town's leading draper, had done a roaring trade in such items, and thus the contemptuous nickname of 'Davie Carroll's Fusiliers' for those who wished to appear what they were not and never had been.

Their masquerades, their play-acting, Bryan thought as he walked along, were only a small part of Ireland's sickness that late winter. After the truce and the treaty signed five months later, the country was confused, fearful and divided. And that mood had undoubtedly spread to Listowel.

But this day political differences would be put aside, he reckoned. It was likely to be a day for drinking and the telling and retelling of the old and not-so-old legends for most, if not all, the townsfolk.

The crowds grew thicker when Bryan and Hannah turned into William Street and reached the junction with Market Street. People on the edge of the narrow, uneven pavements moved courteously aside to allow Hannah an uninterrupted view of the convoy of trucks and tenders parked, engines idling, further along the street.

She had expected the onlookers to be happy and excited. Instead there was a distinct feeling of tension everywhere.

The low murmur of conversation around her died away completely when dozens of Tans and Auxiliaries began streaming from their barracks and boarding the vehicles in the convoy.

Hannah felt Bryan's protective hands suddenly tighten their grip on her shoulders. An irrational pang of fear made her legs tremble. She winced as the baby moved inside her womb.

She wanted so much to shout, to scream at the men in green and khaki. Obscenities, awful words, formed in her brain. Her fingernails pressed sharply into her palms. She saw herself for an instant dashing forward into the street and lashing out with hands and feet at the grim faces. But Hannah did nothing, said nothing. Neither did anyone else.

The spectators watched sullenly, nursing their loathing and bitterness, even luxuriating in the depths of their hatred for these men whose presence had hovered over the town like a malevolent spirit for more than eighteen months.

Smoke from ten exhaust pipes billowed and hung in the air as the drivers revved up the engines. A young officer wearing a fawn trenchcoat stood up in the front seat of the leading tender and waved the convoy forward.

The vehicles rumbled and rattled through the gauntlet of silent hostility. Hannah looked closely into the passing faces but did not recognize any of them.

A single, vehement curse rang out above the noise of the engines. 'May you rot in hell forever!' By then, though, it was too late for others to join in.

The convoy turned into Market Street and headed away from the crowds, safely on its way to Tralee and the beginning of the evacuation of the British forces from Listowel and Kerry.

Listowel came to life again. The crowd began dispersing. Some people stood together in small groups for a while, talking quietly, rather disappointed after what was supposed to have been an occasion to remember, perhaps let down by the strength of their emotions and expectations. The others hurried off to their homes, the shops or the bars.

'Well, they've gone, haven't they?' Hannah remarked as she and Bryan started towards home.

'Aye, and good riddance!'

'Did you really hate them?'

'Yes. Did you?'

'But I didn't recognize any of them, dear.'

'Nor did I.'

'I felt baby move when they came out of the barracks.'

'I'm glad they've gone before he comes into the world.'

Bryan hugged Hannah close for a moment.

'You know, I'd have taken a shot at them if I'd my gun.'

'I would've as well. I really would, Bryan.'

'Your gun?'

'Well, yours . . .'

They laughed together, knowing how much Hannah hated the sight and sound of firearms, even her father's ancient crow-gun.

'Are you off drinking now?' Hannah asked mischievously when they reached the corner of Courthouse Road, near the top of Church Street.

'You know I said I'd meet Grandad Jack in the tavern.'

'Well, while you men are jawing, I'll pop round to Forge Lane and keep Grandma Maude company.'

'You mean you'll have a good gossip?'

Hannah looked exasperatedly at him.

'Why is it men hold discussions and women gossip?'

'Cos you do and that's why,' Bryan smiled, bending slightly to kiss her cheek. 'See you later.'

'And not too much, mind you,' Hannah called sharply after him. 'Or you'll have no bed nor tea tonight.'

Bryan gave an exaggerated shrug of his shoulders, waved and crossed the street towards the family's tavern where his grandfather was already waiting for him, seated as usual at the table nearest the bar.

Jack Aherne had been treated kindly by his sixty-nine years. His mind was clear and retentive, his back straight, his eyes as observant as ever they'd been in the classroom. Only his legs gave him trouble, allowing him to walk, at best, a few hundred yards before a necessary rest.

'Any trouble, then?' Jack asked, pipe between clenched teeth, when Bryan had placed two frothing glasses of porter on the table.

'Not a whisper, Grandad. They seemed as happy to leave as we were to see them go.'

'Hardly surprising, young Bryan, is it? They didn't have much of a time here, did they? Not during the troubles and not since the truce, did they?'

The old man was thinking of the numerous gunfights between the Tans and the IRA Volunteers in North Kerry during the past months of supposed, declared peace.

'Old scores,' Bryan mumbled, totally unrepentant that he had taken part in, even organized, some of the incidents. 'Pity is, we didn't kill any of them, let alone wound them.'

'And what about that police sergeant shot down on the green at Ballybunnion?'

'Nothing to do with us, Grandad. Nothing. Truthfully. Simon Mulvihill was only settling personal accounts for Danny Scanlon.'

'Was he now?' Jack said sarcastically. 'Well, that makes it fine and dandy then!'

'You remember Danny Scanlon and what happened?'

'I do that . . . hot outside the barracks in the riot . . . straight through his wedding tackle . . . I remember, but I'm also remembering how long ago it was. Five years is a mighty long time waiting to settle that blood debt.' Jack Aherne's voice was bitter, his eyes angry. 'If you youngsters want it like that, why they'll be back-shooting all over Ireland for generations to come!'

'It's not that way, Grandad. You know that. Calm down. Calm down, please,' Bryan pleaded, worried that they might be overheard.

Jack paused, gazed round the bar, then nodded resignedly. He emptied his glass and pushed it towards his grandson.

'Bring two more,' he ordered. 'They'll cool us down. And don't be worrying. I'll pay.'

Almost simultaneously, grandfather and grandson broke their silences.

'I'm sorry,' Bryan began.

'So what happens now they've left?' Jack interrupted, tamping down his pipe before relighting it.

'You haven't heard, Grandad?'

'When does it happen, Bryan?'

'I thought you'd heard. I knew you would have!'

'The Tans leave and you IRA, you Republicans, move in? Is that it?' Jack asked.

'Yes.'

'Does anything change then?'

Bryan paused before answering.

'You know as well as I do, Grandad, what's happening.'

'Does that make it right . . . your boys taking over from the Tans?'

'Who knows? But what else can we do?'

'Aye.'

They were silent again, both considering the political events which were dividing their small market town as well as their country, or rather twenty-six counties of it.

The new Irish Free State was to have its own parliament, its own constitution and its own army and navy. Militarily, all Britain wanted was the use, if needed, of four sea ports.

But the Irish delegation at the conference had been completely outclassed on the question of Northern Ireland by the British negotiators.

If the Northern Ireland Parliament asked to stay out of the Irish Free State within a month of the treaty proposals becoming law, then it could do so. It was, of course, a foregone conclusion that such a request would be made. But then, under the British scheme, a boundary commission would begin work considering the border between North and South.

On this issue, Lloyd George used all his cunning to find agreement.

He led Michael Collins to believe that the boundary commission would hand a deal of Ulster back to the fledgling Free State. Collins hoped in turn that this would make Northern Ireland stillborn, not viable politically nor economically.

At the same time, Lloyd George gave the Ulster leader, James Craig, the impression that hardly any boundaries would change.

Within months, those understandings – or rather misunderstandings – were to cost hundreds of lives, many of them totally innocent.

The debate in the Dail was filled with bitterness and acrimony before the treaty was approved by the 121 representatives with a majority of only seven votes.

De Valera resigned as President and went into opposition, being replaced by the ailing Arthur Griffith. Strong differences emerged between those like Collins, who regarded the treaty as a first step towards a full Irish Republic and those, like de Valera, who saw in it the betrayal of all for which the IRA had fought its guerrilla war.

But Collins, as before, controlled the Irish Republican Brotherhood. He threw its weight and influence behind the treaty, however much he disliked the necessary compromises within it. This gave him tentacles spread throughout the IRA but they were not enough to win anything like total agreement for his view.

The IRA split into two. Those who supported Collins and the treaty were swiftly issued with green uniforms, arms supplied by the British, and transformed into the Free State Army. Those against the treaty hid their weapons and pondered the next move.

In Listowel, after much heart searching and anguish, sixteen of the North Kerry Flying Column, originally members of the 3rd and 6th Battalions of the 1st Kerry Brigade, IRA, decided to join the army. Fourteen, including Bryan Aherne, gave their allegiance to the anti-treaty Republicans supporting de Valera.

Both factions actively canvassed support and new recruits. Both had equal success. North Kerry, like Ireland, was tearing apart like a sheet of tissue paper between the Free Staters and the Republicans.

And in the six counties of the north-east, now officially Northern Ireland, the eternally fragile peace between the Protestant majority and the Catholic minority ruptured into vicious sectarian warfare.

The Republicans within the formerly united ranks of the IRA realized that they would soon have to make their first move, that the bloodletting was likely to spread throughout the island.

Their opportunity came as the Auxiliaries and Tans started to be evacuated, the first of the British forces to leave under the terms of the Anglo-Irish Treaty.

What happened in Listowel almost exactly mirrored events in the rest of Ireland. As Bryan Aherne and his grandfather sat in the family tavern in Church Street around midday on February 14th, 1922, groups of anti-treaty Republicans stealthily took over armed occupation of the emptied Tans' barracks in the market town, in Ballybunnion and Ballylongford.

Jack Aherne had a fair idea of what was happening and persisted in questioning his grandson.

'So where does it all lead?' he asked, none too gently. 'If I knew, if I'd heard what your boys were planning to do, surely the Free Staters would have known as well?'

'A bit late now, I'm thinking,' Bryan grinned, perhaps a trifle smugly. 'We beat them to the punch. Now we have to hold the line while the politicians sort it out.'

'Politicians?'

'Mick Collins and Dev and the rest.'

'Do you really think they will . . .'

'Yes . . .'

' . . . because if you do, you've more belief than you've the right to.'

Bryan shook his head tiredly, dispiritedly. 'They have to, Grandad, don't they? For Jesus' sake, they've got to. I don't want any more killing. Oh, yes, I fought the Tans and whatever. You know that. So does everyone else. But I'd never tell anyone else but you that I'd probably damned my soul because of it, because of the killing I did. I don't want any more killing.' He paused, his eyes circling the bar, taking in the customers. He reached into his jacket pocket for tobacco and cigarette papers. 'Sure, I don't like the treaty, Grandad. Nor do you, if you say what you mean.'

Jack's voice was stern, resentful that his integrity might be questioned. 'Don't ever be thinking, young Bryan, that I'm not with you in everything, with all your thinking, excepting, that is, your methods. Those I don't like and never have.'

Bryan grimaced, reddening a little on his cheek bones.

'So what do we do? Nothing? Let it pass by default? After all the blood? Just let it pass?'

His grandfather slammed his glass down on the table, becoming deeply angry.

'The treaty was voted on and passed by the Dail,' he argued. 'Or aren't you believing in democracy? Is that what you're about? Is that what you're about just like the rest of them? The people have to accept what you lot want come what may? Is that what it is? Heads we win, tails you lose? Is that what it is?'

'No, no . . .' Bryan protested, temper rising.

His father, who'd just arrived in the tavern, leaned over the bar, guessing already the subject of the argument, the familiar subject between the two.

'Come on, Dad,' Sean Aherne urged, tongue in cheek. 'Let the boy be. We've enough problems without a scrap in here.'

'It's no scrap, son,' his father snapped back. 'We're talking – or trying to – about democracy . . . at least, the Irish version of it. That's no joking matter these days, is it? Or is it?'

'And sure, what was all the fighting about if it wasn't democracy?' Sean replied.

'Sure it was, Dad,' agreed Bryan.

Jack Aherne rose dourly to his feet: 'Don't you realize that now we've a proper Irish Parliament again, we've to settle differences without the gun? If Irish are to fight Irish over what this word means and that doesn't, why, then, there's little hope for us – nor should there be – for generations and more. The politicians will always be pandering to your man with the biggest gun and that's no good for the rest of us – the old folk, or you'll excuse the expression, the women, the children, the ordinary, wee people – who just want to live their lives the best way the good Lord allows us.'

'Oh, Grandad, it's not . . . you know it's not,' Bryan began again.

'Anyway, I'm away now, having served my purpose as a decoy.'

Bryan placed his hand on his grandfather's forearm, attempting to restrain him, but the old schoolmaster brushed it aside and walked stiffly to the door.

'Grandad!' Bryan appealed. 'Grandad, please come back.'

At the tavern entrance, the old man turned, wagging his head ruefully. 'Here endeth the first lesson,' he called, the merest suspicion of a twinkle in his eyes. 'And God be with you.' He gave a little hop, half twirled his walking stick and went through the door.

The next morning, Bryan Aherne, and most of Listowel, awoke with a hangover to discover that the town was split into two armed camps.

During the night, the Free State Army had rushed 250 troops from Tralee to garrison and fortify the old workhouse at the end of Market Street, by the junction of the road to Ballybunnion.

By midday, the troops were nervously patrolling Listowel. The anti-treaty IRA responded immediately by sending out its own patrol, using some of its most experienced men.

The two groups edged cautiously, watching each other carefully, yet trying to pretend that the other wasn't there.

Bryan wore his revolver in a holster at his waist, the flap conspicuously unbuttoned, as he led the IRA patrol with Con Dee at his side, his rifle in the crook of his arm. Three others trailed behind, carrying Lee-Enfield service rifles captured in raids on police barracks.

They all knew that the patrol was simply a show of strength designed to prove that the IRA wasn't cowed by the official government's troops, was still a force to be reckoned with in the town.

Round and round Listowel they went following each other, first one in front, then the other, through streets and alleys rapidly emptying of people who had sensed the danger themselves.

'We can't be going on like this, Con,' muttered Bryan Aherne to his second in command out of the corner of his mouth. 'It'll be dusk soon and then heaven knows what'll happen in the dark.'

'Aye. I'm so jumpy I'd shoot at moonbeams. What I'm needing is the hair of the dog, not all this nonsense walking around with a loaded gun.'

'Amen to that.'

'Besides someone could be awful hurt. Those Free Staters look like they know one end of a rifle from t'other.'

'And don't I know that. We helped train a few of them.'

'I'm guessing so.'

'So what do we do?'

'Don't be asking me. You're the officer, and anyway, the old leg's beginning to gyp me.'

'That's an awful help, Con!'

'Well, we could just go home, after all.'

'No. That'd be losing face. The big man wouldn't be liking that.'

'Well, what then?'

Bryan looked across the opposite side of the market square where the army patrol was standing, seemingly deep in discussion. Their officer gazed back at him.

'Let's take our own route,' Bryan suggested. 'And if they . . . ' He jabbed his thumb at the huddle of green uniforms. ' . . . don't follow us, we'll go round the town once on our own and then home. That'll show we're not worried about them, won't it?'

Con Dee and the others didn't need a second bidding. With a new spring in their step, the IRA men wheeled out of the market square and began their fifth circuit of Listowel's near deserted streets.

This time, without the irksome presence of the Free Staters, the atmosphere was more relaxed. They exchanged greetings with the few people still around and waved jauntily to those peeking nervously from behind their curtains.

The afternoon became darker, colder and damper. The patrol increased its pace, anxious to be on the way home, preferably after a stop in a warm, friendly bar.

'Back to the square and that's it, boys,' Bryan announced over his shoulder, hurrying down Charles Street, alongside the courthouse, ready to turn right into William Street.

'And maybe a wee jar or two with the officer?' one of the patrol called cheekily.

Bryan turned his head, about to answer before he reached the corner of the street.

'No sodding cha . . . '

The riposte choked away into a gasp. He cannoned into someone coming the opposite way round the corner.

'What the fuck?' he spluttered.

'Jesus!' cried Con Dee, already starting to crouch into a firing position by the wall.

'It's them!' a voice shouted in alarm.

Suddenly, the street corner was filled with a confused mass of men, feet and weapons tangling and jangling together, as the Free Staters' patrol collided with the IRA men.

Bryan heard the click of a rifle bolt behind him.

'No, no,' he screamed. 'Don't fire! Don't fire!'

Automatically, though, his hand darted towards the butt of his revolver.

'Hold your fire, for Christ's sake!' the man beside him frantically ordered.

They looked into each other's faces at close range for the first time.

'Paddy Murphy, as I live and breathe!' Bryan exclaimed.

He realized immediately that the Free State Army Officer, he'd bumped into was an old friend from the North Kerry Flying Column and the 1st Kerry Brigade, IRA.

'Well, well, if it isn't the bold boyo himself,' Murphy replied, smiling hesitantly at Bryan.

'So it's you, Paddy, we've been following around. I should have known.'

'Should have known? Why?'

'By your ragtail formation, of course,' Bryan joked. 'Call yourself an army . . .'

'And wasn't I saying the same about your wee mob of amateurs?' Murphy's grin broadened.

Bryan blew into his cupped hands. 'Jesus, it's perishing,' he complained, his eyes flicking round his men and the Free State troops. They were lowering their weapons smiles of recognition on their faces.

'It is that,' Murphy agreed. 'Haven't seen hide nor hair of you for months.'

'Not since the split up.'

'Well, how are you then?'

'Middling, Paddy. Just middling.'

'And the wife?'

'Two months to go.'

'You should be indoors.'

All around them the men were chatting together, swapping cigarettes and matches.

'Aye, you've something there, Paddy. But, as the man says, orders

452

is orders.'

'Aye.' Murphy scratched his gingerish hair. 'That's the rub, isn't it? Orders.'

'What are yours?'

Murphy looked doubtful for a moment, then shrugged: 'Just to make sure your Republicans aren't taking over any more of the town.'

'Just five of us? Chance'd be a fine thing!'

'So what are you doing then?'

'Simply watching what you're up to. That's all.'

The two men gazed at each other for a second before bursting into laughter, both seeing the black humour of the situation.

'Is it a private joke, then?' Con Dee asked sarcastically.

'No . . . no . . . ' Bryan coughed, wiping tears from his eyes. 'It's just so stupid . . . so fucking stupid . . . that's what's so funny. We've been spending the afternoon watching these boys watching us and they've been doing the self-same thing.'

Murphy nodded. 'A bloody pointless exercise, that's what,' he guffawed.

'Shall we pack it in?' Bryan suggested.

'Why not?'

The two officers shook hands.

'A drink sometime maybe, Bryan?' Murphy asked.

'You know where to find me, Paddy.'

'I do that. Indeed I do,' the Free State officer replied, giving Bryan a mock salute.

'Come on boys,' ordered Bryan, 'The first drink's on me and then we're away to our homes.'

That night, after supper, he held Hannah tightly in his arms as they lay in the warmth of their bed.

'I think it'll be all right, mavourneen,' he whispered, face pressed into her sweet-smelling hair.

She shifted her position, trying to be more comfortable. Her back pushed against him. His arms circled her, gently holding her breasts.

'All the men with guns though,' she worried, voice half-muffled against her pillow. 'Guns and men all over town.'

'They're old friends really. Sure, they've different points of view but they're not wanting a fight. Leastways I don't think so. Why, old Paddy Murphy greeted me like a long-lost brother. All of us have been through a war together. We're not wanting another one.'

His hands slid under her nightgown, running across her smooth flesh. Their lovemaking was less frequent and more sedate because of her advanced pregnancy, but no less passionate nor mutually satisfying for that.

Hannah lifted herself a fraction, offering her body. Bryan slid into her.

Later, not much later, as they drifted off to satiated sleep, his mind wandered back over the past months. They had been overwhelmingly happy together. His decision to move into Listowel rather than live with the Wilmots at Galey Bridge, had been the right one. They might have been stifled under the concern of Hannah's parents for their only child. As it was, Mrs Wilmot visited them twice a week, full of ideas and suggestions.

Nor was he overfond of being so near his own family. His parents were always calling round. It was something he was obliged to accept for the time being, in return for their financial help in renting the house in Courthouse Road and the virtual sinecure of his part-time job at the tavern.

Soon, Bryan knew, he would have to find a proper job. Fatherhood demanded that. But it would have to wait until the tensions had died away and Ireland had finally decided what it wanted to do about the treaty; until then perhaps, he could be released from his commitment to the anti-treaty IRA.

This proved a longer process than he had foreseen. The Republicans and the Free Staters in Listowel maintained the unspoken truce of old IRA comrades but continued their patrols, even strengthening their numbers. The mood of foreboding grew almost daily.

Most of the country, whatever their allegiance, shuddered when de Valera proclaimed that if the treaty was ratified, the IRA, 'in order to achieve freedom, would have to march over the dead bodies of their own brothers.'

'They will have to wade through Irish blood!' de Valera warned chillingly.

As the fear grew, so did the anarchy, particularly by the anti-treaty Republicans, desperate for money and equipment to be able to face the government troops.

Post offices were held up and robbed; goods were stolen from trains; people were terrorized into subscribing to so-called collections. Once again, old scores were settled. The lifeless body at the side of a country road became a familiar sight. It was as if the entire country was talking itself into a war that no one, except the zealots, wanted.

Not that that mattered a jot in the Aherne household in Court-house Road on the morning of April 14th, 1922, with Bryan running for Annie Cahill, the midwife, after Hannah had shaken him awake.

'Baby's coming,' she'd said, her voice trembling, her eyes calm.

'Oh, God!' Bryan cried, leaping out of bed and pulling his trousers over his striped nightshirt, stubbing his toe against the brass bedstead in his hurry.

'Be careful, gosseen,' Hannah exclaimed. 'You'll be falling out the window next and then where'll we be? There's time yet.'

Indeed, Bryan had another four hours of anxious waiting in the kitchen, boiling kettles, fetching towels, trying to shut his mind to Hannah's occasional moans from above, before he heard a sharp slap followed by a thin piercing wail.

He ran to the foot of the narrow staicase, combing his hands nervously through his hair.

'It's fine they are,' Annie Cahill suddenly called, her beaming face appearing round the turn of the stairs. 'Come and say hello to your wee son! It's all done. It's a proud man you should be.'

Hannah smiled palely up at him when he stepped into the room, her hair still damp with perspiration. He bent over the bed to peck her cheek and look more closely at the swaddled baby, at his son's tiny, mottled red face, wisped with dark hair, eyes tight shut.

'He favours you,' Hannah said quietly, smiling to herself.

'Now be off with you and tell your folks,' Annie Cahill ordered briskly. 'There's some women's work to be done yet. Be back in an hour though. I've another confinement due any time.'

'I'll be sending Mam and Grandma Maude,' Bryan whispered to Hannah. 'Love you,' he added.

Her tired eyes, dark ringed, glistened up at him. 'Not too much celebrating, mind,' she murmured, gazing at her baby for a second. 'Remember you're a da now.'

After taking the news to Forge Lane and No 32 Church Street, Bryan headed for the tavern, reckoning he deserved a good drink after the morning's anxieties of fatherhood. He really did feel proud, prouder, he thought, than he had ever been. A firstborn son, he decided, really proved he was a man at last.

Bryan's huge beam told his father immediately of the successful birth. He could hardly stop his son talking after he had burst forth with the good news.

Sean Aherne reached for the whiskey bottle to pour drinks for everyone in the bar.

'To the wee one, God bless him and keep him all his days and may

455

he die in Ireland,' he toasted, gulping the whiskey down and refilling the glasses.

'It's a marvellous feeling, Dad, isn't it?' Bryan enthused.

'So it is, son, but I'm wishing it'd come a better day.'

'A better day? Why? What's happened?'

'It's in the newspaper. Last night the Republicans took over the four Courts in Dublin as their military headquarters. Threw down the gauntlet to Mick Collins and the government.'

Bryan was silent. He emptied his glass, the spirit burning in his throat.

'Slainte,' he said automatically.

'What's that?' his father asked over the increasing hubbub in the tavern. 'If you ask me what it means, Bryan, I'll be telling you. It means fucking war, son. That's what it means. Civil fucking war!'

'Slainte,' Bryan repeated, not quite hearing his father.

## Chapter 9 June, 1922

The sunlight played on the dull grey walls of a town holding its breath. It glinted and sparkled on the dozens of rifle barrels poking out of first floor windows on three sides of the market square. It danced through the dusty glass of the Listowel Arms Hotel in the lower corner of the square, forcing the troops of the Free State Army to shield their eyes, making them feel even more isolated. It warmed Bryan Aherne's face as he strolled round the square with Brigadier Humphrey Murphy, commanding the Republican forces in the area and in charge of Listowel.

'There's been a good job done here, Aherne,' the brigadier said, stopping by the entrance of St John's Church to survey the surrounding buildings.

'We've everything except the hotel,' Bryan replied. He swept his arm round the square. 'All those houses from the hotel to the hardware shop on the corner. Those two bars, Leah's and Danahar's, on this side and the National Bank over there. No one can enter or leave the square without coming under our guns.'

'The machine guns?'

'Two of them here in the square and the other two in those bars in Market Street I showed you, Griffin's and Moroney's.'

'Good. That was a fine capture, so it was.'

'It was that,' Bryan agreed.

Brigadier Murphy allowed himself a smile bordering on self-satisfaction.

'I think we can safely be saying, Aherne, that we can hold this town,' he said. 'And if we hold here, we hold North Kerry. How are you deploying the men?'

Humphrey Murphy liked using such phrases to remind those under him that he'd once held a less exalted Commission in the British Army.

'Twelve hours on duty, twelve hours off.'

'They're happy?'

'They're surviving. There's not much they're having to pay out of their own pockets. The locals are being very generous.'

'Good. And the Free Staters?'

'Miserable and frightened, I'm thinking.'

'They've not much, have they?'

'No, not much. The workhouse. Clancy's in William Street, Latchford's Mill and, as you see, the hotel over there. Not much at all.'

'Well, Aherne, at least no trouble so far, thanks be.'

'No. We're allowing them only one small patrol a day for exercise and provisions. Otherwise, they stay where they are. Mind you, the boys still talk with them through the windows next door.'

'Hard to stop?'

'Don't want to really, Brigadier. Many of them are old friends, after all. It's been a bit tense at times but nobody's fired a shot yet.'

'I wish I had more confidence, Bryan, that they never will,' Brigadier Murphy said, deciding to become informal, heading determinedly for a closer inspection of his forces manning the Castle Bar, trusting to the owner's hospitality.

As Brigadier Murphy ducked through the bar door, he removed his wide-brimmed, high crowned hat, one side pinned in the style of the Anzac troops of the Great War.

Bryan, following, felt rather strange and unmilitary in his normal rather shabby, everyday suit with a mere holster buckled round his waist. But then, he reflected, everything felt strange these days, had done for weeks past.

The results of the election for members of the first Dail of the new

Irish Free State, announced only three days later, on June 24th, added to the feeling.

That 94 of its 128 members were in favour of the Anglo-Irish Treaty served only to heighten the dream-like unreality of what was happening. The democratic voice had spoken but, as before, was rejected by the minority who didn't care for its clear message.

Ironically, Michael Collins, the head of the Provisional government striving day and night to keep the Free State intact, provided the final catalyst himself.

As he had done many, many times before, Collins ordered the death of a man. This time his target was Sir Henry Wilson, lately Director of Military Operations at the War Office in London, now advising the Northern Ireland government on matters of law and order.

The murderers, Joseph O'Sullivan and Reginald Donne, were captured swiftly, mainly due to O'Sullivan being handicapped by the loss of a leg at the Battle of Ypres. Before their trials and executions, they revealed their memberships of the IRA.

An outraged British government mistakenly assumed that the killing was at the behest of the anti-Treaty Republicans. They immediately ordered the commander of the British troops still in Dublin, General Macready, to attack the Republicans' headquarters in the Four Courts. He advised wisely that this would only unite once again both Irish factions against the British.

Thus, Michael Collins, who'd ordered the murder in retaliation for the Catholics' sufferings in Northern Ireland, was given an ultimatum to bring down the Republicans himself or otherwise the entire treaty would be abrogated. He played for time by asking London to provide proof of the Republican links of the two gunmen in custody. Since, as the real instigator, Collins knew that there were none, he gained a short respite. It couldn't and didn't last.

At seven minutes past four on the morning of Wednesday, June 28th, 1922, the first muzzle flash lit the Dublin sky. The shrapnel shell, from one of two British field guns borrowed by Collins, exploded near the outer walls of the Four Courts, ripping into the masonry, shattering windows.

It was one of the better shots by the inexperienced Free State gunners just across the River Liffey.

The Republicans could do little except loose the occasional, hopeful fusillade, huddle in the safest depths of their headquarters, and rue their rejection of Collins' surrender ultimatum.

The pounding barrage continued for nearly two days.

Early on June 30th, a white flag fluttered amid the smoking rubble of the great building. Rory O'Connor, leader of the Republicans stumbled out of the ruins and into captivity with his executive committee and more than a hundred IRA men.

Their surrender after such futile, though brave, resistance lanced into the abscess of bitterness which had been welling and suppurating for months.

The news of the fall of the Four Courts reached the Republicans in Listowel by telephone at breakfast time that pleasant Friday morning.

At first, no one knew quite what to do. The wiser and older barricaded their doors and windows. The bolder and more inquisitive risked a walk through the streets but soon scurried home after listening to the clicking rifle bolts and angry recriminations coming from the Republican positions.

Bryan Aherne tried to calm his men from the command post above the hardware shop at the corner of the market square. 'Wait for orders!' he urged. 'For Jesus' sake, we must wait!'

His men reluctantly obeyed his instructions, their tempers and nerves on edge. The minutes of ominous silence ticked away. Suddenly, a cheer rolled into the market square from the windows of the Arms Hotel. The Free State troops, completely isolated there, cheered once more, reacting to the fast spreading news of the Four Courts' surrender, their side's first victory.

The listening Republicans grimaced sullenly. A few brought their rifles to their shoulders, aiming towards the noise.

Bryan realizing the provocation, dashed to the nearest window and leaned out. 'Hold your fire!' he bawled. 'No firing without my word!'

A sneering voice bellowed back, interrupting him as he started to repeat his orders, 'You fucking rebel! What's the matter? Afraid you'll be tasting the same metal as your friends in the Four Courts? They soon gave up, didn't they?'

The few insults from a Free State Army soldier were all that was needed.

Rifle fire began to crackle from the enraged Republicans. Bullets slapped into the hotel facade, splintering plaster and brick into puffs of dust. Shards of glass smashed to the pavement.

For thirty minutes, the antagonists blazed away at anything that moved and everything that didn't.

The town rang with gunfire, the air cracking and whizzing with hundreds of rounds of ammunition, the four light machine-guns chattering in deadly conversation with each other.

'Stop firing!' Bryan shrieked. 'For fuck's sake, stop it!'

His orders were totally ignored and, as the acrid cordite smoke bit into his nostrils, Bryan too succumbed to the general hysteria. It didn't matter that there was hardly ever a clear target at which to aim. The feel of the revolver bucking and humping in his hand was enough.

Gradually the hysteria ebbed. The shooting slackened. Any attempt, Bryan knew, to storm the Free State defences head on would inevitably mean heavy casualties. He considered burning them out but swiftly rejected that course. A fire would be difficult to contain. He thought of Hannah and their little son, Joseph, of his parents and grandparents on the periphery of the battle. The flames might even spread to their homes.

Around ten o'clock, a messenger arrived from Brigadier Murphy, who was directing the action round the corner in Market street. The scribbled note ordered Bryan to try for a parley with the Free State troops in the hotel.

Without much confidence, Bryan pulled off his white shirt and tied it to a broomstick taken from the hardware shop below.

Gingerly, he pushed the makeshift flag of truce out of the window, waving it up and down.

The sporadic firing in the market square died away when the Republicans saw the signal although the crackle of shots could be heard from other parts of Listowel.

Bryan poked his head over the windowsill.

He looked quickly to his right along the front of the houses and shops towards the hotel, hoping for an answering flag of truce. Instead to his horror, Bryan saw a Free State soldier leaning out of a window, rifle aimed directly at him.

'Jesus!' he cried, pulling his head back into cover.

Two shots rang out. The broomstick jerked in his hand as the bullets ripped through the shirt.

A third shot cracked across the square. Bryan heard a wail of fearful agony followed by a soggy thud. A Free State soldier lay on his back in the gutter, legs twitching. A spreading redness across the front of his jacket showed where the Republican bullet had struck.

'God's mercy,' Bryan whispered.

'It's Eddie Sheehy,' one of his men at another window said quietly.

'You know him?'

'His mam lives next to us. We went to school together.'

'Poor silly fucker,' another man said, shaking his head sadly.

'There's another white flag!' someone called excitedly.

'Where?'

'By St Mary's.'

A young priest had stepped through the doors of the Catholic Church, holding over his head what looked like a white altar cloth.

The firing stopped while the priest walked without hesitation over to the dead soldier and knelt to administer the last rites.

When the priest had finished, he spoke for a few moments to one of the Free State soldiers in the hotel's downstairs window. Then he glanced up at the windows of the buildings held by the Republicans before walking along the pavement and stopping directly below Bryan.

'Are you in charge here?' he called up.

'Who's wanting to know,' Bryan replied.

'I do. I'm Father Troy.'

'Well, Father?'

'Can't you be stopping this slaughter?'

'We tried but they fired on our flag of truce, so they did.'

The priest, not much older than Bryan, dressed in a shabby black suit, spread his arms in a gesture of appeal, 'Will you try again, for the Lord's sake, if I guarantee the Free Staters will respect the flag this time?'

'Aye, if you can.'

'They will. They promised me they will.'

Bryan leaned a little way out of the window, ready to duck back. No shots came. He waved his shirt again. Another shirt answered from the hotel. He lifted himself into full view.

'God bless you!' the priest cried. He flinched suddenly as a stray bullet from the shooting away from the square slapped into a wall about twenty feet from him.

'Be careful, Father,' Bryan shouted. 'The bullets won't be respecting your collar.'

Father Troy smiled ruefully.

'And isn't that the truth?' he called back. 'Will you keep the truce while I'm away stopping the others in this madness?'

'If they will.'

'They will.'

'I'm praying so, Father, for everyone's sake. And, by the by, you'll be wanting the brigadier above Griffin's in Market Street. He's really in charge.'

The priest nodded, waved the white cloth once and hurried out of the square.

His progress along the street could be judged by the way the shooting gradually died away. Within fifteen minutes, it had ceased altogether.

For hour upon hour, the men on both sides stayed tensely on alert while Brigadier Murphy parleyed with the Free State commander, Tom Kennelly. Just before five o'clock, the two leaders walked into the market square with Father Troy between them, white cloth still held aloft.

'They've surrendered,' the brigadier called to Bryan. 'It's all over here for now. The boys can stand down.'

'Thank the Lord,' Bryan murmured as his men cheered and slapped each other on the back.

Bryan left his position and went down the stairs, through the hardware shop and into the square. The priest was standing by the dead soldier. He made the sign of the cross above him before covering the body with the altar cloth.

'Shall we be guarding them?' Bryan asked Brigadier Murphy, nodding towards the Free State troops who were emerging from the hotel, carrying their weapons.

The brigadier shook his head.

'No need,' he said quietly, looking round to ensure that Kennelly was out of hearing. 'They know they're licked. Just keep a close eye on them.'

Under Kennelly's orders, the Free State troops stacked their guns in the square and then formed up into three ranks. Four of them carried Eddie Sheehy's body into St Mary's Church.

Brigadier Murphy waited until they had disappeared from view before addressing the captured soldiers. Kennelly stood by his side, shoulders slumped dependently.

'Lads, you're all as brave men as any commander in the field could possibly want to lead. You fought like Irishmen should and you shouldn't be ashamed that you've had to surrender. Commandant Kennelly here made the only possible decision.'

The brigadier turned to Kennelly, smiling sympathetically. They shook hands.

'You were outnumbered and outgunned and there's the end of it,' the brigadier continued. 'I'm only glad that but one of your comrades died.'

Kennelly leaned towards him and whispered a few words.

'And I'm told, one of you were wounded as well.'

Brigadier Murphy paused, gazing round the square filled with men, faces dark with cordite powder, grime and nervous exhaustion.

'The war no one wanted has begun,' he declaimed solemnly. 'All of us, I'm sure, will fight according to our consciences. But now the war is upon us, some might see the issues differently than before. All around you . . . '

He gestured towards his own troops.

' . . . are men who fought the British in the name of old Ireland. Many of you risked your lives gloriously as well in that struggle. Many of your brothers and friends gave their lives.'

The brigadier pointed dramatically towards the Free State soldiers at ease before him.

'Do you really want to fight against your old comrades? Are you really going to split this brave country of ours in two? Won't you be joining us and finishing the battle for the Republic begun by the Easter Martyrs and the martyrs before them?'

He lowered his voice, speaking almost confidentially. Bryan, twenty yards away outside the Arms Hotel, strained to hear.

'Commandant Kennelly has agreed that as part of his surrender I can ask you to change sides, to rejoin your Republican friends of old. He's assuring me that there'll be no dishonour in this nor any rancour held against any man who does so. What do you say? It'll be your last chance before you go into captivity. Any man now who'll join us on our road to victory and the true Republic . . . well, let him fall out and shake hands with his new comrades. What about it, boys? Who'll fight for the true Republic?'

He folded his arms across his chest and waited.

The Free State soldiers looked round at each other. Some shook their heads immediately. Others whispered together. A few shrugged their shoulders and broke ranks and walked over to those they recognized among the Republican soldiers. In all, fifty accepted Brigadier Murphy's offer. The other two hundred were marched off the next day to Tralee and detention in Ballymullen Barracks.

Within a few days, most of the Republicans had also left on their way to help garrison Limerick where the confrontation between former friends was potentially even more explosive.

Paddy Landers and Bryan Aherne remained in charge of the fifty men still holding the police barracks and courthouse.

The townsfolk of Listowel sensed, rightly, that they'd been spared the worst.

In Dublin, the Republicans' resistance hadn't ended with the fall of the Four Courts. Fighting went on for nearly a week in the capital of the new state, artillery, machine guns and grenades effectively destroying the property in O'Connell Street opposite the buildings ravaged by the British bombardment during the Easter Uprising. The battle was hopeless and the Republicans knew it.

Eventually those still alive surrendered after repeated appeals from priests. The Free State troops led the Republicans off to prison as they emerged one by one through the dust and rubble.

Within five weeks, any pretence that the anti-treaty forces had a chance of winning was gone. Collins sent battalions of newly-recruited men – some former members of the United States Army – in a drive south-west from Dublin at the same time landing units from the sea behind the Republican lines.

On the morning of August 3rd, Colonel Michael Hogan led ashore more than two hundred Free State troops at Tarbert, on the southern banks of the River Shannon. The few 'Irregulars' in the small port decided that discretion was preferable to valour and fled inland, leaving the local coastguard station in flames as a gesture of defiance.

The Free Staters advanced unopposed through North Kerry on their way to Listowel, ten or so miles to the south. Their overwhelming superiority made resistance pointless.

As reports of their progress reached the market town, Bryan Aherne's depression grew. He knew that if the Republicans made a stand, then the main loser would be Listowel itself. For an hour, he, Paddy Landers and Con Dee talked of various strategies which might halt or slow the Free Staters – a series of ambushes, perhaps – but by early afternoon they accepted the inevitable. They would retreat south-east to Abbeyfeale leaving the town undefended. While the Republicans gathered their equipment and 'requisitioned' £1,658 in notes from the National Bank in the market square, Bryan hurried home to give Hannah the news.

'How long will you be away?' she asked dully after he'd told her. She stood by the fireplace, baby Joseph cradled in her arms, pressed against her white apron.

'Not long,' Bryan assured her.

He stepped towards Hannah, wanting to hold her and his son, but she turned away.

'How long?' whispered Hannah, automatically patting the baby's back to bring up his wind.

Bryan breathed in the baby smells pervading the small home, the odour of milk, powder and drying nappies. 'Not long,' he repeated quietly. 'A month or two at most. The fighting won't last. Mick Collins'll settle it quick enough now his army's front and back of us.'

'You've lost?'

'Aye, I'm reckoning so.' To his own surprise, Bryan felt neither disappointment nor anger in conceding defeat. Perhaps, he thought, it had always been an impossible dream. Perhaps it always would be.

'I'll be going back to the farm,' Hannah said flatly. 'We'll be safe there.'

'Safe?'

'From your friends in the proper army or, rather, the people you used to call friends. They'll be after looking for you.'

'They'd not be hurting you.'

'It'll be safer.'

'Aye, it may be,' Bryan conceded reluctantly. 'But this is your home.'

'Only when you're here.'

'Oh, Hannah!' he exclaimed, made guilty by her deep unhappiness. He slipped his hand round her narrow waist and pressed her back. He hoped she wouldn't feel the revolver belt strapped round his waist. 'I'm so sorry. I'm sorry, mavourneen.'

'Why should you be? You've always been fighting for something, haven't you? We've always come second.'

'You haven't. You haven't.'

She twisted in his arms to face him. Tears streaked the dusting of powder on her cheeks. 'Just for once, Bryan Aherne,' she said bitterly. 'Just for once, will you be after telling me why the fighting? Just be telling me so I can be explaining to babbie when he's old enough and asking what his da did in his awful short life.'

'You're thinking I'll be dead?'

'And why not?'

Bryan gripped Hannah around the shoulders and almost forced her to sit down on the narrow sofa. He knelt before her on the rug, his arms embracing her and their son.

'Don't be thinking that,' he pleaded. 'Don't be.'

'And are you so special then?'

'I'm not . . . but I'll not be doing anything reckless. I've both of you to live for.'

'Then, why? Why all this?'

'Because . . . because . . . ' he hesitated, shaking his head slowly, before the words came in a torrent, words half remembered from

IRA pamphlets and indoctrination lectures, words that sounded angry because of Hannah's use of emotional blackmail.

'Because what I'm wanting is for you and Joseph and all my family and the families of Ireland. It's not for me alone, Holy Mary knows, it's not for me. If this country is to be free – truly free – then its affairs must be changed. That's what we're meaning by the Republic and our need to fight for it. The Republic is the very symbol of what we must be having. It's not enough that Irishmen should form a government in Dublin. It never has been. What's important is how we're governed. It's not enough that an Irish landlord should replace a British landlord. There should be no landlords. Don't you see the land is ours, belongs to everyone? Don't you understand that no one man should have the right to control this or that part of it? It's not enough that our business houses should be run by Irishmen instead of Englishmen, each growing wealthier in turn from the sweat of their workers who produce their riches but have no share in them. Don't you understand that a country's wealth belongs to all its people and should be shared equally amongst them? It's not enough to change British privilege for Irish privilege. There'll be no privilege in the Republic, not of position, land, wealth, health or education. Doesn't your heart tell you that the Free State is just another name for part of the British Empire with all the evils of imperialism and privilege and decadence that that contains? It's not the Republic of Pearse and the Martyrs. We've simply exchanged one set of masters for another. Don't you believe that in the Republic the only masters shall be the people with all having equal rights – Catholic or Protestant or Jew – as well as equal opportunities? What we have now only maintains the old social and economic system and brings us nothing. You ask why the fighting, Hannah? Then I'm telling you that there'll always be fighting until there's the Republic. Not a republic. The Republic. That's what the boys died for, standing alongside me in the field at Gortaglonna. Ireland may be the country of dreams and dreamers, but at least they're dreams worthy of your own life and at least there are plenty of dreamers prepared to sacrifice that. While there are, there'll be fighting and bloodshed. And if, one day, there's no one ready to die for the Republic, why then Ireland'll be no better than Britain and the Irish people no better than the slaves of imperialism that they've always been and not deserving to call themselves Irish . . . not deserving at all, God help them.'

Bryan's passionate, jumbled words ended as hesitantly as they'd begun.

Hannah listened, eyes widening, trying to comprehend his whirling thoughts about the Republican philosophy.

'And will this fighting make a better life for Joseph here?' she said finally, turning the gurgling baby towards Bryan so that he could look fully into his chubby face.

'I've said it will,' Bryan said gently. 'Believe me, it will.'

'But what you've been saying sounds an awful deal like what those terrible men in Russia are saying and you know what the Church thinks of them.'

'Communists, you mean?'

'Aye, like them.'

'They only believe in what Jesus Christ himself basically preached.'

'Then why does Father O'Connor call them the servants of the anti-Christ?'

'Because he's not understanding what they're trying to achieve.'

'You're knowing better than the Father?'

'No.'

'And they're killing people as well,' Hannah said reflectively. 'And most people don't want killings.'

'Nor do I.'

'You're fighting aren't you and people are killed in fighting?'

Hannah started to sob, realizing the futility of it all. The baby sensing the distress and tension around him, began to cry too.

'Oh, Jesus!' Bryan exclaimed. 'I've not the time for all this now. No time at all.'

He went upstairs, pushed a few clothes into his old rucksack and returned downstairs and took half a loaf and a hunk of cheese. All the while, the baby howled and Hannah sobbed.

Flooded with misery, Bryan walked to the front door. 'I'm off then,' he called. 'I'll be at the farm when I can.'

There was no reply. He opened the door as noisily as he could, rattling the latch.

'Bryan! Wait, Bryan!' Hannah shouted suddenly. Her slippers pattered across the sitting room and then she and Joseph were in his arms. Bryan felt the wetness on both their cheeks as he held them close.

Hannah's voice whispered, bedroom soft, against his chest, 'You can't be going like this.'

'No. Nor could I,' he replied, relief surging through him. 'No, I didn't want to.'

'You have to do it? You're certain? Whatever anyone thinks?'

467

'I have to.'

'Then go with our love and blessing.'

She lifted her lips to his. Their long kiss stifled for a moment each other's uncertainty and fear.

'Take care, avourneen,' cried Hannah as he swung down the street.

'I will that,' he called back.

'For both of us,' she murmured, waving him out of sight. She turned back into the house, still speaking as if the baby could understand her every word.

'They'll not be learning that all we're wanting is peace and quiet, a house to call home, and someone to love. They'll not be learning that, will they, babbie? And will they ever?'

Joseph Aherne belched sleepily, ready for his afternoon nap.

Outside, flames began to lick into the sky over Listowel from the fires set by the retreating Republicans in the police barracks, the courthouse and the workhouse.

The gathering pall of smoke was visible a mile away to the advance scouts of the Free State Army.


## Chapter 10 January, 1923


On a raw morning, Kevin Christopher O'Higgins, Vice President of the Executive Council in the first Dail and Minister for Home Affairs, looked imperiously down from the first floor window of the Arms Hotel at the crowd of three hundred, held back by a rank of Free State troops, bayonets fixed to rifles.

'People of Listowel,' he announced, 'I speak to you at a time when the future of our beloved country is at stake. The question,' he continued in a Queen's County accent, 'is whether Ireland is to be a nation governed by constitutional principles or whether it is to be a mob dictated by an armed minority. To resolve that question, the nation is entitled to act on its own intuition of self-preservation. My friends, that nation's life is worth the life of many individuals.'

Hannah Aherne shivered when she heard those words.

There above her, was the man whose sworn aim was to hunt down Republicans like her husband; a man who, with the military, had instituted and implemented the death penalty, without proper trial, for anyone found in possession of a gun; a man who'd authorized the execution without trial of his life-long friend, Rory O'Connor, the anti-treaty Republican leader captured at the Four Courts in Dublin six months before.

'I venture to say,' O'Higgins added, his sharp voice carrying against the wind, 'That this country of ours has more heroes to the square mile than any equivalent country in the world. That is, if you're foolish enough to name as heroes those in militant opposition to your constitutionally elected government.'

'They are heroes. They are,' Hannah whispered to herself.

'Sshh,' hissed Jack Aherne beside her.

Hannah blushed slightly, looking round to check that no one else had overheard.

'It would be a generous estimate to say that twenty per cent of that militant opposition is idealism. It would be a generous estimate also to say that only twenty per cent of it is crime. And between those twenty per cents, there flows sixty per cent of sheer futility. We are presented in Ireland with a spectacle of a country steering straight for anarchy and chaos. If this country fails to get through, if this country fails to win out to democratic government, that will be unfortunate.'

O'Higgins' voice was quieter now, but no less lacking in determination and resolve. The crowd stood like statues.

'I do not think that any of us hold human life cheap. But when you must balance the human life against the life of the nation, that presents a very different problem. When the nation is threatened, as it is now, then human life does become cheaper and the fate of individuals of less importance. If the nation's survival demands blood, then blood it shall have.'

The statement was so bold, so chilling that Hannah heard Bryan's grandfather draw breath in surprise.

'There can be no turning back, people of Listowel,' O'Higgins concluded. 'You have seen what measures the nation is prepared to adopt, and, indeed, has adopted to preserve itself. Those in militant opposition have a choice. To surrender or to continue their futile fight. Let them make their choice. But also let them clearly understand what the consequences of a wrong choice shall be.'

Hannah suddenly felt trapped in the crowd by her own panic at the politician's message. There was no doubt any longer in her mind that those carrying weapons against the Free State Government were doomed. O'Higgins had been unequivocal. There would be little mercy for such as Bryan and his friends.

She pushed blindly through the dispersing crowd, away from Kevin Higgins, away from his stony words.

'Hold fast, lass,' the old schoolteacher called, having difficulty in keeping pace with his grandson's wife. He put a hand on her shoulder, drawing her back towards him.

Without warning, Hannah turned and flung her arms round his neck, bursting into tears. 'Oh, Grandpa!' she sobbed. 'What's to become of us? Bryan'll be dead by the Free Staters. I know he will. They'll get him in the end, so they will.'

'Hush, hush, child,' Jack Aherne murmured, patting her hair. 'Not here. They're all after watching you.'

'I'm not caring,' Hannah wailed, lifting her face to look into his wise, calm eyes.

'I know you're not, lass,' he smiled reassuringly. 'But just be thinking what your tears are doing to my nice clean shirt your Grandma Maude ironed only this morning.'

He reached into his inside pocket and produced a white linen handkerchief.

'Here,' he said. 'Dry your eyes and let's be home to see how your wee babbie's faring.'

She nodded, gulped back her sobs, trying to smile a watery smile at the same time.

'And what was so terrible about your man?' Jack asked lightly when they were half-way to his home in Forge Lane where Hannah had left baby Joseph.

'Just his words and the way he was saying them.'

'And sure and what was so new about that? He's been putting it in the newspapers for weeks past.'

'But it's the way he spoke . . . you know . . . here, in the flesh.'

'Aye, he looks an awful hard man and there's no mistaking he means business. I wouldn't fancy being on my own keeping with him after me.'

'And isn't that how Bryan is? He's a gun and you know what the Free Staters'll do to him if they catch him.'

'Don't be worrying. If the Tans couldn't get your Bryan, I doubt if this lot will.'

Jack Aherne put as much confidence into his voice as he was able, trying to hide an emptiness of fear within himself. He looked sideways at Hannah. She was biting her lower lip.

'You're right, of course, Grandpa Jack,' she exclaimed. 'They'll not be taking my . . . our Bryan.'

Her voice was bright but her eyes were heavy with threatening tears and ever-present foreboding, an emotion constant to her in these days of Civil War, in its last, most horrific stages.

The Repubicans opposed to the Anglo-Irish Treaty had ceased to exist as a force of any substance after the Government offensive the previous August.

Cork and the other remaining large centres of population in the south and west of Ireland had fallen to the Free State Army within a matter of weeks.

Ironically, Michael Collins had not lived to savour the victory, if any event in a civil war can be termed as a victory. He had died, like so many of his proxy victims, with a bullet through the back of his head in a roadside ambush during the offensive.

The mopping-up operations were now being conducted by his successor as President of the Executive Council, William Cosgrove, and Kevin O'Higgins.

Their orders allowed virtually no quarter. Nor was any offered in return.

Few bolt holes used by IRA men in the Tan War were open to them any longer in their guise of anti-treaty Republicans. The ordinary people were loath to give sanctuary or even food except in pockets of support. And if hiding places were still available on the lands of friendly farmers or landlords, they also held the terrible danger of being known to a fugitive's former comrades, now wearing the green uniform of the Free State Army.

Many a Republican had thought himself safe for the night in his secret place in a hay rick or barn until he had found himself blinking into the light of a lantern and the barrel of a rifle held by someone who had served alongside him in his old IRA unit. Loyalty to the Free State often meant treachery to friends, even blood relations. There was no mercy.

Sometimes, the fugitive died where he was discovered. Sometimes, he was interrogated with the aid of hammers and lighted cigarettes before being shot in a ditch. And quite often he was used as a human metal-detector to clear a road mined not many hours before by his Republican colleagues.

Each new tale of horror reaching Hannah at her family's farm at Galey Bridge increased her fears. In her nightmares, she would see Bryan dying every imaginable death at the hands of the Free State Army. She would wake wet with perspiration, staring into the dark with the awful images vivid in her brain.

Since Bryan had left Listowel with the other Republicans five months before, he'd managed to visit her and Joseph on only three occasions. Each time, he had stayed just the night but those short hours together had been some of the most precious of their marriage.

After passionate and repeated love-makings in Hannah's narrow bed, they had lain awake whispering quietly about their childhood memories, their hopes for the future, their feelings for each other.

All the time, though, Bryan had refused to tell her about his activities in the Civil War and how he was surviving on the run. The less Hannah knew the less she could divulge, however unwillingly, if the Free Staters ever came to interrogate her.

She could guess that her husband was virtually living off the land by the feel of his thin body under her caresses. His ribs and shoulder blades seemed ready to burst through his skin. The black rings under his eyes told of nights sleeping rough. His nicotine-stained fingers with nails bitten to the quick showed the nervous stress of his existence.

On his last visit, just before St Stephen's Day, she had noticed that he had developed a nervous tic high on his left cheek. She had begged him to stay longer – a day or two, perhaps – but Bryan insisted on slipping away in the half-darkness of early morning, saying that any delay might bring his capture and the chance of harm to herself, their child and her parents.

The ecstasy and relief of each of his visits had soon faded to be replaced by loneliness and nagging fear. Hannah found her parents relatively unsympathetic to Bryan's plight, urging her to persuade him to give up the hopeless fight. Thus, she found herself seeking comfort and reassurance from Bryan's parents and grandparents. And, as the weeks of worry continued, she discovered a particular affinity with Jack and Maude Aherne and Aunt Brigid. Their serenity in old age and apparent acceptance of God's will in all things helped soothe her troubled mind. In their company, Hannah could stop brooding, for a few hours at least, about her husband's fate.

In fact, Bryan was near the limit of his endurance. The Free State Army's advance had decimated the Republicans in North Kerry. It was impossible for them to act as a unified force so they had split into small groups which, one by one, had been picked off by the government troops. They had fled into the Stack Mountains between Listowel and Tralee just as they had done in the days of the flying column. Now, however, the rocks and crags and valleys were not so safe. Their pursuers, led by Tom Kennelly and Paddy Murphy, knew the old hiding places from their own service with the column and harried the fugitives without respite. Eventually, Bryan and his companions had been driven out of the mountains and towards the coastlands running down to Kerry Head, above Ballyheighe Bay, north of Tralee.

By April 1923, Bryan's unit numbered only four, including himself. The others, a dozen or more, had vanished to their homes after burying their weapons, preferring the dubious mercy of the Free Staters to the harshness of life on the run.

The unit had to content itself with occasional skirmishes with small Free State patrols which usually consisted of a few shots fired at long range and then a dash to safety. Most of their time was taken up with finding food and shelter, an increasingly difficult task as more and more of the population shut their doors to the Republicans.

Bryan's unit was lucky to some extent, though, because one of them, Jinty Fleming, had a widowed sister living in a cabin at Ballynaskreena, a mile from the dark impregnable cliffs confronting the Atlantic near Inshaboy Point.

The four of them would travel inland for their forays against the Free Staters and then retreat to the coast where they knew they could find a hot meal of sorts and at least one night's sleep under a dry roof.

By April, Bryan had virtually decided to give up, to set just one more ambush and then disband. He did not know whether to surrender personally to someone like Tom Kennelly, his old commander in the North Kerry Flying Column, or whether simply to hide out near Listowel until the Civil War formally ended.

They were returning one evening to the cabin after an abortive attempt to mine a road used frequently by a Free State Army cycling corps. For some reason, the troops had not followed their usual route and after two hours and no sign of the soldiers, Bryan decided to blow up the mine by rifle fire.

They walked back towards their refuge in single file, rifles slung across their backs, disonsolate and tired.

'Come on, boys,' Bryan urged as they neared the small cabin. 'We'll crack a bottle of the hard stuff if you like and drown our sorrows.'

'Fuck that!' said Jinty Fleming, a small, wiry man, normally full of optimism and humour. 'I'm thinking it'll be better for us to drink some fucking rat poison.'

'With our fucking luck,' Paddy Swift grunted behind him, 'The fucking rats'll have drunk it first.'

'And fucking enjoyed it too!' Tom Reagan added.

The four laughed humourlessly.

'Nearly there,' Bryan called from the front.

'Thanks be,' Swift panted rotundly.

'You'll be skin and bone soon,' Reagan joked. 'Your mam'll not be recognizing you, Paddy.'

'For Jesus' sake,' Bryan exclaimed. 'Will you be quiet!'

The four quickened their pace, anxious to be indoors, feeling on their faces the first drops of rain from which they knew there would soon be a torrential downpour, an almost nightly occurrence in Kerry at that time of the spring, a season known locally as 'scoriveen', 'the rough weather of the cuckoo'.

In the distance they could hear the Atlantic breakers pounding away at the base of the cliffs.

Bryan was only twenty yards from the cabin, whose beckoning light was shining round the edges of its ill-fitting door, when he stopped suddenly.

Another sound had reached his ears.

He thrust out his hand, signalling the men behind him to be still. He cocked his head, listening intently, unsure of what he had just heard from the darkness ahead.

'What's the . . ?' Fleming began to whisper.

'Shut up!' Bryan muttered.

A second later and the sound came again, borne on the wind from the ocean. A definite clink of metal upon stone. Paddy Swift heard it too and, for all his bulk, dropped noiselessly to the ground. The others immediately did the same. They were only too familiar with the noise made by a rifle butt against a loose pebble.

Bryan gestured again and the four of them slid into the shallow ditch beside the track. Fleming's rifle clattered against stones lying under a broken wall.

Immediately, the beams from half a dozen powerful torches pierced the night, searching towards them. Somewhere behind their blinding glare rifle bolts clicked.

'Can you see 'em?' a voice called.

'Not yet. They're not far though.'

The beams crossed and re-crossed, probing and sliding across the uneven ground, illuminating the steadily falling rain. A voice called again; 'Come on out, boys! We know you're there. You're surrounded. Come out with your hands up and there'll be no harm to you!'

Fleming's fingers jabbed into Bryan's leg.

'Let's fuck off,' he whispered fiercely.

'Where, for Jesus' sake?'

'Out of this bastard ambush!'

A rifle cracked and flashed to the front and right. The bullet whined harmlessly over them. More rifles began firing. From the muzzle flashes, Bryan saw that they were, in fact, encircled.

Suddenly, behind him, Tom Reagan began firing back, aiming at the flashes in the darkness.

'Shit!' Bryan exclaimed not bothering to lower his voice. He shouldered his rifle and returned fire as well.

The torch beams converged on the four men crouching by the wall. Bullets from the Free State troops began whizzing and snapping off the stones around and behind them.

Fleming scrambled on all fours alongside Bryan.

'We'll be massacred here!' he cried. 'Let's away now.'

'We're surrounded, fuck it!'

'Not if we go down the cliffs.'

'In this weather?'

'I know it blindfold. Come on else we'll be plugged where we are.'

Bryan shrugged. The only alternatives were surrender or death, perhaps both.

'You lead then,' he told Jinty Fleming. 'And you better know what you're at!'

'Right. Over the wall,' Fleming ordered. 'We'll have to run their fire.'

The four of them scrambled over the wall, stones collapsing about them, bruising shins and elbows, and began running across a field.

They crouched low, rifles thrust before them, firing at the flashes all around. The rain beat into their faces, chilling and spiky, soaking through their thin, torn clothes.

'Watch ahead!' Bryan screamed at Fleming, noticing the flash of a rifle directly in front.

'At him, boys!' Fleming shouted back, fear lost in the exultation of mortal danger.

Their weapons jumped in their hands as, somehow, they fired and reloaded, feet tripping over the sodden tussocks in the field.

Ahead, someone screamed in agony. The shooting all about them seemed to grow quicker and fiercer. People were cursing at the top of their voices. A whistle blew shrilly. Torches weaved and bobbed as the Free Staters gave chase. The sounds of the waves below the cliffs became louder.

'Stop! Stop!' Fleming shrieked, flinging both arms out, but Bryan's momentum carried him on, and the two collided, desperately trying to keep their balance, swaying together on the edge of the cliff. When they looked down they saw the phosphorescence of the breaking, swirling waves.

Following Fleming, they dropped to their hands and knees and crawled along the edge of the cliff.

They crawled for perhaps twenty yards before Fleming found what he was seeking, the start of a narrow path leading steeply downwards. The sounds of pursuit behind were drowned by the angry seas below.

'On your bums,' he whispered. 'Slide easy but hang on for your life! It's mighty slippy.'

Down and down they went, the path nearly vertical in places, their fingers and heels digging into the wet mixture of soil, sand and pebbles. Once, they seemed to be hanging directly over the sea foaming and beating against the outcrop of rocks below.

'Watch it! Be careful!' Fleming called after almost two minutes of frantic slipping and slithering, their fear and exertion mingling perspiration with the rain plastering their faces.

'We're nearly there!'

Seconds later, Fleming vanished from sight.

Bryan was left with his legs dangling over a ledge with, apparently, nothing between himself and the sea.

'Drop down!'

Fleming's order came out of the blinding, stinging rain.

'What? Where? Jinty, where, for God's sake?' Bryan called. 'I'm not seeing a thing.'

'Just drop. There's a ledge below. Just drop. I'll be catching you . . . maybe.' Fleming laughed gruesomely, regaining his usual humour now he considered himself safe.

Bryan sucked in a deep breath, closed his eyes and pushed himself over the edge.

Although the fall was shorter than he had expected, his knees still gave way with the impact on rock.

Fleming grabbed him and pulled him into the stygian darkness of a cave, its mouth high enough to be entered without stooping.

Paddy Swift and Tom Reagan quickly followed. All four rested against the wet rocks of the cave walls.

Once or twice, a curtain of spray lashed across the cave entrance but they were so wet already that they didn't bother to move away.

'What now, Jinty?' Bryan asked after a few minutes. 'We'll perish with cold where we are.'

'Don't worry,' Fleming replied cheerfully. 'Just follow me. Hang on to my arm.'

He led them ten paces back into the cave and round a slight bend.

'Right. Here we are,' he announced. 'As far as we go.'

'It'd be fine,' Bryan said sarcastically. 'If only we could see where the fuck we were.'

'Hang on,' Fleming replied grumpily. 'Just hang on.'

The others listened while he scrabbled around the cave, swearing loudly when his knuckles scraped painfully against rock. Then they heard the sound of matches striking, before a flickering, yellow light suffused the cave. Fleming lifted the stub of a candle and held it above his head.

'There!' he said proudly. 'Have a look at the safest hide-out a man ever had.'

They could see that they were standing upright in a squarish cave about six feet wide and five feet long, its roof a comfortable foot higher than Bryan, the tallest of them. It's deep brown walls were shinily damp. Water plopped down steadily from several parts of the roof. In one corner, presumably the driest, there was a small pile of sacking.

Bryan nodded, half-doubting, half-approving.

'Where did you get all this luxury, Jinty?' he asked. 'Candles and bedding?'

'And sure haven't I been using this place since I was a wee 'un. Came in mighty handy when the Tans were around, so it did.'

'I can imagine,' Swift said drily. 'So what do we do now?'

'Wait for the Staters to get tired of looking for us. That's what we do.'

'Won't they find us?' Bryan asked.

'They might and then again they might not. And if they do . . . well, you'll see at first light what problems they'll have.'

The four of them spent the night huddled together for warmth, the sacking wrapped round them. In the early morning, when the sky was turning from black to grey, Jinty Fleming led them to the entrance of the cave.

'Holy Mother, Jesus and all the Saints!' Bryan exclaimed, truly awed, when he gazed out at the landscape above and beneath the cave.

At the foot of the cliff, long ridges of rock ran out, finger like, to meet and split the foaming breakers. The cave was clearly a mixture of a rock fault and a small hollow beaten out of the cliff by the wind and rain of centuries. It stood ten yards above the apex of a horse-shoe-shaped creek with high lichen-covered boulders flaunting their invincibility above the dashing sea. Above, ledges of rock jutted and arched out, effectively shielding the mouth of the cave from all but a few dangerously exposed parts of the clifftop.

The position, Bryan realized immediately, was totally impregnable except from the narrow path or from the ridges of rock within reach of the breakers.

Fleming pointed down to the huge boulders running out from the creek.

'That's our way of escaping if they should be finding us,' he remarked. 'At the end of them . . . see, there . . . there's another path winding round the cliffs to the next headland. It's difficult but I've made it before.'

'In daylight?' Swift asked dubiously.

'Yes.'

'Not in the dark?'

'No.'

'We'll see when the time comes, if it should,' Bryan said. 'Right now I'm just wishing we had some food.'

'How long do we wait?' Reagan asked seriously.

'Until we're certain the Staters have gone,' Bryan replied tersely.

The four sat in the cave entrance watching the breakers below, marvelling at their power and rhythm, drawing the salt-tanged air into their lungs, trying not to think of their hunger.

Then all at once, a shower of pebbles clattered on to the narrow ledge in front of them.

'Jesus!' Fleming exclaimed, jumping up and reaching for his rifle. 'Someone's coming!'

The others scrambled for their weapons.

But before Bryan could give any orders, Fleming and Reagan had stood on tiptoe, thrust their rifles over the overhanging arch of rock and fired upwards.

The Free State soldier sliding down the path from the clifftop grunted like a stuck pig, rose to his knees, one hand reaching for beardless cheek and tumbled headlong down the path and over the edge.

A drawn-out scream echoed against the cliff-face while he turned in mid-air, frightening the birds who fluttered off their nests, mew-

478

ing and screeching. Their cries continued, a requiem for the hapless soldier as he smashed onto the jagged boulders at the water's edge.

The sea gathered up his limp, shattered body, cradling it, rolling it back and forth gently, drawing it through the pinched mouth of the small creek and into the boundless ocean.

'There's another!' Reagan cried, working the bolt on his rifle, forcing another bullet into the breech. He and Fleming fired again.

The second Free State soldier was, by this time scrabbling back up the path to safety, digging frantically into the earth for a hold.

He arched upwards when the two bullets ripped into the back of his green uniform jacket and was dead before he, too, tumbled down the cliff, spinning and twisting in the air, bouncing sickeningly off the boulders and into the spewing foam.

As Bryan watched the two soldiers fall to their deaths, he realized that something quite irrevocable had occurred in his life. He was now committed, as were his companions, to the final fight. He could find no words of reproach for Jinty Fleming or Tom Reagan.

'Inside!' he cried. 'Get inside! There'll be hell on earth let loose now!'

It took some minutes for the Free State troops at the top of the cliff to fully appreciate what had happened.

The commander of the cycling corps who had laid the ambush, Bryan's old comrade, Paddy Murphy, had merely sent his two soldiers on a reconnaissance down the path. As far as Captain Murphy was concerned the fugitives had vanished. The path was one of the last places for a routine check before calling off the search.

Now, he was both angry at his men's deaths and excited that at last he could get to grips with an elusive prey. He wasn't even sure who was in the cave. Jinty Fleming was one, he knew from interrogating the Republican's sister. But the others? She wouldn't say. The original information about four armed men frequenting the Fleming woman's cabin had been too sketchy to give any further clues about identities. Perhaps, Murphy thought, the others could be important? Perhaps one of them was even Eamon de Valera himself? After all, the Republican leader had been reported to be skulking around the West.

Murphy's first action was to send his junior officer into Bally-naskreena with instructions to wire divisional headquarters at Tralee that, as Murphy termed them, 'prominent irregulars' were in the cave and that reinforcements were needed.

Next, he gathered his senior men around him and worked out a plan of attack. Clearly, an assault down the cliff was tantamount to suicide. Other tactics were needed.

In the cave itself, forty or so yards below, Bryan and his companions grimly readied themselves for battle. None of them had any illusions about their chances of survival. In daylight, they were trapped, unable to move. They would have to take what was coming.

Bryan did tentatively offer an alternative. He felt, that as leader, he was honour bound to do so.

'We could be showing a white flag,' he suggested. 'Maybe they'd take us prisoners.'

'Fat chance,' Swift grunted, his round, freckled face set with grave determination. 'They'll pot us like clay pigeons!'

'I was only thinking last night we'd had too good a run for our money,' said Reagan.

'Aye,' Swift added, grinning maliciously at Bryan. 'And now we've nowhere else to run to, even if we were wanting to.'

'Maybe, before those soldiers, we could have given up,' Fleming said. 'But they'll be awful mad now, I'm thinking. Awful mad.'

'Can you be blaming them?' Bryan replied. He squinted out to sea through the sights of his rifle.

'You're saying we did wrong?' Reagan asked bitingly.

'No . . . no . . . I'm not saying that, Tom. I was only thinking there'll be some weeping mothers before this is over,' Bryan said simply, moving to the cave entrance.

An image of Hannah breast feeding baby Joseph flashed into his mind. He thrust it away, irritated at his own sentimentality.

From above he heard shouted orders, indistinct in the moaning wind of 'scoriveen', followed swiftly by the clatter of pebbles falling on to the ledge.

'They're here!' Bryan shouted, lifting on to his toes and peering over the protective arch above the cave. The others dashed to join him.

To Bryan's amazement, all he could see was a wall of orange and black flame trundling down the path towards him. It took a full second for him to realize that, in fact, the Free Staters had set light to bales of hay and pushed them over the cliff.

'Holy Mother!' he shouted 'Back, boys! Back into the cave!'

He cannoned into his companions as he dropped down. Jinty Fleming had to grab Reagan by his jacket lapels to stop his teetering over the narrow ledge.

They cowered at the back of the cave. The flaming bales, parcelled with sods of turf, slid over the arch and hit the ledge just outside. Most disintegrated and continued their blazing way to the rocks below, again disturbing the gulls and cormorants.

But two of the bales wedged themselves into the mouth of the cave, spitting red-hot sparks and billowing smoke.

The onshore wind drove the smoke into the back of the cave, blinding the fugitives, cutting deep into their throats and chests.

'Oh, Jesus!' Bryan choked, eyes streaming and raw.

'We're suffocating,' wailed Paddy Swift, burying his head in his hands, twisting back into the cave walls.

'Hang on!' Bryan cried.

He grabbed one of the pieces of damp sacking, pulled it over his head and crawled towards the cave entrance, now invisible in the smoke and flame.

With his rifle barrel outstretched, he pushed and prodded at the burning bales, shoving them inch by inch out on to the ledge. Sparks singed the hairs on the back of his hands.

Finally, when he thought his lungs would burst, first one bale and then the other toppled away towards the rocks below.

Within a minute, the keen wind from the sea had chased the smoke from the cave. They were safe again for the time being.

In the next eight hours, however, while daylight held, the Republicans had to resist three more attempts to smoke them out or, perhaps, burn them alive. The Free Staters used burning hay once more before throwing down blazing bedsheets, presumably gathered from nearby cabins, soaked in oil, tar and a sulphurous compound.

Some of the local people watching from the clifftop thought at times that the very cliff itself would be consumed in the raging flames and their cloying, clinging, creeping smoke.

But, to everyone's amazement, the wind miraculously changed direction and blew the flames out to sea.

Captain Murphy was as baffled and frustrated as the fugitives were surprised and thankful.

That night, the Free State Army officer placed snipers in positions along the top of the cliff where they could gain a slight view at an extreme angle of the cave entrance.

Then, by rope, he lowered a lantern hoping to illuminate an unsuspecting target.

Paddy Swift showed himself for just long enough to place a bullet through the lantern before the snipers could sight him properly.

It was stalemate.

That night, the Republicans slept reasonably well in their cave.

perceptibly warmed by all the flames which had danced around them during the day.

They were woken at first light by the crash of a grenade detonating by the ledge. It was the first of many. The Free State troops hurled down mines as well as grenades and constantly peppered the entrance with bullets from a machine-gun position established on the clifftop. Some bullets whined and cracked inside the cave, ricocheting from wall to wall.

The Republicans huddled at the back, unable to speak in the cacophony of violence, ears deafened by constant explosions, terrified by the hissing, whirling splinters of rock.

To make their ordeal worse, an onshore gale began to blow, driving the sea into a frenzy, smashing great spumes of spray up the cliff-face, drenching the cave. Soon, inches of salt water slopped round the Republicans' refuge.

By late afternoon, Bryan was ready to concede defeat.

The bombardment had slackened off with grenades exploding at only ten-minute intervals. Even those were warnings of what would come when the onslaught was renewed.

It was a miracle that none of the four had been injured so far by bullets, shrapnel or rock but their physical damage could hardly have been greater.

Nerves were in shreds. Bodies ached with damp, cold and hunger. Eyes were bloodshot and raw from lack of proper rest and the continual barrage of salt spray piercing inwards to every cranny of the cave.

Their safety matches were sodden.

They faced the night without light, without a comforting cigarette.

The four looked at each other, despair in their haggard, unshaven faces. None of them wanted to be the first to state the obvious.

'We'll have to go,' Bryan said finally flatly. 'We can't be taking this any more.'

'Surrender, you mean?' asked Fleming dully.

'Whatever you want. Whatever you think best. We're all equal now. There are no more leaders.'

'What are you wanting then?' said Swift, his hunger so acute that it no longer pained him.

'It's not for me,' Bryan replied. 'We either give up . . .'

' . . . and get murdered,' interrupted Reagan.

' . . . or we try Jinty's escape route.'

'It's a chance anyway, isn't it?' Fleming said eagerly. 'One way we're certain dead. The other, we've at least a chance.'

'You're agreed then?' asked Bryan. 'An escape?'

'Aye,' the three chorused wearily.

They waited until late into the evening before setting off, leaving their rifles covered with sacking in the furthest corner of the cave.

The night was dark and without stars. The gale had abated. But the sea was still in torment when they crept out of the cave and lowered themselves gingerly over the edge.

They slid as noiselessly as they could down the steep incline of the cliff-face until their boots crunched into the thin strip of pebbles at its base. Any sounds they made, Bryan reckoned, would be masked by the grinding surge of the breakers dragging the shingle back and forth.

The four stayed close together in the impenetrable blackness of the great cliff's shadow.

Jinty Fleming led them on to the first of the large, flat boulders curving out into the ocean.

At first, it was easy going, jumping from one boulder to the other, but soon the rocks became slippery with seaweed. And then they came to the boulders washed by the breakers at low tide. The possessive, seeking sea lapped and tore at their precarious footholds.

First Fleming, then Reagan overbalanced and splashed up to their thighs in the icy water. Each time, they were hauled back on to the ring of boulders which would eventually lead, they hoped, to safety.

By now, the four of them were freezing and exhausted. Fleming was becoming increasingly distressed, taking the brunt of the wind and the waves.

He paused more and more often, gazing this way and that, clearly uncertain of his way in the darkness lit only by the sea's murky phosphoresence

'Are you fine, Jinty?' Bryan shouted from the back. 'Can we be making it?'

He wasn't sure that his voice carried against the elements. He looked around and thought he saw, high up, the glowing fires warming the Free State Army troops on guard on top of the cliff. They vanished when the clouds moved again. The blackness descended.

Jinty Fleming half-turned. In profile, Bryan could see him mouthing some words. Then he leaned, bent, sideways and toppled off the boulder and into the breaking waves. He uttered no sound, simply lifted an appalled, white face, upwards, eyes closed, before disappearing from view, before the ravenous sea closed over him.

Bryan spun round instinctively, looking for an escape from what he now saw was a death trap. There could be no escape in this darkness, in this weather. He didn't think of Paddy Swift and Tom Reagan, men who had shared so much with him. He thought only of self-preservation in this wilderness of wind and sea and spray.

When he turned back to the two men still in his charge, they were no longer there.

The breakers had dragged them down, without a sound.

Suddenly, above and to the side of him, a searchlight beamed out from the top of the cliff, cutting through the night.

Its single tentacle reached out to Bryan and embraced him as he stood motionless amid the torrent.

He was so weary and so cold that he hardly felt the sniper's lucky bullet rip down through the rib cage on the right side of his chest.

The crushing impact pushed him sideways into the sea. For a second, he panicked, trying not to take the water into his mouth, attempting to keep breathing.

The effort was too great.

He only had time to wonder why the stars had appeared in the sky. One of them had the face of his wife, smiling.

## Chapter 11 April, 1923

In the morning, when the Free State Army soldiers looked over the cliffs near Ballynaskreena, they saw two bodies rolling in the swell of the horseshoe-shaped creek.

They knew that their sniper had probably hit one of the Republicans. The second body suggested to them that all the fugitives had been trying to escape when disaster overtook them. But they remembered what had happened on the first day of the siege and were loath to descend the cliff.

Eventually, Captain Paddy Murphy ordered the launching of a boat from the inlet just round the headland. Five soldiers were rowed round to the head of the creek, directly opposite to the cave.

Two of them held iron shutters for protection.

They waited nervously for a couple of minutes, backing oars, but all was silence except for the waves, the sighing wind and the seabirds' cries.

Machine-gunners and snipers on the clifftop covered what little they could see of the ledge outside the cave while the boat manoeuvred into the creek and came alongside one of the bodies.

Only then did the tension relax. The troops knew that the siege of Ballynaskreena Caves was over. They cheered with delight and congratulated each other as the bodies were landed at the base of the cliffs.

Ropes and blankets were lowered down the cliff-face. Amid joking and ribald remarks, the bodies were secured and hauled to the top, banging limply against the rocky outcrops.

They were laid on the grass and the coverings pulled from their faces. Captain Murphy looked at Jinty Fleming's cut and bruised features impassively, wondering who the dead man was. He decided to show the body locally for identification.

He moved to the second body. At first he didn't recognize the swollen, yellowish face with open mouth and staring, salt-rimmed eyes. Then he gagged with nausea and turned away to vomit his breakfast on to the ground.

The excited chatter around him was stilled.

'You're knowing him, sir?' someone asked quietly.

Captain Murphy nodded, wiping his mouth with a handkerchief. He gazed down at the body again.

'It's Bryan Aherne from Listowel.'

A soldier whistled through his teeth. 'One of the big 'uns, eh? Jesus, he looks so young.'

'He does that,' the captain replied. 'But he's been fighting an awful long time. Since he was at school, I hear tell. He was in gaol too and then at Gortaglonna.'

'Aye, a miracle that was.'

'Yes, he's fought all the way for the Republic. You have to give him that, the Lord have mercy on him.'

'Amen,' the soldiers muttered in unison.

'Was he a friend of yours then, sir?' one of them asked curiously, sympathetically.

Captain Murphy straightened up.

'At one time, he was close . . . when we were together in the flying column. But you can't have friendships in a civil war. I won't be remembering him as a friend: I've been chasing him too long for that. But, by God, I'll be telling my children about him. You can't be forgetting a soldier like he was.'

He clicked to attention and saluted, standing motionless by the body for nearly a minute, the ocean breeze ruffling the skirts of his trenchcoat.

Later, the soldiers placed Bryan's body carefully in the back of a truck, covered it with a tricolour and took it to the mortuary in the old workhouse at Listowel.

Captain Murphy himself drove out to Galey Bridge to break the news to Hannah. She didn't cry, merely clasped Joseph tighter to herself.

She didn't speak during the journey to the mortuary, just listened as the captain outlined what had happened at Ballynaskreena.

She didn't flinch even when they asked her to formally identify her husband, simply nodded and stepped up to the coffin.

Baby Joseph, a year and a bit old, wriggled in her arms as she looked down at Bryan.

Captain Murphy moved beside her, offering to take the child. Hannah shook his hand away angrily.

'Let him see his da,' she said bitterly, thrusting the baby over the coffin. 'He'll have precious little else to remember 'cept his dying. And I won't be letting him forget who caused that.'

Joseph began to cry.

Hannah left dry-eyed, a deal of her weeping done in the months of anticipation of this day and this scene. She refused to hold a wake and buried Bryan in Listowel graveyard two days later.

The same day, April 27th, 1923, Eamon de Valera signed a proclamation on behalf of the 'Republican Government', ordering a suspension of all offensive action by the Irish Republican Army.

*BOOK FOUR*

# Chapter 1 January 11th, 1971

A foghorn sounded mournfully from the murk of Belfast Lough. Flurries of snow whirled off the Black Mountain looming above the city and whipped stingingly down the mean little terraces huddling between its dark shadow and the curving shore of the lough, dominated by the shipyard's huge mobile crane.

An occasional car drove cautiously through the yellow-streaked slush, bumping over one of the ramps built into the road at strategic intervals. The driver deliberately didn't look up at the firing slits in the Army sentry posts, standing like children's tree-houses by the ramps, covered with brown and green camouflage nets and wire mesh to stop a well-directed nail or pipe bomb. He didn't want to appear too interested in the dark gun barrels which moved fractionally to cover his progress until he was out of sight. Menace so pervaded his life that, for life to be at all bearable, it had to be ignored.

Above him, watchful, the soldiers stamped their feet to keep passably warm and offered a year's pay to be anywhere other than the capital of Her Majesty's Province of Northern Ireland on this freezing night.

The boredom of barracks in West Germany, the humidity of Hong Kong, the drill sergeants of Aldershot and Catterick Camps, the insects of Belize, were preferable to Belfast. And the cramped billets in draughty halls and overcrowded police barracks were infinitely preferable to those isolated vigils, peering into the night, nerves stretched, watching and noting every movement in a city divided against itself by centuries of hatred and blood.

A light flashed on the switchboard of the information room on the ground floor of Army headquarters in Thiepval Barracks just outside Lisburn.

The duty information officer leaned wearily forward, picked up the phone and flicked down a switch. It was a friendly journalist, someone who could be trusted, not hostile to or questioning of the Army's job.

'Hello, old boy,' the information officer murmured. 'Don't you fellas ever sleep?'

'Just a final check, old man.'

'What was the last number then?'

'Thirty-six.'

The information officer ran his finger down the list of numbered entries for the day's incidents. There had been one more since that particular journalist had called a couple of hours earlier.

'Right, old boy. Just one. Thirty-seven. Not much, I'm afraid. Bit of stoning in Cupar Street after a Saracen ran over someone's dog. All quiet now though.'

'Prod or Taig?'

'What, old boy?'

'The fucking dog! Protestant or Catholic?'

The information officer flushed momentarily before he realized the journalist was joking.

'Doesn't say, old boy. Sorry,' he laughed.

'Must be Jewish then . . . and tell your boys always to get the fucking religion otherwise we're all up the pipe in this last outpost of Western civilization.'

'Too true, old boy.'

'Anything else in the wind?'

'Quiet as the grave. They won't be out on a night like this.'

The information officer suddenly remembered a conversation he'd heard around the bar in the officer's mess. 'Hang on,' he added. 'There might be something early afternoon so keep in touch.'

The journalist's slightly slurred voice sharpened with interest.

'What's that?' he demanded.

'Can't say yet.'

'Come on, old man. Give us a clue.'

'Can't really. Not yet. Don't know much about it myself but they're quite excited upstairs about some capture they've made.'

'Arms?'

'Don't know. Really, old boy. Just keep in touch, there's a good chap. I'm only giving you a word to the wise.'

The journalist sighed, not unduly disappointed. He had more pressing business than cross-examining a friendly contact.

'Okay, old man. Thanks for the tip. Sleep tight.'

'In this bloody office with every newshound from here to Timbuctoo around my neck? You must be joking!'

'Just think of the overtime, old man,' the journalist guffawed, putting down the receiver on the phone on the reception desk in the Midland Hotel, next to York Street railway station, near the centre of Belfast. He winked familiarly at the girl behind the desk, picked up his glass of Bushmills Black Label whiskey and sauntered across the hotel's lounge towards a discreet table in the corner.

There he resumed his courteous, though unnecessary, wooing of the pretty wife of a far away merchant navy officer, affectionately nicknamed by more than one of his colleagues as 'The Glengormly Gobbler'.

At Army headquarters, the information officer, slightly refreshed by his latest conversation, put his feet up on the nearest desk and carried on reading a green-covered booklet, issued by the Ministry of Defence, entitled 'Aid to Civil Power'.

It was the distillation of Army wisdom gained in emergencies from India to Kenya, from Aden to Cyprus. The booklet laid down the guidelines of how soldiers should behave when dealing with, for instance, rioting civilians. Its advice was academic and useless to the Army in Northern Ireland. New rules had to be learned, ever since the province's Prime Minister Major, James Chichester Clark, had officially asked the British Government on August 14th, 1969, to send the Army to the aid of his government, to aid the civil authorities. After weeks and months of rioting between Catholics and Protestants, that well meaning farmer turned somewhat unwilling political leader had decided that the police could no longer cope with the extreme situation of civil unrest which was being fanned and exploited by a hitherto almost extinct Irish Republican Army. However, the information officer on night duty found the booklet's contents reminiscent of the great days of Empire, of long-lost certainty and confidence and conviction, when the enemy invariably had black, brown or yellow faces.

Not far across the road from Thiepval Barracks, down a cul-de-sac of identical houses, Major Stephen Gates, Senior Ammunition Technical Officer (SATO) of the Royal Army Ordnance Corps in Northern Ireland, stirred fitfully in the front bedroom of his two-storey married quarters. He eased his arm across the back of his wife, Elizabeth, neither of them yet fully asleep, both conscious of the presence next door of their youngest daughter, Mary.

The major clasped a gentle, if unusually large hand around his wife's right breast and pressed his lower body against hers. These days he found it difficult to fall asleep straight away, always waiting for the telephone to summon him to give advice about a difficult bomb discovered by one of his Explosive Ordnance Disposal (EOD) units.

Apart from the problems of bomb disposal, he was also wondering about the interview planned for next morning with the man captured by 1st Battalion of the Parachute Regiment.

From previous experience, he'd found that such interviews with known bomb-designers like Seamus Aherne always caused frustration and disappointment. His scientific skills allowed him to deal well enough with their explosive devices. His personality, however, often abrupt, sometimes arrogant, rarely helped him understand their motivations, despite his own family's distant Irish connections. After the interviews, the major knew, he invariably drank two too many pints of Bass bitter in the mess, which inevitably led to a whiskey or three. But his position as the senior bomb disposal officer demanded the interview and he was never one to shirk his duty, however unpleasant.

The ways of a terrorist bomber also occupied the mind of Edward S. Aicheson as he pushed through the heavy plastic doors leading to the children's medical ward in the Royal Victoria Hospital, on the corner of Grosvenor Road and Falls Road in Belfast.

The young surgeon had stayed on late, rather than returning to his rented flat in the suburb of Dunmurry, to monitor the condition of the two-year-old boy rushed to the hospital that evening after the explosion in a car in Bedford Street, just outside the local, fortress-like headquarters of the British Broadcasting Cororation.

He walked quickly up to the night sister's dimly lit desk in the middle of the ward.

'How's he going?' the surgeon asked softly.

'The wee 'un from the bomb, sir? He's holding his own. Staff Nurse Anderson's with him.'

'I'll take a look.' The nasal tone of his Massachusetts voice cut through her broad Ulster accent. The surgeon pulled aside the flower printed curtains and gazed down on the small figure lying motionless in the high sided cot. For an instant, rage seared through him as he saw the bandaged head and the tiny face, parchment pale and pitted with angry specks of gravel and glass.

'He's quiet, sir,' the staff nurse by the cot whispered.

Aicheson nodded and leaned over the boy, noting his shallow breathing and the slight tremor in one of the small hands lying outside the coverlet. He gently rolled up one eyelid and then the other, peering into the boy's pupils. He was deeply unconscious. The surgeon grimaced. Was it brain damage needing surgery, or merely a deep concussion, serious as that might be in one so young?

That had been Aicheson's concern ever since the boy had been admitted. The superficial injuries caused when the explosion flung him and his mother through the window of the Chinese restaurant had been quickly cleaned by the nurses in the casualty department. They would heal in time. The worry had been the slight sign of pressure on the boy's brain shown by the first X-rays. There would have to be further tests in the morning. For now, Aicheson decided, rest and quiet would do the boy as much good as anything.

'Tell Sister of the slightest change, Staff,' he said.

'Of course, sir.'

Immediately, Aicheson realized he might have sounded tactlessly patronizing. The nurses at the hospital were among the most experienced in the world. They had to be to cope with the appalling carnage brought daily to the 'Royal Vic'.

'Of course you will, Staff,' he added with a half-apologetic smile. 'Good night.'

Edward S. Aicheson, graduate of Harvard Medical School, intern and then surgeon at Peter Bent Brigham Hospital on Huntington Avenue in Boston, drove home, tired and despairing of human nature.

For the umpteenth time, he asked himself how any person could knowingly plant bombs which caused such indiscriminate and dreadful hurt to ordinary, innocent people like the little boy he'd just left. What kind of men and women were these?

He thumped the steering wheel of his car angrily. 'The bastards!' he cried out loud. 'Just who the hell do they think they are?'

Not ten miles away, in his basement cell at Holywood Barracks, a slightly different question of identity was keeping Joseph Aherne's son Seamus from much-needed sleep. He was wondering exactly which two IRA men had been killed when their Cortina car exploded by the BBC while they were trying to deliver their bomb to its target.

He shuffled through mental photographs of members of the Active Service Units of the three IRA battalions in Belfast. After a few minutes he decided it was fruitless trying to guess who the unfortunates might be. He knew that he'd be told soon enough if that sergeant had been telling the truth and his next sleeping place was really to be the Republican wing of Crumlin Prison. His fellow inmates would know. Seamus just hoped the bomb's premature explosion hadn't been caused by a fault in his design. The vast majority of bombs in Belfast at that moment had been made – and were being made – from his blueprints.

Seamus was fairly cynical about how blame was apportioned by the IRA's hierarchy whenever a bomb went wrong.

He, as designer, was top of the carefully worked-out pyramid of responsibility. Below him were the bomb electrician who wired the circuitry to his instructions and the bomb carpenter who built the wooden or metal container, designed to make the task of the bomb disposal officer as difficult and dangerous as possible. From them, the half-finished bomb would be passed on to the bomb officer whose job was to supply and insert the explosive. He would pass the completed device to the bomb-layer, responsible for getting it to the target. But Seamus knew that at the base of the deadly pyramid and the most expendable were the youngsters recruited to steal and drive the vehicles carrying the bomb.

Seamus guessed it was the latter who'd died earlier that night. It usually was.

The IRA's formal committees of inquiry, court martial and memoranda would undoubtedly push some of the blame for the disaster back up the pyramid to the designer, even if he had been in Army custody when it exploded.

He sighed at the thought.

## Chapter 2 January 12th, 1971 (a.m.)

Major Stephen Gates sat at the desk in the interrogation room in the basement of Holywood Barracks perusing the slim, orange file containing all the intelligence and background information that the Army and the Royal Ulster Constabulary had gathered about Seamus Aherne.

Beside him, Captain Charles Briance, a young Ammunition Technical Officer recently posted to Northern Ireland, leafed through the preliminary report supplied by the officer of the 1st Battalion Parachute Regiment who'd detained Seamus.

'Anything there?' the major grunted, brushing an errant lock of pepper-and-salt hair back off his forehead.

'Not a lot, sir. Picked up watching that bomb scene in Botanic Gardens. Smart piece of work by the patrol sergeant . . . '

'Cheeky sod!'

'Sir?'

'Presumably trying to see how we dealt with his brutes.'

'Presumably.'

'Shouldn't have been so nosey, should he? Has he said much?'

'Not a lot. Seemed a bit surprised that we had a snap of him from his days at the Irish Post Office training school at Dublin Castle.'

'Uh-huh.'

'Mentioned his father apparently. Asked for a call to him.'

'Joseph Aherne?'

'Affirmative.'

'Well, old Joe's in my book of words too. Into bombs from way back when. In and out of internment like a yo-yo.'

'Hardly a surprise, sir.'

'Runs in the family.'

'Not an offence though, is it?' the young officer said tentatively.

'Don't be naive, Charley,' the major replied wearily, striking a match to light a slim Panatella cigar. He blinked his pale blue eyes as the pungent smoke curled round his face. 'We've known about Aherne for a year or more from the usual sources. He's not much good at present but with his technical training from the Post Office and the right instructor he could be a proper pain in the you-know-what. That's why he's got to be nipped in the bud now.'

'Of course, sir. Shall we have him in?'

Captain Briance walked to the door, straightening the sleeves of his olive-green pullover. On his right sleeve, as on the major's, was the tiny flash of orange and yellow flame rising above a black circle that identified them as bomb disposal officers.

The captain opened the door and gave an order to the sergeant outside.

'Just wait one,' the major called from the desk. 'Let's have the sarn't in.'

'Suh?' barked the NCO standing at attention in the doorway.

'At ease, Sarn't,' murmured the major. 'Tell us what the skull's been like while you've had him.'

'Bit pushy at first, suh, if you know what I mean. Usual guff about his rights when he got over his first fright. He's settled down now. . . good as gold really. Hasn't had much sleep, of course, suh.'

'I see. Do you think he'll talk?'

'Not really for me to say, suh. I can tell you though he doesn't like being hurt.'

The major looked up sharply, lips pursed around the glowing cigar.

'Hurt, Sarn't?'

The sergeant reddened slightly. His eyes fixed on an imginary dot on the wall above the officer's head.

'Stumbled once or twice when we picked him up, if you know what I mean, suh.'

Major Gates shook his head slowly from side to side, glaring from under heavy eyebrows. 'Yes, I do see what you mean,' he said with deliberate irony. 'Fetch him along now and make sure he doesn't stumble again.'

'Suh!'

The sound of the sergeant's boots clacked away down the corridor, a door clanged open, and then the boots returned, accompanied by the scuff of a softer tread.

'Aherne, suh,' the sergeant boomed, propelling his prisoner into the room before shutting the door and resuming his vigil outside.

Major Gates surveyed Seamus's laceless shoes, the unbelted trousers he was holding up with his hands, and his unshaven face and tired eyes.

He saw a dark-haired young man with thin, symmetrical features that gave an impression of experience combined with youthful vulnerability. His eyes met the prisoner's and held them for a moment, before he looked down to his file again.

'Sit down, Aherne,' the captain muttered, embarrassed as always at meeting an enemy face-to-face.

Seamus lowered himself wearily into the chair in front of the desk, not once taking his eyes off the stockily-built major with his ruddy, outdoor complexion.

'I'm Major Gates, SATO, and this is Captain Briance, one of my ATOs.'

Seamus opened his mouth to reply. The major interrupted coldly.

'Just shut up, laddie, for the moment. I'll tell you when to talk. Right?'

Seamus nodded. The major's authority was so clearly paramount that, for a split second, he thought he was back before his old headmaster at the National School in Listowel.

'Now, young Seamus, you probably realize that we know all about you and your little tricks. We've been trying to meet you ever since you arrived on the scene here – when was it? Fifteen months ago? . . . but we've waited patiently for the pleasure and now here

496

we are. Do you know I've a ruddy great map in my office with lots of little pins stuck into it? They're coloured green just for you and your bombs, laddie. Every last one of them. Your handiwork is quite unmistakable, you know. Very neat way with the wiring you have, just like they taught you to wire telephone bells at Dublin Castle. Very good. And your bomb officer?' The major shrugged. ' . . . well, he really should try to find some new explosive. That Quarrex stolen from the Enfield munition factory is much too obvious. As soon as we see that sandy muck, we offer up a small prayer of thanks to you and your Third Battalion quartermaster.'

Seamus shook his head, truly puzzled.

Major Gates smiled knowingly, perhaps patronizingly.

'Once we discover whose little device we're dealing with, the rest is kid's play. By the book, that's your work, laddie, and by the book is how we kill the brutes.'

There was silence full of unspoken thoughts. Seamus lowered his eyes.

'Ever thought of building bigger and better bombs, laddie?' the major asked, a perceptibly harsher tone in his voice.

'I don't . . . '

'Shut up, young Seamus, and listen to your Uncle Stephen, will you? I'm just asking if you've some more designs you're working on.'

Seamus shook his head again, becoming somewhat baffled at the direction of the questions. He hadn't expected such a conversational, roundabout interrogation.

'Not even those new pipe bombs your boys are tossing around. Very nasty, they are. Very unstable. Put in the old co-op mix – your dad used to call it Pax, I wouldn't be surprised – stick in a fuse, crimp one end and away you go. Bit dangerous though, isn't it? Quite a few have lost their fingers and hands, haven't they? Quite a few wingies on your company's pension scheme, aren't there?'

'I don't know anything about these!' Seamus blurted out, needled that he should be connected with such notoriously shoddy devices.

Major Gates leaned back in his chair, face wreathed in cigar smoke and a benevolent smile.

'Good boy,' he sighed. 'Just knew you could be relied upon . . . '

'What do . . . '

'Nothing, laddie. Thought all along the pipes couldn't be your work. Shipped up from the south like the nail bombs, aren't they?'

The certainty in the major's voice, its very confidence, his own uncertainty, made Seamus begin to nod his head in agreement before he could stop himself.

'I'm not saying anything,' he said defiantly, angry at having been tricked.

'No need, laddie. A nod's as good as a wink, isn't it Captain Briance?'

'Indeed it is, sir.'

'I don't know . . .'

'Shut up, laddie . . . tell me, are you religious?'

'Yes,' Seamus replied without reflection. A clear image of Monsignor O'Sullivan came to him, standing before the altar of St Mary's Church in Listowel, the sun shadowing a cross down the nave. Before he could think about the switch in questioning, the major spoke again.

'No, I mean religious religious, young Seamus,' Major Gates persisted. 'God knows, I'm a padre's man myself but I doubt if I'd claim I was religious.'

'I'm a member of the Church.'

'And you believe in the Church's teachings? Say, your Church's?'

'Indeed and why not?' Seamus replied, somewhat bewildered.

'In the sanctity of human life?'

'Oh, Jesus, do we have to go into this?' Seamus exclaimed, genuinely offended.

'Why not, laddie? This is all about religion, isn't it? Protestants against Catholics? Paisley versus the Pope?'

'We're not against Protestants. No way are we.'

'Why are you killing and maiming them then?'

'We don't.'

'But you do. You know you do.'

'Not deliberately.'

'That makes the difference, laddie?'

'Yes. The IRA are only against the forces of British imperialism.'

'Imperialism? That's balls, laddie! You mean you're against us and the RUC?'

'Yes. No one else.'

'And what happens to those who get in the way?'

'That's unfortunate. We don't mean to hurt them.'

The accents beat against each other like tennis balls in a fast doubles rally.

'But if they are hurt?'

'Fortunes of war.'

'What war? Have we declared war? Have the Irish Government? Have you?'

'We have.'

'Bit one-sided, isn't it? We came in here with your people, your Catholics, cheering us to the rooftops. We were the great protectors. Now, suddenly, you say we're the enemy.'

'You are. You're the occupying forces.'

'But we've always been here. Just like the Protestants have.'

'You're in part of Ireland. You're keeping the Border!'

'When did the pure Irish ever run Ireland? Hundreds of years ago. It's like us English saying to the Americans, "Sorry, we've decided we still run your country." It's like the Red Indians telling the Americans to give them the whole continent back. It's like the Aboriginees saying they own Australia. Or the Maoris, New Zealand. For a people who seem to live in history, you're pretty poor on the subject. History, as they say, having writ, moves on, brother!'

'What's this about, anyway. You're talking rubbish. I don't have to . . .'

'You do what you're told, young Seamus or you might stumble some more against the toe-end of a filthy big army boot.'

Major Gates was conscious of the captain's surprised, sideways glance. He lit another cigar, not taking his eyes off Seamus.

'Recognize these names – Frankie Sharpe, Donal Card, Alby Walsh?'

The question speared into Seamus's brain. He ran a hand through his dishevelled hair, trying to gain time, his mind exhausted, whirling at the change of direction.

'Of course, you do, don't you, laddie?' the major persisted.

'No.'

'Oh, is that so?'

The major slowly picked up some photographs from the file on the desk, their backs to Seamus, and peered at them closely.

'You're sure?' he asked again. 'Mind you, it's not the best likeness but I'd have sworn it was you, Seamus, going into the Collins club in Andersontown with our Frankie.'

'I don't . . .'

'You know our Frankie, don't you?' Major Gates went on casually. 'The big man in the Rodger McCorley branch – Cumann, don't you call it? – of Sinn Fein in the area. Before he split with the official IRA, of course.'

'I don't . . .' Seamus began to repeat but again he was inter-rupted.

'Of course not. You wouldn't would you, laddie? Not a good religious boy like you.'

Seamus, brain numbing with confusion, hardly able to think

499

logically, held up his hands, palm upwards and outwards, as if surrendering.

The bomb disposal officers looked quizzically at him.

'May – may – may I say something, for Jesus' sake?' the young man stammered.

The major shrugged. 'Go ahead, laddie.'

Seamus thought for a moment, sucking in a deep breath of stale air mingled with cigar smoke. 'It's clear you think you know everything there is to know about me,' he said. 'You've me down as someone who helps the bombers and nothing's going to change your mind, is it?'

'It'd have to be good,' Captain Briance said drily.

'A southern Irishman up here,' Major Gates interrupted, flicking through the file. 'A man with your Republican background; the whispers in the pubs about you and your bombs; the photographs of you with known Belfast IRA; getting arrested at the scene of a bomb incident . . . Yes, it'd have to be good, young Seamus. Bloody good!'

'In other words, you're just playing cat and mouse with me. Nothing I say is going to convince you that I've sod all to do with this. All you want is for me to shop my friends . . .'

Major Gates rubbed his hand over his firm, jutting jaw.

'. . . and I wouldn't be doing that even if I was who you say I am and I'm fucking not.'

The major sighed as if Seamus's use of swear words distressed him.

'Just once more,' he said quietly, 'I'm interested really. If one of your bombs kills an innocent Protestant, say a little boy, can you go to your priest and ask forgiveness in the confessional?'

'I could ask.'

'Will he grant it?'

'Most would.'

'Most?'

'Yes.'

'But how? You've taken life, innocent life.'

'I wouldn't have meant to. And I'd be truly sorry that it had happened. And I'd ask forgiveness and accept a penance . . . Jesus, why am I telling you this?'

The major leaned over the desk and offered Seamus a cigar from the brown packet.

'I see you smoke from the colour of your fingers. You better have it now before you head for the Crumlin. I don't think they'll be having them there.'

He took out a box of Swan Vestas matches, throwing it to Seamus who lit the cigar.

'Last one, laddie?' Major Gates said, almost apologetically, when Seamus had taken his first puff of the cigar, coughing once as the smoke reached his lungs. 'This is hypothetical. You know what that is?'

Seamus's look was sufficient.

Captain Briance, a non-smoker, rubbed a surreptitious knuckle across his right eye, discomfited by the smoke filling the room.

'Say, if the Pope declared that he'd excommunicate all members of the IRA. Say, if he announced that it was a mortal sin for anyone to belong. Do you think it'd make any difference to you?'

Seamus puffed on the cigar again, admiring the glow at the tip, the way the grey ash still clung.

'No,' he replied after a second's silence. 'It wouldn't make any difference.'

'That's what I . . . '

'Because His Holiness would never do it.'

'And that's what I thought as well.'

They looked at each other. Major Gates leaned his right elbow on the desk and covered his eyes as if in prayer.

'We'd protect you if you talked,' the officer said quietly. 'You could leave the country with a new passport and maybe enough money to start somewhere else – Australia, New Zealand or the States even.'

Seamus felt his left eyelid begin to quiver. He couldn't stop it. He shook his head, rubbing the eye, trying to rid himself of his tiredness and confusion. He smiled bitterly.

'You really don't know, do you? If I was telling you anything and then skipped, I might be safe for a year, maybe two, but they'd be finding me. They've friends wherever there are Irish, and that's about everywhere since you fucking Brits ruined this country. I'd have no chance. None at all.'

'And what about your chances if we picked up the boys who've been calling round to your place in Andersonstown to see where their favourite bomb designer has vanished to? They might even get the idea that you'd shopped them. They'd be wrong, of course, laddie, but mistakes can happen. And in your case, I promise you they will.'

Seamus slumped down in his chair, trying to evade the major's piercing stare. He was trapped and he knew it. He looked up at the ceiling, allowing the intensity of the mesh-covered light bulb to burn into his brain. 'No names,' he whispered. 'No names, not one at all.'

'All right then,' the major continued, his voice low and insistent. 'Who's your instructor?'

'Instructor?' Seamus grinned. 'I go by the book just like you said. The American Army manual. It's all in there.'

'Smuggled in?' asked Captain Briance, clearly surprised.

'No way. You just fucking buy them in Dublin. Most bookshops have them.'

Major Gates coughed, flushing angrily at the captain's ingenuousness, knowing the answer was true.

'Right, laddie,' he said menacingly. 'Your last chance. Where are the bomb factories? Where are the bombs armed?'

Seamus bit his lip and then sighed deeply.

'I'm only knowing one and that's all you're having. Nothing else. Okay?'

'You're hardly in a position to bargain, laddie, but all right . . .just one thing . . . for now.' Major Gates put both hands on the table, locking the fingers tightly together.

Seamus hesitated for a moment before muttering the address of a house off Cromac Street in the Markets district of West Belfast.

'What is it?' the major asked calmly, trying to keep his inner excitement from showing in the question.

'A factory. They've a weekly delivery of the stuff . . . '

'Explosive?'

'Aye . . . and I'm not knowing where that comes from!'

'How much?'

'Depends on what they're making.'

'You haven't been putting much in the brutes recently.'

'Maybe they're saving it up. I'm not knowing either way.'

In fact Seamus did know but he wasn't going to tell about the plan, involving a large bomb, to ambush an Army patrol guarding a BBC transmitter in Co. Tyrone.

The major nodded, unsure. He thrust back his chair and stood up. 'Show me,' he ordered, walking over to the large street map of Belfast, coloured orange and green, which had been on the wall during Seamus's first interrogation.

Seamus shuffled over, one hand holding up his trousers and gripping the cigar at the same time. With his free hand, he ran a finger over the map until he reached the street he'd mentioned, hard by the city's docks. The area on the map was coloured green, denoting a Catholic enclave.

'Number Four, you said, laddie?'

The young man looked sideways at the major. He smiled faintly. 'If you like . . . but I thought I said Number Seven.'

'Right. Sit down again,' muttered Major Gates.

'Now, young Seamus,' he began when he'd resumed his seat. 'If you've told the truth, we'll keep our side of the bargain. We'll let it be known that you said nothing, that you were a proper little hero. But if you send us on a wild goose chase, then . . .'

The major shrugged his shoulders.

Seamus nodded, understanding the implied threat. He wasn't too worried since he'd given a correct address, although it was for a bomb factory which was due to be moved elsewhere shortly.

In all probability, he thought, the Army would find an empty house with enough traces of explosives to satisfy the major that he'd been telling the truth.

The major slapped the file on the desk. 'Come on, Captain,' he said impatiently. 'We've heard enough.'

'And me?' Seamus ventured.

'You? You'll be off to the Crumlin like you've been told.'

'On what charge?'

'Nothing to do with us, young Seamus,' the major replied, adjusting his black beret.

'The RUC'll be going into your place in Andersonstown about now, I should think. They'll probably find a detonator under the mattress, I wouldn't be surprised. Possession of explosive material contrary to the Act, I suppose. That sort of thing, anyway. You know the score, surely?'

'But there isn't any!'

The major tapped the side of his prominent, rather hooked nose with a finger. 'Who knows what they'll find, laddie. I don't. It's nothing to do with us. We're just army . . . not police.'

Seamus lifted his head to the ceiling as if in supplication, then leaned forward to stub the cigar out in the metal box serving as an ashtray.

'Don't do that,' Major Gates called from the door, half-opened by Captain Briance. 'Don't waste it. The sergeant will let you finish it.'

His voice fell to a whisper, barely reaching Seamus.

'After all, laddie, never let it be said that the British Army never rewards its informants!'

He flicked his stick against his beret in a mock salute before gently shutting the door.

Seamus sat there with the cigar in his right hand, its smoke turning sour in his throat. He stubbed it out viciously on the desk top.

'Was that really necessary, sir?' Captain Briance asked earnestly as the two officers walked out into the icy air of the barracks' parade ground and headed for their Land Rover.

'The last crack about informants, Charley? Yes, it was necessary. Keeps the skull on tenterhooks, you see. Reminds him of what he's done. Maybe he'll talk some more.'

'Do you really think so?'

'Frankly, no . . . '

'And all that religious chatter, sir? I thought we were supposed to stay off that.'

'We're supposed not to do many things, Charley, but we have to if we want to stay in this fight. The religion's an old trick. Used it in Cyprus. Keep switching from bombs to some subject near their hearts like religion or their families. Makes them lose track of the real questions. Funny, they try to be truthful about personal matters then find themselves doing the same about their other activities. You'll get the knack when you've handled one or two skulls on your own, Charley.'

They reached the vehicle. At the wheel was the major's personal driver, Corporal Arnold Green, a genial, overweight man in his mid-thirties.

The two officers scrambled into the back seats and clipped on the specially-adapted seat belts.

'Where to, suh?' asked the corporal, his voice nasal with a thick Midlands accent.

'Home, Green, and put the light on. We're on our way to put a bomb under some skulls . . . we hope.'

The driver grinned broadly as he started the vehicle and switched on the siren. These were the sort of journeys he liked. Despite his overhanging belly and permanently rumpled appearance, he was a driver whose reactions would have been envied by many professional racing men. The Army, despairing of ever making him an infantryman, had discovered Green's latent skills and put them to their best use.

The Land Rover screeched left out of the barracks and hurtled down Holywood Road towards the M1 motorway leading to Lisburn. Even though the siren forced other drivers to the side of the road, it wasn't enough for Green. He jumped traffic lights and even drove straight over a small grass-covered roundabout. Behind him, he left motorists with palpitating hearts and shattered nerves.

'Quite successful, don't you think?' Captain Briance said loudly, bouncing in his seat, as the Land Rover slowed a trifle to negotiate the city centre traffic.

'Better than I could have hoped for,' the major replied, twisting sideways in his seat to watch an Army foot patrol wend its way through the shoppers. The Land Rover skidded round a corner by the City Hall, sternly Victorian, narrowly missing two elderly ladies hovering on the edge of a pedestrian crossing.

'Christ, Green, watch it!' the major interrupted himself for only a second, quite used to his driver's near-misses. 'A good address and confirmation of our theory that the pipes and nails were coming from the south.'

'Do you trust him then?'

'The skull? Funny, I was just thinking that. Maybe he was just too eager to tell us things, though I think he'd rather talk to anyone other than the Paras. Did you see that sergeant? Built like a brick shithouse. Wouldn't like to meet him on a dark night. I'd say our Seamus had principles but he's also very scared of what his own mates will do to him. Probably heard some grisly tales from his old dad. I'd say it's a fair chance he's giving us some real gen.'

'So what's the next move, sir?'

'Tricky one that,' the major replied, his voice competing with the vehicle's rattles at high speed and the wailing siren. He saw that there were well on to the almost deserted motorway.

'Shut the ruddy noise off, will you, Green?' he shouted to his driver. 'Can't hear myself think . . . that's better.'

He turned again to talk to the young captain, still on the familiarization part of his posting. Major Gates believed his ATOs in Northern Ireland should be eased carefully into their dangerous work of defusing bombs.

'Yes, it's tricky, Charley. The brigadier, bless him, wants to make an announcement about capturing the skull. You know the sort of thing . . . "Army smashes bomb ring" . . . that kind of guff . . . But if we do, we might alert the skulls using the bomb factory and they'll clear the place. Yet again, if we tell the press boys once we've the factory under surveillance, then the publicity might drive the skulls right into our hands. That's one thing to learn, Charley. The press can be a bloody nuisance but it can also be a great help if we manipulate them tactically. That's one lesson I soon got under my vest when I arrived here. The skulls were playing tunes on us because we didn't have the press properly organized. Now we have, they're a jolly useful adjunct to intelligence.'

'You mean, we lie to them sir?' Captain Briance asked.

'Good Lord, no!' the major replied indignantly. 'No need to do that. But there are a few key journalists – particularly on the box and in the quality papers – who get very private briefings; they get little tit-bits about the skulls which cause mayhem all over the place. You know, we might pick up so-and-so . . . well, they might be told that chummie was living with a girl we suspect to be a leading skull as well but that she escaped our net. If chummie's married with his wife and kiddies south of the Border, that sort of gen in the papers can cause quite a deal of grief. Good psychological warfare that. Our skulls don't like their right hand with a rosary in it to know that their left hand's up some female's knickers!'

The two officers laughed. The corporal gave a lewd chuckle which seemed to come all the way from his ample belly.

'Shut up, Green!' the major said evenly. 'We all know where your brains are.'

'Nearly there, suh,' Corporal Green replied, in fine humour after his hair raising drive.

'And when we are, make sure this heap of yours is cleaned, Corporal. I'll want to see my face in the polish or you'll be driving a dustcart,' the major warned gruffly.

'Suh,' said the corporal without resentment, knowing that, in reality, the major regarded him as almost indispensable to the bomb disposal operation, often bragging affectionately about his skills as a driver to other officers in the mess. Green reciprocated the admiration in his tales about the major.

When they reached Army HQ Major Gates vanished into his filing cabinet of an office and made three telephone calls before reporting to the senior officers manning the operations room along the corridor.

Ninety minutes later, he joined the weekly general operations meeting in the conference room on the second floor, overlooking the helicopter landing area and the sports fields.

He looked round the rectangular table at the half-colonels, colonels and brigadiers, all superior in rank to himself, red brevets on their shoulders.

He was quite at home. He knew that they held greater power over a greater number of soldiers than himself. But he also knew that these men envied, perhaps feared, his own nerve and expertise in walking up to a bomb and defusing it. He played often on the buccaneer, one-man-to-a-bomb aspect of his job to get his way. He was usually successful. The GOC invariably treated his problems with some deference.

'If we raid the place tonight, Stephen,' the general asked, 'What do we win? What do we lose?'

'I would think everything and nothing, sir. We have to go as soon as possible. I'm pretty sure the skull's telling the truth as he knows it at this moment in time. And with the proper publicity, we might get the bonus of other skulls flooooding into the area.'

The general, a florid, square faced man with curly hair parted down the middle, winced. 'Please just call them the enemy,' he said, a trifle testily. 'I had this problem of different names in Aden. Just call them the enemy and then we all know, don't we?'

'As you wish, sir . . . anyway, I think we can draw them in if we time it right. Might have a bigger bag than we hoped.'

'It'll give us the chance for a thorough sweep through the Markets area, sir,' volunteered the officer commanding No 42 Heavy Brigade (Royal Artillery), the unit holding responsibility for the centre of Belfast.

'You can always lay on a sweep if you want one, Frank,' remarked the GOC.

'But without good reason it always causes resentment. We're usually on the streets half the night afterwards with the rioters – as are your chaps, Fergus.'

The district inspector of the RUC liaising with the Army, a grey and wise man, nodded agreement.

'It's always different, sir,' the policeman said quietly, 'if we can give the locals a reason, like a bomb.'

The general lit a menthol cigarette, all his wife allowed him ever since the luncheon at the Palace where his nicotine-stained fingers, according to her, had drawn disapproving glances from Prince Philip.

'And precisely how do they know there's a bomb situation?' the general asked. 'How do they know it's not a phoney?'

'Oh, they're pretty wily, sir,' said the brigadier commanding No 42 Heavy Brigade. 'If they see SATO and his EODs, blue lights flashing, they reckon we're not fooling about.'

'Any press releases to coincide?'

The chief information officer smiled rather secretively like someone in possession of mysterious skills.

'No problem, sir. Bell of the BBC and Seymour of ITN are both in town. Both frontline chaps. I'll let them know too late for the network early evening news which'll guarantee the local news on

BBC and UTV will run it as their leads at six o'clock.'

'Sure, John?' asked Major Gates.

'Well, if not at six, very shortly afterwards. It won't be their end item for sure!'

'And what do we say?' asked Major Gates.

'Simple as you like. A major break through in smashing the bombers? Army questioning bomb ring leaders?'

'Not that!' interrupted Gates. 'Keep our sku . . . man out of it for me. He could be valuable.'

'What about us then?' asked the RUC officer. 'What do we do with our friend who's talked so much.'

'Anything found in his lodgings?'

'Enough for a charge, they say,' the RUC man replied enigmatically. 'They weren't too specific though.'

'Well, pick him up from Holywood,' suggested Major Gates, 'and hold him incommunicado in the Crumlin remand wing till you get the wire. He could do with some more questioning before any charge.'

'You don't want him connected?'

'Not if possible. Keep him totally under wraps. Let's say the operation in the Markets area follows a long observation job. Why not say it's down to the RUC. For God's sake, Fergus's boys need some encouragement after what they've been through.'

'So what do I tell Bell and Seymour before six o'clock?'

'Just tell them something big's happening which might smash a bomb factory. Tell them to bring the cameras to the east end of Cromac Street and we'll look after them. They'll give their local newsrooms enough to get their teeth into before they rush out.'

'Can you provide the men, Frank?' the general asked the brigadier commanding No 42 Heavy Brigade.

'No problem, sir. It sounds a good 'un to me. Let's see who we flush, eh?'

'Right!'

The GOC made a few notes on his pad and then looked up.

'Stephen, you've got your operation. Hope it works.'

# Chapter 3 January 12th, 1971 (p.m.)

Glistening wet tarmac reflected the knowingly winking red and blue lights of the Army and police vehicles parked in the tiny side streets surrounding the Markets area of West Belfast.

Messages crackled back and forth on the radio sets.

Soldiers and policemen, rifles and submachine guns at the ready, protective flak jackets buttoned high, redirected the late rush hour traffic into a tortuous detour avoiding the area. Firmly and politely, they parried the inevitable questions from office and shop workers on their way home.

'No, nothing happening. Just a routine check,' they'd say in accents which were a vocal map of the United Kingdom.

A few men, who'd spent the afternoon between bar and betting shop were moved along with less tact. One drunk went off into the drizzly darkness whining like a hurt dog after a rifle butt on his toes ended the argument he was trying to pick with a young soldier.

Three television film crews huddled down into their dark anoraks, almost invisible against the soot-grimed walls of a tall Victorian warehouse, wondering if they'd be back in their hotels before dinner finished or whether they'd have to survive yet again on curled sandwiches from the night porter.

'Sod this for a lark!' one cameraman remarked morosely, adjusting the 16mm Arriflex camera on his shoulder, forgetting the overtime pay he was due.

'Too bloody true, mate,' agreed the sound recordist.

The lighting technician started rubbing his hands together to keep them warm and accidentally switched on his portable light, his 'handbasher'.

The strong beam flicked across startled, white faces of the security forces, now perfect targets for any sniper lurking in the deep shadows.

'Turn that fucking thing off!' a policeman roared.

The gloom descended again. There wasn't much excitement and

the atmosphere was more one of tight reined fear and deep down tiredness.

'Oscar one calling Felix. Over,' the radio called. 'Come in, Felix.'

Major Gates, standing by a Land Rover pressed the switch on his radio.

'Felix receiving Oscar One. Over,' he said, using his new call-sign of the cartoon cat who always walked backwards. He'd thought that more appropriate for bomb disposal than the previous call-sign of 'Jelly Baby'.

'Area secured, Felix, Over.'

'Any skulls, Oscar One? Over.'

'Possible three sighted at scene. Over.'

'We'll move then, Oscar One? Over.'

'Affirmative. Out.'

They'd been waiting for more than an hour since the local news bulletins on television and radio had briefly reported the setting-up of road blocks near the Markets area. The information released by the Army Information office had been designed to set IRA alarm-bells ringing, but was so deliberately vague and noncommittal that, hopefully, no one determined to enter the area would be totally scared off.

All the while, the suspected house off Cromac Street had been kept under surveillance through night binoculars. Now, with people apparently at the house, the sweep could begin. Whatever there was to find, would be found.

Men of the Welsh Guards, faces blackened, moved silently into the narrow cobbled alleys to reach within a thirty yard radius of the house named by Seamus Aherne. They clambered over walls leading to the small yards serving as gardens in these 'back-to-backs' and negotiated past dustbins and rusting bicycle and pram frames to enter the kitchen doors.

The startled occupants, most finishing high tea and watching television, were told that there was an unexploded bomb nearby. They were hurried into warm clothes and led quietly out of the area, across Ormeau Road to the public swimming baths where police-women had arranged temporary accommodation for them among the changing cubicles.

An officer's whistle shrilled into the night when the evacuation of the houses had been completed.

In counterpoint, dustbin lids began clattering rhythmically as the people in the Catholic enclave signalled to each other that the troops were coming.

'Go!' ordered Major Gates, slapping the bonnet of his bomb disposal team's Land Rover.

The vehicle, carrying Staff-Sergeant Blundell and Corporal Jefferson, his assistant, hurtled down the narrow streets, headlights blazing, and screeched to a halt behind a 'pig', an armoured troop carrier, blocking one end of the evacuated street.

Two groups of six soldiers started edging towards the target house from either end of the street, keeping well into the shadows and walls of the houses on the same side. They were covered by four marksmen with light-intensifying sights on their rifles.

Soldiers in groups of three began to search the houses in adjoining streets.

They hammered on front doors and barged in once they were opened. One man would stay with the family while the other two went quickly through the house, opening drawers and cupboards, looking into attics and under beds – often knocking over and breaking furniture and prized ornaments in their haste.

Those who were slow to their front doors, sometimes the elderly had their locks kicked in. Women screamed and sobbed with fear and shock. Men cursed with anger and frustration. The soldiers paid little heed.

Overhead, a small Army helicopter circled, noisily, insistently, its powerful searchlight flicking and darting through the steady curtain of rain.

All was noise and frightened confusion, shouts and pounding boots.

A voice magnified by a loud hailer sliced through the skein of sounds. 'You in Number Seven. Come out with your hands raised. The house is surrounded. Come out now!'

A light in the front room of the house flicked off.

For a moment, the street was in almost total darkness until a searchlight stabbed out from one of the 'pigs', lighting the front of the house as bright as day.

The soldiers dropped to the uneven pavement and wriggled on elbows and knees until they were only two dozen feet from the front door.

A window shattered in the upstairs of the house, glass tinkling on to the streets below. The soldiers at the front and back heard a woman cry out, seemingly protesting. Instinctively, they hugged closer to the wall and pavement.

'Crack . . . peeww! Crack . . . peeww!'

Two revolver shots echoed along the street, bullets whining off the concrete pavement, yards away from the troops.

Another shot, flatter and faster, cracked out, its firer's position in the window clear from the tiny flash of flame. The bullet clanged and ricocheted off the side of the armour-plated 'pig', not feet from the bomb disposal team.

'Three rounds CS! Fire!' shouted the captain sheltering behind the vehicle, directing the raid.

A sergeant spun round the nearest street corner, raised his weapon to his shoulder and fired. Immediately, he pulled back into cover to reload.

'Thummm . . . !'

One grenade round of CS (Composition Smoke) gas smashed harmlessly against the outside wall of the house, falling into the gutter, billowing its fumes.

'Thummm . . . !'

Another gas grenade.

'Thummm . . . !'

The third grenade followed the second into the house, crashing through a window.

Within a few seconds, the soldiers could see the smoke begin to drift out. They heard someone coughing, a man shouting obscenities, a woman screaming shrilly. The smoke with its irritant chemical compound, fret-sawing at throats and eyes, continued to billow out of the house.

'Marksmen, ready! Prepare to return fire!' the captain shouted. 'Fire on definite target!'

The soldiers, picked as battalion marksmen because of their natural reflexes and ability with a weapon, peered through their sights. The east wind blew the CS gas into the faces of those at the furthest end of the street. They lowered their weapons, eyes smarting, unable to see clearly.

One of the marksmen at the other end of the street, detected a solid shape moving behind the curtain of smoke. He waited a split second to be sure, then squeezed the trigger.

A man, his back to the street, slumped through the broken upstairs window, twisted slightly in mid-air and thudded to the pavement.

The second marksman at that corner, rigid with concentration, saw the dying man as he came through the window. His high velocity bullet, fractionally off target, smashed into the upstairs room.

'Kerrumpp . . . !'

The fireball of the explosion billowed outwards and upwards, fierce and yellow black and frightful and orange.

The ground shook.

Soldiers lying on the pavement were lifted six inches into the air, choking for breath, lungs frozen with shock.

Almost in slow motion, the walls of the house, front and back, lifted off their foundations and buckled outwards with the explosion's force, dragging the walls of the adjoining houses with them.

Windows for two streets around shivered out of their old putty surrounds and sharded on to the pavement.

Inside the house itself, the people who'd been trying to evacuate the bomb factory were ripped limb from limb.

The energy waves entered their mouths, trying to suck breath, and took the tops of their heads away. Their arms and legs were torn from their trunks, and, finally, in those micro-seconds of carnage, their flesh was ripped from their very bones and scattered this way and that.

On the perimeter of the search area, fifty or so yards from the explosion, Major Gates felt the shock waves travel up through the soles of his boots to punch him, as a boxer's punch, in the solar plexus. He bent forward, struggling to keep some breath in his body.

'Felix One to Felix Two! Come in, over!' he coughed into his two-way radio, still searching for breath. And again, 'Felix One to Felix Two! Come in!'

There was no reply, simply the crackle of static noise.

Other radios uttered half-strangled messages as troops and police, winded and shocked by the explosion, tried to report back to their superior officers.

Major Gates was conscious of passing a woman at one house. She stood on the front step shrieking hysterically and pointing, index finger quivering, towards the plume of fire in the sky.

Major Gates skidded round the last corner and cannoned into a soldier who was staggering about, rubbing dust filled eyes, slightly concussed. 'Fucking hell! Fucking hell!' the soldier kept repeating with changing emphasis on the same two words.

'Blundell!' the major called moving towards the scene of devastation: 'Staff-Sarn't Blundell!'

Suddenly, to his horror, he saw four soldiers begin picking their way through the pile of rubble which was all that remained of the bomb factory and the two houses either side of it. 'Get back!' he screamed. 'Get the hell out of it, soldiers!'

The privates turned and saw a stocky, dust-covered figure waving his arms frantically at them. They stood still for a moment.

'I'm SATO,' Major Gates bawled. 'Move back to cover. The area's not cleared! Move!'

There could be no mistaking his authority. The soldiers withdrew round the corner shouting to others to do the same.

'Well, that was a bang and a half, sir,' a voice said quietly behind the major.

'Blundell!' sighed Major Gates with relief. 'And just where the. . . where have you been?'

'Seeing to Corporal Jefferson, sir. When the roof fell in, he was lying under the pig. Got a crack on his head when the shock wave lifted him.'

'How bad?'

'Couple of aspirins and an early night.'

'Serves him right for lying under pigs, what? Anyway, for one ghastly minute, I thought you'd moved in.'

'Without telling you, sir?' asked the young staff-sergeant matter-of-factly.

'Of course not, Blundell,' the major said reassuringly, smiling.

The staff-sergeant began slapping the dust out of his combat fatigues, then took off his rimless spectacles and wiped them with a handkerchief.

'Christ!' the major muttered. 'I almost had heart failure when the brute blew.'

'So did we, sir. Thought the whole street was going.'

'How much do you reckon?'

'Good 100 lbs. Maybe more. They wouldn't have felt a thing,' Blundell said.

'More's the pity,' grunted Major Gates. 'Anyway, how many of them?'

'From the shooting, two men. Marksman got one skull before she blew. And, from the screaming when we arrived, there might be a female.'

'Right. Get the area taped off and let's have a look.'

'Sir!'

'Guardsman! Here!' Major Gates shouted. 'Help ATO run out the tapes.'

'Suh.'

'And where's your officer?'

'Injured, suh.'

'Badly?'

'No, suh. He was pretty well the one nearest the explosion. He's

514

spewing his . . . he's feeling a little shaken, suh.'

'Good. Send one of your lads to find him and tell him that SATO requests his presence here as soon as possible.'

Less than a minute later, a young captain, whey-faced, shakily approached the major who was now standing by the 'pig', establishing his command.

'You wanted me, sir?' he asked, obviously still suffering from the after effects of the explosion.

'Son,' said Major Gates quietly, so quietly that he couldn't be heard by other than the captain, 'Lay a cordon round this area, establish perimeter defences against possible snipers, then report to the nearest M.O. Right?'

'As you say, sir.'

'Good man. First class.'

Soon, white tapes had been secured at waist height across each end of the street, effectively warning people from going near the scene of the explosion. Some troops guarded the street while others resumed searching homes in neighbouring streets.

Corporal Jefferson, a bulbous swelling on his temple, approached the major, now conferring with an RUC inspector.

'Sir!' he said. 'The television people want to know if they can film inside the tapes.'

Major Gates swung round and saw one cameraman with his eye already to the camera's viewfinder, his left hand adjusting the focus on the special lens capable of filming with the minimum of available light.

'Just the thing,' said Major Gates cheerfully. 'Ask them in on the usual conditions and we'll use their hand-bashers. Save us rigging lights.'

For the next hour, bomb disposal and forensic searched through the rubble with the aid of the camera crews' hand-held lights. The cameramen were allowed to film on the strict understanding that they never took identifiable close-up pictures of the EOD unit or their equipment.

The unit checked first that there were no more bombs or explosives in the rubble. Then they picked carefully through the shattered bricks, glass and wood of what was once three dwellings. They searched for the smallest piece of electrical wire or a fire seared brick which might contain the impregnation of explosive, or the smallest slivers of human flesh. Each of the searchers wore rubber gloves and carried tweezers and each placed their finds in small plastic bags. There was only one substantial find and that a street away. A forensic detective, gagging a little, identified it as a human thigh. A young soldier picked it up on a shovel and pushed it, quivering like jelly, into a large transparent bag. He later surprised himself by being sick only three times.

The search resumed at first light and by mid-morning the pathologist at the Royal Victoria Hospital was able to begin his post-mortem examination of what few remains there were.

While he worked, Major Gates and Captain Briance watched from the next room, through a large rectangular window.

Normally, curtains were drawn across the glass but the major wanted the young captain to undergo a final experience of Northern Ireland's awful realities before he was assigned to his own bomb disposal unit.

Major Gates did the same with all his young officers. His intention was not to shock them but to try to save their lives and the lives of those around them. He reasoned that if they saw the effects of an explosion on the human body then they wouldn't take any chances whatsoever in their work.

The major knew from his long experience that to stay alive as he had an ATO had to be especially cautious, meticulously prepared and an absolute stickler in following the laid-down procedures for defusing bombs. He had little time, if any, for individualists, innovators or improvisers. To him, bomb disposal was a precise science in which the slightest mistake invariably meant death. His own surival had proved that.

'Caution and concentration,' he always told his men. 'Never take a chance unless it's irrevocably necessary. And then don't. Brothers, never hurry to your own funeral!'

His teaching had succeeded until now. Since he'd arrived in the Province late in 1969, not one of his charges had died, though some had had lucky escapes.

But, as he'd often said in the officer's mess, 'You either have bad luck or you get what you deserve!'

Captain Briance, tight-lipped, tried to concentrate on the minutest, least significant details of the gruesome scene before him, hoping in that way his mind wouldn't accept the wilder thought that the pile of raw, bloody meat on the white, slightly inclined, slab in the next room had once been a human being, maybe three.

'Stay with it, there's a good chap,' Major Gates said encouragingly patting him lightly on the shoulder. 'Stay with it!'

He turned and winked conspiratorially at the RUC sergeant sitting stolidly in the corner of the same room, waiting to take a statement from the pathologist.

The sergeant, a veteran of such duties, smiled ruefully. 'The first's always the worst,' he said in his unmistakable Belfast accent.

Captain Briance drew a deep breath, his face grey. He swayed slightly, steadying himself by leaning forward with his palms against the glass.

The door to the observation room opened. A man of about thirty strode in, white coat flapping. He paused when he saw the three men in uniform.

'Not interrupting anything?' he asked.

'Not at all. Come on in,' Major Gates said with a welcoming smile. 'Always room for another.'

Edward S. Aicheson nodded and moved to the window, standing besides Captain Briance. 'Last night's explosion?' he asked over his shoulder.

'Affirmative,' replied Major Gates.

'Sweet Jesus, what a mess!' Aicheson muttered, shaking his head.

'Seen one before?'

'Once, back home, major, but nothing like that.'

'American, aren't you?'

'You got it.'

They introduced each other, shaking hands. The major used his masonic grip but it wasn't reciprocated.

'What are you doing over here?' Major Gates asked conversationally. 'Last place I'd volunteer for.'

'You gotta be where the trade is,' Aicheson grinned, mocking his accent for a moment. 'No, seriously, there was a visiting fellowship available, and since I'm specializing in neurological surgery I reckoned this was where it's at. There's some tremendous work being done here on new techniques because of the troubles.'

'Out of bad comes good.'

'That's right, Major. I can learn more here in a month than in a year back home, though, mind you, we've gotten our fair share of fellows shooting bullets into each other.'

'Where's home exactly?'

'Boston, Massachusetts.'

'Where the Irish come from.'

'Go to, more like. Scratch most anyone in the old town and you'll draw a drop of Irish blood.'

'You?'

'Oh, yes. There's a fair amount in me, so the family say.'

'Where from originally?' the major asked more courteously than inquisitively. As he talked, he watched Captain Briance, weighing him up for the future.

'Somewhere deep in the west, I'm told. Apparently on the female side. Some place I'd doubt you'd ever heard of. Listowel.'

'In Kerry?'

'That's right.'

'Funny, but I'm supposed to have some distant ancestor from round that part of the woods.'

'You? You, Major, with Irish ancestry?'

'Most of the British Army have, actually. Certainly most of the field-marshals anyway. Right down to Wellington.'

'Small world.'

'Affirmative, and yet your Irish-Americans, maybe three cousins removed from my lot, keep wittering on about us moving out from here and allowing a blood bath.'

'Some, Major. Just some. The Kennedys and so on aren't exactly typical. They might like to think they are but they aren't. Sweet Jesus, I wish we had your young soldiers running things back in Boston. They make things work!'

'They're trained to. It's the best army of its size in the world.'

'No doubt there, sir.'

'Thanks. Nice to know someone appreciates us, isn't it, Charley?' Major Gates said, warming to the American surgeon.

'Sir?' gulped Captain Briance, still staring through the window.

'Oh, come away, Charley,' the major said. 'Don't make a meal of it. I only wanted you to have a peek after all.'

'May I be excused then, sir?' asked the captain, moving swiftly away from the observation window.

'From that, yes, Charley . . . hang on, though, I think he's finished.'

The pathologist was removing his near-transparent rubber gloves. He tossed them into a waste-bin and left the mortuary.

'Interesting, gentlemen, to say the least,' he remarked strolling into the next room, still wearing his blood-streaked gown. 'How many did your people think, Gates? . . . Oh, hello, Aicheson.'

'Good morning, sir.'

The police sergeant fumbled in his breast pocket for his notebook.

'Two males and a female they reckoned, professor,' said Major Gates.

'Well, certainly, two males . . . left their undercarriages.'

The pathologist peeled off his gown, revealing immaculately

tailored waistcoat and trousers, and tossed it casually into a corner of the room.

Captain Briance stood, transfixed.

'Undercarriages?' interrupted Aicheson.

'Their cocks, young man,' said the pathologist: 'Always count the genitalia. Can't go wrong like that. One of the softest parts but always seem to hang on to the last I find. We've a problem on the females, though. Certainly one. Definitely one. But I do think another one as well.'

'How, sir?'

'Because I've got three tits in there, that's why. One pair and an odd 'un. And, unless we've a freak, that's two females, isn't it, Aicheson?'

'Even in Boston, Mass . . . ' the major interrupted.

'Shut up, Gates,' the pathologist said, not at all put out. 'Or I'll order a perch in there for the vulture you really are.'

'Jesus,' murmured the police sergeant, used to most anything. 'Three! That'll be problems!'

'I thought it might,' said the pathologist even more smugly.

'It will,' agreed the major.

'The bumf'll be something awful,' said the police sergeant disconsolately. 'They'll not be at all happy at headquarters. Any chance of identification, sir?'

'None at all,' replied the pathologist. 'I've taken the measurements of what bones and limbs I could. When I've worked them out, you might have some idea of height and build. Best I can do, I'm afraid, Sergeant.'

'Long and short of it, eh? Looks as if we'll have to wait for the death notices in the *Irish News*.'

'As you say, Major,' the pathologist murmured. He walked through the door and then turned. 'By the way, Aicheson, how's the child?'

'The one from the bomb? Holding his own, sir, but still unconscious. I've decided against operating, though. I reckon it's a deep concussion and he'll pull out given time.'

'Good decision,' the pathologist nodded. 'I've had more clients on the slabs down here from surgeons who insisted on meddling than from those who let good old Mother Nature take her course.'

'We must meet again,' Major Gates said to the young surgeon as he too prepared to leave. 'Perhaps a noggin some time? Discuss our Irish ancestors, eh?'

'Pleasure, Major. And take care now,' Aicheson replied.

'You can bet your life on it,' smiled Major Gates. 'And mine for that matter.'

Outside he found Captain Briance standing in the corridor, as pale as the cream painted walls.

'Come on, Charley. What you need is a stiffener in the mess.'

When they arrived back at Thiepval Barracks, the two officers went first to the major's office. There, on his desk, was a report detailing the finds made during the previous night's search of the Markets area.

'Look at this!' exclaimed the major, quite excited. '862 rounds of Kynoch 9-millimetre in all. Our stuff made in '56 and '58.'

'Decent haul, sir.'

'Yes, but see here. Look at where the bullets were found. Most in one house but they've spread the ammunition around seven places in just two streets next door to each other. I'd bet a year's pay there's a skull in every one of those houses. Classic sign of a terrorist cell, Charley. Remember that. Precisely what they used to do in Malaya and Cyprus. They all learn off each other. The brotherhood of international terrorism, that's what we've got here. Not a little local difficulty as some of these bloody politicians seem to think!'

'You'll mention it at the briefing?'

'For the Home Secretary? For my sins, I'm afraid so. Waste of an afternoon but there we are. Just thinking of it gives me a thirst. Come on, Charley!'

They walked out of the headquarters building, turned half-left and approached a high wire fence guarded at its only gate by two soldiers. This was the inner compound, containing the commanding general's house, tucked away within evergreen shrubbery, and the officer's mess.

The mess was reached down a narrow outside passage leading to the wooden front door of what was once a grand old house. Immediately inside, the large sombre hallway was all brown veneer panels. Half-a-dozen officers sat around, waiting to have lunch in the adjoining dining room, thumbing through copies of *Punch*, *Country Life*, and the *Illustrated London News*. The atmosphere was of disciplined order and comfortable calm, a haven from the nasty, untidy events of the world outside.

The actual bar was a smallish rectangular room off the hallway with a curved dispensing counter set in the corner nearest the door. It was fairly empty at this time of day.

'What's yours, Charley?' asked the major. 'A drop of brandy to settle the stomach?'

'Why not, sir, seeing it was upset on duty.'

'Quite right. A large brandy, steward, and a pint of Bass for me.'

The elderly steward, a retired soldier, served the drinks while Major Gates wrote out and signed the chit of paper which would place their cost on his monthly mess bill.

'Nice one last night, Stephen,' another major remarked, standing at the other end of the padded bar counter.

'The own goals? Even better than we thought. Four instead of three.'

'Another one, eh?'

'That's what the old prof says. It's either that or there's a lop-sided female skull in town.'

'Like that, was it?'

'And some, brother! It'll be in ops. briefing notes.'

'Look forward to reading them.'

'You callous devil!'

'What about you then, old man?'

'Me? Can't you see my tear-stained cheeks?'

They laughed cynically.

Major Gates, still smiling, carried the two drinks over to a table by the large sash windows and sat down. He took a long pull at his beer, sighing appreciatively.

'Well, our Seamus certainly came through,' Captain Briance remarked quietly, warming the brandy glass in his cupped hands.

'He did that, Charley. In spades. I wish he'd been there to see it rather than snug in his cell at the Crumlin, and preferably in the house when it blew!'

The captain raised his eyebrows. 'Don't you feel anything at all about the skulls? About their families when they die? Anything?'

'Nope,' Major Gates grunted, lighting his third Panatella of the morning. 'It's their choice if they want to play games. They pick the game. They pick the rules. Not us.'

'Odd though, isn't it?' Captain Briance said reflectively. 'Our Seamus seemed a nice enough young fellow really, yet he throws up a perfectly decent job to come up here and take us on.'

'Very odd. When I first arrived here, I couldn't understand it either. Not one iota of it. Oh, yes, I could see why the Catholics were upset all right. They'd had the muddy end of the stick in Northern Ireland for mumble-mumble years and not one blessed person had done anything about it. They could hardly get a job if they were up against a Protestant who wanted it as well. They couldn't vote in

521

enough of their own councillors even if there were more of them in a town than Protestants. The plural voting system fixed that . . . dammit, a helluva lot of them weren't even entitled to vote. And, of course, if they couldn't get control of a council, they didn't have the houses allocated to them. Hardly a Protestant went begging for need of a council house. Thousands of Catholics did. I mean to say, it was bloody ridiculous. Take Derry for an example. Twice as many Catholics there as Protestants yet, thanks to the gerrymandering, the place kept returning a Unionist M.P. to Stormont. No wonder there was trouble. Those civil rights youngsters were on the ball about the carve-up going on. But that's all being put right now. As you'll guess, I'm no admirer of your darling Harold when he was Prime Minister but he was spot on in telling Stormont to pull its finger out and sort out this nonsense with the Catholics. Should have been done years ago! The Protestants brought a lot of this trouble on themselves, make no mistake, but now it's being sorted and everyone's equal under the law etcetera, etcetera, what do we have? Still more bombs and bullets. And what do they want? They want the Brits out, the very people who set it back on the tracks again. And who, might you ask, are precisely they? Not Dublin politicians, on your life. They know they couldn't afford to subsidize this place like the poor old British tax-payer does. The Catholic population in Northern Ireland then? No way! They know they'd be worse off if they were run by Dublin. Where would all the subsidies for jobs come from, the social security, the old age pension, the dole money? So, as I asked myself a long time ago when I stepped off the boat, just who are "they" and what's it about?'

The major swallowed the last of his beer and edged the mug towards the junior officer.

'Christ, Charley, talking to you always gives me a dry throat,' he smiled.

'My round, sir. Same again?'

'You'd better watch the old cognac. You're in ops this afternoon while I'm with our beloved Reggie.'

'I'll just take a dry ginger.'

'Good man!'

Captain Briance returned with the drinks and set them on the table. He glanced through the window at the well-kept lawns and shrubberies outside and thought it a rather incongruous scene in relation to what was happening many miles away. 'You were saying, sir?' he asked tentatively.

Major Gates laid down his beer mug, brushing a knuckle against the side of his mouth to remove a speck of froth.

'Well, I was telling you about "they", wasn't I?'

The captain nodded.

'International communism, that's "they". simple as that. Marxist anarchists. Just like they've got in Germany and Italy. Same sort of mob. Sure, this lot call themselves the Provisional IRA but that's just window-dressing. Should be prosecuted under the Trades Descriptions Acts among other things.'

Captain Briance looked doubtful.

'You mean someone like our Seamus? A communist?'

'Him?' the major smiled and shook his head sadly. 'No, they just wind up boys like him: just wind up most of the poor punks with stories of the old IRA. It's a very convenient name to use. After all, it's worth some mileage. All the top boys, those who really matter in the Provo's Army Council, are about as near to the old IRA as Moscow is to Washington. They're always vanishing off overseas for their conferences and indoctrination lectures. If they can bring about a total breakdown in law and order, then they'll be in. They won't be satisfied till the whole of Ireland's a Democratic Republic like the ones behind the Iron Curtain. They'll make Ireland as threatening to Western Europe as Cuba is to the States. That, Charley, is what it's about.'

Captain Briance was still doubtful.

'You mean there's no old IRA in this at all?'

'There's a bit. Of course there is. After all, it's a basic principle of the IRA to have a united Ireland one day. That's what pulls the suckers like our Seamus in. Another glorious campaign just like dad and grandad and great-grandad fought. What they don't realize is what's behind it all. And, let's face it Charley, the only way they're going to have a united Ireland is to throw us out. It'd mean another civil war and I'd put my best shirt on the Protestants to win every time.'

Major Gates stubbed out his cigar and finished his beer.

'I think a last half before lunch. What about you, Charley?'

# Chapter 4 May 1971

His eyes didn't flicker when he heard the keys chink and rattle the locks turn, the murmurs and the footsteps further along the landing.

After four months, fifteen days and twelve hours of imprisonment, Seamus Aherne could time the warders' approach almost to perfection.

They were four cells away.

His gaze remained fixed on the light in the ceiling. By concentrating upon it, he could enter, for a moment at least, a world of aloneness.

He wished it could stay on throughout the night. If it did, he thought its trance-like effect might even shut out the sounds of his three cellmates as they evacuated their bladders or bowels into the tin bucket in the corner by the door, or panted and sighed and snorted as they exorcised their sexual fantasies by masturbating.

The warders were opening the door of the next cell but one.

If the light was with him through the night, thought Seamus, he might also avoid the nightmares, which persisted despite the tranquillizers prescribed by the medical officer.

Awful images of people torn limb from limb by bombs of his own making. They were always people he knew, his family or friends from the National School in Upper Church Street in Listowel.

They were next door now. The sounds of them echoed off the stone and metal of the Republican wing of the Crumlin Gaol in Belfast.

Sometimes, in his dreams, he ran towards the people trying to warn them. Always, a figure in khaki uniform, grinning, blocked his path. He would lie winded on the ground, watching the bomb victims disintegrate in the blast. Major Stephen Gates would be cackling with laughter.

The tiny spy hole, recessed into the cell door, clicked back. They key clunked in the heavy lock. The warder's voice was flat with boredom.

'Slop out, you Ras! Come on now, move it!'

Seamus swung his legs over the edge of the bunk, stars and blobs swimming liquidly before his eyes as they readjusted to normal light.

'Another day, another dollar,' he muttered, his stockinged feet striking the harsh matting on the floor.

'Do you always have to fucking say that?' exclaimed the man in the bunk below, an IRA veteran from the early 1960s, Andy McCann.

'Why not?' Seamus answered. 'And what else?'

He knew it was his turn, and he quickly dressed himself in the prison's blue denim uniform.

'It's all shit,' he said lightly, picking up the tin bucket in the corner and walking out on to the landing.

Nobody argued about him pushing into the queue of prisoners waiting to 'slop-out' the contents of the night-buckets. The essential thing for all was not to spill a drop, not to be ordered to spend the morning scrubbing down that landing and the landing below.

It was almost a social occasion: there was a camaraderie which lifted the participants above their menial, evil-smelling task.

'Good night, Vienna,' Seamus murmured when he eventually reached the sluice basin and up-ended the contents of his cell's bucket down the waste pipe. Then he moved sideways to wash it out in the adjoining basin.

The prison officer standing by the door, fresh on duty, usually averted his eyes rather than watch what was happening in the sluice room. His early morning bacon sandwich was too valuable to risk.

Thus that part of the prisoners' daily routine became a favourite time for relaying messages and instructions.

Seamus had been approached while slopping out only two days after receiving his five-year sentence for possessing explosives from the court directly across the Crumlin Road.

'Second landing. Cell thirty-four,' the man slopping-out beside him had muttered from the side of his mouth, his lips hardly moving. 'Ten o'clock.'

Seamus had begun to protest, believing that the warders wouldn't allow such movement from landing to landing.

'Don't worry about the screws, cunt,' the man urged. 'Just be ready.'

To his surprise, at a few minutes before ten o'clock, his cell door opened, a prison officer motioned him out with a flap of his wrist and he was escorted down the circular iron staircase to the landing below and to Cell 34. Nothing was said. Nothing remarked upon. It appeared simple routine.

'Thanks, Mr Allen,' a prisoner, standing casually outside the cell, said to Seamus' escort. The prison officer merely nodded and turned away.

'Through there,' the prisoner ordered Seamus, opening the unlocked door and pushing him inside.

Cell 34 resembled a bed-sitting room rather than the overcrowded, squalid cell which Seamus had just left.

Along one wall, there was a single bunk covered with a flowery blue bedspread, transforming it almost into a sofa. Large coloured photographs of idyllic scenes of the Irish countryside covered two walls. A table, bearing a radio and what were obviously family photographs, was set at an angle under the high, barred window.

The middle-aged man behind the table waved Seamus inside.

'Come in, son,' he said in a flat, nasal Belfast accent. 'You'll excuse me for not standing, but the old legs are playing up today.'

'I'm sorry,' Seamus replied automatically, surprised at the cell's appearance. There was even a strip of carpet on the floor.

'Sit down,' the man invited, gesturing towards the bunk. He pushed a pack of cigarettes and a box of matches across the table. 'Smoke?' he asked.

Seamus nodded and opened the pack. It was nearly filled with proper cigarettes, not the scraps of hand-rolled tobacco he'd become resigned to since beginning his sentence. He raised his eyebrows.

'Living in luxury, eh? That's what you're thinking?' the man at the table went on. 'Just perks of the job, son, for the officer commanding the Republican wing.'

'Then you're . . .'

'That's right, son, I'm Charley McCool.'

'Of St Matthew's?'

The man grinned. 'You know the local history, then? Yes, I was with Billy defending the church against those fucking Prods. Unlike Billy, I got bullets in both legs. Still, they're all right now unless they pick up a wee bit of damp. I can always tell from the legs when the rain's coming!'

Seamus looked with undisguised admiration at the older man, legendary for his exploits in protecting Catholic areas from rampaging Protestants during the riots of 1969. He saw a man with steel-grey hair brushed straight back, deep lines on his forehead and around his mouth, and eyes which seemed both penetrating and kindly.

Seamus lit his cigarette.

'I thought, Mr McCool we weren't due any political privileges in here.'

'We're not, officially, Seamus. But the governor and the Home Office accept realities if they're not flaunted in their fat civil service faces. They negotiate conditions and whatever with me and that way we can both get things done. It's a two-way deal.' McCool shrugged. 'It's the same in the Loyalist wing though, things being what they are, there are less of them.'

Seamus leaned back against the wall, beginning to relax.

'I'm told you refused to recognize the court at your trial, Seamus.'

'Sat with my back to the judge. It didn't really matter what I'd said. They'd me colder than Monday's snap. They put up the evidence and that was that.'

'It's a worthwhile gesture anyway.'

'Traditional, so my da said.'

'You've seen him?'

'In the cells afterwards.'

McCool nodded approvingly. 'Keep the family links. They're important. We'll help with the cost of their travelling, if you like.'

'They'd appreciate that. Money's pretty scarce back home.'

'Isn't it everywhere? My wee wifie's still got three at home. Three away, but still three at home. Sounds like the football results, eh?' McCool stopped for a moment, perhaps thinking of his family. His hand slapped down on the desk. 'Anyway, son,' he resumed, 'I've heard good things about your work with the Third Battalion.'

'Uh-huh?' Seamus murmured doubtfully. He looked round the cell and particularly at the door and ceiling.

McCool smiled reassuringly. 'We'll not be overheard,' he said. 'It's part of the arrangement that they don't bug our cells. We don't take any chances anyway. The fellow you saw outside can sniff a microphone from thirty yards, so he can.'

'So it's safe to talk?'

'In here at least. But be careful anywhere else. Better safe than . . . '

'Right.'

'Well then, your work with the Third Battalion?'

'Fairly routine, Mr McCool. All the old stuff. Actually, I was working on a new 'un when they picked me up.'

'At a bomb, wasn't it?'

'I liked to watch them. If I could see what they were doing, it gave me an idea sometimes of what might give them problems. Careless, I suppose.'

'Pity. You were getting results. Lived in Andersonstown, didn't you?'

'A room in Slievegallion Drive. Three quid a week and walk the landlady's dog.'

'Deliberate?'

'The area? Yes. As you know, it's the First Battalion's patch – that Ballymurphy and the Falls – so the Brits might get a wee bit confused finding me where I was rather in the north or east of the city where we're supposed to operate.'

'Your da train you?'

Seamus shook his head. 'He's not the man he was. He took ill during his last spell in the Curragh. He told me a wee bit, but it was Jack McKay who filled in the details.'

'Where's he at?'

Suddenly, Seamus had the strong impression that McCool already knew the answers to the questions he was asking. It was more of an interrogation than a friendly chat. 'Where he usually is. At home in Swords Road, Dublin. Works in his garage mostly.'

McCool nodded, evidently satisfied. 'Nice fellow?'

'A hard man and then some, to be sure.'

'When did you join?'

'Late '68. After the first Derry.'

'A lot did. Suppose they singled you out?'

'They knew of my family, Mr McCool. Probably helped.'

'It would. When did you come north?'

'When I was sent. September '69.'

'No qualms?'

'Not really. I liked my job but . . . '

'Post Office, wasn't it?'

'You know a deal . . . yes, the Post Office . . . but once I became involved, once I joined, it didn't seem to matter that much.'

'Willing volunteer then, Seamus?'

'You could say that.'

'Inevitable, perhaps.'

'Aye. Suppose so.'

The chat-cum-interview between Seamus and Charley McCool continued for another half hour before it became clear that both had exhausted questions and answer.

Seamus came away surprised that the destruction of the bomb factory in the Markets had not been mentioned at all, remembering the coincidental date of his arrest. He also took away the feeling that, because of his particular skills, he was regarded as someone special among the IRA prisoners.

'The door of Cell 34 is always open to you, son,' McCool had said at the end. 'If you want anything, come here. If you feel the bonk coming on . . .'

'The bonk?'

'Depression. A special kind. Prison depression.'

'Does everyone get it?'

'Most. If you do, drop in here before you see the medical officer. Like to know what's happening.'

'Thanks, Mr McCool.'

After that interview, Seamus's life in the Crumlin Gaol was as pleasant as any prisoner's could be. Most of his fellow inmates deferred to him, though he insisted on taking his share of the menial jobs like slopping-out and peeling potatoes in the kitchens. He found it a time of thinking and, perhaps for the first time, a period of reassessment. His mind constantly returned to the question of the inevitability or otherwise of his chosen path. With his inherited background, he knew it would have been nigh-impossible to escape from adolescence without a leaning towards republicanism. He'd been well indoctrinated by Grandma Hannah and his father, Joe.

Strangely, he thought, he always connected his father with a bed, probably because of all these weeks and months he'd spent over the years by his bedside, listening to him. That's where he'd learned it all, wasn't it? At his father's bedside. Not that he didn't also remember his father as a lean, energetic man always ready with a laugh or a hug. But those days had been before Seamus really understood what Joe Aherne's life was about, before the four men from the Special Branch had called at the farm at Galey Bridge and taken him away into internment for the second time.

The first time had been in 1941 when Joe Aherne had joined 2,000 other IRA men at the Curragh Camp. He'd become active in the movement in the border campaign of the 1930s before acquitting himself well as the quartermaster during the IRAs bombing campaign in London during the early part of the Second World War.

Like many others, Seamus's father emerged from internment, thinner and sadder. True, he had a better understanding of the Gaelic language and culture from the classes he'd attended in the detention camp as well as a more sophisticated knowledge of bomb-making gained in other instruction groups. But, he used to joke later, if it hadn't been for that spell behind barbed wire, Seamus might never have been. As soon as Joe was released, he proposed to his sweetheart of schooldays, Bernadette Burns, flushed with renewed longing for soft femininity. They'd married in the autumn of 1945 and Seamus had arrived in the summer of the next year. Joe concentrated on bringing the farm back to some sort of production after his time away, and on enjoying his new son, soon to be joined in successive years by two sisters, Shelagh and Mai.

He still attended IRA gatherings in North Kerry whenever work or domestic duties permitted and continued to take part in the Bodenstown march every June when Republicans gathered at the grave of Wolfe Tone, one of the leaders of the uprising in 1798 who committed suicide in prison after being sentenced to death.

This occasion in County Kildare, thirty or so miles from Dublin, was perhaps the most important in the IRA calendar, always ending as it did in speeches from the leadership which spelt out future policies.

Joe Aherne was among the IRA detachments at the Bodenstown Rally in 1949 to hear the IRA's new post-war policy put into public words for the first time by Cristoir O'Neill.

'The aim,' he announced, 'is simply to drive the invader from the soil of Ireland and to restore the sovereign independent Republic proclaimed in 1916. To that end, the policy is to prosecute a successful military campaign against the British forces of occupation in the Six Counties.'

The new policy attracted recruits in plenty. The problem was to arm them. To do this, the IRA staged half-a-dozen daring raids on British Army Barracks in England and Northern Ireland in the early 1950s. A campaign began late in 1956 which soured relations between London, Belfast and Dublin. And in its initial stages in 1957, it did help the return to power of de Valera.

Once more de Valera, IRA hero of 1916, turned the full force of law and order against his old organization by reintroducing internment.

Joe Aherne, who'd designed a number of bombs exploded during the border campaign, was picked up along with 60 others, during the first Special Branch sweep on July 8th, 1958.

Most were to stay for ten months behind the five barbed wire fences at the Curragh but Joe was released before Christmas. Although conditions within the detention camp had improved considerably since the wartime days – some IRA men likened it to a holiday camp – Joe contracted a chest virus which needed medical treatment of a degree only provided in hospital.

The illness left him virtually a cripple for the rest of his life. The slightest damp and chill brought on bronchitis which kept him in bed for weeks on end. Worse, his weakness effectively barred him from all but the lightest work and the family farm, handed down by the Wilmots, gradually declined without a grown man to shoulder its grinding and necessary routine.

Seamus, in his own captivity, remembered that period of his life as one of its blackest. Barely in his teens, he couldn't escape the deep misery pervading the farmhouse.

He would lie awake listening to his father's angry, self-reproachful words during parental arguments about lack of money and, most usually, Joe's drinking bouts in Listowel at his relatives' tavern in Church Street.

The seeming injustice of it all drew him closer to his father. When he assumed, in his mid-teens, the position of virtual head of the family, the person who could do the heavy work around the farm, he became increasingly protective towards the semi-invalid.

After all he reasoned, his father was not alone in suffering the after effects of the detention camps. One man had been so depressed following his release that he'd shot himself. Another was so psychologically diminished that he couldn't bear to cross the road any more.

Often, when Seamus was mucking out the cattle shed or feeding the pigs, he would glance round and find his father watching him, a dreamy, envious expression on his face.

Eventually, the teenager came to realize that his father was living out his dreams of a better life through him, that he saw in Seamus everything he couldn't and wouldn't be.

Sometimes he would sit up late with his father, talking, after the women of the household had gone to bed.

Joe Aherne would sneak a half-bottle of whiskey from his back pocket and pour his son a nip to be drunk with a deal of water.

'Just a drop to help you sleep, son,' he'd wink, lifting the bottle to his lips and taking a swig himself.

'Slainte,' they'd whisper to each other.

On such occasions, they'd discuss life in general and Seamus's future in particular. His mother and grandmother wanted him to become a farmer, to stay at Galey Bridge. His headmaster, Mr Macmahon, thought he'd enough technical aptitude for another occupation. And Seamus himself was adolescently unsure about almost everything. Finally, it was his father who forced the decision.

'You get away from here, son,' said Joe Aherne when they were talking one night. 'We've had enough farmers in this family already and look where it's taken us. The country's full of small farmers, so it is. What Ireland needs is more people with brains and modern skills, so she does.'

'But what about you?' Seamus protested. 'You can't be working the farm on your own.'

'And don't I know that? But we'll muddle along all right. Your sisters will be wed soon enough – pray to the Holy Mother! – and then they'll bring someone into the family to work the farm. Good catch they'll be. You just see, son. It'll be fine. Don't be paying any attention to the women. I'm not, although they're always sticking their little poison darts in me. Just don't pay any attention to them. You listen to your teachers and do what they say. They're knowing better than any of us.'

Reluctantly, after much argument and heartsearching, Seamus took his advice. When he was sixteen years old, in 1962, he sat an examination for the Post Office and was accepted as an apprentice technician. He had the choice of three training centres, Dublin, Cork or Sligo, and, without much hesitation, chose the Irish capital.

Rather to his own surprise, because of his rural background, he proved to be among the best of the apprentices at the technicians' training school sited within the walls of Dublin Castle.

For three years, he learned the intricacies of building and maintaining telephone switchboards, assembling delicate switching gear, indeed everything about a modern telephone and telecommunications system. When he wasn't in class or at the Post Office hostel, Seamus busied himself in discovering the delights of Dublin as well as those of the opposite sex.

His life, even after he became qualified and remained to work in Dublin, was almost totally self-centred, although he continued to be aware through newspapers and magazines of what was happening in the Republican movement.

The IRA, disappointed at the public's antipathy towards its six-year bombing campaign moved even more to the left in the middle 1960s. Many who believed that violence was the only way to win back Northern Ireland left the movement, frustrated and disillusioned, to be replaced by those of subtler political thinking. The Army Council went so far as to appoint a well-known Marxist as education officer despite rumblings from the Irish-Americans in Clann-na-Gael who distrusted any form of socialism.

But the old traditions managed to survive and in 1966, the fiftieth anniversary of the Easter Rising, several bombings showed that there were still IRA Volunteers who believed in action rather than words. The most spectacular explosion toppled the statue of Admiral Lord Nelson off its plinth in O'Connell Street.

Behind the scenes that year, however, the IRA leader, Cathal Goulding, secretly committed the organization to support an embryo civil rights movement in Northern Ireland during an informal meeting at the home of a Derry solicitor.

And the next year, in his Bodenstown oration, Goulding revealed publicly the IRA's shift in policy when he admitted that the movement's narrow aim of ending partition by violence had been a mistake. In future, he announced, the IRA would campaign to end social and economic ills, retaining at the same time the right to use force when necessary.

His policy succeeded beyond the IRA's wildest dreams. In little more than a year, the searchlight of world opinion swung on to Ireland following a march by civil rights supporters in Derry on October 5th, 1968, which was broken up by the Royal Ulster Constabulary with a series of baton charges.

The incident would normally have received scant attention outside Ireland but the dramatic television news film, satellited from country to country, roused indignation everywhere. The problems of Northern Ireland became the major topic of debate.

The IRA had stumbled at last upon a new cause. It didn't matter that few knew of its connection with the civil rights activists. Suddenly, Republicanism was almost respectable again cloaked, as it was, by the shining, radical zeal of university students like Bernadette Devlin, Kevin Boyle, Michael Farrell and the rest, all protesting about the undoubted discrimination of Protestants against Catholics in the fields of housing, employment and political representation.

Seamus Aherne, like many of his generation, was jolted from his complacency by those flickering television images of young people scattering this way and that from stick-wielding policemen, grotesque in their riot helmets. The marchers looked so innocent and defenceless; the police so menacing and cruel.

Like the IRA, Seamus had found a cause.

It appeared entirely natural to Seamus for him to want to join the IRA rather than the civil rights movement. What was good enough for his grandfather was surely good enough for him? After all, wasn't the IRA the shadowy influence behind the civil rights demonstrations?

He felt totally at home from the first. The words of his pledge of loyalty were almost second nature to him.

'I, Seamus Aherne, do solemnly declare that, to the best of my knowledge and ability, I will support and defend the Irish Republic against all enemies, foreign and domestic, and that I will bear true faith and allegiance to the same. I do further declare that I do not and shall not yield a voluntary support to any pretended Government, Authority, or Power within Ireland, hostile or inimical to that Republic. I take this obligation freely without any mental reservation or purpose or evasion – so help me God!'

He attended a couple of desultory weekend training camps in the Wicklow Mountains, and, more importantly, began taking instructions from Jack McKay, a veteran bomb-maker from the 1940s.

All the while events in Northern Ireland were moving as inexorably as an Alpine avalanche.

In the May of 1969, with anarchy almost total, the IRA leaders in Belfast hurried down to their senior colleagues in Dublin. Their worry was how to protect the families in the Catholic ghettoes. They couldn't hope to match the undoubted firepower of the Protestants who managed to gain firearms certificates from magistrates on the flimsiest pretexts or, sometimes, acquire weapons temporarily from their fellow loyalists in the 'B-Specials', the part-time constabulary.

The response in Dublin was disappointing. The IRA's Northern Command was told there were hardly any guns to be had, pretty well the whole armoury having been sold to the Welsh Nationalists. The commanders from Belfast and Derry left Dublin empty-handed and unhappy.

The summer heat increased. The police, weary and hard-pressed, continued to dodge and skip stones and guttering pipes but now the sounds of shots were heard in the Belfast night. Protestant gunmen began hunting their Catholic rivals just as they'd done in decades past.

The IRA men, who could only muster a dozen revolvers and rifles in the entire city, defended desperately.

Finally, on August 12th, 1969, the point of no return was reached when the Northern Ireland government rashly authorized a march by the Apprentice Boys of Derry, a virulently Loyalist organization.

The rhythmic thudding and wailing of the Protestant drums and fifes pierced through the thick walls and ramparts of old Derry, reaching, challenging the Catholics penned into their housing estates, the Bogside and the Creggan, outside those walls.

Trouble began with sharpened coins being flicked at the marchers in their solemn bowler hats and garish sashes. Then small stones beat down on to their heads followed by large pieces of brick and concrete. The police charged the mobs of Catholic youths, driving them with flailing batons out of the old city and back into their Bogside ghetto. For once, the Catholics stood their ground in the maze of narrow streets, ambushing the constables on street corners with hails of missiles. Policemen fell under the barrage and were dragged away by their colleagues, riot shields held above their heads.

'Fuck King Billy!' the Catholics jeered. 'Fuck the Prots!'

'Up the IRA!' they shouted. 'Up Free Derry!'

As the news of the action spread across the Province to Belfast, Protestant mobs stormed out of the bars in their own ghettoes off the Shankhill Road, inflamed with drink, infuriated at the Catholic's defiance in Derry. Petrol bombs set houses ablaze in the neighbouring Catholic areas.

Catholic families fled for their lives or huddled under their beds and sofas while revolver and rifle shots smashed through windows and doors and whined down deserted streets.

Armoured tenders of the RUC growled down the street, constables blasting away at the snipers with the 30-calibre Browning machine-guns mounted on the vehicles' turrets.

Rioting, murdering and burning continued into the next day and night with both factions hardly breaking for food or rest.

On August 14th British troops swept out of their bases in Derry and Belfast to take up positions between the factions. Catholics ran waving and cheering into the streets, clapping the soldiers as if they were a liberation force, their apparent saviours against the onslaught of the Protestant mobs.

Between them, politicians in London, Belfast and Dublin – by their vacillation, obstinacy and opportunism – had created a situation where the only winner could be the IRA.

Since the Dublin Government was unable to help the Catholics in Northern Ireland over whom it still claimed constitutional sovereignty, then the IRA would have to protect the minority.

The Dublin government, preferred not to notice as various individuals and organizations provided the IRA with thousands of pounds with which to purchase arms in Europe and the IRA in the South despatched to Ulster what men it could. Among them was Seamus Aherne, who arrived in Belfast by train on September 22nd, 1969.

By this time, the Army had constructed what it called a 'peace line' in the city from Cupar Street to Coates Street. This ugly strip of corrugated iron and barbed wire, searchlights and sentry posts, was supposed to be a barrier between the Catholic and Protestant ghettoes, between the Falls and the Shankhill. It satisfied no one except the Army and the world's media who took it as the final acknowledgement that Northern Ireland was a hopelessly divided community.

Seamus obtained lodgings with a family in Merrion Street, just off the Falls Road, not far from the Long Bar in Leeson Street which was used as an information centre by the Republicans.

Each night, he helped mount the patrols guarding the Catholic enclave from any sneak attacks by Protestant gunmen.

By early October, the IRA had obtained two dozen more weapons and Seamus was issued with a .38 calibre Smith and Wesson to carry during the long nights.

It was a time for the IRA, like the British Army, to build up its strength and review its tactics. Many politicians on mainland Britain, still refused to see the hand of the IRA behind the civil unrest and recommended, on October 10th, the disbandment of the Protestant part-time B-Special constabulary.

The Protestants were so infuriated that they poured on to the Shankhill, attacking police and troops, even trying to roll a lorry into them. Their gunmen flitted behind the mob, sniping at the security forces, eventually fatally wounding one policeman.

For the first time, on October 11th, the Army was given orders to return fire. It was a delightful irony for the IRA that the first two to be killed by the forces of the British Crown were Protestants whose entire *raison d'etre* was to remain subjects of that Crown.

The IRA had the chance to seize the initiative totally but, as so many times before, its leadership was split and in disarray.

Cathoal Goulding and his supporters on the Army Council and in its political counterpart, Sinn Fein, wanted the movement to recognize what it termed 'the partition parliaments' in Dublin, Stormont and Westminster and to resume using political methods to bring about change in Ireland. They also suggested the possibility of amalgamation with the Southern Irish Communist Party.

This idea of a switch away from direct action was anathema to many IRA men who believed in the movement's traditional aims and methods. They banded together to form the 'Provisional Army Council' which held fast to the old IRA philosophy that only physical force, not class politics, would bring about the re-unification of Ireland.

Sinn Fein and IRA groups, north and south of the Border, split. Most stayed with what was now called the 'Official IRA'. The others, usually more militant, pledged themselves to the new 'Provisional IRA'. Seamus Aherne, with his family's history, found it more natural to side with the Provisionals.

For a time there was vicious animosity between the two sides which manifested itself in a sharp, nasty shooting war in Belfast, centred mostly around Leeson Street, before a priest arranged a ceasefire.

After that, the Officials continued to man the barricades while the Provisionals adopted a more offensive policy.

Seamus was set to work designing crude nail grenades for throwing at Army foot patrols. These consisted of a dozen six-inch nails fixed through thick corrugated paper, a small amount of explosive and a detonator on a burning fuse taped to the contraption. They were simple but effective in confined spaces like narrow alleys. Later in 1970, he worked on bigger bombs which were laid at public utility targets – gas-holders, water pumping stations and electricity transformers.

His great problem was lack of sophisticated equipment. The supplies of stolen explosives were adequate enough but he had no access to modern timing devices. He fell back on methods used long ago in the Fenian bombing campaigns, tying wire round clockwinders or pushing tin-tacks through wooden clothes pegs.

It was simple but dangerous. Seamus knew that there could be no accuracy about the timing.

At least three of the bombs designed by Seamus went off prematurely, killing four IRA Volunteers, but that was a fact he didn't mention to his cellmates in the Crumlin Gaol whenever he discussed his work with the Third Belfast Battalion.

He did tell them briefly about the new device he'd designed which used a metal rod to arm it but they weren't particularly impressed.

To his chagrin, they regarded a bomb-designer as someone on the periphery of IRA active service. Their stories were all of gun battles with the security forces or the Protestants and, occasionally, of murdering informers.

'You southerners don't know what it's about,' his cellmate Andy McCann would jeer.

His face had the pinched expression of a hungry rat. When he was excited, his high nostrils twitched and quivered like a rodent on the scent of food.

'You came up here, Seamus, believing it was about politics and civil rights, my son,' he'd continue, unpleasantly patronizing. 'Just like all the big brains down in Dublin. About civil rights and politics, that's what you thought.'

Seamus would half-nod, perhaps agreeing slightly, certainly not wishing to give offence. Each of his cellmates carried the unmistakable stamp of men long accustomed to direct physical violence. Seamus knew that he was hardly capable of that himself except in the most extreme circumstances. It worried him and made him feel inferior in such a place as this prison where brutish violence simmered so near the surface.

'In Belfast, my son,' McCann would continue his lecture, 'it's always been about the survival of the hardest. Your own da helped bomb the customs posts on the Border for God knows how long and thought it was all about bringing workers' power to a united Ireland. Up here, down the Falls, it mattered as much as a limp prick waving in the west wind. Up here, we had to fight or die. It didn't matter or not whether you were IRA, though most of us were. Just being Catholic was enough, believe me, my son. In the Thirties, we tunnelled under the houses and garden walls just so the womenfolk could get from street to street, from house to shop without being plugged by a bullet. Why, the Prods would just as happily loose a few rounds down a Catholic loanin as they'd buy a packet of Woodbines at the corner shop. And all the while, you boys in the south were happy having your fist-fights with the Blueshirts or picketing some building site or other. Did you know, up here the Prods took out a whole family and shot the menfolk dead down to the wee-est boy? We went to a Proddie factory and hit all them. We even asked them to pick out the Mickies first so we knew who wasn't to be dealt with.

'Mind you, all that stuff ended back in the 30s when none of us had any work. Then the war came and we both got bombed, Proddie or not. But you still picked which bar you supped in 'cos we weren't that friendly. In those days, though, we both had to make the best of it so there wasn't too much energy left for fighting. And anyway, those bastard Bs were everywhere. They knew who was who and what was what and they carried the guns that mattered. Christ, in the old days, if they'd had a wee party at their barracks, they'd end up for an encore driving down the Falls and tossing a couple of grenades through a window just for the hell of it. No, Seamus, my son, up here it's always been a wee bit of a private war, whatever the hell you fellas in Dublin might've been doing. We've admired your political principles but they've meant fuck all to a fool as far as the Belfast boys are concerned.'

Always, it seemed to Seamus, his cellmates had forgotten the fear, the sheer terror, of their gunfights and bombings, only immortalizing the bravado involved. They had no regrets about what they'd done and, actually, were loath to place their legends within the framework of IRA history. It was somehow a private war.

To them, he realized, shooting and being shot at was regarded as almost an everyday part of life in the Belfast ghettoes. He wondered if their children would have a similar attitude when they grew up, would live out their fathers' legends once more.

He, at least, had experienced a fairly normal upbringing despite its deprivations and strong Republican overtones. He had not had to become involved. He'd had free choice, unlike many of the Belfast and Derry IRA, and the realization of that made him feel more able to withstand the ordeal of imprisonment. Seamus also knew that he could take a more detached view of what was going on outside the prison walls than men like Andy McCann, who cheered every shooting, riot or burning as a new victory.

Seamus wasn't so sure, couldn't share their enthusiasm for the news reaching the prisoners within Crumlin Gaol that late spring and early summer of 1971.

The first British soldier had been killed, and the tempo of violence had increased. Seamus's bomb laid by the BBC transmitter on Brougher Mountain had been partly instrumental in that. Instead of killing the Army patrol charged with guarding the transmitter, the bomb had devastated three BBC workmen.

That incident, along with others, had raised the political temperature. But Seamus's guess was that none of the mayhem and destruction had yet begun to affect those people in Westminster and Dublin with power to make decisions about the future of Northern Ireland.

He pondered the question during his first months in prison, walking round and round the exercise yard, watching the helicopters buzzing into Girdwood Barracks nearby, standing in this queue or that, or simply laying on his bunk gazing into the light or the darkness.

And when he'd plucked up the nerve, the confidence, to voice his ideas, he was surprised at how matter-of-factly they were received at first by Charley McCool in his Republican commander's cell on the landing below.

'So you think the tactics are wrong, do you, son?'

'Some, Mr McCool,' Seamus replied hesitantly.

'And why are you telling me now? Why now?'

'I've been thinking of it for some time.'

'Strange, son. Strange now, when I was about to send for you myself.'

'Me. Why?'

'Doesn't matter for the moment. You just be telling what's wrong for the present.'

Seamus took a deep breath, wondering how to begin.

'Well, Mr McCool, I think the emphasis on guns and rifles is wrong. We'll never beat the Brits in a shooting war. We'll never match them like that. They've the training and they outnumber us thousands to one.'

'Who says there's emphasis on the gun?'

'That's all the boys along the landings talk about. When they laid such-and-such an ambush on an Army patrol, fired a few rounds and skedaddled, or when they knee-capped some poor sod or gave someone a head shot.'

'Guns are necessary sometimes.'

'We'll never hurt the Brits enough with them and that's for sure!'

'Guns are necessary for discipline, for raising money, even for finding recruits. There's nothing like the sight of a pistol of his own to give a youngster a powerful urge to fire it at someone,' McCool said flatly, almost dismissively.

'I agree that. I agree all that,' Seamus replied, searching desperately for the right arguments. 'But the guns aren't hurting the right people where they should. Bombing can do so much more damage.'

McCool nodded.

'If we blow up a factory, we hurt all the people with money in that business. We cause unemployment and that costs the government a fortune here, let alone the social upset caused with people without jobs. If you ruin the industry, then you ruin the country. That's what we want, after all, isn't it?'

'Not totally,' McCool smiled. 'We want to hurt the Brits so much that they'll want to get out of this place. Not total ruin.'

'Bombs are still the answer, not bullets. Don't you see? A few pounds of mixture, a detonator for 5p, a bit of wire and a battery, and we've a bomb for about £1 which'll cause hundreds of thousands of pounds worth of damage. And also, there's nothing like a bomb to put the shit up the civilians.'

'So?' McCool shrugged. 'We're using bombs, aren't we? Christ, son, you should know that if anyone.'

Seamus shook his head: 'You can hardly call them bombs! We've not the proper equipment to build real good 'uns and if we had I'm doubting if I'm well enough trained, or the others are, to make proper use of it. My Post Office training just about got me to a simple circuit and a makeshift arming rod.'

'So what do you suggest then, son?'

'We find proper timers, maybe even remote control stuff, and we put bombs on top of the list of priorities. Not just fart about with them. And, last but not least, we also dig up a proper instructor from somewhere.'

McCool looked at him for a moment, narrowing his eyes, then grinned broadly.

'You're right, of course, son. Dead right.'

Seamus stared with amazement.

'Just testing the strength of your convictions, if I can use that word in here!'

McCool stood up and limped round to the bunk where Seamus was sitting. He leaned over him, speaking not much above a whisper: 'Now listen . . . the Army Council agree with what you've been saying. They've been thinking the same. That's why I was wanting to see you . . . to tell you they've decided you're to get out of here.'

'Escape?' Seamus whispered back.

'That's what I said. You'll be on a break-out in a fortnight or so.'

'Jesus, that's good, Mr McCool.'

'Maybe so. Maybe not. It won't be so good for you if you're caught. Nothing's guaranteed, mind.'

'I'll take the chance.'

'You will, son. You will that.'

He placed a hand on Seamus's shoulder in a paternal gesture.

'But one word of warning and I'll not be mentioning it again. There are still some not happy about the word on that bomb factory down the Markets a few months back. They're wondering awful hard where the Brits found the info on it and how they did when they did.'

'That! Christ, I was inside here at the time, wasn't I? Why put me with that fuck-up.'

'No idea, son. I'm just thinking. They're just guessing. Only you're knowing what happened if anything happened at all.' He paused. 'Let's leave it like that, shall we? Any three ways, the big men are thinking you're more useful out than in so you'll be going.'

'That's something, isn't it?'

Seamus hoped his voice sounded calm. Inwardly, he felt sick with shock at the mention of the bomb factory, at the clear warning.

McCool clapped him on the shoulder again.

'Don't worry, son,' he said. 'You'll be a big man one day. And that I'll guarantee or . . . '

He paused, his eyes harder, his mouth tighter, his grip harder, claw-like, on Seamus's shoulder.

' . . . or you'll die in the trying, so help me!'

## Chapter 5 June 1971

The young housewife, slim and dark in sweater and jeans, stood at her kitchen sink listening to the birds singing and chattering in the small copse just outside the window. Tree branches, high up, swayed and dipped as a red squirrel foraged relentlessly. A patch of sunshine crept into the far corner of the courtyard surrounding the small, isolated cottage, once the stables behind the Victorian mansion fifty yards nearer the road.

Sharon Ayres thought there was little that could add to her contentment. It was a lovely day; baby Oliver, nearly three months old, was fast asleep in his pram out in the courtyard; and her husband would be home that evening.

Later on, she decided, she would walk Oliver down to the pine woods and sand dunes at the end of the road. They'd feed the squirrels, plentiful and nearly tame along the Lancashire coast, north of the Mersey.

Perhaps, by accident or design, she'd stroll past that particular dune where she and Roy had made love under a full moon on their way home from a late party. Her grey-blue eyes always softened at the memory of that and the shared bath afterwards when they'd tried to rid each other of intimately embedded grains of sand.

She took a deep breath and smelled the fragrance of the pine in the air. Then she grimaced to herself, smiling, as her nostrils also took in the earthier smell of dirty nappies soaking in their bucket by the sink. Anyway, Sharon decided, she wouldn't let that unpleasant chore spoil her mood. She bent down to lift the bucket and heard the voice at the same time as she saw the trouser legs and shoes.

'Don't cry out, lady! Don't scream! Don't do nothing!'

Something cold and hard jabbed into her back, into the gap of bare flesh between sweater and jeans.

'Slowly now!' the voice commanded, gruff and low yet strangely lyrical.

Her body went rigid with shock. She couldn't move. Her hands in their rubber gloves clenched tight beneath the scum of the soaking bucket.

'Up, lady! Up!'

But she couldn't. Her eyes, wide with fear, were fixed on the scuffed suede of the man's shoes.

'Come on,' the voice urged.

A hand slid under her armpit, encompassed her full left breast and pulled upwards. She jerked straight and began turning her head. A snatch of breath rasped in her throat. Her heart fluttered out of rhythm. It had to be a nightmare.

There, close by her, in her kitchen, were two of Snow White's dwarfs.

'That's right, lady. Easy now,' said a red-nosed Grumpy, so close that she could feel his body-heat.

'Don't be feared now,' echoed a lop-eared Dopey over by the door.

And then Sharon realized that the men were wearing coloured Disney masks.

'Who? Who?' Her voice was high-pitched and quavering. She saw the revolvers in their gloved hands pointing unwaveringly, black and shiny, at her midriff. She turned fully round, gasping again, and pressed back against the sink. Instinctively, she clasped the dripping wet gloves across her breasts as if to shield them from attack. 'Wha . . .a . . . a?' She tried to ask something but her tongue had thickened and dried.

An image of Oliver, eyes tight shut, little fist near rosebud mouth, flashed into Sharon's mind. She lurched towards the door. 'My baby!' she cried.

Dopey didn't move from the doorway. His gun was steady.

Sharon stepped back, clutching herself in anguish.

'The wee 'un's sleeping sound,' said Grumpy, a surprisingly reassuring tone in his thick Liverpool-Irish accent. 'At least he was when we slipped in and found you day-dreaming out of the window. Just wait till you calm down, lady, and then you can bring him in.'

The young woman knew she had to regain copntrol of herself. She took a few deep breaths, eyes flicking from one dwarf mask to the other. She couldn't understand. Why hadn't she heard them? She must have been too lost in her happiness.

'Right,' said Grumpy, seeing her compose herself. 'Go and get the wee 'un and bring him in.'

'But he'll cry if I wake him,' Sharon protested automatically. 'He always does.'

Grumpy shook his head as if in amused despair. 'Then, sure we'll be after helping you carry the pram in, lady. Anything to oblige.'

He stood by the front door, just inside the glazed porch, while his companion lifted one end of the pram gently up the three steps, through the porch and into the large square hall which doubled as a dining room.

'Now sit yourself down, lady,' said Grumpy when the pram had been manoeuvred indoors and wheeled alongside the small, extendable dining table.

Sharon sat down warily, stiff-backed, by the table, one hand pressed into her lap, the other grasping the pram handle. She noticed the rubber gloves still on her hands and began irritably to peel them off.

'That's right, lady. Relax,' murmured Dopey, sitting down opposite her, gun casually in hand.

'Now we can talk,' said Grumpy. 'In about an hour you'll be having a phone call from your man . . .'

'But he's away on a job,' Sharon interrupted. 'He won't ring till he's back at the airport this evening.'

She heard her own voice as she spoke and realized that her natural Scouse accent, nasal and sing-song was reasserting itself over all her elocution lessons.

'Don't worry, lady. Don't be worrying at all,' said Grumpy, leaning over the table. 'Believe me, he'll be ringing all right.'

'And when he does,' Dopey continued, rubbing the barrel of his gun against his wobby rubber ear, 'All you have to do is tell him that you've two nice gentlemen here for coffee who'll go away when he does what he's told.'

'What's that supposed to be?' she demanded, beginning to feel anger rather than fear.

'Nothing to do with you, lady,' said Grumpy.

'All you have to worry about is staying calm and looking after your wee 'un. We're not criminals. We're not after harming you.'

'Then who are you then? What are you doing here?'

Sharon began to rise from her seat. Dopey motioned her down again with a wave of his gun. 'Can't you tell from our accents?' he asked teasingly.

'Oh, my God!' Sharon exclaimed, suddenly understanding.

'That's right, lady. We're an Active Service Unit of the Provisional IRA. We're soldiers, not criminals, though I suppose you mightn't guess that from our masks. But we wanted to wear something which wouldn't frighten the babbie too much. Don't want him crying a storm.'

'You see,' said Grumpy, 'All along we want to do what we have to do without hurting anyone. We're not enemies of yours.'

Sharon nodded, her mind whirling with questions. 'And if Roy doesn't do what . . . ?'

Grumpy shook his head. 'He will, lady. Never fear. He will.'

She sunk her head in her hands and started to sob.

'Put the kettle on,' Grumpy muttered to Dopey. 'Maybe a nice cuppa'll put her right.'

He touched Sharon gently, almost paternally, on the shoulder. She reminded him of his own teenage daughter.

At that moment, Captain Roy Ayres was 2,000 feet above the Irish Sea in his charter firm's Bell 206 Jet Ranger helicopter, GTAX-4. Beside him was the client who'd hired him from Speke Airport in Liverpool to the Isle of Man for the night and then on to Belfast.

The customer, a florid, balding Irishman nearing middle age, called Black, had explained that he wanted the helicopter for his urgent business trip in preference to a small aircraft because he wanted to test the machine's performance, possibly to buy one himself for his own company.

Ayres had guessed that his client was probably connected with the gaming industry. Certainly, he'd spent most of the previous evening at the tables in the small casino at the Palace Hotel in Douglas, the Manx capital. Not that it was any of the pilot's business how a client spent his money. He seemed a nice enough chap, though lacking the usual Irish loquacity, and had even given Ayres £10 pocket money to spend at the hotel.

The pilot noticed the grey, indistinct smudge on the horizon. He tapped his passenger on the forearm and pointed. 'The coast, Mr Black. Another ten minutes,' he said into his microphone.

The Irishman nodded, smiling and reached for the briefcase by his seat.

'Any further orders when we land?' asked Ayres.

Mr Black fumbled for his mike button before replying.

'I'll let you know when we're on the ground.'

'Enjoying it?'

'Fine. Just fine, Captain.'

Soon, the helicopter dropped lower on its approach to Belfast

Lough. Its shadow danced across the small silvery waves and the decks of two coasters making their sedate way back to England.

The city could be seen clearly now, sprawling round the horse-shoe shaped lough, the huge shipyard crane of Harland and Wolff's raised above the docks like a yellow offering to the sky.

'Merseyair helicopter Golf Tango Alpha X-ray,' Ayres called. 'Request clearance to land at Sydenham.'

'Roger, Alpha X-ray. Affirmative to land,' crackled back the reply. 'Nothing in the circuit. Wind north east, twelve knots. Visibility good.'

The helicopter whirred over the factories on the reclaimed land on the east side of the lough, across the perimeter fence of Belfast Harbour Airport and descended gently on to the grass about fifty yards from the main buildings. The rotor blades driven by their 317 hp Allison engine turned ever more slowly before drooping to a halt.

'Right, Mr Black, what now?' the young pilot asked, removing his headset and turning cheerfully to his passenger. 'Shall I . . . ?'

'I'm sorry about this.'

'What? . . . Oh, Christ alive!'

The Irishman held a small revolver in his lap pointing directly at the pilot's chest. It was shielded from all but Ayres by the briefcase.

'Don't do anything silly, Captain. Please. For your own sake – and your family's.'

Ayres struck a clenched fist against his thigh. 'You're hijacking me?' His voice was flat and angry.

'Something like that. We want you to perform a wee service for us.'

'I don't suppose I have to ask who you are?'

'Probably not.'

'You realize you'll never get away with it.'

Ayres sensed he was speaking like a character in a second-rate film. He looked into Mr Black's eyes, calm and alert, and knew that, indeed, he could get away with it. He shrugged despondently.

'Well, what now?'

'A phone call, Captain. Just a phone call. We want to be sure you'll cooperate fully. There's to be no mistakes, no sudden errors of judgement.'

'A phone call?'

'To your home, Captain.'

'Sharon!'

'We want you to realize it's not only your future at stake if you decide to play hero.'

546

'Bastards!' Ayres exclaimed venomously.

Mr Black was unconcerned. His voice continued flat and hard, no longer jaunty and appealing.

'Possibly. But let's just get on with it, shall we? This gun'll be on you all the way so let's not be stupid.'

To the men in the control tower, the sight was perfectly normal, simply a businessman and his pilot walking towards the main airport building.

When they neared the building, past three airport workers pushing a trolley, Ayres readied himself to attack. It was an animal feeling. His deep anger allowed no fear for himself or anyone else. He stiffened his muscles, about to swing round suddenly. But it was as if the gunman could read his thoughts.

'Don't, for Sharon's sake,' he murmured quietly. 'And the babbie's.'

Ayres' shoulders slumped fractionally, the threat registering. He shook his head slightly and pushed through the building's glass doors towards the grey public phonebox set on the wall a few yards inside.

Mr Black stood so close to him while he dialled the nine digit number that he could feel the gun pressing against his chest. At the other end of the line, the phone rang only three times before Sharon, his lovely Sharon, answered.

'Darling,' he cried urgently before she could finish giving the phone number.

'Roy!'

'It's all right, darling! It's all right!'

'What's happening, Roy?' she almost shrieked.

He could sense that she was near to hysteria.

'I don't know, darling, but are you and Oliver all right?'

'There're two men . . .'

'I know. But are you all right?'

He'd wanted to be calm and reassuring but his frantic worry was clear in his voice.

'Yes. They haven't . . . .'

'Are you sure?'

'It's horrible. They've guns and mas . . .'

Mr Black leaned across and pressed down the phone rest, cutting off the call.

'That's enough, Captain,' he said harshly. 'We've work to do.'

Ayres replaced the phone receiver slowly. He felt drained and weak. 'If anything . . . if you hurt them . . . I'll . . . I'll . . .'

'Nothing will,' the Irishman interrupted. 'Now let's get on. The quicker we're done, the sooner you'll see them again. Once you've done what we want, they'll be left alone. You've my word on that.'

'And what's that worth?' Ayres asked bitterly.

The gunman looked stonily at him for a moment, then jabbed him in the ribs with his briefcase and nodded towards the door. They walked quickly back to the helicopter and clambered into the cockpit.

'You know we can't take off without clearance and without filing a flight plan,' Ayres remarked, settling back into his seat. 'So it's no use going on.'

'Uh-huh,' Mr Black replied, unconcerned, pulling three large coloured photographs from the briefcase with his left hand. The other held the gun, pointing without the slightest quiver.

He handed the photos to Ayres who immediately realized they were aerial survey views of Belfast.

'See where we are?'

Ayres nodded. He could easily identify the airfield jutting out into the middle of the harbour.

'Right. See the big crane over there?'

'You can't miss it,' said Ayres.

'Well, you fly directly over that, come down to 300 feet and head on the same bearing over the city until you see the first large piece of greenery. It's there on the photo. Girdwood Park. I'll tell you where to put down.'

'Is that all?'

The sarcasm was ignored.

'It'll take no more than three minutes. Probably less.'

'But I told you, we've no clearance.'

Mr Black's voice hardened.

'Fuck clearance! If they query, just stall. Got it?'

'Okay,' the pilot sighed. 'Shall I start up now?'

The gunman looked at his watch. It was ten minutes to eleven o'clock. He shook his head.

'Dead on five minutes to. That's when we go. Start the rotors a minute before.'

The two sat in silence, occasionally glancing at their watches. Roy Ayres thought of his wife and child and if he'd lose his job after doing what 'they' wanted. He had no doubt who 'they' were. Mr Black waited impassively, hoping that the others would carry out their orders as well as he'd done. His main worry was the £55 he'd lost in the casino the night before. He would have to refund that if he wasn't to risk a bullet through the calf muscles of one leg, perhaps both.

Not three miles away, Seamus Aherne trudged round the exercise yard of Crumlin Gaol, hearing the monotonous tread of dozens of boots upon paving stone, the sound of men walking for the sake of walking with little enjoyment and no expectation of getting anywhere. It was a sound even more redolent of prison life than keys turning in locks.

He counted the prison officers on duty: six of them, with three more holding dogs in the far corner where workmen were repointing the main wall, not twenty yards from the nearest cell block.

Every time Seamus looked at that wall, he thought it had grown taller and thicker. He wondered idly if the remote-controlled television cameras ever relayed close up pictures of the exercising prisoners and, if they did, how he would appear on the screen. He brushed a hand through his black, greasy hair.

Suddenly, from a cell above, he heard the distinct sound of metal striking metal once. It was the signal to begin counting.

'1 . . . 2 . . . 3 . . . 4 . . . ' he muttered under his breath, glancing sideways at the two men walking with him, Frankie O'Riordan and Mickey Quinn, both veterans of gun-battles along the 'peace line'. They were counting too, just as they'd practised together after Charley McCool had arranged for them to share a cell.

It took exactly a minute to circle the yard at the accepted pace, to be in the right position at the right time. And timing, as McCool said, was all.

' . . . 49 . . . 50 . . . 51 . . . ' they muttered to themselves.

Seamus noticed the prisoners on the opposite side of the yard starting to bunch together.

' . . . 54 . . . 55 . . . 56 . . . '

They were nearly in position.

' . . . 57 . . . 58 . . . 59 . . . '

'You Provo bastards!'

The cries rang out around the yard, swiftly followed by the thuds of fists upon flesh.

Seamus looked quickly across. At least half-a-dozen men had begun fighting with more joining in every second. Already two prison officers had been drawn into the brawl while others were hurrying towards the disturbance.

'Kerrump!! . . . Kerrump!!'

Two loud explosions echoed round the yard as 'shipyard

spaghetti' grenades containing nuts and bolts, thrown from a passing car, detonated against the Army sentry-post at the Crumlin Road entrance.

These were followed by a fusillade of shots from a machine-gun while the car accelerated away into the busy morning traffic. The bullets cracked and whined against the outer walls.

Inside the yard, all was panic and pain. The warders fought baton-to-fist with the prisoners, fearing a concerted, full-scale attack on the prison. The alarm siren wailing from high on the cell-block wall added to their desperation.

Seamus and his two companions waited a moment, backs pressed against the yard's inner wall, until the warders with dogs had charged past them towards the brawling scrum. Then they dashed towards the outer wall.

'Quick!' called O'Riordan reaching the wall first.

Seamus already had the two half-sticks of explosive in his hand.

He thrust them into the gaps left between the bricks by the workmen, and immediately lit the short, dangling safety fuses.

The three flung themselves to the ground, covering their heads.

Automatically, Seamus counted away the seconds.

'1 . . . 2 . . . 3 . . . 4 . . . 5 . . . '

Kerrump!!

The explosions came together, lifting the three men off the ground, partially deafening them, momentarily winding them.

They forced themselves to their knees, coughing and spluttering in the cloud of dust and powdered cement. Around them they could hear broken bricks clattering on to the yard's paving stones.

Seamus pushed himself blindly into the cloud, arms outstretched. His knees crashed agonisingly into a pile of rubble but, through the clearing dust, he could see that the explosions had done their work. Before him, at thigh level, was a jagged hole about four feet high and three feet wide. He launched himself through it, rather like a diver entering a swimming pool, and tumbled on to the grass bank on the other side, the side abutting the open spaces of Girdwood Park.

For a moment, he lay there, gazing up at the cloudless blue sky. It had never looked so blue from inside the prison. He felt totally calm, almost disorientated, until first Quinn and then O'Riordan dived through the hole and landed on top of his legs.

The prison siren continued to wail and the sounds of the fighting could still be heard even from outside the wall. Then, overpowering every noise, came the battering cacophony of a helicopter flying low.

Seamus looked over towards the nearest clearing, now used as a sports pitch by the troops who'd taken over most of the park, and saw the red-and-white helicopter hovering with its landing skids about two feet off the grass.

'Come on, for Christ's sake or we're all done for,' panted Quinn.

They pushed themselves to their feet and began running. Seamus felt weary. Perhaps, he thought, it was the mental exhaustion of the previous twenty-four hours when he'd been unable to rest properly, always rehearsing the routine with the explosives, smuggled into the prison in plastic bags hidden in women's vaginas. He heard shouting behind him.

Before he could look back, O'Riordan shouted a warning: 'They've loosed the fucking dogs!'

The thought of the German Shepherd dogs bounding over the grass, fangs bared, lent them speed. No one dared turn his head.

To his left, about a hundred yards away, Seamus saw a group of soldiers, apparently unarmed, break into a trot towards them. Ahead, closer with every stride, was the helicopter. The pilot was rigidly straight in his seat, concentrating on the controls. A man hung out of the door nearest to them, gun pointing, mouthing something that was lost in the roar of the machine's engine.

As they ran, the three prisoners ripped off their denim jackets, trusting in Charlie McCool's advice that the dogs would break their progress to sniff and harry the cloth.

Quinn reached the helicopter a yard ahead of the other two. He tumbled through the doorway and on to the wide bench-seat at the back. Seamus and O'Riordan collided in their haste to get through the narrow door. O'Riordan's greater bulk pushed Seamus aside. He slipped on the turf and fell full length. The helicopter began rising while Seamus scrabbled frantically to his knees. He gazed round wildly, thinking he was about to be abandoned.

The soldiers came nearer. One of them was obviously carrying a weapon. Seamus saw him drop to one knee and aim a rifle. The prison officers were still a good way off trying to disentangle their dogs, grouped and snarling and tearing around the discarded jackets.

He heard a shot ring out close to, clear above the helicopter's thumping, beating blades. He scrambled upright and felt a hand reach out for a grip on him, then another. Somehow, slipping and twisting, he hauled himself up. The helicopter banked sharply to the right and lifted. Somewhere on the fuselage, a bullet pinged off metal. Hands gripped Seamus under the shoulders and pulled him finally, safely, into the cabin. The door slid shut. He grinned up into the sweating and triumphant faces of Quinn and O'Riordan.

The middle-aged man beside the pilot was shouting above the noise. At first, Seamus couldn't hear him. He shook his head. The man leaned further towards him between the front and rear seats.

'For Jesus' sake,' he roared. 'Where were you? Did you think this was a fucking scheduled flight?'

Seamus shook his head again, too breathless to answer. The man broke into a wide grin. O'Riordan gripped Seamus round the waist and lifted him on to the seat. At last he was able to see out of the windows.

The helicopter was flying at about 200 feet straight along Crumlin Road towards the hills surrounding the city. It was so low that Seamus could clearly see the people's faces as they peered up at the machine. The houses and shops below resembled large models, complete in every detail even to the washing on lines in gardens and courtyaards.

In the pilot's seat, Roy Ayres took a peek at the aerial survey photo as his hijacker traced the route with his finger. Within a minute, they were away from the city streets and flying over the heather and gorse of the hill slopes and the scattered homes on the outskirts near Ligoneil.

A message crackled indistinctly on the radio. Mr Black leaned forward and flicked up a switch on the control panel, turning off the transmission.

The pilot banked away from the road below him, flicked across a spinning mill and descended even lower. Seamus thought at first that the helicopter was preparing to land in the open but then he saw, over a gentle rise, a large quarry deserted except for two cars.

Mr Black jabbed his thumb downwards. The helicopter swung to the left and began its descent, sinking to the ground only ten yards from the waiting cars, its rotors swirling up a cloud of earth and small pieces of gravel.

No one waited for the blades to stop. They tumbled gleefully out, shaking hands in self-congratulation at the success of their escape so far.

Two men jumped out of the cars, shielding their faces from the stinging gravel, and waved the prisoners over.

'You, in here!' one ordered Seamus, pushing him into the rear seat of a large lrey Volvo. 'And keep down!'

Quinn and O'Riordan jumped into the other car, a red Austin Maxi.

Seamus looked back at the helicopter, blades now stopped. Mr

Black was handcuffing the pilot to one of the struts of the skid undercarriage.

The middle-aged man patted Roy Ayres consolingly on the shoulder before trotting over to Seamus's car and jumping in the front seat. 'Let's go,' he called.

In convoy, the cars screeched away down a hard-rutted track.

'Listen, Aherne,' Mr Black called over his shoulder. 'We're dropping you off in a minute. You'll hide up for the rest of the day and then be picked up again tonight. You'll find new clothes and the necessary instructions where we're leaving you. Okay?'

'Fine,' Seamus replied. 'I'll be on my own?'

'Uh-huh. The other two are decoys to lead the bloodhounds off the scent.'

'Do they know that?'

Mr Black shrugged. 'They've a chance,' he said blandly.

When they reached the end of the track, the vehicle carrying Quinn and O'Riordan turned to the left, tyres screaming, while Seamus's car went to the right.

The Volvo sped along the narrow country road, green hedges blurred on either side, for little more than half-a-mile before it spun into a small car-park behind a squarish, grey-stone building. Seamus lifted his head above the back window. The car skidded to a halt close to the building.

'In there!' shouted the driver, pointing at the nearest door. 'Lock it behind you. Your stuff's in the next room through.'

Seamus was out of the car and into the building in a second. 'Thanks,' he called, closing the door, reaching for the key, but the Volvo was already in motion. All he could see was Mr Black with his hand half-raised as if saluting or waving farewell.

He locked the door carefully. He was standing in a narrow, dark passageway. He walked quietly along it to a room leading off to the right, a largish kitchen. By the sink, he saw a suitcase and a large envelope weighed down on the tiled floor by a bottle of milk and a quarter-bottle of Paddy whiskey. Seamus smiled, silently thanking someone's thoughtfulness. He picked up the whiskey and began unscrewing the top. Suddenly he stopped and listened. The silence was slightly disconcerting. It was the first time he'd heard silence since the Army had picked him up five months before.

'Slainte,' he murmured, taking a swig of the whiskey. The spirit made him gag and splutter. 'Jesus, it's been too long,' he reflected.

On the wall, by a mirror, was a tiny notice. He took another mouthful, more carefully this time, while he read the instructions about how to switch off the livhhs in the building. He grinned when he saw the heading 'Masonic Hall'.

Seamus sat down on the floor, resting against a set of drawers, and tore open the envelope. Inside were two closely-typed sheets of paper and a leather wallet.

He checked the contents of the wallet first. Apart from a few receipts from restaurants in Belfast, there were currency notes totalling £64, rail and sea tickets, a driving licence and a rectangular piece of plastic about two inches square.

'So that's why,' he muttered, remembering how Charley McCool had somehow acquired a Polaroid camera, presumably from a friendly prison officer, to take two photographs of him. His hair had been smarmed with grease and parted down mhe middle; he'd worn thick-framed spectacles borrowed from another prisoner and he'd been told to puff out his cheeks. Peering into his shaving mirror, he'd been surprised at how much these touches of disguise had altered his appearance.

Now, seeing the finished product in the plastic identity card, he guessed that his old friends in Listowel, perhaps even his family, would have great difficulty in recognizing him from the photograph.

The typwritten instructions confirmed that he was to disguise himself once more, using the materials and clothes in the suitcase, and provided details of his new temporary identity.

He was a textile engineer called Alan Anderson, Courtaulds employee, on his way to its Lancashire mills for a conference. The plastic card was a Courtaulds identity pass for its factories in Northern Ireland. Clearly, Seamus decided, sometne must have had friends within that organization who'd laminated his photograph into a genuine pass.

Next, he opened the suitcase and lifted out a smart, lightly checked grey suit on its hanger. He hooked this behind the door to allow any creases to drop out. There was a complete change of clothing, shoes, a wash bag with toilet gear, a wristwatch, properly set and wound, even a pack of cigarettes and a well-used lighter.

Finally, there was a packet of cheese sandwiches, the bread cut thick, and a documents file. He leafed through this and saw a number of letters, memoranda and instructions booklets, each bearing the distinctive Courtaulds' heading, many with his alias typed upon them.

Seamus settled down to eat the sandwiches and drink the milk, studying at the same time the instructions for the next stage of the escape.

The plan was as daring and simple as the actual break-out from Crumlin Gaol. On first read, he thought it almost too simple, perhaps suicidal, but the longer he read, the more he could perceive its chances of success.

Although he felt mentally and physically exhausted, Seamus didn't dare sleep during the next six hours or so spent in that kitchen. He was too afraid of missing the pick-up. Instead, he busied himself by washing the dust from the explosion out of his hair, shaving carefully, changing his hairstyle and checking the spectacles, memorizing his instructions and studying the Courtaulds documents.

The last thirty minutes dragged interminably. He kept examining the watch on his wrist but its hands seemed hardly to move.

He dressed in his new clothes and walked up and down, becoming used to the feel of them. Then he took the suit off again for fear of it being stained or creased. He packed the suitcase with his prison uniform and any rubbish, everything except the documents file and the near-emptied bottle of whiskey. He wanted a last drink before setting out.

But still there was time to spare, time to worry.

By now, he supposed, the news of his escape must have reached his family. Probably the Garda had already been round to check that the helicopter hadn't spirited him by some miracle to Galey Bridge.

Seamus wondered how they'd all taken the news. His father would have been excitedly proud, he was sure, and perhaps would have made it an excuse for a trip round the bars in Listowel. He could see his mother and Grandma Hannah being inwardly pleased as well, yet showing a stern face to any outsider. It was a strange feeling, wishing to know what others were saying but, at the same time, not wanting to know in case their opinions were hurtful.

Seamus read the instructions for the last time before burning them in the sink and flushing away the ashes. He wiped every surface clear of possible fingerprints, finished the whiskey, packed the suitcase and finally put on the suit once more.

He took a last look around the kitchen to make certain that there were no signs of his stay. Satisfied, he walked to the back door with the suitcase in his hand and the file tucked under his arm.

At exactly six o'clock, he turned the key in the lock and stepped outside just as a cream Belfast taxi pulled up. Seamus locked the door behind him before climbing into the back seat. The young man sitting beside the driver smiled nervously.

'Any bother?' he asked, a deferential tone in his voice.

'Quiet as a Croke Park crowd when Dublin lose,' said Seamus lightly, handing him the key to the hall and the suitcase. Another suitcase lay on the seat beside him. He noticed it was monogrammed 'A.A.'

'Away we are then,' said the driver, a grey-haired man with the inevitable paunch of a veteran cabbie.

The taxi moved out of the car park and turned left into the main road a hundred yards away. To Seamus's surprise, it braked only another hundred yards on outside the Glen Inn, a bar nestling just off the road. The young man in the front seat jumped out, waved once to Seamus and walked into the bar carrying the suitcase with its wealth of incriminating evidence. The taxi set off again.

Seamus wondered if the driver knew that his passenger was an escaped IRA man and whether he should talk with him. He decided silence was wiser. He rubbed the tiredness out of his face and turned casually to gaze out of the car window.

'Jesus!' he exclaimed, realizing for the first time that the taxi was heading directly down Crumlin Road towards the centre of Belfast. 'Hey!'

The driver glanced back at him through the rear-view mirror. 'No worry at all, sir,' he said over his shoulder. 'I always take the quickest route.'

'But . . .' Seamus began to protest when the all-too-familiar shape of Crumlin Gaol loomed up on the left.

'Just settle back nicely and enjoy the ride,' the driver interrupted, seemingly unconcerned.

Seamus risked only a quick peek as the taxi passed the prison. Workmen and soldiers were busy stringing more barbed wire across the entrance.

'Wee bit of trouble there this morning with this escape,' the driver announced cheerfully. 'And a fair palaver when two of them were captured at Coleraine.'

'Was there?' Seamus replied as innocently as possible, grinning a sickly smile into the driver's mirror.

'So I hear, sir.'

'Ah, well,' Seamus sighed, re-opening the documents file on his lap, thinking for a moment of Quinn and O'Riordan back in the hands of the security forces.

In ten minutes, the taxi had threaded through the tail of Belfast's rush hour traffic and arrived outside the ferry terminal at Donegall Quay in the docks.

'Got your tickets, sir?' the driver asked.

Seamus pulled out the wallet from his inside jacket pocket.

'Aye, and the cabin reservations.'

'Well, have a safe crossing and take it easy now.'

'Thanks.'

Seamus got out of the car clutching the suitcase and the file stamped 'Courtaulds' across its cover. A thought came to him. He leaned into the driver's window.

'How much do I owe?' he asked.

The driver laughed shortly. 'It's on the company's account, sir, the old company. And sure, didn't you know that?'

'Of course. I thought it might have been.'

Seamus slapped the taxi's bonnet lightly before walking into the terminal building. His nerves tightened when he saw an Army foot patrol by the ticket barrier and another patrol, with a group of policemen carrying sub-machine guns, by the queue of passengers waiting to have their baggage searched before boarding the ship.

He started to veer away from the queue towards the men's toilets, then sensed that even that might be suspicious behaviour. Instead, he quietly joined the line of passengers, each shuffling forward with their suitcases and shopping bags, either lifting them or pushing them with their feet.

'Reserved cabin, is it, sir?' the man at the barrier asked automatically, already noting the answer in his hand.

Seamus nodded.

The man clipped together his ferry ticket and the cabin reservation. 'There's a baggage check tonight, sir, if you don't mind. Just wait by the tables. It won't take too long, Mr . . . ' He peered at the tickets again. 'Mr Anderson.'

Seamus nodded again. His instructions, now memorized, had emphasized that he should speak as little as possible in case anyone recognized his Kerry accent.

He touched his spectacles, pushing them further up the bridge of his nose and joined the second queue beyond the barrier. His finger began to reach for the spectacles again. He pulled it away realizing the gesture might draw attention to himself.

'Is the suitcase locked, sir?' the constable asked at the examination table.

Seamus hesitated, unsure. He bent forward and pressed the catches. They sprang open.

The constable opened the lid.

Seamus tried to look anywhere except into the suitcase or at the

557

young Army corporal standing behind the constable, rifle nestling in the crook of his arm.

He realized he was under the closest scrutiny. He adjusted the file under his arm, hoping someone noticed the lettering on the front.

'That's all right, sir,' the constable remarked, closing the suitcase lid.

'Any identification with you, sir?' he added.

Seamus coughed chestily.

'Driving licence, maybe, sir?'

Seamus fumbled for the wallet. In his nervousness, he spilled some of the contents on the floor.

The corporal moved forward. 'Excuse me, sir.' He picked up the driving licence and the Courtaulds identity pass. He looked at them both, examined Seamus and then handed them back to the policeman who nodded.

'Mr Anderson?'

'Uh-huh.' Seamus, nodded, coughed.

The policeman looked closely at the two documents. 'From Ligoneil?'

'Wolfhill Gardens,' Seamus answered without pausing, remembering his instructions, blessing his own good memory.

'Thank you, sir,' said the policeman, apparently satisfied, snapping shut the suitcase. 'Have a good journey, Mr Anderson.'

Seamus nodded, coughing again.

He lifted the suitcase off the table and began walking towards the gangway leading to the ferry. A sense of release was already flooding through him.

'Mr Anderson . . . ?'

The voice came from behind him. He stopped. His knees bent, losing strength.

'Mr Anderson!' the voice called again, closer.

He turned slowly, reluctantly. After all there was nowhere to run except up the gangplank.

'Yes?'

Behind him, beaming, the Army corporal held out the Courtaulds pass and the driving licence. 'You forgot these, sir,' he said pleasantly.

Seamus tucked them away in his breast pocket.

'Wouldn't do to lose those, sir,' the corporal went on, the muzzle of his rifle swinging near Seamus's midriff. 'Not your licence and your identity.'

'Right,' Seamus murmured.

He walked up the gangway on to the ferry and handed his reservation tickets to the steward. PFive minutes later he was safely into cabin 3A.

'Fucking hell,' he swore, tossing the suitcase on the bunk. The locks snapped open on impact. There, lying on top of a pair of striped pyjamas, were a tube of Alka-Seltzer tablets and a half-emptied bottle of Bushmills whiskey, aids common to many travellers across the Irish sea.

Seamus sniffed, feeling rather humble. At the Masonic Hall at Ligoneil, he'd been grateful, but now, after the penultimate stage of his escape, he truly realized how much trouble and thought had been invested in the entire operation.

He stayed in his cabin, its door locked, sipping whiskey, until the thumping and vibration told him that the ferry had slipped its moorings and was heading towards the open sea. Then he left the cabin and walked along the narrow passageway to the open deck.

The last rays of the setting sun were orange and deep red on the slate roofs of the older houses near the docks and glinting piercingly off the glass windows of the larger office blocks rising behind.

From the rail of the ferry, Seamus thought Belfast looked benign and comfortable in its huddling, Victorian sprawl. Certainly, from this perspective, the city gave no hint of the embracing terror and hatred within its deepest core.

'See youse,' he muttered thickly, knowing he was a bit drunk and very tired, turning away from the rail and making for his bunk and hoped-for sleep.

As the ferry sailed into the enveloping darkness of the Irish Sea, en route for Liverpool, Roy and Sharon Ayres shut the door of their small cottage on the last of the newspapermen who'd been waiting, clamouring, for the story of their experiences.

While they'd given their interviews and posed for photographs, eyes blinking into the electronic flashes, their sense of unreality about the day's happenings had heightened.

Roy remembered his feeling of foolishness when the firemen had come to saw through the handcuffs linking him to the helicopter. He'd thought himself so stupid, sprawled there in the gravel, surrounded by men in varying uniforms, all asking him questions.

Sharon had felt equally lacking when the police had come to release her and baby Oliver from the bathroom where they'd been locked in an hour previously by the men in the Disney masks. The police, of course, had been very kind and sympathetic but Sharon had sensed their mutual embarrassment that the forces of law and order had known nothing of her plight until the anonymous phone call, presumably from Grumpy and Dopey.

The young couple, shaking their heads in unison, walked into the kitchen to prepare their supper.

'I was just doing the nappies,' Sharon began again, disbelief still clear in her voice.

'And I was just flying a client,' her husband went on.

Suddenly, the horror returned to them, their hours of fear alone overwhelming them once more.

They clung together by the kitchen sink, holding each other tightly and rocking slightly.

'Dear God!' Roy breathed. 'Oh, dear God, what a day!'

## Chapter 6

Like New York or Boston, Seamus thought, Liverpool was a place familiar to any Irishman whether or not he'd ever seen it before. Its history was part of Irish history, its skyline marking the traditional gateway for emigrants seeking work, any work, in the richer industries of Britain.

He began whistling tunelessly to himself, swinging his suitcase, as he stepped onto the covered gangway with the other passengers after the ferry had docked under the splendour of the Royal Liver building with its two stone birds perched atop, sprigs in their thin beaks.

And then he saw the two uniformed policemen waiting at the bottom accompanied by three men in rumpled suits, clearly detectives.

He cursed himself for having become too casual: he'd forgotten his instructions to appear inconspicuous and remain on his guard at all times. But it was too late to do anything other than brazen it out, to continue playing someone who was literally on top of the morning.

He imagined eyes boring into him, following his every step. He cursed himself again for having packed the Courtaulds documents file in his suitcase. He puffed out his cheeks, still whistling, feeling naked and helpless inside.

The file of passengers stopped suddenly. There was a murmur of excited voices. Seamus lifted himself on to his toes and peered over the shoulder of the man in front. A small, old man, wearing a light fawn raincoat was being held around the forearm by one of the policemen while a detective read from a piece of paper. Another detective joined the group and, together, they hurried the man off, one arm held high behind his back.

Passengers started moving slowly along the gangway again towards the remaining constable and detective.

Seamus elbowed himself alongside the man in front, hoping to give the impression that they were travelling companions. 'What was all that about, for God's sake?' he asked loudly, flattening and sharpening his natural accent, ignoring the policemen.

'And how the divil would I be knowing?' the man alongside him replied. 'Ask your friend in blue here,' he added, nudging his suitcase in the direction of the constable.

'Nothing to concern you, gentlemen,' the constable interrupted, his eyes blank with boredom and tiredness. 'Just move along and don't hold the other passengers up.'

The two men walked on to the deck, across a narrow bridge and into the bustle of Liverpool's commuters from the Wirral, all hurrying for buses after disembarking from the cross-river ferries.

'Going far?' Seamus remarked casually.

'The station. Lime Street.'

'So am I. Share a taxi?'

The other man, older than Seamus by at least ten years, shrugged, swaying slightly. 'Why not?' There was little enthusiasm in his voice.

When he reached the station, Seamus walked over to the book-stall next to the buffet, looking for something to read during the journey. The headlines on the newspapers leapt out at him, biting into his complacency. His eyes darted round, alarmed behind the plain-glass spectacles.

Was that policeman over there looking suspiciously at him? Were they playing cat-and-mouse with him, just waiting for the right moment to pounce?'

'One of each,' he mumbled to the girl by the papers, proffering a £1 note.'

'Every one?' she queried, surprised.

Seamus nodded, stuffed the bundle of newspapers under his arm and moved off quickly towards the train without waiting for his change.

He picked a corner seat and huddled into it, not daring to gaze out of the window nearest the platform where the station porters were busy trying to appear busy.

It wasn't until the train pulled slowly out of the station and into the Edge Hill tunnel that he begun to relax once more. He spread out the newspapers one by one.

'Security tightens after IRA escape,' thundered *The Times*.

'Prison probe after IRA flight to freedom – MPs furious,' announced the *Daily Telegraph*.

'Ordeal of IRA hijacked pilot,' cried the *Daily Mail*.

'He slept through IRA hijack terror,' screamed the *Daily Mirror*, featuring a large picture of a small baby in a pretty young woman's arms.

'My ordeal – by wife in IRA terror,' declared The *Sun*, showing a similar picture.

Seamus shook his head in disgust. Only three of the papers concentrated upon the actual escape and the subsequent row in the House of Commons, the others being more interested in the human-interest story of Sharon Ayres and her baby.

If that was how the English press covered events in Northern Ireland it was no woonder the English had little understanding of the situation. In some ways it was a blessing. There was hardly a mention of his police description and the few photographs of him were smudgy and virtually unrecognizable. He was flattered, however, to be called 'No 1 IRA bomber', 'top of the wanted list', and 'IRA's leading bomb-maker'. Not strictly accurate of course, but it was enjoyable to be a personality again rather than an anonymous number in Crumlin Gaol.

'Reading the free publicity of those bastards, are you?'

He glanced up, startled. The man he had met while disembarking leaned over the orange coloured table offering him a miniature bottle of Bell's whisky. The man slid down into the seat opposite, pushing the newspapers aside.

'Bit early, isn't it?' Seamus said nervously, looking at his watch.

'And when the hell is it too early? If they're selling, I'm buying.'

Seamus was far from happy at the intrusion. The man was a virtual alcoholic. He fumbled in his pocket for a cigarette.

'So what're the rags saying?'

'Not a lot. Usual things.'

'All rubbish. All of it,' the man went on aggressively, his voice already slurring.

Seamus unscrewed the small bottle, toasted the man and took the merest sip. 'Why rubbish?' he asked curiously.

'Because the boys are just gangsters these days, and these press boys make them out like fucking Robin Hoods!'

'But you're from the south, aren't you?' spaid Seamus, thinking he detected a Dublin accent.

'That I am, but now I've the northern territory, sod it!'

The man finished the bottle in his hand, thrust it under his seat and simultaneously pulled another from his coat pocket.

'For what?'

'Shoes,' the man sighed. 'Used to be at head office in Dundalk before they moved me. Office politics, that's all. And, anyway, what's that to do with it?'

'What?'

'Whether I'm a southerner or not. Whether I'm from Howth or you're from Limerick. Does it matter? I've seen what's going on in the North and it's sheer bloody gangsterism, so it is.'

'You're a wee bit strong, aren't you?' Seamus said apprehensively. He'd noticed that people in the seats across the aisle, probably businessmen, were beginning to cast curious looks at them, even craning to hear better.

'Look, sonny. I've seen 'em. I've seen what they're doing.'

'I'm no stranger to Belfast. Everyone knows.'

'Not the bombings, sonny. The way they're robbing the people their own people, our people if you like.'

Seamus began to rise from his seat. 'The bog,' he said by way of explanation, although the need wasn't particularly pressing.

The man shoved him in the chest, returning him back into the seat, and swigged at his bottle. 'You're not understanding anything, are you?' he whined. 'How d'you think they came by the money to put down a deposit on that chopper they used yesterday? How did they pay off the prison officers?'

Seamus shuffled into the next seat, the one next to the aisle, ready to make his escape, thoroughly frightened at the way his 'travelling companion' was drawing attention to them both. The drunken man gripped him by the right wrist, clasping his hand over his watch. Seamus tried gently to shake himself free but only succeeded in fluttering some of the newspapers to the floor. 'I must . . . ' he protested.

'No. No, listen. I've seen 'em. I've watched 'em. I've seen the gangsters with their collection boxes for this and that, their bingo tickets, their shoddy bits of wood carving or weaving. 'Buy this,' they say, 'and help the boys behind the wire!' And God, who's going to refuse 'em when everyone knows they'll be back with a bullet through the window – or worse – if you don't pay out? Look at their taxi service. You've got to use it since they've burned out most of the Ulster buses. It's the biggest protection racket since Al Capone. The poor bastards caught in between them and the Army haven't a prayer, though they're offering a wee few to be rid of each pack of vermin. I know. I've talked to the shopkeepers down the Falls when they can't settle their bills. I know where their money's going and every last penny begrudged, so it is! Many of them are just packing their traps and stealing away for the ferry rather than pay the extortion. What's the point of carrying on, they say, and, you know, they're bloody . . . '

'Excuse me,' Seamus exclaimed, at last wrenching himself free and side-stepping into the aisle. He hurried through the automatic doors and into the nearest vacant toilet, to relief in more ways than one.

He remained locked in for more than half-an-hour. He thought about what the drunken man had said and dismissed it. He'd never met a Catholic in Belfast unwilling to subscribe to the Republican cause. In fact, he'd always found them only too happy to do so. After all, he'd never carried a gun while rattling the collection box at various functions.

When Seamus emerged from the toilet he peeked gingerly into his compartment. The shoe salesman had vanished, presumably to find more convivial company in the buffet car. Seamus took no chances though. He lifted his suitcase down from the rack and moved to another part of the train settling down to read the newspapers for the rest of the journey.

After the train reached Euston Station in London, Seamus didn't follow the signs to the taxi rank in the basement but wandered nonchalantly into the busy road outside to hail a cab.

Only when the taxi was lost in the traffic did he feel truly safe. He directed the first cab to Oxford Street, paid it off, then switched to another one which was cruising for business along the crowded street.

He paid this off at Paddington Station, and strolled into the Great Western Hotel.

As instructed, Seamus went to the reception desk, identified himself as Alan Anderson, and asked if any messages had been left for him.

The girl behind the desk flicked through the notes on a clipboard. 'Mr Anderson . . . Mr Anderson . . . ' she murmured. 'Ah, yes, sir. Captain Black phoned for you earlier. He said he'd meet you at this address.'

She handed him a slip of paper. Seamus checked that no carbon copy had been taken of it, and turned away.

'Aren't you booking in, sir?'

'Not yet. Later.' Seamus lied, now knowing where he was to stay. It would have been too dangerous if he'd had the information before. He glanced down at the address. It was in Paddington itself, obviously not far away. He walked out of the hotel and into the pub across the road to ask directions. He had plenty of money for a few large whiskeys to celebrate the success of his escape.

Seamus's name, and the escape, figured prominently at that day's General Operations meeting at Thiepval Barracks.

The first item was a progress report on the construction work at Long Kesh. Ostensibly, this was to provide more military accommodation. But senior officers knew that in reality the barracks blocks were being prepared to house prisoners in case the government reintroduced internment. Most of them guessed this was likely to happen some time that summer.

As the brief discussion ended, the commanding general warned once more of the need for extreme secrecy. 'If anyone gets wind of this,' he smiled without a trace of humour, 'Then all hell will be let loose – and not only in the streets. A number of promising careers, gentlemen, including mine, will take a very sudden and very prominent nosedive. And that I wouldn't like to happen. Right, next business. Yesterday's escape. How do you read it, Stephen?'

Major Gates squared up the file lying on the table in front of him, glancing up at the coloured photograph of Her Majesty the Queen on the wall. 'Fairly ominous, sir,' he began. 'I think we have to assume that the basic intention was to spring Aherne. The other two escapees were merely false leads to pull our attention away while Number One Johnny did his vanishing trick.'

'You think he's away?'

'I'd bet my pension on it, sir. Wherever he is, he's not in Northern Ireland now. Probably south of the Border, but who knows?'

'If he is,' interrupted the senior intelligence officer, 'Then we'll soon hear from the usual sources.'

'I hope so,' retorted Major Gates, rubbing cigar smoke from eyes ringed with tension and tiredness. 'They're obviously pinning high hopes on the laddie and that means some nasty bombs sooner or later.'

'Is he that good, Stephen?' queried the general anxiously.

The major nodded, opening the file. 'He has the technical background, that's the worrying point. Given a good instructor and some decent material, he could be a real problem. My hunch is that's why they've sprung him. Their other bomb designers are pretty hopeless. All old-fashioned stuff.'

'So what are we doing?'

'Well, I've warned the EOD teams to treat all devices with kid gloves. Otherwise, we'll just have to play it by ear until the new product is launched on the market.'

Later that week Major Gates, his wife and daughter took Saturday lunch with the young American surgeon, Edward S. Aicheson and his wife. It had beenh a long-standing appointment, twice cancelled at the last moment when the major had to rush off to examine a bomb.

The families ate in the half-filled dining room of the Conway Hotel in Dunmurry, one of Belfast's more select suburbs. They exchanged social pleasantries and shared experiences of life in the Province, each a trifle unsure of the other.

Elizabeth Gates, slim and capable, dark elfin charm hiding an independent mind, swopped shopping tips with Lindy Aicheson, blonde shininess and chattering veneer masking deep uncertainty.

Mary Gates kept silent, concentrating like a twelve-year-old should, on finishing every last morsel of her roast chicken.

The two men attempted to keep their copnversation from the grimmer realities of their respective jobs.

It wasn't until their wives took Mary for a paddle in the ornate swimming pool at the end of the hotel's garden that the major and the surgeon settled down to a real talk.

They sat drinking brandy on the terrace overlooking the gardens, both able to pretend that the hotel had reverted to its previous existence of a private – and decidedly stately – residence, all pillars and Georgian windows.

'It's strange sitting here, Ted,' remarked Stephen Gates, using as requested, the familiar version of his companion's Christian name. 'We could be anywhere in Britain . . . '

'Or Massachusetts . . . '

'Or Massachusetts, yet not five miles away pretty well every crime in the book is being committed in the name of one cause or the other. They've come from all over the world – the soldiers, the media, people like you – and all because history has decreed that two factions should beat the living daylights out of each other and anyone who tries to stand between them. It's so bloody unreal in this day and age that sometimes I feel more like an actor than a soldier.'

'You've gotten that feeling as well? Many a time I've looked at the mess of flesh on the table and had to pinch myself that I'm not in the middle of a bad dream.'

The major grinned, smoothing the lapels of his houndstooth sports jacket. 'I just pat my back pocket . . . '

. He did so. The American heard the chink of something metallic.

Stephen Gates rose slightly out of his seat and lifted the flap of his jacket. The butt of his personal revolver, a specially tailored .38 Smith and Wesson poked out.

'Always with you?'

'Always. You can bet the one time I'm not carrying it is when some skull will come after me.'

The waiter poured more drinks from a bottle of four-star Hine.

Aicheson realized that behind the major's urbane manner, there was the calculating ruthlessness and arrogance of a man dedicated to the destruction of his country's enemies. He tried to change the subject.

'You know when we first met and you said you'd some Irish ancestors? Well, don't you ever think that you're fighting your own people?'

'No way. The skulls are no more representative of Ireland than my left tit. Sure, they've supporters, a hard core of maybe a thousand or two, but the majority who go along with them do so because they're scared witless.'

'Do you think your Irish relatives suppport them?' Aicheson asked rather tentatively.

'That's a curious thought. Frankly, I don't know, Ted. I've never bothered to trace them back or even find out whether there are still any left over here. Way back, they're supposed to have been land-owners in Kerry, apparently thrown out during the Land League troubles near the end of the last century. Always been a bit of a mystery, not really talked about in the family. They say great grandpa on my mum's side was a bit of a sod with the local girls on the quiet. He had to change his name from Sanders or something like that because he was afraid of getting the chop even when he'd

567

moved over to Hampshire. Drank most of the money, they say. Certainly none came down to my dad. He lived and died a farm foreman.'

'You've never wanted to find out more?'

'Not really,' the major smiled, hoping he didn't sound patronizing. 'What's passed is past. Leave that sort of thing to our American cousins.'

Aicheson laughed. 'Not me, brother. Or should that be cousin? My Lindy's the expert in our family. She's given up trying to prove she came over in the Mayflower so she's making me the direct descendant of the old kings of Ireland.'

'Much luck?'

The surgeon shook his head in a mock-sad way.

'Not much. I reckon my folk were just like the rest of the Irish-Americans. Poor farmers who became poorer in the bad times. But Lindy's clipping all the papers like crazy. Our apartment down the road's looking more and more like a library. Funnily enough, I thought of you the other day, Stephen, when she surfaced with that guy who skipped gaol in that chopper. She swore he'd the right name and address to be a distant cousin. Aherne, wasn't that his name?'

'Affirmative.'

'Well, I know for a fact my great-great-whatever grandpa married a girl back in Boston whose sister married someone called Aherne, who came from around where this guy comes from.'

'Listowel?'

'Right in one, Stephen. Listowel. You know of him?'

The major nodded ruefully.

'Oh, yes, I know him all right. But, remember, there must be hundreds with the same name.'

'That's what I tell Lindy, but you know women. She's all for spending part of our vacation down there searching parish records and digging around churchyards.'

Seamus hadn't stirred in four days from his small bed-sitting room in the back streets of Paddington, about half-a-mile from the cavernous, glass-roofed railway station.

When he'd arrived there, the owner of the lodging house, an elderly Wexford man, had asked no questions and clearly expected no answers. The lodging house provided no food but, each morning, the owner offered to buy groceries, drinks and books which had to be paid for in cash.

568

After four days of baked beans and sausages, cooked on a small gas-ring in the room, washed down with tea laced with whiskey, or cans of Guinness, Seamus began longing for a change of diet. He was also extremely bored with his own company and his only means of entertainment, a 9-inch black and white television set, which, like the room, had seen better days.

His instructions had been clear: stay out of sight for at least a week. Seamus decided, however, that a quiet evening out would do more good than harm.

He waited until early dusk, just after seven o'clock when the shadows were softening, checked his disguise once more and then went out. The streets were empty except for a few children playing ball on the pavements. Seamus wandered into the first pub he came to and ordered a large whiskey with a beer chaser, followed quickly by a second. The bar was virtually deserted.

'Where's everybody?' he asked the barman, ordering his third round, at last feeling some effect from the alcohol.

'Too early yet, Paddy,' the barman answered cheerily. 'We only get the locals here in the evening. If you want some action, try the places nearer the station.'

Seamus took his advice and wandered out of the quiet side streets into Praed Street, the main road running alongside Paddington Station, and past St Mary's Hospital, whose bulky ugliness disguised one of the finest medical facilities in the world. The opposite side of the road could hardly have been a greater contrast.

The cheap takeaway cafes jostled for space with sex-aid shops, pornographic bookshops and scruffy hotels. Red 'Vacancy' signs leered into the gathering dusk, others simply winked out the two words 'Sauna Massage'.

The air was filled with the smells of spicy cooking, car fumes and the promise of forbidden sin.

Seamus found it irresistible. He'd never seen such a street before. They didn't exist in Dublin, and if there were similar establishments in Belfast, they were well-hidden.

He bought two more large whiskeys in a pub opposite the hospital's main entrance, then risked a kebab in the adjoining cafe. It was surprisingly tasty and filling. By now, though, his stomach was fluttering with other than hunger for food and drink.

Seamus walked out of the cafe amd into the next street, towards a beckoning 'Massage' sign. He slunk past the converted shop window. The heavy brown curtains allowed no sight inside. He strolled over to the opposite corner and lit a cigarette, watching the doorway below the sign. He waited a good few minutes, wishing he'd taken another drink, before striding over to the enticing door and pushing it open.

An auburn haired woman in her early thirties smart and clean in a white overall, stood behind a counter in the narrow, curtained hallway. She smiled brightly at him. 'Good evening, sir.'

'Hello' he said hesitantly, not sure what to say next.

The woman was used to nervousness. 'A sauna and massage, sir? The VIP service, sir?'

'Oh . . . yes, then. All right.'

'That'll be £10.'

Seamus gave her two £5 notes which disappeared beneath the counter. The woman handed him a numbered ticket as she called through the hatch beside her. 'Rebecca will look after you, sir.' She pointed to the inner door with a long, painted fingernail.

Seamus opened the door and stepped into a large room scattered with low chairs. In one corner, there was a tiny, curved bar with a half empty bottle of Yugoslav Riesling on the counter. A colour TV flickered silently on a table.

A tall, suntanned girl, dressed in a tight fitting blue gingham overall, stood at the head of a flight of carpeted stairs spiralling downwards. She was not much shorter than himself, with a swirl of black hair. A fluffy white towel hung over her bare forearm. She beckoned encouragingly to him.

As he walked down the stairs behind her, Seamus felt totally at a loss. 'I'm in your hands,' he murmured.

Inane pop music filled the basement area, little more than a square of threadbare carpet surrounded by numbered doors.

Seamus was shown to a small cubicle lit redly by a combined light and heater in the ceiling. One wall was covered entirely by a coloured print of a Mediterranean landscape, the others with wallpaper simulating pine panels. The space was dominated by a waist high couch covered with towelling and a wide strip of absorbent paper, leaving little room for a fawn bath, shinily clean.

Rebecca pointed to the only chair. 'You can put your clothes there, sir.' She placed the towel on the edge of the couch and took the numbered ticket from him. 'The sauna and shower are just across the hall. I'll be back in ten minutes or so to see how you're getting on.'

With another encouraging smile, she turned on her high heels and left the cubicle, closing the door gently behind her.

Seamus was as excited as he was uncertain while he undressed.

He slipped his diminishing wad of £5 notes into one of his socks and stuffed that into his jacket pocket. He'd read court reports in the *News of the World* about what could happen in places like this.

He tucked the towel round his waist and left the cubicle. The sauna was empty and hot. Seamus reckoned it would seat four at the most. On the floor was a discoloured saucepan, filled with water and a ladle. He picked it up and dashed the liquid on to the glowing heating unit. Steam hissed up into the wood-panelled room.

Seamus took off his towel and sat down on the wooden, slatted bench. 'Jesus!' he exclaimed, immediately jumping up. The wood was burning hot to his bare flesh.

He folded the towel on the bench and sat down again. Within a few minutes, he was gasping for breath. He noticed globules of sweat forming among the fine hairs on his forearm. It really was becoming unbearably hot. He stood up, picked up the towel and crossed a narrow passage to the shower where he lathered himself with soap and stood under the fine spray of cold water. Refreshed, he went back to the sauna again. This time he felt the sweat forming under his hair.

'All right, sir?'

The door had opened suddenly. Rebecca smiled inquiringly at him. Seamus crossed his legs, trying to hide some of his nakedness. The young girl seemed totally unconcerned.

'Another five minutes, sir, and then we'll be ready for our massage, won't we?'

Seamus nodded without speaking. Rebecca shut the door once more.

'Gentleman in Number Four, Jane,' Seamus heard her call to someone outside.

'How's yours?' another girl asked.

'Be done in ten minutes.'

'There's one waiting upstairs.'

'Okay. I'll start him off.'

Seamus realized that if he stayed in the sauna any longer he might hold up the finely-tuned workings of the establishment.

He took a last shower and padded back to his allotted cubicle to begin drying himself, ready for he didn't know what.

The door opened quietly behind him and Rebecca entered as smilingly brisk as ever.

'Let me dry your back, sir.'

She took the towel and gently wiped his skin, even patting his buttocks dry. Seamus looked down at himself. To his amazement, there were no sexual stirrings.

'Now, on to the couch, sir. On your front.'

Seamus scrambled up and lay there naked.

He turned his head, watching Rebecca open a low cupboard beside the couch which contained a box of coloured tissues and some clear plastic bottles.

She picked one up and sprinkled the contents along Seamus's back. The slight perfume of the oil filled the cubicle. It was cosy now, almost homely. Seamus felt the whiskey reach his brain again after its temporary retreat in the sauna steam. He began to relax as Rebecca started massaging him. Her hands were strong, kneading the muscles at the back of his neck.

'Hard day, sir?'

Seamus nodded, his head resting on a small paper-covered pillow. Rebecca had an Irish accent. Strangely he hadn't noticed it before.

'Soon have you relaxed, sir,' Rebecca prattled on, massaging away. 'Is this your first time here?'

'Uh-huh.'

'Recommended, were we?'

Her hands were now rubbing and stroking his buttocks. She paused to pour more oil onto him. A hand slipped between his buttocks, a fingernail lightly scraping him before flicking between his legs and moving on to the back of his thighs. Seamus twitched.

'No, I was just passing when I saw the sign.'

'You've a scar here.'

'Yes,' he replied, thinking for a moment of that bicycle accident when he was a small boy.

'Are you a mercenary? We get a lot of mercenaries here.' Her hands dug into his calf muscles.

'No.'

'You're not a copper, are you?'

Her questions sounded automatic with no particular curiosity behind them.

'God forbid!'

'What do you do then, sir?'

'This and that. Mostly that,' Seamus joked.

She slapped his buttocks. 'Turn over now, sir.'

Rebecca begun running her clasped hands up and down his legs, each time moving them closer to his crotch.

'And what part of the old country are you from?' Seamus asked. He felt his penis beginning to thicken and lengthen. He didn't dare

572

look down at it. He turned his head to the side, seemingly by accident.

'Galway, sir. The far west.'

Her hands slid down once over his penis as she started to knead his stomach.

'I'm Irish too.' Seamus's voice was strained. He'd never felt so naked before, spreadeagled there on the couch. It was delicious.

'I know.'

'Kerry.'

'Oh, yes.'

Rebecca didn't sound that interested. She leaned over him, to massage his chest briefly. Suddenly she stopped and tapped his flat stomach with her long fingers. 'Healthy, aren't we, sir?'

'Try to be.'

'I mean this, sir.'

Her hand closed gently around his penis, now fully erect. Seamus didn't answer. He looked directly into her dark brown eyes. They smiled mischievously back at him.

'Any extra services, sir?'

'Extra?'

'Straight relief is £5; topless, £10, strip £15.'

'Well, strip, I suppose.'

'You've the money?'

'Of course.'

Rebecca nodded. She unbelted her overall and deftly removed her brief, light brown bra and matching panties. Her slim, honey-coloured body was firm, breasts slightly pendulous, nipples pointed and hard. She sprinkled some more oil and then began masturbating him, using both hands, fingers linked to form a tunnel.

'Can I touch?'

'Yes, sir.'

Seamus fingered her right nipple before sliding his hand under her small, tight buttocks. She was open and wet although she gave no visible response as he caressed her wiry curls, even thrust a finger inside her velvetness.

'Too much to drink sir?'

'A bit.'

'Can't be all night, can we?'

Her hands moved more urgently.

'Why not climb aboard then, Rebecca?'

'Oh, no, sir,' she said quite severely. 'No sex here.'

She worked over him for another minute, the only sounds the slurping of her oily hands and his quickening breaths.

'You'll have to hurry up, sir,' she said, exasperation growing in her voice. 'My shift finishes in ten minutes. Please try, sir.'

Seamus tried. Soon he felt his climax approaching.

'That's it,' Rebecca said encouragingly. 'I can always tell when your toes begin to curl.'

And then it was on him. He groaned with pleasure. Rebecca covered him with tissues and wiped him dry, holding him until he began to soften.

'That's it. Always like to see my gentlemen come.' There was a genuine note of achievement in her tone.

'A bath now?'

'Bath?'

'You're VIP service, aren't you sir?'

Seamus nodded weakly.

'That means an assisted bath but I won't be able to stay, sir. I'll run it for you though.'

She turned on the water after squirting some foam into the bath, bending naked before him, unconcerned at totally displaying herself.

Seamus sat up, swung his legs over the couch and reached for the sock holding the money. He counted out £15 and then added another £5. He turned back to her, offering the blue notes. By some miracle, she was already dressed.

'Oh, thank you, sir.'

'Can I see you again?' Seamus asked intently.

'Whenever you call, just ask for me,' Rebecca said as she left the cubicle, bright, brisk smile back again.

'Goodnight, sir.'

'Goodnight.'

He bathed, dried and dressed quickly. He took a last look round the cubicle, grinning ruefully to himself, before tramping upstairs.

Rebecca was standing at the bar talking to the woman who'd been at the entrance.

Seamus walked swiftly to the door.

'Goodnight, sir,' the women chorused.

'Goodnight,' Seamus mumbled as he went into the street.

# Chapter 7 July, 1971

'Will you write?'

Her voice was muffled in the pillow.

'And phone,' he answered, his lips moving against the fine hairs at the nape of her neck, his tongue tasting salt.

'Every week?' Rebecca begged, turning over, pressing her smooth warmth against him.

'Twice a week at least,' Seamus assured her, feeling his excitement growing again, sliding a hand down her back pulling her even closer, index finger slipping between tight valleys of flesh.

He raised himself slightly and kissed her. Her lips were still moist. He lifted his face a few inches and looked down on her beauty. Her eyes were shut, black hair spread on white pillow. His free hand followed his gaze slowly down her body, shaping, tweaking, caressing, stroking. And when she sighed deeply in her throat, ready, he moved gently over her and entered slowly, inch by inch until they were one body, thrusting and receiving in unison, quicker and quicker, deeper and deeper into the whirlpool of their pleasure from which there was no escape but inevitable flooding, overwhelming release.

They panted, foreheads damp, into each other's shoulders, still close, before he pulled away and lay next to her, one arm draped limply across her soft breasts. She shifted a fraction and nudged his arm lower, lifting his hand and placing it between her thighs, wanting him to feel their wetness there.

'Was it nice?' she murmured.

'For you?'

'Oh, yes.'

'And me.'

The tone of her voice changed.

'I wasn't easy, was I?'

'No.'

'You didn't think I was just because I work there?'

'No.'

'Sure?'

'You proved it, so you did.'

'I did, didn't I, so I did?' she mimicked affectionately.

'You did.'

'Sleepy?'

'A wee bit.'

She kissed him on the cheek, then shifted decisively to her side of the bed.

Seamus turned on his side but shuffled back towards her so that their buttocks touched. He rubbed provocatively against her once. She linked her feet with his and was instantly asleep, satiated.

No, he thought, peering into the gloom of the bedroom, she certainly hadn't been too easy. Quite the contrary and she'd made that clear from the outset. He smiled to himself, seeing the trail of clothes leading from the door to the bed, laying where they fell or were tossed. No, she hadn't been easy.

It had taken two more visits to the massage parlour before Rebecca would even tell him that her surname was Fahey. And, during his next visit, she'd only agreed to meet him for a drink afterwards if he foreswore the 'extra services'. Even in the pub, she'd been very doubtful about spending her day off with him. He had had to promise never to go near the massage parlour again and to put their previous sexual intimacies firmly out of his mind.

'Outside that place,' she'd said adamantly, 'I'm just like any other girl. I'll not be having you think I'm easy because of what I do in there.'

Actually, Seamus had been only too happy to accept her conditions. His visits to the massage parlour were already too expensive and his growing familiarity with the establishment had begun to breed self-disgust.

He slid a hand behind him and ran it over the curve of her hip, marvelling at the silkiness of her skin. The even rhythm of her breathing didn't alter. Suddenly, he felt extremely possessive towards her.

On their first date, they'd talked deliberately of inconsequential things. But each was aware of the other's probing, the gathering of titbits of family history here and there, the eliciting of scraps of information, the tossing of tastes and opinions back and forth, discovering those which matched, discarding those that didn't or filing them for future reference.

But it hadn't been until the early evening when they were eating curry at Veeraswamy's near Piccadilly Circus that Rebecca had found enough trust to speak of her past.

'It's so huge,' Seamus had said. 'I thought Dublin was big compared to Listowel – well anywhere's big compared to there – but London . . . ' He spread his arms expressively, nearly knocking over his frosty glass of lager.

Rebecca smiled. 'It took me months to find my way around. I kept losing myself on the tube and having to surface to take a taxi.'

'Do you still?'

'Even after eighteen months, I'm unsure.'

'You regret coming at all?'

'No, not really. I had to come and that's all there is to it.'

'Had to?'

'I couldn't stand it there any more.'

'Galway?'

'Not the place so much. It's beautiful and all but it's so damned small. That's the trouble. You see, I was courting a boy for two years and he apparently was going round the bars and bragging away, when he was in drink. Well, one Sunday, I was coming away from mass when I overheard these two biddy women talking about me, jawing away they were, saying what a shameless hussy and all I was and what a wonder it was that I wasn't showing yet and not banns fixed.'

Seamus almost choked on his chicken biriani.

'Showing?' he spluttered.

'Showing . . . they thought I was carrying his babbie, that I was pregnant.'

'And?'

'Of course, I wasn't,' she said indignantly. 'It was their dirty minds, that's all. Even Father O'Donovan, our priest, heard the talk and came to see me. He was just panting for all the details and whatever, God forgive him. Anyway, after that, how could I stay? I took what money there was and left. I'd heard they wanted nurses bad over here but my Leaving Certificate passes weren't good enough and I could only be a ward orderly polishing the bedpans and helping old men take a pee. I wasn't having that at all and then when I was near broke I met this girl in a Wimpy Bar, Geraldine, my flatmate, and she offered to fix me up at that place in Paddington. And there you are . . . The money's good, the work's all right when you're used to it.' She paused, looking down on the table, crumbling a poppadom into her meal, a korma. 'And I'll only say this once, though I'm not wanting to right now. I don't think I'm doing any wrong to anybody by doing what I do. I'm not selling myself like some of them are. I just shut my mind when they want me to . . . those things . . . you know . . . and when they want something else, something more, I simply tell them I won't.'

'Have you ever tried for another job?'

'No, nor will I till I'm finding what I want.'

'And what's that when it's at home?'

Rebecca shook her head, leaning across the table and brushing Seamus's lips with the index finger on her right hand. 'Enough secrets for one day,' she whispered. 'Enough of mine anyway!'

'I've none,' he lied. 'Just a businessman trying to do business.'

In the cosiness of her bedroom, after their frantic love-making, that falsehood still preyed on his mind as part of the deception he'd played on Rebecca. He'd wanted to tell her his real name and his work even on that first date, but that would have been stupidly dangerous. As their relationship deepened, such a confession became too difficult. Simply, he'd been frightened of losing her, of scaring her away.

Twice a week, sharp at eight o'clock in the evening, he went to specially selected public telephone boxes around central London, waiting for the phone calls from Dublin, certain that he would be recalled shortly. After all, he'd believed, the situation in Northern Ireland was deteriorating quickly with the British Army arriving in ever increasing numbers to combat the IRA's campaign.

Despite the growing funds from bank and post office robberies, augmented by money from Clann-na-Gael in the United States, the movement had struggled to maintain its offensive with hit-and-run shootings and small-scale bombings, as well as continually promoting inter-community incidents to keep the temperature high on the streets.

Undoubtedly, however, the Provisionals' bandwagon of violence had been gaining an awesome momentum of its own, exposing the years of political mismanagement and neglect in Belfast and White-hall, tearing away once more the thin veneer of civilization which cloaked the ugly hatreds and suspicions of centuries.

Everything indicated that something climactic was about to occur. Yet, in call after call, Seamus had been ordered to continue his aimless existence. He'd been puzzled and resentful at the Provisionals' attitude, his unhappiness deepened by Rebecca's desire to have him as a drinking and eating companion but nothing else.

Thus, on July 28th, when he was given his long-awaited orders to return to Ireland, he was eager to obey. They supplied a valid reason for saying goodbye to Rebecca without ever having to own up to his deception.

The next day, he sat with Rebecca at a corner table in the hotel bar, nibbling crisps and gherkins, his rail and ferry tickets already in his wallet. Outwardly, he'd been as attentive as ever. Inwardly, he'd been feeling rather empty, awaiting the chance to breach his news.

'Rebecca,' he'd begun tentatively. 'I've something to tell you and I'm not sure how . . .'

She had glanced at him a secretive smile around her lips. 'And I was going to tell you something,' she had said.

'Women and children first, I suppose,' Seamus had shrugged.

'Well, you know my flatmate, Geraldine?'

'Uh-huh.'

'Well, she's going home to Manchester for a few days to visit her dad in hospital.'

'So?'

'Well, I thought you might like to see me home tonight when I've finished work and maybe have a takeaway.'

Seamus had straightened up in his chair, not sure if he'd heard correctly. 'Tonight?'

Rebecca had nodded, eyes twinkling mischievously. 'I couldn't let you there with Geraldine around,' she'd explained. 'She's had her boy-friends there in more ways than one but I couldn't. Not with someone listening in the next room. But tonight, there'll be no one.'

Instinctively, he'd held out his hand to take hers.

'And what's your news?' she'd asked brightly.

He sighed and shook his head sadly. 'I've to return to Ireland tomorrow. Definite orders from the boss man.'

Her face had shown her disappointment. She'd pulled her hand away from his and gazed down at her lap.

'When did you hear?' she'd asked dully, not looking at him.

'Late last night,' he'd replied, his heart sinking, anticipating she would change her mind now about their evening alone at the flat.

'You can't be putting it off?'

'No way.'

She'd raised her face, eyes glistening with held-back tears. She smiled, wanly at first, then more happily. 'Then your last night'll have to be one to remember, won't it?' she'd said determinedly, returning her hand to his and squeezing gently.

Twelve hours later, snuggled beside her, Seamus regretted not being frank with her. He'd half-suspected that he was in love with her. Now he was certain.

He slipped out of the bed and padded, naked, into the lounge next door to search for a pen and paper. Then he settled down to write a note to Rebecca, explaining everything and assuring her that he would phone soon from Ireland, begging her love and understanding.

Seamus placed the note prominently on the sideboard and went back to bed, eventually falling into a fitful, dreamless sleep.

He awoke to the caress of Rebecca's fingernails scraping lightly up and down, lengthening and hardening him. He luxuriated in the sensations from her practised hand before turning hungrily, pulling her close.

'Last time?' she whispered.

'For a while, but there'll be many more, I promise you.'

Their love-making was slower and surer, more a mutual celebration of their finding each other than a lustful snatch at momentary pleasure.

Afterwards they remained entwined in their oneness, loath to break apart.

'Don't you wish we could stay like this for ever?' she breathed against his cheek, arms folded round his neck.

'Aye,' he murmured. 'And let the whole bloody world go by.'

'Then why don't we?' she teased.

He slapped her buttocks slightly and rolled away from her. 'Because I've a train to catch in an hour,' Seamus replied. 'That's why.'

He jumped out of bed and hurried into his clothes while Rebecca lay on the bed, making purring noises like a contented cat and offering lewd suggestions about what they could do if only he'd return to her arms.

Finally dressed, Seamus leaned over the bed and kissed her once, deeply.

'I love you,' he declared, looking into the depths of her eyes.

'This isn't all?' she asked mournfully. 'Not just last night?'

'No, no. It's the beginning, you see.'

When she heard the front door close, Rebecca turned her face to the pillows and began sobbing. 'Oh, you bastard!' she cried. 'You bastard, leaving me like this!'

It wasn't until early afternoon that she found Seamus's note and understood. For nearly an hour, she sat on the sofa reading it again and again, hardly believing its contents yet knowing they were true.

'You stupid, stupid, lovely, lovely Kerryman,' she crooned, pressing the note to her lips, realizing that his 'confession' was as great a commitment as giving her a wedding ring.

By that time, Seamus was aboard the British Rail ferry some thirty minutes out of Fishguard and headed across the seventy or so miles to Rosslare in County Wexford. He'd spent much of the train journey from Paddington in the buffet bar, attempting to stay awake with a mixture of black coffee and whiskey. On the boat, however, he felt comforted by the Irish accents all around him and nodded off to sleep, swaying to an unusually gentle swell across St George's Channel.

When the ferry docked in early evening, he went directly to the tiny bar on the railway siding by the quay.

'If you've a long journey, sir,' said the young barmaid, serving him with a pint of Smithwick's, 'you'd better be buying what you want here. There's no refreshments on the train.'

'No, thanks,' Seamus replied, 'I'm waiting for a lift.' He nodded wearily at the middle-aged priest standing beside him, firmly clutching a plastic bag filled with bottles of spirits.

'All right, Father?' he said conversationally.

'And isn't all this travel the very divil?' complained the priest, downing a brandy.

'It can build a thirst, so it can,' Seamus smiled, presuming that the priest had been on holiday in Britain and wasn't looking forward particularly to resuming his encompassed life in an Irish country parish.

'Mr Anderson?' a voice asked at his side.

Seamus turned and nodded.

A young man, possibly still in his teens, cloth cap almost hanging off his right ear, held out his hand for the suitcase.

'I'm your driver.'

'Right,' Seamus said, swallowing the last of his beer.

'To Dublin?' he asked when they were out of earshot in the car park.

'No. You'll see.'

After an hour's driving, Seamus had lost his bearings totally. He knew they'd headed north and inland, probably into County Carlow, but he didn't recognize the villages and townlands through which they sped.

Eventually, late in the evening, the car turned into a pair of high, wrought iron gates. By the lights of the headlamps, Seamus saw two men standing by them, both carrying what appeared to be sub-machine guns. A mile further on, the car scrunched to a halt on a wide patch of gravel in front of the pillars and terraces of a substantial, early Victorian mansion.

'Well, I see we've gone up in the world since I've been travelling away,' Seamus joked.

'Only the best for Mr M,' the young driver answered, mentioning the name of a prominent member of the Dail.

'This is his?'

'He's lending it, so he is, while he's away in the States on some lecture tour or other.'

Seamus whistled through his teeth in amazement. He knew that the politician had Republican sympathies but he'd never dreamed of him actively supporting the Provisional IRA.

'You'll be going to your bed now,' said the driver, leading the way into the house with a swaggering, natural authority beyond his years. 'No reception committee?' asked Seamus.

'Tomorrow. Be ready at nine.'

The next morning, thoroughly refreshed by a deep sleep, Seamus stepped down the wide, winding staircase and followed the chatter of voices into a lounge overlooking acres of lawn and fields. He waited awkwardly in the doorway for a moment, recognizing none of the eight men sitting around the room.

Their animated conversation died away when they noticed his presence. A stout man in early middle age heaved himself out of a deep chair and walked over, smiling broadly, greeting Seamus with a vigorous handshake.

'Seamus!' he exclaimed genially. 'Your timing was never better.'

'Timing?'

'Your arrival here. It couldn't have been better!'

'And why not?' he asked, puzzled, entering the lounge.

'The Brits went into Derry this morning. They smashed right through the no-go areas, so they did. Troops all over the place. Enough pandemonium to wake the dead.'

'So there's no more Free Derry?'

'Was there ever? Did it matter, son? This means more volunteers than we can handle. It means an end to the milk-and-water Republicans like Fitt and Hume and Currie. From now on, they're either with us or agin us, and that's it. Oh, by the way . . . sorry . . . I'm the commandant here, Matt O'Neill.'

They shook hands again. Seamus had heard of this man's reputation as a gunman during previous Border campaigns. He'd been credited with at least half-a-dozen killings, two of them especially callous. Matt O'Neill's avuncular, cheerful manner belied his true ruthlessness and dedication to the movement.

Seamus was introduced quickly, cursorily to the other men. Two had North American accents. Two were gutturally mid-European. And the remaining three bore familiar southern Irish accents.

He was waved to a seat and handed a steaming mug of coffee.

'Now let me explain again briefly for the benefit of our new friend,' O'Neill began, standing close by Seamus, patting him encouragingly on the shoulder. 'You're all here for training or, in some cases, just to sharpen up what you already know. You'll be finding out about each other in time but it'll be better if none of you say too much about yourselves or what your jobs'll be when you leave. That way no one'll be too embarrassed with too much information.'

O'Neill patted Seamus again, then wandered over to one of the large sash windows and looked out at the countryside.

'We'll not be disturbed here,' he continued. 'The Garda won't be nosey if we don't go scaring the locals. That we've agreed.'

He turned and beamed at the seven men in the lounge.

'Well, finally, before we all get down to work, just a word about the importance of your week or two here. According to our intelligence – and it's mighty high-grade, thanks to some friends in Dublin – Operation Motorman in Derry is only the start of a crack down by the Brits. A lot of the boys have already skedaddled underground. When the balloon goes up, we want to be able to hit them hard where it hurts. They've started doing our work for us. Let's be sure we can finish it!'

After a further desultory conversation, the others drifted away, leaving Seamus alone with Matt O'Neill.

'You're seeming a wee bit worried, son,' said O'Neill. 'Didn't I make myself clear?'

'It's not that, Mr . . . '

'Call me Matt, but don't be forgetting the rank.'

'I won't . . . Matt . . . nor your reputation.'

O'Neill nodded, smiling. 'I thought someone with your background might have heard.'

'I have that.'

'Well?'

'What I'm wondering is why, if all hell's going to be let loose, I was left kicking my heels in London for so long.'

O'Neill chuckled. 'Didn't Charley McCool give you a few wee words of advice before you jumped the wire from Crumlin?'

'He did that, Matt. Oh.'

'Yes. Oh, son. That's why. You were being watched in London.

Sure, they wanted you out of the nick for your bomb skills but they also wanted to check whether you were an informer or not.'

'And?'

'They must be satisfied or you wouldn't be here – or anywhere else, come to that. Mind, I hear that one or two of the Army Council didn't approve of your girlfriend. Bit puritanical. But I wouldn't let it worry you. Her family's known to us.'

'Rebecca's?'

'That her name? Well, her da's helped in the past so she's in the family, like.'

'Since you know, I might as well tell you I promised to phone her.' O'Neill smiled bleakly.

'Not from here, you won't, son. The local guards might not be unfriendly but the Special Branch will have the phones tapped as a matter of course. Write a letter and I'll see it's posted. But don't lick it down: I hate steaming them open. And why not one to your folks in Kerry? We're hearing you're awful famous down there.'

There was enough sarcasm in Matt O'Neill's voice to tell Seamus that, despite his recall to the Provisionals, he was still on probation.

'Thanks, I will,' Seamus answered, rather subdued.

'And, son, start growing your whiskers. You'll be needing all the disguise you can get when you head north again. Make that one of your jobs here. Okay?'

For the next three days Seamus was taught how to fire and maintain handguns and automatic weapons, using a miniature shooting range in the basement of the country house. He was also sent on an assault course built in a large copse next to the market garden.

'Toughen you up, son,' O'Neill said pointedly. 'After all your soft living.'

Every evening after supper he listened to lectures about Irish history from O'Neill and talks on the tactics used by revolutionary organizations throughout the world. These included various off-shoots of the PLO, the Basque organization, ETA, the Baader-Meinhof group in Germany, the Red Brigades in Italy, and even a cell of Croatians waging a campaign against Yugoslavia. Seamus hadn't realized that revolution was so interconnected.

His classroom work, as O'Neill termed it, began on the fourth day with the appearance of a man in his early 30s, introduced merely as Captain Jan. Although it took some time for Seamus to gather that his instructor was an East European army officer, attached to an embassy in Dublin, it was immediately clear that he was an expert on bombs.

Hour after hour till his eyes were red with tiredness, Seamus watched and copied 'Captain Jan' as he built complicated circuits for activating explosives.

Seamus was taught how to construct trembler switches; how to set false wiring to confuse a bomb disposal officer; how to wire bombs into cars using pressure detonators which would trigger an explosion once the victim sat down in the driving seat; how to conceal circuits in a bomb; and, perhaps most deadly, how to set off bombs remotely with radio signals. These devices could be employed as 'sleeper bombs', being placed in position long before their intended use and then detonated days or weeks later by someone miles away.

After ten days of intensive study, Seamus's notebooks were filled with diagrams and designs. He studied them with detachment, not relating them to the death and destruction they would cause. He deliberately fostered his detachment, glad that it was unlikely he'd ever have to meet his victims face to face.

He was content in his world of technical theory, even though it would soon end, particularly after internment, the detention of citizens without trial, was introduced into Northern Ireland.

Dozens of IRA supporters and activists, Provisionals and Officials, were arrested along with their counterparts in the Protestant para-military organizations like the UDA and UVF.

The British Government had found a use for the Nissen huts on the disused aerodrome at Long Kesh, ten miles west of Belfast.

Nightly, Seamus and the others watched the scenes in Belfast and Derry transmitted by Radio Telefis Eireann: rows of burning houses, young rioters attacking the Army, empty streets crackling with gunfire, barricades of gutted buses, refugees in church halls ineffective appeals for calm by politicians who'd helped light the fuse and wondered why the powder keg had exploded.

Four days later, with the whole of divided Ireland in torment, Seamus sat in the back of an estate car on its way through County Donegal to the Border.

Beside him was one of the Americans, a deserter from Vietnam, a native of Detroit called Teddy Block. In front was a German with an unpronounceable surname known simply as Hansi, and the driver who'd met Seamus at Rosslare, Brendan Donaghy.

The mission, according to Matt O'Neill, had two objectives. One was to drop Seamus back into Belfast, the other to kill policemen or soldiers or both. But Seamus rightly suspected that the mission had a third objective, to test his own commitment to the Provos and, perhaps, to provide them with another hold over him.

Two of them, the American and the German, were mercenaries, pure and simple, each due £1,000 for every murder of a soldier or policeman on the mission. It had been quite clear at the country mansion that they were feared and despised by the IRA: feared because they were so much better murderers than IRA men: despised because they killed for money rather than ideals. Young Brendan of the smiling face and nineteen years was equally feared and despised. A superb driver, he was also a psychopath who delighted in taking life and causing pain.

Early in the morning of August 13th, the four entered Northern Ireland along one of the hundreds of the unguarded country lanes which crossed and recrossed the length of the border.

By ten o'clock they were parked in a side street about a hundred yards from the police barracks in Strabane, a small town just inside the border.

No one was near when the American leaned into the back of the car, lifted a horse blanket and pulled out two Colt .45 automatic pistols which he handed to Brendan and Seamus and then a Thompson sub-machine gun which he kept on his own lap.

'Don't suppose you're joining in, Hansi?' he said to the German in the front passenger seat.

'Is crude, Teddy. Too crude. I shall wait for the real shooting.'

'Thought so.'

'Too crude?' asked Seamus.

'Hansi doesn't like shooting anyone at under a quarter-of-a-mile range and then only one round in the breech,' explained the American with a grim smile. 'Reckons it's unsporting otherwise. Me? I take anything that moves.'

Seamus felt a slight dampness on the gun in his hand. Was it oil or his own sweat? He didn't dare look.

'You get to the corner,' the American ordered, 'And give us the nod when the patrol's coming. Okay?'

'Sure, and then what?' Seamus tried to keep his voice steady.

'Just finish 'em off when we've done. That's all O'Neill wants. Simple. Okay?'

'Sure,' Seamus repeated, climbing out of the car and walking the ten yards to the corner, pistol in the waistband of his trousers, hidden by his sports jacket.

He peeked round into the town's main street. It was quiet and unhurried as ever it was. There were no more than two dozen people in sight, mostly women with shopping bags.

Seamus looked back to the car and shook his head. He lit a cigarette, waiting, rubbing a hand over the beard stubble on his face.

Two or three minutes went by, long minutes during which he tried not to think of what was about to happen. He was alone and frightened. His life was shortly to be changed. There could be no going back. Until now it had been unreal, playing at history to please his father. Bombs hadn't been personal. Bullets were. And so were the men in the car. There were no false heroics about them.

Seamus glanced back at the vehicle, noticing all the windows had been wound down. He knew the three inside would have been ordered to dispose of him if he failed this test, if he tried to run away. He guessed that was why they'd hardly talked to him during the long journey to Strabane.

He began murmuring a well-remembered novena, 'Oh, Most Holy St Jude Apostle and Martyr, great in virtue and rich in miracles, near kinsman of Jesus Christ, faithful intercessor for all who invoke you, special patron in times of need, to you I have recourse from the . . .'

And then he saw the flashes of blue uniform on the pavement, glimpsed between the shoppers, coming closer.

' . . . from the depths of my heart, and humbly beg you, to whom God . . . '

Two RUC men, one a sergeant, the other a constable, were now in clear sight, perhaps thirty yards away.

Seamus suddenly felt stupid mouthing words which long ago had lost their power for him, ritualistic phrases meaning little in his heart.

He waved his left arm behind his back, signalling the car to be ready, gripping the pistol butt with his right hand before he risked another peek round the corner.

The policemen were only ten yards away. Seamus could see that the constable was young and nervous, staying close by the sergeant, fingers constantly playing near the holster on his shiny belt.

His left arm waved again, motioning the car forward. It eased quietly into second gear and drew level with him.

The barrel of the American's sub-machine gun glinted suddenly in a ray of sunlight, poking just above the rear window.

At that moment, the car accelerated, jumping on to the pavement at the corner. Seamus glanced round the brick wall once more, ready to draw back from the line of fire.

The policemen had stopped six feet away, their backs to him.

'Oh, Jesus!' he exclaimed aloud.

Between the blue uniforms, he saw a young woman standing in the doorway of the house just round the corner, a baby in her arms, presenting it to the policemen for their admiration and approval.

It was too late, much too late.

The machine gun began to thunder as the RUC men turned, alerted by the noise of the car.

The American had squeezed the trigger immediately the uniforms had come into view, not knowing that they shielded the young mother from his position, crouched low in the back seat.

Seamus instinctively took a step forward although there was nothing he could do.

He was so close that he thought he heard the bullets thudding into flesh and the strangled cries of the policemen.

Holes exploded jaggedly across their uniforms, replaced an instant later by spurting blood, first at their waists, then up their sides and backs, eventually tearing open their cheeks and foreheads.

Bullets smashed into the windows and bricks behind, adding to the awful sound of carnage.

Seamus noticed an old woman further down the street, watching with mouth wide in horror.

'Aaaagh . . . !'

The young housewife, in apron and fluffy pink slippers screamed a split second before the policeman started to fall away from her, pushed forward and sideways by the smashing impact of bullet upon bullet. The air around them was pink, darkening into red, with spraying blood and flesh and chips of bone.

'Aaaagh . . . !'

Her scream rose, piercing, and then gurgled away as the bullets stitched across her breasts and neck, wrenching the baby from her arms, tossing him high with the reflexes of her convulsive agony.

She was lifted bodily off her feet and thrown back into the shattered doorway of her home.

Her baby spun to the ground and rolled into the gutter, white shawl billowing, already spotted and stained with crimson lifeblood.

As suddenly as it had begun not ten seconds before it was over.

The silence was harsh with the smell of cordite and the echoing screams of shoppers across the road.

Everything seemed to be moving in slow motion.

The young constable's feet drummed against the pavement with the last frantic orders from a brain mostly smeared on the wall, dripping down.

Glass still tinkled from the windows.

The baby began to whimper in the gutter, kicking its legs and arms, miraculously unharmed but for bruising.

'Finish 'em!' the American shouted from the car. 'Finish 'em!'

Seamus dragged his eyes from the twitching, ripped bodies and looked at him.

'They're done,' he shouted back over the noise of the revving car engine. 'All of them. They're done for! Oh God, didn't you see her?'

'Fucking finish 'em!' the American roared back, lips drawn tightly over his teeth, staring, eyes glazed, over the smoking barrel of the sub-machine gun.

Seamus's mind went blank. He dragged the heavy pistol from his waistband, took two steps forward and fired at point-blank range into the back of the constable's head, watching, almost microscopically, the hair part as the bullet struck and the shattered skull distended once more, quite perceptibly bouncing against the paving stone. He took another half-step and looked down into the sergeant's face, eyeballs white, rilled back, blood dribbling from both sides of his open mouth, displaying stumps of splintered teeth and gums. Seamus shut his eyes quickly and pulled the trigger again. A third eye appeared, blacky-blue, on the bridge of the sergeant's nose. The last suck of air ballooned the dead man's cheek and hiccupped in his throat.

He moved towards the woman as in a trance. She lay on the linoleum of her narrow hallway, skirt hitched around ample thighs, long dark hair obscuring her face.

'No, no!' called the American. 'Leave her for fuck's sake. In the car!'

Seamus turned slowly, shaking his head, trying to clear the sounds, the sights. He ran back to the car and clambered in the opened door, falling across the seat.

Brendan shoved his right foot hard on the accelerator. The back wheels spun for a moment in the growing pool of blood in the gutter, then gripped. The car screeched away down the main street of Strabane, missing the baby's waving hands by less than six inches.

'Oh, Jesus!' cried Seamus. 'Did you see her? Did you see her?'

'Tough shit,' said Teddy Block, the American, barging his shoulder into him as the car lurched broadside round a corner, heading for the next rendezvous and, hopefully, a fresh vehicle.

Spent cartridges rolled back and forth on the floor, tinkling.

'Trust a Yank!' Hansi, the German, shouted over his shoulder.

'I didn't see her, goddammit you krauthead! I didn't see her till it was too late!'

'Anyway,' Brendan chimed in, hugely enjoying the argument, relishing the drive and images of murder, 'Your man did well enough for a backroom bomber, didn't he?'

'Is one good thing from fuck-up,' agreed the German.

'Two down already,' Brendan chortled, spinning the steering wheel, 'And not even lunch time yet. That's really something! That really is!'

He'd already dismissed the young mother from his mind. After all, he'd thought, the Provisional IRA always issued a statement of regret after a mistake had been made, sometimes even paying the funeral expenses. Everyone, he knew, had heard the movement was generous in such matters.

'Christ!' exploded the American, feeling a sudden dampness, gazing down and seeing Seamus vomit bile all over his new trousers and shoes.

## Chapter 8 August, 1971

'Sod that for a game of Indians!' exclaimed Major Stephen Gates. 'Just come and look at this, Charley.' He was in a foul mood, standing by the large map of Northern Ireland covering one wall of his tiny office at Army HQ in Lisburn.

'What is it, sir?' asked Captain Briance, skirting the clutter of chairs and filing cabinets, to move beside his Senior Ammunition Technical Officer.

'Another abandoned car with those bloody French bullets in it. All .45 calibre and all with the SF headmark. Has to be the same gang of skulls.'

'The ones who got Green?'

'Must be. And look at their route, curse 'em!'

Major Gates ran a finger along the line of coloured pins stuck into the map, each indicating where a recent shooting had occurred and where stolen cars had been found abandoned, littered with spent cartridges of similar French manufacture.

From Strabane where the policemen and the young mother had died so horrifically, the pins traced a course through Coleraine, where the police barracks had been sprayed with bullets, Andersonstown in West Belfast, where a soldier had been killed with a single shot through the head, near the M1 motorway, where the major's personal driver, Corporal Arnold Green, alone in a Land Rover, had been hit by bullets from a passing car, and finally Strabane again, where a fifth stolen car had been found.

'They've gone in a circle, sir.'

'Affirmative, Charley. The cheeky bastards used the same border crossing to go out as they did to come in. We might as well cancel the alert for them. They've long gone.'

The major knew it was simply bad luck that his corporal had been attacked. Incredibly, Arnold Green's bulk had saved him from death despite being struck by nine of the thirteen bullets which had riddled the Land Rover. But Major Gates viewed the incident as a personal insult. He vowed grimly that the score would be settled.

'Strange that,' mused Captain Briance, interrupting the major's dark thoughts.

'What, Charley?'

'Why did they come right over to Belfast? The more travelling, the more chance of being picked up.'

'Who knows?' said the major. 'One of the skulls might have wanted to see his granny.'

'Or deliver something or someone?'

'Could be, but we've missed 'em for sure, and I'm short one helluva driver.'

Major Gates, like other officers, was under extreme pressure in these weeks following the introduction of internment under the Special Powers Act, approved by all political parties in the House of Commons at Westminster. Within a fortnight, thirty people had been killed, bringing the total deaths to more than a hundred since the beginning of the IRA campaign, and the bomb disposal units had been called to their 600th explosion since the start of the year.

And by early September, 1971, the major's problems had increased even further with the discovery of bombs clearly aimed solely at the disposal officers.

The earliest were cardboard shoe boxes with a burned out safety fuse laid on top to suggest that the bomb had failed to explode. In fact, they were still 'live' and even contained anti-handling devices to cause detonation if they were moved at all.

Then came a spate of bombs made out of a sugar and weedkiller mixture packed in salt containers which again had switches on the bottom to set off the devices if they were picked up.

'Hell's teeth, Charley,' the major complained to his assistant on the fourth day of a new bombing offensive, 'They really are having a go this time.'

He sat wearily at his desk, sipping a mug of tea and puffing his usual small cigar, wondering how long his EOD teams could stand the pace. They'd virtually been on round-the-clock duty dealing with the wave of new bombs and Major Gates had hardly left his office, busy coordinating movements and offering advice.

'One good thing, sir, is that we know these brutes are fairly straightforward. At least we're pulling them over like nine-pins,' said Captain Briance smoothing back his dark hair and rubbing his black-rimmed eyes.

'So we can make 'em go bang and save some lives,' the major shrugged. 'But these are the best we've seen so far, Charley. One of their designers must have learned a new trick with anti-handling switches and they're churning 'em out like Model-Ts. Let's hope they get fed up when they realize we're on top.'

The red phone on his desk rang, the direct line from the operations room.

'Here we go again, Charley,' the major sighed, lifting the receiver.

He listened for ten seconds and scribbled an address. 'Right! Wilco!'

Major Gates looked up at his assistant, nodding towards the door. 'On your bike, Charley,' he muttered. 'A package on the steps of the Orange Hall near Lambeg. There's no one left so you'd better buzz along.'

The captain saluted and hurried out of the office, picking up his flak jacket from a chair.

Major Gates smiled wanly to himself. He could hardly remember ever being eager to reach a bomb incident. He supposed he must have been once, years ago.

Still, he admired Charley Briance's spirit. He could guess how near his men were to breaking point. He knew he was. He'd even sneaked a pre-breakfast whiskey that morning 'to wake himself up'.

The major leaned back in his chair and blew a smoke ring, gazing at the small board on the wall, showing the disposition of the EOD units. He shrugged. If there were another emergency he'd have to attend himself and that wouldn't please his wife. They'd arranged to have a rare evening out: dinner at a new restaurant at Holywood called the Pepper Mill. The King Prawns Andalusian were said in the mess to be a special treat.

The major ran a hand through his prematurely grey hair and settled down to study the incident reports piled in his in-tray. Each was a meticulous account of how particular bombs had been defused the previous day. They formed the basis of all the briefing notes carried by the ATOs.

He wasn't aware of time passing until his green phone jangled. It was a friend at 39 Brigade headquarters in Belfast.

'Have you heard?'

'Nothing.'

'An explosion! First flash on our net says one of your boys has bought it, Stephen. Sorry.'

The major stiffened in his chair, clenching his pen. His chest suddenly felt very tight. 'Where?'

'No details yet. Somewhere between you and Belfast, I think. It's a bit confused. It's only just happened this instant.'

'Right. Thanks, chum.'

'And sorry again, Stephen.'

'Right.'

With his free hand he was already dialling the EOD unit in Belfast, at Girdwood Park. They'd just returned safely from an incident outside the Law Courts.

Stephen Gates slapped his palm against his head in anguish. It had to be Charley Briance, his newest ATO, the one with the young wife and baby back in North Yorkshire, the one . . .

The red phone rang. An impersonal map reference from the duty officer in the operations room.

It was Lambeg!

The major grabbed his hat and ran out of his office, down the slightly winding staircase, past startled military policemen, through the front hall and round to the car park.

His temporary driver, a young corporal, was slouched in the Land Rover's driving seat. The orders were swift, shouted and direct. The driver simultaneously started the vehicle, threw a cigarette out of the door, engaged first gear, and switched on the siren and flashing light.

A torrent of thoughts went through Major Gates' mind as they roared through the traffic towards Lambeg. What had gone wrong? How near had Charley been to the explosion? Was it possible he'd been simply badly injured? What had he done wrong, if anything? Not Charley, surely? Not young Charley who'd begged him for a chance to join bomb disposal? Why not himself? Why hadn't he gone to the bomb? Had his briefing been good enough? Was it his fault after all?

Some of the answers were all too clear when the Land Rover shuddered to a halt outside the Orange Hall near Lambeg, less than fifteen minutes after the first alarm.

An infantry patrol stood around the building keeping about thirty of the local people back from the scene. Four marksmen were crouching by the dry stone walls along the road, vigilant against any ambush. A military ambulance, red crosses prominent, waited, engine running, rear doors wide open. Two men in white coats were wrapping something in deeply red blankets.

Major Gates took a deep breath, already knowing the worst, as he jumped out of the Land Rover. He looked towards the young infantry officer who'd started doubling towards him. Then he saw the ladder perched against a chestnut tree by the hall and a medical orderly clambering up gingerly towards one of the higher branches.

'Up there?' muttered Major Gates, half gesturing with his right arm.

'Fraid so, sir,' said the infantry lieutenant.

'Thanks, chum.'

He turned away having seen the medical orderly lift Charley Briance's head off the angle between branch and tree trunk and place it gently in a black plastic bag.

His grief would come later, probably after he'd formally identified the body. It was more important for him at that moment to discover what had gone wrong. The lives of all his other men depended on that. Emotions couldn't be allowed to interfere.

'Any witnesses?' the major asked brusquely.

'Plenty, sir,' answered the lieutenant. 'Try the postman. He used to be in the ranks himself.'

The postman had been the first to raise the alarm. He described the device as a box, standing on its end, about 12 inches high, 7 inches wide and 7 inches deep.

'Certain it was on its end?' queried the major.

'Definite, sir.'

The major nodded, worried. He had never encountered a bomb in Northern Ireland placed in that particular way.

'Well, tell me in your own words what happened.'

'Well, you see, your man arrived in his jeep like a bat out of hell.

Bold as brass, he walked straight up to the thing on the steps of the hall. He crouched by it for a good minute, then he tied a line round it. He took the line out to the wall over there and pulled it. I could see the thing move a foot maybe but nothing happened. Then he walked up to it again, reeling in the line. He seemed a wee bit worried, like something was puzzling him, but not afraid in the least. Brave as a . . .'

'Just go on,' the major urged testily.

'Well, then he took the line out in the opposite direction and gave the thing another pull. It moved again, I could see that from where I was. Then he told the lads to keep us all well back, took up his tool bag and went to the bomb again. I could see him fiddling around deciding what to use. I reckoned he picked a wee fretsaw. He knelt right over it and seemed to start cutting into the top or maybe a corner. That's when it went. A big crump. A sort of bluey-white flash and . . .'

Major Gates cut him short. He'd heard enough. 'Thanks, Postie. I'd like you to give a full statement to the lieutenant here. All right?'

He took one last look at the scene; at the door of the hall, splintered and hanging off its hinges; the small hole in the concrete steps; the shocked people standing by; the pleasant rural setting.

Involuntarily, he glanced up into the green foliage of the chestnut tree, at the darker patch. He wanted to say something to himself, maybe a prayer, but there was nothing except hate. 'Fuck it!' screamed in his head. 'Fuck it and fuck them!' his mind repeated. His fingers scratched against his trousers like the claws of a new-landed crab.

The obscenities didn't help.

Back at headquarters, he managed to calm down. He didn't blame Charley Briance for disobeying orders, for tackling something outside his experience and training. He couldn't even feel bitter about the man who'd designed this latest bomb so cleverly. He'd lulled the RAOC into believing that he was only capable of building one trick into a bomb and then he'd put in two or three. Gates had to accept responsibility for the Corps' first fatality, for the waste of a promising young officer. All his anger was directed against himself.

He quickly flashed a warning to every disposal team to be on the watch for a new type of bomb, not very big, perhaps 15 pounds of explosive, but with an unknown number of anti-disturbance switches.

The orders were simple and to the point: lay sandbags around the bomb to muffle its effect, try to take an X-ray picture, a radiograph, of its innards, and then topple it complete to cause detonation. Until the bomb's secrets were discovered, Major Gates could only wait, pray and stall.

'What's gone wrong, Stephen?' asked the General Officer Commanding, expecting questions from the high politicians.

He was glad that night to shut the front door of his married quarters and infinitely grateful that Elizabeth was an experienced enough Army wife not to bombard him with questions and recriminations about one more cancelled night out.

After a makeshift spaghetti bolognese and a bottle of red wine, they talked quietly about Briance's death and what the RAOC wives could do for his young widow.

Young Mary sat listening, eyes wide, cuddled against her mother on the sofa. The Gates had never hidden the realities of a soldier's life from her. She knew it could have been her own father in the mortuary of Lisburn Hospital.

'If you've heard nothing about me,' Stephen Gates would tell his wife, 'that means it's all right. No news is good news. The bad news is going to come from a guy in uniform knocking on the front door.'

For the next few days, the tension remained high in Army HQ, and in the married officers' estate just across the road, as the EOD units continued to joust with the new bombs.

By the twelfth explosion, Major Gates was convinced that the Provos had an unusually potent bomb-designer.

The Army had obtained radiographs of the devices, now christened 'Lambegs', but they were useless because of the amount of decoy wiring inside the bombs.

But eventually a bomb disposal team pulled over one of the devices without it exploding. Within hours, Major Gates had had an exact replica made, minus the explosive, and that evening carried it home.

Elizabeth Gates took one look at it and smiled. She was well used to her husband's routine. 'Coffee and sandwiches in the kitchen?'

'Affirmative, darling,' he replied, kissing her on the cheek, wondering at her patience after so many years.

'Don't be too long. You've had an awful lot of late nights.'

'As long at it needs. That's all. And I'll clean up the mess. Promise.'

'Just see you do,' she said, touching his arm affectionately.

He cleared off the table and settled down to work while Mary finished her homework and his wife watched television.

This was the challenge he relished, pitting his brains against another's cunning. He was confident of the outcome. He'd always been mechanically minded, forever tinkering with the farm machinery where he'd been brought up. He'd been going to study science at university, but that dream had been ended by compulsory conscription at the end of the Second World War. However, as he'd progressed in the Corps, he'd spent periods studying at the Royal Military College of Science but had never qualified for a degree. But then academic degrees couldn't save anyone who bungled a bomb!

To his dismay, though, the mocked-up 'Lambeg' proved too good for his delicate work with pincers and screwdrivers within intricate circuitry. Time after time, the little light bulb, substituting for the explosive, flashed on, telling him he'd failed, that, if it had been a real bomb, he would have been as dead as Charley Briance.

He got up and walked round the kitchen, gazing at the 'Lambeg' from every angle, peering into its chipboard interior with its tangle of switches, taped over batteries and curling, striped wiring.

Major Gates poured himself a generous measure of his wife's cooking brandy in the pantry and sat down again. There had to be a way, he knew, but he couldn't see it. Whenever he broke one circuit, another would become live.

'Oh, bugger!' he murmured, tempted to give up the task.

He wondered about the man who'd designed the 'Lambeg'. Clearly, he thought, his object was to trick and confuse, to lure the bomb disposal officer into the maze of inter-connected circuits, to his doom, wanting to make him believe that there lay the solution. No, the major decided, lighting his fourth cigar of the evening, there was no way to dismantle the bomb quickly enough to avoid activating the detonator and thus the explosive.

And then a memory came to Gates from his days at grammar school, from a lesson by his science master, Mr Ladd, nicknamed 'Stiffy' because of his artificial leg. There might be one substance which could stop the bomb's relay of switches before they did their deadly work.

He rushed out of the kitchen and began a search of the house, calling excitedly to Elizabeth for help, waking Mary, before he found what he wanted in a small cupboard upstairs and returned to the 'Lambeg'.

Two hours later, he'd succeeded.

Not once but three times, he'd dripped the substance into the 'bomb' and three times he'd managed to disrupt the wiring without the light bulb coming on.

'The brute's dead,' he announced triumphantly to himself. 'We've got to stun it first before killing it. That's the secret.'

# Chapter 9 September, 1971

The Republican Club in Andersonstown in West Belfast was smoky and noisy. A couple of hundred people sat round the tables in the converted warehouse, drinking and talking, flirting and arguing. Others stood three deep at the bar, elbowing, pushing, apologizing in their haste to reach the counter. A local showband beat its way towards exhaustion on a small stage. Men's faces grew redder, women's voices shriller, as the climax of the evening approached.

Unnoticed and unmourned, the music faded away. A roll on the drums drew eyes to the stage. The chatter and clatter died.

A rotund man in a cheap, creased suit heaved himself on to the makeshift stage and stood under the Irish tricolour draped across a romanticized portrait of Michael Collins. He raised his arms for total silence. Some of the drinkers felt for their wallets to check how much cash was left.

'Right, friends and fellow Republicans,' the fat man boomed through the microphone. 'You've had a good time tonight. I've had a good time tonight. But now's the time to remember those who're not having such a good time; those who can't be with us because of British imperialist suppression; those who're suffering in their agony while we've been enjoying ourselves.'

He paused while a silence, heavy with guilt and drink, settled over the club, then his tone of voice rose, more vehement, almost evangelical. 'Yes!' he shouted. 'Yes! This is the time to remember all our boys behind the wire!'

Applause rippled out.

'Yes!' the voice echoed and reverberated. 'This is the time we remember our debt to them and repay it by putting our hands in our pockets!'

The applause grew.

Four blushing girls in their early teens, wearing the berets of Na Fianna Eireann, the IRA's youth organization, trooped on to the stage with trays filled with an assortment of goods.

The MC signalled to the band, wet-shirted behind him. The drums rolled again.

'Now, friends,' he began, lifting a piece of embroidery off the nearest tray, 'This is from Johnny Hughes in Hut 6.'

He held up the scrap of cloth so that the audience could see the words embroidered crudely upon it, green upon white – 'Long Kesh 1971 – The fight goes on.'

Clapping hiccupped and was extinguished by disapproving glances.

'Now, isn't that great, friends?' the fat man continued, undaunted by the interruption. 'What a message! What a momento to take pride of place in your front room!'

Stamping feet boosted clapping hands.

'Yes, a tremendous effort . . .'

The microphone began whistling. He tapped and slapped it back into audibility.

'Tremendous, but before I start the bidding, are there any of Johnny's folks here tonight?'

He shielded his eyes to look into the audience against the glare of the lights.

'Ah, yes!' the fat man announced triumphantly, gripping his fast-sagging trousers, pointing to a pinched-looking woman who'd stood up nervously by a table in the middle of the room.

'Mrs Hughes, isn't it?' he called. 'Johnny's mam, so it is!'

She nodded, haggard face lightening as even more clapping broke out around her.

'Well, that's the sort of brave lady we'll be helping out tonight, friends,' the MC cried, sweat beginning to drop from wobbly dewlaps. 'We'll be buying Johnny's mam a wee something as well as providing comforts for her gallant boy behind the wire!'

He held the cloth above his head, a hand still clutching his trousers.

'Now,' he said, even more triumphantly, 'what am I bid for this fine work done by Johnny Hughes in Hut 6 of Long Kesh concentration camp?'

'A pound,' a voice called.

The fat man frowned menacingly at the bidder.

'And if that's who I think it is,' he warned, 'I'm not appreciating the jape . . . nor will Johnny's friends.'

'Three pounds!' the same voice called again.

'Make it five!' another shouted.

'That's more like it,' the MC encouraged.

'Seven!'

'Eight!'

'Nine!'

The bidding continued briskly until the rectangle of cloth sold for £15.

The fat man's perspiring beam embraced everyone. The standard for the evening had been set.

In quick succession, he auctioned more embroidery, metal ash trays, lumps of wood burned with Republican inscriptions, drawings and paintings, even miniature tricolours made of toilet tissue.

Seamus Aherne, standing close by the bar, drinking Guinness, estimated that the sale raised more than £500.

Certainly enough to provide some small luxuries for the relatives of the IRA internees and the internees themselves.

Other, more discreet collections from factories and shops who preferred not to be bombed out of business, would help bring in his own pay and that of all on full-time IRA active service.

In addition, since internment, Seamus had heard, considerable funds had been raised by Irish-Americans, supposedly to help the Catholics in Northern Ireland who'd been burned and terrorized from their homes. He knew a goodly proportion of this money from the Northern Ireland Aid Committee, NORAID, had already been earmarked for the Provisionals' use. After all, the movement claimed, one of the Provos' main jobs was to protect such unfortunates, forgetting that their unfortunate circumstances might never have arisen but for the IRA's campaign.

'Another one?' the head barman asked, breaking into his thoughts, noticing his near-empty glass.

Seamus nodded. 'Might just as well. I'm reckoning they'll be a few minutes yet.'

'The big men?'

'Aye. Their meetings take longer and longer.'

They smiled at each other, realizing they were among the few who knew that, while the audience enjoyed their evening's entertainment, the senior leaders in the Provisionals' Belfast Command were meeting in a room behind the stage.

The Republican Club was safe enough: in the unlikely event of a raid by the security forces, there was sufficient people around to provide a screen of protest and panic behind which the IRA leaders and activists could escape.

Seamus's nervousness that evening had nothing remotely to do with his personal safety. Since returning to Belfast, his beard had grown thick, his hair long, and he had put on at least two stone through a deliberate diet of Guinness and chip sandwiches.

His confidence in his new appearance had grown so much that he now moved freely in and out of the Catholic enclave with little fear of identification.

'Evening, Mr Aherne.'

Seamus acknowledged the greeting from an IRA Volunteer in his late teens who'd shoved his way to the bar for a round of drinks.

His self-confidence had increased as well, partly due to the deference shown to him by younger Provos, after his role in the Strabane shootings and the success of the 'Lambeg' bombs.

Indeed, his increasing status in the movement had helped ease his mind over those bloody shootings. The policemen's faces returned to haunt him in occasional nightmares, but after all he'd only fired the gun when the two men were beyond all help.

'A drink, Mr Aherne?' the young Volunteer beside him asked.

'Thanks but no thanks. I've business shortly.'

He wanted all his wits for his chat in the backroom with the officer commanding the Belfast Provisionals.

He had a personal matter to raise and was unsure how his CO would react. He was hopeful of success, though, because he'd always got on well with the IRA leader, particularly since that bomb disposal officer had been killed.

Seamus had felt only elation when he'd heard of the RAOC's first fatality. Of course, he'd conceded a tinge of sorrow for the dead officer's family, wishing they could have known that it wasn't a personal attack by him on their loved one. He'd remember what his IRA lecturers had taught during his indoctrination, that the movement didn't attack British soldiers and policemen as people. It merely attacked what they represented.

Thus Seamus could divorce himself, as did his colleagues, from reality. If a member of the security forces died, it didn't matter because he or she was only a cypher of the authority standing between the IRA and its aims. If an innocent civilian died, it was simply bad luck. If a Provisional was killed, then he or she was a martyr to the struggle, a person to be singled out and transformed into myth.

The barman flicked Seamus's glass to gain his attention.

'They say they're ready for you,' he whispered, leaning over the bar as if to polish it. 'You know the way.'

Seamus grinned. 'Wish me luck,' he winked and began threading his way past the crowded tables towards the small room behind the stage. Two young Volunteers stood on guard outside, hands tucked into their jackets. They nodded to Seamus and pushed the door open.

'Come in, son,' invited the CO seated behind the trestle table, shuffling some papers into a brief case. A haze of cigarette smoke hung over him.

'Evening, sir,' said Seamus, standing to attention.

'At ease,' the older man muttered, pointing at a chair. 'Take a seat. I won't be a second.'

Seamus watched as he finished putting away his papers. He wasn't a particularly impressive figure with his glasses and thinning, brushed back hair. But his reputation commanded total respect. He was revered among the Belfast Provos as a man of fairness and integrity who'd never send his men on any mission he wasn't willing to undertake himself. He also had an encyclopaedic knowledge of Belfast from his former occupation as a bookie's runner, taking bets in factories and bars. He was also a person who wouldn't hesitate to be totally ruthless.

'Now, son,' the Provo leader said, putting the briefcase by the side of his chair. 'What d'you want?'

'It's a wee bit personal.'

'So I gathered, but I must tell you we've been talking about your bombs in the meetings.'

'You saw the new designs?'

'They look good.'

'Thanks,' Seamus smiled.

'But the priming?'

'That's the trick!'

'You'll do it on the first one?'

The query sounded rather like a command.

'To make sure?' asked Seamus.

'Well, yes. It'll make the layers more confident when they take the others.'

Seamus thought of the spotty teenagers who had laid his bombs up till then and had to agree. 'I don't mind,' he said, an image flashing into his mind of the two killed outside the headquarters of the BBC at the corner of Bedford Street and Ormeau Avenue.

'Good,' the officer nodded. 'That'll be tomorrow.'

'Yes, I heard from the bomb officer.'

'Fine, that's settled. Now, what's all this personal stuff?'

Seamus hesitated a moment, unsure of how to begin. He took a deep breath. 'Well, sir, when I was away in London . . . '

'That girl?'

Seamus shook his head admiringly.

'Yes, the girl. How did you know?'

'It couldn't have been your landlady, could it? Mrs McGuinness, isn't it? Nice widow-woman so she is but as plain as the nose on my face.' He spoke brusquely, obviously eager to be away to the bar or his bed.

'I spoke to the girl – to Rebecca – two days ago, and she says she's pregnant!'

His commander tilted his chair back, sighed and closed his eyes for a moment. 'Son, son, son,' he murmured. 'Will you boys never . . . ?'

'I didn't mean . . . '

The leader of the Belfast Provisionals gestured despairingly. 'If you were a married man, son, you'd know excuses don't count. If she is, she is. And if you're the one, it's down to you.'

Seamus felt himself reddening around the cheekbones. 'I didn't mean excuses!' he exclaimed. 'I just meant I didn't mean it to happen.'

'Do any of us?'

Seamus shrugged. 'Well, it happened and she says . . . '

'You're not doubting her?' There was a warning note of disapproval in the CO's rasping voice.

'No, no!' Seamus said hastily. 'Of course not. If she is, then it's mine.'

'And so?'

'She wants to come over here.'

'And?'

'Stay with me.'

'And marriage?'

'Who knows?'

The man began to laugh. 'I do, son. I know even if you don't.'

'Can she? Will it be all right?'

The CO stood up, tucked the briefcase under his arm and moved round the table. He clapped Seamus between the shoulder blades.

'I appreciate your asking, son, but I don't want to interfere. You know the dangers as well as I do. Just you do what you think best.'

He looked closely into Seamus's face.

'But remember your work and the oath you swore to the movement. We wouldn't be wanting anything to get in the way of that, would we?'

Seamus understood the implied threat.

'Nothing will, sir,' he promised.

'Grand. Then, son, it's up to you.' He took Seamus by the arm and led him into the club. The two guards followed, flanking them. 'As long as you invite me to the wedding, eh? Now, what about a jar? All the yammering's given me an awful thirst.'

'Just a quick'un,' Seamus replied. 'I've a phone call to make.'

'Break the good news, eh?'

Seamus smiled. 'Something like that.' Ten minutes later, he was in the public call box round the corner from the club, speaking to an overjoyed Rebecca at the massage parlour in Paddington.

'You're sure it's all right?'

'It is. Don't worry. The big man okayed everything.'

'And your landlady, darling?'

'No problem. She's already said you'll be company for her until we find another safe house on our own.'

'You're sure you don't mind?'

'Me? Mind? Don't be silly.'

'I'm not being silly. I just don't want you to feel trapped. You don't, do you?'

'No, of course not,' he said, trying to fill his voice with reassurance.

He did feel slightly enmeshed however. His first reaction to the news of Rebecca's pregnancy had been one of shock. They had spent such a short time together and now, suddenly, there was a child on the way. It seemed an awfully swift way to be landed with such a huge responsibility. But later, after a few reflective drinks, he was rather pleased at the prospect of fatherhood. It would mean marriage, of course, but then the weeks of separation and longing, the letters and phone calls, had made him even more certain that he was in love with Rebecca.

'Are you sure?' she asked again.

'I'm sure I'm sure.'

'When can I come then?'

'Soon as you like.'

'I'll take the boat.'

'Hang on!' Seamus called, hearing a noise outside the phone box. 'What?'

'Hang on!' he repeated, pushing the door open and listening. In the distance, there was the wail of approaching sirens.

'I'll have to go!' he shouted down the phone to Rebecca. 'Write me when you're coming and I'll meet you.'

'What's happening?'

'Nothing to worry about but I'll have to go.'

'But . . .'

'Love you!' he called, slamming down the receiver and darting off down the road towards the club, hoping to raise the alarm.

But when Seamus turned the corner, he saw people already hurrying out the entrance, urged on by two policemen.

'What the hell's on?' he demanded of a man and a woman who almost cannoned into him.

'A bomb!'

'Bomb?' he said incredulously.

'Down the side alley.'

'Oh, Jesus!'

'Must be the Prods.'

'Well, it won't be one of ours, for fucks's sake. That's for sure!'

Within minutes, the club and all the neighbouring shops and houses for a hundred yards around had been evacuated.

Seamus stood as close as he dared to the police cordon, watching the Army bomb disposal team begin its work.

At that distance, he could barely distinguish the figures of the Ammunition Technical Officer and his assistant moving cautiously in and out of the pools of light thrown down from the street lamps, going back and forth to the bomb with equipment. He thought he saw one of them carrying a long, cylindrical object, probably the radiograph machine for photographing the device's innards.

From the care and time they were taking, Seamus reckoned that they must be dealing with a particularly well-made and dangerous bomb.

After almost an hour, a whistle shrilled its warning to the silent and deserted street. The ATO scurried back to the protection of a Saracen personnel carrier, unwinding wire as he ran. Police and a few onlookers like Seamus moved back even further, seeking what cover they could.

Crack!!! The sound echoed along the street and round the buildings. A cloud of dust puffed out from the alley where the bomb's mechanism had been shattered by the tiny explosive charge laid by the ATO.

The emergency was over.

Policemen muttered into their radios and then started to wave people back to their homes.

Five minutes later, traffic was moving along the street as if nothing had ever happened.

'I wonder who the fuck designed that one?' Seamus muttered to himself, scratching his beard and heading off towards his lodgings.

Until now, the Protestant bombs had been even less sophisticated than the IRA's. They must have discovered a new man with enough talent to worry the Army.

The bomb designer's identity was also worrying Staff-Sergeant Warren Palmer of the RAOC as he talked to Army HQ from his office in Girdwood Barracks. 'Never seen one like it out here before, sir,' he told Major Stephen Gates.

'Sure, Palmer?'

'Not out here, no. It was almost like the ones we handled in training.'

'Really?'

'Whoever put it together knew what they were doing. A bit of a craftsman with a neat line in soldering. I'd swear he'd had professional training. And, if I didn't know better, I'd swear I'd seen his work somewhere before.'

'But it was straightforward? You had no problems?'

'No, not really. I just took my time and followed the book of words.'

'Well done! Well, have a quiet night.'

'Sir.'

In his office, Major Gates slumped back in his chair, smoking a cigar and sipping a large whiskey. It had been a gamble, an awful gamble, but it had seemed to work.

He rubbed his chin and smiled when he saw the black smear of boot polish on his fingers. He'd have to wash before going home to Elizabeth. He was glad he had arranged the roster so that young Palmer had been on duty to deal with the bomb. Anyone more experienced might have recognized his handiwork from the bombs he had made for training purposes back in England. And Major Gates had spent a great deal of time on the bomb for the Republican Club.

It had taken him more than two days to build it after that phone call from the secret Army intelligence unit, which wasn't supposed to exist, and didn't on paper.

He had been extremely careful to ensure that the device had been within Palmer's capabilities yet difficult enough to force him to work carefully and provide the time needed for the intelligence mission inside the Republican Club.

The major had even insisted on laying the bomb himself so that

Palmer would face precisely what his senior officer had planned for him.

Earlier that evening, as dusk turned to darkness, Major Gates had been driven in an unmarked Army car along the M1 motorway leading into the heart of Belfast.

He'd hunched low in the back seat, feeling a trifle ridiculous with his blackened face, black beret covering grey hair, and black sweater, trousers, socks and plimsols.

The men from Intelligence had even provided a knife with a black lacquered blade. Major Gates had refused the offer of a gun. He reasoned that the entire mission was doomed anyway if he ran into a shooting match on his way to the club. The whole district would be alerted and on guard.

'Good luck,' his driver muttered, allowing the major out of the vehicle just by the motorway intersection at Kennedy Way on the edge of the Andersonstown district.

'Just you be here, chum, when I get back,' Major Gates had replied, starting over the rough ground beside the motorway, the bomb tucked safely in his rucksack, knife clenched between his teeth.

Once he'd started, he had no time to feel any nervous tremors. He tried to skirt as many houses as possible by ducking down alleys, but eventually, he was forced to make his way through back gardens, weaving in and out of their gates and clambering over wooden and wire fences.

His worse moment had been when he'd trodden on a pair of copulating cats. Their screeches of anguish had brought a woman to her window, bawling for quiet. As she'd pulled the curtain to see out, a square of light had jutted across her small garden, catching the major in midstride. He'd frozen still, quivering inwardly, praying that he wasn't silhouetted.

'Just like a ruddy oversized plastic gnome,' he'd murmured grimly to himself when, after a seeming eternity, the cats had vanished into the bushes and the woman had closed her curtains again.

For the last hundred yards, the major had taken his directions from the lights and music flooding out of the club. To his surprise and relief, the entrance to the building had been deserted except for a courting couple who were too busy with each other to notice the figure slipping into the alley beside the club.

It had taken only a few seconds to prime the bomb and lift it from the rucksack before the major was on his way back towards the motorway.

The further he moved from the club, the more he abandoned his previous caution. Finally, he'd run at full pelt to the waiting car, tumbling gratefully and breathlessly into it.

'Move it, chum,' he'd called to the driver.

The car sped away.

'Something scare you?' the driver'd asked casually.

'Just myself,' Major Gates had panted.

The bomb had been discovered and the alarm raised before he'd reached his office. Then the worst part of the operation began for Major Gates, the waiting to hear that his EOD unit had been successful in defusing it. He'd had to resist the temptation to wash and change quickly in order to sit in the operations room and monitor radio transmissions from his men.

Anyway, that would have been a change from his normal routine and policy of leaving them well alone unless they requested advice and help. And the men from Intelligence had emphasized that everything should appear normal. Not only should those around the Republican Club believe it was a genuine, though routine, bomb disposal operation, the Army headquarters staff should also have no suspicions to the contrary. No one who didn't already know was to learn that it had, in fact, been a diversionary action to empty the club and allow the intelligence unit free access. Thus the call from Staff-Sergeant Palmer had eased the major's mind considerably.

He poured himself another drink from the bottle in the filing cabinet, smiling to himself, imagining the row if any hint of the secret operation should ever leak out. His career would be finished for certain and he didn't fancy life as a civilian just yet, life in the unordered, disorganized world outside where few knew their place and most were forever dissatisfied, not understanding their proper role in society.

That was one of the attractions of service life, he'd always thought, beginning to relax now. It was the certainty of it all. Sergeants saluted officers and officers saluted generals. The salutes went up, the orders went down. And if you did what you should do to the best of your ability, then there was a real chance of a contented mind.

The green phone on his desk rang.

'SATO,' he replied unhurriedly.

'Thanks for the help, old boy,' said the voice at the other end. It was from the unit that didn't exist.

'Everything go well?'

'Fine. And your chap at the sharp end?'

'He coped.'

'Good.'

'Enough time to do all you wanted?'

'Plenty. If any of the boyos so much as farts, we'll have him on tape. That particular watering hole is well and truly bugged.'

## Chapter 10 September, 1971

It was the middle of the afternoon and life in the hotel was as it usually was at this time of day.

In his eighth floor suite the general manager, Bryan Green, was dozing on his bed, gathering his strength for the evening's drinking, eating, greeting and placating, an ordeal which would last until the early hours.

Two floors below, in a bedroom, a middle aged London businessman who'd drunk too much was desperately trying to achieve an erection while his thin blonde companion helped with growing despair, worried about collecting her children from school.

In the small alcove behind the cocktail bar, the barman counted his tips and considered a customer's complaint that he was putting too much ice into his drinks instead of spirits.

On the same floor, the chef was in his office, locked in a heated conversation over the phone. It concerned a sub-standard side of beef and the chef's commission from that particular supplier.

In the reception area on the ground floor, the hall porter announced that he was away for the afternoon newspapers, and set off for the betting shop up the road.

Behind the desk in the corner, the duty receptionist was telling the switchboard girl about her encounter with a journalist the previous night and her post-coital promise to provide him with an inflated bill for his expenses sheet.

It was an entirely unremarkable mid-afternoon in the hotel until the revolving glass doors began to swish round violently and noisily.

'Everyone stand with their hands in the air!' two voices bawled before the staff and half a dozen guests in the reception area could react.

Two men in athletes' tracksuits, balaclava helmets covering faces, stood there, sub-machine guns at their hips. One moved a pace at a time towards the reception desk. The other stayed by the doors, covering the lifts and the curved stairway leading to the first floor.

The switchboard girl, dark haired and pretty, began screaming hysterically as the gunman advanced. Slowly her eyes, wide and bulging, were fixed on his weapon. Her hands closed and opened convulsively over her breasts.

'Shut your gob!' the gunman shouted but her screaming grew louder, shrilling higher and higher, until her eyeballs suddenly rolled upwards and she slid untidily to the floor in a faint.

'Thank fuck for that!' the gunman by the revolving doors exclaimed moving aside to allow two more hooded men through the entrance. Between them they carried a wooden box about two feet wide and eighteen inches high.

'Where?' muttered one to his fatter companion.

Seamus Aherne looked quickly around the lobby, sweating profusely. 'Over there,' he said, nodding towards the two glass phone booths at the end of the lobby furthest from the door to the coffee shop and bar. The bomb would be more difficult to deal with if laid in a confined space.

'Gently,' he urged as they began lowering the box on to the brown and cream patterned carpet.

He slid his right hand underneath, feeling for the tiny, protruding metal rod. He pushed it in and then held a coin over it while the box was finally laid on the floor. The device was primed.

Seamus stood back to check that the bomb was pushed tightly into the corner of the phone booth. He looked at the wording, now revealed, on the wooden casing. He smiled under his mask, wondering if his instructor, 'Captain Jan', would have approved of his attempt at psychological warfare.

On the one side, he'd daubed in red paint, 'Ha-Ha-Ha'; down the front 'Bomb'; and on the other visible side, 'Tee-Hee-Hee'.

Yes, he decided, it was definitely a message to worry any bomb disposal officer. The words would be a challenge to him, perhaps even unnerving him. At least, that was what 'Captain Jan' had taught. The officer would certainly be uneasy from the very start and that was half the battle.

Buzz . . . zzz . . . zzz . . . zzz!

The insistent noise was growing louder as more incoming telephone calls stacked up on the unmanned switchboard.

'Come on!' Seamus shouted. 'It's set. We're away.'

The duty receptionist began crying hysterically, thinking the bomb would explode in a few seconds.

'You've plenty of time to get out,' Seamus called, almost at the door, wanting to give the impression that the bomb contained a timing device.

But the screaming became even more piercing, swelled by shrieks of fear from a middle-aged American woman at the foot of the hotel staircase.

The noise unnerved the gunman by the reception desk. He turned to run out of the hotel and dashed straight into one of the floor-to-ceiling panes of glass by the entrance.

'Fuckin' hell!' he swore, bouncing back off the thick glass. He fell to his knees, half-stunned. His sub-machine gun clattered to the carpet.

A hotel guest, standing by a jewellery display counter, started to lower his hands and took a tentative step towards the weapon.

Seamus saw the movement from the corner of his eye. 'Don't move!' he bellowed. 'Don't anyone move!'

The second gunman swung the barrel of his weapon round to the guest who, in that split-second, thought better of his impulse.

The injured IRA man, nose bleeding, scrabbled for his gun, cursing loudly, then staggered to his feet.

Grabbing him by the shoulder, Seamus pushed him through the revolving doors and into the stolen car waiting outside, with its engine racing.

Two patrolling policemen, about a hundred yards up the road, spotted the hooded men bundling into the car. They started to run, barging aside shoppers, unslinging their sub-machine guns.

But by the time they were anywhere near firing range, the vehicle was in the heavy traffic of central Belfast heading for the comparative safety of the nearest Catholic enclave, the Falls Road. There, another car would be waiting.

'Done it!' Seamus exclaimed triumphantly, pulling off the suffocatingly warm hood.

'Jesus, my ears are still ringing with all those caterwauling women,' one of the IRA Volunteers complained.

'And that bloody switchboard! What a fucking racket!' said another.

'It'll be nothing to the noise when that bomb blows,' Seamus added. His hands were trembling now the raid was over.

Behind them, the Provisional IRA's bomb gang had left scenes of total confusion and panic.

The two RUC officers were trying to push through the revolving doors into the hotel while frightened guests and staff jammed into the doors attempting to leave.

The switchboard continued to buzz away. The duty receptionist's screams had subsided to sobs but still she stood behind the desk, transfixed with fear, one hand over her mouth, the other pointing, wavering, at the large wooden box in the telephone booth nearest to her.

Once inside, the policemen saw the words on the box and moved swiftly. One ran behind the desk, slapped the receptionist back to her senses and pushed her towards the door, before lifting up the telephonist, now moaning, and carrying her out.

The other radioed his operations room, then picked up the Tannoy microphone lying on the switchboard.

'This is a police emergency,' he broadcast, trying to sound calmer than he felt. 'Please evacuate the building. This is an emergency. Please evacuate the hotel immediately.'

Lights began flicking above both lifts bringing down chambermaids from the upper floors. Staff in white jackets ran down the staircase from the first floor.

The policeman saw the red button on the wall by the switchboard with a small hammer hanging below its glass case. With a swift jab, he smashed the case and pushed the button. Bells clanged their urgent, deafening warning throughout the hotel.

The general manager in his suite stirred and turned over restlessly, thinking for a moment he was in a dream. A second or so later, he jerked upright, fully awake. 'Christ!' he exclaimed and reached for the phone at his bedside. The RUC men looked at the mass of lights, switches and plugs on the switchboard, shrugged helplessly and hurried out of the hotel to join an Army patrol which had just arrived.

In his room, the London businessman struggled into his clothes. He cursed the noise, his impotence, his wasted money and the threat of publicity if photographers were in the neighbourhood. The woman from the escort agency slipped her dress over her head and stuffed her underclothes and tights into her handbag. It wasn't the first time she'd had to leave a hotel room at a moment's notice.

Major Gates heard the news of the bomb before the last of the staff had clattered down the outside fire escapes.

'Right – on my way!' he barked down the phone to the operations room, realizing that, for once, he'd have to abandon his policy of not interfering with his men. The tower of shining glass was so prestigious a target that the bomb demanded his presence.

His driver, Corporal Hosken, got him to the hotel just after five o'clock, travelling the last hundred yards down a deserted road, cordoned off and evacuated by the police. The bomb disposal team had already set up a temporary command position in a bar opposite the hotel.

'Well, what's the bad news?' the major asked the two RAOC captains, Alan Campbell and Derek Madeley.

'You can see it from here, sir,' said Campbell, handing him a pair of high-powered binoculars.

They briefed him on how the bomb had been laid, mentioning the remark made by one of the bombers that there was time to evacuate the building.

'Time means timer, eh?' grunted Major Gates.

'Could be!'

'We'll see about that. Everyone out anyway?'

'Everyone.'

Major Gates peered through the binoculars, focusing on the box in the phone booth. He smiled grimly when he saw the lettering.

'Cheeky sod!' he murmured. 'How much do you think?'

'Pretty big, maybe 15 pounds, enough to blow the lobby and the windows,' said Madeley.

'I'll buy that,' the major nodded. 'Thank the Lord, the place's build round the lift shaft. Chummy's put his package too far away from that to do any structural damage.'

'Shall we just let it cook, sir?'

'Nope. We'll have the brute out without cracking a single pane, that's what we'll do. And then we'll kill it in full view. Chummy's thrown down the gauntlet. He's challenging us. So we'll show him what's what.'

The major checked the lay-out once more. He pointed to the bar next to the reception area.

'Call up the sappers,' he ordered. 'We'll have sandbags between that bar and the bomb. Then we can work from there, from inside, and even move the guests back in there. At the worst, they'll have sand in their coffee if it blows. Okay?'

The three officers in their work clothes of camouflaged fatigues, sweaters and combat jackets, walked out into the road, one of Belfast's main thoroughfares. The major looked at the surrounding buildings, noting that four television crews had set up their equipment in the first floor windows of a bar along the street.

He strode over and called up to one of the cameramen.

'If you boys want to stay there, make sure none of my chaps faces are on film, right?'

'Fine with us, sir,' the cameraman replied.

'I'll let you know when anything's about to happen but settle down for a long wait.'

'Understood. Thanks . . . and good luck!'

The major waved casually, rejoining his officers.

'We've all the equipment?'

'Everything.'

'Right. Alan, you sort out the radiograph and, Derek, you brief the sappers. I'll have a sniff round the brute.'

Major Gates pushed through the revolving doors and entered the deserted hotel. He felt suddenly cold and lonely. He always did when approaching a bomb. It was the moment of truth, the last few steps up to something unknown which contained the power to rend limb from limb to totally obliterate in one second of awful heat and energy.

Someone had asked him once if, in those moments, he thought about the family or the insurance or whether the gas bill had been paid.

He had replied that he thought of nothing except the bomb in front of him. Every time it was the same, the sense of walking down a narrowing, darkening tunnel with only the bomb at the end. All else was outside his vision and hearing.

The major squatted outside the phone booth, his eyes searching for any hidden wires. There were none.

He dismissed the words painted on the box. He knew they were meant as a distraction. Instead, he noted the location of the screw holes, the flush fitting of the sides, the dimensions.

He listened, head pressed almost to the bomb, his absolute concentration filtering out the interminable buzzing from the switchboard and the clanging of the fire bells.

Was there a timing device in the bomb? It was a possibility. And that meant it would explode at any second whatever he did. That was one of the risks.

There were no sounds of whirring or ticking from the box. He doubted it contained a timing device. The IRA had already lost too many men through timers going wrong. He reasoned that this bomb was something a little special because of the target. It was probably laid by one of the Provisional's more experienced units who wouldn't have taken risks with their lives.

Major Gates sat back on his heels, teeth nibbling his lower lip, thinking. 'Yup,' he declared to himself and stood up. He began the long walk back out of the lobby, all ten yards of it, terribly conscious of the menace behind him.

But it wasn't until he was going through the revolving doors that he felt any fear. Then, it was so strong, so embracing, that his skin shivered under his uniform. Again, that was something that always happened.

'Sappers here?' he asked Captain Madeley rhetorically, seeing the Royal Engineers already unloading sandbags from their lorry and into the side door of the hotel.

'Just arrived, sir.'

'Let's get on then.'

He sketched the bomb on a pad, illustrating its main details.

'It's going to be hellish to get a picture because the brute's right against the metal of the phone box but we'll have to try.'

'Who d'you want in first then?' asked Campbell.

'You and me, Alan, but not till the sandbags are up. Then Derek can watch us from there in case we make a cock-up.'

'Do we need lights?'

'Better alert them but there seems plenty available in the lobby. Should be enough for the closest work.'

Major Gates paused, scratching his forehead.

'And that reminds me; all those glass windows. We're not only sitting ducks for a sniper but we'll be giving free bomb disposal lessons for anyone who cares to watch.'

'Screens then?'

'Yes, whistle up the manager and we'll borrow some of his sheets.'

The hotel's general manager Bryan Green and Major Gates were old acquaintances. They had shared an interest in the hotel's security since its opening. They both had a taste for good champagne and cigars. And they were both Freemasons.

Captain Madeley, a rather gauche officer unversed in most things except his work, shepherded the hotel executive over from the far side of the road.

As always, Bryan Green looked dapper with his pomaded hair and immaculate morning suit. Somehow, however, his rasping Belfast accent clashed incongruously with his appearance. The major, perhaps snobbishly, always expected this stoutish man to speak with an upper class English voice. Yet, he liked him immensely, respecting his courage and professionalism.

'Bryan, my dear chap,' he greeted him, offering the masonic handshake, pressure on the second finger joint. 'What did I tell you?'

'What, Stephen?'

'When we talked before about security?'

'You said there wasn't much to do except the best we can.'

'Affirmative, old chum. And that's what we're going to do with your help. The very best we can.'

He outlined his plan and, with an encouraging pat, sent Bryan Green scurrying into the hotel through the bar entrance to gather some of the establishment's largest bedlinen.

'Now,' he told his two captains, rubbing his hands eagerly, 'When the glass is covered and the sandbags in place, we can really get down to it.'

After the large white sheets had been securely taped over the outside of the windows, Gates and Captain Campbell moved into the hotel with the radiograph machine.

'This is going to be the very devil, Alan,' the major remarked as they tried to maoeuvre the cylinder into the small phone booth.

They tilted it this way and that, stood it upright, placed it flat on the floor, taking exposures all the time, ignoring safety precautions against radiation. Eventually, after half an hour, with sweat dripping from their brows, they'd covered the bomb from every possible angle.

By the time the two officers reached the fresh air again, their heads were splitting with concentration and all the buzzing and clanging inside the lobby.

The X-ray negatives were rushed to the radiology department at the Royal Victoria Hospital for developing.

Major Gates looked at his watch. The time was nearly seven o'clock. 'Let's have a break, chaps,' he said, longing for a cigar. They sat in the sandbagged bar, drinking coffee and smoking, until the developed plates arrived back from the hospital.

'Jesus H. Christ!' the major murmured as he began studying them. 'Someone's been putting in overtime! Look at this!'

At first, all that the bomb disposal officers could see was a jumble of wires, switches and taped-over batteries with sticks of explosive fixed to the bottom of the box, lying on a metal plate. Then, perusing other X-ray plates, they began to trace the various circuits inside the box.

'At least six, possibly seven,' the major concluded ruefully. 'Some of them are dummies, of course, but which?'

'Can we cut into it, do you think, sir?' asked Alan Campbell.

'Possible. Look there and there. He's put clips on the joints at both sides with wives to the batteries. They'll either trip if we go in through the sides or else they're total decoys inviting us to go in through the top or the front where the real ambush is.'

'I can't see any wires either to the top or the front.'

'Neither can I. I think Chummy wants us to use the front door to get at the innards and when we do the circuit'll trip. So we'll go in at the top.'

'Steam it, perhaps?' Captain Madeley said tentatively, suggesting the use of high-pressure steam to dissolve the explosive.

The major shook his head.

'Wouldn't be able to get at it. That's why he's used the metal plate under the stuff. He knows that trick well enough. No, the only good thing about this is that I can't see any sort of timer.'

'Neither can I, sir.'

'He's taped everything but they all look like simple batteries to me. No, he wants us to think it's on a timer so we'll get a move on and make a boo-hoo. This bomb's meant to bring the hotel and the whole area to a standstill. It'll only blow when you try to move it or kill it. So we'll assume there's no hurry then?'

'Affirmative, sir,' his Ammunition Technical Officers chorussed.

'You know,' the major said reflectively, rubbing his tired eyes, 'I reckon this brute's just a tarted-up "Lambeg". If we pull it over or move it, it'll go. Likewise, if we cut into the sides or front. I reckon Chummy's simply thrown in a couple more switches and a helluva lot of wire to confuse us. Otherwise, it's fairly plain sailing.'

'Could be.'

'We'll know soon enough anyway.'

'Before we start, sir, can't we do something about the bloody noise? My head's throbbing like a tom-tom.'

'You're right. So's mine . . . Bryan!' He called the manager over to the table. 'Bryan,' he said, gesturing at the empty coffee cups and the stubbed-out cigars. 'Your hospitality is appreciated. So were the sheets for the windows. But, old chum, if you want us to go on, you'll have to stop that infernal din in the lobby. Can you fix it?'

'It's by the switchboard.'

'You're not going through that lobby, friend. That's all we need. Mr Green and his hotel going kerboom at one and the same time!'

'I can reach the switches through the back, through the luggage store.'

'Then do so, Bryan, if you can. Derek, go with him.'

The two set off into the labyrinthine corridors behind the hotel's shiny façade.

'Where's the equipment, Alan?' the major asked, squinting through the smoke of a second free cigar.

'In the bag, sir.'

Suddenly instead of the cacophony of buzzes and clangs, sweet music from a violin orchestra flooded the building.

'That's better,' laughed Major Gates. 'Music to defuse by!'

Bryan Green hurried sheepishly back into the bar. 'I pulled every switch I could, Stephen,' he explained, 'And the Muzack just seemed to come on. I couldn't switch it off.'

'Don't worry,' the major replied, standing up from the table and waltzing a few steps on the carpet as if he'd a partner in his arms. 'As long as it doesn't play the "Dead March" or "The Wearing of the Green"!'

His hawk-nosed face lost its forced smile. The lines around his mouth and chin set deep once more.

Captain Campbell recognized the signs and walked over to the sandbags laid three deep from the ceiling to floor, blocking the bar off from the reception lobby.

He picked up the bag of equipment and the neck-radios they would wear so Derek Madeley could hear every word and sound while they tackled the bomb. If anything went wrong, at least one of them would have an idea of what might have happened.

They walked out into the fresh air again, day turning to dusk, and back into the hotel through the revolving doors.

'Well, at least no one's pinched it yet,' Alan Campbell joked as they approached the bomb again behind the cover of the white sheets.

The major's eyes flicked up at the clock above the reception desk. It was nearly ten minutes past eight. He knew the night's work had barely started.

They laid out their tools on the floor by the phone booth, checking everything was in place.

'This one, d'you think?' asked the major picking up an extremely fine hand drill and bit.

'Will the liquid get through?'

'Should do, Alan. Let's try anyway.'

Major Gates knelt before the box as if in prayer to the God of bomb disposal, hands clasped around the drill. He took one deep breath and lowered the tool to the surface.

The specially hardened bit cut easily into the chipboard of the box precisely at the point calculated by the major from the radiographic plates. He drilled slowly, hardly exerting any pressure, continually blowing away the shavings so that none might drop down inside. After two minutes' careful work, the drill met no resistance. The hole was made.

The major left the bit in the hole for a second. He took another deep breath. If the bomb contained a light-sensitive switch, then this next second would be when it triggered the bomb. He lifted the drill slowly and permitted himself a quiet smile. The bomb had been penetrated.

He looked back over his shoulder and winked at Captain Campbell.

Next, the major leaned even further over the bomb, shining a slim, powerful torch into its workings. He could just see two of the soldered connections amid the maze of green and white striped wire.

Like a surgeon in an operating theatre, he held out his right hand and Alan Campbell placed a thin glass pipette in his palm, all the time talking quietly into his neck-radio, relaying each of the major's moves.

Major Gates slid the glass tube into the opening, released thumb over the top and allowed six drops of liquid to fall into the box, hopefully on to some of the electrical connections.

He waited a few seconds before using the torch again, right eye pressed nearly to the bomb casing.

'That's two knocked out at least,' he said quietly, straightening up, sighing, rubbing the aching muscles in the small of his back.

He shuffled round on his knees. Captain Campbell held a shadowy radiograph plate up to the light of the lobby's false chandeliers while they both checked the position of the other contacts and switches.

Three more times, the major drilled holes into the casing and dripped through the chemical whose bomb disrupting powers he'd proved in his kitchen experiments.

He studied the radiograph plates constantly as he worked, always checking the work with Alan Campbell.

'Just there,' the major murmured, another drop of liquid slithering into the bomb's innards. 'That's right.'

'Watch it, sir. That wire's a bit fine.'

'Is that enough? Should be.'

'I reckon that's okay, sir.'

'Let's wait a mo. We're in no hurry.'

'That should do it.'

'Let's look at that plate again, Alan.'

'This one?'

'Uh,-huh. Now here's that other wire to the detonator. There's the connection.'

A few more drips fell through the hole in the casing, effectively jamming the bomb's electrical circuits.

'Right. Got it.'

'I think that's the lot, sir.'

The major hadn't been conscious of the passing minutes and hours until he eased himself back out of the phone booth.

He brushed a hand wearily through his grey hair, feeling the strands sticky with sweat from his scalp.

The clock above the reception desk showed it was nearly fifteen minutes past ten o'clock.

'It's stunned, Alan,' Major Gates muttered, smiling lop-sidedly at his ATO. 'Better tell Derek to organize the pulling line.'

Captain Campbell spoke briefly into his radio.

'He's already got it prepared and made a plan.'

'Good man. Let's have a smoke.'

The major stood up and stretched, pulling the front of his trousers away from the sweat-stickiness of his crotch and thighs.

'And so ends the second act,' he murmured, glancing down at the bomb.

There was an acute sense of expectancy when the two officers walked back into the bar next door. Bryan Green hovered near them, unsure, with two steaming cups of coffee.

The major waved him over.

'You can bring your guests back in here, chum,' he said, taking a cup. 'Got any grub for them?'

'Toasted sandwiches?'

'Why not, as long as you don't charge them? And make mine a ham and cheese, eh?'

'Can I pull it out, sir?' asked Captain Madeley anxiously. 'I've hardly done anything all evening.'

'All yours, Derek. Through the luggage door, down the ramp and into the car park. Have the sappers build a sangar there and we'll finally kill the brute once it's inside.'

The captain turned away, enthusiastic.

'And, Derek,' the major added, 'Better put some sand down outside to help it move. I don't want the bastard tipping over. It's safe when it's upright but I won't give a five-year guarantee in any other position. Let's not lose the game now, eh?' He beckoned to Bryan Green. 'Fix me a line out on the receptionist's phone, will you?'

Back in the lobby, the pulling operation had begun. Inch by inch, the bomb, secured by a strong nylon cord, was moving across the carpet towards the luggage door which was wedged open by a single sandbag.

After every six inches or so, Captain Madeley, his normally puce features growing redder, crawled along the carpet to check the box's progress.

Once the bomb was outside on the ramp leading to the car park, Major Gates walked jauntily over to examine the phone booth. It was exactly as he'd thought. He picked up the coin on the carpet, the piece of metal holding in the anti-disturbance switch, and wrapped it carefully in his handkerchief in case it might yield some finger-prints.

Smiling to himself, he walked over to the reception desk, jumped up to sit on the counter, then dialled the operations room at Army headquarters.

'Where are you, Stephen?' asked the major on duty, surprised at the call. 'I can hear music your end.'

'I'm in the hotel. About twenty feet from the bomb. It's just leaving by the front door without paying its bill.'

'God! Be careful!'

'Don't worry. Simply wanted to let you know we're winning. Anything else happening?'

'Quiet as the proverbial, old boy.'

'Good. I'll see you later then, chum.'

As he walked outside to watch the bomb's movement, the Muzak tape changed to the melody of 'Moonlight Becomes You.'

'Like hell it does!' he murmured.

The major tossed back his head and sucked in the night air, gazing momentarily at the stars and their shredding cloud cover.

He sensed a desperate weariness around him and within himself. His Explosive Ordnance Disposal teams were near the limit of their endurance.

By now, the bomb was sliding over grains of yellow sand, approaching the beehive of sandbags, the sangar, built in the car park by the Royal Engineers.

The major and Captain Campbell, munching sandwiches, drew up their final plans, checking again and again the radiographic plates.

'First charge here, Alan?' asked Major Gates pointing to a cross on the diagram he'd drawn on the back of a bar menu.

'Should open it at the very least, sir.'

'And if it blows, well, it's in the sangar.'

'Should save the windows.'

'I bloody well hope so. I'm getting a little obsessional about them.'

They grinned at each other, relishing a conspiratorial feeling about their expertise and shared danger this long evening.

'Half an ounce?'

'No more.'

'Can I lay it, sir? I don't reckon I've earned my corn so far.'

'Don't be silly!' the major protested, secretly pleased at the captain's modesty. 'Of course you have and of course you can!'

Captain Campbell positioned his tiny, wedge-shaped lump of explosive against a particular joint in the bomb casing once the box slithered into the protective shield of sandbags.

He walked unhurriedly back to the new command position behind an armoured personnel carrier, carefully laying down the wire connecting his detonator to the electrical circuits.

'When you're ready, sir,' he said.

Major Gates shook his head. 'Wait one, Alan.'

He stepped into the road, cupped his hands and shouted up at the windows occupied by the television crews. The major wanted the triumph of the Royal Army Ordnance Corps to be properly recorded.

'Count down starts at five,' he called. 'Five . . . four . . . three . . . two . . . one . . . '

Alan Campbell twisted the key which connected the circuits.

Kerr--rr--ack!

The explosion, red and angry, leapt out of the half-dark, silhouetted against the steady yellow lights of the hotel.

Dust blew up into the strengthening breeze, wafted away and settled.

'Come on!' the major said, gesturing his two captains forward.

In the light of the major's torch, they saw that the bomb casing was virtually shattered, its front and back hanging on by mere splinters of wood. Inside, switches and batteries swung gently, torn from their connections.

'Let's have another go,' urged Major Gates, grinning broadly, almost totally satisfied. 'We'll have a total victory!'

Captain Madeley, somewhat nervous, laid the second small

charge inside the far corner of the casing. His walk back to the firing position betrayed quickening anxiety.

He looked, kneeling, at the major for permission to turn the key.

'Not yet,' said the major.

In the darkness, he'd sensed people beginning to move across the road, presumably thinking that the bomb was safe after the first dismantling charge.

'Keep clear,' he shouted. 'Keep well clear. There's another charge. Five . . . four . . . four . . . three . . . two . . . one . . .'

The flash and crack of the explosion burst into the night.

Major Gates walked to the bomb alone this time, torchlight bobbing on the tarmac of the car park.

The breeze from the Black Mountain brooding invisibly above Belfast's sprawl grew into a sharp wind. Its gusts whirled down side streets, tinkling plastic cups and empty Chinese takeaway containers along the gutters.

Now, the loneliness was to be savoured, a time for the inner communion between hunter and prey after a long stalk and successful kill.

The inside of the bomb was completely exposed, broken wires flapping harmlessly, batteries hanging off threads of black tape.

The major shone the torch on his watch. It was thirty minutes past midnight and the bomb was dead.

The major walked slowly back to his men, kicking at fragments. He saw their eyes shining in the hotel's light.

Suddenly, six feet from them, he smiled broadly and ran forward to shake their hands.

'We stunned the brute,' he cried exultantly. 'We carted it out and now we've shot it! We've won!'

They hugged each other without any self-consciousness and slapped shoulders and backs before the major called a halt. 'Right, chaps,' he said, perhaps a trifle curtly, 'Pick up the pieces and I want your reports on the desk in the morning.'

He left his men to gather up the remains of the bomb, ready for forensic examination, and drove down the road to Lisburn, blue light flashing on the roof of the Land Rover.

Just before one o'clock in the morning, he crept up the staircase and to his bedroom, determined not to wake Elizabeth.

But, as always, she seemed to sense his presence even in sleep.

'There's a message for you,' she grunted, lifting her head off the pillow, pointing towards the phone by his side of the bed.

He picked up the piece of paper and read the Belfast telephone number scrawled upon it by the light of the night-bulb on the landing.

'I'll call from downstairs.'

'It doesn't matter,' Elizabeth replied, smiling blearily at him and scratching her head. 'I'm awake now.'

The major began dialling the number.

'How did it go, darling?' his wife asked.

'We won, hands down.'

'I can see that.'

'Ssshhh!'

The number rang and was answered within seconds. Major Gates recognized the voice immediately.

'You called?' he said shortly.

'Ah, SATO. Thanks for ringing back after such a busy night.'

'It's late.'

'Is it? Of course it is. Sorry,' said the man from the intelligence unit which didn't exist, sounding indecently wide-awake. 'Anyway, old man, I hear hearty congratulations are in order.'

'Thanks, old man,' the major replied with some irony. 'But what do you want at this hour?'

'Sorry . . . but you did say to give you a bell if we heard anything.'

'And?'

'Your fans were getting a blow-by-blow account while you and your boys were hard at it . . .'

'And?'

'They were more than disappointed with the result.'

'You heard?'

'Clear as a bell. They seemed to be blaming a chap called Seamus. Apparently, he as good as guaranteed that little package you unwrapped.'

'Did he, by God?'

'Thought you'd be interested, old boy. To quote one of their happy band when the news of your win came through, "We should have left that fucking Aherne in the Crumlin".'

# Chapter 11 September 1971

'Zip me up, darling,' asked Lindy Aicheson as she stood before the mirror in their room at the Listowel Arms Hotel.

'Uh-huh,' Edward S. Aicheson murmured from the chair where he was reading that day's *Irish Press*.

'I said, zip me up, will you?' she repeated.

'Sure thing,' he replied, still engrossed in his paper.

She sighed to herself and slapped the front of the newspaper. 'I said, zip me up, will you?' she demanded once more and smiled warm and soft and fragrant from the bath she'd taken after their unexpected love-making.

Ted Aicheson jumped up, apologetic, and reached for the zip at the waist of her black cocktail dress. He slid it half-way up, then leaned forward to kiss the smooth skin just above her bra-strap.

'Hey!' she protested, wriggling. 'Enough of that, Aicheson. Remember I'm a respectable married woman.'

He slid his hands round her and squeezed her full breasts.

'Respectable women don't screw in the afternoon,' he teased, breathing into her long, blond hair.

She rested against him for a moment, rubbing her bottom against his groin, covered only by his thin dressing gown, before pulling away, pretending annoyance. 'You're nothing but a horny, dirty-mouthed old man,' she exclaimed, flattered by his renewed desire. If she hadn't moved away that very instant then they would have ended up in bed again.

'I'm on holiday,' he said lightly.

'And we've to meet your relatives in an hour.'

'Suppose so,' he sighed, making a last, playful grab at her. She twirled easily from his clutch.

'What was so interesting in the paper then?' she asked, deliberately changing the subject.

'Oh . . . that? There was a big bomb scene in Belfast last night. In that hotel where we ate last week.'

'Oh, no! It's not blown up, is it?'

'No. The Army defused the bomb. The paper says it took them hours.'

'Our intrepid major with the gun in his hip pocket?'

'Doesn't say but I guess he'd have been in the action somewhere.'

'Seems so far away, doesn't it, Ted?'

'Another country, another century.'

'Another planet?'

'That too.'

'Glad we came?'

'Just now?' he smiled lecherously, slipping off his gown and posing before her like a body builder. She threw his underpants and trousers at him, sparkling eyes savouring his nakedness.

'Now stop that! Just stop it!' she ordered laughing. 'You know very well what I meant.'

He shrugged resignedly, beginning to dress.

They'd arrived in Listowel three days before expecting to find another quiet and unhurried market town. The reality was different. Listowel had been packed with people attending the last day of the town's September race meeting.

The market square had been jammed with cars and only the help of a police sergeant had enabled them to double park outside the Listowel Arms Hotel in the corner of the square.

'From the North?' he'd remarked, noticing the vehicle's number plates.

Ted had nodded.

'Well, don't you worry, sir,' the sergeant had grinned. 'You'll be finding a wee difference here.'

And so it had proved.

The hotel had been a scene of controlled chaos when they'd booked in. Their room had not been ready and the bar had been too crowded with racegoers for comfort.

'Come back in an hour,' the receptionist had said, apologizing fulsomely. 'By then, they'll all be at the track or drunk and we can sort you out.'

Ted and Lindy had wandered out into the square, smiling to each other at the frenetic bonhomie pervading the town.

They had admired the two churches and the ruins of Listowel Castle, not quite knowing what they were, and then had decided to try their luck in Buckley's Bar, diagonally opposite to the hotel. This, too, had been packed with racing men, mostly dressed in checked sports jackets and brown trilby hats.

Ted had left Lindy standing by the grimy mirror covering one side of the room and pushed to the bar through the rising gabble.

'And didn't the man tell me so himself?'

'It's a three-legged donkey, so it is . . . '

'Four more Paddys, Pat!'

'I'd have had the forecast but for that one-armed jock . . . '

'Away with you! You wouldn't know Vincent O'Brien from Father Mulcahy!'

'Two gin and tonics, please,' Ted had heard himself order.

'What's that, sir?' said the man behind the bar, expertly flicking Guinness froth from a glass with a plastic spatular.

'Two gin and tonics!' he almost shouted.

The exchange of misinformation around him died away as his nasal Boston accent registered.

Faces had turned towards him, friendly but curious.

'It's an American you are?' the tiny, gnomic man at his elbow had asked.

'Uh-huh. That's correct.'

Ted had reached for his drinks on the counter.

'And here for the races?'

'Nope,' he'd replied, handing a glass through the customers to Lindy. 'Just a holiday.'

'A holiday it is?' another man had chimed in, evincing total disbelief.

'That's right.'

'In Listowel?' they'd chorused incredulously.

'Looking for ancestors,' Lindy had volunteered, pushing to her husband's side amid a general touching of hatbrims.

Ted had shaken his head slightly, but it had been too late. The forthcoming races had been forgotten.

Questions had come from every corner of the bar. Their replies had brought more questions and even more answers until the Aichesons were overwhelmed with information about this family Aherne here and that family Aherne there.

Eventually, an old man sucking a sticky pipe had been ushered forward. All the information gathered by Lindy had had to be repeated in a loud voice because the old man's hearing aid battery was run down.

He'd ruminated through most of a pint of Guinness bought by Ted, who suddenly noticed that his hand was dipping into his wallet with increasing frequency.

'If it's you are after a Mary Aherne,' the old man had finally pronounced, 'who married in Boston and ran a bar, then you're after wanting . . . ' He had counted on his fingers. ' . . . her great-great-great-grandson, Michael, at Aherne's in Church Street.'

'Ah, that's your man,' everyone had agreed immediately with much nodding of heads. 'You'll be wanting Michael Aherne.'

'And where's he?' Lindy had asked, delighted at everyone's willingness to help.

'Well, he won't be there anyway!' the barman had declared, leaning his elbows into the spreading slops of beer on the counter.

'Where?'

'He'll be at the races with Johnny O'Hara from Ballybunnion,' advised the little man still at Ted's side, now drinking the American's gin and tonic. 'Always together,' he'd added. 'Inseparable they are except when Johnny's away on business and then they're not seeing each other.'

'Hold on,' Ted had said, lifting his hands. 'Now just hold on.'

There'd been a momentary silence.

'Now where will this Michael . . . '

'Aherne,' the little man had interrupted needlessly, taking another sip of gin and tonic.

'This Michael Aherne be when he's not at the races with Johnny O'Hara?'

'At his place, of course,' the barman had declared between two gulps of Guinness which emptied his glass. Somehow, in putting it down, he edged it invitingly towards Ted's side of the counter.

'O'Hara's?'

The little man drained the glass of gin and tonic, shaking his head. In doing so, he caught sight of the yellowing watch on his wrist.

'Dear Mother of Heaven!' he'd exclaimed. 'It's twenty to, boys! Sorry, friends!'

Elbows had risen. Mouths had opened. Drinks had been swallowed.

Within a minute the racing men had left the bar. Some of them ran out, pushing each other through the door in their eagerness to reach the track in time to bet on the first race.

Ted and Lindy had leaned on the bar, carefully avoiding the damp patches and looked at the barman expectantly.

'Now, what were they saying?' Ted had asked.

'Well,' the barman had started. 'There's this . . . '

The door had opened and the police sergeant who'd allowed the Aichesons to double-park walked in.

'Ah, so there you are at last. I saw you walking this way,' he'd said, removing his peaked hat, rubbing his palms together.

Ted had winked at his wife and reached for his wallet again.

'Just a pint, sir,' said the sergeant, not waiting to be asked. 'It's terrible thirsty with all those cars.'

'Must be,' Lindy had agreed.

'Well, no rest for the wicked,' the sergeant continued, before downing most of his Smithwick's bitter. 'It's after . . . '

The door had swung open again, this time more violently. Through it staggered a beefy man, more than six feet tall, cloth cap over one side of his head. The barman had started towards him, alarmed. The sergeant showed little interest.

The big man had swayed to the bar, face ruddy and sweating.

'And where the divil is this?' he'd slurred.

'Buckley's,' the sergeant had answered, not even turning his head.

'Buckley's where?'

'Listowel.'

'Grand!' the big man said, weaving his head, clearly sodden drunk. 'Not far away then!'

'And where are you headed?'

'Tralee!'

'Well, you'll know the road then,' the sergeant had said dismissively, supping his pint.

The man turned and, in turning, almost fell.

'He's drunk!' Lindy had whispered indignantly as the door slammed shut again.

'He's been in Dublin,' the sergeant had explained.

'Dublin?'

'The All-Ireland Final.'

'The Final! When?'

'Four days ago but your man's nearly safe home now.'

'Can take more'n a week when Kerry win,' the barman had added.

'And it's been known they end up in Liverpool,' the sergeant added, visibly refreshed by his beer.

'Even Rome . . . in St Peter's Square,' the barman had breathed in some awe.

'Don't blather,' protested the sergeant. 'That's just old stories and can't you see our American friend here is wanting to buy another drink?'

In the next hour, the bemused Aichesons were treated to a rendering, for fifty pence, of 'Danny Boy' by an old woman who'd wandered into the bar; an incomprehensible explanation from the sergeant about how he'd been transferred from his normal work in County Donegal and why he was drinking and not on duty; and finally, from the barman, a fairly lucid explanation about Michael Aherne and his bar in Church Street.

Slightly drunk, they wandered out into the square, now somnolent and quietly sedate in the warm afternoon sunshine. They drifted arm-in-arm past the banks and shops, drawn towards the occasional, distant sound of cheering.

'Isn't that the cutest!' Lindy had exclaimed, pointing to the narrow alley, Tay Lane, sloping mysteriously downwards from the rounded junction of William Street and Market Street.

They picked their way carefully along the cobbled surface, badly needing repair, turned a gentle corner and saw the river at the end of the lane.

Ted laughed aloud.

'Look! That's their racetrack!' he'd said, pointing across the narrow, meandering river to the wooden rails circling the large island on the opposite bank. In the distance, they'd seen a small grandstand and some white marquees.

Suddenly, as if from nowhere, they'd heard the pounding of hooves. A dozen horses, jockeys in multi-coloured silks, had swept into view, staying as close as possible to the rails.

For a moment, it had seemed that they would gallop headlong into the river, that their momentum wouldn't allow them to manoeuvre round the bend.

Lindy had stepped back, frightened, hand to mouth, sensing the tremendous power in the horses only yards away.

'Sweet Jesus!' Ted had muttered, alarmed himself.

And then, in a flash of colour and noise, the horses were out of sight, away down the far side of the track in the middle of the River Feale.

Ted had shaken his head in astonishment, laughing nervously. 'Crazy!' he'd exclaimed. 'They're absolutely crazy!'

The Aichesons' experiences in the next three days did little to change that opinion. They could hardly believe the contrast between the easy-going, exuberant, almost overwhelmingly friendly people and those they'd left behind in Northern Ireland.

That first night, they were greeted by Michael Aherne as life-long friends when they called at his bar. It was clear that the heavily built, crinkle-haired man in his late 50s was extremely busy with all the departing punters but business was dismissed from his mind immediately he heard of the American couple's relationship with his family.

He'd insisted over many drinks on arranging a family reunion party at his own expense and sent Ted and Lindy on their unsteady way back to the Arms Hotel well under the influence of the town's hospitality.

For the next two days, they had explored the country and coastline of North Kerry, relaxing more and more with each sight and sound: the old man plodding along the straight country road beside his donkey laden with bricks of peat; the four nuns paddling on the shining sands at Ballybunnion, habits clasped demurely at mid-calf; the farmer's wife who invited them into her cottage for fresh made apple pie when they'd merely stopped to ask directions; the sudden hush in a crowded bar as Radio Telefis Eireann broadcast the Angelus; the gypsy children, tanned and cheeky, begging outside shops with their mother, babe in arms; the priest, on holiday himself, telling Bible stories to a rapt audience of small children on the terrace of the Greenmount Hotel, perched above the beaches at Ballybunnion; the sunsets, orange and dark purple above the hills; the quiet and sweet of empty, stone-walled fields, high clouds dancing shadows across them; the curious, gentle smiles of the elderly; the bold, inquisitive gazes of children.

Ted and Lindy Aicheson fell under Kerry's spell. No longer did they attempt to organize their time. Indeed, time was of no importance. They relaxed as they hadn't done since their student days, surrendering totally to each other and the people of North Kerry.

It was like their courtship in Boston when everything, visible or unseen, had been made fresh and exciting by their love. Then, the flower sellers along Newbury Street had seemed magically romantic and the pavement cafes so intellectually chic. The Charles river, dit-dotted with sailing craft and rowers, had looked as wide and important as the River Shannon, particularly when the dying sun reflected off the windows of the sky-reaching office blocks. They talked of those times when they'd viewed the town from Cambridge across the river, when it had appeared that new Boston was growing perceptibly upwards from the old, rough-bricked buildings, from the gold glittering dome of the State House nestled comfortably among the dips and rises of Beacon Hill, its narrow alleys and streets offering continual glimpses of water. They held each other's hands like they'd done those years before on the Common or in Harvard Yard or when they'd strolled through Quincy Market, sipping fruit cups and wondering how clever or banal any trader could be to name his stall 'Boston T. Baggs'. They ate snacks not formal meals, love-filled just as they'd done when they'd motored out to Medford on a Sunday for the 'dim sum' savouries at that Chinese restaurant.

And they'd talked again of smells and sights and colours, just as they'd done during their honeymoon at Rocky Neck on the jutting arm of Cape Ann, living in a friend's wooden holiday home among all the other wooden houses painted blue-green, white, red or grey.

They remembered their loving in a huge bed, how they luxuriated in each other, despising the previous grabbing and groping, the zipping and unfastening in the back seats of cars or borrowed-for-an-hour apartments.

They stopped to look at flowers in hedgerows, recalling the scarlet maples of September in New England and the fresh picked butter-cups and ox-eyed daisies in the vases on the tables at that little restaurant at West Wharf, the one called The Kitchen, where they'd eaten late breakfasts during their honeymoon, eggs and bacon and muffins, sex-tired eyes adoring each other.

The guarded suspicion, fear even, generated by the ugly bruta-lities of Northern Ireland slipped from their minds. They no longer felt embarrassed about their presumption in claiming kinship with these Kerry folk.

Now, the Aichesons found it natural to stroll rather than stride purposefully, to nod to passers-by rather than avoid their eyes as they did in Belfast.

'A fine evening!' Ted called to an elderly couple as he and Lindy walked slowly along the west side of the market square, deep in slanting shadow, towards the tavern and the reunion party.

'It is that, thanks be,' answered the strangers.

'Thanks be,' Lindy echoed softly, clutching her husband's arm, feeling, like him, totally familiar with Listowel. Its peace of mind was deep within them.

When they reached the bar, simply signed 'Aherne's', the chatter and juke-box music suggested that they were among the last arrivals.

Slightly uncertain, they pushed the door open and immediately saw the beaming face of Michael Aherne, his paunch finding the gap between waistcoat and trousers.

'Hello there!' he cried, hurrying over. 'So it's yourselves are here!'

He clasped Lindy in his arms and kissed her damply on the left cheek before vigorously pumping Ted's right hand up and down, pulling him into the bar.

The narrow room was crowded with more than thirty people

632

sitting or standing by a number of round tables covered with white tablecloths. Two girls in their late teens, faces shiny with exertion, bent and bobbed behind the bar counter, serving drinks with practised speed.

'Quiet now!' Michael Aherne called, clapping his hands three times. 'It's the guests of honour are here.'

Faces, freshly young to wrinkled old, turned to the Aichesons, smiling, assessing. For the next ten minutes, Ted and Lindy were led round the bar, shaking hands or kissing.

'This is Joe . . . he's my nephew . . . the son of Bryan Aherne, my elder brother killed in The Troubles . . . his wife Bernadette . . . their girls, Shelagh and Mai, and their husbands, Sean and Patrick. . . and this is Hannah, my sister-in-law . . . Bryan's wife . . .Grandma Hannah . . . and my sister, Sinead, who'd be your Mary Aherne's great-great-grandaughter just like you're her great-great-grand nephew . . . and here's Kevin, my second older brother . . .his wife, Maggie . . . '

The names and faces circled round them, too many to remember at once, until Michael Aherne called a halt.

'Enough of that,' he announced, pushing Ted and Lindy to the counter. 'They'll be having a wee drink before meeting the rest of you.'

With glasses in their hands, the Aichesons had time to look round the bar again.

'I didn't realize there'd be so many,' Ted remarked ruefully.

'So many?' said his host. 'And sure isn't this just the half of them? The others are scattered over the world.'

'I'll never remember them all.'

'Don't worry, Ted. I've had them all written down.'

He beckoned to a gentle-faced woman in her early seventies, sitting quietly in the corner.

'Now this is Miss Quinlan . . . Mai Quinlan,' he said. 'She's not a relative, a neighbour really, but she knows who's who in Listowel.'

'I wouldn't say that, Michael Aherne,' the woman said softly, brushing back a stray lock of grey hair, smiling deprecatingly behind her spectacles, the epitome of an educated spinster.

'Oh, come on now,' urged the bar-owner, respect clear in his manner although Miss Quinlan was obviously of the same generation.

'Well,' she admitted. 'I have been talking to one or two since you asked.'

'Then you can tell them about it over supper. You'll be sitting with us.'

Miss Quinlan smiled and accepted a glass of sherry, duty overcoming modesty.

There were more introductions before everyone was called to a meal of porterhouse steak and salad with potatoes boiled fluffily in their skins. The tables were so filled with food that the bottles of wine and pints of Guinness were relegated to the scuffed linoleum on the floor.

While the Aichesons and their host ate and drank heartily, Miss Quinlan pecked bird-like at her food, telling the story of the Ahernes of Listowel, the joys and tragedies of each generation, their achievements and failures.

As she talked, Michael Aherne pointed out the relevant branches of the family at the various tables.

And as the story went on, told with the disinterest of amateur scholarship, Ted and Lindy became increasingly aware of its Republican overtones. They looked uneasily at each other, wondering if questions would be welcome, particularly about that Aherne who'd escaped from Crumlin Gaol and who, according to the newspaper, came from near Listowel.

After his fourth glass of wine, Ted Aicheson, replete with food, decided to broach the subject indirectly.

'And are there Ahernes all over Ireland, Miss Quinlan?' he asked.

'All over the globe, Mr Aicheson,' she answered.

'As Michael here's probably told you, I'm working right now in Belfast, at the Royal Victoria, and I've heard of Ahernes up there. Would they . . . ' From the corner of his eye, he noticed the glazed look of cheerfulness on his host's face suddenly change. ' . . . be related as well?'

Miss Quinlan's smile tightened.

'They could be. Oh, yes, they could be,' she conceded.

Michael Aherne hunched forward over the table, pushing aside the condiments.

'Is that what brought you here?' he asked bluntly, expression hardening.

'What?' Lindy said, all innocence.

Their host shook his head, then tapped the side of his nose knowingly. He laughed in the back of his throat, relaxing again.

'The Ahernes in Belfast? Or rather, should I say the Aherne in Belfast?'

'But we knew about the Ahernes in Listowel before we left Boston. . . ' Ted began to say.

634

'Sure you did,' the bar owner interrupted. 'Sure you knew, but I'm reckoning it was newspaper stories about a certain Seamus Aherne which brought you down here finally.'

He winked shrewdly.

Ted Aicheson spread his hands upwards on the table, shrugging, smiling a trifle sheepishly.

'Well, seeing as you're family now,' Michael Aherne continued. 'I don't suppose you shouldn't be knowing.'

'About Seamus?'

'He's Joe's son. My great-nephew.'

Michael Aherne pointed to a table further down the room. Ted looked quickly and saw a thin, sickly man in the act of swallowing a glass of, presumably, whiskey.

'And he is in the Provisionals?'

'Oh, yes. He's one of the boys all right. Joined them after Derry, not long since he finished his apprenticeship with the Post Office.'

'Don't you mind?' Lindy asked, ingenuously.

'I mind,' Michael Aherne replied, a trace of bitterness in his voice. 'Oh, yes, I mind enough. We all do. But then, after all, he's his own man now.'

'You worry then?' Lindy persisted.

'Worry? Worry? Of course, we bloody well worry, but he's doing what he thinks right by himself and the family and that's that. He's a good boy, Seamus. Always helped out round the farm when Joe had one of his turns. He was well liked. You see, down here we stopped fighting a long time ago. At least most of us did. Let's face it, there's precious little to be fighting about except income tax and not enough jobs and the pill. We've forgotten in one generation what it's like to have the troops marching up and down the street, right outside your own front windows, scaring the wee 'uns half to death. Miss Quinlan here . . . well, her da used to barricade the windows all day and all night so that Tan bullets wouldn't be coming through when they were out drinking and raping and looting. Why, some of them even pulled their funny business with Grandma Hannah before she was wed. In those days, the only good British was a dead 'un. Now, the only bad Britisher is the one who doesn't come here on holiday spending money. Oh, yes, we've forgotten what it was like down here. And maybe we'll be forgetting even more in that Common Market. Then we'll be Europeans not Irish. Sometimes, it's seeming to me that you Irish-Americans remember more than we do. But then, you can be affording to. You're far away enough to be enjoying the luxury. We've forgotten and maybe we shouldn't have. But they've not been able to forget up in the North with all those Protestants sitting on their necks and maybe it's a good thing that some Southerners like Seamus and the rest of the boys haven't forgotten either and are giving them a hand to get rid of the Brits and . . .'

He stopped suddenly in mid-sentence, sensing that his words were coming too fast and with too much anger. He shook his head and sighed deeply.

'And don't you see how it sets me off at the mouth and this supposed to be a celebration?' He rubbed a large hand over his face, wiping away globules of sweat.

Ted lowered his voice, sympathy evident, glancing a warning at Lindy. 'Have you heard how he is?'

'Seamus? All right as far as we're knowing. But there's not much we've heard since the prison break. One letter and a brief phone call, that's all. He's worried that if he gets in touch, then Joe and Bernadette will be in trouble. We already reckon the security boys have a tap on the phone but who knows what's happening? We're presuming he's back in the North but we just don't know. That's the worst of it, not knowing.'

'None of you've seen him then?'

'Not since he broke out.'

'It must be very difficult,' said Lindy Aicheson, realizing how embarrassed Michael Aherne was to talk about his young relative in the Provisional IRA.

He patted her hand, shaking his head again.

'Most things are difficult in Ireland, lass, particularly being able to forget. That's why this place makes a good living. That's why there're more bars in this town than food shops. We're not serving pleasure and company here, just oblivion.'

There was silence at the small table and an awareness that the conversation had gone on too long and that those at the nearby tables had also been listening to the bitter words.

'Anyway,' said Michael Aherne, regaining some joviality of manner, 'How are you two finding Belfast, the city of ten thousand bigots?'

Ted coughed and cleared his throat. 'It's different,' he joked grimly. 'Definitely different. You have to live everyday as it comes. You can never get yourself away from the tension. Most times, some tiny part of you is afraid. Coming down here is like having a huge weight lifted from your brain. Lindy and I haven't gotten to understand yet how the people who live there all the time manage to cope

636

without ending up on the funny farm. I know we hand out tran-
quilizers at the hospital like candy but that still doesn't explain it.
You simply have to go on living, praying to the Almighty, or Dr
Paisley or the Pope that there's not a bullet or bomb round the
corner with your name on it.'

'D'you see a deal of it?' Michael Aherne asked, all previous
aggression absent from his voice.

'I see the results of it pretty well every day in the operating
theatre.

'You must despair.'

It was a statement, not a question. Miss Quinlan nodded agreement.

Ted took a long sip of wine, looking over the rim of the glass at his
host. 'To be truthful, sometimes I do,' he sighed. 'It's as if the whole
world's gone mad up there. I can see both sides of the question, sure,
even three sides, but I just can't figure that it's worth all the killing
and maiming. No one's winning, everyone's losing.'

'And isn't that the God's truth,' Michael Aherne replied. 'I'll only
be saying that you've had to live through the last fifty or sixty years
in Ireland to make the slightest sense of it all. It's gone on and it's
still going on and you don't know whether you're proud or ashamed
that you've a relative like Seamus involved. Most times, it's a bit of
both.'

He paused, then called to one of the girls behind the bar for
another bottle of wine, obviously wanting to end the conversation
about Seamus Aherne.

Ted turned to Mai Quinlan, suddenly remembering an unasked
question.

'Have you ever heard of a family round here called . . . oh, what
was the name, Lindy?'

'Who's?'

'Stephen's old ancestor.'

'The . . . '

'Yup,' Ted interrupted quickly not wanting his wife to mention
Stephen Gates' military rank.

Lindy nodded and thought for a moment: 'Sanders, wasn't it? He
said it was Sanders.'

'That's right. Miss Quinlan, have you ever heard of anyone with
that name in Listowel? Apparently he owned land hereabouts at the
turn of the century. A friend of ours thinks he's related.'

The town's unofficial historian shook her head doubtfully, repeating the name softly to herself. 'Sanders, no. I don't think so. Not

Sanders. In Father Gaughan's book about Listowel there's mention of a land agent called Sandes but I don't remember Sanders.'

'That Sandes was a real bad lot,' Michael Aherne interrupted. 'I remember stories about him from my own grandfather. In the end, he had to leave town or else. A lot of people ran foul of the Sandes family. Awful drinkers and womanizers they were while they drove hundreds of poor devils into the ditch.'

Ted smiled. 'Doesn't sound like my friend's ancestors,' he said. He wondered how Stephen Gates would take it when he heard that the only family bearing a name remotely like Sanders was one of the most notorious in the district.

The evening continued with toasts and singing until the floor of the bar was littered with empty bottles and glasses.

Ted tried to talk quietly with Joe Aherne, wanting to discover if any help was needed about Seamus, but found him too drunk to be coherent. His professional eye noticed the well-developed signs of someone who'd die in a year or so from cirrhosis of the liver. The realization sobered him slightly for the walk back to the hotel.

'Well, that was one hell of an evening,' he remarked, putting his arm around Lindy's shoulders to steady her. She'd never had a head for strong drink.

'I guess we got what we deserved for prying. I thought Michael was really going to blow his stack.'

'Uh-huh. At least we understand a bit more.'

'Are you sorry?' Lindy asked, nestling her head to his chest.

'A bit. Stephen's going to have a real laugh when he hears we're related to the IRA.'

Lindy giggled. 'I'd have sorta liked,' she said, 'to have gone on thinking of your people over here as . . . well, like the stage Irish. You know . . . Barry FitzGerald and Victor McGlaglen in "The Quiet Man" . . . all begorrahs and bejabers and shillelaghs.'

'They're happy to play it that way if they think you want them to be like that.'

'Till you scratch them. Then they're different.'

'Then you see why the Irish are some of the saddest people in the world. Really helpless melancholics.'

'But they enjoy it, their sadness,' Lindy suggested.

Ted smiled wanly, holding open the front door of the hotel. 'They've had to learn to,' he said.

# *Chapter 12 October, 1971*

Everyone kept telling him not to worry, not to be nervous, and to act naturally. As Edward S. Aicheson sipped a weak whiskey and water, young men and women with clipboards and large stopwatches kept dashing in and out of the hospitality room on the top floor of Broadcasting House in Belfast.

Their remarks to the man sitting with him ranged from the profane to the incomprehensible.

'The Derry film's gone down in the sodding soup!'

'The two-way from London's okay after Manchester has the first five!'

'Billy can't VT his piece so he'll have to go live at the top after your intro. Okay?'

They all smiled at him in passing but it was mere courtesy, not real friendliness. When he'd first arrived at the fortress like building the television people had gone out of their way to make him feel special, thanking him profusely for coming. But now that he was securely in their clutches, safely within their peculiar world, he had become just another titbit to be fed into the medium's voracious maw.

'You're down for four minutes,' someone had told Aicheson and that was precisely how he felt at that moment, merely a time-unit, a face and a voice capable of filling a slot in 'Scene Around Six', the nightly television programme broadcast by the BBC to the people of Northern Ireland.

The knowledge of his own temporary unimportance made him even more upset at having allowed himself to be persuaded into this by Major Stephen Gates.

'A fine pal he turned out to be,' Aicheson murmured to himself.

'Pardon?'

His companion, the presenter of the programme, thought the half-heard remark was directed at him.

'Sorry,' Aicheson smiled, reddening slightly. 'Just talking to myself.'

'Don't we all over here?' grinned the presenter, a chubby, cheerful young man. 'And isn't it the only way of not offending anyone?'

He returned to the yellow pages of his script, underlining words here and there, leaving Aicheson to his dark thoughts.

It had started out innocently enough over lunchtime drinks at their flat on the Sunday after he and Lindy had returned from their holiday. They'd regaled Stephen and Elizabeth Gates with their impressions of country life in County Kerry and then teased him about the possibility of his being related to the despised land agent Sandes.

'Wouldn't surprise me in the least,' the major had joked. 'Always was attractive to women. Always was a bit of a rake, eh, Elizabeth?'

'Not that you'd notice,' his wife replied, trying to look severe but only breaking into giggles.

Ted Aicheson was so absorbed in describing all his distant relatives in Listowel that he failed to notice a certain thoughtfulness come over the major when he mentioned his relationship to Seamus Aherne.

'I feel sorry for his father,' said Aicheson, pouring another round of drinks. 'I guess he's headed for an early grave with a bottle in each hand. And having a boy in the Provos can't help much.'

'Can't,' agreed Major Gates, tugging the lobe of his right ear. 'All the worry and whatever must have some effect.'

'Sure does,' said Lindy. 'And they all reckon he was a fine son before he got mixed up with the IRA.'

'Probably was,' the major agreed again. 'He threw up a good job to go in with them and now he's about as popular as a barman with no arms.'

'What's happened?' Aicheson asked. 'What've you heard?'

The major smiled mysteriously, shrugging. 'We hear things, you know. Apparently, your Seamus isn't too popular with his friends right now. He promised more than he could deliver and lost the Provos a fair number of brownie points. They don't like being left with egg splattered all over their faces.'

'You won't tell me what it's about?'

'Not won't, Ted. Can't. Official Secrets Act. But I can say your precious relative isn't too high on the totem pole at present. In fact he could be in deep trouble.'

'D'you know where he is?'

'Somewhere in town, that's all. If we did, we'd lift him and stick him back inside. Probably the safest place for him.'

'Oh, I do wish we could help the boy,' Lindy remarked, looking appealingly towards her husband.

'He's not much younger than you,' said the major. 'He's no boy. He's an extremely dangerous terrorist.'

'But his folks are real nice,' protested Lindy. 'Real nice.'

'So was Hitler's mum by all accounts,' the major replied, sharpening his voice, an idea forming in his mind. He cupped his jaw in his hand, little finger flicking at his lower lip. The Aichesons waited expectantly.

'It might be worth trying,' the major mused, deliberately allowing the sudden tension to increase. 'Yes, it might . . .'

'What?' Lindy pleaded.

'Well,' he said after another pause, 'It'd have to strictly be unofficial, of course, but how about if we plant a story in the newspapers about how ill Seamus's dad is, quoting Ted, asking chummy to think about giving himself up? After all, you say his family have hardly heard from him. At least, I reckon there's a chance he'd contact you, Ted. You know, long lost American cousin and all that guff. It might give you the chance of talking him round.'

Aicheson looked doubtful.

'He'll probably think it's a trap.'

'Almost certainly,' agreed Major Gates. 'You'll just have to persuade him otherwise.'

'And what'll you be doing while all this is going on, Stephen?'

Major Gates looked hurt and innocent. 'It'd be nothing to do with me,' he said. 'Nothing whatsoever. Any advice from me is strictly on the old-pals basis. After all, you might have the police sniffing round, asking questions, and I can't be involved with that.'

'Police?'

'They'll probably want to know what you're up to, if you can give information on chummy's location. That sort of thing. You have to remember he's an escaped convict.'

'That'd be difficult.'

'Shouldn't be, Ted. Not necessarily. Just plead the big hearted, open-handed Yank who wants to help and you'll get away with it.'

Aicheson sniffed, still doubtful. He took a long pull at his glass. He suspected that the army major had an ulterior motive behind his suggestion but more important to him was the thought of trying to help Seamus, and thus, his new-found friends in Kerry.

Like many in a closed profession where years of intensive study were obligatory, Aicheson wasn't particularly worldly-wise. He guessed that one of his faults, if it be a fault, was to take people too much at their face value but had not yet acquired enough natural wariness to protect himself from his weakness.

He looked across at his wife, raising his eyebrows quizzically.

'Oh, can we please try, darling?' Lindy pleaded in response.

'It's up to you, of course, old chum,' the major intervened. 'But it might be the only way of saving the poor sod. Even if it doesn't work and you never hear from him, well, at least you can say you tried.'

He leaned back in the easy chair, smoking his cigar, apparently disinterested and unconcerned. In fact, his mind was seething with plans and theories and thoughts. Mentally, he crossed his fingers.

'How would I get in touch with the press boys?' asked Aicheson, still undecided.

'Don't worry about that, Ted,' the major replied, smiling encouragingly. 'The chaps in our information room can pass the word. It'll be quite painless, you see.'

'Uh-huh,' Aicheson muttered, clutching hands to head, thinking. Finally, after a minute's silence so intense that the major thought he could hear his watch ticking, the American looked up and grinned. 'Okay then, Stephen. We'll have a go. Will you fix it?'

Lindy clapped her hands with delight.

'Leave it to me, old chum,' said Major Gates, trying not to appear too pleased nor too smug.

He was as good as his word. Two days later, at the start of the second week in October, 1971, Ted Aicheson was interviewed by a journalist from the *Belfast Telegraph*. The story appeared the following afternoon, headlined 'SURGEON'S PLEA TO 'IRA RELATIVE':

'An American surgeon working in Belfast made the dramatic disclosure today that he has a relative in the Provisional IRA.

'And the surgeon, Mr Edward S. Aicheson, 31, appealed to the man: "For your family's sake, quit the terrorists".

'Mr Aicheson, who's working at the Royal Victoria Hospital on a two year fellowship, made the appeal in an exclusive *Telegraph* interview.

'He declined to name his relative but said that the man came from County Kerry and that his parents' given names were Joe and Bernadette.

' "If he gets in touch with me at the hospital," said Mr Aicheson, "I'll give him enough proof that we are, in fact, related.

' "I'll also provide as much help as possible if he wants to start a new life away from all this senseless and terrible killing."

'Mr Aicheson, from Boston, Mass., made the discovery about his relative during a recent holiday in the South.

'He said: "My wife and I traced a family in a small town in Kerry who are related distantly to us on the female side.

' "It was great meeting them but then, at a reunion party, I learned that one of the younger men in the family was a Provisional, supposedly in Belfast.

' "I was very upset at the thought that while I'm trying to save lives, he's trying to take them. It seems quite ridiculous.

' "I'm sure if he realized just how ill his father was and how worried the rest of the family were, then he would reconsider his actions."

'The surgeon, specializing in neuro-surgery, said that he wouldn't name his relative for fear of the Provisionals blocking any contact between them.

' "I don't want to cause any trouble for him," added Mr Aicheson. "I simply want to help and maybe save someone's life. After all, that's what my whole existence is about." '

The tone of the newspaper article hardly pleased him. He realized that to many in Northern Ireland he would appear to be a naïve meddler. Indeed, this was one of the first comments made to him by the two detectives from the Royal Ulster Constabulary who called on him that evening at the flat at Dunmurry.

They told Aicheson that they'd already identified Seamus Aherne in their files from the scant details in the newspaper and then proceeded to threaten and wheedle and bluster, making it very clear that they expected to be told if Seamus should make contact.

The next morning a telephone call came from the BBC, inviting him to appear on its local television news programme. He changed his mind about further publicity, deciding that if he gave his appeal the fullest exposure then no one would be able to accuse him of acting secretly. He would adopt Stephen Gates' advice and pose as the disingenuous American that he appeared to be. He had had time to regret his decision during the seemingly interminable wait in the small BBC hospitality room.

Eventually, though, he was led into the television studio along narrow corridors, past a canteen, and up and down flights of steps. The journalist who was to interview Aicheson was all smiles and reassurance under the hurtfully bright lights of the studio.

'Just take your time, sir,' he advised while a girl dabbed powder on Aicheson's nose and forehead, even combing his hair. 'Don't think of all the people out there, watching. Imagine you're simply talking to a nice old lady alone in her front room.'

The interview began gently with Aicheson being allowed to explain how he'd discovered his relationship with a member of the Provisional IRA. Then, to his discomfiture, came some sharp, almost impertinent questions.

'You're absolutely sure this man is a terrorist?'

'His family tell me so and I have read about him in the papers.'

'Then why do you want to help him, Mr Aicheson?'

'I simply want to meet him, to try to talk him round, to have him stop what he's doing.'

'You say you don't want to cause any trouble for him?'

'That's right.'

Aicheson felt sweat forming high on his brow. He hoped the camera, red light glowing, couldn't detect it.

'Why not?' the question snapped back.

'Why not what?'

''Cause trouble for him. After all, you say he's a terrorist.'

'I think he needs help.'

'What sort of help?'

'I don't know precisely,' Aicheson replied, realizing how weak his answer must have sounded.

The interviewer lifted one eyebrow, hoping the cameras would catch the expression. He'd been practising it.

'Don't you think some people, like the relatives of IRA victims, will be upset that you want to help an IRA man, even though he's your relative?'

Aicheson shrugged, trying to think, conscious of the lights and the curious stares from the others in the studio.

'They probably will be,' he conceded. 'But, you see, my whole object is to have this man stop . . . '

'Isn't that rather the job of the security forces?' the interviewer said coldly.

'They haven't gotten far,' Aicheson snapped back, anger growing.

'You're not saying that you can succeed, Mr Aicheson, where the forces of law and order have failed?' the interviewer asked curiously more quietly, a somewhat smug expression on his face.

'No, I guess not,' Aicheson floundered. 'No way.'

'You're not in sympathy with this relative of yours?'

'Again, no way. I abhor violence.'

'Then why bother with him? Aren't your motives as misguided as those of your fellow-countrymen who raise cash for the IRA?'

'No, they're not. I think they're wrong too. Just like I think the

IRA is wrong. All I want to do is simply help the guy. Is that . . . '

'Mr Aicheson, thank you.'

The interviewer cut him off smoothly, ending the interview before Aicheson could finish his statement, protest clear in his voice. Off camera, he gestured with his palms and smiled at the American as if disclaiming responsibility for the public humiliation.

Aicheson, emotionally drained, was ushered quietly out of the studio as the programme's next item was introduced.

'Fancy a drink before you go, sir?' his guide asked, leading him back down the corridors, one of them decorated with originals of cartoons about Ulster politicians.

'Uh-huh. I surely do.'

This time, he took the generous glass of whiskey without any water, wanting the jolt of neat alcohol.

'You did very well,' the BBC man said conversationally, helping himself to a drink as well. 'Our Don can be a wee bit hard at times.'

'Don't I know it? He really chewed me up and spat me out.'

'Oh, I wouldn't say that, sir. I thought you came over very sincerely.'

Aicheson shook his head.

'I came over as a fool,' he said. Adding quietly, 'But maybe I guess that's no bad thing.'

'Oh, I don't . . . '

'Can I use your phone?'

'Of course,' said the BBC man, indicating the instrument on a corner table. 'Just pick it up and ask for an outside line.'

He told Lindy that he was about to start home before asking rather tentatively what she'd thought of his appearance on television. Her hesitation provided a more truthful answer than her guarded reply.

Aicheson drove down Lisburn Road towards Dunmurry blaming Stephen Gates for the entire idea, angry at having been made to look so mixed-up during the interview, too angry to understand that the aggressive, one-sided interview was exactly what he should have hoped for.

Major Gates, to the contrary, was feeling rather pleased with himself as he drank his second pint of Bass in the officer's mess at Army Headquarters. He reckoned that Ted Aicheson had portrayed perfectly a well-meaning American blundering into a situation which was none of his business. No one could have mistaken the young surgeon for anything else. Certainly, someone would have to be extremely cynical and far-sighted to think that the American was the key figure in a plan that'd been hastily put together by the major and his acquaintance in the clandestine intelligence unit.

Indeed, the major's professional judgement was absolutely accurate as far as Seamus Aherne was concerned.

His first reaction had been one of shock when he'd seen the story in the *Belfast Telegraph* the previous evening. He guessed immediately that it referred to himself and thought instantly of telephoning Michael Aherne at the bar in Listowel to find out what was going on. But he'd quickly rejected that as too risky in case the Irish security branch had already tapped the line.

He'd spent that night and the next day in an agony of indecision worried that his superiors in the Provisional IRA might have recognized him from the article although he knew they dismissed anything in the *Belfast Telegraph* as anti-Republican propaganda. However, the last thing he wanted after the ajbect failure of his new bomb at the hotel was another question mark against him. He'd already noticed the doubtful looks and taciturn remarks from some of the other members of the Active Service Units who occasionally frequented the Republican Club of Andersonstown.

Seamus's only comfort was that since Rebecca Fahey's arrival in Belfast he was able to discuss his dilemma with someone trustworthy. Her advice was to the point.

'Give the fella a call. What harm can it do?' she said, smiling up at him as she sat on a cushion on the floor of the front room of the house off Lenadoon Avenue, lazily comfortable in the heat of the hissing gas fire.

'None really,' Seamus agreed, stroking her long hair. 'On television he looked a right clown. When I first read that thing in the paper I was thinking that it smelt like a pretty obvious trick. I don't give a toss if he's related to me or not. All I want to know is what he's saying about our dad.'

'You're sure you can't get in touch with them at home?'

Seamus sighed deeply. 'If our dad is ill, or rather, iller than he usually is, then having the special branch boys sniffing round the farm won't help. He really does hate those bastards.'

'Then ring this fella,' Rebecca urged, scraping a long fingernail against the palm of his hand.

'I'll sleep on it,' he replied.

'We'll sleep on it,' she whispered, now moving her fingers to caress the inside of his thighs. He looked down at her, feeling a stir of excitement in his loins. Their appetite for each other's bodies had been nigh insatiable ever since he'd collected her from the ferry terminal in a borrowed car.

Thankfully, the Provisional commanders knew of her arrival and hadn't bothered him since. Seamus suspected that they were quite relieved to have an excuse for leaving him alone while they considered his future as a bomb designer. He'd already submitted a new design based on the hotel bomb, the improved 'Lambeg', but this time containing a delayed timing device. He thought that his drawings were being shown to other, more experienced and trusted designers for their opinions, perhaps even his first instructor, Jack McKay in Dublin. Seamus didn't mind. He was thoroughly confident of his new work.

Meanwhile, he welcomed the chance to be alone with Rebecca, alone that is except for his landlady, Mrs McGuinness, who'd shown surprising tact in leaving them alone, always off to bingo or a bar or shopping. Not that they would have noticed her presence, so rapt were they in a rediscovery of mutual passion and affection. Even the thought of the tiny being developing inside Rebecca had not affected the uninhibitedness of their loving.

For the first time in his life, Seamus experienced living with a woman, watching one in the intimacies of toilet and dressing and make-up, discovering grips and tiny brushes on the dressing table, noticing her clothes pushing his own to the most distant cavities of the drawers and wardrobe, smiling ruefully at her bland illogicalities and her refusal to acknowledge them, and, most of all, accepting her downright untidiness.

Far from upsetting him, Seamus was totally fascinated by these glimpses of the female world, wondering all the time if his mother had been the same.

That night, after repeated lovemaking, they did, in fact, sleep on Seamus's dilemma, awakening in the morning to the same conclusion that nothing could be lost and, perhaps, peace of mind gained, if Seamus should contact the naïve American who claimed to be his relative.

In mid-morning, he walked to a phone box six streets away and dialled 40503, the number of the Royal Victoria Hospital. He listened intently when the hospital switchboard answered, alert for any clicks or changes of tone which might have signified that the telephone line might be tapped. He could hear none.

'Dr Aicheson, please,' he asked.

'Mr Aicheson, you mean,' the man on the switchboard corrected, using the correct prefix for someone who was not only a doctor but a consultant surgeon. 'Connecting you.'

There was a pause for a few seconds before Aicheson – his New England accent unmistakable – came on the line from his office.

'Mr Aicheson?' Seamus queried.

'This is he. Who's calling?'

'Maybe a relation,' Seamus said guardedly.

There was an audible intake of breath at the other end of the line.

'It's you then?' asked Aicheson.

'I saw you on the telly last night. You said our dad was ill.'

'He is if it's your father.'

'Tell me about him then.'

'He lives on a farm near a stream at a place called . . . '

'Don't say it,' Seamus warned urgently. 'Where did you meet this man who might be our dad?'

'At a party at a bar in the town run by your great-uncle Michael.'

Seamus knew then that the American had met his family. He wasn't particularly concerned that this man was almost certainly a relation. What really interested Seamus was that this American might have news of his father.

'How is he?' he asked.

'Sick.'

'Badly sick?'

'Sick as anyone can be, I reckon.'

'Tell me.'

'Not over the phone. Let's meet,' Aicheson suggested, anxious to gain an opportunity to persuade Seamus to leave the Provisionals.

'Why the hell should we?' Seamus answered impatiently. 'You could be setting me up.'

'I'm not setting anyone up,' Aicheson protested vehemently. 'I simply want to help. Remember we are related.'

Seamus lit a cigarette with his right hand, pushing the match box against the side of the shelf in the phone box. He thought furiously.

'You say you only want to help?'

'That's right. I only want to help.'

'How?'

'Maybe get you out of the fix you're in. Maybe stop your family worrying, particularly your father.'

'He's really bad?'

'Really.'

'I'll not come to you,' Seamus said, finally making up his mind. 'That'd be as good as cutting my throat in public.'

'Then I'll come to you. Anytime. Anywhere. You name it.'

'Maybe,' Seamus conceded, desperate to hear about his father, worried by the American's opinion of his condition. 'I'll be ringing you back,' he added. 'I'll have to work something out.'

'When?'

'Tomorrow. Same time,' Seamus said, putting down the phone and hurrying out of the booth and away down the road. His wrist-watch told him that the conversation had lasted barely ninety seconds but he knew from his work with the Irish Post Office that that was long enough for a tracing operation to be well under way. To prolong the call any longer would have been inviting trouble.

'Blast it!' cursed the officer from the secret intelligence unit when he heard the news. 'Just Andersonstown, that's all we know?'

'Just Andersonstown. He rang off too quickly,' confirmed one of the unit's sergeants who'd been at a telephone headquarters watching the attempts to trace the call.

'But he's calling back?'

'He said he was.'

'Well, we'll just have to wait, won't we?'

'Suh,' answered the sergeant, who was bored with the job. He would have preferred to have been out in the unit's new undercover van, touring the Catholic enclaves, the IRA's heartlands, masquerading as a street laundry.

The next call from Seamus to Ted Aicheson was even briefer, allowing no chance of his location being traced. He didn't even phone at the appointed time. In fact, Aicheson and the unseen phone tappers had almost given up hope that he would make the contact. The surgeon was about to leave the hospital for home when the call came just before six o'clock.

'Be at the Elbow Room in the Ormeau Road in fifteen minutes,' Seamus ordered briefly, not even introducing himself.

'Will I need my car?' Aicheson asked.

'Maybe. Just be there.'

Seamus put down the phone.

The intelligence officer cursed again when he heard his sergeant's report a couple of minutes later. He knew there'd be no time to tap the phone at the bar and hardly any time to mount a proper surveillance operation. He rapped out some orders, rather pessimistic about their successful outcome. He knew he should have taken more account of Seamus Aherne's knowledge of telephones. He should have realized just how wary his quarry would have been about talking on open lines.

Despite Belfast's chaotic rush hour traffic Ted Aicheson reached the bar, diagonally opposite the BBC studios, with two minutes to spare. He felt empty to the depths of his stomach as he pushed through the grimy, though finely etched, glass doors, wondering if Seamus would be waiting for him inside.

Immediately, it was clear that that couldn't have been the plan. The bar was deserted except for three elderly, down-at-heel men whose clothes were as dirty and as ravaged as their faces.

Aicheson walked to the horse-shoe shaped wooden counter, instantly sensing an aura of despair about the establishment. It was a gaunt, bare room, offering no concessions to comfort or attractiveness. Like so many similar bars in Belfast, this was no place where young people or courting couples might gather. This bar was dedicated to those who wished to drink seriously without any frills. Its atmosphere was pervaded with the loneliness of its habitues for whom alcohol was the only escape route from the disappointment and emptiness of their own lives.

The barman, as spare and unwelcoming as the bar, wandered over to Aicheson, noting his well-cut suit and mistaking him for a broadcaster from over the road dropping in to see how the other half lived.

'A drink?' Aicheson asked, his mind on Seamus.

'Yes, we do sell 'em,' the barman sneered.

Aicheson flushed. 'Sorry. A Jamieson Crested Ten, I guess.'

He picked up his whiskey, poured into a cheap, thin glass, and sipped. Somewhere in the cavernous recesses of the bar, a phone shrilled.

'It's for someone called Aicheson,' a gin-thickened woman's voice called to the barman.

He looked disapprovingly around his four customers. 'Anyone called Aicheson?'

The American nodded. 'That's me.'

'The phone. Take it upstairs,' said the barman, jabbing his thumb towards a door at the side of the bar. 'And tell your friend not to make a habit of phoning here.'

Aicheson nodded, embarrassed by the barman's animosity, and walked over to the door. He pushed it open and saw it led to a carpeted stairway going upwards.

As he went through, the main door of the bar opened behind him and a young man in a long, light brown raincoat entered quietly.

'So you're there?' Seamus said straight away when Aicheson picked up the dangling phone.

'Hardly a cocktail bar you chose.'

'It is that but you won't be having a second drink'

'Good.'

'Go out through the side entrance, the one at the bottom of the stairs from where you're talking. Turn right and walk twenty yards. You'll see a battered old blue Anglia, registration EKU 316D. Get in. The keys are under the front seat in an envelope along with your instructions. Got all that.'

'A blue Anglia?'

'Right. A banger. I'll talk to you in a wee while and then, for Holy Mary's sake, check you're not being followed.'

'Check.'

The line went dead.

Aicheson leapt downstairs, loath to leave a fine whiskey unfinished, gulped it down and hurried into Bruce Street through the side entrance of the Elbow Room.

He turned right, as instructed, and could just make out the blue Ford Anglia car in the gathering gloom.

A young man with rather piercing blue eyes, wearing a long, light brown raincoat, brushed past him on the pavement, apologizing in a thick, rasping Belfast accent.

Aicheson walked quickly to the car, noting that the narrow street was now deserted, opened the nearside door and pushed up the driving seat. There was the envelope.

Inside were some car keys and his written instructions. He had to drive to the Post Office in Andersonstown, wait ten minutes, then ring a phone number from the call box outside the building.

Aicheson shrugged to himself, noticing that the handwriting was scrawled and uneven: the writing, he thought, of someone under fairly severe mental pressure.

The drive took about twenty minutes in the decrepit car, minutes in which Ted Aicheson couldn't help but wonder if he was doing the correct thing, whether he should simply return the vehicle to its original parking place and then go quietly home to Lindy.

Aicheson remembered suddenly Seamus's instructions to check that he wasn't being followed. He looked guiltily in the rear view mirror, driving along the Falls Road, and could see no headlights behind. He steered the car to the side of the road in front of the dark and wire shuttered Post Office, just opposite what seemed to be some sort of park with tennis courts.

'Sweet Jesus,' he sighed, nervous tiredness beginning to grip him. The Post Office looked more like a Second World War fortification than a place of business. Just a sign of the times, he knew, with the IRA often choosing such establishments for fund-raising robberies.

When the allotted ten minutes had passed, Aicheson walked over to the public phone box and dialled the number on his sheet of instructions, ready to push in a 2p coin when the connection was made. As the digits tumbled, he heard a helicopter above but dismissed the noise as merely a routine sound of the troubled city.

'Anyone follow you?' Seamus asked immediately, breathing hard, not bothering with any greeting.

'Not that I saw.'

'And not that I saw either.'

The remark surprised Aicheson.

'You're near then?' he said. 'Were you watching?'

'You arrive? Yes, from the sports club across the road. That's why I wanted you to wait before calling. So I could get where I am now.'

'You're surely careful,' Aicheson said.

'I'm alive and free, so I have to be.'

'A poet too, I guess,' Aicheson grinned into the mouthpiece, encrusted with grime and flecks of tobacco.

Seamus grunted unappreciatively.

'Now drive the car straight down the road, past the church on your right, keep to your right at the junction and keep counting roads leading off to your right. You want the eighth on your right. Turn up there and pull in when you see a light flash twice. Got it?'

'Real James Bond, eh?' the American said dryly, now beginning to savour the danger. His tiredness fell away. He was very awake, very alive.

'It's my life,' Seamus growled. 'For fuck's sake, watch for anything and everything and if you don't see my signal just drive off and forget tonight.'

'Bit late now,' Aicheson drawled but the phone was already dead.

The helicopter was still above when he pushed through the door of the phone box. He glanced up, picking out its navigation lights among the darkening clouds.

He waited a moment, watching the few passing cars. None slowed, quickened, turned, or did anything to suggest their occupants were at all interested in him.

The ill-used Anglia coughed and spluttered on its way again along the almost deserted road. It passed under the eyes and rifle barrels of an Army Observation post, wired and netted and camouflaged, before reaching the eighth turning on the right, a road leading into a fairly new housing estate.

652

Aicheson peered carefully into the rear view mirror, no other vehicle had turned behind him. Nobody, he was sure, could be following. He looked back through the windscreen. A light winked twice about thirty feet ahead on his nearside. He changed down and rolled to a stop by the kerb.

No one approached. His eyes tried to penetrate the darkness, flicking left and right. He could see nothing but the glow of lights behind curtained windows further up the road. He switched off the car's lights and continued to wait, nerves taut.

The rap at the window on the passenger side came so suddenly, unexpectedly, that his body actually lifted an inch or so from the driving seat. His head switched to the left. All he could see was a hand beckoning urgently to him before vanishing into the darkness. Aicheson scrambled out of the car, not thinking even to remove the ignition keys.

'Come on, for fuck's sake,' a voice whispered hoarsely from a patch of stygian shadow. 'Up this alley and quick about it!'

The American broke into a trot, following a bulky, dark clad figure he assumed to be Seamus Aherne.

They turned two corners, crossed a well-lit road, loped across what seemed to be a playing field and ran through two more alleys in another housing estate before stopping outside the back door of a house identical to all those they'd already passed. Seamus knocked softly three times. A key clicked in the lock and the door swung open. He pushed Aicheson into an unlit room, took one last look around and then followed him.

The light flashed dazzlingly on and Aicheson saw that he was standing in a rather small and untidy kitchen.

By the inner door, a slim, attractive young woman, her long hair in a pony tail, stood with a hand still on the light switch. He turned his head, eyes adjusting to the light, and saw a tall, youngish man, bearded and thick round the waist, leaning, panting, against the back door.

Aicheson wiped a layer of sweat from his forehead, smiling, unsure, thinking that his immaculate grey suit was hardly the ideal clothing for a jog round the back streets of Andersonstown. 'Phew!' he exclaimed, wiping his face again, not quite knowing what to say.

'So you're my American relative who wants to help?' Seamus said a trifle sarcastically, looking intently at Aicheson, still breathing hard.

'That's right. So you must be Seamus?'

Aicheson pushed out his right hand. Seamus looked at it for a moment, then slowly extended his. The two men shook hands.

'And this is Rebecca,' Seamus said. 'She's my fiancée.'

'Congratulations,' Aicheson smiled, shaking her hand, feeling the fine bones and long fingers.

Rebecca blushed and looked down at the floor.

Aicheson turned back to Seamus who was still leaning, winded, against the back door. 'I guess you've taken a helluva risk in seeing me,' he said. 'Thanks.'

Seamus shrugged non-committedly. 'We haven't much time,' he said shortly. 'No time for jawing about nothing in particular. You said that our dad's a very sick man. What's the trouble with him?'

Aicheson gazed round for a chair. He couldn't see any. Seamus nodded and pulled out a stool from beneath the kitchen table.

'Well, Seamus,' Aicheson began, sitting down, 'you have to realize that I didn't make a formal examination of your father but I did have a pretty close look at him at that hooley your great-uncle Michael threw for Lindy and me . . . '

'What's the matter with him?' Seamus interrupted impatiently.

'I don't suppose it's any news to you that he's got a drinking problem.'

'He's always liked a drop. Maybe it helps him forget.'

'A drop?'

'Well, sometimes more than a drop if he had the cash.'

Aicheson nodded, noting the dark rings under Seamus's eyes and the almost imperceptible tremor in his fingers. This was a man, he could see, living on his nerves.

'Well, to be frank,' he sighed, 'I'd say the booze is near killing him. Right now, I'd guess he should be hospitalized and treated for cirrhosis. And, right now, I'd wonder if it's even too late for that.'

'Too late?'

'His liver's shot to hell. Soon it'll pack up altogether and then his body will simply poison itself. I tell you, it's not exactly the method I'd choose to shuffle off the mortal coil.'

'You're certain?'

'Well, as I said, I didn't . . . ' Aicheson paused, shaking his head. 'Yes, I'm certain.'

Seamus rubbed the back of his hand nervously across his mouth. 'What can I do?' he asked.

'Go and see him,' Aicheson urged. 'Talk to him. Persuade him to be hospitalized. Get out of this thing you're in and stop him worrying. Your family said he listens to you.'

'We always got on well,' Seamus conceded. 'That's true. Maybe, if I asked, the big men might let me off for a wee while. But then, if I go home, the Garda would probably snap me up. It's a bad choice.'

'Maybe for you. Not for your father.'

Aicheson fumbled in his jacket pocket for a handkerchief to mop his forehead, feeling a drop of slithering sweat on his skin.

Seamus gazed down at the floor, then looked appealingly across at Rebecca.

'If they did arrest you, they wouldn't extradite you from the South,' Aicheson continued, pressing his argument as he sensed Seamus's resolve weakening.

'They might. After all, I did break gaol. It's mighty uncertain if that's a political offence.'

'Well, it's your choice but anyway that's what I wanted to talk to you about, your family and you leaving the Provos,' Aicheson said, finding his handkerchief at last and pulling it from his pocket.

Seamus laughed humourlessly. 'Leaving the Provos? You must be . . . '

Aicheson shook his handkerchief. A round, shiny disc, not much bigger than a coin, entangled in the handkerchief's folds, fell on to the cracked linoleum covering the floor. It tinkled metallically as it rolled a few feet before settling just by the stained gas cooker. Aicheson gazed at it with amazement.

'Fucking hell!' Seamus snorted, starting towards it, eyes blinking with fear.

Aicheson's groping fingers reached it first. He held the disc up, turning it, gleaming under the light. Seamus tore it from him. He threw it to the floor and ground it under his heel, crunching it into a tangle of metal, plastic and wires.

'What . . . what?' Aicheson stammered.

'A fucking bug' Seamus screamed. 'You were fucking bugged!'

'But . . . but how?'

'How the fuck should I know?' Seamus cursed, his eyes wild. 'They must have . . . '

A boot crunched into the lock of the back door. It splintered open hitting Seamus on the right shoulder, spinning him round, pushing him forward. Another crash came from the front of the house, through the small hallway.

A crouching figure in combat fatigues, face smeared with black, burst through the back door, stubby machine gun covering all three in the kitchen.

Another soldier slid round him, thrusting Aicheson roughly aside. He threw the inside kitchen door open as Rebecca cowered in the corner. The American could see more troops running through the front door, some beginning to take the stairs two at a time. He began to protest, shouting incoherently.

'Shut it, cocker,' called the first soldier, through the door, ramming his weapon not too heavily into Aicheson's buttocks, forcing him against the gas cooker.

Seamus's face was white and shocked, his mouth moving soundlessly, as he was spreadeagled against the wall, hands and legs thrust apart in a position only too familiar to him.

Rebecca started to sob, both hands covering her face, dropping to her knees as if in prayer.

'Well, this is a nice place for a family reunion,' murmured Stephen Gates, stepping into the kitchen, dressed incongruously in a tweed sports jacket and flannel trousers. 'Hello, Ted,' he nodded towards Aicheson, who was speechless with surprise. The major flicked a suede shoe against the remains of the electronic device which had been slipped into the American's pocket outside the Elbow Room, enabling the Army intelligence unit to monitor his movements from the helicopter.

'Tut-tut,' he sighed. 'Damaging government property . . . still, there's always the one in that old heap of metal you drove up here, Ted.'

'Bastard!' exclaimed Aicheson. 'You limey bastard!'

The major looked evenly at him, shaking his head. 'All's fair in love and war, old friend,' he said, disregarding the insults. He turned to Seamus who was squinting viciously at him over his shoulder. 'Nice to see you again, laddie,' the major said heartily but without a trace of a smile. 'Been a long time, eh? You were bloody careless for a phone man. You should have remembered that phones in most bars have extensions.'

Seamus spat before the soldier behind was able to crash the stock of his weapon between the prisoner's shoulders. The gob of saliva spattered harmlessly on to the linoleum.

# Chapter 13 October, 1971

Major Gates reckoned he had a thicker skin than most, but his memory of the searing row with Aicheson after the raid on the house off Lenadoon Avenue was to remain with him for months afterwards.

When Seamus Aherne and Rebecca Fahey had been taken away in handcuffs – she to be released in the morning without being charged – the major offered to give the American a lift back to his car, still parked outside the bar. Aicheson had looked coldly at him before holding out both arms in front of him, wrists close together.

'You'd better put the cuffs on, Major,' he said bitingly.

Stephen Gates understood how deeply upset his former friend must be. 'Maybe even the leg irons too, Ted,' he said wryly. 'That's what the tough boyos sometimes need though we're not supposed to use them.'

'I'm not bloody joking,' Aicheson continued, a chill in his voice. 'You've treated me like a criminal so why stop now, you bastard?'

The major stepped towards him, in the small kitchen, wanting to put a friendly hand on his shoulder, wanting to calm him.

Aicheson twisted away. 'You really took me for an idiot, didn't you?' he murmured bitterly. 'You talked me into this all the way. You saw what I was doing and let me go on. You used me to capture Seamus. You betrayed me, for me to betray him!'

'It was necessary, Ted,' the major said quietly, hooking out a stool and sitting down at the kitchen table, willing to listen.

'Necessary?' Aicheson snarled, unsure whether he was angrier with himself or Stephen Gates. 'Necessary to stamp all over someone who thought you were a friend, who trusted you? Necessary to follow me, to sneak in the shadows, to plant your bugs on me? Necessary to set me up as a Judas goat?'

'It was necessary,' the major repeated patiently. 'If we . . . if I could have done it any other way . . . it was a chance, an opportunity, I had to take and it came off.'

'And sod everything and everybody?'

The major nodded reluctantly. 'Yes . . . if needs be.'

'Even a friend?'

'Yes.'

Aicheson swung round, pointing an accusatory finger. It actually quivered with indignation and rage.

'Just who the hell do you think you are? Almighty God? How can you play with lives like this?'

Major Gates hunched over the table, pressing his thick fingers together. Under the stool, his ankles were clenched tightly together. His head seemed bowed to the scorn and insults. He said nothing.

'Let me remind you, Major,' Aicheson went on, 'That I'm an American citizen carrying a United States passport. Not one of the poor Catholics you seem to enjoy kicking from pillar to post!'

The major rubbed a hand wearily across his eyes.

'You had no right . . . '

'Shut up,' the major murmured.

' . . . to do what you did. Legally you had no right to plant those devices on me, no right to break into the house, no right to stick a gun up my nose, no right . . . '

'Shut up,' the major repeated, more loudly this time.

' . . . to tap phones without a warrant, which you must have done, no right . . . '

Major Gates' unusually large hands banged down on the flimsy table, the vibration lifting it off the floor. 'Now, just shut up and listen, Ted,' he roared, his voice startling a soldier still posted in the hallway, mid-way between front and back door. 'Don't you tell me what I can or cannot do in this town. Don't you dare tell me what I can or cannot do about some hairy skull who's already murdered innocent people with his bloody bombs!'

Aicheson opened his mouth to interrupt. He saw the fury in the major's hooded eyes and decided otherwise. At that moment, the Army Officer resembled more than ever a hawk in the wilderness about to swoop on its prey.

'Do you think I wanted to do it, Ted?' the major exclaimed vehemently. 'Do you think I even want to be here, losing my friends and my sanity and my sleep? No way, soldier. No way. None of us want to be here. The British Army have learned the hard way about running colonies and provinces and whatever and trying to back gracefully out of them without getting our throats cut. You bloody Americans think you know the lot. Well if you don't learn a lesson from that cock-up in Vietnam, you'll learn it in some place, believe me . . . '

'What the hell has . . . ?' Aicheson tried to interrupt. The major waved him to be silent.

'Listen and I'll tell you something. Listen and you'll learn, my New England friend,' Stephen Gates continued angrily. 'The bloody natives haven't spears any more. They've bombs and rifles and bazookas and know-how and a world-wide supply organization run from Moscow or Peking or just down the road as far as I'm concerned. It's not so easy, chum. To even hold them to a draw, we've got to play their game. The name of the game is survival and that's what we're going to do. There's no way Her Majesty's imperial bloody troops can solve this one. We bloody well know we can never win and, anyway, who wants us to? All we can do is hold on until the bigwigs in London and Dublin get it into their thick heads that the only solution is for people to get used to living and working together, north and south of the border. But that'll only happen when they want to. Some maniacs say that everything will be sweetness and light if the British Army pulls out. Well, shall I tell you what'll happen then? A very bloody, nasty civil war, that's what. The Prods'll bash the Catholics and they'll call in the Provos to defend them. It'll be the greatest thing since sliced bread for the IRA. And don't you bloody Americans realize what they want? It's not simply a united Ireland. We all want that one day. It's the only thing that makes sense. No, what they want is a communist republic of Ireland, and that's what you freedom-loving Yanks are supporting them for. You're not only mad, you're pathetic!'

Aicheson looked incredulously at the major, hardly believing what he'd just heard. 'I always second-guessed you for a hard bastard,' he said, sitting down opposite Stephen Gates. 'But I never realized how twisted you were.'

'Twisted?'

'Yes, twisted and downright wrong. You're like all professional soldiers: you don't give a tinker's cuss about the people you're dealing with. You don't really think about what you're doing over here, the harm you're doing, the enemies you're making for generations to come. God, why do you think those young kids are out on the streets most nights throwing stones and bottles at soldiers and policemen . . . ?'

'Because their uncles in the Provos tell 'em to,' snapped the major.

'You're wrong. So wrong. It's because they think that if they don't attack first, then they'll be attacked themselves. You raid their

659

houses, smash their belongings, search the family car, take their dad away for questioning and beating, all in the name of security. Haven't you ever thought of winning their hearts and minds? Not you especially – that'd be asking an elephant to dance a minuet – but your government, your politicians sitting on their arses and pontificating about this Irish solution and that through their well-oiled rectums.'

'Save it for the social workers!'

'That's why you're winning a battle and losing the war.'

'Just like your people are doing in Vietnam,' the major jeered.

'Maybe. But at least we're learning from our mistakes. You British never learn anything. You're behaving like this is the Irish revolt of '98 that these people, these Catholics, have no more rights than the peasants had then . . .'

'Nor should they if they support the skulls.'

'Let's face it, you don't give a shit about the Irish!'

'You're probably right, old friend.'

'Don't call me that! Don't you patronize me! Our friendship ended in this house tonight!'

'As you like. But as I said, you're probably right. Why should we give a shit for the Irish anyway? They've meant nothing but trouble for us for hundreds of years. You see, Ted, it's true that we recognize the Irish have charm and wit. Oh, yes, they can be extremely charming and witty, but their attraction is seedy. Over the years, I'm afraid we British, maybe even we English, we Anglo-Saxons, have treated them like a slightly crazed maiden aunt. Of course we were bloody grateful when they fought for us and of course we've given them enough to keep them in genteel poverty. But when they have a mad spell and turn against us, well, we shake our heads sadly at their ingratitude and wait till they come to their senses again. Sometimes a course of electric shock treatment is necessary and we administer it, naturally telling them that it hurts us more than it hurts them.'

Aicheson shook his head, fascinated. 'Unbelievable,' he murmured to himself. 'Absolutely unbelievable.'

'Really, historically,' the major continued sarcastically, 'it would have been kinder if we'd treated the Irish like you Americans treated your Red Indians, simply wiped them out and put the survivors in the prison camps you euphemistically call reservations. Then we could have sent round coachloads of tourists to buy their souvenirs and admire their out-of-date culture. The simple fact you have to grasp is that the Irish, just like your Red Indians, are a total anachronism. Their great times were the times when Christianity carried a flaming sword, when it was a blessed thing to slaughter some poor sod who happened not to agree with the prevalent idea of God. Sad, maybe, but those times have passed. No, it's all about compromise, live and let live, abstentions at the United Nations. And that's the rub. It's all or nothing here. You Americans deal with the Irish believing that they will and do compromise. We British know they're incapable of even understanding the word.'

Aicheson raised his arms in disgust, then clasped his hands behind his shaking head. 'You're talking balls. Wild generalizations, bloody wild ones.'

The major sniffed and grinned, taking a small cigar from a crumpled packet. 'Of course I am. I know that. But what I'm telling you is what most British people on the mainland believe. Okay, so most of the Northern Irish want to remain in Britain. I'd wager my hard-earned pension that the majority of the British don't want the Northern Irish. They might not want to do the dirty on them by breaking all the politicians' promises, but the truth is that they don't particularly care. The Northern Irish are costing the mainland, ordinary Briton an awful lot of money and lives. The time may come when they say to the smart politicians in Dublin who're always ready to play the problem for a few votes come election time, "Right, chums, we've had enough. You claim the six counties of Ulster. Well, brothers, here's your chance. You sort 'em out." And then you'll see the fur fly, my angry young American. It'll be the biggest bloodbath since I don't know when, say since Genghis Khan first lifted a horse's tail. And then all your politicians after the Irish vote in the good old US of A can really start wringing their hands and shedding the crocodile tears.'

Aicheson recognized truths in the major's vicious statement. But he was still outraged by what had happened that night. High on his cheek bones two red spots glowed. 'You think that excuses your conduct tonight,' he glared. 'Weaseling your way into my confidence purely to use me as a decoy. It's bloody unforgiveable.'

'Christ alive!' the major exploded. 'I've been trying to make you understand. It's a love-hate relationship, deeper than any we have with you Americans. Sometimes we love the Irish, sometimes they hate us and vice-versa. We're like Siamese twins except we're bound together by history and geography and economics. The Irish are the flea in our hair. We're the dog nipping at their ankles. Christ, don't you understand we could have played it hard tonight, done a street-to-street, house-to-house search for your precious Seamus, turned Andersonstown into the Warsaw ghetto till we found him. If we took the gloves off, we could end this little emergency in a matter of weeks. You Americans have to remember that if we didn't have the Irish as neighbours, we'd have to invent someone like them!'

'And invent friends like me?'

The major smiled, conceding the point. 'Yes, and friends like you. But remember, you didn't get hurt tonight.'

'There're other kinds of hurt than an accidental broken jaw, you bastard!'

'The only thing hurt tonight, here tonight, Mr Edward S. Aicheson,' he grated, 'were your delicate Boston bloody feelings.'

'I'll never forgive you,' Aicheson cried. 'I'll never bloody forgive you.'

'So break my heart,' said Major Gates, standing up and tangling his feet in the stool. He kicked it aside and moved towards the back door.

'You'll be in deep trouble because of this!'

The major stopped by the door, leaning tiredly against the frame for a moment. His voice was angry no longer. 'Don't threaten me, Ted. Just don't,' he said quietly. 'You could still spend the night, or perhaps two, under interrogation. You could even be charged. You know that.'

'And then I'd tell 'em what happened,' Aicheson said defiantly. 'By Christ, I would.'

'Spitting out your teeth and holding your broken ribs, you would,' the major growled. He felt tired, so tired, and depressed, very depressed, when he knew he should be feeling exactly the opposite after the night's capture. 'So d'you want a lift or are you going to walk?' he added, turning back to Aicheson, attempting a weak, conciliatory smile.

'Is there a choice, goddamnit?'

'No.'

Ted Aicheson shrugged and followed the major through the back door. The RAOC driver took the surgeon back to his car in Ormeau Road before driving Stephen Gates on to Lisburn. During the journey, the British officer and the American said not a word. Nor would they ever again.


'That bastard Gates really stitched you up, Seamus,' commiserated Mickey Quinn, one of Hut 8's occupants in the gaol at Long Kesh.

'Does it matter, Mickey?' answered Seamus, 'I'd had a good run. They were bound to get me in the end and put me back behind the wire.'

'Bad timing, though,' Quinn smiled. 'Just when you'd moved your girl-friend in.'

Seamus shrugged. 'In more ways than one with a wee 'un coming along.'

'Aye, it is that. Maybe they'll allow you to wed her. You know, special parole for the ceremony.'

'Maybe, but I doubt it. Not straight away at least, not with the escape.'

'Maybe not, Seamus, but if I were you I'd give it a few weeks and then have a word with Charley McCool. He can fix it if anyone can.'

Seamus nodded agreement. That had been his second surprise after arriving at Long Kesh, discovering that McCool was an inmate too.

In fact, it was rumoured that McCool had been asked if he would transfer from Crumlin Gaol to Long Kesh since he was respected as someone who could bring the younger, unrulier IRA internees under control and make the prison routine more manageable for both the guards and the guarded.

Charley McCool was not a collaborator, but he was astute enough to recognize that there had to be a tacit deal with the prison administration if the IRA was to maintain control of its members in the internment camp. McCool had set up a command structure in the Republican compound which was the envy of the Loyalist internees in an adjoining compound. In return, the prison hierarchy left him virtually in charge as far as discipline among his men was concerned.

The camp presented a bleak landscape of Nissen huts and barbed wire, fences and watchtowers, reminiscent of Second World War prisoner-of-war camps. McCool furthered the military comparison by ordering parades and drills and physical jerks, setting strict timetables within the Republican compound. His lieutenants organized lectures about the history of Ireland, classes to teach the Irish language, and various courses aptly termed 'vocational'. These were, in fact, instructional classes about the tactics of guerilla warfare, about weapons, using replicas modelled in wood, and, with Seamus's arrival, about bombs.

'Might as well make yourself useful, son,' McCool had told Seamus at their first interview, about a fortnight after he'd come to Long Kesh.

'I don't mind at all, Mr McCool,' Seamus replied, smiling enthusiastically, 'But how can we get away with it without the screws finding out?'

'Like we get away with everything else in here. By keeping our mouths tighter than Paisley's mind. Okay?'

'Suits me.'

'And, son,' McCool added, sitting at the desk in the small anteroom to Hut 9 which served as the IRA commandant's office and private bedroom, 'no more disappointments, eh? A lot of people invested time and money in you, your training and your escape, and, frankly, they don't feel they've had too much return on that investment.'

'I tried my best, for Christ's sake, Mr McCool,' Seamus protested alarmed at the sudden menace in the older man's rasping voice.

'Sure you did but some of the big men are wondering real hard if you've the stomach for the job, whether you may be just a wee bit of a paper tiger. Indeed, I tell you straight, son, there's some who reckon you need a proper whacking for what's been going on.'

'They're still upset about that hotel bomb?'

'Not so much upset. Mighty resentful, I'd say at us being made to look fools. The big 'un and what happens? The Brits make heroes of themselves and we get our noses rubbed in it. And then you get yourself picked up like that. Personally I'd never have allowed you to bring that lady over here. Distractions, that's what's led you astray. Maybe this is all just a wee bit of fun for you, a way of keeping up the family traditions.'

Seamus flushed, stung by the criticisms. 'I'm as committed as ever I was, Mr McCool!' he exclaimed. 'True, things haven't been going my way lately but you're forgetting the "Lambeg". That had the Brits over a barrel.'

'Aye, for a while. But what since then? Very little, I'd say.'

Seamus bowed his head, licking his lips, realizing the truth of the statement. 'You know,' he said, 'I gave up a lot to volunteer, Mr McCool.'

The Provisional's commandant in Long Kesh sighed. 'Oh, dear, son. You gave up a job. No more. I'm wondering if you'd ever be prepared to give up your life or whether the Republican blood in your family has run a bit thin.'

'I'm prepared . . .'

'No, listen, son. I don't want your assurances and promises on the spur of the moment. I want you to go away and think and work I want you to consider that maybe, in the not too distant future, we might be asking some of you boys behind the wire to take up a hunger strike, to starve yourselves to death like Terence MacSwiney did during the Tan Wars, God rest him. I'm not asking you now. I only want you to think about it son. Okay?'

Seamus nodded, hardly daring to speak. The concept of actually starving to death was too horrific. He thought about it for the next days, particularly at night, just before sleep. He couldn't see himself being able to go through with such a thing. He realized, not for the first time, that he might be a physical coward. He hated himself for it.

The phase of self-doubt passed gradually, however, as late autumn became winter at Long Kesh, and everyone's main purpose in life became keeping warm and occupied. Seamus's classes in bombs and bomb-making were well established. He enjoyed passing on his expertise. It gave him a sense of confidence. The pupils were only too willing to learn and Seamus discovered that he had a fair knack for teaching.

He looked forward to his weekly visits from Rebecca. At first, they were emotionally trying but soon – he wasn't certain why – the pangs of longing dulled. He went through the motions of reassuring her that he would try to arrange a marriage before their child was born but somehow, after she had left to return to Belfast, the minute-to-minute effort of simply existing in the camp was of greater importance. After a few weeks, it was hardly mentioned, neither of them wanting to plan ahead when there appeared so little chance of an immediate future together.

'It must be the bromide in the tea,' Mickey Quinn joked one night. 'You're forgetting what your old plonker's for!'

Seamus laughed but continued to wonder why he was feeling so apathetic towards Rebecca. The only thing they had in common, it seemed, was the unborn child.

His greatest joy came from the infrequent visits from his mother and father. His father looked comparatively better than he'd been led to expect after Ted Aicheson's dire statements. His mother explained that he was being more careful in his drinking habits, now that his worry about Seamus had partially lifted. At least, his mother said, they knew now where he was and that he was safe from any immediate danger.

Yes, Seamus often reflected that life in Long Kesh suited his purpose quite well. He knew precisely how to behave within the strict rules laid down by Charley McCool. He was still a Provo, demonstrably so with all the parading and ritual. He could preen like a peacock in front of the warders and watching Loyalists, sometimes even noticing a gleam of slightly fearful respect in their eyes.

For the first two months, he felt comfortably remote from the dreadful conflict continuing outside the closed world of the camp. Then, on New Year's Day, 1972, he was called to Charley McCool's room in Hut 9 to be given the news about Jack McKay, his first bomb instructor and probably the Provisionals' most important bomb-supplier.

'He died like the hard man he was,' said McCool sombrely. 'By God, he was a hard man!'

'Do they know what happened?'

'Oh, yes. Jack McKay wouldn't allow himself to die without giving that information and him with his eyes and balls blown clean away by the explosion.'

'And?'

'Well, it seems he was mixing the stuff in his garage.'

'On the Swords Road?'

'Yes, at his home, and the shovel hit the floor, scraped it like, and put a spark into the explosive. Whoosh! That was that!'

'Terrible, terrible,' Seamus muttered, picturing the scene of bloody carnage. 'He was an awful decent man.'

'Well, he's gone to his reward now,' McCool shrugged. 'And that means you've proper work to do, son, until someone else outside can be trained up.'

Seamus looked surprised.

'What on earth can I do behind the wire?'

'You can start drawing some proper designs again and we'll smuggle them out. Keep on with your lessons but make the designs your first priority.'

Seamus did as he was ordered and within a few weeks his designs were being put into production.

And those early weeks and months of 1972 were to bring the movement to the edge of success, not only through its own efforts but through another gigantic misjudgement from the authorities, handing the Irish Republican cause yet another day to be commemorated in its bloodstained history.

On the afternoon of Sunday January 30th, thirteen people in Derry were shot to death when British soldiers opened fire on the remnants of an illegal, though comparatively inoffensive procession under the civil rights banner.

The dramatic TV films cause horror and recriminations and

questions throughout the world; the bodies lying in pools of blood; the soldiers with rifles aimed and firing at seemingly unarmed and fleeing civilians; a Catholic priest, later to be a bishop, frantically waving his white handkerchief as he escorted a group carrying a fatally-wounded youngster through the horrible, deadly confusion.

Another 'Bloody Sunday' had been added to that one of 52 years before when twelve civilians had been shot at Croke Park, Dublin.

The reaction was swift. The British Embassy in Dublin was stoned and burned by a mob and the bombing campaign moved to the British mainland. A car bomb exploded outside the Old Bailey in London. One-hundred and eighty people were injured, many horribly.

Within a fortnight, the British Prime Minister, Edward Heath, dissolved the Northern Ireland Parliament at Stormont. He was angered by the mistaken advice from the Northern Ireland Premier, Brian Faulkner, who'd demanded internment, promising it would curtail the violence. From now on, Northern Ireland would be ruled directly from London.

The backlash came from the furious Protestants with riots and shootings and bombings.

It was a nightmare time for Major Stephen Gates and the RAOC bomb disposal teams. They worked with hardly any respite as the bombs grew bigger and better. The previous year, nearly 11,000 lbs of explosives had been detonated in terrorist bombs and 3,000 lbs successfully defused. The scale of the warfare increased so much that, in 1972, 50,000 lbs exploded and nearly 20,000 lbs were defused.

The major was under constant pressure from the weekly General Operations meetings to stem the tide of destruction but he was too busy actually dealing with the devices and deploying his men to analyse the backlog of bomb reports. When he did, late on a relatively quiet Sunday afternoon, the pattern immediately became clear.

The Provisional bombers were using new timing devices. That was to be expected. It was the method of wiring that interested him. Stephen Gates shuffled through the reports from his Explosive Ordnance Disposal units, placing them into three piles.

The first was for those about which he had a growing suspicion; the second for bombs clearly of Protestant origin; the third for those of indeterminate manufacture.

After scrutinizing the bomb reports once more, the major had twelve sheets of paper in the first pile. He picked them up from his desk and read them through again. 'If it's not him, it bloody well ought to be,' he muttered to himself. He leaned his elbows on his desk in the small office and lit a cigar.

He sat thinking for nearly five minutes before re-examining the bomb reports for the third time. In his own mind, he was certain. Most of the bombs being laid by the Provisional IRA were wired in an unmistakable way. They were, he knew, to the particular method of wiring equipment and connection used by telephone engineers in Britain and Ireland. They had to be the work, somewhere along the line, of Seamus Aherne.

The major rang his acquaintance in the secret intelligence unit. He had heard whispers that the Provos were running bomb-designing courses in Long Kesh.

'Thanks, chum,' said the major, replacing the receiver.

He looked up at the wall bearing all the maps and charts. 'The silly sod!' he remarked. 'What a silly sod!'

He prepared his plan before the next G. Ops meeting. The commanding general was, as usual, in full cry about curtailing bomb warfare. But, for once, Major Gates had a suggestion.

'I'm pretty certain I've identified one of the Provos designers, sir,' he said, gazing round the conference room at the weary and grey faces of the other senior HQ staff.

The general perked up visibly. 'Well done, Stephen. Is he accessible?'

'Extremely, sir.'

The general lit his third menthol cigarette of the meeting and took a deep puff. At all times, he was an extremely careful and even-handed man. That was why he held his position. 'You mean,' he said, slowly inclining his head, 'You know where he is?'

'Affirmative, sir.'

The general leaned back in his chair and gazed at the ceiling. 'Do you have a plan, Stephen?' he asked quietly.

'Yes.'

'Will it involve us?'

'Not necessarily, sir.'

'Publicity?'

'Shouldn't be too damaging. Not as damaging as chummy's bombs or those made to his pattern.'

'Take him out, Stephen. The whole bloody place is falling apart so we've got to get down on the carpet with them. Take him out, Stephen, if necessary with maximum prejudice. We just can't afford to keep that sort of type around.'

Major Gates looked evenly at the general. The general shook his head slightly, his eyes despairing.

'As you say, sir,' the major replied.

The major didn't even use the special intelligence unit to implement the operation. Two nights later, Corporal Hosken drove him along the M1 motorway towards Belfast. When the unmarked vehicle approached the Kennedy Way intersection at Andersonstown, the corporal slowed it on to the hard shoulder.

Major Gates pushed open the back door and tossed a load of files and papers on to the bank at the side of the motorway. The car sped away into the night.

'And that's your lot, your murdering bastard,' the major murmured, settling back in his seat and lighting another small cigar.

At first light, the local Provisionals were gleefully examining a pile of Army documents which had apparently fallen from a lorry while in transit.

Some of the papers were deliberate forgeries. Most were out of date and useless. Only one was in any way genuine and confidential. It was the official record of Seamus Aherne's interrogation at Holywood Barracks.

Two days later, during a glorious, early April mid-afternoon, Seamus was summoned to Charley McCool's office in Hut 9. He strode across the compound, whistling cheerfully, hoping he was about to receive a reply to his request about marrying Rebecca.

In the last few weeks, as her advancing pregnancy became more obvious with each visit, he'd decided that marriage was the right and proper thing. McCool had seemed fairly sympathetic, privately thinking that such a ceremony might attract favourable publicity for the Provisionals, and had promised to press the application with the prison authorities.

When he first stepped into the IRA commandant's office, Seamus was certain that everything had been arranged, noticing straight away the file and papers on the desk. 'Afternoon, Mr McCool,' he said, rubbing his hands together theatrically. 'It's come through then . . .'

The door slammed shut behind him. Suddenly two men were at either shoulder. One of them was a grim-faced Mickey Quinn.

'What the . . . ?'

'Shut up!' rasped McCool, his eyes boring into Seamus. He held out a flimsy sheet of paper. 'Read that!'

At first Seamus couldn't take it in. An official notice convening a court martial, with his name on it. 'I . . . I . . . ' he stammered, fingers quivering.

'Read it again!' snapped McCool.

And on the second reading, Seamus understood. His eyes flicked to the official looking file on the desk, its cover turned towards him. He could read the wording on the front. He shivered, feeling very cold.

'You're confined to this room under close arrest until the court meets this evening,' McCool announced, limping towards the door, avoiding even a glance at Seamus. 'You've the right to study the evidence.'

For the next four hours, Seamus stayed in the office-cum-bedroom with Quinn and another Volunteer called Billy Fogarty. They didn't speak to him and, after a couple of vain attempts at conversation, Seamus kept his own silence as well.

He felt numb and physically sick reading and re-reading the meticulous record made by Captain Charles Briance of his interrogation all those months ago. Seamus smiled wryly at the thought that the dead Ammunition Technical Officer, killed by his 'Lambeg' bomb, might actually revenge himself from beyond the grave.

Just after eight o'clock, Seamus was led into the next room and pushed into a chair in front of a trestle table covered with an Irish tricolour fashioned inside the camp.

Charley McCool was hunched forward over the table, flanked by his two closest lieutenants, Raymond McCartney and Terence Walsh. He looked expressionlessly at Seamus, then swept his eyes along those grouped behind the semi-circle of chairs before the table, themselves forming an arena for the participants in this much-respected IRA ritual.

'Now before this court martial comes into session,' McCool said solemnly, 'let me emphasize that it will be conducted in a proper way and according to the rules laid down by the Army Council. The legal officer here . . . ' He gestured towards another of his lieutenants, a gunman named Donal O'Hare. ' . . . will be advising the court if there is any question of the interpretation of the rules. The accused has declined by his silence the opportunity to be represented by a defending officer and will therefore conduct his own defence with the guidance of the officers of this court martial. He has been given a copy of the charge sheet, a copy of the order convening this court and unrestricted sight of the main exhibit to be used by the prosecuting officer.'

Seamus gazed at the bulb swinging gently above McCool's head, reflecting off his grey hair, emphasizing the deep lines on his face. The meagre, yellow glow reached just far enough to illuminate the principals grouped in the middle of the hut. He was unable to see the spectators, his comrades in the deep shadows, though he thought he could detect eyes gleaming with expectation, lips moistened with anticipation.

Strangely, Seamus's fear had vanished now that the court martial had begun. He felt numb still but hoped that he possessed enough strength of will to endure the ordeal with at least an outward semblance of courage. He knew the verdict would inevitably go against him. All he could hope for was leniency. But, however foregone the conclusion, Charley McCool insisted that the proceedings be run with the trappings and particular nuances of a legal court of law. His brooding presence invested the room, tatty and shabby, with a semblance of dignity and pomp.

'The legal officer will now read the charge,' McCool announced.

Donal O'Hare stood up and cleared his throat before reading from a light-blue writing pad. 'Seamus Aherne, a sworn Volunteer of the Irish Republican Army, is accused of giving vital information to the enemy on January 24th, 1971, contrary to the terms of his sworn oath.'

'How do you plead?' McCool asked quietly.

Seamus opened his mouth to reply.

'Stand up,' the legal officer ordered harshly.

Seamus pushed the chair back and stood slowly. His legs almost refused to obey. They felt like rubber. Mickey Quinn, by his side, held his elbow, seeing his unsteadiness.

'Guilty,' he said hoarsely, his left eyelid starting to twitch.

There was a gasp around the hut.

'Guilty?' queried McCool, raising his eyebrows,

'Yes,' Seamus muttered, 'But I'd like a chance . . . '

'You can talk after,' McCool rasped. 'Sit down!' He addressed the entire hut, his voice carrying and echoing off the wood. 'Since the prisoner has pleaded guilty there's no need for the prosecuting officer. The facts are simple.'

McCool went on to explain the circumstances of the raid on the bomb factory off Cromac Street in Belfast and how four Volunteers, two men and two women, had died in the subsequent explosion.

'Until only a few days ago,' he continued, his voice rising and sharpening, 'it was not known how the enemy obtained their information. There were suspicions, of course, but it was assumed to have come from their own intelligence sources, through their own cunning and observation and not through the word of a self-confessed traitor.'

He picked up the file recording Seamus's interrogation by Major Stephen Gates and Captain Briance.

'And then this . . . ' McCool slapped the file on to the table. ' . . . came into our hands, discarded by chance or choice, but discarded nonetheless. It is here in black and white, the enemy's own document, showing that the accused, Aherne, told the Brits where the bomb factory was and was therefore directly responsible for the deaths of four of his comrades.'

'I don't . . . ' Seamus began to protest, rising.

McCool waved him down sternly.

'Do you want to ask any questions about this document?'

'No.'

'You've read it?'

'Yes.'

'What it says is true?'

'Mostly. I just want to say I never intended . . . '

'Quiet!' McCool said menacingly. 'That makes no difference to the charge.'

Somewhere behind Seamus a spectator sniggered.

McCool peered into the gloom. The snigger became a coughing fit.

'The accused admits his guilt and admits the truth of the document which conclusively proves that guilt . . . ' McCool paused, waiting for the coughing to stop. ' . . . but before the court's decision is made and announced, the accused has the right to address this court. Do you want to, Aherne?'

Seamus stood up again. For a moment, he swayed. Quinn steadied him again. 'I just want to say I never wanted anyone to die. I wanted to lead them off the track . . . '

His voice was hard and desperate. ' . . . For God's sake,' he said more boldly, 'I'd been beaten and kept without sleep for days. I hardly knew what I was saying at the end when these officers began hollerin' and hammerin' . . . '

'Did the officers hit you?' McCool interrupted, his tone concerned, his face grave.

'Not exactly,' Seamus hesitated. 'But the sergeant would have done and I could hardly stand up from the beatings and no sleep and not being able to think stra . . . '

'Did they or didn't they hit you during this interrogation?' McCool persisted.

Seamus swayed again, his eyes suddenly mesmerized by the colours of the tricolour, knowing how much danger he was in, unable to help himself. 'Well, no,' he mumbled, shaking his head. 'No they didn't have to. I'd already taken all I could. I had to tell them something. They threatened . . . '

His voice died away as he slumped back in his chair.

McCool picked at his fingernails, gazing down at the notes he'd been making. Terence Walsh, to his right, began exploring the cavities in his teeth. Raymond McCartney puffed out his cheeks, leaned back and inspected the hut's cross-beams and rounded ceiling.

The silence in Hut 9 was tangible. It lasted more than a minute while everyone looked at Seamus and he looked sullenly at the floor.

'The officers of the court will retire,' said McCool eventually. 'We're doing this properly but we can't be here till the crack of doom.'

They walked solemnly and in step to the anteroom. The discussion was brief once the door was closed.

'Agreed?' said McCool.

'Have to,' the other two chorussed.

'But how?' asked Walsh.

'Hanging?' McCartney whispered.

McCool shook his head.

'It's been arranged. Let's face it, Aherne's been set up by the Brits. We all know that but the fact is he has to be hit. It has to be for morale and discipline. Dammit, he's as guilty as sin, wherever the information came from.'

The other two nodded.

'Well,' McCool continued, 'it'll be done in such a way that we'll be able to claim that the Brits did it. They'll argue but they'll not try too hard to disprove it. After all, I'm guessing they'll get what they want. Your man dead.'

'But won't that make him a martyr?' McCartney asked, surprise in his voice.

'I don't give a fuck what it makes him,' McCool said viciously. 'As far as I'm concerned when he's dead he can be anything he likes. His family can think he's the greatest hero since his grandfather. That'll be no bad thing. But the main point is that the boys'll really know what happened. Maybe the truth'll filter out, maybe, but in the meantime it'll keep them strictly in line. Agreed?'

'You know best, Charley,' said Walsh.

'Aye,' agreed McCartney.

The whisper of conversation died away as soon as the three men trooped back into the main hut. They stood behind the table. Quinn urged Seamus to his feet.

Charley McCool took a deep breath. 'Seamus Aherne,' he began huskily, then coughed to clear his throat. 'By your admission to this properly constituted court martial, you are guilty of the offence as charged. By powers from the Army Council, this court sentences you to death. There is no appeal.' He swept out his right hand in front of him. 'Take him out,' he ordered curtly.

Seamus's eyes widened. He wanted to speak but no words came. Quinn and Fogarty grabbed him by the wrists and hustled him into the anteroom pushing him down into a chair with its back to the door.

'Wha . . . wha . . . what?' Seamus stammered, his mind blank.

Fogarty shrugged and pulled out a hip flask. He unscrewed it and handed it to Seamus. He took a pull, nearly choking on the raw spirit, a sample of the secretly brewed camp poteen. 'Jesus,' he muttered, feeling the raw alcohol explode inside him. He took another pull, gasping again.

Fogarty held out his hand and took the flask back.

With tears in his eyes from the emotion and the poteen, Seamus peered up at the two men on either side of him. They gazed back inpassively. He wondered if this was how a beast in an abattoir felt. He didn't know what was happening, what was about to happen, when it would happen. 'Oh, Mother of Mercy, keep me through this night . . . ' he muttered.

His mind was full of images now.

They flickered back and forth: scenes of childhood; playing on the sands at Ballybunnion; the market at Listowel; Grandma Hannah leaning over his sick bed; a glass shining and filled with whiskey; Rebecca's face in ecstasy beneath him . . .

So much, he thought. So much and so little. But it was true. Your life did . . .

He didn't hear the third man, Donal O'Hare, enter the room behind him, didn't hear anything, felt nothing until the thick blanket was pulled down over his head and shoulders. And then it was darkness and struggling panic.

All images vanished from his brain.

'Aagh!' he cried agonizingly, the sound muffled to a groan, as the first blow struck the side of his face and glanced down, breaking his right collar bone.

And again.

He whimpered and groaned twice more as two lead-filled pipes and a chair leg spiked with nails crashed down in close succession on his skull. Then he felt nothing. His body's reactions were independent of his stunned, bruised, lacerated, dying brain.

Seamus slumped slowly sideways off his seat and on to the floor. The light in the room was strong enough to reflect the shadows of the men bending over him, raising their arms, unnaturally extended by their weapons, and striking down in rhythm, each in turn. Their arms rose and fell. At first there was a sharp, cracking noise as their blows connected. Within a minute or so, however, it was a sound akin to a housewife mashing potatoes. When the blanket was becoming sodden with blood and other pinker and greyer substances, the blows ceased.

The three executioners carried Seamus's body to the window, opened the shutters and the frames, waiting to observe the search lights bathing the compound outside in a pale, creamy light. Then, with a sudden heave, they rolled the body through the window, hanging onto the blanket so that it stayed inside. Carefully, they closed the window and shutters before checking the floor for bloodstains. There were none to be seen. The floor would be thoroughly mopped over before the guards discovered the body outside and the wrangle would begin about how Seamus Aherne had died. Charley McCool would claim he was beaten to death by the guards; the prison authorities would say it was by his own colleagues. And nothing would ever be officially admitted or decided.

The three men walked back into the main room of Hut 9. McCool was still sitting at the table, his hands outstretched across the tricolour. 'Well?' he asked.

'It's done,' Quinn nodded, wiping a hand across his face.

Charley McCool looked round the hut at the men standing silently, at their expressions of awe and fear. 'He never stood a fucking chance, boys. Never!'

McCool closed his eyes. His lips moved in a silent prayer for Seamus Aherne and, perhaps, himself.

# Chapter 14 April, 1972

It was an impressive funeral. The furore in the newspapers had ensured that, the accusations and counter-accusations, the charges and denials about an internee beaten to death in Long Kesh. Everyone, north or south of the Border, Protestant or Catholic member of the security forces or rank and file IRA, believed what their heritage, upbringing and duty demanded they should. Truth was swamped by rumour and, therefore, what was believed came to be the truth.

By their numbers alone, the people of Listowel demonstrated their certainty that Seamus Aherne had died at the brutal hands of the authorities and, thus, was worthy of elevation to the pantheon of Kerry's Republican martyrs. They stood in their hundreds, silently lining the streets of the small town as the cortege moved circuitously from St Mary's Church, across the market square, down William Street, into Courthouse Road and then into Upper Church Street to the cemetery.

Police snapped to attention and saluted when the gleaming black hearse inched by, coffin draped in the green, white and orange Irish flag, a black beret and a pair of black gloves on top to denote the dead man's service in the Provisional IRA.

Seamus's family walked behind. His mother, Bernadette, snivelled quietly into a shoulder pad of Joe Aherne's Sunday-best suit. He looked straight ahead, staring blindly at the coffin. The sisters, Shelagh and Mai, clung on to their husband's arms, weeping copiously behind borrowed veils.

Only Grandma Hannah walked alone, scorning all support but her stick, silver hair peeping beneath black shawl, stern and unyielding in her seventies, clutching a sprig of hawthorn.

Ted and Lindy Aicheson paced hand-in-hand behind Seamus's aunts and uncles, cousins, cousins by marriage, second cousins and schoolfriends. They looked totally out of place. It wasn't their expensive clothes. It wasn't their hair cuts. They simply appeared different from the other mourners because they knew themselves to be different. They knew they had no feeling for this particular ritual of death. They had been brought up to believe that a funeral was an occasion for remembrance of a person's life, an expression of regret at the death, and the declaration of trust in the everlasting life.

But this funeral was a celebration of death. Beneath the Ahernes' natural grief, there was a feeling of grim pride in the way of Seamus's death, as if his dying was more important than his living.

Suddenly, as they'd left the church and begun walking in the procession they'd felt their prized links of kinship with these people snap. The Aichesons realized that tenuous family history was not enough. They were no more a part of these people and their beliefs and culture and town than any other outsider. They were American, perhaps even Irish-American. But these people were Irish.

Their sense of awkwardness was heightened by guilt about Rebecca Fahey. Immediately Seamus's death had been announced amid fulsome tributes in the *Irish News*, Ted Aicheson had hurried to the house off Lenadoon Avenue, hoping to give comfort.

Rebecca had only allowed him into the dingy hallway. Through the slightly opened door to the lounge, Aicheson had glimpsed three men sitting down, obviously drinking from a bottle of whiskey placed in the middle of the rug in front of the gas fire.

'How are you?' he'd asked, sniffing alcohol on her breath, noting her eyes reddened from tears, smudged through lack of sleep.

'How d'you expect?' she'd shrugged.

'Have you had anything?'

'From the doctor?'

'Yes.'

'Some tablets but they're not much of a help.'

'Do you need anything then . . . anything else?'

She'd glanced round towards the door to the lounge.

'No. They're looking after me all right. A woman's staying and they've given me money.'

'The funeral? His . . . are you going?'

'Yes, if I can.'

His professional gaze had assessed her shape beneath the grubby maternity dress. 'Look, Rebecca,' he'd said, almost pleading. 'We'll be travelling down to Listowel, my wife and I, can't we give you a lift?'

She'd shaken her head emphatically, lifeless hair swinging at her neck. 'I'll be taken, I'm told, and brought back. Maybe taken to my folks in Galway, if they'll have me, though that's an awful long shot.'

'What about Seamus's family?'

'I'll not be imposing on them if I go. I'll stay away in the crowd.'

'Imposing?'

'They've enough grief, so they have. They're not knowing about the . . . the . . .' She tapped her stomach lightly. 'Well, they're not knowing and I'll not be telling and I don't want you telling either!'

'You sure?'

'Yes. I'll not be wanting their sympathy or whatever. I'll cope. I've had to so far.'

Aicheson's hand had stretched for the lock on the front door. He'd heard no noise from the lounge. Clearly, the men there were listening to the conversation. He was frightened of them without knowing precisely why.

'Maybe when we start off, we can call round for you, check if you need a lift?' he'd suggested.

'If you like,' she said without much enthusiasm. 'But really, they're looking after me. They say they'll take me.'

Aicheson had known better than to inquire who 'they' might be.

'So we'll call,' he'd added lamely.

'As you like.'

'You know . . . you do know . . . I'm really sorry.'

'About leading them here that evening?'

He'd felt regretful that she'd brought it into the open. 'Yes.'

'Don't be,' she'd smiled tiredly, 'If it hadn't been you, it'd been someone else.'

'I'll see you then,' he'd said, stepping on to the path.

'You can.'

'And yourself?' he'd asked finally, inclining his head downwards.

'The lump? He's fine. Any day now.'

'I can guess.'

'You can? Of course, you can. You're a . . .'

'Yes . . . when I'm not interfering.'

'Goodbye then,' she'd said with some finality, shutting the door.

The next day, Seamus's body was released by authority of the Home Office after two post-mortem examinations and driven to Galey Bridge. There, it lay in an open coffin for viewing in the front room of the farmhouse, heavily bandaged head just visible, the rest of the body shrouded and covered with Mass cards.

That same day Edward S. Aicheson resigned his fellowship at the Royal Victoria Hospital, pleading immediate personal problems, settled the difference on the lease of his flat in Dunmurry, booked two Aer Lingus tickets to Boston, and said what few farewells he deemed necessary.

He and Lindy barely discussed his decision, both realizing it was inevitable and irrevocable after Seamus's death. They did talk about what could be done for Rebecca and her child when it was born, even mentioning the possibility of adoption, but somehow the conversation petered away to nothing. The responsibility was too much for them and they recognized it. Soon, they hoped, they would start their own family and that would be more than enough.

After Seamus's burial, they spent the briefest time possible at the wake at Michael Aherne's tavern in Church Street, muttering appropriate words, issuing half-hearted invitations to Boston, making empty promises to return to Listowel one day.

They hurried back to the hotel, collected their suitcases and set off towards Shannon Airport. The town was almost deserted in the mid afternoon, bathed in a warm April glow, as the Aichesons drove out of the market square, between the shops and bars in Church Street and past the neat houses in Upper Church Street. Lindy slid a comforting hand on to her husband's thigh, pressing lightly. She recognized of old the haunted look in his eyes. She'd seen it first when one of his early patients had died.

He smiled at her with as much warmth and reassurance as he could summon and slowed the car to a halt by the metal swing gates of the cemetery.

Seamus Aherne's grave was only a few yards into the burying ground beside the last resting place of a young gypsy girl who'd died a year earlier. Her grave was covered with flowers sealed into boxes of clear plastic. The fresh flowers heaped over Seamus's grave seemed alive and blooming in comparison. Among them they noticed Grandma Hannah's sprig of hawthorn and wondered.

The masons had already done their work. The cross of the head-stone was simply inscribed – 'Seamus Aherne: 1946–1972'.

Underneath were three words – 'Killed Serving Ireland'. The unequivocal statement brooked no argument.

'Was he?' wondered Aicheson.

'What?' Lindy queried.

'Killed serving Ireland.'

'They think so and that's all that counts surely, darling?'

'I guess so.'

They crunched back along the gravel path towards the car. Aicheson stopped suddenly.

'Whose Ireland anyway?'

'Darling?'

'That he was serving. Whose Ireland?'

'Who knows? Does it matter now?'

'It sure as hell might one day,' he said, thinking of Seamus Aherne's unborn child.

E. V. Thompson
## The Music Makers £1. 95

In the troubled countryside of Ireland, the 1840s were the bad years, when the potato crops failed and the spectre of hunger stalked the landscape. Against this backdrop, prize-winning novelist E. V. Thompson spins the tale of Liam McCabe, one-time fisherman of Kilmar, who turned his hand to politics and offered his hungry fellows a gleam of hope. Never far away, the women in his life, Kathie the winsome fiddler's daughter and Caroline, dazzling lady of the aristocracy, whom he would need as he faced a host of enemies and a web of corruption – the source of a nation's torment . . .

## The Dream Traders £1. 95

The China opium trade of the 1830s was a maelstrom of greed, intrigue and misery – the way to power and wealth for the men who traded in drug-steeped dreams – and it spawned a conflict that would change the course of Asia's history. Luke Trewarne was a young Cornishman who came to China to make his fortune, but he fell in love with a country, an ideal, and a beautiful Chinese water gipsy . . .

## Harvest of the Sun £1.95

A magnificent saga of passion and conflict in Africa a century ago . . . The ship was bound for Australia. Aboard, Josh Retallick and Miriam Thackeray, prisoners destined for the convict settlements – until their vessel was wrecked on the Skeleton Coast of South West Africa. Far from their Cornwall origins, the two strangers in a hostile land meet Bushmen and Hereros, foraging Boers and greedy traders in an alien world of ivory tusks and smuggled guns.

'A host of characters and adventures' MANCHESTER EVENING NEWS

## Jack Higgins
## Touch the Devil £1.95

'Touch the Devil and you can't let go – an old Irish saying which fits Frank Barry, 100-per-cent a terrorist; his ideology is money and his track record is the best. When the Russians want review copies of the latest NATO missile system, Barry's the man to deliver them. The only man who can stop him is Martin Brosnan, poet and scholar, a killer trained in Vietnam and polished in the service of the IRA, currently a convict rotting in the French prison fortress of Belle Isle. To get him out of there and working for British Intelligence is a job for his oldest friend, Liam Devlin . . .

'Higgins . . . knows what he's about and does his job with skill, speed, sang-froid' NEW YORK TIMES

## A Prayer for the Dying £1.75

With a gun in his hand, Fallon was the best. His track record went a long and shady way back. This time the bidding came from Jack Meehan, an underworld baron with a thin varnish of respectability you'd only got to scratch once to watch the worms crawl out. The job was up North, but when Fallon got there he found himself changing sides, which put him in opposition to Meehan, a place where life expectancy was very short indeed.

'Tough, bitter, superbly written' NEW YORK TIMES

## Solo £1.95

'A brilliant but psychotic concert pianist who murders for pleasure in his spare time makes the mistake of killing the teenage daughter of a tough Northern Ireland SAS soldier, a trained and vicious killer himself. As soldier stalks maestro for vengeance, the tale builds to a tense, shattering climax' SUNDAY EXPRESS

## George MacDonald Fraser
### Mr American £2.50

When Mark J. Franklin stepped ashore from the *Mauretania* in Liverpool in 1909, his luggage included a pair of Remington .44s, a Mexican saddle and a fortune courtesy of a silver mine in Tonopah, Nebraska. Tall, rich and handsome, he soon found that money talked in Edwardian England. From Shaftesbury Avenue to Sandringham he cut a dash through society, and married the ravishing jewel of the county set. The mysterious Mr American – a man with a shadowy past and some very sinister enemies . . .

'Every page is sheer pleasure' THE TIMES

'The sort of book that can keep you armchair-locked all day' NOW!

### The Pyrates £2.50

What have we here? Out yonder on the high seas of adventure are Pyrates! Can our impossibly handsome hero redeem the treasure and rescue his lovely lady from the lascivious clutches of Akbar the Damned? Read on, and all shall be revealed.

'It's all there, right down to a dead man's chest, cleavages that are everything they should be and characters in seaboots who say nothing but 'Arr' or 'Me, hearty!' THE FINANCIAL TIMES

## Thomas Tessier
### Phantom £1.75

Ned was only a kid, but he knew. There were forces that stalked the night. Like that night in Washington when his mother almost died and he heard them. In the house, at dead of night he heard them. Then they moved to the tiny seacoast town of Lynnington, and he still knew, even there, something was coming after him. In the end Ned must face the terror alone. He must seek out the phantoms on their own ground and fight them for his very soul. Through a long night of cataclysmic battle . . .

## Susan Howatch
### The Sins of the Fathers £3.50

From Wall Street to the quiet of an English country churchyard,
Susan Howatch's magnificent narrative traces the fortunes of the
Van Zale dynasty through two decades of wealth, ambition and
struggle, until the sins of the fathers are finally visited upon the next
generation.

### The Rich are Different £3.50

A great fortune and the struggle to control a worldwide business
empire; an ambitious and beautiful woman who is one of the most
provocative heroines in fiction; a love that spans ecstasy and
anguish and a story that reaches from the quiet Norfolk countryside
across the ocean to the New York of the Roaring Twenties.

'Love, hate, death, murder and a hell of a lot of passion . . . DAILY
MIRROR

### The Devil on Lammas Night £1.75

When Tristan Poole moved to a remote Welsh village, was it to form
a nudist group? Or was it, as Nicola Morrison suspected, for
something much more sinister? What was the hypnotic effect
Tristan had on her mother? What was the cause of the sudden
accidents and deaths at Colwyn? And what was Tristan planning for
Nicola? As Lammas night approaches, the true, supernaturally evil
nature of the group is revealed and Nicola is drawn into deadly
danger . . .

## Piece of Cake £2.50

Their flying was breathtaking, they played God in the sky. They lived as they flew – reckless, flamboyant, no time to lose. For Hornet Squadron even dying was a piece of cake. From the early days of the war in France to the Battle of Britain's 'finest hour' the squadron fights on through terrible losses and triumphant victories.

'Destined for a place in the literary clouds' PRESS AND JOURNAL

## Ira Levin
## The Boys From Brazil £1.95

'Ninety-four men have to die on or near certain dates in the next two and a half years . . . The hope and the destiny of the Aryan race lie in the balance'

'Superb . . . the plot moves so fast. The scene shifts constantly through three continents and the episodes are so tightly packed' WASHINGTON POST

'You won't stop reading . . . his best since *Rosemary's Baby*' AMERICAN PUBLISHERS WEEKLY

## Derek Robinson
## Goshawk Squadron £1.95

Wooley was a professional, in business with death – flying with him is like living with a maniac. Brutal, callous and obscene, without manners or morals, he moulds green young pilots into ruthless killers. By 1918 chivalry had been a long time dead.

'One of the most powerful indictments of war I have ever read. . . savage, funny and heartbreaking! SUNDAY TELEGRAPH

## Brian Garfield
**The Paladin** £1.95

A warrior who will show no emotion and question no order; a warrior who fears only the showing of fear: in the darkest days of the Second World War, Churchill needed such a warrior. His task was to pass unsuspected in the deepest territories of the enemy, to carry out missions that must remain shrouded in silence when the war histories are set down for generations yet unborn . . .

'The most incredible war story of them all . . . one of the most amazing books of this year. Or any year' DAILY EXPRESS

## Lewis Grassic Gibbon
**A Scots Quair** £2.95

From the years of the Great War to the hungry thirties, Lewis Grassic Gibbon's magnificent trilogy spans the life of a woman and the story of a people. This powerful saga of Scottish life through three decades is now published in one volume.

'His three great novels have the impetus and music of mountain burns in full spate' OBSERVER

## Nevil Shute
**Lonely Road** £1.75

The deadly cargo of a burning lorry leads a pretty dance hostess and a rich ex-naval officer into a dangerous web of intrigue. A compelling story of adventure which blends haunting romance with the sustained suspense of a gun-running drama.

## Fiction

| | | | |
|---|---|---|---|
| ☐ | **The Chains of Fate** | Pamela Belle | £2.95p |
| ☐ | **Options** | Freda Bright | £1.50p |
| ☐ | **The Thirty-nine Steps** | John Buchan | £1.50p |
| ☐ | **Secret of Blackoaks** | Ashley Carter | £1.50p |
| ☐ | **Hercule Poirot's Christmas** | Agatha Christie | £1.50p |
| ☐ | **Dupe** | Liza Cody | £1.25p |
| ☐ | **Lovers and Gamblers** | Jackie Collins | £2.50p |
| ☐ | **Sphinx** | Robin Cook | £1.25p |
| ☐ | **My Cousin Rachel** | Daphne du Maurier | £1.95p |
| ☐ | **Flashman and the Redskins** | George Macdonald Fraser | £1.95p |
| ☐ | **The Moneychangers** | Arthur Hailey | £2.50p |
| ☐ | **Secrets** | Unity Hall | £1.75p |
| ☐ | **Black Sheep** | Georgette Heyer | £1.75p |
| ☐ | **The Eagle Has Landed** | Jack Higgins | £1.95p |
| ☐ | **Sins of the Fathers** | Susan Howatch | £3.50p |
| ☐ | **Smiley's People** | John le Carré | £1.95p |
| ☐ | **To Kill a Mockingbird** | Harper Lee | £1.95p |
| ☐ | **Ghosts** | Ed McBain | £1.75p |
| ☐ | **The Silent People** | Walter Macken | £1.95p |
| ☐ | **Gone with the Wind** | Margaret Mitchell | £3.50p |
| ☐ | **Blood Oath** | David Morrell | £1.75p |
| ☐ | **The Night of Morningstar** | Peter O'Donnell | £1.75p |
| ☐ | **Wilt** | Tom Sharpe | £1.75p |
| ☐ | **Rage of Angels** | Sidney Sheldon | £1.95p |
| ☐ | **The Unborn** | David Shobin | £1.50p |
| ☐ | **A Town Like Alice** | Nevile Shute | £1.75p |
| ☐ | **Gorky Park** | Martin Cruz Smith | £1.95p |
| ☐ | **A Falcon Flies** | Wilbur Smith | £2.50p |
| ☐ | **The Grapes of Wrath** | John Steinbeck | £2.50p |
| ☐ | **The Deep Well at Noon** | Jessica Stirling | £2.50p |
| ☐ | **The Ironmaster** | Jean Stubbs | £1.75p |
| ☐ | **The Music Makers** | E. V. Thompson | £1.95p |

## Non-fiction

| | | | |
|---|---|---|---|
| ☐ | **The First Christian** | Karen Armstrong | £2.50p |
| ☐ | **Pregnancy** | Gordon Bourne | £3.50p |
| ☐ | **The Law is an Ass** | Gyles Brandreth | £1.75p |
| ☐ | **The 35mm Photographer's Handbook** | Julian Calder and John Garrett | £5.95p |
| ☐ | **London at its Best** | Hunter Davies | £2.95p |
| ☐ | **Back from the Brink** | Michael Edwardes | £2.95p |

| | | | |
|---|---|---|---|
| ☐ | **Travellers' Britain** | ⎫ Arthur Eperon | £2.95p |
| ☐ | **Travellers' Italy** | ⎬ | £2.95p |
| ☐ | **The Complete Calorie Counter** | Eileen Fowler | 80p |
| ☐ | **The Diary of Anne Frank** | Anne Frank | £1.75p |
| ☐ | **And the Walls Came Tumbling Down** | Jack Fishman | £1.95p |
| ☐ | **Linda Goodman's Sun Signs** | Linda Goodman | £2.50p |
| ☐ | **Scott and Amundsen** | Roland Huntford | £3.95p |
| ☐ | **Victoria RI** | Elizabeth Longford | £4.95p |
| ☐ | **Symptoms** | Sigmund Stephen Miller | £2.50p |
| ☐ | **Book of Worries** | Robert Morley | £1.50p |
| ☐ | **Airport International** | Brian Moynahan | £1.75p |
| ☐ | **Pan Book of Card Games** | Hubert Phillips | £1.95p |
| ☐ | **Keep Taking the Tabloids** | Fritz Spiegl | £1.75p |
| ☐ | **An Unfinished History of the World** | Hugh Thomas | £3.95p |
| ☐ | **The Baby and Child Book** | Penny and Andrew Stanway | £4.95p |
| ☐ | **The Third Wave** | Alvin Toffler | £2.95p |
| ☐ | **Pauper's Paris** | Miles Turner | £2.50p |
| ☐ | **The Psychic Detectives** | Colin Wilson | £2.50p |
| ☐ | **The Flier's Handbook** | | £5.95p |

All these books are available at your local bookshop or newsagent, or can be ordered direct from the publisher. Indicate the number of copies required and fill in the form below      11

..........................................................................................................

Name_____
(Block letters please)

Address_____

_____

Send to CS Department, Pan Books Ltd, PO Box 40, Basingstoke, Hants
Please enclose remittance to the value of the cover price plus:
35p for the first book plus 15p per copy for each additional book ordered
to a maximum charge of £1.25 to cover postage and packing
Applicable only in the UK

While every effort is made to keep prices low, it is sometimes
necessary to increase prices at short notice. Pan Books reserve
the right to show on covers and charge new retail prices which
may differ from those advertised in the text or elsewhere